GOOD MORNING, YOUNG LADY

GOOD MORNING, YOUNG LADY

ARDYTH KENNELLY

HOUGHTON MIFFLIN COMPANY

BOSTON · The Riverside Press Cambridge

To the memory of my father
James D. Kennelly

AUTHOR'S NOTE

One of the characters in this book is a man who really lived: Butch Cassidy. He was a cowboy, rustler, robber and the leader of a gang that would have made Jesse James's outfit look sick: The Wild Bunch. He was a great fellow and pulled off some great stunts.

He lived, all right. Still does, maybe.

You are told this so that should his image amid the feigned and fictive here (like the actor Grossmith at Madame Tussaud's one day fooling the customers) all of a sudden give a wink and begin to poke its hand out to you smiling, you will not get scared out of seven years' growth.

❦

My foot in the stirrup, the reins in my hand,
Good morning, young lady, my horse he won't stand. . . .
— Old Wyoming Refrain

1

THE DOCTOR SAID THAT THE BABY WOULD LIVE
but that Mrs. Leaf would not, and he was right. The baby was only
two hours old when her mother died. Mr. Leaf, an emotional man,
had a tear for everything; the flag, Major General Crook on horse-
back, "Tenting Tonight," "Her White Bosom Bare," "Backward,
Turn Backward, O Time in Your Flight," or the sight of a boyhood
friend, so it is not to be wondered at that he was much affected by
the loss of his wife. The girls felt bad, too, the Leaf daughters,
Madge and Wanda, but somewhat embarrassed at the same time.
Mother had had her family: Madge, now twenty, Wanda, now seventeen, and Willie, who would be fifteen if he had not died of
swollen glands at the age of four. That should have been enough.
She was after all a woman of forty-two! a grandmother.

She looked quite young in her casket and her long-packed frock
still fitted her like the paper on the wall. Madge thought she would
want to be wearing the wedding gown and Papa agreed. It would be
nice to see her in it when he joined her in their eternal home, an
event he predicted for early spring, or summer at the latest. Wanda,
who had expected to wear it herself, if and when she married
Thomas Diltz (it had been too small for Madge), ventured to suggest that Mother's black ottoman with the braid and the jet buttons
would have been as appropriate, but they overruled her. Both girls
joined forces, however, against Papa giving the baby the name
Mother had picked out for a boy, Dorncy, her maiden name, but
Papa went ahead and gave it to her anyway. He wrote it in the
Bible with a fancy D and a fancy L: Dorney Leaf.

Wanda, the young sister, was afraid maybe Madge would want to
take Dorney home with her, to give her a start, being the experi-
enced mother of two girls aged one and three, but when Madge's
husband, 'Dair Yandle, came for the funeral and to take her and
the children back out to Reliance, she did not mention it. She
may have thought Papa would refuse to let the baby go, and she
may have considered that she already had her hands full. Whatever the reason, Madge merely left orders to keep the child warm

1

and said that if cow's milk did not agree with her, goat's milk would.

As it turned out, neither one would do. Dorney grew smaller instead of bigger, turned blue and ill-natured, and after some days of despair a wet nurse was secured. She was a young woman of Bohemian descent, with a pair of white-haired twins plucking at her skirts and a gigantic infant in her arms, and Dorney flourished at her breast until for a brief period her milk was poisoned with grief occasioned by the accidental death of her husband. She lived only down to the corner and around in back of the Feed Store, so it was easy to take the baby to her. Wanda used to make the trip as often as necessary, but when January came and she was confined to her bed with quinsy, Papa had to leave the forge and come and take Dorney back and forth himself. Snow was already deep on the ground, icicles had grown to the size of clubs, and when the big blizzard of the winter came, Papa had the sensible idea to invite the mother and her children to come and stay awhile, at least until the weather cleared.

He married her on Easter Sunday, when Dorney was five months old.

Madge refused to come to the wedding. She thought it was a disgrace, and Wanda thought so too, although she was present at the ceremony. Papa was quite overcome because Madge stayed away. He blew his nose and wiped his eyes and said he certainly thought she was a daughter who could forgive and forget. Mother would have been the last, he said — and indeed she would, having been a most clement, judicious and regardful lady — who would want to see him waste away with grief. Also, if he took three fatherless children to feed and raise, was that such a terrible crime? There was plenty in the Bible about being kind to widows and orphans. Besides, would not his own motherless babe now have a mother's love and affectionate care?

She would, but at the hands of her sister, not her stepmother, Benedicta by name, who almost immediately conceived a profound dislike for the "motherless babe." Benedicta complained that Dorney bit her nipples and pinched her breasts in a cruel way between thumb and forefinger while she sucked, that she cried, dawdled, dreamed, kicked viciously with her heels, and took three times as long to nurse as did her own son Jan. Not only that, she expected too much attention, wanted to be rocked, walked with, sung to and wouldn't sleep through the night. That was the way it always was with the child of an old mother, Benedicta, herself coralline and young, said. An old mother had no business to put on airs and have a baby. Wanda said she had no business to say such a thing. Her stepmother said she most certainly had, in

2

her own home! It was that. She had made it so almost on the day of the wedding, replacing pictures, changing the furniture all around, hanging a crucifix in Mother's bedroom. Wanda reached out and slapped her for what she said. She was slapped back so fast, it was like getting hit by lightning!

Father didn't take Wanda's side. When he came home just before supper and tiptoed into the dark bedroom where she lay crying, he said that was a terrible thing to do, haul off and slap somebody. She even thought so herself and could not imagine what had got into her, but she would not admit it. He wanted her to apologize but she said never.

That night after the house was still, she took Dorney off the lounge in the dining room where she slept behind chair backs, wrapped her up and stole out, leaving the back door ajar. She made her way through the crooked streets of Rock Springs and out the sandy, rutted road to Reliance, where Madge lived. The moonlight was bright as day so she was not scared, but sometimes the sagebrush or greasewood would look like a man crouching and then she would pick up her skirts with one hand, and clutch Dorney against her shoulder with the other, and run for all she was worth. Peering back over her shoulder, though, she would see that no one was following, that the crouching man, a mere speck now, was right where she had left him, and then she would stop running and walk, swallowing two or three times down a parched throat. She might have feared a horseman, for Wyoming was full of outlaws, even some of Jesse James's old gang, they said, but none came along. Coyotes howled over in the mountains and the jack rabbits were out but otherwise she had the place, the moon and stars, all to herself.

Madge was married to a horse buyer named 'Dair Yandle and she had a snug house on a fenced lot in Reliance. She was sixteen when 'Dair rode through Rock Springs, heard there was going to be a dance and stayed to it. That was the night they met, to the strains of "Old Joe Clark, the Preacher's Son." 'Dair thought Madge was a sight for sore eyes and she thought the same about him.

When they got married, they went to live in Reliance, where 'Dair paid cash for a house. The first year, Madge had a little girl they named Crystal and two years later a little girl they named Jetta. Madge had just about everything a woman's heart could desire, and a few things besides! A new dress every year, a cupboard always filled, a fashionable kitchen stove, a complete set of dishes for twelve. The only drawback was, 'Dair's business took him away the biggest part of the spring, summer and early fall, and in the winter, when he was at home, he grew restless and always had to be going to Rock Springs or Green River where something was doing,

3

sometimes staying away two or three nights at a time. Madge didn't mind him being gone on business, but when it came to the pleasure trips she used to sulk considerably and then he would have to buy a cameo pin or something to make peace in the family. He came from up Johnson County way, a cowboy turned horse buyer, and everybody said Madge had made a very good catch.

Madge was careful to peek from behind the kitchen curtains when a knock came at nearly three in the morning, before she opened the back door.

She could hardly believe that Wanda had walked all the way from Rock Springs carrying the baby, but when she heard the reason why, she didn't blame her.

Wanda might have stayed on with her sister if Papa had not come to Reliance in a livery stable wagon with such a fair proposition, and also if Madge had insisted. Madge didn't, possibly because plump Wanda, at seventeen, was about as pretty as she was ever going to be, and 'Dair would be home for the winter, or possibly because two more in the small house would be too much of a good thing.

Father's proposition was for Wanda to come home. She could take complete charge of Dorney, as though her stepmother did not exist. He would buy her what she needed to get started on her hope chest, and with taking care of the baby, embroidering and crocheting, she would be busy enough not to collide with Benedicta and all should be well. He wiped away several tears. Wanda was never a girl to be vindictive or hold a grudge, and when Papa broke down, it always touched her, so she said she would try it and let bygones be bygones. She was not asked to apologize, but did, and meant it, too.

Bendicta's milk giving out a short time later, both Jan, her son, and her stepdaughter had to make other boarding arrangements. Again Dorney had to contend with the cow's milk, then goat's milk, again fail to endure them. From a sunny girl, she became a notable misanthrope, and Wanda hardly crocheted a foot of lace in better than a week. Of course, she would be past the milk stage in a few months, if she survived. In the meantime, it was a sorry trial. Benedicta, an indefatigable cook and housekeeper, did her work with cotton in her ears, giving her already blank face a look of idiocy. Her own children, of whom Wanda could not help but grow fond, were good and quiet, any one of the three an example in decorum to naughty Dorney.

One cool evening, after a hot day, Wanda carried out her fretful charge for a walk. First she went past Diltz's Drygoods and General Merchandise, the smallest such establishment in town, and paid a formal call on Thomas Diltz (never called Tommy or Tom),

4

her undeclared suitor, who helped out his father. Thomas was in the process of saving $100 before he proposed and had got as far as $58. Since he now "put by" at the rapid rate of $1 a week, Wanda could almost figure to the day when his offer would be forthcoming. While they talked together, rather formally, though they had known each other from childhood, Wanda had to jiggle the baby, pat her back and change her position, while Dorney whimpered and complained.

On her way home, Wanda tried something. She walked past Grandpa Bannon's house, where tethered Beauty cropped the grass in the front yard.

"Dorney," Wanda said with a serious note in her voice. "I want you to look there at that little cow right over there by the tree."

The baby, suddenly quiet, turned her head and looked where Wanda was pointing. The cow looked back, then began to come forward, chewing, forgetting to chew, quite quickly and curiously, to the very fence.

Dorney shrank against her sister, but gazed into the cow's soft gaze, not crying.

"This here's Beauty," Wanda said gently. "She's a Jersey. She gives milk. Her milk agrees with *anybody*. You can drink Beauty's milk and you won't get sick. She's the only cow, that you can drink her milk. Now you pay attention because that's true." Dorney looked wonderingly at her sister and back at the little brown cow.

Sure enough, when they started taking Beauty's milk the next day, it agreed with Dorney! She drank it and kept it down. She can understand things, Wanda told herself in surprise. Here she's only a little past six months old and I took her and showed her Beauty and explained about the milk, and it almost seems as if she understood all about it. Wanda never told anybody, though, except Grandpa Bannon. He was the one who suggested in the first place that there wasn't a young one living that wouldn't thrive on Beauty's milk and that they'd ought to put Dorney on it. He thought it the most natural thing in the world that the baby should be introduced to the cow and the cow to the baby.

A year later, when Thomas Diltz had saved up his hundred dollars and married Wanda, they rented the cottage next door to the Bannons, so Dorney and Beauty became neighbors.

Wanda took Dorney to live with her. In fact, she said she would rather not marry Thomas than have to leave her little sister behind, now that she had taken care of her for so long. Anyway, Benedicta was about to have another child and Papa was talking seriously about going out to California to live. His wife's brothers had a vineyard out there and she had been after him to go. When the new baby arrived, he thought they might sell the house and make the change.

5

Thomas's mother did not approve of her son starting in life with a ready-made family, as she called Dorney, but Wanda took such a firm stand that he knew he had to, or lose his girl. So they had a wedding, Madge and 'Dair came, there was a wedding cake with a man and lady on top, Papa cried — and then Thomas, Wanda and Dorney settled down to live happily ever after.

Thomas Diltz was nobody for a little girl to love, or for that matter anybody. It may have been that he was too busy. As Herrick rightly says, "The lazy man the most doth love." The most *is* loved, too, perhaps. Besides, he was always purging himself, either by medicine or large amounts of cold or hot water, the latter never drunk because of honest thirst but to flush away impurities. Thomas was under the impression that comestibles of whatever nature became highly corrupt and polluted upon the instant of reaching the dark stomach where bitter juices ran. His conviction was that they should be expelled immediately, or a little before that. This program of hasty emptying left him but poorly nourished, as may be surmised, and he was pale, thin, icy cold in his extremities and bluish white about the nostrils. Add to this a natural shortness of temper and the constant endeavor to rise above the natural jollities of life, and it is not to be wondered at that Dorney, even in the toddling stage, learned to make a wide detour around Wanda's husband. One of Thomas's most agreeable attributes was that he was never at home, especially after his father died of a patent remedy and the store fell to him.

Dorney was about four when she began to appreciate Madge's husband, 'Dair Yandle. She did not see him very often as her sister was not much of a visitor and 'Dair seldom came without her. He was reddish brown, so firm within his high boots that you could run against him with all your might and never dislodge him the least little bit. His hands were warm and arid, big enough to stick your own hands in clear up to the elbows. Beneath his mustache, that looked like silk but felt like sun-dried tule grass, his lips were cool. Two kisses Dorney gave him! one for arrival, one for departure, every time. Two kisses took with great delight.

By the time she was five she was faithfully in love with him, and when she was six, and he came to his end, she thought her heart would break with sorrow and disappointment. Wanda was kind to her, there were babies in the house, she had a doll to dress, a wagon to pull, and yet at the time of 'Dair's sudden death she was scheming how she might persuade him to carry her away with him! all up into Johnson County and away into Montana and over the mountains . . . where he was said to go.

Three or four times he had taken her up behind him on his black horse Fiji, much farther up off the ground than it looked. But she

6

was not afraid! though Fiji was so slick and the saddle so slippery, like glass. She just hugged him with her knees and put her arms tight around him and knew she could have galloped anywhere without falling off or even losing her bonnet. She would not be afraid of the dark, either, when night came, or of painted Comanches sneaking out of the bushes by the side of the road, or of rattlers, wolves or outlaws, nor ever think that his revolvers, one on each side of him, might go off by accident. She knew they never would, and if sometime or somewhere 'Dair had to shoot, he would give her ample warning, she could carefully stick her fingers in her ears and shut her eyes tight, and when it was all over, he would touch her arm and she would unstop her ears and open her eyes, laughing. And there would be a dead Indian like a dead rooster in his feathers! or a dead outlaw! or a dead snake! and they would ride away fast on Fiji, with never a glance behind.

It was cruel the way the two strange men brought 'Dair home to Madge in Reliance. They went to the door and had her come out with them to look at him in the wagon bed, shot through the heart and dust all over him and his hat gone and only one of his six-guns. She cried and questioned, but all the men did was to carry him into the house and put him on the lounge. They wouldn't tell her anything, not even what had happened to Fiji, they just left him and drove away in the wagon, one of them calling back, "You ain't the only gal a-bawling today. His sweetheart's a-bawling too!" She didn't notice the red sash wrapped tight around his waist or she would have taken it off long before the neighbors came and saw it. If she had done that, she could have stayed in Reliance or at least in Rock Springs, and wouldn't have had to go where she was not known and nothing could be held against her innocent children.

Dorney asked what the red sash meant, for of course she heard of it, too, and Wanda said it meant their brother-in-law was a horse thief, rustler and outlaw. Up in Johnson County, she said, was a man named Nate Champion. He was the leader of a gang of outlaws and cattle rustlers. All his riders wore red sashes, so his gang was called the Red Sash Gang. 'Dair Yandle must have belonged to it all along.

Madge gave orders that the casket was to be closed during the funeral ceremony in Rock Springs and interred unopened. She did not want to see her husband's face again, or have Crystal and Jetta see their father. All during the ceremony, while Madge kept her black veil over her face and her head bent down and never raised it, Dorney looked and looked at the long box and tried to imagine how 'Dair must look within it. She couldn't imagine for she had not seen him asleep.

If Papa had been there he would have been one of the chief

7

mourners, cut to the quick by youth brought low, but he was long since in California, with new children.

Madge took Crystal and Jetta and went to Salt Lake City to live. She thought it would be easier to get work in a big city than in a little town. She didn't cry about 'Dair. She said she hated him for tricking and cheating her. Wanda reminded her that she had a good living for almost ten years (even if the house was mortgaged to the hilt and she had been left almost penniless) but Madge wouldn't listen to a word in her dead husband's favor. The life of outlawry she might have forgiven, yes, but the weeping girl, no, never.

Right after that, the Bannons' Jersey died. Dorney had not drunk her milk for quite a while, as the Diltzes had a cow of their own, but she knew well the story of her first meeting with Beauty and they had long been friends. She picked a bunch of cabbage roses and printed upon a board with charcoal the words: *Beauty, age 9, gone to her reward* (Wanda helped her with the spelling) but she could not raise it, because the Bannons had the dead cow carted off.

2

"WHAT YOU SIGHING FOR?" GRANDPA BANNON asked, coming out through the mosquito-nettinged door onto the back porch with a dishpan full of water. He threw it over the lilac bush, gave the pan a shake and hung it on a nail, wiping his hands on the flour sack tied around his waist. "Nice day like today and you sighing. Why ain't you in school?"

"Teacher's sick." Dorney looked up from the bottom step where she had been waiting for Grandpa Bannon to get through with the dishes and come out and take a seat on the porch.

He took it now, settling into the old rocker with a groan.

"What you sighing for, yourself?" she inquired politely.

"That ain't no sigh. That's a protest."

"What's a protest?"

"Means I'm agin it." He took a small newspaper, folded into a square, out of his back pocket and spread it over his knees, page one on top, but left his steel-rimmed glasses high on his forehead.

"Agin what?" Dorney began to wipe the dust off the toe of her shoe with one finger, in a design, a cross with a circle around it, holding her head back and on one side to get a better view of her work. It kindled ambition within her and she reached for a little stick in order to draw a more elaborate pattern on the ground.

"Well, not agin being so good-looking. I can stand that. Getting so blasted old, I mean."

"Wish I was!"

"Are, ain't you? Seven, ain't you? Pret near as old as me. Add a aught and you would be. Know how to make a aught?"

Dorney nodded and scratched a lopsided one the size of a saucer into the hard ground.

"That's a dandy. About how old would you like to be, say?" He put the question indulgently, with a sly look of eliciting the wish only to grant it.

Dorney thought of Adeline Sproul, who bossed the job all the time and told what games should be played and who should be It,

9

named forfeits, and all that, just as she liked. And could wander all over!

"Ten," she said. It seemed a bold desire and she looked up to see what effect it would have.

Grandpa Bannon pulled his glasses down onto his nose and squinted at her through them, his eyes now half the size they were before, so small it was ridiculous. "Ten! You don't want much, do you?"

"I'd go somewheres, then," she said apologetically. "Wanda'd let me."

"You go somewheres now. Go to school, don't you? Go down to the store, don't you? Run over here when you want?"

"But not down to the crick where the kids play!"

Her sister kept her close to home. A coal-mining town was no place for little girls to be running loose, Wanda said, echoing her mother's words. The off-shift miners were always roughhousing, fighting or coming out of the saloons drunk, cowboys in town on a spree were too quick on the trigger, and some wild-eyed foreigner was always taking out after another wild-eyed foreigner with a long knife. . . . No, sir, the place for children in a town like Rock Springs was home, Wanda thought.

Dorney wanted to roam, but a whipping or two from Wanda meaning business and she stayed where she belonged, unwillingly. Grandpa Bannon never sided with her but could see her point, and his sympathy had a consequence almost as good as Freedom itself. He told her about real travel, and though he but recounted details of the same trip, from Indiana to where they then sat, it never seemed the same but always different, so that he appeared a seasoned traveler, full of knowledge of strange customs, animals, stars, weather and circumstances, like a man who'd been around and around the world, maybe a dozen times.

"Down to the crick," he repeated with disdain.

"The kids is too little to play with." Dorney meant Wanda's children. "Ora ain't, but Grandma Diltz is scared to stay alone and keeps him. Tommy's too little. So's Pearl. . . ." She dropped her stick and sighed deeply. "They still take naps."

"Well, would you look at this here." Grandpa Bannon was holding the paper out at arm's length, the way he had to hold it to read, and was reading something that made him get red in the face. "Of all the everlasting gall." He read the story through, while Dorney watched with some curiosity, then slapped the paper down on his lap and tipped his chair back. "Why, he's a friend of Blufe. Knows him well, Blufe does. Knows all about him. Told me." Blufe, the only child among ten who sent money home, was the son

10

who lived in Star Valley. "He never no more rolled no drunk than a preacher would! But what do they do? Clap him in jail!"

Dorney tried to understand. A drunk was a man who was drunk. Rolling meant to roll. He was stiff as a board, likely, balanced on a slope, somebody gave him a push — and he rolled. But you must never do that, it seemed. Merrily the man, like a log of wood, turned over and over down the long hill gathering speed. . . .

"Claimed he rolled him." The delighted eyes of his small listener made Grandpa Bannon pause to explain. "Means somebody robs some fellow that's drunk, real drunk, dead to the world. Empties his pockets and takes all he's got. Meanest, onriest, sneakingest no-account thief ever was, does a stunt like that."

That was a different story. Dorney sobered at once.

"And here they say George Cassidy done such a thing. Say it right here!" He tapped the paper angrily. "Big as life."

"Who's he, Grandpa?"

"Who's he? Why, he's been working right here in town in a butcher shop the past winter. Honest labor. Seen him once or twice myself. Made it a point to go by and see him. Told him who I was. Blufe Bannon's pa, I says. Give me a big old smile and grabbed ahold of my hand like he was tickled pink to see me. Knows Blufe well. Said so." A pleased look crossed his face. "Makes some of the boys bust out laughing to see *him* working behind a counter weighing out meat. Fellow like him, you see. Kid the life out of him. Got to calling him Butch. He don't care, though. Good-naturedest cuss ever was."

Dorney waited for more.

"What you doing out there, Will?" a voice called querulously from the side window.

"Taking a recess. Can't a fellow take a recess once in a while?" Grandpa Bannon's lips shut tight.

"Who you gabbing with so strong?"

"Dorney."

"Hello, Mrs. Bannon," Dorney called.

"What's she want?"

"Just a-visiting."

"Ain't it time to put the potatoes on?"

"Not yet, Mother. I'm keeping track."

"Well, I'm cold, Will. I wish you'd come in and lay something over my feet."

"All right, Mother."

When Grandpa Bannon came out again, he picked up the rocking chair and making no noise set it down on the other side of the porch, and took his seat carefully, holding the two arms so it would not rock. Dorney slid along the bottom step on the opposite side, twisting around so she could see her companion as well as before.

He spoke softly. "Yes, sir," he said, taking the newspaper out from under his arm, "that they would do a thing like that to a boy like George Cassidy beats me. That's all I can say."

"Did him and Blufe play together when they was little?"

Grandpa Bannon shook his head. "But all there is to know about him, I know. And more than that. I know how him and some of the others got started. And all I can say is, what I've always said, that it ain't to be wondered at, with conditions as they was. But of course, naturally, some of 'em took it up for the hell of it. Young birds, you know, full of the old Nick, r'aring to go, ripsnorting, hell-tooting. In it for the devilment."

"In what, Grandpa?"

"In their line of business. You had a brother-in-law in their line of business. Your sister Madge's husband, 'Dair Yandle."

Dorney beamed. The dear, familiar name could not be mentioned at home, not 'Dair's, nor Fiji's either. Thomas wouldn't allow it and Wanda, too, kept silence.

"Same proposition," the old man said. "Red Sash Gang, McCarthy's Gang, six of one and half a dozen of the other."

"He was a nice man, Grandpa."

"'Course he was. Had many a spiel with 'Dair Yandle. Lot different guy than Tummy-Ache Diltz."

"Lot different," Dorney agreed.

"You don't have no conception," Grandpa Bannon began, and now he was not a lonely and bulldozed old man forced to the extremity of conversing with a little girl. His knowledge of the topic they were about to pursue, redeemed him, put him where he belonged, as if in his rightful domain of street corner, City Hall steps or up against the bar in the Fashion Saloon (where his lady never allowed him to go), face to face with an equal. "No, sir, you don't have no conception," he said, "just what the situation was that was behind the whole thing."

"Twenty-two, twenty-three years ago," he said, "when the railroad come in, why, then's when the cattle barons, as they say in the newspaper, really started to bloom. All the land," he spread his arms in a big circle, "millions upon millions of acres of land, that had been the Indians' stamping grounds — which speaking of Indians, remind me to tell you sometime about old Washakie, the old Shoshone chief that always wore a little casket plate in the middle of his hatband, made out of silver all engraved, that said 'Our Baby' on it. Seen him many a time."

"Where'd he get it?"

"God knows, but I'll tell you about him some other day. This land," he said, again spreading his arms, "that I'm talking about,

12

why, these big boys took it all. Had cattle by the thousands upon thousands shipped up or drove up from Texas, turned 'em loose to graze and then all they had to do was settle back and be millionaires. Easiest proposition in the world. Never paid no attention, never had no work to do, just let 'em graze and fatten up. Couple times a year there'd be a roundup and then these big herds would be drove to some railroad terminal where they could be hauled to markets back east, and that was all there was to it. Only drawback was, it took a pile of money to get in the cattle business in the first place — that was really a case where 'it takes money to get money,' like the old saying says — at least the way it was run in them days, and in these days, too, for that matter. Little penny-ante ranchers, penny-ante homesteaders — 'nesters' — they couldn't get a toe hold no place, didn't have a look-in in the world. Know what them big boys thought? Still think? And always will? Thought the Heavenly Father had went to work and created the land all for their benefit — not for nobody else — and if ever you seen anybody fight tooth and toenail, why, it was them, to keep it so. Now, tell me. How would you do, if you was a little rancher or a little homesteader and you come up against something like that?"

"I'd put 'em in jail," Dorney said defiantly.

Grandpa Bannon laughed. "Good for you! But I'll tell you what a lot of young fellows done instead, if you want to know. They went out and rounded up some mavericks and branded 'em with their own brands. The big outfits done that! Was doing it all the time, so it wasn't new. So that's how these young fellows got started. What would come next on the program, do you think?" He did not wait for Dorney's reply. "Why, next — well, it didn't take long to go from slapping their brand on a stray calf once in a while to honest-to-God rustling, and the first thing the ranges knowed, here was a flock of full-fledged cattle thieves and outright desperadoes. That was about sixteen, seventeen years ago, and they're getting livelier every year. Don't know what's going to be the upshot." He scratched his head and began to rock, softly, with a glance at the right-hand window.

"Is George — who you said — is he — one of them?"

"One of who?"

"What you said?"

"A rustler, you mean? A outlaw?"

She nodded.

"Now, don't you go and blab anything of what I tell you, or I won't tell you *nothing* no more. You be sure."

"Oh, I won't. Hope to die." She crossed her heart.

"Well, you just be sure."

"Is he?"

13

"George Cassidy? Butch, like the boys been calling him? Like to tickled 'em to death. Couple of 'em come by and seen him working behind that there counter weighing out meat and like to busted their sides laughing. George Cassidy? What you want to know about George Cassidy?"

She opened her mouth and closed it.

He hitched his chair closer to the edge of the steps, propped a dusty boot on the low porch railing and cleared his throat. "He was born right down in Beaver, Utah, right in Circle Valley, oldest of seven kids. Twenty-two, I guess he is, twenty-three, maybe, now. Eight or nine years ago his old man bought a ranch. Blufe knows the whole story. Bought this ranch twelve miles south of Circleville, the old Jim Marshall ranch was what it was called. Didn't know it, his old man didn't know it, but that there place had been the hangout — oh, for a long time — for a whole conglomeration of rustlers and horse thieves. Fine spot, see. Laid right where these fellows could get in and out of Bryce Canyon with stock they stole, and guard it good while it was in the canyon, without needing only a man or two for the job. They wasn't no particular gang, but such as they was, they had a kind of a leader, a easygoing fellow named Mike Cassidy. Now, when George's pa bought the ranch, this Mike Cassidy was working on it, so he just stayed on and kept right on working for the new owner. George wasn't named Cassidy in them days. He took that name later on, because of liking Mike so well. His rightful name is Parker, George LeRoy Parker, but he don't never use it no more, except the George. Don't care for it, I guess, or something. Anyhow, like I was saying. George and this Mike Cassidy took to each other right from the start, the way a kid and a grown man once in a while will take to each other and a person will think, What a damn shame they ain't father and son. George was fifteen, sixteen then and Mike was maybe twenty years older. First thing anybody knew, Mike had George under his wing, educating him. By educating I mean learning him all there was to learn about riding, roping, branding and shooting, because if ever there was a expert at them things, it was Mike Cassidy. And George was a A number 1 scholar. Why, before he was sixteen, he was a absolute dead shot, the best in Circle Valley, and that's saying a whole blame lot. Imagine something, Dorney. Imagine that tree over there — "

She looked hard at the budding aspen in the corner of the yard.

"— with a ace of spades nailed to the trunk. That George Cassidy, he could be on his horse, going full tilt, and ride around it, and shoot, and every time he come past he could hit it dead center — bang! bang! bang! all six shots within a inch of the center. Now, that's shooting. Ain't it, though?"

Dorney nodded and her eyes saw the adiaphanous man on the black horse, the horse like Fiji, make his last swoop around the tree and disappear lickety-split behind the corner of the coal shed in ghostly thunder, while the card upon the aspen trunk, smoking, grew dim and fell away.

"Half the people," Grandpa Bannon went on, "half the people that lived around there in Circle Valley, half of 'em was rustlers, at least. The most of 'em, that's the way they got their start in the cattle business. Go out on the desert, see, or sashay into the hills, shoo a unbranded calf away from his mammy and slap a mark on him. What you gopping at?"

She blinked and looked around at him. "Nothing."

"Thought you seen a weasel or something."

She shook her head.

"Well, the way they done — it was kind of like a game, see, that pret near everybody played, whether they was honest men or whether they was crooks. Rustling and that kind of business didn't used to be looked down on like it is now. But to get back to Mike Cassidy — "

"This here George, he liked him?"

"Liked Mike Cassidy? You bet your life he did, and Mike liked George. Them two thought the sun rose and set in each other. But to go on with what I was saying — "

"This here George, you know, Grandpa. I'd like him, too."

" — Mike had managed to collect a pretty big bunch of cattle on his own hook, while he was working for Jim Marshall and then later on for George's Pa, Mr. Parker, and he had been keeping 'em up in Bryce Canyon. Well, after a while when this herd got so big that people started in asking questions, why, then the time had come to move 'em. He hired George, and between the two of 'em, they herded 'em over into the Henry Mountains on the Colorado River. That there is what they call the Robber's Roost country, and George, he took to it like a duck to water. They hadn't no more than got the cattle over there and got settled — Mike was still learning George his lessons and George was still picking up tips, but he had got to the stage where Mike didn't have many more tricks up his sleeve to learn him — when what should happen but Mike run right smack bang up against the law, and had to make tracks for Mexico. That was the end of Mike. . . . Said he'd be coming back, but he ain't come back yet, and maybe never will. George missed him something fierce, for there never was nobody like Mike, I guess, for singing and laughing and making the time pass pleasant, except the kid himself. It wasn't long till George took the name of Cassidy. Dropped the Parker cold. A person can understand that, though. Mike was more of a old man to him than his old man ever

15

was. So here he blossomed out as George Cassidy, which he has been ever since."

"How about if he gets married?"

"How about if he does?"

"What will his wife be called, and his kids?"

"It's catching before hanging. A guy like him." Grandpa Bannon's smile was smug. "He'll be too smart for 'em, George will, or I'll eat my hat." The smile broadened and he laughed aloud. "Well, anyhow." He scratched his cheek. "There wasn't no better cowboy nowhere and he was a pretty fair outlaw, too, for his age, and he wanted to show what kind of stuff he was made out of. Guess he wanted Mike to hear tell of him wherever he was, and be proud of him because Mike was the one had learned him and should get the credit. He didn't do so good, though, that first crack on his own, when he moseyed on back across to Circleville and stole himself a bunch of horses. Less'n a dozen, but their owners was wild! Found out about it right away while the trail was still warm, and started two officers after him with a warrant all swore out. Caught him red-handed, too — "

Dorney held her breath.

" — said, 'You're under arrest,' locked a pair of handcuffs on him and off they went for the county seat, which it was thirty or forty miles away. George went along like a lamb. Never said aye, yes, or no. Not a peep out of him. Noon come along and the officers spied a shady spot where a little crick run by, so they stopped for dinner. George climbed down off his horse, still handcuffed, of course, and commenced to watch them. One of 'em started to kindle a fire and the other one went off to dip some water out of the crick. That was all the chance George needed. He gave the fellow squatting by the fire a good swift kick, grabbed ahold of his six-shooter, and when the fellow with the water come clumping back, George had him covered. Quicker'n I can tell it, he got the guns away from 'em, got the keys, throwed away his handcuffs, was up on his horse and making tracks, herding his stolen horses! He had two more than he started with, see, these dumbhead officers'! Now, they was a pretty looking sight, wasn't they, them two? Miles and miles from town, sun boiling down, no mounts, no nothing — and their prisoner vanished off the face of the earth! What comes next, George never breathed a word of, never, not to nobody, but them officers told it, and that's how come it's known. All of a sudden here he come tearing back again in a cloud of dust! Never said nothing, just grinned and tossed first one fellow his canteen and then the other. Had spotted 'em on their saddles, see. That was desert country. . . . Desert country ain't no place to be without water. So he come back, to bring the canteens. That was him for you, every time."

16

"What does he look like, Grandpa Bannon?" Dorney asked. Light dust obscured him now, on the hot badlands, under the sun. . . . Before, his horse had gone too fast around the aspen tree, disappeared too soon behind the coal shed.

"Look like? Well, let me see." Grandpa Bannon pondered, his lower lip caught between thumb and forefinger.

"Ain't it about time to put the potatoes on?" the voice whined from the right-hand window.

"Just about, Mother." The old man took his foot off the railing.

"Who you gabbing to out there?"

"Just Dorney."

"Ain't she gone home yet?"

Dorney's little face flushed and she stood up quickly.

"She's been a-visiting." Grandpa Bannon gave her a friendly wink.

"Well, I wish you'd come in, Will. I know you've let the fire die out."

He got to his feet, clasping a hand to the small of his back. "Hear that?" he said. "Sit five minutes and happen to get up and damned old bones creak like a windmill. Hear 'em?"

Dorney giggled.

"It's time for my medicine, Will."

"I know it. I'm coming." Still holding his back, he started for the door. Behind him, the chair rocked a time or two, and once more, before it stood still.

"Will you tell me the rest tomorrow?" Dorney pleaded.

"The rest of what?"

"The story?"

He turned. "Why, that ain't no story, honey. That's the living gospel truth."

Dorney hopped across the yard and through the gooseberry bushes. Wanda, with Pearl on one hip, was adding more salt to the stew.

"Where you been?" she asked.

"No place. Over on Grandpa Bannon's steps."

"No place else?"

Dorney shook her head, but as ever when she told a fib she did not look straight into Wanda's eyes. She really had been no place, but it didn't seem so. She had a feeling she had never strayed so far from home before.

17

3

WHEN DORNEY CAME HOME FROM SCHOOL AND
banged her lunch basket down on the bureau by the sink, all Wanda
made her do was change her muslin apron for her old one. She
didn't make her fill the wood box the way the Irish kids' mothers
made them fill theirs, and do other chores besides. In fact, Wanda
was so good, she didn't make her do anything, not even rock the
baby unless she wanted to. She just gave her a piece of bread and
jam and asked her how school was, and Dorney told her about the
spelling, the reading, what she had added and took away, how mean
the boys were, who had got caught passing notes and so forth. Then,
if Dorney was still hungry she would have another piece of bread and
jam, and after that, if the weather was good (which was always,
unless in the dead of the winter) she could wander outside. No use
to ask if she could go down to the — because, no, Wanda would
say. Or to the — because, no, most assuredly not. Or to — because,
flatly, No. That was Wanda's only fault. She simply would not let
a person go as far as to the road.

But Dorney could hop, skip and jump over to Grandpa Bannon's.
It wasn't every day, though, that Grandpa could come outside and
sit. Lots of times, in the hours between school and supper, when
Dorney was free to pay her call, he was kept busy inside. She never
went to the door and knocked, but merely sat on the bottom step
or wandered by the window or swung on the gate or stepped in the
dusty coal shed and stepped right out again, and waited. He knew
she was there, always. When he could come out, he did, but when
old Mrs. Bannon kept him too busy, he just stayed without making
an excuse.

He said often that Mother had worked for nearly fifty years for
him and the family, and now she was collecting what wages she
had coming to her, with interest. A high, a very high rate of it.
She was not entirely bedfast, but nearly so, with a disease that was
supposed to be turning her to stone, or something so similar that
you could not tell the difference. Far from affecting her eyes and
ears, however, her malady seemed only to make them brighter and

18

sharper. Break a cup and try to hide the pieces! Accidentally stir
a gnat into the pancake dough! Throw an eggshell in the stove
instead of saving it for the hens to peck on! Forget to dust under
the clock! Let a drop of spit land on the porch sometime instead
of out in the yard! No man living could put anything over on her.
He could try it, but old Mrs. Bannon had more than two ears, for
she seemed to hear with parts of her body as well, like a grasshopper;
and more than her two eyes, for she retained quite adequate vision,
even when her eyes were shut tight. Her one voice was filed, thinned,
honed like a hunter's knife, and she used it as such within the
house. Without, it was a whine and whimper, dishonored as a
child sent out to beg.

Grandpa Bannon called his servitude "being dinged at." "She
dings at me," he said, "from morning till night." This was not entirely true, as sometimes during the day she quit bossing the job
and drifted off into uneasy slumber, but her naps were short and
she woke up more alert than ever.

Old Mrs. Bannon was napping today. When Dorney came across
the bare yard, Grandpa Bannon was sitting in his rocking chair, and
he hailed her. "They couldn't hold him!" he said, waving the paper.
"Couldn't hold him," he repeated, as she approached. "Knew they
couldn't. Had to let him go. Says right here."

"Who?" Dorney dropped down on her usual seat, the bottom
step.

"Why, Cassidy, of course."

It all came crowding back.

"They ain't got him in jail no more?" Dorney asked.

"No, sir. Had to let him go. Craziest thing, in the first place.
Fellow like him. Rolling a drunk! *He* turned the air blue or I
miss my guess, and I wouldn't blame him."

"Did he go back to work?"

"Cassidy? Work?" Grandpa Bannon looked puzzled. "Oh, you
mean in the butcher shop." He rocked, smiling. "Oh, that was
just some devilment to start with. Joke on somebody or something."
He stuck his foot up on the railing. "No, he didn't."

Dorney's heart sank. She had been thinking that when she got
big, maybe ten or eleven, she would get to see him, because — But
it was hard to explain why.

"Hell, no," Grandpa Bannon said with great satisfaction. "Rode
out of town without looking back, madder'n a wet hen, I guess.
Turning the air blue. And I wouldn't blame him."

"Now where's he going?" she said disconsolately.

"Him? Lord only knows. Somewheres, sure. Liven things up
wherever it is, you can bet. This town! Ain't worth setting a match
to."

19

Dorney looked down at her hands. She put them together for the game of Here's the church, here's the steeple, open the doors and see all the people, without thinking of the words. Then she put them in her apron pockets. She felt as sad and forlorn as if a picnic had been called off on account of rain. Postponed, indefinitely. "What did he do after he give them two officers back their canteens?" she said. "That time?" Something put off, she could not have told what, very nice, very wonderful . . . and when would it ever be? (Postponed till what fair day?)

"Today I ain't got much time to gab," the old man warned her. "Mother wants I should write a letter and I got to sew on buttons and clean the lamps, but — "

His eyes wavered before her steady gaze.

"That time?" he said. "When he got away from them officers on the desert? He rode off and that was the last they seen of him!"

"Where did he ride to?"

Grandpa Bannon resigned himself with little struggle.

"Now let me see," he said. "Let me just see, a minute."

She waited.

"Circle Valley," he said, "was a locality that was a little bit warm for him right about then. So him and a couple of friends of his thought they'd try Colorado for a change. One of these fellows had chewed off some other fellow's ear in a friendly tiff, and this other friend of Cassidy's, there was some reason why he wanted to make himself scarce, too. So anyhow the three of 'em went up to Telluride. That's in Colorado. Telluride had a big boom on right about then. George got put on at the mines driving mules down the mountains loaded up with ore. Right then's when Blufe got acquainted with him. Knows him well. Never sore at nobody, Blufe says. But I bet Cassidy's sore now! At these numskulls around here. Rolling a drunk!" He snorted in derision.

"No, he ain't," Dorney decided. "I bet he ain't sore." She could not bear to think that he was, at Rock Springs, because if so, then he was sore at her and she was not going to have that if she could help it.

"Well, the time went along," Grandpa Bannon said, "but that driving mules, that was pretty tame stuff for a kid like George Cassidy. First thing you know he was riding again! For the McCarthy's." He cast her a significant look. "And then, robbing a train."

Something cold went down her spine.

"Now you go blabbing what I say and I'll never tell you *nothing* no more."

Silently she crossed her heart.

"You mind now, because anybody that blabs ain't worth a nickel,

20

not a nickel, and people go miles out of their way so as not to even see 'em."

"I won't tell nobody," she murmured. "But Blufe told you, though," she added as an afterthought.

"That's a entirely different proposition. And the only reason I happen to be telling you all about this is because — " He did not know the only reason why he happened to be telling her all about this, the small girl from next door, so he stopped, coughed sternly and spat upon the obstinate lilac, full now of tiny tight sweet blooms.

"Go on, Grandpa," she said meekly.

"Well, next on the program come the big bank robbery in Denver!" Grandpa Bannon said briskly. "That was pulled by Tom McCarthy and George Cassidy, all alone."

"I won't tell," she promised before she was asked.

"This has already been spread all over the newspapers."

"But anyhow."

He smiled at her. "Next come the Telluride Bank robbery — and that was a entirely different proposition. First, though, for a while, they hung around Star Valley. That's a pretty spot! Lays partly in Idaho, partly in Wyoming. Ain't very long but it's wide and deep, with the Salt River running along. Good place to disappear. Of course, lots of decent folks live there, ranchers and settlers, but a good many of 'em — " He let the sentence die out.

" — is outlaws, maybe."

"Who said so?" Grandpa Bannon looked stern.

"What did they do there?" Dorney asked contritely.

"Who?"

"Oh, George Cassidy and the McCarthys."

"Where?"

"In Star Valley," she pleaded.

"There, you mean. Well, they took different names," Grandpa Bannon said, relenting. "Lived around. Mixed with folks. Everybody liked 'em. Matt Warner opened a saloon, Tom McCarthy bought a ranch — George, I don't know what George done except have a ripsnorting high old time like always. Went to the dances Saturday nights. George, he's a fellow that's very light on his feet, ain't a dance that stumps him. One little lady up there — rancher's daughter — she was pretty far gone on him, I guess. Very near had her heart busted. Same way with several."

Dorney lifted up her chin.

"Put a claim on George yourself, huh?" he teased, eying her. "Got your dander up, huh?"

She looked down.

"Because just as well try to catch the wind, is all the advice I can give you."

She looked up again. (Not catch, you know. Be, you know. Somebody on the go, Grandpa. No more no, no. Nobody on the watch. Going, Grandpa. Person's own boss. World spread out all over. Horse a-flying. Catching, Grandpa? *Being.*)

"When I get big," she began, and stopped helplessly.

"Yes, ma'am."

"I'll —" She stopped again.

"Yes, ma'am."

"I'll certainly —"

He waited a moment. "You better not," he said. "There may be a law agin it." He smiled at her. "But on the other hand, there may not be."

"Are you out there, Will?" Old Mrs. Bannon's voice whined from the window.

"You know blame well I am. Where else would I be?" Grandpa Bannon stopped rocking with regret and prepared to rise.

"Who you talking to?"

"Dorney."

She, too, began to desert her place.

"Don't that look weak in the head to you?"

"Don't what look weak in the head?" he answered back, not looking at his visitor.

"Three score years and ten," the voice droned. "Supposed to be so know-it-all. And gabbing away out there for three quarters of a hour to a little kid six years old."

"Seven," Dorney called quickly. She looked at Grandpa and looked away again when she saw his face was dark and strange.

"How a man in his right mind . . . a little kid six years old . . . nothing gets done . . . everything goes to rack and ruin . . . lay here . . . can't get no medicine . . . fire goes out . . . bread runs over the pans . . . and out on the porch sits Will Bannon, seventy-one his next birthday . . . gabbing away to a little first-grade kid."

"I better go home, Grandpa," Dorney whispered.

"You ought to feel very foolish, Will Bannon. Very *foolish.*"

Grandpa did not say anything.

Dorney fled without a glance around, for this was a time when she knew he would not want to be looked at, and she did not want him to look at her, either. Even Wanda she did not want to have look at her, because she had been shamed, so she stayed around at the shady side of the house for quite a while.

Dorney knew, even without seeing her and without being told, when one of the gray-haired Bannon girls, as they were called, had come on a visit. Grandpa Bannon was about half a head taller, for one thing, and for another, he would open the gate and walk right down the street. He was not allowed to leave the premises (the grocer's boy brought their few supplies and Wanda or Mrs. Stroble on the other side made what other purchases were needed), for old Mrs. Bannon, since stricken by her illness three years before, had a deadly fear of being alone. Blufe, she suspected but did not know for certain, had once "put Will up to" going out and leaving her by herself for an hour, to prove to her that she would survive the ordeal. She showed him something that time! Her husband came home to find her lying flat on her back on the floor, only the whites of her eyes showing, blue in the face, chilled, rigid, and *that* taught him a lesson! Since then he had been, as she confided to her indignant daughters, a "good dog," but it was a month before she was herself again.

It was too bad that Nila Bannon had come for a visit! Dorney would not be able to converse with Grandpa now until Nila went home again. The time ahead looked long and empty. Grieving, like the child who has had *Kidnapped* torn from his hands in the best part and the book cruelly hidden away, Dorney longed to hear more about George Cassidy, the young outlaw.

Long since, 'Dair Yandle had faded from her mind, grown yellowish and dim, but love of him and all he was — and Fiji too — and for the country where they roamed, that stayed, not like something, but like nothing, like emptiness, like hungriness. It did not always make itself felt, this subterrane, for she had many joys and satisfactions, but sometimes it did, when durance angered or she was balked by authority or when her imagination gave out and left her stranded on the reefs of boredom. Then, how echoing it was, the heart's cranny, till Cassidy came and went. He did not camp long anywhere! By a little blaze beneath massive stars, rolled in his blanket, or squatting and smoking while his black horse cropped scarce grass and drank from a dish-deep stream. They brought back 'Dair, but never brought back Fiji, and Dorney had taken the whim to imagine that Cassidy rode him under a bright new name over the Outlaw Trail.

All of blue-skied April, Cassidy and the McCarthys and the other riders stayed in Star Valley. Cassidy then was often at Blufe Bannon's cabin where he played with Blufe's little baby and talked courteously with dovelike Mrs. Bannon. Sometimes they all sat on the warm ground outside, under the tall pine, and watched the stars come out, one by one, and the moon come up, and Cassidy would sing, when his turn came, in a true light voice, "Billy Venero," "Hard Times" or "Love in Disguise." There were other cabins to

23

visit, other bare dooryards, and Matt Warner's Saloon, such as it was, and four or five girls, daughters of the scattered ranchers, and at least one pretty girl with sturdy curls and a skin not rough as a nutmeg grater. But two months is a long time there (even with the Saturday night dances that ended not with "Home, Sweet Home" but with "Goodbye, Old Paint, I'm a-leaving Cheyenne" when the fiddle kept still and the dancers chanted all together) and May beckoned Cassidy away. He wanted a little excitement for a change. Many a night till morning, midmorning, even afternoon and evening again, he played cards for high stakes, and oftener won than lost, but the gambling that signified was not for money and he longed to be gone again to play a game that had a little real excitement connected with it.

He liked the people in Telluride, Colorado, when he was there working in the mines as a mule driver. He and the two young men who went with him from Circle Valley, Heber Wiley and Eli Elder, had been treated well, made friends. Now he was going back to help rob the Telluride San Miguel Valley Bank, and might be thought by some to be about to repay hospitality with treachery. Not so, however. Would the bartender at Ole's, the bartender at Scotty's Corner suffer loss? Would orange-haired Madame Laverne in her papered parlor where Em, Rhea, Ruth and Lillian tripped in the light of coral lamps be bilked? Others? The good-hearted dealer at Anderson's with his dilapidated stomach and the green eye shade far down upon his death's head? Mrs. Peipenbrink, who served her boarders the best grub in town but charged less than anybody? The old soak against the side of the livery stable, growing there? Pete, with his round horses and dusty rigs for hire? The lazy firemen in their hot red shirts? Banks and railroads did not belong to any of *them* in Telluride, or their friends or friends' friends. They belonged to a perfect stranger, one man in thousands, known to no one who mattered.

"It's well-heeled," George Cassidy said of the San Miguel Valley Bank. "It's worth the trouble."

The McCarthys figured it and thought it might be.

Toward the last of May, Cassidy rode into Telluride and took his old room back at Mrs. Peipenbrink's. She was glad enough to see him to put three kinds of dessert on the supper table instead of two, as though it was Sunday. "Where you been, George?" she said. He told her of dreamlike travels, long celebrations, the "funny ducks" along the way, for he was one who kept his eyes and ears open to what stood off by itself, picked the finicality and left the abstraction to bigger, airier heads.

Mrs. Peipenbrink laughed over, but respected because George respected the "funny ducks" — the white man with his long hair

24

braided into twelve separate braids, one for each moon, the cross-eyed squaw, the skinny fellow who could sing a song in every language under the sun and count up to ten in every language, the old squatter who shot at an antelope, and hit her, and cried because she turned out to be someone he knew.

Madame Laverne in her rosy grotto was glad enough to see Cassidy to open a sixteen-year-old bottle of brandy while Em, Ruth, Rhea and Lillian saluted him with a kiss. Everybody was glad to see him wherever he went. The first thing he did was to renew old acquaintances. Where you been keeping yourself, George? Look who's here! As I live and breathe! Where did you blow from? They greeted him all up and down Main Street. If he shook hands once, he shook hands forty times. Cassidy. You old son of a gun. What do you know?

He is but a young man of twenty-two, a wandering cowpuncher, rancher and miner, nobody, nothing, but eyes light up when he walks in, the heart feels lighter. He smiles like a beam of sun, but it is not that. The curious, honoring, improvident eyes shine with good intent, but it is not that. What, then? Why is one man loved and another scorned? For what he gives or withholds? What he thinks or thinks not? Is it not rather "the harmony within" that steadies like the sight of the Pole Star?

Cassidy rode in one day on a black horse called Little Dipper, and the day after, he set about teaching Little Dipper a trick. The two practised it for hours out on the flats back of Mrs. Peipenbrink's. The lazy firemen used to watch them and so did a lot of people who didn't have anything else to do, even some who had. It was a simple trick. Little Dipper had to stand like a horse carved out of wood, not move an inch, scarcely twitch his eyelids, while George Cassidy, sometimes from far off, sometimes from near, came running for all he was worth with his spurs rattling — gave a big spring! — landed in the saddle! — and grabbed the reins. Instantly, off Little Dipper would tear like a blast of east wind for a mile or more, slow down, circle back and start in all over again. The lazy firemen hollered out comments from time to time and so did other people, and George took off his hat and waved it and hollered something back. It didn't amount to much as a trick but at the same time it was interesting to watch, for the black horse *might* make a bolt for it sometime or sashay off to one side when George came loping — or George might soar clear over him and land on the other side. But Little Dipper never did and neither did George.

Over in Colorado, Tom and Bill McCarthy and Matt Warner and three or four others were teaching their horses the same frivolous trick. On a fine June morning they came into Telluride, not intending to stay, and George was ready to go with them.

Bill and the rest rode leisurely out of town, but George, with Tom McCarthy on one side of him and Matt Warner on the other, had a little unfinished business to do.

Only the bookkeeper was in sight when they entered the San Miguel Valley Bank with black bandannas over the lower halves of their faces and said "All right," said "Reach," said "Keep quiet." The bookkeeper sent his white hands up and his paper cuffs rustled like dry leaves. "Up means up," Tom said. "He's doing fine," George said, and winked at the bookkeeper. Before the minute hand on the big bald-faced wall clock went around once, the bandits were backing out, all the money in sight scooped up in a sack; they turned, ran, jumped on their motionless horses and thundered off in a cloud of dust. Not a shot was fired.

It does not take long to get out of sight in the country between the Dolores and Mancos rivers. The posse, full of heavy breakfast, pounding along a trail two hours cold, never caught a glimpse of them! and the trail faded away like Happy Birthday on the frosting that didn't spin a thread, so there was nothing for them to do but turn back and let the robbers hightail it for Robber's Roost.

Tom McCarthy divided eleven thousand dollars between them, share and share alike, while Matt Warner grumbled that Cassidy should have made sure about the Telluride payroll, not waited till it was gone to the mines. Cassidy promised to go to school to the Pinkertons, and graduate, and hang his diploma on his saddle horn. They stayed awhile together there and then began to drift. The Mccarthys and Matt Warner went to Oregon and Washington, not to settle down, though, and the other riders drifted. . . . Only Cassidy stayed some days on the high plateau on Sam's mesa. In boulder shadows he took his ease or sat and viewed his neighbors, rough old Green River to the east, five black peaks of old Henry Mountains to the south. Then he, too, down one of the three dim trails out of Robber's Roost, drifted. . . .

From that time to this, over three years, he has been an honest man in southern Utah and Wyoming. He has got on as cowhand at various ranches, once or twice has been foreman. Nothing to complain of there! Maybe he will go straight, this Cassidy. The past winter he has done Rock Springs the signal honor to work in its butcher shop, a notion he took, has got the affectionate name of Butch — and Rock Springs in return has outrageously arrested him but released him for lack of evidence. He has cantered away, turning the air blue. Where did he go, this Cassidy?

Dorney wondered sometimes. She tried to guess, looking far away, which direction he had taken once he was out of town but who could tell?

26

When she saw Grandpa Bannon coming home she ran out to the path and waited for him. His chest did not rear out so far now and he did not lift his feet so high off the ground.

"You want something?" he said, pausing. He lifted his hat far enough up to loosen it from the red ridge in his forehead and then tugged it down again. "Hot, ain't it?"

She shook her head.

"Ain't hot?"

"I mean, I didn't want nothing."

"Oh, you sure? Never seen a woman yet that didn't." He began to walk again and she hopped first on one foot and then on the other to his front porch.

"Nothing excepting you tell me the story about him."

"About who?" Grandpa pretended he did not know, his foot on one step.

"You know."

"I've told you already. There ain't no more. Besides, he's gone away now and no telling if anybody will ever hear tell of him again!"

Her heart felt heavy. "It don't have to be — more. You can tell me what you told me before," she suggested, not looking up at him. "The same thing over."

"You won't learn nothing thataway. That's how they do with parrots."

"I don't care."

"Soft spot for old Cassidy, huh? Don't blame you. Son of a gun gets out and travels. Nothing holding *him* down. Won't let nothing."

"Pa!" Nila Bannon called in a voice that could hardly be told apart from her mother's. "Is that you?"

"You know blame well it's me."

"Mother wants you to come in and help turn her mattress."

"Please, Grandpa?" Dorney asked.

"Please what?" He frowned down at her mightily but she did not take offence.

"Tell me again?"

"Trade with him any day . . . " he muttered to himself as he hobbled up the stairs.

Dorney walked lonesomely across the sun-baked yard. This very minute, while Grandpa Bannon had to toe the line and she had to toe the line, the bold outlaw was riding Fiji, called Little Dipper, through a cool canyon or 'cross a rippling plain. They were trotting right along. And Cassidy — Cassidy would pull on the reins and take his hat off and let the fresh breeze blow through his hair while Little Dipper halted, and he would look off to the right or off to the left or straight in front and think, I'll go towards there, and then he'd nudge Little Dipper and off they'd go. Towards there!

She used to wish she was up on that horse behind 'Dair, holding on to him with both hands and her knees pressed in, herself going, with him, two separate people who loved and watched out for each other, father, child. The wish was different now — not to go along but to be going, all alone, up in that saddle on clever Little Dipper, spacious, towering, quick as a flash on the draw, powerful, wonderful so that everyone said YOU are here, and stay, oh, stay. But she would never stay. And Cassidy would never. Other people had to toe the line. Not him!

Grandpa Bannon did not now have to repeat the ancient story of the outlaw from the beginning, when he made friends with Mike Cassidy and learned to shoot and ride, to the end, when, as Butch Cassidy, unjustly accused, he rode out of Rock Springs turning the air blue. After many repetitions Dorney knew it herself by heart as other children knew the story of Jason and the Golden Fleece or Jack the Giant Killer. Grandpa Bannon had not had to tell it to her for a long time past.

Because she did not wheedle, he thought she forgot or did not care, but she did not wheedle because she herself could think of him any time, think thoughts more real than pictures Grandpa could conjure. Any time she wanted, Cassidy could just be bringing back the canteens, be riding into Star Valley, Blufe could just be catching sight of him and waving, smiles all over his face; he could be fording the Colorado, plunging right in not scared a bit to cross; slumping down in his saddle while Little Dipper side-stepped the stones and boulders on the way up, up to Robber's Roost; he could be riding into Telluride again, all on a fair May morning. . . . Traditional as the scenes in an ancient drama, these for Dorney, no word, no gesture ever changing.

Grandpa Bannon did not know about this. He thought she did not care any more.

She had a friend now, a girl her own age, with whom Wanda let her play, a homely little girl named Bernice, with rusty braids. It was not every summer day that she ran across to old Grandpa Bannon, who was getting grumpier all the time, or even every other day.

The truth was, Grandpa Bannon not seeming to set the store by her company he once had done, she did not set the store by his she once had done, either.

Old Mrs. Bannon "dinged" at her husband more than ever, even Wanda said, and Blufe, who might have changed things, never came, and Grandpa Bannon could not go anywhere except on the rare occasions when his daughters were visiting (neighbor women had offered to sit with old Mrs. Bannon so her husband could go out but she refused to avail herself of the service with so much rancor that they were sorry they suggested it). All that, and then his age, too, for he was growing older quickly, worked on Grandpa and changed him into something different from what he had been. Dorney's loving allegiance, so long his, had been recalled and went now to Bernice. Perhaps if Cassidy had kept on . . . hadn't quit, hadn't dropped from sight . . . if Blufe's letters had borne news of exploit and spectacle by him and of him, month after month, year after year, Dorney and Grandpa Bannon would never have grown apart. But not a word of Cassidy from that day to this, only the one little legend to hold the two of them together . . . and it was not enough.

"Grandpa Bannon, I just want to ask you something. Where do you suppose he *is*?"

"Cassidy?" The old man thrust his leg up onto the porch rail and groaned absently. Then he smiled and looked about the same as ever for a minute. "Having a high old time like always, I guess. Raising the dust. Going. . . . Lord, Lord only knows."

Dorney was eleven when the word came, where he was. He was in the Wyoming State Penitentiary! But no, because when Blufe wrote to his father, Cassidy was out again. Had just got out. Had been sentenced for two years for horse-stealing, but the Governor let him out a little beforehand. Even the Governor liked Cassidy!

Grandpa Bannon hollered to her to come over and hear *that* news.

Dorney, at twelve, not only had Bernice, she had a friend named Opal, for another respectable family had moved into the neighborhood, and while she couldn't "run loose," as Wanda persisted in calling the most constrained elbowroom, she could at least go to both their houses, in sight of her sister at all times, no latitude to boast about but better than none. Less and less did she perch upon the bottom step of the Bannon house and talk to Grandpa about anything. He did not seem to miss her. In fact, he seemed just as glad not to see her — she would wave to him when running over to Bernice's or Opal's and he would wave back, but not call, not say, Dorney, ain't you forgetting your old friends?

Sometimes she thought that she was, herself, would feel sorry and ashamed, and rush over, but then Grandpa Bannon as often as not would be cross as a bear.

"What's your teacher learning you?" he would say quarrelsomely. She would tell him and then he would say, "What good's that going to do? Why put something like that in your noggin?"

Dorney would not know, except that it was very pleasant to have knowledge of a palace, the Alhambra! of Japan where they hated

29

cats because the cat and the snake were the only creatures who did not cry when Buddha died! of Buddha himself, the statue, with the six-inch-long earlobes (from wearing such heavy jeweled earrings when he was a rich man before he gave everything away) and the pot belly. Very delightful to get something like that into your noggin, something about the Mound Builders, the planets lined up around the sun, names of flowers, saxifrage, bend with the gales, brabas nod, Jacob's ladder globeflower; names of birds, white-throated swift, flycatcher, magpie, greentailed towhee, pygmy nuthatch and willow thrush.

"What good's it do you?"

It *felt* good, that was all. Dorney tried to tell Grandpa Bannon how good it felt to have been taught, to have learned these things.

"Must be crazy," was all he would say, grumpily. "That teacher!"

But when Dorney told him about knights going to war in gold and silver armor, with shields and plumes and sticks in their arms as long as a telephone pole, he liked to listen to that and said, "Well, go on," irritably, when she quit because she didn't know any more.

"I guess you don't remember your old friend Butch Cassidy no more, do you?" He had called her over this April afternoon and now he was looking severe and put-upon as she came running across the yard.

"Don't care nothing for *him* no more, I guess. Rather hear some damn foolishness about some king or something. All got a screw loose in the head, fellow told me once. As soon marry their own sister as look at her. Sooner. Guess you lost all interest in *him*." He scowled.

"Who said so?" she said, beaming.

"Well, ain't you?"

"Who said so?" She took her old seat on the bottom step.

"Well, listen then. You used to wonder what become of him —"

She sat upright.

" — after he rode outa Rock Springs. Didn't you used to wonder?"

"Sure," she whispered. Not so much, not so often, not what became of him. Not wonder. Rather, think of what he had primigenously *been* until the hour he went away — that was Dorney's classic.

"Thought he set the world on fire, I bet," he sneered. "Thought he — no telling *what* you thought."

"I didn't think of anything," she said defensively, "really I didn't."

"Old Cassidy." Grandpa Bannon fingered Blufe's letter, and the mention of the name somehow softened him. "All he done," he said, "all he done when he left here, was, he went back to cow-

30

punching. Course," he confided gently, "he rustled just a little on the side."

Of course he did.

" — but never from the folks he was working for — never — for that would of been something he couldn't stomach — bosses never had anything to complain of, on that score — "

Of course they didn't!

" — and, in fact, he was the best hand they had. But you know how Cassidy was. Go along so long, and then — he'd get restless."

Of course, he'd get restless. Little Dipper, too. . . .

Cassidy played cards with a red-bearded man named Al Hainer (a young fellow who had been going to kill himself over a girl at one time but changed his mind) and soon they were partners. When autumn came, they went to the Wind River country in Wyoming, bought a ranch north of the town of Lander, close to the little settlement of Dubois, became ranchers and horse dealers, the kind who never buy, only sell, but nobody paid any attention to that.

Beside a trickle of water they had a cabin with a cookstove in it, a table and two benches, a lamp and a few dishes.

Nights, they wrapped up in blankets and slept on the floor. In that region, it was easy to round up cattle, horses, easy to get rid of them (nobody the wiser till it was too late). They did fine.

It looked desolate, uninhabited, that gnarled country, but it was livelier than it looked. Once the two young ranchers roped a mountain lion and once a grizzly bear, yellow eyeballs smoking, and both times, Butch wanted to turn them lose!

The winter, after so soft an autumn, surprised the partners by starting off with a blizzard the like of which nobody could remember to have seen before in those parts.

It started with a blizzard, ended with a blizzard, nothing but blizzards between — the meanest winter ever to hit Wyoming! Thousands upon thousands of stock froze or starved to death. There was no way to rescue them, would not have been even if able-bodied men had been about, to try it, but they were few and far between. Then, everybody took sick, a fine state of affairs in a community without a doctor! They were not without medicine, however, for on a ranch fifty miles away from Cassidy's, the widow Mrs. Simpson lived, and she brewed a remedy that seemed to help the sufferers. The difficulty was, to get it to them. Al Hainer was sick too, so Cassidy went alone while the epidemic raged, to Mrs. Simpson's time and again, and from her place through the great high drifts to the isolated cabins with her medicine. When he could, he lent a hand with the stock.

In April, the partners pulled out and sold their ranch to the first bidder.

Nobody ever wanted to see another winter like that one. There was hardly an animal left on the range. Dozens of penniless cowboys were given their walking papers, set roaming, and many took to rustling. It was the poorest time in the world to do so, for the hard-hit stockmen, once so indifferent, now stood guard like an elderly mother over one toddler, memorizing and tallying every animal they owned. When even one was gone, let alone four, seven or ten, they set up a holler that could be heard for miles. These stockmen organized against the rustlers (who might be anybody! including sheriffs and deputies) and vowed to rid the country of them or bust.

One day not far from Lander a bunch of sixty horses turned up missing and the owner offered a big reward to get them back. A deputy started out to try to locate them — and did, in the McCarthy's old hide-out in Star Valley. The nearest little town was Afton, and the deputy went to the postmaster there and asked him if a couple of men by the name of so-and-so and so-and-so (he made a good guess) were getting their mail there. The postmaster said yes, they were.

The daughter of a nearby rancher, named Kate, rode in every week and got the family's mail and picked up their mail, too, at the same time.

When next Kate, a pretty girl, called at the post office and started back home, two men trailed right along behind her, the deputy and a Montana officer who was also on a hunt for stolen horses. When they thought she was getting close to her destination they rode up and stopped her, and after she had got as red as she could get, and then as white, she told them where they could find the men they wanted. They had a cabin right in back of that little rise — there, to the left. One of them was working at a sawmill off to the east about a quarter of a mile. The other one was not feeling so well and had stayed home.

The deputies took the girl, crying, along with them for safekeeping, and went after the man at the sawmill. He wasn't expecting them, was unarmed. They overpowered and tied him to a tree, then went back to the cabin for the other fellow.

Butch Cassidy was taking a cat-nap, no more. He heard them instantly, knew it was no light girl that came up on the porch! He grabbed for a gun in the holsters hanging over the chair back . . . but the deputies were quick, bold, too, had the door wide open before he could blink. If he had been one to shoot first and ask questions afterwards! but he never was. . . . He went out like a light, and when he came to, a few seconds later, with a fiery furrow plowed along his scalp by the bullet that had stunned him and buried itself in the cabin wall, the officers had him right where they wanted him.

They took him and Al Hainer back to Lander where he had so many friends that surely no jury would convict him! Never in this world. But the Stockgrowers' Association, with plenty of money to spend, saw that a jury was sworn in, who would, and they did. Butch Cassidy was sent up for two years!

The night before he was to be taken to Laramie City to the state penitentiary, he asked the jailer if he could go out for the evening, and the jailer said he could if he would promise to come back.

He promised, and at ten past three in the morning he rapped lightly at the rear door of the jail. While waiting to be let in he sang a song:

> "Half a score of cabins there,
> And in one a maiden fair
> Held the heart of Billy Venero,
> Billy Venero, Billy Venero,
> Held the heart of Billy Venero,
> Billy Venero's little Bess. . . ."

He had served a year and a half of his sentence when the Governor of Wyoming inspected the prison, and Cassidy saw him and had a few minutes conversation with him. Right after, he was given his pardon. Too bad the Governor didn't make his inspection sooner!

Riding a black horse, Cassidy went up the old Outlaw Trail on a freezing January day, heading for Brown's Hole, one of the great hide-outs, a cliff-rimmed valley in three states, Wyoming, Utah and Colorado. Matt Warner, married now, lived there, but the McCarthy gang, after Bill McCarthy and his son Fred were shot down on the streets of Delta and Tom had gone nobody knew where, no longer existed.

He built a cabin high up on Diamond Mountain on a sandstone ledge with cliffs like walls to three sides of it. . . .

And there's where he was this minute!

"What do you suppose he'll do now?" Dorney asked concernedly

Grandpa Bannon put the letter he had not read aloud from but only consulted from time to time, back in his pocket.

The pain lingered, that had clutched her when hearing the news that Cassidy, who never had had to stay anywhere or do anything he didn't want to do (not like her, not like Grandpa Bannon), had been put in prison behind bars.

But it was all right now! He was up there on Diamond Mountain, he could light out and go, any time, even stay, for it sounded a high,

33

wide, handsome place. She turned to Grandpa Bannon. "You never did tell me," she said, "how he looks, exactly. You were going to once, but then you didn't. How does he?" All of a sudden it was important to know.

"Why, he's about —" Grandpa began, and stopped. His habit was not to look at her, to scowl just above or around or beyond where she sat, but he looked this time, curiously and kindly, as kindly as for a long time, with wild old parrot eyes. "What's your own guess?" he said. "What would you imagine?"

She shut her eyes a minute and tried to picture long-dead 'Dair Yandle. . . .

It is possible to see but the dim outlines of the truly beloved, or one part at a time: the eyes, glinting and knowing; a quick flash of the lips; the hand, one hand, handling a fork, a pipe, lying on the chair arm, lifted to the face; the damp hair, combed for Sunday; the fine ear, the foot in the narrow boot. . . . Never all these together at once, never, never. The dim outline, the large all-over shadow — or the vivid glints, the flashes. There is a disease which acts this way: the sufferer may read a page of print, read and recognize every word of every line, but never may he connect the word he reads and recognizes with the word which went before or the word which comes after. Thus are the lost, the dearly beloved, remembered, tantalizingly, the sense of them gone.

She opened her eyes in disappointment.

"Well," she said slowly, "he's real tall — and he's got brown eyes — and his teeth are white — and he's got black hair — curly — and he's —" She could see him very certainly for the first time. "Is that right?" she asked.

"I've saw him," Grandpa Bannon reminded her, still curiously and kindly, still looking at her and not around and beyond.

"I know!"

"I can tell you just exactly."

"I know you can, Grandpa Bannon. Is he —"

Grandpa cupped his chin in his hand. "You know, it's a funny thing —" he said.

"Real tall," she repeated pleadingly, "real, real tall, with brown eyes and black curly hair and white teeth and —"

" — but I declare you've hit the nail right on the head!"

"I have?" She hugged her knees joyously.

"Yes, you have. That's Butch Cassidy for you, right to the life."

4

DORNEY, CONFIDED IN BY THEM, CONFIDED ALL IN
return to her two friends, Opal and Bernice, except mention of Butch
Cassidy's name and word of the fame she and Grandpa Bannon had
bestowed upon him. Whether now, after the years of Miss Littley's
moral training, Dorney was ashamed of the hero of her little girl-
hood (as she was to say that 'Dair Yandle was once her brother-
in-law), whether because she had solemnly promised Grandpa Bannon not to blab, or whether, at a time when life itself was so full
of marvels (longer skirts, autograph books and graduation coming),
the old saga had paled beside them — Bernice and Opal were spared
it. They were unimpeachable little creatures, duteous and inerr-
able. Possibly Dorney feared they would bob about in such a buoyant wind, and it may also have been that, though seldom recalled
now, his image was yet too great a treasure to be disesteemed or set
at naught. Whatever the reason, they chattered about a good many
things, those three little friends, but not about Cassidy.

Grandpa Bannon, watching Dorney go about her small affairs
with malevolent old eyes — when he had time to watch, for his
tyrant, entirely bedfast now and grown worse in all ways, let him
stray less and less to the porch or sit undisturbed by the window
without calling him in — considered letting Dorney go uninformed
about the famous Montpelier Bank robbery that had taken place
in the past week. It would serve her right, with her snippy little
friends. But Grandpa Bannon recalled her eyes going dark and how
she would change from the bottom to the top step if he told something interesting enough. The ambition of the bard, long denied an
audience, again stirred within him. He called out to her irritably to
come over and hear something! if she wasn't too high and mighty.
When she came running, he told her that Butch had a gang of his
own now — The Wild Bunch, named so for the wild things they
did — with headquarters on Diamond Mountain! told her that
Cassidy and two of his young lieutenants rode down to Montpelier,
Idaho, and cleaned out the bank there of $7500 without turning a
hair. Nobody got put out of commission when Butch was running

35

the show! Mind you, his own gang. No more taking orders from somebody else. HE was the boss now.

Dorney's eyes did go dark in the old way but she did not move to the top step.

"What's the matter with you?" Grandpa asked contentiously.

"Nothing, Grandpa." Would it not have been much better for Butch Cassidy to stay up there on Diamond Mountain and — be honest, she thought, not hold up banks, not have a gang of his own? For the first time, she wished that she could get to him and tell him all the many things she herself had been told about right and wrong. It would be early in the morning. Diamond Mountain. . . . Oh, how easily she would run up, up it under the pink sky, with flowers whose names she had learned (they bloomed at home but seldom) to either side of her feet, with birds whose names she had learned (but saw most rarely) singing and flying in the green bushes, the green trees. As she gazes, stock-still, the door of the cabin opens, and he comes out . . . comes smiling, comes welcoming. It does not matter that never did she go with Grandpa Bannon into the butcher shop when he was there and have a proper introduction. She says quickly, I am Dorney — Dorney Leaf — Miss Dorney Leaf, and a house does not have to fall on *him*. He knows at once. I'll tell you why I came, Mister Cassidy. I came because — but it does not matter why! He tells her it does not with that look that makes the woman put three kinds of dessert on the table when he will sup, makes the great Governor let him out of prison. And he forgets why, says where's old Fiji anyhow, that Little Dipper? Him? says Cassidy. That old son of a gun? He puts two fingers to his lips and gives a whistle and look at him, here he comes!

"If you don't care about nothing no more, why, it's no skin of my nose," Grandpa said. "Keep these things to myself, should of. Should of kept 'em to myself anyway. When you used to be — why, you used to come over and a fellow could — but now — kids sure change. People sure change. Getting so a fellow ain't got nobody no more. . . . no satisfaction out of nobody. . . ."

Dorney blinked up at him.

"What's the matter with you, anyway?" he said viciously. He meant, Why am I so lonely? Why have I grown so old?

"If you can't be civil," he said — and his face shook all over like a mountain that is going to erupt, and sure enough it did and tears ran down its crevices, "why — stay *home*, where you belong."

Dorney stood up, indignant. "I haven't said a word," she said. "Not a word."

"You have too," he said furiously, rubbing his horny hands over his wet face. "Wrangling and talking back, just like everybody, 'stead of using manners."

36

She stared at him open-mouthed.

"Now gop. Stand there and gop!"

She turned and fled.

Wanda said, when Dorney told her, crying, that she would never speak to Grandpa Bannon again as long as she lived, that of course Dorney would. All that was the matter with Grandpa Bannon, he was in his second childhood again. Why, he was seventy-six years old! He didn't mean to quarrel and run his friends off — he just couldn't help himself. Besides, he had had almost ten years of you-know-what on earth, with old Mrs. Bannon, and that would surely change a man's nature.

"Why does he *let* her boss him around like that?" Dorney asked.

"He lets her, that's all," Wanda said, making the careful cuts on the folded round of thin piecrust which would, when laid over the bumpy apples in the crust-lined pan, show three half moons above, three below, and a daisy in the middle. "They say, when the Bannons was young, he was the boss and she was the one jumped to his bidding. But somewhere along the line the tables got turned, she got the upper hand some way, and there you are. Maybe he thinks about her having his ten kids one after the other, and working her fingers to the bone when she was able, and now she's flat of her back, helpless. Maybe she couldn't of got the upper hand no way else. A person never really knows how such things happen."

"I wouldn't let her do to *me* like she's done to poor Grandpa!" Dorney said sternly. "I'd leave her lay right there, and go away, and never come back, and see how she liked it *then*."

"You don't know what you'd do," Wanda said, crimping the edges of her pie.

Dorney went back that very day to beg forgiveness of Grandpa, just before supper, when she saw him come out to throw away the potato peelings. She slipped over, not afraid of his ill temper, for, as Wanda said, he was in his second childhood and that meant he was only someone younger than herself disguised as a sour old man. He said he would grant pardon, after some frowning thought, if she would mind her manners better, and she, having no idea how she had transgressed, promised that she would.

"Remember old Beauty?" he said suddenly, shaking the empty pan as if there were some more peelings in it to fall on the cinder heap. "Used to tie her right there." He pointed through the gathering twilight. "Stood you on your feet, for one. You just remember that sometime, when you get to feeling high and mighty."

"I sure wish you had a nice cow like Beauty now," Dorney said gently.

"I don't!" he said. He began to walk back to the house and she followed along beside him, as tall as his bent self.

"Grandpa, let's you and me not quarrel any more, shall we?"

"Ain't *my* fault," he said. "*I* never done no quarreling."

She wanted to say, Why, Grandpa Bannon, it was TOO your fault, it always is, because most of the time you're as cross as a bear! but she didn't.

"Let's always be nice to each other, and friends, like we used to be, shall we, Grandpa?"

"*I* ain't got no objections. It ain't *me* that runs with two little know-it-alls and don't care nothing for nobody no more!"

She walked to the house with him, saw the lamplighted kitchen through the open door. As clean as a pin, Grandpa kept it, but it looked lonesome inside there. Long ago, the neighbor ladies had stopped coming, wounded, each one, by old Mrs. Bannon's sharp tongue, and nobody else came, only a sharp-tongued daughter now and again, none of the boys, who had scattered like geese, only Blufe, and it had been years now since he was here. But he was coming soon! Grandpa Bannon said that he was. "Blufe'll be coming this fall. Bet you don't remember *him*, do you?"

"Oh, yes, I do," she said.

"Blufe's a boy that — " he began.

Then the voice broke in, coming from just beyond his shoulder, through the dark half-open window.

Dorney had not seen old Mrs. Bannon for a long time as the lady did not like children very well ("young ones," she called them, "traipsing-through-a-person's-house-and-getting-into-everything"), but old Mrs. Bannon sounded just the same.

"Who you gabbing with out there, Will?" she whined.

"You know very well."

"Answer me, Will Bannon."

"Just Dorney."

"Why ain't she home helping her sister with the work once in a while?"

"Why ain't you — ?" Grandpa stopped without finishing the question.

Dorney began to edge away in the blue darkness. "Well, I got to go," she whispered. "Remember what we said."

"Why ain't I what?" old Mrs. Bannon wailed. "I heard you."

"Nothing, Mother. Hush a minute. I'm coming."

Dorney started, stopped to wave a hand like a flash of wing, flew homeward. . . .

"Why ain't I what?" the voice droned on.

"I'm coming."

"Answer me this minute, Will Bannon!"

"I *am* answering." He stood very still with his empty pan dangling down beside him and looked at nothing on the dark porch.

"Why ain't I WHAT? I heard you. I heard what you said."
He said something under his breath.

Supper tasted good to Dorney. The whole evening was good, even with Thomas's scolding about the ink stain on her challis dress and then later snoring on the couch in his sock feet. Tommy and little Pearl went to bed charmingly with no argument, heard charmingly the story of Snow White and Rose Red, went charmingly to sleep. The dishes were easy! No pans! at least, none that had to be scoured. Light as a feather does he sail in the air who comes together again with his disaffected friend, and Dorney, light as a feather till bedtime, was glad she had begged forgiveness.

"You went over and made up with Grandpa Bannon, did you?" Wanda asked, sitting down by the center table when the kitchen work was done and reaching for her mending.

Dorney nodded.

"What did you and him happen to fight about anyway?"

"I don't know. He just got mad and told me to go home. I don't even know."

"What was you talking about anyway?"

"Oh — nothing. Just talking."

"Poor old soul," Wanda said, pulling out a black thread from her needle and poking in a white one. "Day after day and month after month, she keeps on living, and he seems to stay about the same. I wonder how long it will last?"

It lasted until school started, till fall came, and then, it ended.

Early one morning, just when the lamps had been lighted in the cold dark kitchens and the matches set to the fires in the stoves, while whoever was first up in a given household stood yawning and scratching and trying to get warm by the initially but ornamental flames, a commotion started in the Bannon house. First — it sounded like a crazy man screaming in an asylum, and then like a crazy woman, and then, like both of them together, and then, like a dog or a coyote with its leg caught in a big bear trap, and by that time Wanda, for one, in her old wrapper and flapping slippers, was racing over there, and Mrs. Stroble, for another, was racing from the other side, and somebody from off the daybreak streets, a man or two with lunch buckets, were racing through the gate — and then the shots rang out from the old gun that nobody remembered Grandpa Bannon had owned — one! two! three! four! — five! came after an instant's pause.

When they found her, shot four times, floating on a red puddle in the middle of the feather mattress, old Mrs. Bannon didn't have her sharp tongue any more, or her two sly eyes or her two pricked

39

ears. She didn't even have a head — at least it seemed not at first, it lolled back so far above the red slit in her throat.

They found Grandpa Bannon dead in the kitchen, stretched out with his head amid the lumps of coal by the overturned scuttle and his feet under the table and the old six-shooter beside him. They thought he was dead, speechless and horror-struck Wanda, Mrs. Stroble and the two men, each with a lunch bucket they started to put on the table, but didn't, it was so neatly set (for the breakfast of oatmeal mush, now bubbling on the stove, that would be cold, congealed, scraped out by a solemn neighbor), and instead they put one on a chair seat, one on a bureau where a well-wound clock struck that instant six times. They knelt beside him, felt gingerly with fingertips to one side of the sticky stain on his faded shirt front and found that his heart was still beating. Then his eyes opened, scaring Wanda as if a corpse's eyes, shut for hours, had opened, opened wider, closed again. . . .

His heart beat for three days, until the evening of the day old Mrs. Bannon, not fit to be seen again even by the six of her ten children who lived close enough to be on hand, had been buried after rites at Smutz's Funeral Parlor attended by nearly all the white populace in Rock Springs. Then it stopped. Everybody was glad because it would have been a terrible thing to have to arrest an old Rock Springs citizen seventy-six years old for murder, try him and either hang him by the neck till dead or put him in prison for the rest of his natural life.

The fact that Grandpa Bannon was so old was what stumped everybody. His life, his trouble and torment was so nearly over! Ten years at the very utmost, probably less, much less, such a little while. Surely, he could have waited. It was Wanda who said that second childhood was not very different from first childhood in this, perhaps: the way time seems. She said, take a child, he thinks it's forever till his birthday, till Christmas, he thinks he can't stand it till summer comes, the Fourth of July. Say it's Monday and you promise him you will take him down and buy him a new pair of shoes and a sack of candy on Saturday — and Saturday, why, that's till the end of the world! It must have been like that with poor Grandpa — time looked like that, different from the way it looks to us — and he waited and waited, impatient, as a child will wait, and then couldn't wait another minute. . . .

Wanda went often over to the Bannon's conspicious small house full of relatives and neighbors, taking a pie or cake and offering to do this and that, but she would not let Dorney go and see the scene, see Grandpa Bannon suffering.

Dorney cried nervously every day until Grandpa died — she was so afraid they would arrest him and put him in prison. She knew

40

which one of the three sons Blufe was and she wanted to go and talk to him, but Wanda said no. She did not know what she would have said to him anyway, exactly. (So much must not be said: even if you didn't like your mother, Blufe, you should have come home sometimes and visited poor Grandpa because he thought such a lot of you. He got lonesome. Anything you wrote about in your letters, he took right up, as if he was the one it happened to, he took up your friends like he had known them for years. Butch Cassidy, that Grandpa spoke to only once that time in the butcher shop, never had a better friend in his life than Grandpa because Butch happened to be your friend. He said — oh, really, you should have come home!) Dorney wanted to run to Butch Cassidy's friend, she looked over there often, sniveling, in the hopes to see him, great Blufe, Grandpa Bannon's great son, but he came and went and did not know she existed. (And what would she have said?)

She asked if Mrs. Blufe Bannon had come with her husband and Wanda said she couldn't come as she was tied down at home with a little baby, their third child. Wanda said that Blufe, by the way, looked like a sick man, not just from grief and worry but from some ailment. At times he was yellow as saffron. Dorney caught a glimpse of him at both his mother's funeral, and two days later at his father's, and it was true that he looked yellow and ill.

Bernice and Opal went to Grandpa Bannon's funeral and sat beside Dorney. When she dabbed at her eyes with her handkerchief, they did the same thing with theirs, but they did not really grieve, for, as they said later on, Grandpa Bannon was nothing but a cruel, wicked murderer just like Bluebeard and had no more chance of getting to heaven than a snake.

That was what caused the big quarrel between the three friends. Dorney flew off the handle and told them Grandpa Bannon was worth the both of them put together, their mothers, fathers and all their relations, all put together, and that he was, was, WAS in heaven. It took several days for them to make up, Bernice and Opal, and Dorney, and after that they were never quite the same again.

She did not completely miss him until spring when she read (for now she was a big girl of thirteen, and read the paper by the advice of Miss Littley, who told all her girl scholars that if they ever wanted to be "emancipated" — whatever that might mean — they would have to read the news) about the big robbery at Castle Gate, Utah. Butch Cassidy was suspected, it said so plainly right in the newspaper! She stared at the name for a long time, for it was the first time she had ever seen it in print with her own two eyes. Butch Cassidy, down off Diamond Mountain again, riding Little Dipper! The Wild Bunch right alongside him. It mentioned them here,

41

Butch's gang — The Wild Bunch. She read it over marveling: ". . . suspected to have been perpetrated by the notorious George LeRoy Parker, alias Butch Cassidy, and his gang, The Wild Bunch." They got $9000! The payroll for the big Castle Gate coal camp had just arrived on the Denver & Rio Grande train from Salt Lake City, the paymaster had picked it up and started up the stairs to his office, located over a store, when Butch took the satchel away from him . . . just stuck his gun in the paymaster's ribs, said "All right, mister," and took it! Then leaped on his horse and galloped away, six riders following. Posses had been organized, were on the trail . . . would probably soon catch the criminals. It said!

Too excited to sit, she got up and walked to the window, stared at the Bannon's empty house. It came, then, the blank, gulping feeling of loss, of grief, for the very first time. Wouldn't she have ran across the yard, though, to talk this over? Maybe old Mrs. Bannon would have kept him so busy up to then that he wouldn't have had time to see the paper with its story, and when he came out through the door to take his seat on the porch (it was spring now, warm spring), sighing over his old back, and pulled his glasses down off the ridge in his forehead, and opened up the Rock Springs *Evening Herald*, she would be watching and waiting! Would fly over there, say, "Grandpa Bannon! What do you guess? What do you think Cassidy has gone and done?" while Grandpa, poor, miserable lost old Grandpa Bannon, would brighten all up and say — and then she would plump down on the bottom step and say — and they would say — say to each other — For the first time she knew what it meant to be bereft: *You had something to tell, and the only one in the world to tell it to, was gone.* Her throat got a bigger and bigger lump in it, and while she gazed through the window, the old house wavered and blurred like a house beneath running water.

5

DORNEY, WITH BERNICE AND OPAL, AND A BOY
named Herman, and a boy named Sam, and two Scandinavians
named Hilma and Oscar, was graduated from the eighth grade in May.
Wanda made her a very pretty dress of white lawn and put up her
hair the night before, in rags. It stayed in curl for an entire week,
long after the two little crêpe paper baskets of flowers she got (and
had her picture taken with) had withered, the stiffly rolled diploma
had been unrolled, looked at, rolled up again and the white satin
ribbon band slipped back on with the elegantly tied bow intact,
fifty times, and Dorney, tired of it at last, had put the famous
document away in a drawer.

Nobody suggested that she go on to High School. In the first
place, there wasn't a High School near enough for her to go to, and
in the second place, what would be the good of it? That was what
Mrs. Diltz said, and Thomas, too.

Wanda had indulged her from babyhood (except in the matter of
letting her "run"), imposed few tasks — in fact, all she generally had
to do was dry the supper dishes, iron the handkerchiefs and doilies
and help keep an eye on the children. However, now that her
charge's formal education was at an end, her elder sister thought that,
in preparation for womanhood and a home of her own, Dorney
should have lessons in housekeeping and learn how to cook something besides molasses candy and gingerbread men. She also had
plans of a social nature. From hence, Dorney would attend the
weekly meetings of the Ladies' Quilting and Sewing Society, be allowed to accompany Wanda on all shopping tours, few though they
were, enroll in the Young People's Debating, Literary and Shakespeare Club and go to Christian Endeavor. That way, she would be
sure to meet the best class of "young people" and in three or four
years would find a nice husband with a good steady job. Besides,
Wanda and Thomas would start taking Dorney to the dances.

After Christmas, she was taken in as a bona fide member of the
Ladies' Quilting and Sewing Society, so old an organization that
even her mother had belonged to it. Bernice was taken in, too

43

(Opal's mother did not attend). They were the youngest members. The ladies always looked about for them before they made certain statements, to see if they were out of earshot, and if they were not, leaned and half whispered whatever it was, said it behind a hand or garbled it radically. This always made the youngest (or unmarried) members blush, not for what was said but how the sayer had said it.

Thomas flatly refused to take in the dances, but he let Wanda go with Dorney in the company of Mr. and Mrs. Stroble, two globular people who liked nothing better than dancing with each other round and round in a rub-a-dub-dub three-men-in-a-tub fashion. Dorney learned to waltz, two-step and polka. At home, her domestic education was progressing, too. She learned how to iron a starched shirt, how to keep a fruit pie from running over in the oven (but this never got past the theoretical stage), and how to make a ruffle and sew it on.

She had not yet a sweetheart, for at the dances, Christian Endeavor and the Debating, Literary and Shakespeare Society, she was so backward that if a boy spoke to her, she grew dumb, but Wanda saw how the "young people" looked at her and knew that it would not be long before one of these would come who would loosen her tongue. Then, it would hang in the middle and wag at both ends! Wouldn't it, though! All he had to do was show up.

Wanda did not live to see him do it.

She took sick on a Monday (though Dorney hung the wet clothes out in the windy March weather), was worse on Tuesday, better Wednesday — so she said — much, much worse on Thursday and terrifyingly ill on Friday. Saturday, at noon, Wanda died.

She was buried on Dorney's fourteenth birthday.

Mrs. Diltz at once took poor Thomas, Tommy and Pearl into her own home to live with herself and Ora. Her house was bigger than theirs. After her first grief for Wanda had spent itself (the first day Mrs. Diltz cried a pintful, the second day a wineglassful, and the third day just enough to dampen her handkerchief, like cologne) she seemed born anew — bigger, taller, years younger, and looked so exactly as she had looked when her son Thomas was her grandson Ora's age that everybody was astonished. Her friends said she was equal to the crisis, rising from her ashes, living to fight again, weathering the storm — which only went to show what a real mother could do when her son needed her! (Nobody suggested that all this store of vigor, power, and exuberance might have been called on all along to benefit somebody besides that one lone child). She took Dorney into her house, too, along with her son and grandchildren, when Thomas gave up the house and moved the furniture over to his mother's, but not to stay.

44

Mrs. Diltz had never approved of the way Wanda let Dorney "have it so easy." She said now — and it was perfectly reasonable — that why should Thomas be saddled with the responsibility of feeding and clothing a big girl like Dorney Leaf, when she wasn't even related to him? No, she said, the thing to do with Dorney was, she ought to either go out to California and live with her father and that foreign stepmother, or else she had ought to go down and live with her sister Madge Yandle in Salt Lake City.

Mr. Leaf, when contacted, wrote sorrowfully that he was not doing by any means as well as he had hoped in California. Benedicta's eldest son was working, but her twin girls were still at home and it was to be feared that they and Dorney might not get along together. Besides, he and Benedicta now had four children of their own, besides Benedicta's son who was Dorney's age, seven in all. Much as he would like to have her, he said, he felt that under the circumstances it might be better for all concerned if Dorney went down to Salt Lake City and stayed with Madge. He would keep in close touch with them, he said, and begged that they would keep in close touch with him, Dorney, especially, who, being his first wife's last child, was very dear to his heart. He sent his condolences, his true love and his best wishes that everything would work out the best way possible for all concerned. If Dorney had ever known him, she would have known that the blots all over his letter were where real, warm tears had splashed upon the notepaper, not where he had spilled water or raindrops had accidentally fallen. A second letter, however, he did not answer; at least not for a very long time.

Madge could not come to the funeral but she wrote a long letter to Thomas "and all" and said what a shock it was and how sorry she was to hear that her beloved sister Wanda had died when she was still so young and they had all needed her so much. Then, some days later, she sent an answer to Thomas's and Mrs. Diltz's letters about what to do with Dorney. She had two girls of her own, she said, and she thought it was Papa's place to let her come and live with him and his wife out in California. If, as they said, Papa could not see his way clear to do it, why, she supposed she could take Dorney into her own home. But it did seem somewhat of an imposition, to take over a responsibility which belonged to Papa. Of course, one redeeming feature was that Dorney was practically grown, it was not as if she was a child. . . . Yes, she could come, if she would hold up her end of the bargain. Madge would meet her at the station.

"Surely you remember your sister Madge," globular Mrs. Stroble said, when Dorney dropped in to say goodbye. "You ought to enjoy living with her and her daughters, although Madge was never a bit like Wanda or your mother either. How much older are they than you anyway? Madge's girls?"

"Crystal is three years older and Jetta is one year," Dorney said. She remembered her sister, quite well. Madge was not one to whom one ran, upon whose lap one clambered, but she had looked pretty and had reddish hair. She also remembered her nieces — white-skinned Crystal and small and wizened Jetta, who was suspected to have worms or at least something that made her a little different from other children.

"You must of been about six when they left here and went down to Salt Lake, wasn't you? That would make the oldest girl nine and the youngest girl about seven, then," Mrs. Stroble said cutting a slice of cake and giving it to Dorney to eat with her fingers. "After 'Dair Yandle was shot over that woman or whatever it was, when they brought him home and dumped him down in front of poor Madge, wearing that red sash. Madge took the kids and left right after, didn't she?"

Dorney nodded.

"Funny she ain't been home, not even to her own sister's funeral, but then I suppose — "

"Well, she couldn't come, because she's got a good job, where she can be home nights, instead of having to stay there," Dorney apologized, "and she hasn't had it very long, she said in her letter."

"Stay where? What kind of a job?"

"Stay at the people's house where she works," Dorney said. "She's the cook, and she says that generally cooks have to live on the premises, but these people let her come in the morning and go home at night. She likes to go home, of course, to be with the girls, and besides, she gets good pay, and she likes it. It's some judge she works for, and his wife. She likes it."

"I guess you don't remember *him* a-tall, do you, Dorney?"

"Who?"

"Wanda's husband, 'Dair Yandle."

The name was one that had not been often spoken in Thomas Diltz's house, he was so against dishonesty. Even when Thomas was not by, Wanda was careful not to speak of the brother-in-law who had "disgraced" them (though she had been fond of 'Dair, too, and grieved at his funeral). Grandpa Bannon was the only one who had mentioned him from time to time, to Dorney. Mrs. Stroble never had, until now.

"I can still see him ride up on that big black horse of his — Blackie, or something, he was called — " Mrs. Stroble said.

"Fiji," Dorney said softly.

" 'Dair Yandle was a little too good-looking for comfort, I always said. No wonder Madge was jealous."

"He let me ride up behind him once or twice, on Fiji," Dorney added, still more softly.

46

"Well, God rest his soul, anyway. It's nine years now. I wonder if Madge's girls are much like him?"

Mrs. Diltz, temporarily her guardian, did not care if Dorney took a long stroll through Rock Springs the day before she left, and she went first to bid her friends goodbye and then, heavy of heart, for a walk. She went past the butcher shop where Butch Cassidy had worked — how many years ago was it? and glanced in at the sawdust-covered floor, saw the shadowy red and white carcasses hanging on the big hooks, the chopping block, the glistening implements. Back of that counter, that very one, in the shadows, he had stood, laughing, being a butcher for a joke — everybody knew him — and through this very door, that time, Grandpa Bannon had walked, went up to Cassidy, told who he was, shook hands. . . . Out of this door Butch Cassidy came when he got through work at night. He stood right here a moment, thinking where to go, as she was standing. Dorney looked down at her feet, up again. And down this street, that ran right along in front of her, down this very street he rode on Fiji — on Little Dipper — leaving Rock Springs forever, that one last time, turning the air blue. Never again would she stand where he had truly stood, for she was leaving too. She had lost them all — 'Dair Yandle and Grandpa Bannon and Wanda — but she had not lost Butch Cassidy. She looked as far away past the shafthouses and black smokestacks as she could, past the edge of town, past the horizon. He was alive somewhere, off in that direction, or that, or that, and so she still had him. Not only did she have him, she could see him, whenever she wanted, not flashes only, not a dim outline, as with the known beloved dead, but see him plain as we can see the unknown, see him forever. Her heart was not so heavy when she started down the street again and turned the corner.

But tears came, that she blinked away, when she went past the only home she had ever had, beheld it empty, next the Bannon's empty house. She wanted to open the gate and go and sit on Grandpa Bannon's bottom step once more, twist her head and look upward, but a sudden flickering chill ran down her back and she stayed on the path. Gone forever, Grandpa Bannon to whom she might have been so kind. Gone forever, Wanda, at the back door, calling her away from the old gray blanket amid her doll rags to have some jelly and bread. Gone forever, the golden time, the happy time.

But Butch Cassidy was still alive! She stopped suddenly and turned and looked back at Grandpa Bannon's alder tree where the target had been tacked. The young outlaw had ridden round it in a dizzy circle, firing shot after shot. A dream, of course, not true, just

47

something Grandpa had pictured to astonish her long ago. But it seemed true. It seemed so true that while she stared even now, it was there, the tiny white oblong, the target, and she had the feeling that if she walked up quite close to the trunk and looked, she would see the bullet holes, see where Butch Cassidy had hit that ace of spades dead center, every single time. . . .

6

DORNEY, IN THE MIDDLE OF THE DENVER & RIO Grande Station in Salt Lake City, was looking in every direction but the right one when a hand was laid on her sleeve. As if unexpectedly accosted, she whirled blushing, although she had known that some- one would meet her.

"You're Dorney, I suppose," said the someone with formality.

It was not Madge. It was a thin young lady with a puff of modish black hair above a heart-shaped face with a high small nose and a high small chin, like a picture tilted far back on its frame. She was wearing tight kid gloves and had a furled parasol with a long ivory handle coming forward under her right arm. This, and a large stylish purse, made it difficult to approach her, but Dorney, in the flood of relief that followed the hearing of her own name, stubbed her toe on her heavy satchel and made an attempt to embrace the speaker, handle and purse or no, and somehow managed to plant a hearty if clumsy kiss upon one cool cheek.

"I bet you're Crystal!" she said. She had been met, was not to be left friendless and alone in a big strange city (as she had feared for some twenty minutes). Overjoyed by this fact she was not dis- tressed by the way the young lady had held so stiff a pose and bent a little backward instead of coming forward for the warm salutation. "Or else you're Jetta." A tear or two gathered in her eyes because she was *related* to somebody once more and she brushed them away smiling. "Oh, I'm so glad to see you!"

"I'm Crystal," the beautiful girl said. "Mamma don't get off till seven, so I was elected to meet you."

"Where's Jetta?" Dorney asked happily. Her blush had faded, leaving a stain of pink at her temples. Jetta, being but a year older, was going to be her own particular friend, she had her plans all laid, better and dearer than Bernice and Opal put together. Jetta was the one she was most anxious to see.

"She's home," Crystal said. She looked down at the telescope suitcase, once the property of old Mr. Diltz, long before he took his last fatal dose of medicine. "Is that the only luggage you've got?"

Dorney nodded, her gladness (for no reason) evaporating like perfume when the stopper is left off the bottle, grief coming, grief for Wanda, and homesickness, so that for an instant she could not speak.

"In that case, we can carry it. It isn't so far to the streetcar." Crystal made no move to take one of the handles.

After the darkness of the cool marble station, the bright yellow afternoon waiting outside was hardly to be looked at for a moment, and they had gone some little distance before Dorney could see without winking and blinking. It was hot, too, ninety in the shade, an early spring — better say summer, for though it was only April it had all the earmarks of summer — in the first big city Dorney had ever viewed. Not the heat alone, however, or the heavy burden she had to carry, shifting it first to one side and then the other, accounted for the breathlessness which kept all her questions in air like feathers borne on an eddying breeze. Forgotten now was sorrow, loss and homesickness. A city! The capitol of Utah! Streets as wide as four or five ordinary streets put together, narrow gutters on either side full of fast-flowing icy green water, fluttering poplar trees, linden trees on the grassy curbs, mansions of great size in flower-decorated lawns, high stone buildings.

While they waited on the corner of Main Street by the shady Temple wall for the Waterloo car to come, Crystal consented to make a few amused explanations. This wall encompassed, she said, what was known as Temple Square, where the Tabernacle and Temple were. The gold angel on top of the spire (Dorney craned her neck around and stared up wonderingly) was somebody from the Book of Mormon. He was supposed to be made of solid gold. And right ahead down the street there, to the left, that gray rock house with all the gables, and the white one beyond it, at the corner, those were two houses that had once belonged to Brigham Young, where he had lived himself and where he had kept all his wives. In fact, some of them still resided there, if Crystal was not very much mistaken. Of course, they were very old. Further on, in the next block, was the house where Mamma worked, Judge Alexander Tower's, but it couldn't be seen from here. Catty-corner there, she said, the store there with all the windows (she had been late to the station because she had loitered looking into them) — that was the Z.C.M.I., which meant Zion Co-operative Mercantile Institute. You could buy *anything* at the Z.C.M.I.

On the streetcar Crystal was not so communicative. Dorney, after a timidly put question or two had been answered with "Wait, I'll tell you later," lapsed into silence and looked out of the dusty panes opposite as well as she could for the hats and shoulders in the long seat underneath them. Little gusts of cool wind meantime came in through the open windows and soon the red tingling hands on her lap paled to ladylike white. Several times she glanced at her companion who stared straight ahead with her nose and chin lifted, and felt she was quite stuck-up. She smiled and turned impulsively. "I bet you think I'm a funny aunt," she said. "Don't you, Crystal?"

"Shhh," her companion said, giving her a quick look and then staring straight ahead again. "We'll talk when we get off the car."

They got off on the corner of Fifth East and Eighth South. Crystal nudged her to take her suitcase and start up the aisle (not such an easy matter) and then she rang the bell and followed.

Crystal gestured with a small gloved hand to the left. "We go that way," she said.

"I'm anxious to see Jetta," Dorney confided, not knowing what else to say. The suitcase now, after the long ride, seemed even heavier and it had begun to bump her often about the region of the knee.

"Dorney," Crystal said, "I couldn't tell you, but it's better not to talk to each other on the streetcar, and I don't look at anything either, if I can help it."

"Why not?" Dorney asked, blowing a wisp of hair off her damp cheek.

"It attracts attention, and the last thing a lady wants to do is attract attention. A person does enough anyway, heaven knows." She shrugged resignedly, rolled her eyes and pursed her lips.

Dorney's already hot face turned hotter and she swallowed something in her throat as big as a plum, while her vision began to blur with tears. She was silent so long that her companion looked at her curiously. "Good heavens," she said. "You're not crying, are you? Set your suitcase down and get your handkerchief out and dry your eyes. What in the world are you crying about, you foolish girl?"

Dorney did as she was bidden, blowing her nose as well. "Because you said I — attracted attention — " she said, "because I guess you're ashamed because I'm your aunt." She saw that a man was approaching and of course it wouldn't do to stand like a big booby from the country and cry right there on the street. He would think her a perfect fool.

"I said that? Why, I never said any such thing!" Crystal said impatiently.

"You did, but I don't blame you." Dorney made a valiant effort and her lip stopped quivering, the tears stopped coming. She eyed the steadily diminishing distance between herself and the man to see how much time she had to look decent again before he could get a good look at her.

"Why, Dorney Leaf," Crystal said, giving a little laugh. "I wasn't talking about you at all. I mean, if a girl happens to be pret — I

51

mean, well, if you *knew* how it was to ride on the streetcar or walk down the street and have all the — have everybody *stare* at you, you'd know how I feel about — "

"Oh," Dorney said. "I didn't know you meant yourself. I thought you were talking about me."

"It's why, sometimes it's just *terrible*," Crystal said delicately.

Dorney had stopped listening. She did not mean to gape at the man but there was something so strange about him that she had to, she couldn't help herself. He was not merely walking in their direction — he was making straight for them at full tilt! Hastily she stuffed her handkerchief away, picked up her suitcase and bounded over to the edge of the sidewalk. She appealed to Crystal with round, scared eyes but her niece did not seem to be taking the least notice. He came closer and closer.

A tall, thin, gray-haired man, he had a woman's tan straw hat on with a flying streamer behind and a quill in the front, stuck in the band. Dorney wanted to run through the nearest gate and hide behind a house but she stood her ground, staring in utter fascination. When he got in front of them, he halted, like a horse pulled up short by a tug on the reins and Dorney gave a very slight scream. Then he sashayed off to the right — three large sliding polka steps — lifted the lady's hat and made them a sweeping bow. "Friends," he said. Then he gave a skip and proceeded on his way.

Dorney turned her head and gazed after him until he disappeared around the corner. When she shut her mouth she realized that it must have been hanging open.

"That's just Schooner Bill Cursoe," Crystal said. "He lives in that house right over there. Nobody pays any attention to him."

"Which house?" Dorney asked, swallowing.

"The second one from the alley. He boards there with a lady. He's a porter in a saloon somewhere uptown. Everybody calls him Schooner Bill. *I* never speak to him," she said, strolling on again. "Silly thing. Although he can't help being silly, of course. He's crazy, that's why."

Dorney did not mind the heavy suitcase now. "Does he always wear that hat?" she inquired with bated breath.

"I didn't notice," Crystal said. "I was looking at you, you looked so funny. He's always got on some silly hat. When he gets ready to leave the saloon at night, somebody puts a hat on him — a fireman's helmet or even a wreath of flowers or just *anything* — and he wears it home. Then he wears it back to the saloon the next day, and then the next night when he gets ready to come home, they do the same thing again, put something crazy on his head. I don't know how they got started doing it. Nobody pays any attention. I just ignore him. He dances off to the side like that and bows every time he sees

52

a lady, no matter if he knows her or not. He leads the parades, whenever there is one, like on the Fourth of July."

"He *always* does that?" Dorney asked, overjoyed. "And never wears the same kind of a hat?"

Crystal nodded. "Nobody pays him any mind," she said, "except maybe strangers."

Dorney drew a deep breath and her eyes sparkled. At home, everybody one knew was just like everybody else, or else they were the "foreign population." Here a man could be rhapsodic, unprecedented, prodigious, one of a kind, an only begotten! "This, then, is a book," said a born reader, laying by in ecstasy the first volume ever to fall into her hands, "and there are more of them." Thus felt Dorney about the individual who had met them, gone on and turned the corner. This, then, was Schooner Bill Cursoe, with his strange headgear and three polka steps to the right. She shot a beaming glance at her niece. The true reader with her first book, Dorney with her first *exalté* — there was not much difference between them. ("And there are more of them!") She breathed a happy sigh.

"I just ignore him," Crystal repeated. "Oh," she murmured, putting out a restraining hand. "Wait a minute. Walk slower. Maybe we'll get to see Mrs. Morelewski." She looked hard in the direction of the large cream-colored house ahead of them and to the left. "I thought — I'm not sure — I saw her on the side porch, but maybe — don't pretend you're looking, though. I wouldn't want her to think — yes, she's there — look, Dorney, and for heaven's sake don't let her see you're looking — "

Following these instructions faithfully, Dorney could glimpse out of the corner of her eye a golden-haired young woman in something lavender rocking back and forth in a wicker chair on the shady veranda. She waited until they had got past the long fence like upright iron lace that enclosed the beautiful green yard where a hose was arranged to sprinkle the lawn by itself without human guidance. Then she opened her mouth to speak.

"Be still," Crystal hissed. "Wait till we get past."

"We are past."

"Shhh."

Her alarm infected Dorney and she did not persist although she was burning with curiosity.

"Isn't she beautiful?" Crystal said, when what she considered the zone of safety had been reached. "Did you ever see anyone like her?"

"I didn't get to see her very well. Who is she?"

"The Queen."

Dorney stopped dead still. "The Queen?" she said. "The Queen of what?" Her heart speeded up. Notional, scenic, never-to-be-for-

53

saken city, what will you offer next? First a madman — now a queen. She shifted the suitcase to her left side, brushing her hot right palm across her forehead. "Where did she come from?" she asked stupidly. What land of palaces, with caskets of jewels, with long lines of sweating slaves?

"Imagine." Crystal sighed, ignoring the ridiculous question. "Here she was," she said, "working at Auerbach's just two years ago! And look at her now! She's got that great big house — everything in the world she wants — even a carriage. She had a sealskin cape last winter. *Real sealskin.*"

Dorney waited a moment before she ventured to ask, "If she was working at Auerbach's, how did she get to be — the Queen?"

"Don't you know about the Jubilee?" Crystal cast her a withering look as they began to walk on again.

"No," Dorney confessed.

"Didn't you hear anything about it?"

"No." Dorney was embarrassed, as well she might be.

"Why, we had it two years ago! It was in all the papers, even back east. Two years ago, it was fifty years since Salt Lake was settled, and so there was the big jubilee. It lasted a whole week, there were grandstands built on the sidewalks clear from the City and County Building to Third South — eight tiers, some of them — and bands, and just thousands of people, and — "

Light began to glimmer.

"She was the Queen of the Jubilee," Crystal continued emphatically. "There was a throne and everything and she wore a gold crown with diamonds in it, and a white satin dress — and she rode in the Queen's float! She had a scepter in her hand, too, of silver with a big knob on the end simply covered with diamonds. You never saw anything like it. She got the most votes, you see, in the contest. People got votes when the bought things in the stores — they could vote for whoever they wanted — and she won!"

"I'll bet she was proud," Dorney said, trying hard to recall more than she possibly could, after such a cursory peek, of the golden-haired image, swathed in lavender, who rocked back and forth on the cool porch. "I guess she had to work hard before, didn't she?" she added.

In spite of her enthusiasm, all Crystal had said so far about the Jubilee's fair sovereign had been tossed off with airy nonchalance, as though one could be excited if one chose, or not, if one chose. But now her voice and manner changed to something that betrayed real excitement. "She doesn't have to work hard now," she said triumphantly. "Because did you notice that restaurant on Main Street between First and Second South when we came by on the streetcar? The one with the fringed awning and all the plate glass and the flowers, and the little pig in the window? Well, that's called the Paris Café, and a very rich man owns it, named Mr. Morelewski — and Mr. Morelewski fell in love with her and married her right after the Jubilee was over! They went to San Francisco by Pullman on their honeymoon and when they came back he bought that house and had it all fixed up, papered and painted and new rugs and everything. They've got electric lights. A woman comes in and cleans for her. She can send her washing out." Crystal stopped to catch her breath, rushed on. "And she wears the most *beautiful* clothes!" She batted her eyes. "You should see. Imagine — all she has to do is dress up, and go in her carriage wherever she wants — uptown — shopping — through Liberty Park — or to the Paris Café — "

"Or sit on her porch and rock," Dorney offered.

"Oh, she don't very often sit *there*," Crystal said disdainfully. "Why, do you know how much a supper at the Paris Café costs? I'd hate to tell you, you'd faint right here in the middle of the street — and she can go there and order *anything* whenever she wants!"

"Queen what, is she called?"

Crystal looked at her companion but did not see her. "Queen Alma, but of course people only call her Mrs. Morelewski now."

"Is Mr. Morelewski good-looking?"

"Why, yes," Crystal said as if she were arguing with somebody. "*I* think he is. He's just as good-looking as anybody *else*. At least, *I* think so."

Madge's small red brick house on Eighth South, off Fifth East and halfway to the alley, stood between two others just like it. It was square, with a square stoop at the left. There was not enough yard on either side of the sidewalk that lead up to the steps, for grass, or it was the wrong kind of earth, smooth and glazed on the surface like pottery, but rich ivy crept up the porch, completely screening one side, and went over the porch roof where it hung down here and there in tendrils over the white gingerbread trimming. Nearly centered in the right front wall was the parlor window under which a bush with glossy leaves grew. The house and yard had a clean, swept, rather prosperous appearance.

"We'll go in this way," Crystal said, running up the three front steps and pushing open the varnished front door. "But generally, we go in the back."

Dorney nodded. Inside it was too dark to see much, only that the hall was narrow and high-ceilinged. Through a pair of double doors on her right pushed slightly apart, she could glimpse the parlor (and smell furniture polish) with its glistening upright piano set crosswise between two narrow windows, the glistening stool that could be twirled up or down, some painted cattails. Wanda had not had a real parlor. Dorney was glad to see this one, felt proud of it.

Crystal opened the door at the end of the corridor and said, "Come on in here. This is the kitchen."

Dorney remembered Jetta now, and she went quickly, anxious to meet the long-wished-for friend.

The large, clean kitchen, furnished by a cold polished stove, a brown cupboard with glass doors, a round table with a red-and-white checked tablecloth and a fine cruet as a centerpiece, four chairs stuck in around it, was empty. Jetta was nowhere to be seen.

"She's out on the porch," Crystal said as if Dorney had put the question on her eager face into words. "She sits out there when the weather's good." She went to the open back door and pushed the screen outwards, "Come on," she said over her shoulder, and Dorney followed.

The back porch ran the whole width of the house, and at the right-hand end was a swing in motion — not a porch swing, but a child's swing. Perched on the board seat, holding tight to the two stout ropes fastened to iron rings bolted into the ceiling, a little creature swung backward and forward, came at them with a rush, went far, far back, came at them again.

"Stop swinging, Jetta," Crystal said. "Get down out of the swing now." She did not make an introduction, did not say, This is Dorney. Dorney, this is Jetta. The little creature stopped, giving the floor a push with her feet every time she went over a certain spot, swung more slowly, more slowly, finally let the old cat die. Then she jumped down, losing her balance in a lurch and a stagger but recovering it again.

The sight of her suffused Dorney's face in a deep blush, she could not have told why. "Hello, Jetta," she said. She cleared her throat and then, hardly knowing what she did, put her arms out and came forward a step.

The little creature took an odd, stiff, tottering step backward (when she went forward, she did not tread but stomped and dug, as though each little bird-leg with its bird-foot was a wooden stilt), poking her tiny hands behind her. She cocked her head on one side and looked at the stranger not curiously but watchfully.

Dorney stopped where she was and dropped her hands to her sides. Embrace and kiss in greeting a squirrel, a quail, not her. Would she not stomp out of reach, give a shrill chirrup? Scarcely higher than the porch railing against which she stood, flat and stick-like, she wore a high-necked long-sleeved dress of dark red wool merino, her full skirt swinging just to her high black shoes, laced together as tightly as they would go, yet leaving gap enough at the tops to thrust a hand in. She stared with dark protruding eyes that could

56

be seen through at the sides like a cat's bubble-eyes, under hooded lids. "Hello," she said. Nose, mouth and chin were too close together at the far end of her tiny yellow face, too great a space stood blankly between them and the wide-set orbs above. Her dark hair, fine as fur, was gathered in a scanty handful atop her small head and tied round with a black ribbon.

"Has she been sick a — long time?" Dorney asked at random, again clearing her throat. Now she recalled the Jetta of long ago, the dim playmate of a Christmas day, a jolly Fourth picnic.

"Oh, she isn't sick," Crystal said. "She just seemed to more or less stop growing when she was about seven, when we first came down here to live. Something sort of stunted her growth, we don't know what."

Jetta, her head still cocked on one side, listened, as though the topic was one of great interest to her. "I am a big girl," she said distinctly, smoothing down her skirts.

"Why, she can understand us, and talk," Dorney said, trying to sound hearty and cheerful. This . . . the friend, the confidante, for whom she had yearned. She had not changed at all in the years, only to be caricatured, parodied by whatever weird ailment had fastened on her. Blank disappointment engulfed Dorney. Jetta might seem a kind of pet in time, like a pug dog or a kitten (if she didn't scratch and bite), but never anything else. Not the ally, the intimate, for whom her heart longed. She looked at Crystal, who was taking the hatpin out of her hat, removing it and smoothing her puff of hair, looked wistfully. Perhaps — ? Maybe — ? If one tried hard to please and to be worthy — ?

She gave Dorney a sudden glance. "I'll show you where you're going to sleep," she said, and something in her eyes answered to what had not been asked aloud.

Dorney picked up the telescope suitcase and followed her, forlorn. Behind them, the little creature took a stiff step forward, another, another, and climbed into her swing.

It was a slanting room, got to by a narrow flight of steps little better than a ladder, slanting upward on all four sides, like a tent, where it was possible to stand upright only in the middle. The unfinished walls were not papered and the floor was bare. A small window looked upon the front porch roof and front sidewalk. There was a washstand and a narrow bed made up with a patchwork quilt over which a threadbare white sheet was turned. A round pillow (an old sofa pillow) in a threadbare case was propped against the wooden headboard. In the corner, a faded hanging concealed a nail or two where garments could be hung.

"Mother and Jetta sleep in one bed in the bedroom," Crystal said. "And I sleep in the other." She did not add that she did not

57

occupy this room because it was like a furnace in summer and the inside of an iceberg in winter.

"It's — fine," Dorney said, looking around her. "I didn't expect to have a room all to myself and a bed to myself and everything. At home, Pearl and I slept together." She thought fleetingly of that pleasant chamber in whose wide bed she had slept so long against Wanda's soft feather pillows, her small bedfellow a round ball beside her. It seemed a great distance away, that shadowy refuge, and far back in time, years instead of weeks.

They ate, at five-thirty, a good supper, which Crystal prepared quickly and deftly, as one long accustomed to the job — baked potatoes, fried beefsteak, a dish of stewed rhubarb. A small oilcloth-covered box was placed on Jetta's chair for her to sit on, in order that she could reach the table. Dorney assisted the ungainly wooden little thing onto her perch, noting that she was very cold to the touch instead of hot, as one might have expected, like a bird. She ate a very small amount of food with such extreme slowness that the two girls had not only finished their meal but cleared the table and washed and dried the dishes before she got to her dish of fruit. Her plate and sauce dish, knife, fork and spoon, Crystal stacked neatly on the drainboard to wash with the breakfast dishes.

Madge, a thin-faced much older Madge with streaks of white in her reddish hair, came home at her usual time, half past seven. She gathered her young sister into her arms and cried quite brokenly. Later, she said Dorney looked like Mamma's side of the family, although her height was more a characteristic of the Leafs. She seemed very much surprised that she was bigger than Crystal. She asked if Crystal had played the piano for her yet and Dorney said no, she hadn't. Then Madge took up the lamp and they all went into the parlor that did not lighten up much because the wallpaper was of so dark a green and the furniture so dark, and there Jetta sat stiffly on the carpet with her little legs spread wide.

Madge and Dorney took slippery seats on the sofa. Crystal twirled the piano stool up three turns and down one, then sat upon it, a book of music before her, and began to play. The piece she played was so long she had to turn twenty pages or more, and it was full of a great many notes for the upper end of the piano, never touched singly but in clusters, with no slow parts. Dorney liked it very much and thought her niece an exceptional musician. Madge said she was sure that in a year or two Crystal could set up as a teacher and although Crystal said, "Oh, Mamma, I've got loads to learn," she had a complacent look as though she thought she could, too. Dorney ventured upon the statement that possibly Crystal could teach her, as a start. She would practise extremely hard! It must be such a wonderful feeling to be able to play all up and down the keyboard,

58

not just a few keys in the middle. Madge smiled but all she said was, "If Crystal could only learn to play by heart, she could be in a recital," and Crystal did not say anything, but sighed a little. She had been taking lessons for five years from Miss Millie Falk (married last month, so now Mrs. Million) and it was a great disappointment to her, her mother and teacher that she could not memorize her pieces and thus could not be presented to the public, but every hope was held that this gift would descend upon her in time, which no doubt it would, for she practised on and off many hours of the day. She looked very pretty at the piano as her thin shoulder blades met together as they ought and her neck was proud and long.

Before she went to bed, Dorney arranged her small possessions in the washstand drawers and hung her clothes behind the faded hanging. Mamma's few things, such as her silk shawl and the fan-shaped vase and the china bluebird, Mrs. Diltz thought it was no more than right that Pearl should have when she grew up, but Dorney was allowed a velvet pincushion of impenetrable hardness and a combing dish that said *Jenny Lind* in gilt under a nearly vanished painted face of ashen pink. She had brought her doll, Leola, not because she had ever greatly loved her, but because sentiment crept in when the time came to pack and she could not leave her behind. She meant to put her away in a closet on the shelf, but there was none, so she sat her (resembling more than a little Jetta as she had sprawled on the parlor rug while her sister played) gently down on the floor, in the corner.

After the light was blown out, Dorney could see Leola's face beyond the shaft of moonlight. She gazed, blinking, then threw back the cover, got out of the squeaking bed and tiptoed barefooted across the floor, coming back with the doll in her arms. Just tonight! for she was far from home, in a strange house, amid strangers, blood relations or no. She settled down in bed and rested her chin on the top of Leola's dusty-haired head, holding her tight against the heartache for Wanda, for her old neighbor, for Jetta, too, as if she had lived, been true and today was dead. Nobody, was there? Nobody left. But when she squeezed her eyes shut and a tear or two trickled out, there was someone . . . streaking across a moonlit landscape on a cloudless black horse. She could have followed swiftly and far . . . but did not, in the peace and quiet that settled upon her at the sight of him, of them. Friends, friends . . . said Schooner Bill, making his bow. Beneath the memory of his word, she smiled. Beneath it slept, in soft consolation.

7

THAT NIGHT, HE WAS NOT STREAKING ACROSS A moonlit landscape. While his black horse cropped the mountain grass in the darkness outside, Butch Cassidy lay on his cot lazily and watched Elza Lay finish his letter at the table, fold it, stick it in an envelope and seal it up. "Tell her you love her?" he inquired.

"Who says you got to tell 'em?" his young lieutenant asked, laughing. He hitched his chair around and leaned back in it.

"Knowed one once you didn't — after she drowned in the crick."

"I told her," Elza Lay said.

"She's a mighty pretty girl."

"I'd take her kind of serious, if we didn't have so much on our hands right now."

"We ain't got so much on our hands right now," Butch said. "But we may have, later on."

"I don't know what you call it."

"Talking about the ladies, I wonder if the one Neibauer was so set on ever come over from the old country the way he wanted," Butch said idly.

"The one he kept showing us her picture?"

"She was a mighty pretty girl."

"Mighty hefty, she looked to me like."

"Everybody to suit his own taste, as the old woman said when she soaked her glass eye in milk."

Elza Lay rolled a cigarette and tossed the tobacco sack to Butch who caught it, turned over on his side and up on his elbow to prepare a smoke for himself with the right hand, as though the left were useless.

"It sure must be something to see, that there old country."

"The only place I'd like to go to," Butch mused, "would be South America."

"Why there?"

"Best damn cattle country in the world," he said. "Take a lot of cash to get started there, though. That's the only trouble."

"That suits me fine," Elza said, after some thought.

"Me, too. But I wouldn't want to grow a long gray beard in Brown's Hole. Not if I could help it, I wouldn't."

There were worse hide-outs, as he had reason to know. Few better, at least in the month of April. Brown's Hole was one of the "stations" along the trail known to the scores of outlaws traveling for their health that ran through Montana, Wyoming, Utah, Arizona and New Mexico, down to Mexico. Situated in three states, Wyoming, Utah and Colorado, it was a mountain-rimmed valley, thirty miles long by five miles wide, running east and west. From the west, through an abrupt canyon, the wild Green River crashed and dashed along the foot of Diamond Mountain for miles until it found a cramped exit through the crystalline cliffs of Lodore Canyon. The Hole could be entered from the north or south, but only if one knew the two or three secret trails that lead dangerously down to it.

Since the robbery at Castle Gate the previous spring, Butch Cassidy to his amused surprise, found himself a famous man among his confrères, whose fancies had been tickled and imaginations fired by what he himself considered no very special stunt, that of taking away a nine-thousand-dollar pay roll from an armed man without firing a shot. For some mysterious reason, it so gratified them that they repeated it over and over, till every bandit, rustler and homeless cowboy on the range knew the story. Then the fad starting up of its own accord, the legends of his earlier adventures began to be dug up and recounted, big-sounding, optimized to the extent that they were hardly recognizable — the Grand Junction train robbery of long ago, the Denver, Telluride and Montpelier bank robberies. In every tale, Butch Cassidy, though he was ignorant of the matter, played the great hero, until his fame resounded all along the Outlaw Trail and reached even the pricked ears of the Pinkertons way back east.

Dusty and sweat-stained riders began to come into Brown's Hole from everywhere, to join the Wild Bunch under Butch Cassidy. The Logan brothers rode in, those handsome killers from the tough old Powder Springs Gang, now leaderless and scattered to the four winds. Gay Sundance Kid came, and Polecat (a name he did not know he had — he thought it was Bill) Carver. So did sly Deaf Charley, the Tall Texan, villainous Flat-Nose George Curry. They begged him to take them on and tell them what to do, fearing the anguish of having to do their own figuring worse than deadly poison, as many a better and wiser man has feared before them, feared since and will fear. "Take us on, Boss. Tell us what to do," they said.

He took them on, calling these few, himself and Elza Lay "the inner circle," took on others as they came riding in, more than he knew what to do with. They settled down, full of good humor and

61

high hopes, in the valley, made the nights merry and the days, too.

In his cabin high up on Diamond Mountain with Elza Lay and Sundance Kid, Butch organized the Train Robbers' Syndicate, laid plans, sent riders out to scout gold shipments and bait the hooks of such railroad employees as would take a bribe. As he also took personal command in foray after foray, riding at the head of his men, he could be said to have his hands full.

He had done well as leader; everybody was satisfied though nobody was getting rich, including himself. There were so many to divvy up with that the take was always small. But he had put himself on the map, at least, willingly or not, had put The Wild Bunch there, too. The Denver *News* wrote about them hysterically every once in a while, calling them "the greatest organized band of thieves and murderers in the West, with a line of strongholds from Powder Springs, Wyoming, in a southwesterly direction across the entire state of Utah and down into Arizona, giving them easy access to Mexico. The number of outlaws is variously estimated at from fifty to five hundred!" The *News* also said they had almost "depopulated the ranges within two hundred miles of their retreat and farmers' freight wagons have been robbed so frequent as to cause little comment, while the large cattle companies have almost been driven out of business." The boys liked to read about themselves. Passing the papers from hand to hand, they wore them out, laughing fit to kill at the commotion they made.

Butch, quick as he was to see a joke, did not think this was such a laughing matter. Notoriety was all very well in its place but in this case there had been a little too much of a good thing. The result was that their old adversaries, the cattle barons, had come to life again. Let them plead poor-mouth as they would, they still had the influence to buy what they wanted, they still had plenty of say. All they had to do, for instance, was notify the Governors of Wyoming, Utah and Colorado, that they were cordially invited to attend a meeting called for the purpose of deciding what steps to take to "stamp out the lawless element amongst us" and the three big Governors fell all over themselves to get there!

Butch was told that when the Denver meeting broke up, the Governors and the cattlemen came out looking like the cat that swiped the cream, licking their chops. When and how they would strike there was no way of knowing unless a leak could be discovered, for whatever had transpired at the meeting was kept a deep dark secret, but "steps" had been fixed on, that was sure.

"What trick you think they got up their sleeve?" Sundance Kid inquired. He had been down in the Logans' cabin for some poker and returned with light pockets. They were still jabbering away about the cattlemen's plot, he said.

"The way I figure, they'll get the Army," Elza Lay said.

Butch laughed. "You guys is getting pretty big-headed," he said. "The U.S. Army! You don't expect much."

"They're planning *something*," Sundance Kid said.

"Sure, they are." Butch swung his feet to the floor, stretched, yawned and stood up. "I am, too. A little surprise on the Union Pacific that ought to put us all on easy street."

"How about if maybe they *do* get the Army?" Sundance Kid said. "Just in case?" He tried not to sound as if he cared much, but his eyes gave him away.

"We'll be waiting for 'em with bells on," Butch said. He scratched his right shoulder blade with his left hand but couldn't reach the spot he wanted, so backed up to the door jamb and rubbed himself against it.

"We ain't five hundred men, like the paper says. We ain't more'n a hundred!" Elza Lay mused. "We'll have to — "

"Not here, we ain't, but we got a few friends, remember," Butch said. "What do you think them riders was sent out for Monday night?"

"I didn't pay much attention," Sundance Kid said.

"If the cattlemen can invite the governors, we can do a little inviting, too, I figure. So I sent the boys out to Hole-in-the-Wall and some of the other hide-outs with a few invitations for the guys to come and take tea with us day after tomorrow at Steamboat Springs." His listeners laughed when he pretended to put a very hot cup to his lips, holding the imaginary handle with thumb and forefinger. "We can have a meeting, too," he said. "Us, and anybody that wants to take sides with us. Why not? You don't have to have a couple million acres of grazing land to have a coupla friends. They ain't governors, maybe, but they're quite a bit quicker on the draw. This time we're *really* going to organize."

He took a stroll outside then, for a last smoke, while his companions inside the cabin discussed the coming trip to Steamboat Springs. They were looking forward to the sights and sounds of a real town again, no matter how small, after the days and weeks in Brown's Hole. Butch was, too.

He whistled for his black horse and Little Dipper came up and wandered along beside him, like a dog.

He met the rider on the other side of the cliff. Jack Rorick, back from Hole-in-the-Wall, had walked up, panting, leaving his mount below.

The air was bright enough for the two men to see and recognize each other.

"They coming?" Butch said, with a broad smile of welcome. "How did it strike them?"

"War has been declared!" Jack said.

"That ain't no news," Butch said. "What else did you expect? We'll whip 'em every which war, Army or no Army! How'd they like the invite? Who's all coming to Steamboat Springs?" he asked.

"You don't savvy," Jack said. "Spain, boss. They blew out the bottom of one of our boats — the Maine, she was called — and killed and drowned two hundred and sixty-six people — and they're going to surround the coasts and come up from South America and Cuba — and the President's going to start drafting — and — "

"Spain done WHAT?"

"Went to work and declared war! I'm trying to tell you."

"Oh, they did, did they?"

"April twenty-fifth, as big as life!"

"Oh, they did, did they?"

"This is sure good news for us, ain't it, Butch? Ain't it, though?" Jack fumbled in his pocket for his tobacco. "The boys is all coming to Steamboat Springs day after tomorrow. It's sure a joke, if ever there was one."

"What is?"

"Why, war like this, with Spain. The governors'll be so busy recruiting soldiers to go and fight the dirty Spaniards, that they won't have no time for us no more. Why, I bet the whole thing'll be called off! The boys is turning handsprings."

"What'll be called off?"

"Why, whatever the cattlemen and the Governors was fixing to do, to clean us out. The cattlemen will be so busy selling beef to the army and the Governors will be so busy recruiting soldiers to go fight, that — " What was the matter with the boss? He was just staring straight ahead, at nothing.

"What do you know," Butch said. Very softly, with wide spaces between his words. "Sinking our boat. Drowning our innocent people. Daring to think they could set foot on American soil. Daring to think it. *Daring.*"

"Ain't it rich, though? Now they'll leave us be for a while. They'll have their hands full, sure!"

"It's rich, all right," Butch said, still in that slow, soft, careful way. "But the one the joke is on is Spain, see. Because all I can say is, she must of not never tackled nothing like the old United States before. That's all I can say. She don't know what a hornet's nest the old Land of Liberty turns out to be, when somebody riles her up. We'll wipe up the earth with 'em. We'll mop up the very earth."

"Who will?"

64

"Everybody!" Butch said, rousing as if from a dream. "All of us. The Wild Bunch. Everybody. Every state in the Union."

"But, Butch," Jack said anxiously, "the boys ain't going to want to go and fight Spaniards. Things has played right in our hands. This is just what we been waiting for. The Army and Navy, they can take care of a few *Spaniards*. We don't have to go!"

"We'll have our own troop," Butch said, exultant. "We'll call it The Wild Bunch. We'll ride into Denver and enlist, right from Steamboat Springs!" He turned on his heel and started back to the cabin, saying "Git!" to Little Dipper who scampered on ahead. "By God, we'll show 'em, won't we? Won't we, though?" He went faster, broke into a run. "I'll holler out for the boys to charge and they'll whoop and yell and here they'll come! And them Spaniards — them Spaniards — " A laugh burst from him.

"Hey, Butch — listen! Listen a minute. The boys — "

"We'll show 'em, Jack! Won't we, though? Just what a ring-tailed roarer old America is, once she gets riled!"

In the middle of the night he woke up and wondered what he felt so good about. It took him a while to remember, listening to the quiet breathing of Sundance Kid and Elza Lay across the dark room. They had been hard to persuade, but he had done it! He sat up, wide awake, and pushed the rolled-up blanket he used as a pillow farther down under his shoulders, settling his head back against the mud wall. Hammer and tongs, that was the way to go after them. That was the way he would have to go after them there in the Hole tomorrow. And the bunch that congregated at Steamboat Springs, the same way. Hammer and tongs. What a troop it would be! The Wild Bunch, three hundred, maybe four hundred strong, when they rode into Denver to put their John Hancocks on those enlistment papers. He could see them, bold as the devil, and his chest swelled. The stylish ladies would wave at them when they went past, and the little kids would run along, looking up — and maybe somebody would point him out, some old friend that knew him, maybe from Circle Valley days and say, "That's Butch Cassidy right there up in front, that's him, all right!" And after they got to Spain, or Cuba, or wherever they were going, he would send a postcard to Mike Cassidy, in Mexico (he'd *have* to get his address this time, no fooling about it), say, Mike, you old son of a gun, you don't know what you're missing. . . .

8

DORNEY DREAMED, THAT FIRST NIGHT AT MADGE'S, that she was on a train coming down from Rock Springs, Wyoming, a train just like the one she had come on, only with a swing suspended in the middle of the aisle for Schooner Bill to swing back and forth in. It annoyed the conductor very much, who was wearing a queen's gold crown with points sticking up all around, instead of a conductor's hat. He tried to make Schooner Bill stop swinging but he wouldn't. Every time he swished past, she crowded closer and closer to the window, making herself as small as she could. It wasn't such a bad dream — not as if it had been of a ghost, behind the hanging in the corner — but somehow it was bad enough, and Dorney was glad to wake in a cold sweat, with a pounding heart. She hunted around for Leola (who had been discarded and had rolled to the very edge of the bed in the meanwhile), held her close again, and went back to sleep that way, holding her.

Crystal, sent up to wake her young aunt at half past eight in the morning, found them so: Dorney in a sound snooze, Leola in her arms, and it was her laughter that woke the sleeper. "Do you always sleep with a *doll?*" she asked, when she could compose herself enough to speak. She hurried back to the door and called downstairs, "Mother, you'd ought to come up and see what Dorney's sleeping with! You really ought to, Mother!"

"Tell her breakfast's ready!" Madge shouted from below.

Madge was on an unlooked-for vacation this morning. Having gone as usual to the residence of Judge Towers at quarter to seven, to prepare breakfast, she was told through a crack in the door by Selma Ankerstrand, the sleepy housemaid in nightgown and bare feet, that the folks had been called away, leaving Mrs. Yandle the message that she was free as a bird for the next two days. Some people had all the luck, Selma grumbled, because *she* had not only to do the regular cleaning as usual but was given orders to put away all the winter clothes and blankets in moth balls. However, for the time being she was going straight back to bed, and if she slept till noon it was nobody's business! "It's probably something to do with the war," she

66

added, yawning, "that they called the Judge away for. A telegram come for him before daylight."

"War?" Madge said.

"The war with Spain," Selma said, as though that was no news at all.

Madge looked dumbfounded. "I suppose because they sunk that boat the other day," she said, after a moment's thought. "That was the Spaniards, wasn't it? Somebody was saying."

"I suppose so," Selma said, rubbing her puffy face. "It's declared, anyway. The Judge says it won't last long. Well, if you'll excuse me — " She shut the door politely enough not to offend her fellow servant, inch by inch.

Dorney sat bolt upright without Leola, who had been tossed to the foot of the bed much as if she had been discovered to be a live snake and was lying there with her eyes shut tight. "I do not!" she said helplessly. "I do not."

"I don't know what you call it. You had her right in your arms," Crystal teased. "I saw you. You were hugging her just as tight could be." She laughed again in high glee. "Why, I gave up my doll when I was ten years old!"

Dorney stared at her niece in a panic, not knowing what to say or how to say it. Today was the day she had been going to try to win a place in Crystal's affections, so they could be chums, but now everything was spoiled. Oh, her stupidity! Her childishness! To have been guilty of such behavior! Caught red-handed! A wave very like sickness went over her and her ears buzzed. "Please, listen, Crystal," she begged. "There wasn't any place to put her last night. At home, I had her back on the shelf in the closet, but there isn't any closet. So first I put her down in the corner right over there," she pointed a nervous finger, "and then — "

"And then it got up and walked across the room and climbed in bed with you! I'll bet you still play with it all the time. I gave up my doll when I was — "

"Please, listen, Crystal. Really, the way it happened — first, I put her in the corner, and then — " Dorney's face grew redder and redder and her eyes stung.

"It's nothing to cry about," Crystal said. "You don't have to cry over a little teasing! You really are a baby, aren't you?"

"I'm not crying. Honest, honestly I'm not."

"You are, too."

"I am not." Why hadn't she left wretched Leola back in Rock Springs or, bringing her, why hadn't she stuck her under the bed, far back against the wall, so far back that she would never, never be seen? The painful thought came then! A nice way to treat your friends, a fine way to do, a fine way, a fine way (as Grandpa Bannon would say it). . . . She looked at laughing Crystal, at the disheveled doll — at one, at the other, and she couldn't help it. Something proud and defiant came and she reached down for the doll's arm, dragged her up over the quilt to her arms again. Let Crystal laugh if she wanted. Let her!

"What's the matter up there?" Madge called, mounting the stairs. "Because there's not going to be any quarreling in my house, I can tell you that, not when I open my house and offer my — now, what is it?" she said, coming into the little room. "What's the matter up here?"

"Not a thing in the world, Mother," Crystal said smoothly. "I came up to get Dorney up, the way you told me, and she was sleeping with her doll, and I just said to her all in fun, I just said . . ."

"You wouldn't let me explain!" Dorney said. "You just stood there and laughed, and when I tried to explain — " Her lips trembled.

Madge spoke gently. "You are our guest, you know," she said, "and guests don't get into arguments with the people they're staying with. Now, Crystal is three years older than you," she went on, "and I want you to treat her like she was. I want you to apologize. We might as well start off on the right foot or we might as well not start off at all. Ain't that right?"

Dorney nodded, miserably, running one finger backward and forward across the blunt eyelashes on Leola's right eye.

"Wanda was one person that I knew would — many's the time I said to her when you was little — Wanda, I said, if you don't watch out you are going to spoil that child till she won't be fit to live with. Many's the time I said to her, Wanda, if you don't watch out — "

"She never spoiled — I used to mind her," Dorney whispered, "honest I did. If she was here, she'd tell you. I used to do everything she told me, and we had — such a nice time — "

"I want you to apologize to Crystal. She just teased you a little bit about sleeping with your doll. You got to be fair, you know. You was sleeping with it, because you've got it right there in your arms, so you can't deny it. All I expect is for you to go ahead and apologize. That is, if you've got a spark of gratitude in you when somebody opens their door to you and gives you a nice room all to yourself and tries every way they can to suit you. Of course, if you haven't, then that's a different story, of course." She looked over the head of the bedstead and out of the window, mournfully, as one who sees her empty hopes go glimmering. "Of course, in that case — "

"I — apologize," Dorney said, drawing a deep sigh.

"What are you sighing about?" Crystal asked, laughing.

"That's better," Madge said. "I hate somebody stubborn."

68

"All I said to her was —" Crystal murmured.

"I apologize," Dorney repeated, wiping away her tears with the sleeve of her nightgown.

She seemed to have wakened to a kind of nightmare of sorrow and disappointment, one that would last all day, all week, forever, perhaps, or so she thought when Madge and Crystal went back downstairs. But when she got up and dressed, combed her hair, went down into the kitchen and was shown (as though nothing had happened) where to wash her hands and face — and when she sat down to a breakfast of pancakes, jam and milk, and had eaten, she began to think it was not such a nightmare after all, the scene upstairs. But it had not been pleasant to wake to Crystal's peal of laughter and find out what had provoked it.

Crystal had gone after breakfast into the parlor, and now the same tune that had been played last night rippled out, quite loudly, considering that both the hall and parlor doors were closed.

"She plays very pretty," Dorney said, wiping the dishes for Madge and being as agreeable as she could to make amends. Above the piano music, she could hear the light thud of Jetta's feet outside on the porch as they jabbed the porch floor to keep her swing in motion. She had breakfasted early and been swinging ever since.

"Crystal's full of talent," Madge said. "Simply full. And if she can't set up as a teacher before another year is past, I don't know who could."

"I don't either," Dorney agreed. "I would just love to take music lessons from her."

"Oh," Madge said. "You didn't hear the news about the war!"

"The war!"

"We've declared war on Spain!"

"Have we! My goodness!" War on Spain! Dorney thought of it wonderingly as she polished a water glass till it shone. "We'll win," she said, feeling cocky about it.

"Oh, sure," Madge said complacently, her frown having disappeared. "I'm not worried."

In the silence that ensued, while Dorney waited for the coffeepot to be scoured out so she could dry it, she remembered what she had been about to say before this new subject was introduced. "I would just love to learn to play the piano," she said. "As long as Crystal is going to be a piano teacher, maybe she could practise on me! I mean, give me music lessons."

Madge handed her the rinsed coffeepot and then dried her hands on her apron and went and took a seat by the table. She motioned that Dorney was to put the pot on the stove and come and take a chair. Dorney obliged, wondering why Madge didn't throw the dishwater out first and wipe the pan and hang it up, since she was so nearly through with the dishes. Wanda hated to dry her hands only to wet them again.

"Now is a good a time as any for us to straighten out a few things," Madge began. "You know I was left with two girls on my hands to support, without hardly enough to get down here to Salt Lake on. Only about half the furniture here is mine — the rest belongs to the people we rent from. I've had the whole responsibility of bringing up my two girls," she glanced in the direction from which the light rhythmic thud came and then towards the source of the rippling music, "myself."

Dorney nodded. "I know, Madge," she said.

"No help from a living soul," Madge went on. "It all fell on me. At first," she said, "when we come here, I used to leave the girls with Mrs. Luby down on the corner, but pretty soon Crystal got old enough so she could watch after Jetta. We don't leave her alone no more than we can help for once in a while she'll get into things and I'm always scared maybe she'll take a notion to play with the matches, although, of course, I always keep them way up on the top shelf of the cupboard in a tin box. She can be left for a little while, especially when the weather's nice and she can sit on the porch and swing, like yesterday, when Crystal went to the station to meet you or when she goes for her music lessons. But usually we don't leave her alone any more than we can help. It's a mystery to me why she never developed, and all I can think is, it's something she must have inherited from her father's side of the family — "

Dorney opened her mouth to speak of 'Dair but thought better of it and kept silent.

"Well, the burden of keeping care of Jetta has fell on poor Crystal, while I have gone out and worked. She has learned to keep house — I don't allow her to do the heavy cleaning, of course, and spoil her hands, because a piano player has got to take care of their hands, especially if they are going to be a piano *teacher* — but she keeps things picked up, and fixes the meals for her and Jetta and does up the dishes. There are them who love to stick their nose into other people's business," Madge said with some severity, "that say that now Crystal is seventeen years old, *she* ought to get out and work and let me stay home with Jetta! But we don't pay no attention to them."

"*I* can stay with Jetta," Dorney offered quickly. "I can take just as good care of her as could be, really I can. I'll be glad to, and take care of the house, in case you and Crystal *both* want to . . ." she faltered then, for Madge was looking so very displeased and odd, "work," she added, not loud enough to be heard.

"Dorney, listen."

70

"What I mean is — "

"We've got to get a few things straightened out, right now."

Dorney nodded, clasping and unclasping her hands in her lap, knowing she had made a false step but not sure how she had done it or quite what it was.

"I can't think," Madge said, "I just can't think that it was quite fair for me to have to take on the added responsibility of another mouth to — well, of you," she said. "It was Papa's place, I can't help but feel. It was different with Wanda. She had a supporter. But the way I'm situated — well, it's an entirely different matter. You can see that."

Dorney nodded again, full of regret, for it was an entirely different matter, a situation for which she herself was greatly to blame, according to Madge's aggrieved eyes. She tried to think of something to say but could not, except, "Yes," and, after a gulp and a swallow, "I know."

"But for Mamma's sake — " Madge took a handkerchief out of her pocket and touched it to the tip of her nose, "poor Mamma's sake, that having you, cost her her life — "

Dorney shifted in her chair and cast down guilty eyes.

"I'm glad to do it," Madge finished. "I'm glad to try my best to be a mother to you and to do all I can."

Dorney looked up, then, her eyes brimming. "Oh, Madge," she said, "I'm so s-sorry." A sudden impulse sent her stumbling around the table to her sister's lap, an uncomfortable stiff unready place where there was not room for her and on which she found she could not sit with her whole weight. She perched there, though, an instant, wishing she had stayed where she was, and put her arms around Madge and laid her cheek against her hair. "I'll be good — and not be any trouble," she said.

Madge gave out an embarrassed sound that was half a laugh and half a smothered sigh. "That's very well," she said, "but you're a big girl." She hugged her sister, though, dutifully, once, before she said, "Now you go back and sit down, Dorney, because I want to get a few things straightened out, and I can't help but think that the sooner the better."

Dorney, glad the clumsy moment was over, returned to her chair and prepared to listen.

"The thing is," Madge said, clearing her throat, "you're a big girl for your age, and as you know, I haven't got a Thomas Diltz to support me through thick and thin. I've got my two girls you know, and, after all, you're fourteen. Nearly grown, you might say. What I mean is, I might just as well come right out and say it, and not beat around the bush. You'll have to go out and get a job, Dorney, and pay me for your board and room like anybody else would, because all I've got is what I earn with my own two hands and if I should get sick — " She paused. "You can see where I stand."

"Oh," said Dorney, smiling with relief. She had known from Madge's grave tone and grave eyes that something was expected of her and in the midst of the contrition and embarrassment of the past few minutes had found time to worry about what it was and whether she was going to be able to measure up to it. But if that was all it was! To get a job and pay board and room! Why, that was nothing. She wasn't afraid of that.

"You can do a lot of things," Madge said, her brow clearing. "You can get a job right in the neighborhood taking care of kids or something, or doing housework, or — "

"Sure, I can!" Dorney said. "I can do a lot of things." She wouldn't be a burden, then. Her heart grew light at the thought for it was a miserable thing to be a burden, she knew now. She had never known it before in all her fourteen years, but two hours' taste of it this morning had been enough to show her.

"You can ask around. Maybe somebody would take you. Of course, if there ain't nothing right in the neighborhood, why, then I can take you to the employment agency — "

"You mean, go around the neighborhood first."

"That's right. Just knock at the door and say who you are and what you can do, and maybe somebody will give you a job. But try to get on steady somewhere if you can, rather than take little piecemeal jobs like cleaning and ironing. If you can't, then we'll try the agency."

A light of valorous resolve burned in Dorney's eyes.

"I'll go to every house," she promised, "except where that Schooner Bill lives."

"Oh, did you see Schooner Bill?"

"Yesterday, when we were coming from the station."

"He won't hurt nobody. But it's no use to ask at the house where he boards. They got plenty of help already."

"Crystal showed me which one it was."

"Well, that's settled then," Madge said. She got up and returned to her dishpan, threw out the water, wiped out the pan and hung it on the nail underneath the sink. "I just didn't want you to start off with any false ideas, because the way I believe, the best way to do, is to put a person's cards on the table, right at the jump-off."

"I believe so, too," Dorney said.

"So about the music lessons and practising and all that. . . . Well, you're not going to have very much time for practising and all that. You can see that?" She took the towel off the nail on the back door and began to dry her hands.

"Sure, I can." Maybe she could not have learned anyway! Maybe it would not have been such fun to play the piano as it looked. "I don't care," she said, "really, I don't," as though someone had asked her if she did.

"Well, that's settled then, thank goodness. This afternoon, I thought Crystal and me would go uptown. I've got to buy a few things. And you can keep your eye on Jetta. And then tomorrow, bright and early, you can go out and see if you can find a job. By the way," she said, "don't mention 'Dair to anybody. I always just say he was a rancher, and that he died. But you probably don't remember him anyway, or anything about him. Do you?"

Dorney's face lit up. "Oh, I do!" she said. "Every little thing."

"Well, we never mention his name," Madge said.

They left soon after lunch, mother and daughter looking so fair and modish that Dorney felt proud to be their kin as they went out the door and down the walk, promising to be back by five o'clock. She did not know what to do with herself after they left, once the few dishes were washed and the floor swept up. She watched Jetta swing for a while but that was as dull as could be, so she went upstairs and sat on the edge of her bed. That was not much of an occupation either. She went over and drew back the hanging in the corner and looked at her clothes — her two winter dresses, the heavy coat that was too tight and short now, her "graduation" dress and best light blue "summer" dress. What a scanty and countrified wardrobe it was, she thought with dissatisfaction, not fit to be compared with Crystal's! Handling them disdainfully, one after the other, she wished she could throw them all away and have, instead — then she remembered Wanda in a stab of grief, poor good plump smiling Wanda, who had made or bought all these things, with so much love, so many kind words! She gathered up the coat sleeve, pressed it against her cheek and began to cry, while homesickness piled up on grief and overcame her. She would never get used to this room, this house, these people (related or not). She would never laugh again — think how many times she had had to cry just since yesterday — never be happy, never, as long as she lived.

Oh, if she had been a boy, it would be a different story! She wouldn't be here, that was sure! She would travel all around like a gypsy or a hobo, wherever she wanted — she turned over on her back and flung an arm up over her streaming eyes. Oh, no. She wouldn't be a hobo. What she would do was, she would go back to Wyoming and find Butch Cassidy! That's what. Climb right up on Diamond Mountain and find his hide-out. Ask him to let her belong to The Wild Bunch, lie about her age, say, I'm sixteen, Butch — I'm seventeen, maybe — and he'd laugh, the way Grandpa Bannon said. All right, kid, he'd say. She began to blot away her

73

tears with the corner of the pillowcase. He'd be sitting on the steps of his cabin, when she walked up (a boy, dressed like a boy), and he'd keep on sitting there, looking at her with his glimmering brown eyes. She could look down and see the white line of his scalp under the exact part in his wavy black hair. But he'd stand up then, taller than herself by head and shoulders, and put his hand out . . . she'd put her hand in it . . . and they'd shake. She wouldn't be alone after that, be sure, friendless and orphaned, in people's way, having to go out tomorrow and get a job.

Get a job . . . she opened her eyes wider, put her hands under her head and gazed at the ceiling. A job! Why . . . say. She drew a deep breath. She'd have money then, wouldn't she, after she paid Madge for board and room? She wasn't used to money except a nickel now and then, Wanda or Thomas did the buying, even to pencils and paper for school — but if she had a job, and worked, she'd have money, wouldn't she? of her own, to spend! She sat up, hugging her knees. She could buy as pretty clothes as Crystal's — even a fur muff. She could . . . why, say. The thought proved so exciting that she couldn't stay where she was but had to get up off the bed and walk around. She could look just as nice as anybody, once she was all dressed up, be proud, too, like Crystal. Go down the street with her nose in the air.

She turned back to the center of the room, clasped her hands behind her and pursed her lips. But no, sir, she wouldn't go down the street with her nose in the air. She would look beautiful, all right, in the extremely fine clothes she would buy with all the money she earned (after the board and room was paid) but that didn't mean she had to act stuck up! Instead, whenever she walked along the street she would watch for beggars and little children — she took on the look of beatification she would wear at the time — and when she ran across them, she would reach in her purse for change, stoop and put it into their beseeching hands, while they said, "Bless you, lady." Finally, everybody would know her by her acts, the whole neighborhood and half the town. The more beautiful she was, the kinder and less stuck up she'd be. The more she earned, the more she'd give. And finally — she moved slowly and gracefully through the narrow door, went slowly and gracefully down the steep steps and into the kitchen — a young man who had long heard tell of her, would put himself in the way to observe her and beg an introduction. To Miss Dorney Leaf! Somebody tall and black-haired, with white teeth and glimmering brown eyes — in fact, like Butch Cassidy, quite a bit — in fact, almost exactly like Butch Cassidy. And he would say to her, Miss Leaf (holding his hat over his heart), Miss Leaf, I have long desired an introduction to you. . . . Indeed? she would say, looking downward, holding a handful of rustling skirt in one hand. And so . . . I am happy to make your acquaintance, she whispered, going out onto the back porch.

She took a seat on the railing. "Aren't you tired of swinging yet?" she said.

Jetta did not answer, but swung slower and slower, not touching the floor, her broomstick legs thrust straight out. When the swing was motionless, she hopped stiffly out, hopped stiffly over and stood close enough so that Dorney could have reached out and touched her. It was the first time she had come so near.

"I saw the parade out the window," she said.

"Did you, Jetta?" Her skin was yellow-colored and the whites of her dull, protruding eyes were yellow-colored, too.

"I saw the Queen," she said. Every word had to stand all by itself, with no word near by to lean against. "I saw everything out the window."

"Did you know the Queen lives right in this neighborhood?"

Jetta nodded, but it was plain to see she did not care.

"They all went past and I saw." She blinked. "Did you bring me a present?" she said.

"Yes," Dorney lied. "I did bring you a present. I almost forgot."

"What kind?"

"Well, you just wait and see. I'll go upstairs and get it and you just wait and see."

"Why didn't you give it to me yesterday?"

"Today's just as good, isn't it?"

"Because I don't get much pleasure out of life, you know."

"Oh, now Jetta, you do too. You've got your swing and your nice mamma, and your sister, and everything."

Jetta blinked again.

"What kind?" she repeated.

Dorney got down off the railing. What in the world could she give her? Not the combing dish — not the velvet pincushion — not the handkerchief with tatting around (for Wanda had made it). She didn't have a string of beads, a brooch, a ring, a book of fairytales. What would seem like a present?

She came back with Leola in her arms — hers ever since she could remember. She had a strange feeling as she came down the stairs with her, a feeling she could not have described in words for she did not know them, that Leola was less a doll than a time and place, a geographical location, a quinquennium. "Here," she said. "Here's the present I brought you. You can name her whatever you want, and see, she'll go to sleep," she tipped her backward, "or wake up," she tipped her forwards, "and she's got real, human hair."

Jetta lifted her tiny stiff arms. "Thank you," she said, precisely. "Because I don't get much pleasure, you know."

75

She kissed Leola's cheek with a solemn peck.

Then she threw the doll on the floor, hard, and the bisque head broke in twenty pieces.

"Goodbye," she said.

So that was how the eyes worked, that contraption with a small lead weight fastened on it. Dorney squatted down and looked at it curiously. She began to pick up and pile together the sharp bits of dim china face — the tip of the nose, the half a chin with half a dimple, the eyebrow painted on like a feather. (That alone hypostatized, or why was the intact body nothing whatever now?) Upon the tiny heap she laid the wig of human hair, shining with new-fallen flakes of ancient glue, stood up and went to the corner for the broom and dustpan.

Jetta returned to her swing. "Poor doll," she murmured, catching hold of the ropes and lifting herself onto the smooth-worn board.

"You might well say poor doll," Dorney said, industriously sweeping.

"Goodbye, goodbye." Jetta gave a push, went backward, swept forward with an airy rush.

Goodbye, goodbye, indeed. That made Dorney smile instead of weep, the inappealable moment when the door swung shut on childhood. So softly that she did not even hear.

9

MRS. LUBY BEGGED PARDON FOR THE STATE OF
her house, the way the cat shed fur all over the Indian blanket on
the sanitary lounge, Thornton's nose (she wiped it quickly with his
own brief shirttail, nearly dislocating his back in the process), Althea's dress — every button in the wrong hole! (she caught the slick
girl with a practised swoop and forced her to stand still while she
unbuttoned her first, then buttoned her up again), the slobbering
baby's red-faced roars — he was teething — and her own unbeneficed
appearance. "I never *thought* of having company," she said, quite
out of breath from all the hustle she had bustled through in the
five minutes since "company" knocked at the door and been invited
in.

"My sister wanted me to start out early," Dorney apologized.

Mrs. Luby insisted that the guest must take the rocking chair by
the stove, but — "Excuse me," she said — not until a crocheted
shawl, several drying diapers, a sewing basket, some jar lids, a seed
catalogue and a pan of green peas, a few of which were shelled, had
been taken off the seat, arms and back. Mrs. Luby did this rapidly,
putting everything except the diapers, which she threw behind the
stove, onto the kitchen table. It was covered with unwashed breakfast dishes, so she had to make room as best she could by piling
one bit of crockery on another until she had a leaning tower which
she took out of the realm of danger by sticking a spoon in the cup
on top and moving it little by little to one side until a safe balance
was achieved.

Once she had accomplished everything she could think of, and had
seated herself opposite her guest in a chair she hastily disencumbered
of a pair of rubbers (these also landing behind the stove), she
settled down. Thereafter, as though she had been an Eastern ascetic
under a vow of immobility, neither quarrels, cries nor any subse-
quent household crisis could dislodge her from her place nor dis-
tract her attention from her caller. Mrs. Luby, sitting, was a woman
of such downiness that imagination had to equip her with framework.
Her fingernails looked thin as tissue, her hair, the color of pencil

77

strokes on butcher's paper, perched like a cloud on her head and her greatest substantiality consisted of her teeth, two hard white eye-teeth and two or three hard white incisors. "My husband," she began cordially, showing these, "works at night, so he sleeps in the bedroom during the day, till about two."

"Right in there," Althea said, pointing at a closed door decorated by a calendar hanging from a clothes hook and a man's gray sock draped over the doorknob. "He ain't never going to get drunk and throw us out and bust the furniture no more, is he, Mamma? He promised," she added, to the visitor.

Mrs. Luby blew upon her very small daughter as though she had been a layer of dust on something. "You go play," she said.

"What with?"

"With your brother."

"He's too mean, and besides, he ain't here."

"Where is he?" Dorney said, looking about with interest, for seven-year-old Thornton had indeed disappeared from sight.

"Oh, under the sanitary lounge," Mrs. Luby said. "He always crawls in under there when company comes. When he gets better acquainted, though, he'll recite. He knows all the Castoria poems."

"Does he?"

"Blow your nose, Thornton," Althea ordered, raising her voice.

"You go play and mind your own business," her mother said mildly.

"What with?"

"Go look out the window."

"Can't I daub up Herman and give him a feather?"

"Not while he's good," Mrs. Luby said of the baby who now sat nodding in his perilously tall and narrow highchair, with his wet chin on his wet bib. "I sometimes daub his fingers with a little molasses," she explained, "and give him a feather and he'll pick it off first on hand and then the hand for the longest time. Once he got the feather in his mouth and sucked it down his throat and very near choked to death, though. I once knew of a man choked to death," she continued, "in a hotel dining room, on a piece of beef-steak. Got up and got clear outside before he fell down on the street dead."

"When he starts crying again, can I, Mamma?"

"You go play."

Surprisingly, Althea did so. She wandered away to a seat on the floor by the woodbox and began to rattle something in a tin can.

"What they won't say next," Mrs. Luby said. "You'd think her father was a regular old soak. But the truth of the matter is, he's one of the best men in the world. English, you know, born right in Liverpool."

78

"Utah is a long way from England, isn't it?" Dorney said, after a moment's desperate thought.

"Maybe he'll go along for a whole month or even longer," Mrs. Luby said imperviously, "won't touch a drop, won't so much as go near the saloon, and then all of a sudden — he don't come home. Generally he gets in about five in the morning and I always hear him and wake up, but this time I sleep till something else wakes me up and I see the clock says seven, eight, or whatever time it is and I know something's rotten in Denmark. And the whole day will go by and the evening, and maybe along towards the following morning, here he'll come." She drew a deep sigh. "There's some that get deadly quiet when they're under the influence, you know," she said, "like stone statues."

Dorney didn't, but she pretended that she did.

"— and some that gets to bawling their eyes out — and some that lays out flatter'n a pancake wherever they happen to be — but Mr. Luby, he's one of these that all he wants to do, he wants to wake up the dead. Now, if I could just leave him alone till he got through, it would probably all blow over," she said. "I guess he'd just sing and holler to the top of his voice till he got it out of his system, but I get flustered about the neighbors, naturally, and try to shut him up. And then's when the trouble starts. It's the same thing every time."

"Oh?" Dorney said.

"But one thing I will say. If he busts a piece of furniture or smashes something, the minute he's sobered up, or a day or two later, here'll he'll come with something new to take its place, and a lot of times it's better than what he busted, for my husband may be a lot of things, but he ain't stingy. When he buys something, it's the best that money can buy or he won't have it. Won't even look at it."

Dorney glanced nervously at the door shutting Mr. Luby off from the world and back to her hostess.

"What I think," Mrs. Luby confided, "is that his work ain't just what he really and truly wanted, but you see, he got started at it. He's got his own team and wagon and all his equipment — don't owe nobody a dime. He makes a good living, too — good enough to raise seven kids on, all told — that is, two passed on and two is married, and then we've got these three little ones at home — so it would be foolish to try to do something different now at *this* late date, don't you think?"

"I should think so," Dorney murmured.

"But, you see, his father was a letter carrier there in Liverpool, looked up to by everyone, wore a nice uniform and everything, and his mother's folks run a store of some kind, so I guess he wishes sometimes *he* was a mailman, too, or something more on the high-

79

toned order, although he never has said boo about it. But, he makes more money as it is and as long as somebody does as good as he does, wouldn't you think that would be satisfaction enough?" She did not pause for an answer. "You was saying something about a job, wasn't you, seems to me, when you first come in?"

Dorney repeated more slowly what she had said in a rush on the doorstep when Mrs. Luby's door first opened to her, that she was Madge Yandle's sister from Rock Springs, Wyoming, and that she was seeking an occupation as hired girl, with the privilege of "going home" at night.

"How old are you?" Mrs. Luby inquired.

"Fourteen."

"How old would Crystal be? I used to take care of them two kids when Mrs. Yandle first moved in the neighborhood. I said then that Jetta was going to be a midget — or whatever she is — and that she wasn't quite all there. Oddest-acting girl I ever seen."

"Crystal's seventeen."

"Why ain't she out looking for a job?"

Dorney explained about the music lessons, the practising, the career-to-be and how Jetta needed a guardian.

"There's a girl," Mrs. Luby said, "that's going to wake up some fine morning and find herself a old maid."

"Crystal?"

"As sure as you're born. She's pretty as a picture and she's had all kinds of chances — but when a girl sets herself up as better than anybody else, and won't go with this one and won't go with that one, because they ain't good enough — and sits around and waits for I don't know what, whether he's got to be the handsomest man alive or the richest, I don't know which, or maybe both — why, some fine morning she's going to wake up and find her chances has all dwindled to nothing. There's many a old maid been made that way and that's just where Crystal is heading. You mark my words."

"I thought sure she had a beau," Dorney said, astonished. "She's so pretty."

"I'd like to know who," Mrs. Luby said, "pretty or not, you can't shut the door in people's faces and give 'em the cold shoulder at gatherings and turn down their invites cold time after time — just because they're learning the shoemaker trade or their dad happens to haul coal for a living or they ain't this or they ain't that — and expect 'em to keep dangling around. They just won't do it, not when they're as good-looking theirselves as Otto Wogberg and Ralph Mulkey, just to name two, that they're both married now to somebody else after bowing the knee to Crystal and being turned down cold. No, sir. Boys like them — and boys like some of the others she's turned down — don't have to go far for consolation, never think they have, and Crystal ain't got a copyright patent on looks, you know. There's others that don't got to hide in the dark, exactly. You, for one, when the time comes."

Dorney did not ask when that time would be, because she knew approximately when. It would be when she earned money and had a pink silk ball dress and had her hair done up over a two-dollar rat the size of a baby's pillow. Also her ears pierced and genuine garnet earrings screwed in. And a ruffled parasol, not just a black old bumbershoot. It would not be long. It really would not be long! although sometimes it seemed as if it would.

"Let me see now," Mrs. Luby said, putting a soft finger to her temple. "Who would want a hired girl, I wonder. I just can't imagine, in this neighborhood. But let me see, now. Mrs. Tofflemire lives around the corner on Sixth East. Her daughter Clara works in the Palace Laundry. You could ask there, but I don't believe — and then, along the alley, there's the Vertrees family, but I'm sure they wouldn't — they're church people, Mormons, you know. There's lots of Mormons, more than anybody else, here. Have you got acquainted with any yet?"

"No, not yet. But in Rock Springs — "

"They're good neighbors, mind their own business, stick together, though, awful close and don't have much to do with outsiders. This Mr. Vertrees, he's along in his fifties and he's got two wives — "

Dorney felt a little bit shocked, to find it was really true, polygamy, and not just something people made up.

"There's not much difference in age but the first one looks just elegant and the second one looks like a wrinkled old Indian squaw. The kids of both of 'em is growed up and gone away now. Nobody knows if the two ladies fight or not. There's a story told that one of 'em cut off the other one's hair one time and there was a battle royal but I don't know how much truth there is in it. It's supposed to of happened a long while ago. If you go down the alley you'll notice where they live — the house with so many vines over it that all you can see is the door and parts of the windows."

"I won't ask there," Dorney decided timidly.

"There's several new families that I don't know nothing about. But don't ask at Joe Mudge's house, the little green house next to the big red brick house on Seventh South. He's the widower with the four kids that Clara Tofflemire's making herself so silly over. The big flats on the corner, the building that's just been painted, you might ask there, but this neighborhood ain't much for hired girls. I should think your best chance would be to try to get on in some of them big mansions up along Brigham Street."

"Well, all Madge told me was to ask, and if I don't find something, then she's going to take me to the employment agency."

"And how do you feel about all this?" Mrs. Luby asked, tugging at her soft ear.

"All what?"

"Coming to a place one day to live and being sent out to find a job the next? And only fourteen years old?"

"I got here day *before* yesterday, Mrs. Luby," Dorney said earnestly.

A series of muffled sneezes were heard from the direction of the sanitary lounge.

"Come out from there, Thornton," Althea ordered, dropping the tin can she had only pretended to play with while she listened to the conversation. A wooden block painted with a blue S, and three marbles, tumbled out and went hopping away. "Or else blow your nose. Make him, Mamma. Make him blow his nose."

"You mark my words about Crystal," Mrs. Luby said placidly to her guest.

"Well, thank you, I'm sure, for all your trouble!" Dorney had to raise her voice to be heard above the sudden din that broke loose around them, to which her impassible hostess paid no heed whatever. Thornton, sneezing and coughing, now rolled out from under the lounge but did not get to his feet. Instead, he went crawling about on all fours hunting the scattered marbles, while Althea, in a towering fury, danced from one foot to the other, screaming, and when he snatched an agate she stamped on his hand as hard as she could to make him let go of it. He did, bellowing, but he clutched her around the knees and pulled her to the floor, waking dozing Herman, who took one hazy look about and began to howl, thumping his heels against the footboard of the dangerously tottering highchair and banging the tin tray that hemmed him in.

"No, sir, no matter how *pretty* a girl is, if she wants to be popular with the boys, she's got to give them a little encouragement. Pretty is as pretty does. Well, it remains to be seen what she's waiting for," Mrs. Luby said placidly. "And if she gets it." She spoke in her usual voice, so all that could be heard for certain was the word *pretty*.

Dorney got to her feet and straightened her hat, preparatory to taking her departure. She looked in alarm at the door behind which Mr. Luby slept — surely the commotion would wake him and he would come rushing out like a teased dragon, breathing smoke and fire. (Even Thomas Diltz had to be pussy-footed around when he was taking a nap — nobody would have dared break loose like this, though he was a man who never gave a whipping to anybody). "Well, if you'll excuse me!" she shouted. And, horror of horrors, Mr. Luby did come out! or at least his head did, his neck and part of his underwear-clad shoulder, scaring her into holding her breath.

82

But all he was doing was yawning and when he stopped, he had next to no chin and large moist blue eyes, so she began to breathe again as usual.

"How do you do, I'm sure," he said Englishly, nodding in her direction while she slowly nodded back, having no idea what he said, only that his lips moved, for Thornton had meanwhile accidentally bumped Althea's head on the corner of the woodbox and she had accidentally raked a fingernail across his eyelid. Herman had got his second wind and the noise was remarkable.

"I got up to remind you to cook the PEAS," he shouted to his wife's motionless back. "In case you FORGOT again."

"Your HUSBAND, Mrs. Luby," Dorney said, pointing.

"My what?" The soft woman turned and looked over her shoulder. She smiled, not only at him, but at Dorney, too, employing the same smile for both, one after the other, for it lasted a great while, like a dropping star with a long way to go down the sky. "Oh, Mr. Luby," she said. "I couldn't imagine."

Dorney turned the corner and went past the vacant lot where amid the tall weeds and rubbish several children were flying a ramshackle kite. It had gone high and would have gone higher in the blue sky, had not the string, made of strips of cloth tied together, been too short. There was breeze enough to carry it out of sight, all that was lacking was string, and Dorney smiled sympathetically, holding down her blowing skirts and then her fluttering hair, but the children were too busy to notice her.

The first house to her left was a neat frame house with a woolly dog on the porch, fast asleep in the warm sunshine. She opened the wooden gate and went up the walk on tiptoe, hoping not to wake him, but his eyes opened when her foot tried the first step. He did not bark, however, merely looked at her without concern and went back to sleep, as much as to say, Oh, it's only you. He was brown with a black nose and round ears, like a bear cub, so friendly a sight that Dorney could not resist stooping down and petting him a little. If it had not been for his trothless tail, she would have supposed he was unconscious, but it beat upon the floor and gave him away. "You're not asleep," she said, "you old dog."

"He won't bite you. His teeth are wore down to nothing, now." The speaker tarried in the open entry but could not be seen behind the dark green mosquito-nettinged door. Her hoarse voice seemed to come from high up in the air, as though she were standing on a chair.

"I bet he wouldn't, anyway," Dorney said, rising to her feet and approaching shyly.

"Oh, yes, he would," the hoarse voice said. "Once a man tried to steal a quilt off the line and he took the seat right out of his pants, but of course that's quite a while ago. He's fourteen now, Rupert is, and don't do nothing but lay around and sleep. Lazy old thing."

"I'm fourteen, too!" Dorney peeked back over her shoulder at the ancient dog. "And imagine, I'm just getting started, while he's nearly at the — " She broke off, not wanting to wound Rupert's mistress, if such this proved to be, by the heartless word "end."

"Getting started at what?"

Dorney looked upward to the spot on the green semitransparent door behind which the face must be. The dim outline of a human being was beginning to show all down it so sesquipedalianly that she did not believe her eyes. She spoke her piece, wondering if some trick was being played upon her.

There was a silence, and then the green door swung wide open.

"We don't need nobody — but come in, because it may be that Mamma knows somebody that does."

Dorney did not stare, but she had all she could do to keep from it.

Clara Tofflemire was a woman of perhaps thirty-five, trundled to the length of better than six feet and squeezed so narrow that looking at her from the front she did not seem to be more than a dozen inches across at her widest point. Viewed from the side, she looked about the thickness of a stout rope dangling from a beam. Her color was the gray-dark of taffy before it is pulled out white and she appeared (which she was not, for she was just the opposite, never down in bed a day in her life) as deathly ill as anyone may look this side of the grave. The thought of many, upon seeing her for the first time, was first, that she was about to expire, and second, that under the circumstances it would probably be better for her in every way if she did. Dorney looked away and back and away again, in profound fascination. Clara's gray eyes sat in gloomy caverns on the high cliffs of her cheeks, under the overhanging of her brows, like thieves plotting mischief, but when she smiled they did not look that way any more, only innocent, timid and anxious to oblige. She had long gums and short teeth. Her thick hair, parted in the middle and done in a massive knot behind, was the color of the mother in vinegar.

Clara was the best bosom ironer the Palace Laundry ever had.

Widowed Mrs. Tofflemire, in the poor but comfortable kitchen, was a usual, stout sort of elderly woman in good health, and not the faintest resemblance could be seen between her and her daughter. She was glad, she said, to make the acquaintance of Madge Yandle's sister and asked her if she would take a seat.

Dorney said she could not stay long, and Clara told her mother their caller's business.

"Sit down anyway," Mrs. Tofflemire said, "and maybe I can think of somebody, but this neighborhood ain't much for hired girls."

84

"That's what Mrs. Luby said," Dorney replied, taking the edge of a chair. "But Madge wanted me to ask."

"I guess she wants you where she can keep her eye on you, you being such a child."

"She isn't a child," Clara said hoarsely, with much tact. "She's just exactly Rupert's age! Aren't you, Dora? Or, what did you say your name was?"

"Dorney."

"Dorney. That's right."

Mrs. Tofflemire was sewing something of gray flannelette, using material enough for a large tent, which, supposing it to have blown down, it resembled, piled around her feet. "Mrs. Luby is a very fine woman," she said. "Came from a very fine family."

"I liked her," Dorney said, sitting up straight and not touching the back of her chair.

"He's a very fine man, too," Clara said.

Mrs. Tofflemire tossed her head, like a mettlesome horse. "A man that gets drunk and comes home as noisy as he does and throws his wife and kids out on the street and then tosses out chairs and tables and busts dishes," she said, "and the neighbors have to call for the police and when they come he runs and hides in the empty lot and then sneaks off somewhere, may be your idea of fine," she paused ominously, "and it may be the idea of fine of a few other old maids, but it ain't mine, that's sure and certain."

"He don't do it very often," her daughter said stubbornly.

"Once a month, as regular as the man comes around to collect for the life insurance, and if that ain't often, I don't know what is."

"Well, he don't stay away only a day or two, and then he always makes up for the damage."

"I'd damage him, if he was mine." She tossed her head again.

"What kind of work does he do?" Dorney asked innocently.

A painful silence fell. Mrs. Tofflemire looked at her daughter and then back to her work, taking up a needleful of tiny stitches.

Clara's gray-dark began to burn with a winey flush. "Why," she said, "why, he — "

"Tell her," her mother ordered sternly, with a look as if to say, you would mention the man, now go ahead and take the consequences.

Dorney stiffened with embarrassment. What in the world had she asked? She wished she could recall her question, and was thinking desperately how to jump to another topic when Clara came over and took her by the hand.

"Come, I'll show you," she said.

Dorney got to her feet and let herself be led to the long kitchen window. With a skeleton hand, Clara pushed the curtain a little

85

to one side, and Dorney looked under it, somewhat blindly, onto a dismal back yard full of flapping clothes. "I can't see anything," she said.

"Look right there," Clara said gently.

"Where?"

"Right there." She pointed a bony finger.

"Why, that's the — "

"That's right," Clara said. She sounded sad, as though she wished it were not so, but it plainly was, and there was nothing to be done about it.

"But what does Mr. Luby — "

"He takes care of them," Mrs. Tofflemire said with fine irony from her chair. "He cleans them and puts in lime. He's got his regular customers."

Dorney went soberly back to her seat.

"They're good neighbors, though, you know they are," Clara said, to break the silence. "You know very well they are."

"I never said they wasn't."

"Their baby is certainly cute," Dorney put in, after clearing her throat.

The clock on the shelf struck the half-hour.

The winy flush gradually died away from Clara's face. "It's too bad you don't wan't to try the laundry," she said. "There's a very nice bunch of girls works there. I could get you on, I think."

"Well, thank you," Dorney said, "but Madge told me to — "

"What time is his funeral, anyway?" Mrs. Tofflemire asked suddenly.

"The owner of the laundry died," Clara explained to their guest, "and they closed the laundry down today, out of respect, otherwise I wouldn't of been home." She turned to her mother. "He's going to be buried at two o'clock, from his home." To Dorney she said, "I hear it's a mansion. His wife wanted to save him till Sunday but the undertaker thought the best thing was to have it today. I guess she expected relations from back east or something."

"You're not surely," Mrs. Tofflemire said, lifting the gray mass of goods from her right and dropping it upon the floor to her left, "not surely going over to the kids today and that no-account man? How much do you suppose he cares about you running over every night to cook and mend and wash and iron, after a hard day's work? To say nothing of Sunday? He thinks you're crazy, that's what he thinks, and I do, too."

This was what they had been discussing when she knocked on the door, Dorney knew. Mrs. Tofflemire did not broach the subject, she fell back on it as on a familiar sofa from which she arose with reluctance and where she was more contented than anywhere else.

"They need somebody so bad," Clara said, resuming the discussion dully, unwillingly.

"Sure they do," her mother said. "Naturally they do. Who wouldn't? Somebody that works for nothing! A old maid that ain't got no better sense than to trot over and scrub for a no-account widower that don't even know she's alive. And if you think for one instant that Joe Mudge is ever going to be edged over to a place where he thinks he can't get along without you, why, you're very much mistaken. Nor them four kids of his, either. Kids is just as fickle as anybody, no matter how they swarm all over you and blather around and call you Aunt Clara."

Dorney was careful not to look at Clara, or anywhere in her direction. "I guess I'd better — " she said, clutching the arms of her chair and preparing to rise.

"Mamma is talking about a friend of mine's husband, that they live over on Seventh South," Clara said to her with painful courtesy.

"Oh," Dorney said, sinking back. She looked then, at the tall strange young woman, trying to signal her allegiance, but Clara did not look back.

She only stared at the toe of one long narrow shoe as though it had writing on it which she was trying to read. "She worked alongside of me," she said, wetting her lips. "Sophie, her name was."

"A beauty," Mrs. Tofflemire put in cruelly.

"She was," Clara said. Now she looked up, almost happily. "Light hair and dimples, and oh, so full of fun. Had us laughing all the time. And she was going with this Joe Mudge, but couldn't get married for quite a while. She made such a lovely hopebox! And then, about seven years ago, they finally got married."

"And she had one baby after another till the last one killed her," Mrs. Tofflemire said.

"It was the saddest thing." Clara said. "Those little motherless kids . . . so I go and try to help out a little once in a while."

"He'll never thank you, and they won't either."

"I'm not doing it for thanks!" Clara said passionately.

"I know *that* well enough," her mother said. She looked at Dorney and back to her sewing. "He's one of these handsome no-accounts," she said. "No regular job — "

"He's waiting to get back on at the cabinet works," Clara said. "He don't lay around and loaf. He does piecework, builds birdhouses and things like that, that they sell in the stores. I don't know what more you want, if a man makes a living for his family!"

"If you wasn't older than him and if the neighbors didn't know he wouldn't so much as look at you, I'd be so humiliated I wouldn't know what to do, the way you run over there and do for them, that's all I can say."

"It's very kind of her," Dorny said clearly.

Mrs. Tofflemire laughed. "You don't know old maids, I see," she said.

Clara took down an ugly dark blue shawl and draped it across her shoulders. She never went out, even in hot summer, without a wrap of some kind as though she would conceal as much of herself as she could. She looked at the door her mother had pulled shut behind her. "I promised the kids I'd make 'em a batch of muffins for their dinner. It won't take long."

"I bet they sure love you," Dorney said.

Clara sneered. "Sure they do," she said.

"I mean — really."

Clara stopped still and looked at her. The bitterness went out of her face and she smiled. "Oh, well, it don't matter much, I guess," she said. "It ain't a matter of life and death."

What isn't? Dorney, puzzled, wanted to say, but didn't for the sake of the stricken eyes that thought it was a matter of life and death, whatever "it" might be.

Dorney did not turn in at the Mudge's house for the muffin-making but said goodbye to Clara and continued on her way. It was growing close to noon and she thought she had better go home and eat. At the corner she crossed the street and went down Sixth East. Somewhere along here was where the Queen lived, she was almost sure. Yes, there was her palace, that fine cream-colored six- or seven-roomed house with the scalloped awnings above every window, and the sprinkling system that ran by itself, whirling and splashing, on the dark green lawn. Naturally, she could never go there, Dorney thought. What gall she would have to have, how bold as brass she would have to be, to do an impudent thing like that, as though the Queen was no different than Mrs. Luby or Mrs. Tofflemire! But she might look from the side, she thought, disguising her gaze, see if she was in the wicker chair or in the hammock . . . just glimpse her, she might. She began to walk slowly and softly, her eyes sliding more and more to the side. Just see if . . .

Her attention was fixed on the house. That was why the sudden sharp click of a scissors not an arm's length away and the "Hello," that came from the side of the yellow rosebush by the ornamental gate, startled her so. She caught up her skirts with a trembling hand, the other she fastened at her throat, her eyes widened. Worst of all, her mouth fell open . . . while the Queen stepped forward, like any other woman snipping roses in her garden on a fair day. But oh, how she looked! How she looked. Dorney held her breath, and when she let it go, it came out in a kind of gasp, as though she had been shoved.

Queen Alma did not seem to notice. She put her nosegay up to her perfect nose and sniffed. Then her perfect lips parted, and she smiled. "Are you taking a walk?" she said.

"Yes, ma'am," Dorney got the words out with difficulty. "That is, no, ma'am," she said.

No shimmering crown sat on her head, but the undulate hair shed golden rays enough. No seething jewels swung about her, but she scorched enough without, with opaline, with eyes so blue they stained her long lids blue, with sunrise pink and moonrise pearl. Her frock was white voile, pleated and ruffled, with a high collar and simple sash, but no Elizabeth in "frock of cloth of silver, checquered with red silk, like bird's eyes," in "French kirtle of white satin," in "clouds of Venice gold," seemed more of consequence.

"Not taking a walk?"

"I'm . . . looking for a job, ma'am." Dorney told the Queen!

Ten minutes later she flew into Madge's kitchen spouting din like a maddened mynah.

"Why?" Madge inquired. She and Crystal were already at the table eating.

"The Queen! Just imagine! I'm trying to tell you."

Crystal looked at her with disbelief. "Why in the world did you go there?" she said.

"For heaven's sake," Madge said. She dipped a radish in the salt she had sprinkled out on the tablecloth and bit into it. "Well, don't get so excited."

"It's not Queen Victoria, you know," Crystal said. "After all, it's not her."

"She said I could start tomorrow," Dorney said, falling into a chair, "at two dollars a week!"

1o

DORNEY ARRIVED AT THE QUEEN'S EVERY MORNING
at eight o'clock. She always closed the gate carefully and went up
the walk and around the side of the silent house almost on tiptoe,
and she came onto the big screened porch the same way, across it
to the glass-paned door, the knob of which she turned very, very
softly. The Queen, of course, was asleep. In the double bed in the
huge chamber she shared with Mr. Morelewski, who left the house
each morning at seven, she would be lying with her long hair spread
over both pillows, until ten or even later. When she arose and put
on her different colored morning gowns tied with different colored
ribbons, she would come to the kitchen. There she would fix her
own breakfast, going back and forth to the brown ice chest with
the four massive nickel-handled doors, back and forth on her sharp
heels to the row of the glass-doored "built-ins," back and forth to
the blue-enameled stove in which Dorney had built a coal fire and
upon which the bright teakettle sat rocking.

Mr. Morelewski did not breakfast at home, nor lunch, nor even
dine there. The Queen did not dine there, either, but every evening
at six, dressed like a fashion plate, stepped into her carriage and
was driven away to her husband's restaurant. The Queen and Mr.
Morelewski, however, had one meal together in the house, their
"midnight snack" — consisting of what, Dorney did not precisely
know, only that a great many spoons, bowls, the eggbeater and egg
whisk, plates, cups, the pan in the chafing dish — sometimes the
pans in *both* chafing dishes — were discovered to be dirty in the
morning, with something very hard to scrape off. When she told
Madge about it, she said it sounded to her like Welsh Rabbit, a
dish made of cheese, beer and a few other things, to be ladled over
toast. Madge could not imagine what had been made in the biggest
baking pan, when that was found to be used, with powdered sugar
sprinkled all over, but she said, "Morelewski could afford to put on
a little heft, but your famous Queen had better watch out if she
don't want to get fat enough some fine day to go in the circus. Al-

though maybe eating don't have nothing to do with it, I don't know, I guess nobody does."

"Oh, she never will," Dorney said to that, as if Madge had suggested that her employer would someday turn into a Blackfoot Indian squaw. Queen Alma fat? Not wonderful? It could never be!

When Dorney arrived, she put the kitchen to rights first, washed, dried and put away everything that had been used the night before. Then she swept the kitchen floor, the porches, steps and walks and hurried back inside to see that everything was in order for when the Queen should appear. No matter whether Dorney had heard her moving about and was waiting for her to come through the door, it was always a surprise to see her. Preparation did no good, the hand trembled, the pupil contracted, the heart beat faster just the same.

While the Queen cooked her breakfast and sat down and ate it at the kitchen table, Dorney cleaned the bedroom and the only bathroom she had ever seen in her life, a dark one with a mustard and blue linoleum floor, a seven-foot chain dangling from a box near to the ceiling above the water closet, a tiny porcelain tub set high on iron claws, and a mahogany medicine chest. When her highness finished, she left as many dishes as had remained the night before, and after she vanished from the kitchen and went in to dress, Dorney returned to do them, feeling oddly privileged when the thin cup she took up was still warm from the Queen's own coffee, as Egyptologists feel when they take up a vessel and know it was once intimately used by Aah-Hotep.

After that came the parlor work and then the large dining room. Since these rooms were never used, or used as by a light bird a light branch before she considers and flies on, it was easy to tidy them. The Queen sometimes laid down a piece of goods on the dining-room table, pinned pattern shapes upon it and cut out a dress that was never seen made up; or she sat briefly on a parlor chair beside the center table laden with a celluloid-topped album, a large vase of imitation asters, a paperweight and the bronze bust of a woman with bunches of grapes and vine leaves in her hair, but she did not stay long.

When she was not in the kitchen, or dressing, which took longer than anything else, or strolling for no more than minutes at a time about her garden, the Queen was on the side porch in her wicker chair among large loose cushions, her little pointed feet on a footstool, or she was in her bedroom lying on her bed. She always wore a snug, strong corset, however, so the sitting or lying was not for the purpose of relaxation and ease. For the most part she was engaged in reading long articles on fashionable dress and fashionable decorum in *Peterson's* or *Demorest's* Magazines, or in a solid book with yellow covers, the front impressively etched with a classic, laurel-crowned figure in flowing white robes, standing between tall torches burning with ribbonlike red flames under the words printed in gold: THE ETIQUETTE OF TODAY. She read stories, periodicals, and this impressive tome, as the scholar reads his Thucydides and Aristotle's *Rhetoric*, with a frown between her soft eyebrows and her burnished lower lip caught between her even teeth. She often yawned, however.

When her mother and father came driving in from Sugar House in their old farm wagon behind the horse they had got at the time the Queen was a rotund seven years of age (and fell regularly asleep in the ripe strawberry patch as the sun grew hot), she would always pretend to be doing some other thing than what she was actually doing. For instance, if occupied with study she would take up her sewing basket and rummage in it for a piece of fancywork. If sauntering on the lawn she would hastily speed to the wicker chair and sit down; if sitting, she would get up and begin picking the dead leaves off the house plants or busy herself with some other peripatetic task; if lying on her bed, she would jump up and pretend to be eating; if eating, pretend to be reading. Dorney soon observed this and wondered at it. She was sure that if she asked, the Queen could give a good reason for it, but of course she did not presume to inquire.

The old farm wagon gave a particular kind of a screech and groan when it rolled to a stop in front of the gate, which was how the Queen always took warning and could switch from one occupation to another, in time.

They were solemn, shabby old people, the Queen's parents, looking no kin to her whatever. Ever since she could remember, she had fancied that she was left in their hands by genitors far other than they, and as a consequence she did not bother to become very intimately acquainted with them. They did not stay long, for the Queen's father had the chores to get back to. Why they came at all, it was hard to see — not to be entertained, that was sure, not to communicate or learn anything, not to fetch or to carry, not to inquire for their son-in-law, Mr. Morelewski, whose foreign birth they took as a breach of trust and whose money they considered tainted (strong liquors being dispensed at the Paris Café), but something drew them and every once in a while the screech and groan would sound out in front of the house and here they would be. After they had gone, the Queen turned the beauty back on that she had switched out like a string of electric lights when they came, and made herself a cup of strong coffee with plenty of cream and sugar.

The scrapbook of clippings about the great Jubilee lay on the window seat in the parlor, and Dorney might not have seen it for some time had not the Queen one day pointed it out. She said, "You might like to look through this some day. It's pieces from the newspaper." Dorney did not delay. She transferred the oily dust rag to her left hand and thrust it behind her skirt. Her right she carefully wiped on her apron before she turned back the cover and began to read, while the Queen modestly vanished from the scene.

The first clipping told how Miss Alma Carlyle, formerly of Sugar House but now a Salt Lake City resident employed by Auerbach's Department Store and residing at Mrs. Gibson's boardinghouse, had won the big Jubilee Queen Contest over twenty-five other contestants, the most beautiful young ladies in Zion! "She is modest and retiring," it said. "When asked what she thought of being a Royal Monarch, she said, 'I am very happy.' She is twenty years old, five feet three inches in height and weighs one hundred and thirty pounds. She wears a size four shoe and a number five and a half glove. She has golden hair and blue eyes." Dorney dropped her dust rag and took a seat on the edge of the window seat, reading with bated breath the long day-by-day stories of entire splendor. Thanks to a young reporter who squandered adjectives with the largesse of Barnum, all could be seen as though just taking place — the Coronation, the great Jubilee Parade, the royal progresses to Salt Air and Garfield, the visits to hospitals, Liberty Park, the Capitol Building, and finally, the Queen's Ball, held at the vast Salt Palace, where, in tight-waisted white satin, with white satin slippers and her glittering crown, the lovely Ruler danced with this famous man and that one, Mr. Joseph Morelewski among them, while two bands took turns and played. Last of all was the clipping that said Miss Alma Carlyle, formerly of Sugar House but now a Salt Lake City resident, Queen of the world-renowned Jubilee held three months ago, will wed Mr. Joseph Morelewski, owner of the Paris Café, in a simple ceremony. They will spend their honeymoon in San Francisco, California, it said, going there by Pullman, and will return to reside on Fifth East, between Seventh and Eighth South, where Mr. Morelewski has purchased a residence. Where I am right this minute, Dorney thought, in awe. She closed the book and looked around her. Where I am, right this minute! She had to take up her dust rag and rub hard on the taboret until her wrist ached before she could quite believe it, and even then, for the whole afternoon, it seemed much more a dream than something true. I can see her every day, she thought, just as if she was anybody . . . who had been written about in all the papers, who ruled the Jubilee. Dorney blushed, when next the Queen went through the room and through the open door to the vine-shaded porch, and could not bring it over her lips to inquire of one so celebrated and august what to do with the stack of old newspapers in the kitchen, or ask any other simple question for quite some time.

There had been, and was, great need for the Queen to keep informed on the matter of the mode, for every evening she dined uptown in the busy Paris Café, and the hours she put in reading about costume in the *besetting* shades were well employed. Whether the time she used to read about the rules of society was as wisely spent could not yet be determined, for Queen Alma, whose few friends at Auerbach's and the boardinghouse had long since been discarded, was not acquainted with any member of the élite, on whom to practise the rituals she had so driven herself to learn.

She knew, as the passing schoolboy knows the Latin he will never use in conversation, how to make a formal morning or afternoon call and how and when to leave her rigid calling card, but the question was — on whom? Even, how to address the daughter of an Earl, wedded to a man without title! A proposition that would stump a great many, only — which Earl's daughter? She knew how to preside at a luncheon table decorated with hothouse roses in cut-glass vases, pink-shaded candles, ribbons running out to the little place cards, fluted paper cups of nuts and soft mints, but nobody came to lunch. With the institution of tea she was familiar, from beginning to end, how the bread-and-butter should be thin as tissue, the cakes small, the tea leaves steeped for five minutes, what the waste bowl was for, how the ceremonial words "One lump or two?" were intoned above the hovering tongs, but nobody came for tea. She knew how to send, in the mystical unblemished third person, an invitation to formally dine, formally come and dance at a ball, how to write a letter of condolence and what the hastily dispatched page of gratitude should impart for the happy weekend at Winterlair. She knew what R.S.V.P. meant, too, longed to see it down at the lefthand corner of the stiff engraved card so she could repondez s'il vous plait, say yes, of course, with many thanks, but no bid came, to anything, though she watched and waited.

She would have thought that — if she had stopped to think at the time, which she didn't, there was so much excitement — to be elected Queen of the Jubilee, by a majority of thousands of votes, because she was more beautiful and graceful than any of the other candidates, including one of Brigham Young's own granddaughters and a niece of J. P. Kearns, the millionaire, should be enough of a triumph to give a person a start in Society! And then, on top of all that, to be courted and married by Mr. Morelewski, who owned a big restaurant — that should have had some weight, too. On the train going there and while they were in windy San Francisco, she read feverishly at night after Mr. Morelewski was asleep, and every moment she had free to herself during the day she read, until the whole of *The Etiquette of Today* was got through, so that when they returned to Salt Lake City she would be ready for anything and everything in the social line that would be likely to confront her.

Everything would, eventually, she felt certain.

Mr. Morelewski did not know what she was reading on their honeymoon; he thought it was a novel for young ladies, and he did not know about her ambition. It was not really that, perhaps — ambition. It may have been that when innocent Queen Alma discovered there was such a thing as Society, she thought that it would discover her, too, since she was not behind a counter any more but up among them, close enough, in rich clothes, for Society to touch. She could reach out and touch it, now. Would not it, when she learned its little tricks and graces, the language it spoke, reach out and touch her? It seemed but natural. The queer part of it was, it didn't work that way. Proximity had nothing to do with it, nor beauty, either, it appeared. The Queen, however, studied on, rather ploddingly now, her attention often wandering, not with her early zeal, to be ready when the first grand caller rang her doorbell and the first invitation came through the mail. The first grand caller had not rung as yet, and the invitation had not arrived, but there was still plenty of time.

When the Queen and Mr. Morelewski returned from their honeymoon, he went back to work while she, as if her life depended on the speed with which it was done, put the finishing touches on their redecorated house. This kept her occupied for several days and then every single item in the Queen's household stood, hung, lay or leaned in its appointed place. There was nothing more to be done. For two days the Queen admired her own gift for embellishment, walking about from room to room and looking, wishing it was all to be done over again, overjoyed to find even so small a task as to change the wax fruit from the silver bowl where the colors didn't show to the cut-glass one where they did, a big improvement. There was no housework to do, for she had a hired girl to do it, and so the Queen now turned her attention to herself, studying to keep her beauty at its zenith and acquire manners sagacious and fair. This took time, and changing her clothes from skin out twice, and sometimes three times a day, took time, and yet there were many hours that hung heavy on her hands.

Of course, one could always eat. To the Queen, food had ever been the one, true, never-failing source of pleasure in life and she ate often and earnestly, would have eaten more often and more earnestly did not a nagging little voice from the region of her conscience lift itself to say that food *might* be the cause of fat, and fat was the danger of the world to beauty. And what would be so bad as to lose that greatest gift? To the ordinary person, maybe going blind or falling down hopelessly paralyzed might compare, but these catastrophes seemed of small consequence beside that one. To lose one's beauty! As well say, be buried, conscious, under six feet of massive earth, as have that happen. When the voice nagged about food and fat, mostly the Queen heeded. She pushed away the jar of *pâté de fois gras* or the third jam tart or covered but one slice of toast with Welsh Rabbit. But sometimes she argued a little, said to herself, who knew whether it was food that caused the trouble, or whether it was just one's natural bent, the constitution one had, something one was powerless against? Who knew?

Mr. Morelewski, when she brought the subject up for discussion, said that so far as he could observe, as a man who made food his business, heavy eating and obesity went hand in hand. Although he had to admit that one of his best customers, the one with the diamond stickpin as big as a two-bit piece, Alma must have noticed him, who owned so much real estate and had the race horse named Coxey, that never won, ate five times as much as a normal man — would eat three T-bones smothered in mushrooms in a row — and he looked like a living skeleton! There was also a woman like that, in Paris one time. "You see," the Queen said, greatly comforted. "Of course, this man may have a tapeworm or something along that line," Mr. Morelewski said. "His eyes stick out so far and he always feels hot, won't even wear an overcoat in winter. But *I* think it's food," Mr. Morelewski said. "I'm not so sure," said the Queen. "It may be just a person's constitution."

He teased her then. "If you — change," he said, "I'll lock you in a dungeon and put you on bread and water. No more *crêpes Suzettes*, no more Lobster Newburg, no more this and no more that. Then we shall see whether — "

"Wouldn't you love me any more, if I was fat?" she asked. They were sitting over their coffee at their usual palm-shaded table, in a secluded corner of the Paris Café's lofty dining room. It was nearly empty now, for the dinner hour was over. She took a sip and put down the gold-crusted cup.

Mr. Morelewski looked at her. She was wearing mauve, under a white picture hat wreathed with white plumes, and a lace shawl. "You are so beautiful," he said. "When I was a boy, a great Princess came to our village, to visit at the Duke's castle. They hunted and I saw her riding past. They had a tremendous ball and my brother and I, and my little sister, too, we crept up close through the vines so we could gaze in at the big windows. I saw her dancing. There are no words to say how lovely she was. Her hair, and her eyes — I said to my brother and sister, If such a women cannot be my bride, I will never marry. Never, I said, never. I dreamed of her for years.

I looked for her, everywhere, not a day but what I looked. Where is she? I said. Does she exist? No, it seemed, no. The time arrived when I gave up all hope, when I resigned myself — but then came the Jubilee, with its Queen, and when I saw her, I knew the great Princess had been as nothing in comparison, that here before my eyes was the most beautiful woman in all the world! And when you danced with me that night — "

"How old would she be, now?" the Queen asked, frowning a little. She pulled the bracelet that had got up under her sleeve, down where it would show, turned her ring so the stone was in the exact center of her finger.

"Who, my darling?"

"That woman."

"The Princess? Well, I was only a boy of twelve, and she was eighteen, possibly twenty. That was thirty-five years ago, so if she is living now, she would be, well, let me see — "

The frown disappeared between the wide blue eyes.

"I thought I had found you too late," Mr. Morelewski said. "I told myself that you would never — that I was a fool, a man old enough to be your — hair going gray — glasses to see with — but I had to try, anyway. I couldn't give up without trying — "

"You sent me all those lovely flowers, and gave me — "

" — and the night you said that you would consent to be my — "

" — such pretty things and wrote me those letters twice a day, and took — "

" — wife, I knew that I had not one thing left in life to wish for. That night! I did not go to bed at all, but walked the floor. I longed for, I dreaded, the morning! Perhaps you would take back your promise, perhaps when I went to you, you would say — "

" — that box at the Salt Lake City Theatre." She said it dreamily.

"But you didn't," he said. "My dove. You are so sweet, so kind, and you grow more beautiful each day."

"You didn't answer my question," she said.

"What question, dearest?"

"About what we were talking about."

"What was that?"

"About if you would love me any more if I got fat."

"Love!" he said. "Has this something to do with *love?* I am yours — I will love you forever — you, and you alone. But we would not allow it, as we would not allow a beautiful painting to mould in dampness, or a statue to be spoiled before our eyes. Certainly, we would not allow it."

"You'll lock me in a dungeon and give me bread and water." She smiled enchantingly.

"I shall watch over you, and do what is best for you, as long as I

97

live," he said. He took her hand and kissed it, kissed it twice. "That is my promise," he said.

After all, she had only gained eight or ten pounds since her marriage two years before. And she used to say back to the nagging voice that that was nothing to worry about! Her waist was so small, or nearly as small, as ever, though her corset seemed somewhat more tormenting. She took a size six glove now, and couldn't get her wedding ring off except with soap, but she suspected that her hands were a little swollen.

The worst difficulty was the French chocolates in the ribbon-tied boxes. They did make the reading of the long tedious articles on fashion, the dull pages of *The Etiquette* so very pleasant, beguiled one so, turned loose such delightful fancies. One would nibble and then take the whole melting chocolate upon one's tongue, and go on reading, and suddenly one would not see the words any more but be staring through the page as through an open door — on such a scene! Oneself in broadcloth riding habit, riding sidesaddle, over fences and ditches after a fox's bushy tail, while everyone said, Ah, would you look at that seat! (which did not mean what some people might think) or one "received" in a room as big as the lobby of the Knutsford Hotel, wearing a four-yard train, or stepped, an honored guest, wound with furs and gems, across the red sidewalk carpet into the presence of J. P. Kearns and wife, just back from Europe. Alma, dear! they said, kissing her upon the forehead under the courtly coiffure. . . .

One ruse was to lock the box in the lower left-hand compartment of the buffet, and hide the key and try not to be able to recall where it was but this was a failure every time. Alma Morelewski found that the best way to do was, after the box was about half empty anyway, to eat up all the rest of the candy in it at once so she would not have to think about it, and pray that Mr. Morelewski would not be put in mind to bring her any more, perhaps ever. But he did, after a week or two, or three, depending on when he happened to remember, and in spite of her various resolves, she was always more glad than sorry to see the familiar oblong package with Schramm-Johnson's printed all over it.

As she had been informed by her reading and as she knew from two years' personal experience, there was luxury of one kind and luxury of another, but in her opinion, the greatest luxury in all the world, greater than having breakfast in bed, which she had only had in that San Francisco hotel and which made her more nervous than not, greater than going to a chiropodist's, greater than American Beauty roses delivered to your door in a snowstorm so thick the streetcars had all stopped running, greater than any of these, was to have a box of French chocolates all to yourself (Mr. Morelewski wouldn't touch them), and choose one, and bite into it — *and put it back in its pleated brown paper cup if you didn't like it!* Of course you might eat the bitten ones later, as you ran out of the chewy kind with nuts and the brandied cherries, but in the meantime, to bite into, and *discard*, chocolate after chocolate, was splendor such as could not be equaled on this earth.

At four, just before the Queen went to her room to begin the complicated task of dressing for dinner, Dorney finally mustered up courage enough to ask her what to do with the stack of old newspapers. The awe which had frozen her solid after the reading of the scrapbook was beginning to thaw somewhat and she could even look straight at the apocalyptic young woman so covered with fame; not however, without winking a little.

"You can put them out in the coal shed," the Queen said, thinking hard a moment.

"All right," Dorney said.

The Queen turned to go and then turned back. "Oh," she said, "I don't believe either of us brought in the afternoon mail, did we?" She said it as though there was certainly something in the box and the mailman did not, time after time, go by without stopping. With agitation, too, for what was there might be the invitation (she expected it twice a day) auguring all the others, as behind the first bud, summer swarmed.

To Dorney's delight, there was a letter in the box. It was addressed to Mr. and Mrs. Joseph Morelewski, and up in the left-hand corner it said, In five days return to Mr. Teige Desmond, 615X 113th Avenue, New York City, New York. She almost flew back in the house to deliver it, the only letter that had come since her employment began.

The Queen, her face flushed, decided to read it over a cup of coffee at the kitchen table, and when Dorney came back from the coal shed, she said (though she well knew that a fashionable lady did not discuss matters of a personal nature with a hired girl), "It's from Mr. Morelewski's nephew, his sister's boy. He's coming for a long visit."

"His nephew?" Dorney said, considering. "My niece, Crystal, is three years older than me. Now wouldn't it be the strangest thing if —"

"He's young, I imagine," the Queen said hurriedly. "I'll have to send the curtains out, in the spare bedroom. This will change everything, of course, simply everything."

Dorney was curious to learn how it would, but she did not ask. She only said, "When is he coming?"

"Sometime this summer," the Queen said and distractedly shook another spoon of sugar in her coffee. "You see, he graduated from

99

the university quite a while ago and he teaches school. That is, it isn't a school exactly. It's called Columbia or something."

"I just loved our teacher, Miss Littley."

"Mr. Morelewski was telling me about him." She looked worried and, now that her flush had died away, pale. "He's very well educated. He — " She stopped, for the fashionable lady had already said far too much, and yawned delicately in place of a sigh, a habit she had.

She puzzled Dorney. It almost seemed that the famous Queen felt fainthearted about having Mr. Morelewski's nephew come for a visit. Her beautiful eyes looked nervous, unhappy. But could that be? Dorney cast her a sidelong glance, to see if it was true or only a trick that her imagination was playing, and could not determine, for now the Queen, her long eyelashes nearly resting on her cheeks, had bent her head and was reading the letter through again, too busy to be disturbed.

When Dorney came home from the Queen's after her first week's work was over, jingling two exceptionally large silver dollars in her apron pocket, she was full of plans, not only for times to come but for the present as well. At first she thought she would buy a pair of kid slippers with a strap across them, like Crystal's. Then she supposed she would buy a parasol like Crystal's, not merely for the shade but for the delight of opening it, resting the long handle upon her shoulder and twirling it around. Or a jetted shoulder cape or a jar of Recamier Balm, The Magic Beautifier, Made for and Used by Madame Adelina Patti-Nicolini, which she had seen advertised in one of the Queen's magazines (she only took a quick peek). Finally, she could not think what to get first! She even rushed ahead and wondered what to buy with the next two dollars, the next, the next and the next, until she felt hot as an oven thinking of it.

Madge settled the problem quickly and easily when she came home from Judge Towers!

"Look," Dorney said, showing what she had in her hand.

Madge had just got in and was hanging up her hat and coat behind the door. "Oh," she said, turning and looking. "You got paid, did you?"

"Yes," Dorney tried to keep a silly smile off her lips.

"Good." She put out her hand, palm up. She wanted to hold the coins, it appeared, and Dorney let her. "Oh, she'll be good pay, all right," Madge said. "You'll never need to worry about getting your wages from Mrs. Morelewski, and right on the dot, too. There's no collectors hanging around *their* house."

"No, there aren't," Dorney agreed, proud of the Morelewskis' financial integrity and her own connection with them.

Madge took up her stiff black handbag off the kitchen table, opened the large clasp with a loud snap and dropped the dollars into it while Dorney's eyes stuck out and her jaw hung slack. Madge reassured her with a friendly smile. "Hold your horses," she said, fishing down into the depths of the handbag with two fingers. "Just a min-ute." She brought out in triumph a shiny quarter and presented between thumb and forefinger. "Well, put your hand out," she said, when Dorney just stood there.

"Don't you want your spending money?"

Dorney gulped once. "But, I didn't — but, please — " she began.

"My, my," Madge said, "If you aren't a peculiar one! Here," she reached for her sister's stiff hand and dropped the coin into it, closing the fingers over the palm. "Now, that's your spending money," she added, "And it isn't every girl your age that can say she's got her own money to spend. Don't you agree?"

Dorney gulped again.

"Well, don't you?"

"You surely don't think," Crystal said from the window sill where she had been perched watching the transaction, "that a dollar seventy-five is too much to pay for board and room, and washing, and I don't know what all, do you?"

"Well, you see," Dorney began, carrying her tears as carefully as the ladies of Brusa carry water on their heads, where they have to pay a fine if they spill a drop. "You see — "

"She certainly doesn't," Madge said loudly. "She's not a thankless heathen, after all, from off a Indian reservation or somewhere." She sounded as if she was quite cross at her daughter and taking sides with her young sister. "Wanda didn't spoil her *that* much, after all."

"Dorney is going to buy me a present," Jetta announced, making her way at that moment into the room through the back door.

Dorney, still balancing her precarious tears, slid the hand with the quarter into her apron pocket. She would not have thought her heart could sink lower, but it did, saving her oddly enough from the disgrace of childish tears, for it drew her attention away by the sensation of its sinking.

"Bananas," Jetta said.

Dorney nodded while her eyes dried. She had indeed, in her folly, made such a promise. And it wasn't as if Jetta needed consolation, a legimate excuse for such a gesture. Not her. She didn't know what money meant. In fact, when Dorney had held it up for her inspection as she soared past in her swing, Jetta didn't pay any attention at all! That was Dorney's downfall. She did want someone to pay attention! "Jetta, look!" she said. "My wages! My money! The first I ever earned!" And after that, how rashly, "I'll buy you a present!" she said, not so much to be amiable as to get some kind of human response, Crystal being hard at work on the piano and Madge still absent. Jetta stopped swinging.

"What kind of a present?" she said with almost frightening earnestness.

"Why, I don't know," Dorney said. "A — some bananas, maybe. How about some bananas?"

Jetta's eyes glinted and her light lips jerked at the corners, which meant her intention (never carried out at any time) was to smile. "Bananas," she said. "And peanuts, too!"

"No, not peanuts," Dorney said, contritely. When Jetta was swinging she was a theorem, no more to be regretted than a bat upon a rafter, but down on the floor, an arm's length away, her wretchness stabbed the breast, and pity ran for her in streams.

"Then peanuts," Jetta said, coming close.

Two dollars was a good deal of money, or rather, four dollars was.

"You mean next week?" Dorney asked. Because it wouldn't hurt, next week, to buy her a bag of peanuts.

Jetta nodded.

"All right, only," in sudden maturity, she felt called upon to accomplish some moral advancement with her generosity, "if I do, you must be a good girl."

Jetta nodded again. "Bananas now," she said. "Peanuts, then." She went back to her swing. "Nice Dorney," she murmured, hoisting herself into it and swinging herself beyond the scope of compassion.

Nice Dorney! who looked now, as Jetta came through the door, like tragic Fantine about to have the eyeteeth she had sold for the sake of her child, drawn.

"You mustn't promise her things," Madge said practically, "if you don't mean it."

"Oh, I mean it all right," Dorney said. Which, of course, she did. Next day when she left the Queen's she returned home by way of Christianson's Grocery & Drygoods so she could buy the present.

A week later, when she presented her two silver dollars to Madge (without pain this time, for long consideration of the matter had made board-and-room settling a natural phenomenon against which there was no recourse), oddly enough, Jetta recalled the peanuts. To remember required a brain, which her very small and strangely shaped head could hardly be imagined to lodge, and Dorney kept her promise, therefore, with a sensation of having witnessed some sort of miracle. With the twenty cents left over she bought thread, needles and a few other such items as would go in a sewing basket if she had one, for Madge said she would have to see to her own mending. So, the "spending money" for the second week went.

The third week she kept mum about presents, but the day after she had been given her quarter by kindly Madge, she bought four two-for-a-nickel peppermint sticks at the store, one for each member of the family, including herself. Sometimes largesse attacks one, like hiccoughs. The fifteen cents left over, she kept in the Jenny Lind dish on her dresser. There was so little one could buy with fifteen cents! Jetta was pleased. "Nice Dorney," she said, sucking on the stick and swinging, while Dorney nibbled at hers on the porch step, feeling contented that someone thought she was nice, even if it was only Jetta. Crystal, when she received hers, expressed her gratitude with an ironic smile that implied its giver was of a nonage that required humoring. Madge added to hers that anything sweet made her teeth ache, and she said, "Maybe you ought to stop and think before you blow in all your money every week, though. Remember what happened to the grasshopper and the ant that time. Rainy days come along, you know! And if a person is ready for a rainy day, a person is ready for anything! As Grandpa Leaf always used to say, although actually he should of been the last man to talk, for he never could hang on to a dime, and neither could Mamma's family, so you be careful. All the ones that knew how to watch what they had was from Papa's mother's side, that I take after. You and Wanda never got nothing from them, I'm sorry to say."

Under the circumstances, Dorney did not greatly look forward to payday.

The fifth week she bought a stamped doily and a handful of different-colored embroidery cotton, but Crystal teased her so unmercifully about starting a hopebox — and who did she think she was going to marry? Schooner Bill? — that, while she stitched at it doggedly and finished it, too, even to crocheting an edge about it, she vowed she would buy nothing else in that line, and when Madge said it was pretty, she gave it to her. Lately she thought she would just drop the spending money in the Jenny Lind dish every week and when she had enough of it, some interminable years in the future, after her long desired beauty had come and in the course of nature again departed and her soft hair was buried under snow and her eyes dry and small like grapes withered upon the vine, why, then she would buy a silk dress and maybe some beads of jet. But until then . . .

What a stupid day Sunday is, anyway, she thought as she sat on the step biting her thumb. From that, it was only a step to, I wish I had — I wish I could — I wish — I wish. Her eyes went cloudy while she slowly wiped off her thumb on her apron. Wish what? You didn't have to use common sense in wishing, that was certain. There was no limit to what — *I wish I had my old geography book back.*

She remembered the day she packed her suitcase while Mrs. Diltz, poor Wanda's mother-in-law, hovered nearby.

"You're not surely going to take them schoolbooks?" Mrs. Diltz had said. "Books weigh as heavy as lead."

"I thought I would, Mrs. Diltz." She looked at them, stacked at the foot of the bed: Lossing's *Outline History of the United States* (Illustrated), Niles's *Elementary Geography*, the great *Eighth Grade Literary Reader*.

"I am very much surprised at you," Mrs. Diltz said gravely. "To take a selfish, big-I, self-centered stand like that one, when your sister ain't hardly cold in her grave, that done for you — and bought — and give — till if you live to be a hundred, you couldn't never begin to pay her back for all she done for you — and sewed — and worked — and washed and ironed — and here you got the chance to give her three motherless little children a chance at some old wore-out schoolbooks that you're all done with anyway — to save poor Thomas a few pennies, at least — him, that's packed home eats for you and never said boo and give Wanda the money to buy you the books in the first place anyway — and what do you do? What kind of a show do you make of yourself? How do you think it would look to somebody, I want to know? What would anybody imagine? I'm very surprised at you, Dorney." Mrs. Diltz bent a sad look on her as she stood clutching the *Literary Reader* to her breast. "But maybe it ain't your fault. Maybe it's just what you're made of, and besides, I don't believe anybody can expect much from quite a few of them that I see growing up nowadays — no religion no more — no proper respect for nothing — no thankfulness, that's the worst. Expecting, expecting, expecting — but when the tables is turned, when it comes to *giving* for a change — well, you see the performance."

Dorney did not miss the books as much as she thought she would, at first. She went away to Madge's and had only been there a day or two when she started to work at the Queen's. Eight to six was a long time to keep on your feet and keep moving. And by the time she got home and helped prepare the dinner, ate, helped with or did the dishes alone, it was eight o'clock, and then Madge came home and pretty soon it was nine o'clock and bedtime. When could she read? Especially as Madge kept close watch on the kerosene for the lamp and didn't believe in wasting it. But Sunday, that was a different story, and as late afternoon came she longed for a book as the Ancient Mariner longed for that puff of wind in the motionless sail to start him across the sea waters home.

Any book! That old Geography, for instance. "Italy has a delightful climate and clear, blue skies. The plains of the river Po, south of the Alps, produce large quantities of wheat and rice. They . . . pasture great herds of cows whose milk is noted for its richness. There are . . . groves of mulberry, olive and fig. . . . Italy has more sulphur than any other country. We go to Venice for beads, Naples for coral-work, and to Tuscany for perfumery and hats." She knew that much and many other bits and snatches but she should have committed it all to memory, if she had had a lick of sense, so as to be able to enjoy it now.

But the old broad green Reader! That was what she missed the most. . . .

Suddenly she straightened up, her pulse leaping. Why, there were *bookstores* in Salt Lake City! Naturally. There must be. She would take her money — sixty-five cents — no, seventy — and next week would make ninety-five — and go uptown and buy those same books back again! One, at least, or two, for if they were all drawn on and written in and generally abused they would go very, very cheap. They went cheap in Rock Springs, anyway, in that condition, but Wanda wanted nice, clean books and only bought that kind. The others carried chicken pox and one thing and another, she thought. But Dorney wouldn't be that particular. And then . . . she almost stopped breathing . . . she would buy, one by one, *the same books Miss Littley had,* that she used to bring to school and read aloud on Friday afternoons!

Miss Littley came to Rock Springs when Dorney was in the fourth grade, and left the year she graduated. Every Friday afternoon she read from some novel. That was the best part about school! That, and being lent these same books, on the promise they would be well cared for and returned in good order. Cared for! *David Copperfield! The Prince and the Pauper! Old St. Paul's!* Dorney carried them home as though they were made out of Venice glass.

She borrowed book number twenty-seven from Miss Littley the spring she was in the Sixth Grade. That was *Moby Dick* which she didn't think was very interesting after Ishmael meets up with Queequeg, the black man. However, she read along in it, hoping it would begin to improve. Up to page 119, when the terrible accident happened, it didn't, and after that betided, with so painful a consequence, she couldn't bear to take it up again. In fact, she couldn't stand to look at it, it turned such a knife in her breast . . . and that very hour, in the midst of her tears, wrapped it in newspaper to return to Miss Littley.

It would have been all right if *Moby Dick,* accidentally left out on the old gray blanket (because it was *Moby Dick* and not *Lorna Doone*) all through the hardest rainstorm Rock Springs ever knew to fall, had not been found in the horrifying condition it was on a Sunday when old Mrs. Diltz was visiting and Thomas was home from the store! Any other day, Wanda would have worked out something and nobody the wiser. She would anyway, if Dorney, her wits taking flight when she saw what had happened, had not come running with the desolate, soaked, buckling, ruined book screaming "Wanda, Wanda, Miss Littley, Moby Dick!" so wildly that even Grandpa Bannon, way over in the other yard, had opened the back door and stuck his head out to see whether Dorney was being torn limb from limb.

It didn't take old Mrs. Diltz long to find out what the disaster was, nor Thomas either.

Wanda gave Dorney her own handkerchief to mop her tears with and took the book out of her convulsive grasp. "Now, hush," she said. "I'll go to school with you tomorrow, and we'll explain to Miss Littley it was an accident, and then, either buy her another book or give her the money to pay for it. Now, stop crying," she said. "Stop, honey. The world ain't come to a end."

But it had, Mrs. Diltz took it upon herself to see that it had. She said that for the child's own sake, meaning Dorney, she should not be allowed to borrow books that she had not the money to replace, when through such disgraceful carelessness with other people's property, she let them come to rack and ruin. It was all very well to take Thomas's hard-earned money to buy that foolish teacher — yes, foolish, Mrs. Diltz repeated emphatically — another book, but what did Wanda think was going to happen to Dorney's backbone in the meanwhile? What kind of respect was she going to have for other people's property, if when she destroyed it, it was no skin off her nose? What kind of respect for other people's hard-earned money, if when it had to be as good as thrown away on her account, it was no skin off her nose, either? Mrs. Diltz went on and on, growing warmer and warmer. She could always arouse Thomas, soon he was taking sides with her, and agonized Dorney cried harder and harder, until she had to be sent to the bedroom. The upshot of it was, her mother-in-law and husband finally maneuvered Wanda over into the path of righteousness, and very sorrowfully she came and told Dorney that never, under any circumstances whatever and no matter how she promised to treat them, was she to borrow any more books from Miss Littley.

While there were still so many to read! Dorney fidgeted now, on Madge's back porch, as she remembered her old boisterous grief. She grew hot and then cold. Miss Littley would not accept either the money or a new book, but took mishandled *Moby Dick* back and said, "Well, accidents will happen, it seems," in her beautiful, cool, Eastern way. And there was the end of that world. After that, Dorney's guilt would never let her come close to Miss Littley again in the old way . . . and the bridge went up across the moat around the castle . . . and stayed that way . . . and she was left outside. She was outside still! But now she was big enough, and old enough, and had 25¢ a week spending money, and she would get back inside again or bust. She bit both her thumbs now, instead of just one, as she thought on. She would buy, one by one, those selfsame books, and besides them, the Geography, History, the Reader. . . . The rampant passion, so long forgot, came flooding back as she considered. She would buy them all, the schoolbooks and every book she could remember that Miss Littley had had. Let's see, now, there was *The Wide, Wide World* and *The Virginians* and *Rasselas* (but she could very well do without that one) and —

When? The word came like a clap of thunder. When, dear Lord? Every day through the week she had to work at the Queen's, and everything was closed on Sunday. Bookstores didn't stay open at night, did they? And if they did, Madge would never allow her to go out after the sun went down. Oh, my, she moaned softly. Well, I'll have to think of some way.

She stood up restlessly and teetered on the steps. Maybe Mrs. Luby would know about the places in town where they sold books and the hours they kept open. Or Clara Tofflemire would know. Mrs. Tofflemire had asked her to come and visit some Sunday afternoon. Maybe they would even have a book a person could borrow just for the rest of today and this evening . . . oh, what good care she would take of it. What a lesson she had learned from *Moby Dick* that the author never knew was in it! She would buy that first, for it, the one book she had not cherished enough to guard with her life, had caused her not only to lose her Garden of Eden but to know thereby *what* she had lost — today, at least, if never truly before (in spite of all her tears). It did not matter if it was interesting or if it was the dullest book in the world. Suddenly *Moby Dick* was the most important book ever written and Dorney vowed to have it before anything else!

She hurried down the steps and around the house, without a backward look at soaring Jetta, and when she went past the parlor window and heard Crystal commence Mr. Humperdinck again she thought with pleasure that after tomorrow's lesson, she would move on to somebody else.

11

AT THE CORNER SHE MET SCHOONER BILL FACE
to face, and he went through all his motions for her in the usual
way — stopping short, sashaying off to one side, making a bow, tipping his hat and saying, "Friend." She had become used to him in
the past few weeks. He started uptown, wearing his ridiculous headgear, to work in the saloon, at just about the same time that Dorney
left the Queen's to go home at night and while at first she had felt
somewhat uneasy to encounter him, and merely said hello, in reply
to his one unfailing word, when they met now, they often lingered
a moment for a little chat.

"Hot," said Schooner Bill amiably, putting his hat (this time a
Scotch bonnet with fluttering ribbons) lightly back on top of his
head.

"It really is," Dorney agreed.

"The birds is all taking it easy in the shade somewheres. Not a
peep out of 'em. You like the birds?"

"Sure I do."

"Not me." Schooner Bill stuck his bottom lip far out and moved
his head back and forth.

"Why not?"

"You look at a bird sometime," he said, after some thought. "Look
right in their eyes sometime. You know how they look back at
you?"

"Bright," Dorney offered. "Cocky."

"I'll tell you," Schooner Bill said gravely, as though she had not
spoken. "That look they got in their eyes, it just naturally *ain't
human*, that's all. And that's what I hold against 'em."

She refrained from saying that perhaps it wasn't supposed to be.

"No, sir," Schooner Bill said, again sticking out his bottom lip
and shaking his head. "Same way with a cat. They give you a look
and it just ain't human. But you take a horse, now, or you take a
dog . . . But I ain't never done nothing to no bird, and wouldn't, for
the world, because *they* can't help it."

"That's the way to think," Dorney said, feeling sorry that she wanted so much to laugh.

"You got a real human look, I notice," Schooner Bill said. "Can tell by your eyes. What's your name?"

"Dorney." She had told him many times.

"My name is Schooner Bill."

"I know it," she said gently.

"But some people ain't."

"Aren't what, Schooner Bill?"

"Got a human look. Not in their eyes, they ain't. No more than a bird. And that's what I hold against people like them. You notice sometime."

"I will," she promised.

She always felt unaccountably pleased after she had met this strange man. It was very kind of the Lord, she thought once, not to make everybody alike. He could have, as easy as not, but no, He didn't. Why didn't He?

Maybe just for the very reason that we'll think about Him, Dorney decided groping today as she went toward the Tofflemires'. We see somebody like Schooner Bill, and the next thing is, we think why is there somebody like Schooner Bill anyway? And the next thing, we think, well, why is there this and why is there that, and pretty soon, here we are thinking about God, because really who else can you think about, if you come right down to the fine points like that? And very likely that's the reason He went to all the trouble and work to make everything in the first place! So we would think about Him. But why would God want people to? Think about Him? that people, that she here on Eighth South meandering along, must look no bigger to, than ants? Littler than ants, in fact!

A door banging across the street distracted her and she looked to see who was coming out of the yellow house. It was a man in his shirt sleeves who went to the edge of the steps, looked up and down, then turned around and hurried back inside, banging the door shut behind him.

Now why did he do that? Dorney puzzled for a moment, as earnestly, it must be confessed, as she had pondered her Creator. She tossed back her hair and quickened her steps, and if anyone had seen her they would have thought she was out upon a matter of great importance.

The old dog Rupert was outside as usual, sound asleep, Mrs. Tofflemire was paying a call, but Clara was at home, sewing undershirts for the Mudge children. They were very small garments, and she hastened to tell Dorney, welcoming her in with a warm smile and offering her a comfortable chair, that they took almost no time at all to make. In fact, if it weren't for the buttonholes, you might almost say they made themselves, she said. They were going to be a surprise for the family.

"How are they?" Dorney inquired.

"Oh, just darling," Clara said, her homely face looking a good deal less so when she spoke of them. "They are just too darling for words. This morning, I was over and rubbed out a few things on the board, and give the parlor a little going over and baked up a batch of — and I tell you," she said, "them little young ones is just simply the cutest and best little kids you ever want to lay eyes on. Why, I tell you, that Ruby, and that little George, he's the oldest, they just — " She gave up for lack of words, and then for no reason her visitor could imagine, began to flush painfully. The hot color crept slowly from the base of her neck and up and over her face, until even her scalp, if one could have seen under the thick rolls of her hair, must have been red. "Well, you see," she said, "Sophie was my best friend, and so naturally her husband Joe, and the poor little kids she left behind without no mother — " She stopped helplessly, and the long bony hand she reached out for the scissors with, trembled.

"I bet you can't guess what I came for!" Dorney said, staring first at a picture on the wall, a large dumpling of a girl with her head pillowed on a crouching St. Bernard the size of a moose, entitled "Innocence's Guardian," and then out of the window until a shy, surreptitious head-turning told her her hostess had recovered her serenity, if what Miss Tofflemire had momentarily lost could be called so.

"To borrow a cup of sugar," Clara said, trying to sound gay, and hitching her chair around so that her back was a little more to the light.

"No," Dorney said. "I thought maybe you'd know about some bookstores."

Clara looked up in surprise, her needle as far out in space as her thread was long. "Bookstores?" she said, looking down again and bringing her needle in for a careful stitch. "What in the world kind?"

"Where they sell books."

"Oh?"

"Schoolbooks and all. There must be some stores like that uptown someplace."

"There must be, of course," Clara agreed, "but I don't happen to know of any. I could maybe ask Joe, though. He might know. Or somebody. Maybe at the Palace." She never said both words together, Palace Laundry where she worked, but just Palace. "Come to think of it, maybe old Ishmael would know."

Dorney pricked up her ears at the oddly familiar name.

"His name ain't that," Clara went on to explain. "But he's very funny. Down there at the Palace, he'll look at a person and say, 'Call me Ishmael,' for no reason a-tall, and so we all got to calling him Ishmael. It's kind of a joke, like."

"Why, that's the way *Moby Dick* starts," Dorney said, feeling the weird, crawling magic of syzygy down her spine. Because not half an hour ago she had been sitting and thinking of *Moby Dick* again, something she hadn't thought of for months and even years, and now Clara Tofflemire was telling her about a man down at the laundry called Ishmael, called so because he went around saying the very same thing that that very book began with, which she had only today remembered after so long a time! "Can you imagine," she murmured, burning to tell the story of the coincidence but deciding it was, perhaps, with all its ramification, a little too long.

"He reads a good deal, some of the girls was saying," Clara continued, "and I know for a fact he does, myself. Eats his lunch out on the loading platform and always got some book he's boring into. 'Call me Ishmael,' he says," she repeated, coming as close as she ever came to a laugh. "So we do. Sometimes just Ishmael and sometimes the whole thing, like it was one name — Call Me Ishmael. Somebody'll say, 'Where's Call Me Ishmael?' and here he'll come a-running. He's a kind of a roustabout around the Palace, quite a old man. That ain't his name Ishmael, you know. It's really Walter Buckingham or something like that, some of the girls was saying. He might know what you was wondering about. I could ask him. . . . Just what was you going to do with them books?"

"Read them," Dorney said. "And that reminds me. You wouldn't happen to have a book right now I could borrow, would you?"

Clara looked up and off into space, thinking hard. She jerked her thread a time or two as though she was testing its strength. "Why, let me see," she said. "We've got a Bible somewheres around, but it weighs about ten pounds and I don't know whether Mamma would — "

"You don't know whether Mamma would what?" Mrs. Tofflemire said. She had come in through the back door so quietly that they did not hear her and she tiptoed across the kitchen and into the dining room where Clara and her young visitor sat. "You don't know whether Mamma would what?" In her best silk dress and massive brown hat, Mrs. Tofflemire looked much larger than she did in her usual clothes, and when she appeared suddenly that way, as though fallen from the sky, it was no wonder that both occupants of the alcove gave a start of surprise.

"Let Dorney have the loan of our Bible," Clara said.

"I never heard of such a thing," Mrs. Tofflemire said flatly. "What for?"

111

"I didn't ask to borrow it," Dorney hastened to say. "Clara just happened to mention — what I asked was, if you maybe had a book I could take home and read."

"Since when has our old family Bible that belonged to my own father been yours, I'd like to know, to let go out of the house, with all the family records in and no telling WHAT will become of it, if you hand it to this one and that one, I'd like to know?" Mrs. Tofflemire said to her daughter. "Since when have you had the say of the Golightly family Bible, if you please?" She turned suddenly on Dorney. "My maiden name," she explained, as though accusing her of serious crime.

"It's certainly a — pretty name," Dorney ventured, after a jerky swallow.

"Pretty! I should think it was. It should be!" Mrs. Tofflemire wheeled to confront Clara again. "And now if you will kindly tell a person where you got your gall to parcel off the *family Bible*, mind you, that don't no more belong to you than it belongs to Rupert outside there on the porch full of fleas, why, I would appreciate it." She heaved like an ocean.

"Now, Mamma," Clara said, laying her sewing in her lap, "if you will just listen a minute. Dorney didn't ask to borrow the *Bible*. She just asked if we had any books around the house and I just merely mentioned — "

"Don't you now mamma me," Mrs. Tofflemire said. "I know all about you and your now mammas. You can't fool *me* with such things forever, no matter what you may think!" To the amazement of one of her listeners, at least, she dropped into a chair, covered her face with both her hands and began to cry as if her heart would break.

"Really, really, Mrs. Tofflemire," Dorney said, rushing to kneel impulsively down beside her as though she had collapsed in deadly illness, the nervousness he feels who has been moved to pluck the thorn from a wild bear's paw, not sure he will live to tell the tale, following a moment after, when she considered that this was Mrs. Tofflemire and that she was not insensible. But she did feel very sorry and stayed where she was, hoping to make amends. "Why, Mrs. Tofflemire," she said, "nobody would even dream of doing anything like that, that would make you feel so bad!"

"With all our family records in," Mrs. Tofflemire sobbed on, a tear squeezing between her fat fingers and running down her hand.

Dorney cast an imploring glance at Clara who had taken up the scissors and was idly clicking them in the air while her mother cried. She looked at them, not her, and in a little while she laid them down, folded up her work, put it in the wicker basket on the floor, pulled the silk-tufted lid down, fastened it and got to her feet.

"You're just tired," she said, pushing her chair back so she would have room to walk in front of it.

"Just tired!" Mrs. Tofflemire's shoulders shook and another tear squeezed out. "Very, very easy to say, of course."

"That's all," Clara said. "I thought it was foolishness for you to walk all the way over to Second West in all this heat, to see Aunt Nellie's girl, when you could just as well of picked a cooler time and not gone today necessarily. I'll make you some tea," she said, and went out into the kitchen. While she laid the fire, lit it, watched a moment to see if it was going to burn, then set the lid on firmly, adjusted the damper and went to the pump with the teakettle to fill it with fresh water, Dorney kept the cramped position her commiseration like a stiff gale had flung her into, on her knees. She laid a light uneasy hand on Mrs. Tofflemire's heavy skirt. "Please don't feel bad," she whispered, "Mrs. Tofflemire, please don't, you know."

When the lady she so timidly addressed, let her hands fall suddenly away from her puffy face revealing her glowing red eyes, it came as such a surprise that Dorney ducked back as if somebody had tossed something at her.

"Wouldn't you," Mrs. Tofflemire said, "wouldn't you cry if you only had the one daughter, and that daughter," she looked from her perspiring comforter to Clara who now came back into the room and took her old seat back, waiting for the water to boil, "and that daughter," she repeated "aged thirty-two, mind you, and supposedly in her right senses, couldn't rest, mind you, till she had made a fool of herself over a widower with four children? A man that won't even look at her? making herself the laughingstock of everybody till," she said, her voice rising, "I can't even go to pay a visit to my own sister's girl clear over on Second West, but what the news has got there and what should be the first thing Ada says, but is it true that Clara has got some widower on the string? Imagine that. Is it true, she says as big as life, that Clara has got some widower on the string? If I could of said yes, at least, yes, she has, he's popped the question and they're going to get married. But no, I can't say nothing like that! Either I got to keep my mouth shut entirely," Mrs. Tofflemire went on, more and more shrilly, "or I got to say, if you call having some widower on the string what *she* does, you can call it that, but I don't. What I call it is making the worst fool out of herself a woman can make out of herself over a man that don't even know she's alive, that never comes and knocks at the door to make a call, never gives her five cents worth of gumdrops, never takes her even for so much as a walk down in Liberty Park! If she had some gumption to her at least! But what does she do? Every night there she runs to Joe Mudge and them kids of his. She washes, she irons, she cooks. Sunday comes along. What does she do? Offer to go with her mother to see her mother's own sister's girl, in other words, Clara's own cousin, which is what any woman with any feeling to her, if only so much as you could put in your eye, would do? Not her. She stays home and she sews undershirts for Joe Mudge's kids — and if it ain't undershirts, it's something else, and if it ain't that, it's mending. For Joe Mudge's kids, mind you, that he wouldn't even so much as — " She refrained from saying what he would not so much as do, either because of their caller's tender years, or her own ladylike sensibilities, but not easily. She had to pull hard on the reins and snorted and puffed after she had come to a standstill.

"For Sophie's kids," Clara put in quietly.

Dorney did not dare to look in her direction for fear of what she would see.

"And that ain't the worst of it," Mrs. Tofflemire plunged on, ignoring the interruption. "If she didn't pay out the money to buy the goods for them undershirts, I will be willing to eat my hat." She tapped the brim of the one she had on, to show this was no idle threat. "Next on the program, it seems to me, my fine Clara," she said, "why, you'll have to start buying a suit of clothes for your lovely Mister Mudge! Maybe if you do that, he'll kind of forget how he can't see you for dust and start in doing some courting for a change instead of you having to do all the hard work all the time! Why don't you try buying him a suit of clothes?"

Clara stood up.

Dorney shot her an involuntary sidelong glance, the first in several moments, and what she saw was an electrical storm in sultry August buttoned into a taut gray cotton dress. In a moment the explosion would come, the small house burst in a million pieces. Dorney wanted to shut her eyes tight and clamp her hands over her ears, but the lightning did not flash nor the thunder roll, and when Dorney dared look again, Clara was just standing there saying, "Maybe I will," and then, "the kettle's boiling, I'll get your tea."

It never broke at all, that tempest.

After the bullfighter has killed his bull he does not keep stabbing and jabbing away at him. He pulls out his sword and that's the end of the battle. Mrs. Tofflemire's last thrust seeming to have accomplished whatever it was she wanted, she did not reply to this but merely fished for her handkerchief, blew her nose and got back to normal again. She removed her hat, tossed it to the lounge, wiped her damp face and began to run her fingers through her stiff gray hair, making cooling paths through it. "Now what was it you was saying," she said to the rather pale young visitor who had taken a seat on the edge of the rocking chair and was thinking how to make her exit as soon as possible, "about a book?"

"I wanted to borrow one," Dorney said. It seemed a long time ago.

"My father's brother was a great reader," Mrs. Tofflemire said as though nothing had happened. She reached down and unbuttoned all the buttons of her right shoe, and the sides spread wide.

"Was he?" Dorney said, clearing her throat.

"Oh, a great reader, till he lost his eyesight on account of it and couldn't tell light from dark. My mother always used to say, them that reads had just as well take a stick and poke their eyes out. It comes to the same thing in the long run."

When Clara came in with the tea, bringing a cup for Dorney as well, Mrs. Tofflemire drew a sigh of pleasure and said, "Well, this ought to hit the spot," sipping it as if they had been thus amiably engaged the whole time, and that not five minutes before her daughter had been the same as wallowing in her own aortal blood. She began to chat about the relative on whom she had paid her call, while silent Dorney regarded an apparently unmaimed Clara, not quite believing her eyes. The spinster peeped at her sewing box from time to time but she made no move to take up her work again. Something, however, about the set of her jaw engaged that she would finish the little shirts, all of them, sooner or later, and that when evening came, as always, she would take up her shawl and go to the widower's house.

" — and who should I see when I got to State Street," Mrs. Tofflemire said (her narrative had sent her to her destination, accounted for the hours of her visit, and now was concerned with bringing her home), "but that awful Schooner Bill."

"I saw him, too!" Dorney said, pleased to be reminded of the fact.

"He ought to be locked up, I thought to myself when I saw him," Mrs. Tofflemire said. "And I think so, every time."

"I don't know why, Mamma," Clara said.

Dorney stiffened, thinking hostilities were going to break out anew, but Mrs. Tofflemire only smiled painstakingly at her daughter. "Well, I'll tell you why," she said in a gentle voice. "He's crazy as a loon, that's why, and a crazy woman is bad enough, but a crazy man . . . There are ladies and girls on the street, remember. And one of these days somebody is going to maybe regret very much that such a man has been allowed to run loose. Very much! Because the place for a man like him is in a asylum behind bars. That's why!" Her face, full of ominous kindliness, gave off a sort of greenish light, as carcasses are said to do in darkness on the desert.

"But Schooner Bill wouldn't hurt anybody!" Dorney couldn't help protesting. "Why, he wouldn't hurt a fly."

"Now, Mamma," Clara said. "Don't bother with nothing like that. He's been working and earning his own living for years, and everybody knows him by now and nobody's scared of him. In fact, the craziest part about him is the people at the saloon putting them different kinds of hats on him and letting him wear them around the streets. But that's just a joke. So don't you start worrying your head over something like that, now."

Mrs. Tofflemire only repeated, "That's why!" still more significantly, and puckered her lips.

"Goodness," Dorney said in consternation. "Why, that would be — please, Mrs. Tofflemire, don't try to get Schooner Bill put in the asylum, because, truly — " She twisted her fingers together. (Because, don't you understand, Mrs. Tofflemire — who would take his place if you did? What acrobat or dancing bear or gypsy in bangles and colors will come down the dull street instead of him, to liven up the world? because — don't you understand?) She thought of a parrot on a post, saying *Friend*, of passing it each day, of the green bird dying, the post empty, how that would be, while her heart ached. "He's not mean or anything! Really."

"Now, Mamma, Schooner Bill's all right," Clara said. "Everybody has known him for years."

"A crazy man should be taken out of circulation before somebody has the need to regret it," Mrs. Tofflemire said. "But *I* can't do it all alone. A lone woman." She bent down and unbuttoned her left shoe and wriggled her foot in it. "A lone woman," she said again, liking the phrase. On her lips it conjured up a solitary female in a band of hunters, bringing down her leopard with a single shot.

Clara kindly strolled to the gate with Dorney when she left, saying that she would ask next day at the Palace whether anybody knew where a bookstore was. She was sure nobody would but Ishmael. Still, she would ask.

Dorney thanked her, then blurted out, "Didn't you ever want to run away from home?" She was sorry for the question when she saw how alarmed Clara looked and wished she could take it back, but it was said and there was no help for it.

Clara turned her head to gaze at the small house in between the vines. On the porch Rupert sprawled out sleeping. His eyes stayed shut as they passed, but his tail had bumped a time or two. Inside, behind the white curtain, Mamma sat. "Run away?" she said, turning back.

"You know."

"No," Clara said, wetting her lips. "I wanted to *die*, yes, but not run away."

"Why not? Because you didn't want to leave your — Mrs. Tofflemire?"

"Her bark is lots worse than her bite," Clara said. "No, not that. It's just — " She thought for quite a long while, crossing her arms on her flat chest and hiding her lank hands between her body and where the insides of her thin upper arms pressed against it. "I don't know how to say," she said. Her great nose twitched. "It's just — " She drew a quick, deep breath as though to test out if she could fill all her lungs with air, but exhaled little by little. "To do some of the easiest things," she said carefully, "like — like writing your name down when somebody at the laundry gets married and they take up a collection and buy a present and ask you to sign the paper that everybody else has signed, well, some people might not think so, but can you imagine? you got to be — brave. Honestly. Like walking across a empty floor of a big room if there's people all around the edges, or — just going to the butcher shop where the butcher says Hello, Miss Tofflemire, how's the world treating you? The easiest things, like them. You see, when you're ugly," she had trained herself to say the word as the disabled learns to mention his affliction without outwardly flinching, but with the almost imperceptible pause before it, that informs he meets it anew every time, "you ain't brave," she said. "I mean, maybe, you could hit a burglar over the head with a flower pot, or jump in the river to pull out somebody, like Joe or the kids, or even somebody you didn't know — or not need no bandage over your eyes if you was going to be stood up and shot. But when it comes to what some people might think was the easiest things — why, you — I don't know how to explain," she said. "In fact, I don't know how I got started even trying to explain in the first place except that you happened to mention running away." She stopped, apologetically.

"You aren't ugly!" Dorney put in the fervent statement she had been saving for several moments. "Cross my heart and hope to die, if you are."

"You're sorry," Clara, strict and harsh who had been so mild, accused.

"No, I'm not! See, look at me and see if I am!" Dorney said, trying to appear as if she had never been sorry about anything in her life.

Clara watched her a moment, her face softening. "For a girl that ain't only fourteen," she said, "you're — You don't take after your sister, sure, and you ain't like that Crystal." She smiled down. "Well, since I got as far as I did with what I was saying," she said, "all I wanted to end up with was, there ain't no worse coward nowhere than a homely woman that knows she's homely. And there ain't nobody — nobody! — braver, nowhere, than a pretty woman that knows how pretty she is! Not even a broody hen fighting off a hawk. So anyway, about what you happened to mention — unless they're forced to, cowards don't go no place if they can help it. They stay right where they are."

12

FOR A MONTH NOW, OR MORE, WHEN DORNEY CREPT softly into the Queen's kitchen at a minute or so to eight in the morning she found everything in order, just as she had left it the day before. Sometimes a used coffee cup stood in its saucer on the drainboard, or a cloudy glass in the sink, but no more was even one chafing dish, let alone the two of them, found to be used, or the flat bake pan discovered buttery and brown with drifts of powdered sugar like snow upon it, in need of a scraping. Dorney was mystified but relieved. A real midnight snack such as the Morelewskis had been accustomed to feast on caused as much commotion as a whole big dinner and when the dishes were not soaked, it was a job of sometimes an hour to bring the kitchen to a state suitable for the Queen to get her breakfast in.

This meal was not what it once had been. No more did the Queen prepare her golden sticks of bacon, fry large eggs, toast with a fork thick slices of bread, or spoon out crimson or green jam or quivering blobs of purple jelly. She still fluttered back and forth in her floating wrappers, her halcyon hair down around her shoulders, on her sharp heels, to the sink, to the glass-doored cupboard, to the blue enameled stove, while Dorney went on with her work, but it was merely to bring to the table half a butterless roll, a cherry or two in a spoonful of weak juice, and her coffee. Lunch was no better. And the long dim-lighted lengthwise nap of the afternoon from which she had risen as from a bountiful meal, rosy and warm, had shrunk to an up-and-down forty winks she came out of with a chilly little shudder. She would reach out, even on a warm day, for her ice-wool shawl or long spotted silk scarf, and rub her hands together as one does in winter, and gape till the tears ran.

With what Dorney supposed was the Queen's sad loss of appetite had come an unfamiliar restlessness. She no more than got settled in her wadded wicker chair than she was out of it and somewhere else, pacing in the well-tended garden, perhaps, unless the old man who kept it was out there at work, when she stayed indoors, or rearranging the pillows in the cozy corner or doing something else. If she sat, she would stir in her chair, and sooner lay what magazine she had in her lap than read it.

Besides, her carriage often came for her at two now, instead of on the hour of six, so she could shop or visit her dressmaker or milliner, and then Dorney had to lock all the doors and windows herself before she went home. These frequent absences — something new, for in the weeks before, while she had often said she might go shopping — "I may go uptown shopping this afternoon, Dorney, and if I do, will you be sure to bring the mail in out of the mailbox before you go?" — the Queen had not really done it, but stayed at home dozing, reading, helping herself to this or that — were like holidays to Dorney. They gave her a chance after she had rushed like a cyclone through her work, finally to read the magazines stacked here and there about the house and sit in the sacred wicker chair with her toes gingerly touching the footstool. But she breathed easier in the kitchen or on a hard edge of a parlor chair, for the creaking coalshed door and the slapping tendril of vine against the window might signal the Queen's reapproach for money, a lace handkerchief or some other forgotten item . . . and the more uncomfortable Dorney was as she read the less her conscience bit her.

They also gave her a chance to look at the Queen's things! When the Queen was really gone, when after half an hour she did not come back, Dorney tiptoed down the carpeted hall and slipped in through the half-open door to the bedroom!

She knew it well, for she swept, dusted and set it to rights every day. But because its inner reality had never been revealed (the towering closet doors shut) and because she was there under new circumstances, of her own free will and pleasure and for no reason but to find this secret, she might have been landing for the first time on Corsica. Forgotten were the many glimpses of it through this same door as she scurried past in the early morning to dust the parlor (the Queen still sleeping in the half-dark, her hair flooding the pillow), forgotten its look when, the bed tumbled, the spread looming like a tent over the chair in the corner, the tall bolster standing on end, she came in to snap the blinds up on its disarray and make it neat again.

She had never been here before! Stopping still, stepping from rose to ingrain rose, she discovered its essentialness, where the long limp gloves came from, the slipping beads, the tender stockings, the fan with the sea waves on, what pressed against the doors . . .

He dead, she dead, stunning Carlyle and his dark Jane, gone from their house in Cheyne Row, Chelsea, do ought think ill of them who visit there, who touch his tasseled dressing gown, breathe upon his spectacles and lift his books? who handle her pens, her page of household sums, her threadbare basque, then hold her laudanum bottle to the light? These are palmers. Do they pry? Such was Dorney, Respectful to the point of holding her breath like a swimmer under water, light-handed as a shadow, she looked at the Queen's possessions, at everything she could see without disturbing anything else, and if she fingered a velvet sleeve or blew into a plume or rubbed a satin band across her cheek, have not creditable tourists done much worse in Venice, Paris, Dumfries, say?

When she discovered the stack of candy boxes at the far end of the closet, row after row of them, her heart leaped though the sight of them came as no real surprise. If you go through Windsor Castle even under stairs and in dark cabinets, it does not astound you if you perceive precious and costly things! The unusual state of affairs (there) would be if you *didn't*, if you pulled open a door and saw a jumble of old shoes, a split suitcase, a broken umbrella, cracked dishes and a lot of old bunting. Then would be the time to stare! Dorney was dumbfounded only when the many boxes were discovered to be empty!

Whether, if they had not been, she would have sampled their wares, there is no saying. She was not put to the test. While she looked down into the vacant box (wide-eyed with astonishment), her mouth got as liquid as if she was gazing at the fat bonbons themselves that had faintly stained the bottom here and there with transparent gray-looking places, that had left, she bent her head down and sniffed, so delicious a smell of good bright chocolate . . . but she said to herself she would not have eaten even one!

She decided that the Queen at some time or other must have had a great ball and had these boxes standing about here and there, all open, for the guests to dip into as they pleased. What a lovely ball it must have been. It was no wonder that the day following, the Queen had saved these boxes when she cleaned up after the party, for they were beautiful with ribbons of every color in the rainbow, young women's faces, babies, flowers and dogs pictured on their lids. Most had Schramm-Johnson written across their labels, "World's Finest," but some had other names, a few in a foreign language. Dorney hit upon the great ball as the most reasonable explanation for these as she had never seen one of them anywhere about the house, or even seen the Queen eating a chocolate.

There was no doubt about it, many of Alma Morelewski's habits were changing, and while she was pleased to grow more beautiful — for she did, she saw it herself, as the (not seven or eight but) thirty-one pounds she had gained since her marriage began to melt away one by one — still, her days were not so pleasant as they had been. When she opened her eyes in the morning she was happy in the old way, with wordless and satisfying thoughts in her mind. —

house! husband! no job! clothes! young! beautiful! never die! break-fast! — as she stretched as far as she would go all ways and yawned and put her silky hands up to her soft face and then held them off to look at the luminous nails on her fingers. But then came remembrance. No breakfast! Not what could be called that anyway. No taking this or that in the midmorning, either. As good as no lunch. No midafternoon snack. And up at the restaurant, no dinner. For after two years of such collations as she had been used to eating there, a mere slice of beef, a green leaf, a bit of fruit and nothing else could hardly be called a dinner. Worst of all, at midnight, having come home from the Salt Lake Theatre or the Grand or from a drive in Liberty Park, there would be no refreshment prepared by the greatest chef in Salt Lake City, to go to bed and dream on! No more Welsh rarebits, crêpes Suzettes, German pancakes, melting sugar and burning brandy! All this happiness was a thing of the past although Joe had promised her that as soon as she could get into the turquoise blue dress she had worn on their first evening to-gether, and button it all up and cinch the belt in as she used to, he would let her eat again.

Where she made her mistake was to have put the dress on for him, or tried to put it on, when he asked her to for old times' sake. She should never have kept the dress in the first place! cheap thing that it was. If she had worn only her new things, he might not have noticed for a long while that she . . . was . . .

Even now, the word *fat* and recollection of his face as he watched her helpless struggles in front of the mirror, made her feel that terrible clutch of fear in the pit of her stomach all over again. Was it fear? Or what was it? No matter how alarmed Joe might look, she knew she would not really lose her beauty. Not now, at least. Why, she was only twenty-three years old, barely turned twenty-three, and here he had got so frightfully upset because . . .

"My darling," he said, coming up close to her as she stood, flushed, panting and neither in nor out of that miserable dress, look-ing as if he saw the mould of fatal gangrene spreading. "Why, my darling! She cannot fasten her gown. . . . " He often spoke to her as though of somebody else.

"Oh, yes, she can!" she said, giving a desperate wrench to the bodice that cracked the cheap silk. "There, you see!" She began to cry stormily. "Don't look at me like that!" she said. "You look like I've got leprosy! *Lots* of wives can't get into some ugly dress that they didn't like in the first place, and their husbands don't stand and look at them like they were — "

"But, my darling." Joe was pale, as though it mattered very much. "She can't go on like this." He half whispered the words. "She was

122

too wonderful, too beautiful. . . . Shall I see this happen before my eyes?"

She stripped off the dress and stamped on it. "I hate it," she sobbed. "I always hated it! And I hate you!" She knew she lied because, never loving anything, she had never hated anything, either. She flew to the bed and flung herself on it, face down, her arms up over her head. "Go away," she said, when he came and sat down beside her and took up a loose strand of her hair and kissed it and bent down close and spoke into the crevice between her shoulder and ear.

"Alma, my beautiful, listen."

Alma Morelewski did not sulk, though for this doting and indulgent husband to find a flaw in her beauty shocked and pained her, and she did not squabble. She never wanted to quarrel or cry or make scenes.

Alma Morelewski, her mother said, and everybody else who had ever been acquainted with her, was easygoing.

Thus constituted, and because her husband was so aroused at the discovery that she couldn't get into the dress, and because of his promise of so many delightful things when it was all over, Alma Morelewski went faithfully to work to starve herself. She let her husband, who was in dead earnest, tell her exactly what and when and how much to eat every day. It was disagreeable to have to suffer from a constant gnawing in her vitals and she didn't like it a bit, but though she grumbled she did not once go against his orders, not so much as by a stolen mouthful.

And the only time she was happy was when she was asleep.

Sure enough, protest though she might it was one's natural constitution and nothing to do with food, in a few days she could lap the belt of her newest lace skirt over two inches and Joseph Morelewski was proved to be right. Then, her corset, when she pulled hard at the strings, began to meet behind and did not dig at her so viciously as it had the week before. Then, when she tried on older dresses, they almost fastened and only split a little under the arms, and she could see, very faintly, the thin raying bones of her hand.

She had not thought she was any the less beautiful, but she must have been, for she could see now in her mirror that she was growing more beautiful every day. This was fine, like learning she had much more money in the bank than she remembered and could, as a consequence, buy much more of what it took to make her happy than she supposed. Of course, what it took to make her happy was perfect peace and plenty, and that, at the present moment, she was doing sadly without, but the day was not far off when the odious turquoise dress would fit and she could once more enjoy those pleasures without which life was an empty shell.

Joe was ecstatic. Wasn't it odd that a man would think of his wife as if she were a painting or a statue? And preserve her like that? Maybe it was because he was born in the old country. Sometimes her husband's passion for her puzzled Alma Morelewski very much. Yet, it was nice to be made so much of even if you had to go through a lot at the same time. It really was.

When she was dressed and ready to go uptown to meet Joe, it was her habit to look in the glass for long minutes inspecting her costume, to see if it was successful and to what degree. But now, at this hour, waiting for the carriage to come, hat on, gloves on, parasol in hand, when of all the day her beauty stood highest as the sun does in the sky at noon, her attention was all on herself. It is worth any price! she would think ardently of the almost unearthly loveliness that stared back at her from the mirror with vast eyes. Oh, it is. And she would forget the dull ache across her middle that spoiled her nap and took away the joy of life. In the carriage, riding up town, however, she would begin to sigh again and think nothing was worth so much trouble as she was going through, looks or anything else.

Mr. Morelewski sat across the table from his wife, giving her, as usual, his unwavering attention.

"How he is going to envy me!" he said suddenly.

"Who?" she asked, poking with her fork at a bit of green and not looking up.

"Alice's boy Teige," he said.

"Oh, you mean your nephew." His visit had been delayed and she had almost forgotten him, but now she recalled that he was coming next week. She frowned.

"What troubles you, my darling?"

"Nothing." She had never had a House Guest before, and she would have to read up on it in the book, for there was a whole chapter dedicated just to that, and train Dorney to do several things and buy her an apron and little cap. She would have to start in tomorrow, to get ready for him. It would be no end of bother, especially when she didn't feel like herself and everything was so dismal anyway.

"But you frown. Your beautiful forehead . . . We must not have it marred by a frown."

Tears started to her eyes. "Oh, quit it," she said irritably. "I can't eat. Now I'm not supposed to frown. Next I guess I can't breathe. Why don't you just put me in a glass case and put a lock on it and be done with it?"

He reached out to pat her hand but she took it away. "My little tiger," he said. "Always she is the dove and now she is the little tiger. Well, it will soon be over. Soon she will be happy again."

"If I'm not dead," she said darkly.

"Then, I shall bring you what you like . . . the chocolates, yes, my lovely child?"

"When?" she asked.

"Soon, very soon."

"I've got money myself. I could buy some myself if I wanted," she threatened. She did not really mean it, and yet, why not? What was the use of feeling so miserable all day long when life was so short anyway? Just to be beautiful for Mr. Joseph Morelewski?

"Life is too short," she said. "Besides, I never heard of such a thing. You wouldn't starve yourself for me. No man would. So why should I?"

"But you will keep your promise?"

"I didn't make any promise."

"It is only because I love you to madness."

"You don't love me." She stared at him coldly. "I'll keep my promise, as you call it, till next week. Next — next Friday. But that's as long as I will."

"Few women are loved so, Alma."

"Pooh."

"I shall prove my love."

She softened. He had been very, very good to her and for two years she had had every happiness a woman could ask of life. "I love you, too," she said. "I really do, but I mean it about next Friday. I'm going to order everything on the menu next Friday night and whether I get into the turquoise dress or I don't, I don't care because I'm going to throw it away anyway."

Alma Morelewski spent what was left of the following morning, after she got up and breakfasted, reading in The Etiquette of Today the chapter entitled "Visiting and House Parties," from the very beginning, where a house party was defined as "a party consisting of from four to twenty guests gathered in a country mansion for any term from three days to a fortnight," to the very end where it said that "while a hostess may be charmed with some little remembrance from an agreeable and appreciative visitor, she would justly feel hurt and annoyed if after every house party the post and express brought her packets of gifts from tactless guests." She had read the chapter several times before but never when she was going to be required to put its tenets into practice, and now it struck her as very complicated indeed. She began to feel quite cold and nervous, with clammy hands, as she had felt at the Coronation, when the Governor of Utah went through the ceremony of putting the crown on her head.

She reminded herself that she *had* been through such a thing, had been famous and renowned for a time, still was, as a matter of fact, for did not a few people even yet give little jabs and pokes to others and whisper that there was Queen Alma!

The expected guest was only Joe's sister Alice's boy Teige, a mere relation, not the owner of the Comstock Lode! Of course, his father Mr. Desmond was well off and Teige had been through college and now was a professor of something at Columbia, some kind of a school there in New York City and probably imagined he was very smart and used big words and made other people feel about two feet high. That made it unpleasant to think of him coming, but the main reason she felt so disturbed and excited was because this was the first time she would ever have had a House Guest, and could apply some of the regulations in the book that had been her Bible for two long years. Like a man called on to make a speech in a language he has studied by mail but never heard spoken, she was not entirely easy about the performance and thought that the showdown had come a little too soon.

In the afternoon she went uptown and bought some little white aprons for Dorney and some little white caps.

Next morning, when she went out into the kitchen for breakfast she brought them with her. Dorney was to wear them, she said, during the visit of Mrs. Morelewski's nephew, Mr. Teige Desmond, who was coming sometime next week, she did not know exactly when. Dorney put down her broom and propped the dustpan up against the baseboard and tried one on instantly, also one of the caps. When she attempted to see herself in the shiny side of the tea-kettle, the Queen kindly told her to go and look in the long mirror in the hallway.

When Dorney came back, she said it was a very pretty cap and apron, but privately she decided she did not like them very well. They were thin, crisp and full, of fine batiste, and the apron ties made a nice big bow in back, but she did not like them.

She told Madge and Crystal that evening what the Queen had bought, and surprised herself by adding that she would rather she hadn't, somehow.

"You're just afraid of looking like a housemaid," Crystal said.

"I don't even know how a housemaid looks because I've never seen one," Dorney said, "so how could I be afraid of looking like one?"

"That's the Dorney side coming out," Madge said. "That's that old Virginia pride for you. From what I've heard tell, them Dorneys must of had their nose up in the air till if they'd of stood out in a rainstorm they'd of drownded, the older generations anyway.

Prouder than jays, the whole outfit! Scrub their steps in the middle of the night so nobody'd see them do it, after they got poor, and I don't know what all. Papa used to tease Mamma about it sometimes, some of the ways she had. The Leafs wasn't like that."

"That isn't what — " Dorney began.

"There's nothing wrong with being a housemaid," Crystal said, examining a pampered white hand.

Dorney swallowed a saucy retort. "That isn't what I *mean*," she said. She never had minded being a housemaid, because she didn't think of herself as that. In the old days, as she knew from *Kenilworth*, the maids of people like Queen Elizabeth were of noble blood themselves, Duchesses and such like. They were called Ladies in Waiting. And no matter what kind of work she had had to do, she didn't feel lowered down a bit, because she always thought of herself as a Lady in Waiting in service to a Queen. But now, if she had to wear a white cap and apron, why, that was a different thing altogether, and she didn't care for it.

"Well, say what you mean, then."

She couldn't. Something in her rebelled but she did not know what.

"The Dorney side coming out," Madge repeated musingly. "I've been noticing it, and I can't say I'm glad."

127

13

ALMA MORELEWSKI BEGAN THE MORNING, WHAT there was left of it, by bringing a ruled tablet, two pencils which she had cautiously sharpened with a paring knife over the woodbox in the kitchen, and the yellow *Etiquette* to the dining-room table. There she took a seat, laid these items neatly out, opened the book to page 403, pressed her palm down the middle of it to make it stay open, and began to read. All she needed was a pair of spectacles to look like the most serious scholar who ever lived. From time to time she underlined certain words heavily with her pencil though she had never so much as made a light V or ? along the margin of the book before.

She read, "It rests with a hostess to confer blessings of comfort and pleasure by always forbearing to force a guest to take part in any planned pleasuring or expedition," and knitted her brows. Ought she to plan a picnic? She pulled it to her, flipped back the cover of the tablet and wrote *picnic* on the first exposed sheet. If they all went out to Saltair for a Sunday afternoon, could that be considered an expedition? She wrote *expedition* and in parentheses beside it J, which meant that she would have to talk the matter over with Mr. Morelewski, perhaps this evening.

The dining-room chair she sat on was very hard, and the high, straight back had certain knobs and whorls up and down it that hurt her soft shoulders. It made her feel engaged in grave affairs and full of earnest resolve to sit on it. "If the guest be a bachelor or man alone," she underscored, "a quick-witted manservant may be trusted to do the honors at the station." Perhaps old Mr. Sodaquist, the gardener, could be sent. He didn't look very quick-witted with the tobacco juice running out of the corner of his mouth and that one white eye of his like a hard-boiled egg, but looks were deceiving. He was said to own half a block of property over on Third West. After all, you couldn't hire a butler just to meet somebody at the railway station. What would you do with him afterwards? She wrote *meet* on the sheet of tablet paper, deciding to worry some more about the problem later on.

"A maid or manservant may fulfill the office of conducting the visitor to his room, as the hostess does this only in the case of the arrival being of the female sex." Lots of hostesses didn't know that and must look very foolish as a consequence. Alma Morelewski was glad she was not of their number, but felt as if she had escaped by only the narrowest margin.

What did Teige Desmond look like, anyway? She began to edge the paper with little circles, like a string of pearls. Joe wasn't bad-looking with his gray hair and his eyebrows so black like that. His skin being rather dark made his teeth look white. Of course, he was only an inch taller than she was. She thought fretfully of how thin he was, and could eat anything he wanted any time of the day or night. If that didn't show it was a person's constitution! and here she had to go hungry . . . that is, until next Friday night, when she would more than make up for lost time. Now, where was she? Oh, yes, Teige Desmond. His father was Irish, a contractor and builder, married again because Joe's sister Alice had died. The Irish weren't very good-looking as a general rule. That redheaded, freckled, flat-footed girl at the boardinghouse, the one that worked at the Templeton Hotel, named O'Hoolihan or something, she was Irish and she certainly wasn't anything to brag about. They were very staunch Catholics, too, somebody was saying. She tore off the sheet of paper bearing the circles, put it off to one side and took back the first sheet again. On the next line under the word *meet* she wrote *ask*, which meant, ask Joe whether Teige is a Catholic or not, just for the sake of curiosity. No, as far as looks was concerned, if he took after the Irish side of his family he probably wasn't anything to brag about. She pushed the paper away and pulled the book closer, hovering over it to keep out of reach of the murderous chair back.

She put by the page of notes to herself, and took a fresh one on which she printed DORNEY in block letters across the top. She looked at it. Dorney was certainly an odd name to give a child, but she was rather an odd little girl, so it seemed to kind of fit her some way. Actually, she wasn't so little. She must be a good five feet six, possibly a little more, and must weigh about a hundred and twenty. She had probably got her growth now and wouldn't grow any more, except to blossom out. Of course she didn't need so much blossoming, really.

On this page she was going to write down what Dorney would be expected to do while Teige was here. She took up the pencil again and idly drew a little scalloped line around the name, like an oblong doily. It was nice she lived so close and didn't have to go back and forth on the streetcar like the other hired girl did, but could just cut across the empty lot on Eighth South and step over the Fifth East alley. There was such a difference in hired girls. Of course she had only had two so far, Maude, and now Dorney, but that was enough to give her some idea. Dorney must have had a nice bringing up wherever it was she lived before she came here to stay with her sister. It wasn't hard to tell, by the way a person acted and the way they talked. She wasn't somebody that got on your nerves, either, although you knew she was around every minute, while Maude, on the other hand, was just like a chair or a table. In fact, how Maude ever got a man to pay enough attention to her to marry her was a mystery but maybe it was true that there was a Jack for every Jill, the way the old saying went. Anyway, Maude had quit to get married, and Dorney had asked for her job almost the very next day, which saved a lot of bother.

The point of Alma Morelewski's pencil retraced the scalloped line around Dorney's name. What nice thick hair she had hanging down her back like that and what eyelashes. Of course, she'd have to start pinning it up before long because she would soon be fifteen, or was it sixteen? It was a pretty shade of brown, too, really beautiful, not like most brown hair, and her eyes were that funny hazel color. Still holding her pencil, Alma Morelewski with three soft fingers smoothed a wisp of hair up from the nape of her neck. I'm glad my hair is blond, though, she thought. I'm glad my eyes are blue, because blue eyes are the prettiest, really, and so is blond hair.

She bent over the book again and sought out her place. "The hostess must bear in mind that she is duty bound to take every care that her visitor is properly waited upon." She slid the flower-decorated sheet marked Dorney nearer under her hand and began to copy word for word, for here began the list of duties for her to perform. "A skilful maid deftly opens the guest's bags and boxes, quickly lays out the contents on the dressing table and in the drawers and closets, and carries off the travel-stained shoes and dress for a thorough brushing." She tilted her head back to admire the round letters of her handwriting. She had at least learned how to write in school, and learned enough grammar so she didn't sound like a country jake even if Mamma kept her out after the sixth grade because the new Sugar House school was built too far away. Let's see, now, where was she? Oh, yes, right here near the middle of the left hand page. She wrote again, diligently.

"Every morning the capable maid taps at the guest's door, asks at what time and at what temperature the bath shall be drawn, sets the fire going if the weather is chill, opens the windows and to the masculine visitor brings hot shaving water and his cleaned and polished shoes. In the afternoon, when the guests retire to their rooms to dress for dinner, a maid should tap at the doors, ask if any assistance is needed . . . and . . . bring extra lights or hot water when required, and as soon as the rooms are vacated, strip the beds of their sham covers and turn them down for the night, draw shades or close the shutters, lay forth night robes and dressing gowns at the foot of the bed, replenish the washstand . . . and . . . carry out the walking shoes and clothes that show the least signs of dust, to be cleaned and returned in perfect condition the next morning. As a final attention, a small tray bearing a jug of ice water and a tumbler is placed on the bedside table; and the servant makes doubly sure that the reading lamp is filled, the bedside candle trimmed and the match box well filled."

She needed a second sheet before she got done and her hand tingled from the unaccustomed employment. She laid the pencil down and flexed her fingers, continuing to read and turning the pages with her left hand. That seemed to be all there was concerning a maid's duties to the guest, that is, Dorney's. The rest of the chapter had only to do with the obligations of the hostess herself, and taking back the sheet of paper she had started out with originally she printed ALMA across the top, supplementing the few cryptic words already noted there with some more. The list then read:

> picnic
> expedition (J)
> meet
> ask
> cheering and nursing (in case)
> telegraph blanks
> dry biscuit? & sherry
> Joe's alarm
> every other day

to remind her of what she might otherwise forget.

The conference was held on the side porch after lunch. The Queen was sitting in the wicker chair when Dorney went out there, summoned by her call, but she did not have her feet on the stool. She was reading something that looked like a letter.

"You may have a seat on the railing, if you like," she said cordially, looking up.

Dorney backed over to it and sat down, feeling rather awed, for this was the first time she had ever been invited to sit and talk to the Queen.

"I want to go over a few things with you about Mr. Morelewski's nephew coming on a visit," the Queen said. "He will arrive next week sometime, we don't know just when. So you will have to be," she paused, seeking the right expression, "more of a maid then, be-

cause of there being a house guest in the house, you understand."
She said this last in rather a rush and her listener was not sure she
had caught it exactly.

"How do you mean?" Dorney asked with much respect.

"Well, the way I mean," the Queen said, "there are certain
things —" She took up the top sheet of what appeared to be a
letter and Dorney could see a flower through it, drawn at the top,
and some large letters making the word YENROD. "For instance,"
she said. "If the house guest arrives during the day, the first thing
you have to do after he gets up to his room is, you have to open all
his suitcases and his trunk and everything and go through them."

"What for?" Dorney asked, shocked. Madge wouldn't even let
her put the clean ironing away in the bottom drawer of her big
dresser and Wanda had been very particular, too, drilling it into her
never to snoop around in other people's property or open any boxes
or get into cubbyholes of a desk or anything like that, which was why
she felt so guilty when she looked at the Queen's things when the
Queen was out of the house. At this moment she was reminded
vividly of her transgression and the way she had come to discover the
empty candy boxes in the back of the closet. She saw herself opening the wardrobe doors, tiptoeing across to the bureau, lifting the lid
of the jewel case to peek inside, and blushed so furiously at the memory that her eyes stung. Her heart began to pound then, for surely
the Queen must know what she was recollecting. . . .

"Why, because you're supposed to hang everything up and lay
things out on the dresser and put things in the drawer, you see," the
Queen said, missing the fire for she was consulting the handwriting
again. "The guest's things, you know. Mr. Morelewski's nephew
from New York City."

"I never knew anybody should do that," Dorney said when her
flush had died away enough to risk drawing the Queen's attention
to herself.

The Queen took a pencil out of the pocket of her skirt and made
a little x on the paper. "Do what?" she said.

"Go through a person's suitcases and trunks like that."

The Queen put her pencil away. "It isn't exactly going through
them," she said. "I maybe expressed myself — you're supposed to un-
pack them, I mean."

"All right," Dorney said. "If you don't think Mr. Morelewski's
nephew will get mad if I do."

"Oh, he won't get mad," the Queen promised, glancing once more
at the page she held. "Then you're supposed to — carry away his
travel-stained shoes and suit."

Travel-stained. Didn't that sound —? Stained with travel. Like
Butch Cassidy coming back to Star Valley after riding clear up from

Mexico. She could see him and Little Dipper, tired and dusty and ready to drink the bubbling spring dry. What was it the Queen — ?

"Where shall I carry them to?" Dorney asked.

"Why, out to the kitchen," the Queen said, "for a thorough brushing."

Dorney bit the end of her right thumb, a habit she had when in perplexity or deep thought or when she was paying most careful attention. She stopped doing it and hid her hand behind her waist to say, "But suppose he won't take them off? Suppose I ask him to, but he wants to keep them on?"

The Queen considered this. "Well, we'll see," she said finally. "We'll wait and see what happens. But anyway that is what you should do by rights."

Dorney cleared her throat and wondered if she could cross her legs without losing her balance on the narrow rail but decided against it.

"Now, every morning," the Queen went on, tapping her cheek with the paper, "you're supposed to knock on the guest-room door."

"What time?"

"Oh, about nine, I guess. And when he comes to the door you're supposed to ask him when he wants to take a bath and how hot he wants it. You see, you have to draw his bath. Then you bring hot water for him to shave with — no, you don't have to do that because he can shave in the bathroom where Mr. Morelewski shaves. Then's when you bring his shoes all shined and everything."

"Oh," Dorney said. She hooked a strand of hair over her ear, holding onto the end of it.

"And then," the Queen went on quickly, "during the late afternoon when Mr. Morelewski's nephew is dressing for sup— dinner, you're supposed to knock on the door again and ask if there's anything you can do."

"Won't he think I'm quite a bother?" Dorney ventured after some consideration. "Every time he gets in and shuts the door, why, he no more than gets turned around when there I am again, knocking."

The Queen reread the line of writing and shook her head. She read the next few lines rapidly and looked up. "Then," she said, "you're supposed to go back to his room again, this time when he's gone, and take off the spread, fold it up and put it over the chair, turn down the blinds and lay out whatever he sleeps in, and his bathrobe, on the foot of the bed. And you're supposed to take out his shoes and if you see a suit that needs brushing. Then the next morning you're supposed to bring them back again, brushed and shined."

"You mean every day?" Dorney asked. She still had hold of her strand of hair.

"Just before you leave at night you can see that he's got matches and everything, in case he smokes," the Queen said. "You don't have to bother about the ice water in the jug because you go home at six, and it would be stale by the time he goes to bed and he can just as well get it out of the faucet. I guess you'll have to cook," she said, "although you won't have to do it all by yourself because I'll help. Breakfast and lunch. You can serve it in the dining room. We'll eat the night meal up at the Café. Do you know how to set the table for company?"

"Oh, yes," Dorney said. "Wanda used to let me, and she always said — " She stopped with a frog in her throat, and could not continue.

"She was the sister you thought so much of, wasn't she?" the Queen said, having heard Dorney's brief history when she engaged her to work.

Dorney nodded, looking down as if she saw something of the greatest interest on the floor just beyond the tips of her shoes.

"You can use the set of china in the china closet. The one with the little roses," the Queen said. "That was certainly too bad to lose your sister like that, when she was just like a mother to you. And her not being really old, either." She folded the sheets of paper together and stuck them in a magazine on the stand at her elbow. "Well, I guess that's all. Except, that you're supposed to wear those caps and aprons I brought home."

Dorney took a deep breath and moistened her lips. "Mrs. More-lewski," she said, "if you don't mind I would rather just wear my — my dress, if it's all right with you, and not wear those, if you don't mind."

"But they're bought and paid for, Dorney." The Queen looked quite hurt and her beautiful eyes grew larger. "And they are becoming to you. I don't know why you wouldn't want to wear a nice white cap and apron like that. Nobody is going to — " She broke off. "Why in the world not?" she inquired curiously.

Dorney slid down from her seat on the railing and came forward a tiny step. She clasped her hands in front of her. "Well, you see, Mrs. Morelewski," she said, "I can't help it but the way I always think, I always think how I am a — a Lady in Waiting, you know. Because, you see, I never think of you being Mrs. Morelewski. I always imagine this way — she's the Queen, and I'm her Lady in Waiting. You see, Ladies in Waiting, they weren't like hired girls. They were called Duchesses and Marchion — and they had different titles like that. Or else they couldn't even get close to the Queen in the first place, to work for her or anything. Maybe you happened to read a book called *Kenilworth*. Our teacher, Miss Littley, she had — So anyway, you're the Queen, and I'm the Lady in Waiting, and they never wore white caps and aprons, so if you make me, it will just spoil everything, because you'll just be Mrs. Morelewski then and I'll just be the hired girl — and don't you see? Don't you see the difference?"

"But that's silly," Alma Morelewski said. "All I was, was Queen of the Jubilee for a week, and everybody's forgotten." She looked beyond Dorney. "Not everybody, maybe, because a few people on the street still . . . I never heard of such a thing," she said.

Dorney was silent.

"Besides, they might not let me return them."

When her majesty, Mrs. Morelewski, brought back the caps and aprons next day, the Z.C.M.I. was happy to oblige, but she did not tell her Lady in Waiting the outcome of the affair or mention it again.

14

WHEN DORNEY ARRIVED ON THURSDAY MORNING, she knew the famous guest had come and must be sleeping in the room upstairs. The kitchen, as it used to be, was full of dirty dishes from a magnificent midnight snack, and the Queen was already up and stirring about though it was only eight o'clock.

"He arrived last night," she said, coming into the kitchen almost at the same instant Dorney had closed the back door. She was not in her wrapper but wore a pale blue silk dress and her hair looked more intricate than usual. "So I want you to set the table in the dining room for breakfast this morning, and you know, you'll have to do those different things I told you."

"Does he look like Mr. Morelewski?" Dorney couldn't resist asking.

"No, he doesn't," the Queen said. She appeared rather pale and tired and now she smothered a little yawn. "Can you remember everything?"

"You mean what you told me to do?"

The Queen nodded, her face anxious.

"Sure I can," Dorney said. "I'll do just what you told me."

At half after nine when the kitchen was clean, the parlor dusted and the table set in the dining room, the Queen said Dorney should tiptoe upstairs and knock at the door and ask Mr. Desmond about his bath. She herself would meanwhile discreetly withdraw to the porch, as he would have to come downstairs to the bathroom.

There was nothing to be excited about, but Dorney was excited as she stood before the guest-room door. That was why she waited long enough to count quickly up to fifteen before she lifted her hand and rapped on the panel.

She thought someone would say, Who is it? or, Come in, but instead of that the door opened all the way and the young man who stood in the doorway said, "Good morning."

"Good morning." They spoke almost simultaneously. He had a bathrobe on, the first she had ever seen. It was brown and tan and had a silk cord ending in long tassels tied around the waist. "Welcome to Salt Lake City." The Queen hadn't said for her to say that but it came into her mind so she said it.

"Thank you."

"I'm going to draw your bath," she said, gazing not higher than his braid-decorated breast pocket, "and I'm to ask you, do you want it hot or cold?"

"I'll see to it myself," he said. "Thanks just the same."

She looked up, then, at his face and said, "Oh." In the one small sound was surprise, pleasure, discovery — not perfect, but the puzzled affectionate half-rueful recognition that says, I know I know your face but I can't quite place . . . She bit her lips.

He folded his arms and put his head on one side. "Little did you think we would meet again so far from old Ephesus, I daresay. Which only goes to show you that we *should* all be happy as Kings. Don't you agree?"

She smiled and nodded slowly.

"Allow me to introduce myself."

He unfolded his arms and made her a little bow.

"Teige Desmond, at your command."

"I know very well who you are," she said, wrinkling her forehead, "because the Queen sent me up to knock at your door and wake you up, and we've been expecting you a long time. That is, I know your name, but what surprises me so much is that I have the feeling I — " Sudden self-consciousness overtook her and she returned her gaze to the braid-trimmed pocket. "I'm Miss Dorney Leaf," she said.

"How do you do," he said, again making a bow, lower this time. "And now, my dear Miss Leaf, if I may ask, in what capacity do you serve the Queen?"

"I'm the Lady in Wa— I'm the maid," she said.

"And who is this fair Sovereign? for I have been many years a wanderer."

"What was that place you mentioned?" she asked curiously.

"When?"

"When you said that little did I think we would meet again so far from there. When you were joking a while ago."

"Ephesus," he said. "In ruins now and desolation, but once the sacred city of Diana. But this Queen of yours?"

Her lips said *Ephesus* silently, before she replied, "Mrs. Morelewski, of course. Your aunt!"

"Oh, indeed."

"Well, she was the Queen of the Jubilee, you see."

"And my uncle? He was the King?"

"They didn't have any king," she said, laughing. "I wasn't at the Jubilee because I was still in Rock Springs, Wyoming. But it must have been wonderful because it took five hours just for the parade to pass." She paused. "Well, I'll get your travel-stained shoes and suit the next time I come up, when you're not so busy." She started for the stairs but turned back. "Mr. Desmond," she said.

"Yes, Miss Leaf."

"Who was that Diana?"

"Artemis."

"Well, would you mind telling me, who was she?"

"In Rome they called her Diana. In Greece she was Artemis. She was a goddess," he said, "the twin sister of Apollo." Something about his listener's eyes made him go on. "He represents the sun, she takes the part of the moon. Every night she was said to roam over hill and dale while the dews fell, hunting the deer." He added, "She used a bow and arrow, and a lot of barefooted maidens and a pack of hounds trailed along with her."

"Mr. Desmond," she said. She opened her lips, closed them.

"Yes, Miss Leaf."

"Isn't that wonderful?"

He might have smiled if her face had not looked so earnest, but it did, so he kept sober while he said, "It all depends on what you mean by wonderful."

"I mean, I can just see all that, can't you?"

While she was filling the coal bucket out in the coal shed she repeated Ephesus, Diana, Artemis, as one hums over a tantalizing bar of music. She thought, I'll borrow some paper and a pencil from Madge or Crystal tonight and write down what he said, just to see how it looks written down, about the goddess hunting deer. . . .

Back in the kitchen she said, "Mr. Desmond is very nice-looking, isn't he?"

The Queen, stirring the muffin batter, said, "Yes, he is, isn't he?"

"He reminds me of somebody," Dorney said, "but I don't know who."

"Maybe some friend of your sister's or somebody." The Queen let the thin dough dribble off her spoon.

"I just don't know who," Dorney said. She took the lid off the stove slowly and stared into the fire.

Teige Desmond found his uncle's wife already seated when he joined her for breakfast.

"Did you sleep well?" she inquired nervously, seeing at least one more improvement she could have made on the table.

"Like a top," he said. "I suppose a relative may be permitted the truthful statement that you look beautiful this morning?"

"I really don't," she said. "This is last summer's." She fingered a fold of her dress.

"Beautiful," he repeated. "Is Uncle Joe still sleeping?"

"Oh, he's gone," she said. "He always leaves the house before eight. He thinks they can't get along without him up there at the restaurant."

"No wonder! Whatever it was he concocted out there in the kitchen last night when we got home from the station was proof enough for me that he knows his business. I noticed you didn't eat much, though. One gets spoiled, I suppose."

"No, I — I wasn't hungry." She looked down at her plate. "Here, Mr. — Teige, I mean, would you like one of these?" She offered a small platter of muffins with an unsteady hand. "And some bacon and eggs?"

He noted that she contented herself with half a muffin, and asked her if she always ate so little. For some reason that made her change color and she only nodded without speaking. He spoke of the weather then and asked a few questions about the climate which she answered in a low voice. Yes, it was always hot in summer. Yes, it was always cold in winter. Yes, it seldom rained.

He asked other questions, for when he did not a most uncomfortable silence settled down which, partly concealed behind the tall vase of roses in the center of the table, she seemed unable to break. Yes, there were a lot of interesting things to see. Yes, there were a few Indians about but not many. She didn't know what tribe they belonged to. He tried hard to find a common bond since they were to be much in each other's company for the next month. "Do you like music?" he said, shifting his chair some inches to the right so he could see past the flowers.

"Oh, my, yes, I certainly do," she said.

"What kind?"

"Oh, you know." She made a purposeless little gesture outward. "All kinds."

"Anybody's, especially?"

"How do you mean?"

"Well, Schumann, for instance." He whistled a few bars of *Das Paradies und die Peri.*

"Oh, yes," she said, looking anxious, "I heard that once, I'm sure. Joe takes me to the band concerts in the Park quite often. He doesn't like music, though," she added.

"Uncle Joe doesn't? Why, Mother always said he just missed being a musician himself. She said when he was a boy — "

"He really doesn't. Every time, it will be just as good as can be, and the people will all clap and everything, and he says it's just awful. He doesn't say it there, of course, because, like I told him, some of the musicians' relatives might be sitting right around us and why hurt their feelings?"

139

Teige put his napkin up to his lips. "Well, what else interests you?" he said.

"Oh, lots of things."

"What?"

"Oh, lots of things."

"Books?"

"Oh, my, yes."

"What do you do all day while Uncle Joe is up at the restaurant?"

She looked so almost distraught by the question, that he hastened to add, "But I suppose, for anyone so beautiful, that it's enough just to *be* beautiful, like a perfect rose or a perfect diamond. I mean, just to be."

"Oh, I'm not so beautiful."

"You'd have to make quite a long trip to get somebody to agree with you. Do you know where you'd have to go?" He looked at her teasingly.

"Where?" she said, as if she did not believe there was such a place.

"Well, Borneo and Cochin China, for instance."

"Why not?"

"Why not what?"

"I mean, why wouldn't they think I was — ?" She seemed reluctant to say the word.

"Beautiful?" He obligingly said it for her. "Well, in Borneo, the Dyaks have a horror of whiteness. Somebody told Mr. Darwin that they think demons and spirits are white. And you're certainly white enough — you seem to be made out of meerschaum."

She put her fingers up to her cheek and drew them across as though her color was a patina she could feel. "And what about in — ?" She could not remember the name.

"Cochin China? Well, there, when the little Negro boys on the eastern coast saw Burton, they said, 'See the white man! He looks like a snow-white ape!' And do you know what was said of the wife of the English Ambassador? 'She has white teeth like a dog, and a rosy color like that of the potato flower!'"

"Maybe she was homely. Is there any place else where — ?"

"Well, the Indians of Paraguay would much prefer you without eyelashes and eyebrows."

"Why, I'd look terrible!" she said. "Those people must certainly have funny ideas."

"Oh, they have."

"Well, I certainly wouldn't want to go *there*."

"Do you like to travel?"

"We went to San Francisco on our honeymoon," she said. "And

Joe says he might take me to New York and even over to Europe sometime soon."

Teige smiled at her. "You won't have to fear not being appreciated there. In fact, you will make your progress like a Queen. By the way," he said, "who was the child who knocked on my door this morning?"

"That was my maid, Dorney."

"How old is she?"

"Fourteen, or fifteen, I've forgotten which. She's kind of an orphan and lives with a sister over on Eighth South."

"Does she go to school in winter?"

"No, she works. She's my maid."

Teige Desmond, for all that he enjoyed the sight of his uncle's young wife in her pale blue frock against the sunny stained-glass window of the dining room, was very glad when the breakfast came to an end. It was a good deal of an effort to talk to her, and for reasons he could not explain, still more trying an ordeal to sit silent in her company.

He told her that she would be overjoyed to hear what kind of a guest he was going to be. A tourist pure and simple, he said, the easiest man in the world to entertain. He had read up on the locality and all he wanted to do was to go out and see the sights. He expected that would keep him busy.

"But there aren't any sights," she said.

"Oh, come, now, Alma, of course there are, not only right in the city but up to some of the mines, and the canyons, and Antelope Island out in the Great Salt Lake. And I want to see some Indian reservations too. I may be gone overnight a time or two while I'm here."

"Well." Again she made her purposeless little gesture.

"Now, am I not a guest after your own heart, my dear? I cannot call you aunt, as I said last night. You are too young and entirely too beautiful."

"Oh, I'm not so beautiful."

He eluded this morass by casting her a glance full of admiration. "I shall seldom be home to lunch," he said, "and in short, I intend to be no trouble at all. Today I thought I would go up to see the sights around Temple Square and visit a few other places, unless you have other plans? Because of course I am at your disposal." Her face told him she had not. "By the way, we must ask Uncle Joe if I may be allowed to take you with me occasionally."

"Where?"

"You haven't been listening," he accused her playfully. "I'm going sightseeing! We must ask Uncle Joe if you can go sightseeing with me. Would you like to?"

141

"I wouldn't know where to go."

"We'll ask him tonight," he said.

Alma Morelewski did not realize until her guest was out of the house for the day how very tired she was, so tired that even her face was tired, her eyes and nose and mouth. It was only eleven-thirty but she went into the bedroom and shut the door behind her. She went over and pulled down the blinds and then unbuttoned and slipped out of the light silk dress, carefully hanging it up in the wardrobe. She turned and looked at herself in the long glass, going close enough to tip it slightly forward. She would nap this way, in her petticoat. No need to take off her corset. It wasn't tight any more even when it was pulled right together in back — she felt with her fingers — in fact, it lapped over. Her tape measure was on the porch in the sewing basket or she would get it and measure her waist. It had never looked so small! not even when she was Queen of the Jubilee. She could probably get into the turquoise dress without a bit of . . .

The turquoise dress! She hurried to the wardrobe and snatched it out, ducked her head in it and eased it down. It would snap, it would hook, it would button, everywhere! She began to breathe faster as she turned to this side and that before the glass. It was a cheap dress bought before her marriage, but as Joe had said, it was unbelievably becoming — she would wear it tonight and surprise Joe and show Teige how she looked in this particular color. She would have to mend it, though, the rip she had torn in it the day she got so cross at Joe because she was too fat to get into it, but that would never be noticed. Men didn't notice such things. She would mend it very carefully when she got up, before she took her bath. It would give her something to do, to keep from being nervous, for she was nervous, she didn't know why. Maybe because she didn't sleep well last night. She leaned over and fluffed her hair out around her face. She would wear the hat with the paisley crown, and the gold bracelets. . . .

When she first lay down in the hot semi-dark, she was not so sleepy as she had been because she was thinking about how she would look in the dress and hat. She heard the parlor clock strike twelve and rose up on one elbow to see if the little alarm on the stand on Joe's side of the bed agreed with it. It was five minutes slow, but the parlor clock was the right one. Lunchtime! She turned over on her back and the movement made her aware of her slenderness and she twisted sideways to be aware again, putting her arms under her head and staring up at the ceiling. Even yesterday she had counted the minutes to lunchtime, then counted the minutes to coffee and dinnertime. And today noon came along and she didn't care whether she had anything to eat or not, was going to lie right here through the lunch hour and take a nap. . . . She wasn't hungry any more! After six weeks of torment, she didn't care whether she ate or not! Why, I'll never get fat again, she thought joyously. I can't get fat because I haven't got any appetite. It will never come back. Something had taken it away! That dinner she was going to eat tomorrow night, the one she had been looking forward to for the last five days, that lobster and steak — she winced — why, it made her sick to think of it. In fact, it made her sick to think of anything, especially chocolates.

She put her two hands over her eyes, the right lying atop the left, and saw Teige Desmond as he had looked at the table, saw him talking and laughing and glancing across at her. She could hear him, too — the different things he had said about how beautiful she was. But he didn't know how really beautiful she could be! She would show him. Tomorrow she would go up and tell the dressmaker she wanted that blond lace dress with the black velvet bodice, and tell the milliner she wanted a black velvet picture hat weighed down with white roses . . . and she would buy . . . she would get . . . but tomorrow Teige wanted her to go sightseeing with him. Mr. Morel — Joe would of course tell her to go right ahead. And she would wear . . . the gray silk with the shoulder cape, or . . . what?

Alma Morelewski dozed off and had an odd dream. She dreamed she was walking up Main Street and saw to her right a shop she had never seen before. When she stepped inside, it was not to step upon a carpet but into the midst of a dry yet well-kept strawberry patch. She went forward, annoyed by the dust that rose up around her, and found that she was climbing, for the field lay on a hill, just like the one at home in Sugar House. Finally she came to a door like a door on a Pullman car, but on the ground, with no steps up to it, and pushed it open and went into a room where there was a great gold chair like the one they used at the Salt Lake Theatre when they needed a throne, and a long counter with many clerks behind but she could never make out what they were selling, as they were facing the other way from her and besides there were no customers anywhere. She was the only one. She approached and was going to ask what department this was, if she could get someone to turn around, but she discovered she had left her purse at home so she hurried on . . . and was then in a kitchen with an immeasurably high dark ceiling and an open fire in the middle of the floor, burning one unreal flame like a red acanthus leaf. Joe was there. At least, she did not see him at first but he was. He moved toward her with his arms full of something light and beautiful, she did not know what. It was wide circles of chiffon, and while she stood, suddenly very still, like a statue (it was so strange), he tossed one over her head and it fell delightfully all about her, and she saw and

143

smiled through the veiling. Then he tossed another upon her rigidity, another, another, and then she didn't see or smile anymore and got scared and wanted to claw it off, but she couldn't claw it off, she couldn't move, she was made of something so hard she couldn't move an inch — or else was paralyzed — and Joe threw another circle of chiffon and another, and then he tossed something heavy but soft, like a feather tick that tumbled her over — she tried to kick and scream, tried so hard to scream that she could feel the cords in her neck stand like tough roots and her eyes bulge out, but she couldn't move or make the faintest sound. And then he heaved more soft light beautiful things, and more, and more, and under them, more terrible than under earth and stones, she was buried alive. . . .

"Mrs. Morelewski, excuse me, Mrs. Morelewski, but you screamed. At least I think you did. It sounded like it."

She opened eyes that were nothing but the black centers, not blue, to see Dorney standing beside her, and sat up and put a hand to her wet forehead. "It must be too hot in here," she said. "I had the funniest dream, kind of a — a nightmare." She shuddered.

"The most terrible nightmare I ever had," Dorney said, looking away from the Queen in her petticoat with her shoes off, "was when I once dreamed the moon fell out of the sky." If she hoped by this communication to hear what the pale Queen had dreamed, she was to be disappointed for Alma Morelewski said not a word more about it, but only asked if she might have some weak green tea.

When Teige Desmond came home from his first day's sightseeing and went upstairs to his room, he found Dorney there. Both his suitcases were open, almost empty, and Dorney was sitting tailor fashion on the floor between them with a book on her lap. She shut it and jumped up to lay it hastily on top of the teetering pile on the bureau. She turned, her face a picture of guilt. "The Queen said that what I'm doing was one of the maid's duties," she explained.

"Reading *The Ring and the Book?*" He bent sideways to identify the title.

"Unpacking your suitcases and hanging things up and putting things away." She met his gaze with difficulty until she saw that he was not angry or indignant.

"It is most kind of you, I'm sure," Teige said. "I see you are almost finished."

She turned to the books and put her hand on the one she had relinquished upon his arrival. "I couldn't seem to make much sense of this," she said. "Is it a book or a poem? And some of the others, you can read a whole page and when you get done, you don't know what it said. Like the one right here." She stooped and looked along the spines till she came to a strip of bright green. "This one," she said, pointing to it.

"Kierkegaard," he said.

"Mr. Desmond, could I ask you something?"

"Go ahead."

"Mr. Desmond, all together, in New York City, how many books have you really got?"

"Many more, alas, than Mrs. Hibbard can keep properly dusted," Teige said. "In fact, too many."

"How many?"

"Oh, a thousand, I should guess. I never counted them."

She let her knees sag as though she might be about to sink to the floor, but recovered to say, "Why, that's ten *times* as many!"

"As you've got?"

"Me? I haven't got any!" She told him about the Geography, History and Reader she used to have but how Mrs. Diltz had made her leave them in Rock Springs for Ora and Pearl.

He took a seat on the foot of the bed and clasped his hands around his knee and listened. "Go on," he said when she finished.

"That's all, Mr. Desmond. Only I'm going to buy some more books like them, only you see, I never have been uptown yet and I don't know where to go, and Sundays everything's closed and I have to work every day of the week till six. But I am, though, just the same. Clara's going to find out about a bookstore — and the library and everything. And I'm not only going to buy *them*, either."

"You like to study, then?"

She thought. "I don't know if I like to study," she said. "But I like to get something inside of my noggin, because — " She looked shy, wishing she hadn't said noggin. "Grandpa Bannon used to say noggin," she explained, and wished she hadn't said *that*, either, for she had the feeling she was somehow laying blame on him for something, a cowardly thing when he wasn't by to defend himself. "I just loved him," she added loyally.

"And who was Grandpa Bannon?"

She told him.

"Ten times as many books as who has?" he wanted to know after that. So she told him about Miss Littley, the Friday afternoons, the books she read aloud and was even willing to lend, how she, Dorney, had borrowed twenty-seven, one at a time, before the tragedy happened. . . .

"Novels?"

She told him some of the titles and at the mention of every one, he nodded his head and smiled. Then (her ridiculous eyes filling, her

145

ridiculous lips quivering as though it had happened but yesterday) she told him all about the disaster! How finally the day came when she borrowed *Moby Dick* . . . and left it out on the old gray blanket to be rained on all night . . . and how she found it on a Sunday when Mrs. Diltz was spending the day . . . and how Mrs. Diltz and Thomas told Wanda . . . and Wanda forbid her ever to borrow another of the teacher's books . . . and how she could never really get near to Miss Littley again, because she was so ashamed of herself . . . and how . . . But someday she would buy a roomful — a roomful as big as this, or even bigger — of just nothing in the world but books, and read until she was blue in the face!

She did not know what she had said to make Teige Desmond, who had been looking so tender and kind, glower the way he did then. He seemed so mad she thought she had offended him and started to edge to the door, wanting to say, Please, what did I do? but not daring. He stood up and walked in long strides to the bureau and began to look through the books as though he was furious at someone, inspecting the titles, taking them off the teetering pile she had made and building another to the side of it saying, "If I had only known!" or, "I might just as well have!" or, "Nothing here, not for the next few years anyway," while she slipped closer and closer to the open door. She was about to flee through it when he said, smiting his forehead, "What's the matter with me? No harm done!" and faced about to give her the brightest, warmest, beamingest smile she had ever seen.

(Thinking about it afterwards, she supposed that he had jumped up that way because the notion struck him that in his absence and while unpacking, she had harmed the books he brought from New York! anybody who would leave *Moby Dick* out all night that way in the pouring rain, and that was why he had rushed over to look at each one to see if it was all right. Why he had muttered what he did she could not imagine but she supposed the "No harm done!" meant just that, that there was no damage that he could see. She would better have kept silent about *Moby Dick*, she knew now when it was too late, because after such a revelation as that he wouldn't trust her to the corner.)

She felt too disturbed to smile back, and when she spoke it was stiffly. "Mr. Desmond," she said, "please give me your travel-stained shoes and suit now, will you please, because I have to go back downstairs now."

He got them for her, his smile staying. "Where did you get the travel-stained?" he asked. "Out of Scott? I'm curious."

"From the Queen," she said.

"Well, it's delightful. It makes me feel like one of the Three Musketeers. Where did the Queen get it?"

"I don't know," she said. "She had it written down on a piece of paper."

Mending the turquoise dress, with such fine stitches they might better have been displayed than hidden, did quiet Alma Morelewski's nerves during the afternoon, and when she had had her bath she felt almost like herself again. But hearing Teige Desmond come in through the front door and go upstairs at four-thirty made her heart give a plunge and begin to beat fast and that made her a little nervous again, as did seeing herself in the long mirror completely dressed even to her gloves an hour later. This time, she was too absorbed by her own image to pay attention to the inward leap and flutter, though before she had wondered if it might not be heart trouble. The paisley-crowned hat was exactly right and so were the gold bracelets and so were the blue-green earbobs that swung from her ears.

All the way uptown to the restaurant in the carriage, Teige talked to his uncle's wife about what he had seen in Temple Square, about Brigham Young's ability as architect and builder, about the Tabernacle, the phenomenon of Mormonism and which type of human being flourished best under a dictatorship, how handsomely the city was laid out and other such things.

Alma Morelewski said yes and no and I think so, too, wondering how a man could live in the biggest and most wonderful city in the United States, and then come out to a town like Salt Lake City that couldn't even so much as hold a candle to New York, and act as interested in what little there was to see as some clodhopper up from San Pete County that never saw anything before in his life. She didn't understand it, because Teige Desmond was anything but a clodhopper, and decided to mention it to Joe sometime to see if he could explain it, if she didn't forget.

By the time they got to Fourth South and State Street, she began to feel tense and chilly though the sun was still high and the asphalt on the hot side of the street soft enough to take the print of a sharp heel or the point of an umbrella. Teige had said she had looked beautiful when they were sitting in the parlor waiting for the carriage to come, said it again when he handed her into it and followed and sat down beside her, but since, had said nothing else, except to drag on and on with this dreary stuff about architecture and politics and city-planning until she wanted to lean back against the cushions and shut her eyes, so dispirited and miserable did she feel. She scarcely had energy to listen any more, to say yes, no, I think so, too. . . .

"A penny for the thoughts of the most beautiful woman in Salt Lake City!"

She turned her head and said, "I didn't catch what you — "

"A penny for the thoughts of the most beautiful woman in Salt Lake City!"

Most beautiful.

Had she been stark whose softness now would squeeze into a ball? Been cold, so warm? Been mute, thus now resounding?

Most beautiful. . . .

She smiled, her face as ablaze as the Match Girl's over her burning matches. "I'm not the most beautiful, by any means," she said. "Not by any means."

He admired her the rest of the way to the restaurant. "If you're not, I don't know who is," he said, and he stopped talking tediously.

When they got out of the carriage, Teige saw Uncle Joe beckoning to them behind the etched glass doors of the Paris Café, and he waved. But Alma didn't see him till they were clear inside.

Mr. Joseph Morelewski took one look at his wife in the turquoise dress and had every one of her favorite dishes brought to the table. "No need to wait till tomorrow night," he said mysteriously, as the waiters came with *pâté de foie gras*, truffles, glistening olives the size of plums. But she ate almost nothing! As the dinner progressed, the courses were brought (everything she had ever loved! while Joseph Morelewski watched anxiously), she ate crumbs, nibbles, nothing. Yet when the meal was over, and as she sat fingering the gold handle of her coffee cup, she looked soft, rosy, satiated, while their guest talked and she listened. Every now and again she would look softly and rosily in her husband's direction. It puzzled him until he concluded that she must have eaten something beforehand. That was it, of course. She had eaten and wasn't hungry. Slyboots, sly puss, to try and scare him so!

Dorney brushed the suit and hung it over the back of the chair, and then she looked at the large pair of shoes standing on the lid of the woodbox. They did not seem so very travel-stained. Still, they needed a polishing. She hunted around and found a clean rag. Every day. The Queen said every day. She reached out, but drew back, because . . . shoes were an entirely different proposition. The realization came from nowhere, as effectively dissuading her as if a firm hand had been laid on her shoulder, a firm voice in her ear had said, No, don't. She looked hard at them. Work was work, scrubbing, washing the big windows under the scalloped awnings, cleaning out the fruit cellar — she willingly tackled whatever the Queen or Madge wanted her to do — but polishing shoes came under another category altogether and she wouldn't do it, couldn't, because something wouldn't let her. Teige Desmond's or the President's, no matter whose, a millionaire's, Mr. John Greenleaf Whittier's, anybody's, no matter how famous . . . if they wanted a shoeshine they would have to go somewhere else, not come to her! She did not even know she knew the word until she said it half under her breath: bootblack. I will not be a bootblack. Never. Not for anything in the world.

She heard old Mr. Sodaquist dragging the hose around the back of the house and quick as a flash she picked up the shoes and rushed out onto the back porch and opened the screen. "Mr. Sodaquist," she said, "please, couldn't you sit down on the back steps here in the shade where it's cool — and I'll make you a glass of lemonade — and polish these shoes for me?"

Mr. Sodaquist looked up with one blue eye, the white one like a hard-boiled egg closed tight against the bright rays of the sinking sun.

"Lemonade would spoil my supper," he said.

"Well, would you please, anyway?" She held the shoes out. "I'll make you some lemonade tomorrow."

"Ain't got the time."

"Please, Mr. Sodaquist."

"Ain't got the time."

"I'll pay you!" She would have called the rash words back if she could, but they were said.

He opened the white eye now, as though he had been saving it for just such an occasion. "How much?" he said.

"A — a nickel."

He thought a moment, while a little trickle of tobacco juice ran down the corner of his mouth. He spat into the rich grass and wiped off his chin with a hand like a brown bundle of twigs. "Give 'em here," he said.

"I'll bring you the money tomorrow, Mr. Sodaquist, and oh, I do thank you."

"Give 'em here." Mr. Sodaquist knew all about nickels, and pennies, too. He had bought half a block of property over on Third West, had an interest in a farm, was going to buy another half block of property, bought a rooming house — all with nickels. Not dollars, you understand. Nickels, and pennies. He sneered at improvident Dorney as he took the shoes.

15

CRYSTAL SAID THAT DORNEY SHOULD WAIT UNTIL
Mother came home before she went over to Clara Tofflemire's that
evening. Mother wouldn't like it if she started running around after
dark without asking, Crystal said. It hadn't begun to get dark and she
had intended to come right back, but Dorney kept silent and
thought only fleetingly of going anyway, Crystal or no Crystal. The
satisfaction wouldn't be worth it, for when she came home she
would find not only Crystal sulking, but Madge as well, and whereas
Crystal soon got over it, Madge's annoyance (kept green by Crystal,
Dorney was sorry to think but couldn't help it) would sometimes
last a whole week or even longer. This was trying and had happened several times already. Dorney would stand as long as she
could injured Madge's looking everywhere but at her, her monosyl-
labic replies to questions, her frequent heavy sighs, the way she
would sit and tell Crystal all about what had happened up at
Judge Tower's (many interesting things did happen every day) as
though no other listener sat by — and then she could stand it no
longer, would burst into tears and beg forgiveness. And Madge
would grant it not easily or soon, but would grant it, saying always,
"Now no more of that, I want it understood." No more of what,
did she want it understood? Of talking impudently to Crystal, of
bringing home a mangy cat and feeding it milk out of a good pie
pan (luckily it ran away), of scorching Crystal's *toile* shirtwaist,
of taking Jetta out for a walk around the block. . . .

Dorney had been guilty of this last misdeed some weeks previous,
while Crystal, as she did now in the early evening after supper instead of the afternoon, was taking her music lesson and Madge was
still at the Judge's. It had looked so pretty outside and Dorney said
to Jetta without thinking, "Come, let's go around the block, shall
we?" and Jetta had liked it so much! She had gone with such funny
stiff little steps and clung so tightly to Dorney's hand.

"Isn't this lovely, Jetta?"

A bird ran a little way with them along the top of a fence and
the different neighbors had waved from their front porches, the two

Mrs. Vertrees (polygamous) and others. Mrs. Luby came clear out to the front gate to greet them, carrying fat Herman. Thornton and Althea came, too, and Jetta stared and stared at the children, a little scared, half hiding behind Dorney's skirt. Mrs. Luby requested Thornton to say one of his Castoria poems and he went some distance back on the sidewalk to say it so as to seem to be on a stage. In a room it was like pulling teeth to get him to do it (his mother informed the audience in a loud whisper) but outside he must have the feeling he could run away and disappear when he wanted to because he wasn't a bit afraid. Without a hitch he recited,

> "Life is restless, days are fleeting,
> Children bloom but die in teething;
> Warning take all friends and mothers,
> Watch the precious girls and brothers;
> Read the home life of Victoria,
> Children nine all had Castoria,
> No sleepless nights, by baby squalling,
> Like larks they rise in early morning."

When the recitation was over they all clapped, Thornton came forward again and by this time Jetta had got over her uneasiness enough to take a step towards him. He smiled at her very sweetly but backed away and climbed to the top of the fence post where he stayed balancing the rest of the time, looking at her but pretending not to look. Mrs. Luby wanted them to come inside the house to see the set of whatnot shelves Mr. Luby had bought the last time he . . . Luckily, when he smashed the old one, there was nothing on it of any real value. Bless his dear heart, though, he had brought home a red glass vase anyway, and the cunningest china girl and lamb. It was too bad he had that weakness of his! For otherwise, Mr. Luby was one of the best men in the world. She did wish she could think of a way to cure him but she didn't know what.

Dorney said no, thanks, they really couldn't stay, they were just taking a little walk, and they started on in the pink evening. She happened to see the first star, then, and pointed it out. "Look, Jetta. Star light, star bright," she said, and Jetta looked up as high as she could into the sky without seeing it, but then she saw it and stopped dead still. Dorney made a wish and helped Jetta make a wish. "First star I see tonight. . . ." They went on, and Jetta kept turning her head to look at it, to be sure it was still there.

Dorney hoped never again to see Madge as mad as she was when she met them coming up Sixth East hand in hand. She was so mad that her eyes crackled and her nostrils got as thin as tissue paper, but she didn't say a word until they got home and Jetta was put to bed. By that time, Crystal was there to chime in. Crystal cried a gallon of tears. The disgrace of it! she kept saying over and over. Dorney tried to get a word in edgewise and say that surely everybody knew there was someone like Jetta in the neighborhood, it wasn't a secret, and Jetta couldn't help it, it wasn't so terrible, and nobody blamed anybody if they were just unfortunate, but they wouldn't let her. "If I had thought for one instant," Madge said, "that the minute my back was turned, you would take Jetta out as big as life all around the block to show every Tom, Dick and Harry," she choked with anger, "for one instant," she said, "well, I know one young lady who wouldn't of been under my roof this long, I know that much!" And she went on to say that furthermore . . .

That night under the hot eaves Dorney cried so hard her nose swelled till she couldn't get a breath of air up it. She sat up on the sagging bed and pushed her round pillow away, wet as if warm tea had been spilled on it. Poor people with whatever it was that ailed them! The ones who always had to breathe through their mouths, she thought. Poor things, like fish out of water. She groped her way to the small open window, knelt down, crossed her arms on the sill and stuck her throbbing head outside as far as it would go, resting her cheek on the back of her hand. After a little she touched her fingers to her thickly cushioned, hot, slick eyelids and thought, No wonder I can't see anything. But it was not because they were narrow slits from crying, it was because the night itself was so black, near at hand, at least, though far up the street to the east it looked lighter. No evening star now, for sure. . . . She shut her eyes and a little breeze came by and picked up a lock of her hair.

Well, she would pack old Mr. Diltz's telescope bag, of course, and go tonight, run off, not stand it, leave, not stay, go. To Papa, of course, out in California. Right this minute. Get up and pack and start traveling. . . .

It would be a long, long trip and she was sleepy and tired because today the Queen had wanted all the heavy draperies taken down and shaken, and because . . . but she didn't care how long it was if it was a million miles. She could walk and maybe ride in somebody's wagon and maybe ride in a boxcar and walk and then ride and walk . . . and sleep under bushes and trees and in fields of daisies . . . because nobody could stand to be treated like that. . . .

She must have slept quite a while by the window there, leaning against the sill, because when she woke up with a start she felt cold and cramped. After she stumbled back to bed and pulled the cover up over her, she dreamed she was back at the window on the floor again, the same as before, thinking the same thoughts about going . . . and that was when she looked down and saw them, right in front of Madge's gate. Months later, when she was coming home from the Palace Laundry, after work, with Clara, she tried to tell her that dream (something reminding her in the twilight, the early moon, or the stars, or the way the snow gleamed) but it didn't sound like anything. She didn't say who the rider was, that it was Butch Cassidy come to get her and take her away; didn't say who the black horse was, that it was Little Dipper. She just said they came and that she spied them and ran down, and that he had this big hat on and was singing, and that he reached down for her and swung her up behind him in the saddle . . . and that this horse gave a big jump forward as light as air. It didn't sound like anything and she felt sorry she tried to tell it, even to Clara. "It's hard to put into words," she said, "how it was, but I wish I could tell somebody once. . . ." She tried again. "See, everything looked kind of light greenish blue outside and the wind was kind of blowing — and my feet never made a sound on the stairs, and Madge and Crystal were sleeping. . . . I was so glad, Clara. I could run so fast. I wish I could explain to somebody once how it really was. . . ."

Next morning she packed the telescope suitcase before she went downstairs, but she came back up and unpacked it again, because when she went into the kitchen Madge was there and made up with her. For Mamma's sake, she said, and because she knew Dorney didn't mean any harm by taking Jetta out around the block and would never do it again. At first Dorney didn't want to make up, but the dream, still so real, seemed to make other things of very little consequence almost for the whole day, and the first thing she knew she was begging forgiveness herself and promising Madge to be a better girl.

Since, Madge had been in a huff several times for one lapse or another, but for the past week Dorney had not displeased her sister in any way and she had every hope so to continue.

That was why, tonight, she took Crystal's advice and waited until Madge came home to ask if she could go over to Clara's.

"Did the Morelewski's company come from New York?" Crystal wanted to know affably.

"He came last night," Dorney said.

"How old is he?"

"I can't tell."

"Old?"

"No, not old."

"Thirty?"

"Oh, I don't think he's that old."

"Twenty-five?"

"I can't tell ages very well."

"Is he good-looking? You ought to know that."

"Oh, yes! He certainly is."

"How good-looking?"

"Well, he looks like somebody I know," Dorney said. "But I can't think who."

"You don't know anybody. Who do you know?"

"Somebody I used to know then." Dorney put her hand over her eyes and thought hard, then dropped it and looked up.

"*How* good-looking?" Crystal asked impatiently. "You're the funniest person."

Dorney looked at her, was going to say something, decided not to, changed her mind and said, "Don't get mad at me, Crystal, but if you'll do something for me, I think I can tell you just exactly how Mr. Teige Desmond looks."

"Good heavens, it isn't important," Crystal said. "The way you talk, you'd think it was important. *I* don't care, for heaven's sake!" But after a pause she said, "Do what?"

"Well, don't tell Madge, because she might get mad."

"I won't."

"Promise," Dorney said, who was taking no chances. "Cross your heart, hope to die and spit."

Crystal reluctantly did this, spitting into the stove. "All right," she said, coming back. "Do what?"

Jetta had crept in from the porch and now pushed a chair over close to Dorney and climbed up on the seat clumsily.

Dorney smiled at her but she did not smile back, any more than a kitten would, much as it may purr. "Well, have you got a picture of 'Dair?" she asked Crystal. "I mean, has Madge got a picture of your father? Because if I can just look at it, I can tell you in a minute if Mr. Desmond doesn't look like him, because I think, I really think, from what I can remember — "

"You know what Mother would do to both of us." But Crystal went into the bedroom, was gone several minutes and came back with a photograph.

Dorney had never seen a picture of him. She took it very gently and gazed with wide eyes at a hatless young man in a narrow-trousered business suit, sitting stiffly in an ornate armchair with his legs crossed, curling his mustache with his right hand. "He didn't look like this a bit," she whispered after a long silence.

"You mean Mr. Morelewski's nephew doesn't?"

"I mean 'Dair didn't. Crystal, you'd ought to remember." Not like this. He was booted and spurred, wore his guns, he — was always laughing. He looks so pale here, but he was the color of — and he looks cold. . . . He wasn't cold, he was warm. He — Dorney looked down at the picture again. She had remembered all these years, but off kilter, like learning to sing and always singing the words of "A Spanish Cavalier" to the wrong tune. Corrected now, she felt dispraised, dispossessed, insecure and oddly melancholy.

"Well, does he look like Daddy, for heaven's sake?" Crystal said sharply. "Look, and get done with it, because you know what Mother would say if she should happen to come home and see what we're doing."

"Daddy," Jetta said. She got down off the chair and came and leaned on Dorney's knee and looked. "Man," she said. She pointed with a bony little finger at the sober-looking eyes.

"They didn't look like that," Dorney said, looking up from the picture and turning to her. "Not when he'd ride up to Wanda's gate on Fiji and I'd see him and run as hard as I could. He'd — They didn't look like that, Jetta, not how they look here, his eyes didn't. They'd be dancing and glimmering and he didn't have his mouth so serious-looking like this, never, you know. He'd just — But it may be that he really looked like this. I don't just know for sure any more." And never will know for sure again, she thought, I never will know again.

"Oh, good heavens," Crystal said, snatching away the picture, "now don't start telling Jetta about Daddy, if you don't want to get into some pretty hot trouble, I can tell you that much. Don't start doing that, I can tell you." At the door that led into the bedroom, she stopped and looked back. "Well, does he?" she said.

"Does who?" Dorney asked stupidly. She put her hand out to smooth Jetta's topknot of downy hair and began to straighten her little ribbon bow.

"Does Mr. Morelewski's nephew look like — like — " Crystal held the picture up.

"Daddy," Jetta said against Dorney's shoulder.

" — or doesn't he?"

"No," Dorney said, "he doesn't. I thought he did. I was thinking all day in the back of my mind that he did, but he doesn't. He looks like somebody else entirely, but I just don't know who." She didn't, only that somehow, occultly, Teige Desmond looked like someone she had seen, loved, missed, expected and would once more see. . . .

When Crystal came back from the bedroom looking cross, she said, "Well, what color hair has he got, at least?"

"Black."

"Curly?"

"Kind of. But not really. Not exactly."

"What color eyes?"

"Brown."

"Is he tall or is he short like Mr. Morelewski?"

"Oh, he's tall."

"Ugly teeth?"

"Oh, no. Beautiful. Just simply beautiful."

"Does he wear nice clothes?"

Dorney thought of the shoes, and the nickel she would have to take to Mr. Sodaquist tomorrow for polishing them. A nickel every day!

"Well, does he? And what are you looking so guilty about?"

"I'm not looking guilty."

"Well, does he?"

"They look nice to me."

"Do you think he's rich?"

"How should I know?"

"Well, does he act rich?"

"How does anybody act rich?"

"Oh, you know," Crystal said, giving her an exasperated look. "Their manners and everything."

"He's got nice manners, if that's what you mean."

Crystal was staring with narrowed eyes far, far into space. "Mr. Morelewski is rich," she murmured, "owning that Paris Café and all and buying that nice house. He must be. Lots of foreigners are. And I bet anything this other Mr. Morelewski — "

"His name's Mr. Desmond," Dorney put in quickly.

" — well, he must be rich, too, I'll bet anything, coming from New York like that and everything. Has he got a girl?"

"How should I know?"

"Oh, I just thought may be you heard him mention somebody to the Queen or something. Is he married?" She opened her eyes wide and looked at Dorney.

"No," Dorney said positively.

"How do you know?"

"I just know, is all."

"How?"

She considered. "Well, I know," she said, "because if he was married his wife would be with him, because Mr. Desmond wouldn't ever leave the one he loved."

Madge said yes, Dorney could go, but as it was nearly bedtime she should not stay out long and it looked very foolish to her to run over to the Tofflemires' at this time of night, she said.

She met Clara Tofflemire just coming out of her front gate, muffled, as usual, in the shawl in which she blended so with the gathering darkness that Dorney was almost upon her before she looked up and saw the white blur of her face.

"Come and go with me," Clara said. "I'm going over to the Mudges' for a minute." She was concealing something under the folds of knitted wool and she gazed back several times nervously at the black parlor windows of her own house. When they had turned the corner and started up Sixth East she breathed a sigh of relief and threw her shawl back and showed what she had under her arm. It was a quart jar of fruit and a small pair of rubbers. "I bought them for George, for when winter comes," she explained. "I happened to see some the last time I was uptown and you know I don't go uptown very often so I thought I'd better buy them while I had the chance. I sure had a time hiding them from Mamma and watching my chance to sneak them out. She'd want to skin me alive; for taking the peaches, too, but I got them off the back of the top shelf, so I don't think she'll notice, at least for quite a while."

Joe Mudge opened the door to Clara's timid knock. "Oh," she said, starting back, "I thought it would be George. I thought you'd still be working in the shed."

"Come in," he said, and they entered a dimly lighted carpetless room, the parlor.

He gestured to the partly open door behind which the one bedroom lay in darkness. "I promised the kids I'd sit and work in here if they'd go to bed nice. Either George or Ruby got scared about something, and scared Alfred — some darn thing, I couldn't make heads nor tails what. Sophie, she didn't pay no attention."

"She's the youngest. She's only a year old," Clara commented tensely to her companion.

Joe Mudge asked them to be seated and they took uncomfortable straight chairs. The worn plush rocker in the circle of lamplight that had not quite stopped rocking, with tools and a half-finished birdhouse on the floor beside it, was obviously their host's, and neither visitor thought of taking it though he pointed it out to them. He sat down after they did and when he had done so, punctilio, with the powers of a Medusa that could stop whatever she looked at in its tracks forever, came to join them. Clara sat with a back as straight as though she had been strapped to a board, and did not loosen her shawl but stayed muffled in it, her long face agonized. She made no move to display the small gifts she bore. "This is Mrs. Yandle's, from over on Eighth South, her youngest sister, from Wyoming," she said, performing a belated introduction. "And that there is Mr. Mudge, Dorney."

"Pleased to meet you," he said, and gave a nod.

"How do you do, Mr. Mudge," Dorney said. She smiled brightly.

He looked first at one corner of the ceiling, and then at another and then down into the cigar box, full of nails, hinges and miscellaneous bits of hardware on the floor beside and a little to the front of him. He leaned forward with narrowed eyes, as though he discovered some one item in it he either had not known was there at all or thought he had mislaid and now run across again, but made no move to extract it, only looked as if he made a mental note that it was there, in case he needed it in future.

Clara broke the silence nervously. "I sure thought I would of got over here earlier," she said, "before the kids got to bed. Because when I left this morning I told 'em I'd get over sure."

"Say," he said, "I didn't know what you was up to till you'd come and gone this morning. Thanks."

"Oh, don't mention it," she said, reddening. The almost imperceptible shake of her head was for puzzled Dorney, as was the entreaty in her eyes. Please, it said, don't ask now, I'll tell you later, it was nothing.

"I got my coal shed fixed up as a shop in one end, and Clara here, she'll sneak over and be in the house with the kids and I won't have no idea what she's been up to till she's been and gone." This was said to the cigar box. "I won't have no idea."

What he had had no idea about that morning was that Clara had changed the beds, baked a platter of cupcakes and ironed his good shirt, all before she went off to work at the Palace Laundry.

She began to breathe more naturally and act more like herself when he reached down for the birdhouse, placed it on his lap and began to sandpaper it with great nicety.

"I was through there once," he said.

"Where?" Dorney asked when, Clara making no reply, she realized the remark had been addressed to herself.

"He means Wyoming," Clara explained softly.

"Awful dry country," he said. "Didn't care of it at all."

When he was really hard at work, using first this precise tool and then that one, with the birdhouse held as in a vice between his knees, and was no longer paying his company any particular heed, Clara got up and motioned to Dorney to follow her out into the kitchen. It was dark but it took only an instant for Clara to find and strike a match and light the lamp. "If that ain't sweet," she said, looking about the bare and very small lean-to admiringly.

"What is?" Dorney asked.

"He's went to work and polished the stove! Maybe George helped him, or Ruby, bless their little hearts. I would of done it," she said, lowering her hoarse voice to a whisper. "He's wonderful in the house, and knows a awful lot about taking care of kids, but of course he ain't much of a cook or a washer and things would get to quite a pretty pass if I didn't come over every once in a while and kind of straighten things out. You know, like a woman's got to do," she said. "A man can just go so far and that will be as far as he can go." She took her shawl off and hung it over her arm. Going to the scarred cupboard, she put the bottle of peaches on the empty-looking second shelf, and after some indecision concluded to put the pair of rubbers down by the back door. She stood back and surveyed them, then stooped and by bringing the left one forward to the line of boarding in the floor made a perfectly even composition. "I'll tell George tomorrow they're his," she said, raising up. "I wish they would have been boots, is all, but they cost a lot more. Besides, they'd of been harder to hide."

"Aren't you going to tell Mr. Mudge you brought these things?" Dorney asked.

Clara put a long finger to her lips and shook her head, frowning. "Why not?"

She stepped closer so that she could speak into Dorney's ear. "He finds out every once in a while and then he'll thank me, like in there just now, but I don't never let him know if I can help it, and lots of times — men, you can pull the wool over their eyes — he don't never find out, and that's the best."

"The way I'd think, anybody as good as you are ought to get credit."

"Oh, no," Clara said, almost in horror. "People don't care nothing for somebody they got to thank every minute of the day. Not right down deep in their hearts they don't. They get so they can't hardly stand the sight of 'em."

"But it's fun to give credit, Clara."

"People can easier like somebody they owe actual money to than somebody they got to thank, thank, thank for little fiddling favors every minute of the day and night!"

"But they're not little fiddling — "

Again Clara touched her finger to her lips and shook her head. She reached over and the latch clicked when she shut the cupboard door. "Did you notice her?" she asked.

"Who?"

"Sophie. The kids' mother. The one I was telling you I worked side by side with so long."

"You mean her picture?"

"Over by the window in the oval frame. Joe paid four seventy-five for it even after he got laid off, so you can imagine what he thought of her. We'll look at it better when we go back in. . . . ."

They tiptoed past the man in the rocking chair who was now holding the birdhouse at arm's length and sighting along the ridge-pole, for no true woman can skirt in otherwise him who, pensophic, abstracted, is engaged in the world's, that is, man's work. Many thousands of years has she been quelled, cautioned and trained.

The picture was hung very high up on the wall and Dorney had tiptoed too close to it so she moved backwards to another vantage point and raised her eyes.

"Wasn't she the prettiest thing?" Clara said in a hushed voice. "And she was just as sweet and good-natured as she was pretty."

It was out of reach of the light, the thick convex glass more obscured than clarified the mild round face behind it, tinted as by an undertaker's plaintive hand, but Dorney tried hard for Clara's sake to see Sophie Mudge plain.

"She had the prettiest light hair and the steam in the laundry just made it prettier. My hair, it would hang like strings, but hers — You can't see her dimples here because she's not smiling, but — "

"I think I can see one, there, on the right," Dorney said politely. "My right, I mean. It'd be her left. On her cheek there."

"I see the one you mean," Clara said. "Yes, that's a dimple, all right. I'm sure it is." She gazed upwards like a true believer. "Yes, it is."

"You bet your life she was pretty," Joe Mudge said loudly.

Dorney looked around at him but Clara did not. He had stood the birdhouse on the table and taken up a small hammer with which, oddly enough, he was striking light blows on his thigh just above the knee. "You bet your boots and bottom dollar she was," he said. "People talk about pretty! They don't know what the word means."

Dorney wanted to say, Mr. Mudge, won't you accidentally hurt yourself with the hammer? but kept silent.

"Them's the ones die," he said as loudly, still striking the light blows that bounced off the tensed muscles of his leg. "Not some damned old drunkard in the ditch bank, not some ugly old witch, not some son of a bitch of a foreman that lays a man off and won't give him his job back and he's got to peddle a lot of damn birdhouses and odds and ends and stay home and go crazy with a family of kids." He threw the hammer up in the air and caught it. "Not them, you can bet. Never nobody like them. Oh, no! It's got to be the ones that lights up the room when they walk through. It's got to be Sophie. It's got to be somebody that when they're gone, you might just as well crawl in a hole and pull it in after you and be done with it."

While he spoke, Clara flung her shawl back on, crossing it over in front with concealed hands, and when he finished, she took a step toward him.

"Joe," she said, her voice breaking.

"What?" he said, looking straight ahead.

"Would you mention to the kids when they get up in the morning that I come over tonight? Because I promised 'em I would and wouldn't want 'em to think I maybe forgot and didn't do it."

"I'll tell 'em," he said. He blinked his eyes, moved his head and then gingerly as a man tries the floor after weeks in bed, he smiled.

"Sure," he said. "You're a real daisy to them kids." He put the hammer carefully down and took up his task again, not seeing, as Dorney saw, how Clara reeled from his words and from that gift, his smile.

She came to herself and her surroundings once more when the little sobbing cry, "Aunt Clar-a," came from the bedroom. "It's Ruby!" she said, as though she had been waiting several long cramped hours in the cold dew to hear the megarhyncha and but now caught the first sweet note. She hastened toward the sound, motioning for Dorney to follow.

Clara knew. It was Ruby, in the crib in the far corner, clinging to the railing, sobbing forlornly, her feet sunk ankle-deep in the straw mattress. In spite of the darkness of the small room, lit by the dim parlor light shining in through the open door, Clara made her way unhesitatingly to the little mourner, edging past the big double bed, a trunk and a chair with the back off without so much as grazing her skirt. Slower Dorney, feeling as if she had got into a den of warm breathing cubs, bumped her shins two or three times and got a sharp jab on her wrist bone from the knob of the bedpost, but she groped her way to the foot of the child's narrow bed and soon she could see quite well.

"What's the matter with Ruby?" Clara said softly. More than her imperfections, was self-consciousness Clara's imperfections. It lost in love and tenderness, she bent like a willow, the hands she stretched out to cup around the child's soft face were full of grace, her eyes rose stars and shone like them. Her voice, too, wonderfully changed. "What's the matter with Ruby?" she said.

"I'm a-scared, Aunt Clara."

"Why should you be a-scared?" She lifted her up and stood her a little to one side so she could reach into the crib and straighten the crumpled baby who lay at one end, and then smooth the sheet at the other and poke the flat pillow. Gently she pressed the small girl down, first so she sat and then so she lay back, her eyes big and black against the pillowcase.

"George says the boy told him, that's why, and George is a-scared, too."

"And what did the boy tell him?"

"About how ghosts come, and scare everybody."

"They don't do no such thing."

"But they is dead people, Aunt Clara."

"They ain't nothing of the kind."

"George told me."

"There ain't no ghosts, it's just hired girls coming home with ironing boards, or sheets on the line, and they ain't dead people, and they don't scare nobody," Clara said, so that it could not be doubted.

"You ought to know that, a big girl like you that can sweep the kitchen so good and make such a fine loaf of little bread when Aunt Clara gives you a piece of dough. So you go to sleep now, because I give you my solemn promise and you know what that means."

Ruby nodded contentedly.

"Now," Clara went on, "you close your eyes, and I'll tell you something."

They drooped and closed.

"I'll tell you what we'll do tomorrow night after I get home from work and have supper and come to see you. I got a jar full of beads," she said, "and what am I going to do? Bring it over. And what are we going to do? Going to string them. Take a long — long — string — and start a-putting beads on one by one. Make a long — long — neckolace." She named the colors of the beads, their sizes and shapes, melodiously, compared the length of the string to a skiprope, a kiteline, the clotheslines of both Mrs. Vertrees put together. "A long — long — neckolace," she finished. "For Ruby — Ruby — Mudge."

It worked like magic and when she had paused for two or three breaths to be certain it had, she stooped and kissed the curl-draped forehead. "It don't take much," she said to Dorney, "when they been running their heads off all day."

"It's as good as singing," Dorney said. "I got kind of sleepy myself. The baby's darling," she added, looking down at small Sophie who lay on her back with her fists flung out to either side.

"Ain't she, though?" Sophie's forehead, too, was kissed, the small right ball of hand patted, and then Clara led Dorney over to the big double bed where two boys, aged six and three, slept soundly in a tangle. With deft motions she unsnarled them.

"They all look alike, don't they?" Dorney said. "All with blond hair and those round heads."

"That's cause their mother and father was both blond," Clara explained. "Sophie was pretty, and anybody can see what Joe looks like. If they'd of been mine," she looked over her shoulder at the crib and back to the bed, "they wouldn't of been nothing to brag about. I'd sure feel sorry for 'em. They'd of been — some sight, I guess."

"Clara!"

"Well, they would. I'd sure feel sorry for 'em." She spoke in the old hoarse voice again and when she pulled her shawl together, it was in the old graceless way, like a scarecrow.

Outside, it was moonlight as the two started down Seventh South. "He ain't really like he was tonight," Clara apologized. "But sometimes he gets so kind of blue and down in the mouth and feels so

162

bad over Sophie. If he could just get back on at the cabinet works, he'd feel so much better. Although how he can go and leave the kids every day with the oldest only six, I don't know. But just the same, he'd feel so much better."

"Oh, he was all right," Dorney said, to reassure her.

"Dorney."

"What?"

"I just can't help but think it no matter how I try."

"Think what?"

"How handsome he is."

To Dorney, Mr. Joe Mudge's eyes had seemed a little too large and blue, with a little too much white showing about the edges, his chin went back a little too far and crowded his Adam's apple and his golden hair was a little too soft and flying. "Yes, he is," she agreed, however.

"I just can't help it."

"Well, that's all right. A person can think somebody's handsome if they want."

Clara stopped abruptly. "It *ain't* all right," she said. "Because it's just like Mamma says. He can't even *see* me. He don't even know I'm *alive*. Just like she says, I ought to have some pride, I ought to quit going, but what can I do, Dorney? I can't rest, I get set down and all of a sudden I think about them maybe needing their stockings darned or their buttons sewed on or their garters fixed — kids pull them things off so terrible — or maybe coming down with the croup that he won't notice — or maybe wanting a slice of bread and the breadbox empty — and the minute I do, I can't stand it, I make a beeline for the door and over I go. Mamma'll be making all manner of fun, she'll be saying mean things that cut you to pieces like a knife, saying 'em when I go and saying 'em when I come back, but I can't help myself. I go. Morning and evening, there goes Clara Tofflemire, the laughingstock of the neighborhood, but — there I go. Because I love them kids like they was my very own," she said miserably, "and they ain't the only ones, either!"

Nothing seemed right to say. Everything seemed wrong, so Dorney kept quiet.

"Do you think he'd marry me?" bitter Clara said, as though the question had been put to her, whether he would or not. "After losing somebody like Sophie? No, it's just like Mamma says, he'll get over this grief someday and then he'll look around and find some pretty young girl — though, like Mamma says, he ain't no bargain, especially if he don't get back on at the cabinet works. He only rents that place, and all he's got is that little bit of furniture and them four kids. That's no bargain, is it? Is that a bargain?"

She seemed to be demanding an answer so Dorney cleared her throat and said, "No."

"No, you bet it ain't," Clara said. "It's anything but a bargain! Anything *but*." Her voice stumbled and fell on the last word and she tried to bend her head to her own shoulder like a flamingo, to weep upon it.

Dorney put a hand on her arm. "Don't cry," she whispered. "Why, I bet you could get him just as easy, if you wanted."

Clara looked around, a moonlit tear running fast down the side of her nose. "How?" she said. "Can a woman go to a man and say she loves him and ask him to marry her?"

"Well, maybe in certain cases, like for instance — "

"If I was pretty," Clara said. "But you seen him tonight. You seen how he acted. What chance would I have? Why, I could get down on my knees to him and it would be just like Mamma says — he wouldn't have me at any price." She began to walk on and Dorney caught up with her. "No," she said. "I might as well give up because I ain't got no more chance to marry Joe Mudge than Schooner Bill's got to be President of the United States. Not as much. But I'll keep on going over there, making a worse and worse fool out of myself, I guess, until — "

"That little Ruby loves you," Dorney put in quickly. "Anybody could tell that. I'll bet they all do. I'll bet Mr. Mudge does, too, only he just doesn't realize it. Maybe if you could just make him *realize* it."

"Never," Clara said. "Never." She dug her heel in the ground. "Oh, well, it ain't a matter of life and death. It might seem like it sometimes, but it really ain't. I — suppose."

16

HER HUSBAND'S PERMISSION HAD BEEN GIVEN THE
night before, and when they had risen from the breakfast table,
Alma Morelewski told Teige Desmond that it would only take her
a minute to get ready to accompany him on the day's sightseeing
tour. The way she flew into the bedroom, he believed her and stood
turning his hat about in his hands, but when after some minutes
she did not reappear, he began to look for Dorney, whom he found
in the parlor. "Good morning," he said. "How does the Lady-in-
Waiting do today?"

"I'm fine, thank you," she said, dusting for a second time the
bronze bust with the grapes and the vine leaves on the center table.

"I saw evidence of your fine Italian hand last night."

She stared critically at the slick celluloid album, took it up,
breathed on it, dusted it a second time, too, and laid it down exactly where it had been before. "The only book I even *looked* at,"
she murmured, trying not to change color, "was that blue one, and
all I read was a little bit over in the middle." It did not occur to
her that he might be speaking, as he was, of the shoes Mr. Sodaquist
had shined, or of the bed she had turned down according to instructions.

"Why didn't you start at the beginning?"

"How do you pronounce his name?" she asked suddenly, looking
up.

"Nietzsche?"

"No, that other one."

"Zarathustra?"

She took a deep breath. "Mr. Desmond, would you mind telling
me, why would anybody want to write a book like that in the first
place?"

He pulled a chair forward for her, she took it shyly, and he sat
down across from her. "Well," he said, "I'll tell you. It's a long
story."

Alma Morelewski meant to hurry, but whenever, unseen by others,
she stood before a mirror, time played tricks upon her. A hundred

years did not go by in the twinkling of an eye, as for the wood-chopper in the old legend who saw an angel come and go, but half an hour, even longer, could pass and she be unaware of its passing. So it was now, eager as she was to rejoin her guest. She was wearing pearl-gray silk, with a little shoulder cape, and for the first time to-day her new corset, the most uncompromising and certainly the tightest she had ever worn. It gave her a waist so small she could span it with her two hands, but of course it was small anyway now that she weighed so little and had got out of the habit of eating.

Having tried on several hats last night, in her nightdress, before she climbed into bed, she knew which one she was going to wear, the white gypsy bonnet with the cherry-colored ribbons, out of its wrappings and ready on Mr. Morelewski's bureau. She put it on with confidence now, stuck a rhinestone hatpin in firmly and started for the door, but something forced her about and sent her back to the mirror. She looked in pedagogically, stepped back, sighed, looked again, and knew beyond a question of doubt that the bonnet was impossible with the gray silk dress, so she took it off and tossed it on the bed. There was nothing to do but start over and go through all her hat boxes again!

When she emerged from her bedroom, she heard Teige say to someone in the parlor, " — and so one may conclude that Friedrich Nietzsche, paradoxically, is a kind of brokenhearted optimist and at the same time a beaming crêpe-hanger who thinks that every cloud has a silver lining. You see, what he is actually driving at is to define — "

Had company come, for heaven's sake? But he was only talking to Dorney, who rose respectfully when her mistress came into the room.

"Class dismissed," he said, smiling. "Same time tomorrow." He turned to his uncle's wife. "My dear Alma!" he said. "For such a vision as now stands before me, I would willingly have spent," he flipped out his watch and looked at it, "nearly an hour twiddling my thumbs and chewing my mustache — if I had one — ought I to have, do you think? — but this young lady," he smiled at Dorney, "has helped me to pass the time much more profitably; a graceless thing to say, considering that I have been talking the whole while, and she has done nothing whatever but put me a question or two."

The Queen narrowed her eyes. "I don't believe you should," she said, studying him bravely, her chin tilted.

"Should what?" he asked in surprise, and his hand went to his upper lip where her gaze was fixed.

"Grow one," she said. "They don't look so bad when they're small, and turn up at the ends, but the thick ones that hang down are just terrible."

166

"What do you think, Dorney?" he asked.

She brought her eyes back from far away with difficulty. "What I think," she said, "I think he must have quite a bad disposition to start with, but of course a person can't help that, and nobody should remember that, only how smart he is to figure out all those things."

"I don't believe you should," the Queen repeated slowly. "But still, if it was small and turned up at the ends, it might look rather nice."

The carriage had been waiting for some time out in front, and when Teige put her into it, he repeated that she looked a vision. She smiled and said that if it was true — which she by no means believed, of course, she would have him know — why, then perhaps he wouldn't mind if she stopped at Madame Blanche's for a moment before they set out for Fort Douglas. She had to call for a dress. And she would also stop at Colette's on State Street, if he wouldn't be too cross, because her hat was ready, this being Friday. Colette had said Friday, she was quite sure, and it was no use to get the dress without getting the hat. To Teige's surprise, she pushed open Madame Branche's silver-knobbed door and came out with an impressive pink box he hastened up the walk to take out of her arms not ten minutes after it closed behind her, but the visit to the milliner's was not so expeditious. At five minutes to twelve when she tripped out of Colette's with the hat, he was, of all places, up beside Mr. Jump in the driver's seat. His head was bent and he was getting a light for his pipe from the coachman so he did not know she was there until she gave a little cough. She had to cough once more to make herself heard above their earnest conversation, and that made him turn quickly, smile and climb down saying "I'll have to take your word for it."

"For what?" she said flirtatiously, pretending at the same time by a little gasp and a rolling of her eyes that she had been through a tremendous ordeal.

He took the round ribbon-tied box out of her grasp and opened the door. "Why, Mr. Jump here was telling me that the Crows, contrary to popular belief, were gentlemen and scholars," he explained.

"Crows?"

Mr. Jump edged across the seat, and twisted around and looked down. "They fought like white men," he said. "Up against them, a fellow had an even chance. In fact, they was the whitest Indians in the whole blame country. Don't know how they might be now, though. Ain't seen none in a long time, and in fact I wouldn't put it past 'em to all die off eventually."

Since it was so late, Teige suggested that they lunch before going out to the Fort and Alma agreed, confessing that she was starved. At the Paris Café, however, where she insisted on being taken — people would gossip if they went anywhere else, she said — she ate a cup of jellied broth and nothing else. Her husband watched her anxiously and tried to ask her in a whisper if she had already eaten at home, but she shook her head and grew so red and then so pale that he desisted, assuming that she had. She puzzled him, laughing aloud as she did, when she had been content to smile before, and her eyes sparkled so, as if she had a fever. He took her hand to feel if she had, but it was clammy cold, not hot, in spite of the torrid weather. He should never have started this thing of making her go without food to take weight off. But then he had never expected her to be so docile and actually follow his orders. He kept his worried eyes on her while she listened to his nephew try to answer her question about how the ladies dressed in New York and if they were very beautiful. Teige was a nice boy to reply that way without levity and go into what details he could for his aunt, Joseph Morelewski thought. A nice, handsome, goodhearted boy, the spitting image of his black Irish father, except that Danny Desmond had blue eyes. I wish to God he'd been mine, he thought, teaching his English or whatever it is he teaches right here in Salt Lake City, except that I'd be so proud, I'd never be able to get my hat on, and every customer I'd tell how my boy's a Professor up at the University, my boy's a whiz, till I got to be a joke. . . .

Teige spotted the bookstore on Second South and Second East and called to Mr. Jump to be so good as to stop there. Gay Alma — and if she had never been truly gay in her life before, she was no more to blame for it than the iron nail without the adducing loadstone, for not leaping up of its own accord — gay Alma, then, said she would love to go with him and did, hanging charmingly on his arm, laughing up into his face and wondering he didn't get enough of books during the school year, without needing more in the midst of his vacation.

The first book he bought was for herself! A big, flat, worn-looking book full of costume drawings which she liked very much for they were tinted in pink and green. The only trouble was, they would be of no earthly use to her, as the fashions were all out of style and in any case quite hopeless. *Modes Directoire*, the title was. The date she happened to run across on the front page she considered some sort of mistake, 1799. But she hugged it to her all the same and was pleased, although the book was dirty and made a smudge across the front of her dress that she tried unsuccessfully to rub off with her handkerchief. It was so nice for him to want to stop off at a bookstore just to buy her a book! She looked about for him. He had wandered away somewhere while she was examining the pictures, or pretending to, for she couldn't really seem to see them, except that they were all out of style and nothing that one would want to have Madame Blanche copy. Where was he? Oh, there he was, talking to the soiled owner, an old man with steel-rimmed glasses and black fingernails who now reached around, took a book down off the shelf and handed it to him. Still clutching her *Modes Directoire* she went between two untidy tables of precariously stacked books, trying not to dislodge any or rub against anything, and over to his side. "Now what?" she said gaily, as though he had just performed some clever sleight of hand and was about to astonish her with more of the same.

"This history will do," Teige said, laying it down on a book that said *Geography* across the front, "and now if I might see the *Lamb's Tales* and *Moby Dick* — " He turned to Alma. "These are for your little Dorney," he said, smiling.

"No Melville, sir, I'm sorry to say," the bookseller said.

Alma heard the words though there was such a rushing and roaring in her head, and could see with astonishing clarity the tufts of hair growing out of the old man's nostrils, the pinpoints of moisture in the large pores of his nose, even while the whirlpool spun her and empty black space yawned underneath. She laid Teige's gift down and clutched the edge of the bare wooden table that served as a counter. "Dorney?" she breathed, and her lips felt as if they had sparkling lights in them.

"Why, yes," Teige said. "The child is a born student, I'm convinced, if she had half a chance, but naturally she's got to have access to some books. There's something extraordinary about her, some — I don't just know what it is. I was thinking about it last night and then this morning. She's — "

"Here's the *Lamb's Tales*, sir," the bookseller said from up front, and Teige, asking her please to excuse him a minute, went forward.

Little by little, the rushing and roaring stopped and by closing her eyes and holding tight to the table, Alma found she could keep from being pulled down in darkness. Gradually the twinkling lights died out of her cold lips and she could open her eyes again, first on the lace-edged corner of the handkerchief clutched in her gloved right hand, then on the book-lined wall before her, and finally, by turning her head sideways, on the outline of Teige against the pale front window. . . .

She received many admiring glances at Fort Douglas, but it was hot up there on the tableland high above the city in spite of the green gardens, shade trees and blowing wind. The gravel paths hurt her thin-soled feet and she was glad when the full regimental post had all been seen, buildings, barracks, parade ground and jail with nobody in it, and Teige said to the smart young corporal who had acted as their guide that they would just stand here on the parapet for a little and look at the view and then go back to town. She did not see how the soldier, after he had received their thanks and good-byes, glanced wistfully back at her, tugging at his cap, walked on a few steps and could not resist looking back again, or she would have given him another smile and perhaps a little wave of her hand, or perhaps not.

She felt very tired and was beginning to long intensely for her soft bed and dark room. She wondered if they would get home in time for her to have a nap before she had to dress and go back uptown for dinner. She must tell Joe about the peculiar attack of faintness she had had. Or, no, perhaps not. He might mention it to Teige and she didn't want Teige to know. Luckily, he hadn't noticed, and once she had got back into the carriage and Mr. Jump gathered up the reins and the horses started off, she was all right. She was fine now, except that her knees quaked a little under her, and the sight of the Great Salt Lake glittering off in the distance made her eyes pain sharply.

"Tomorrow I should like very much to go out to Big Cottonwood Canyon," Teige said. "Would you care to come with me? By the way, have you ever visited the Shoshone Indian reservation? I'd like to go there if possible. Does Uncle Joe ever take time off?"

"He takes off Sundays," she said. A serge walking skirt, she thought, a cashmere jacket and a little Czarina cap. That would look best. Better than something flimsy. She began to feel out of breath with happiness and excitement, as when the returns came in and she knew she had been elected Queen of the Jubilee, gay as before they went into that awful bookstore so Teige could buy her that book of costumes. Funny, she had been past it so often and never even noticed it was there, but he noticed. It was kind of him to think afterwards of buying those books for Dorney, really it was, now that she thought of it. Of course, when one considered, he would be apt to do something like that, being a teacher.

She had a vision of herself among the Shoshone tribe, the contrast of her white and gold against their black and bronze. She ought to wear light blue because that made her eyes look even bluer than they were, or else pale pink . . . no, blue, because then the pink would come as more of a surprise when they went to Saltair, and took a picnic supper — the pink foulard with the Spanish flounces. It would still be daylight when they got there, so she would need her parasol, but when the orchestra started to play in the big pavilion and couples started swirling, it would be night. She could see Teige turning to her on the balcony under the Japanese lanterns and asking, would she care to dance? See herself nodding, debating whether to wear her scarf or leave it behind with Joe — leaving it behind — and going with Teige up the steps, his hand on her elbow. At the edge of the great dance floor that appeared to be lower where they were standing and higher across the room, so polished as to seem in motion, he would put his arm around her waist and she would slip her hand into his and they would begin to waltz . . . and whirl . . . on the already spinning, glittering disk where so many dancers like black dots, were dancing and spinning and whirling. . . .

"Wonderful, isn't it?"

She blinked, the black dots didn't go away but flocked more thickly, zigzagged, and her stomach turned over. "What is?" she said, wanting to hold on to something with a detached and far-away hand.

"The view. Those mountains over there — the Wasatch, didn't he say? Or the Oquirrh, I've forgotten which."

"Please," she said, wanting to move a detached and faraway foot and go home and lie down because otherwise she would certainly be very ill.

"Alma! Are you all right?"

Where was he? Because she had to tell somebody — quickly — "I think I'm going to . . ."

She was. He caught her as she fell.

17

DORNEY DID NOT HEAR THE FIRST RAP AT THE front door because she was out in the coal shed getting some newspapers to spread down where the scrubbed linoleum was most walked on, till it should dry enough not to take footprints, but she heard the second knock, or third. It startled her so much that instead of laying them down in the kitchen, she carried the newspapers with her to the door. Nobody ever knocked! except once before, a man in a plaid suit wanting to enlarge photographs (the Queen ordered one of herself and one of Mr. Morelewski, tinted, but had never hung them up), and one other time, when an ugly boy selling Fairy soap said he was trying to collect enough coupons to get a 21-jewel watch.

The caller was Crystal, and if it had been a Tigré lady in black cowrie-trimmed goatskin, her feet and hands stained with henna, her eyelids with antimony and four sets of amulets around her neck, Dorney could not have been more amazed.

"Well, aren't you even going to say hello?" Crystal said, laughing. "You look like I was a ghost or something."

She sounded extraordinarily pleasant and good-humored, was wearing the pretty red and white striped dress Madge had put the hem in, last night, and she wanted to be asked in, Dorney knew as well as she knew that the flowers on her red straw sailor had been taken off Madge's summer felt and the garnet brooch out of Madge's pincushion. If only she had given fair warning, so some way could have been found out of the predicament! for it was that. Crystal, at the Queen's, and the Queen absent! What else but a predicament? "My, you look nice," Dorney said, to gain time, trying to take up as much of the doorway as she could. If Crystal once got in, there was no telling what she would want to do, see and handle, and the more she was requested to desist, the more she would do whatever she liked. And it was so late, the parlor clock had struck three a long time ago. The Queen and Mr. Desmond would be coming home any minute.

"I decided to go uptown," Crystal said. "And when I came past here, I said to myself, as long as I'm going uptown anyway, why not go in and ask Dorney if she wants something?"

"Why, no," Dorney said. Maybe the Queen wouldn't like it a bit, finding company! "What do you mean?"

"You silly." Crystal's sweet smile vanished and she looked contemptuous. "I'm going uptown and I wondered if you wanted me to pick up anything for you, that's all. I wanted to be nice. I wanted to do you a favor. Now, do you want me to draw you a map?"

A favor, today of all days. Why? Dorney felt in her pocket for the two coins she had brought from home this morning. Mr. Sodaquist generally came and worked from four to six in the Queen's garden, and when he arrived she intended to pay one nickel as agreed, for shining Mr. Desmond's shoes yesterday, and the other for shining a second pair today. If she gave the money to Crystal, she would have to make some excuse to Mr. Sodaquist or else slip home and get another dime, but that wouldn't be much bother. Trying to appear grateful and pleased, she shifted the papers under her left arm, and drew her right hand out of her pocket.

"Why, yes, I really do need something I wish you'd get me," she said.

"You haven't any money, have you?" Crystal put her hand out doubtfully and Dorney dropped the warm coins into it. "What do you want me to get?" she asked haughtily, and opened her purse.

"Why, a — " Dorney wrinkled her forehead. "A tablet and pencil!"

"All right." Her eyes slid downwards. "What in the world are you doing with those newspapers under your arm like you were selling them on the street corner?"

"I just scrubbed the floor," Dorney explained nervously, "and I was going to put them down till it's — but it's probably nearly dry now, because I've been standing here quite a while, and if you don't mind — "

"Let's go see," Crystal said, coolly pushing in past her. "What floor? Which way? The kitchen?"

Dorney stuck her head out to look both ways down Fifth East and see if the carriage was anywhere in sight and then shut the door with reluctance.

"So this is your famous Queen's parlor. . . ." The caller ran her hand through the wine and green bead portière as though it had been harp strings.

"Yes," Dorney said, "it is."

Crystal dropped lightly into a plush armchair but got up almost at once to walk to the center table and stare at the bronze bust. "That's not very expensive," she said. She turned and took a step

173

forward. "Where's the cozy corner you were so excited about? And the Turkish water pipe — Oh, I see." She smiled as though something was very amusing.

"Crystal," Dorney said firmly but in a soft voice. "We can't stay here. We'll have to go out in the kitchen because the Queen is asleep and she might hear us, otherwise." The lie came out in spite of her and sounded so true she almost believed it. "The least little thing wakes her up, and then she gets — she doesn't like it."

"Where?" Crystal craned her neck towards the alcove.

"In the bedroom." As she went through the hangings into the long hall, Dorney prayed that the Queen's door would be closed. It was a little ajar but she ran on tiptoe to shut it very quietly as though a sleeper really lay beyond it. "Come this way," she whispered loudly, and Crystal, looking to both sides, followed her.

In the kitchen she laid the newspapers on one chair and pulled out another. "Sit down," she said, "unless you can't stay and have to go."

But Crystal took a chair she liked better nearer the blue-enameled stove, and sat down elegantly, arranging her skirts. "Oh, I'm not in any particular hurry," she said. Her eyes traveled slowly about, to the big brown icebox, the glass doors of the cupboards full of chinaware, the dark pantry opening off to the left, came back to Dorney who was trying to decide whether to sit or stand. "Where's your apron and cap that the Queen supposedly bought you? I thought you had to wear them!" she said.

Dorney had never told them at home how the Queen had changed her mind and taken them back. "Not — all the time," she said lamely, and braced herself.

But Crystal did not pursue the topic. She got up and went to the window to look out at the side garden, stood there a moment glancing up and down. Then she came back and resumed her seat.

"How's your famous Mr. Desmond?" she inquired.

"Oh, he's fine."

"Is he asleep, too?"

"Oh, no. He's gone sightseeing today."

"Where?"

"Out to Fort Douglas."

"What for?"

"Just to see it, I guess."

"There's nothing up there!"

"Oh, yes, there is."

"How do you know?"

"Well — "

"When is he coming back?" Crystal leaned over and looked at

174

herself in the shining teakettle, tucking in a stray lock of hair beneath her ear.

As plainly as if Crystal was telling her in so many words, Dorney now knew the purpose of this visit. Crystal wanted to see Mr. Desmond! Her inquisitiveness of last night came back, her unusual willingness to sit and chat. She wanted to be introduced to him! That was why she made Madge finish the red and white striped dress before she went to bed, that was why she switched the flowers from the summer felt and came knocking at the front door pretending she wanted to do a favor, so she could get acquainted with Mr. Desmond! And the purpose of *that* was to see if she could make him fall in love, propose, marry her and take her away to New York City! What else? Dorney felt stunned. Nobody around here was good enough for her, as Mrs. Luby had said, she had turned everybody down right and left. But Mr. Desmond might be good enough, handsome, a college professor, related to the owner of the Paris Café. He might very well be, and that was what Crystal had dressed all up for and come to see because, naturally, she couldn't wait *forever*. Dorney, stricken, looked at her, until the thought came that after all, Mr. Desmond would have something to say about all this. Maybe he wouldn't any more propose, and marry and take Crystal to New York than he would take — well, Clara, in spite of her black pompadour and heart-shaped face and the way she looked in this dress and red straw hat. But of course maybe when he found out how well she could play the piano, that would make all the difference, and he would. . . . She could see the pretty white hands flying over the keyboard and hid her own hands behind her. Maybe he really *would!* And then Crystal would get to hear all the funny, teasing, educated jokes, the explanations about — what did he call them? — philosophers, like the man this morning, Nietzsche — the wonderful big words, and she would get to handle the rows upon rows of books. . . .

"Do you stand around and moon like that all day?"

"No."

Why, Crystal would be a terrible wife for Mr. Desmond, even if she could cook pretty well and had to have everything as neat as a pin around her. Just terrible! Because she always laughed at the wrong places, and besides — practising the piano all the time like that. When Mr. Desmond wanted to get his mind on anything, he'd have to go into another room and shut the door and the windows, and nearly have to stuff his ears with cotton! Of course she might not practise so much if she got married. . . .

"Where is the guest room?"

Dorney pointed upwards. I wish he *was* here so she could meet him, she thought suddenly, because what good would it do her? Suppose he just happened to say how do you do and nothing else, and went upstairs — what could Crystal do? She couldn't lasso him.

"Is it carpeted?"

"A flower design with roses and green around the edge."

She'd do something, though, never fear. I'd like to know what, Dorney thought. For the sake of curiosity, I wish he would come home, so a person could see just what she would do. I'd like to know. She recalled then, with acute discomfort, that when he came the Queen would be with him! And she had told Crystal that Mrs. Morelewski was asleep in the bedroom. Crystal would be outraged about being lied to, would tell Madge, Madge would say things about how Wanda had brought her up, she might answer back. . . . She heard the half-hour strike and wondered, How can I make her go before they come? How can I? She excused herself, got the basin off the back porch, brought it back in and filled it with water at the sink. "I've got to wash the windows," she announced, hoping that task would bore Crystal. She rummaged for clean cloths, rolled up her sleeves and set to work on the clean window nearest the door, saying a silent prayer.

Crystal sat watching a few moments discontentedly, and then got to her feet. She walked over to the icebox, fingered the long nickel handle, moved to the cupboard, stood on tiptoe and examined the high-piled china through the glass, lifted the cover of the blue glazed dish on the drainboard (there was nothing in it), set it back on and announced "Well, I'd better go, I guess."

Drying her hands and hardly daring to believe her good fortune, Dorney walked with her to the front door — she had declined to go out the back — and opened it. "It was nice to have you stop by," she said politely.

"Oh, don't act like you were Mrs. Morelewski. After all, you don't live here." Crystal eyed her crossly and then looked at the shadeless street beyond the green hedge. "It's hot, isn't it?" she said.

"I should say," Dorney agreed, swallowing a sharp retort.

"Too hot to go uptown," Crystal decided. She opened her purse, took out Dorney's two nickels, handed them back to her and shut it with a loud snap. "Maybe I'll go tomorrow instead, or the next day." She adjusted her wrist ruffles and took up a handful of skirt.

When she shut the door, Dorney leaned against it, drawing a deep sigh of relief and feeling she had escaped she knew not what calamity. But had she escaped? At that very instant she heard wheels and the Queen's carriage ground to a stop in front of the gate. She flew to the window. There was Mr. Desmond, out of it already! And reaching in to give his hand to his companion. Where, where, was Crystal? There, alas, at the corner of the hedge! Dorney could see the red straw hat, and her heart sank down to her shoes. Crystal deliberately turned as though she had made a mistake in direction and deliberately strolled back down the sidewalk, this time heading toward Seventh South. She did not appear to be doing it, but she was taking everything in, Dorney knew, the carriage, the bays, Mr. Desmond, the coachman, who had unaccountably got down off his seat and was taking the pale drooping hatless Queen by her other arm. . . .

The pale drooping hatless Queen! Forgetting Crystal and any and all aggravations, she ran from the window to the bedroom, where with lively hands she turned down the bed. Something had happened to Mrs. Morelewski! The Queen was sick.

Mr. Jump went back to town immediately to fetch Mr. Joseph Morelewski from the Paris Café, and when he came he brought the doctor, a man six and a half feet tall, with a black overcoat on. Dorney had to hang it up on the clothes tree and she wondered he hadn't cooked in it, but he was not even perspiring. His hatband wasn't damp, either. This was Dr. Bacon, famous for his lectures and for other things as well.

He excluded everyone from the room while he examined the patient, not excepting Mr. Morelewski who, after he had gone out in the kitchen to tell Dorney to put the kettle on, did nothing but walk up and down in the parlor, clap his hands to his head, groan aloud and between times ask questions of Teige who had taken a seat on the tufted ottoman. How was it, once more? he said over and over. Start at the beginning again. How had it happened? Teige told him patiently. They were standing on the parapet up at Fort Douglas looking at the view of the city, when Alma fainted. How, fainted? Well, she had paled — but she had such a white complexion anyway, it was hard to notice. She had groped with her hands, swayed, mumbled something and swooned, but he had turned and caught her in time, so she didn't fall and hurt herself. And then what? Well, he put her down on the grass and people started gathering around, some officers and enlisted men and two or three women, one of whom, when she saw Alma, went through the preliminaries of fainting herself and had to be led away, and the sergeant who had escorted them around, he was the one who brought the tin cup of water. Did he dash it in her face? No, he just knelt down by her and dipped his handkerchief in it and dabbed at her temples, while Teige was rubbing her wrists. How long was she unconscious? Not long, not more than a minute or two, just a few seconds, really, and then she opened her eyes. What then? Well, the sergeant carried her over to the carriage, he was a strong, quick boy and gathered her right up into his arms and didn't want any help, he said, she wasn't heavy, and then the coachman Mr. Jump brought them home! That was all there was to it.

"It seemed best to get her home at once and then send for you, Uncle Joe," Teige said.

"It was, my boy, it was," Mr. Morelewski admitted, clapping his hands to his head and taking a step to the right so as not to bump into the table. "It may be her heart. That's what worries me. It may be that. Heart failure. The beginning of heart failure. And her so young. Well, the good die young — there's a lot of truth to those old sayings, they don't get started if there's not a lot of truth to them, those old sayings. That's what worries me. I must keep it from her, by every means in my power. I should have warned the doctor not to . . ."

"Oh, no, Uncle Joe." Teige took his pipe out, tapped it on the side of his shoe, but put it back in his pocket without lighting it. "Women faint all the time, everybody knows that. You must have noticed. They drop like flies, honestly they do, in hot weather. At least that's the way it is in New York. Every concert, every time you go to the theater, every time you get in a crowded department store, at church. I'd like to have a dollar for every — " He broke off and smiled. "Honestly, I don't think you have to worry."

"Worry!" Mr. Morelewski moaned, clutching two handfuls of distraught hair. "Worry. Teige, you don't seem to understand. That girl is my life and soul, my very soul. If I lose her, I'm dead, that's all, I'm a dead man. I looked for her, waited for her, ever since I can remember, I never expected — you don't know, Teige."

"Sure, I know," his nephew sympathized. "I can imagine."

"You admit she's beautiful? The most beautiful woman you ever saw in your life?"

"She's very beautiful," Teige said gently.

He had a moment of sharp apprehension when the doctor came out of the bedroom and stalked into the parlor. As for Mr. Morelewski, when he saw the man's sober face, in expectation of the blow that was to fall, he took a tottering step backward and groped behind him for support other than the elephant-eared begonia which spread so far afield that two sidling steps to the right barely took him out of reach of it to a stretch of picture-strung wall against which he could sag if need be under what was coming without harm to his surroundings.

Grave Dr. Bacon surveyed him, the tip of his nose pinched between thumb and forefinger.

"Is she — ?" Mr. Morelewski whispered, and could say no more.

"An hour ago, up at the City and County Building, it was a hundred and two in the shade!" the doctor proclaimed, no Ione of Puzel

178

more solemnly. "I myself am not affected by the heat, but some people are. The hottest day, I pay no attention to, whatever. Never have. But," he said, "if I, like the females of this city, yes, and I may say this state and this country, this entire country from ocean to ocean, if I, like these selfsame misguided females whose folly will without fail be visited, not only on themselves, but on the innocent heads of unborn generations, if, as I say — "

Mr. Morelewski's eyes popped open. "Unborn gen—?" He straightened, grew, and the beam of his smile shot light clear out into the dining room.

Dr. Bacon quenched it with a cold glance and a positive shake of his head. "If, as I say," he repeated sternly, "I — yes, or you, or you," turning to Teige and then to Mr. Morelewski, "or for that matter a Roman gladiator — what other consequences do you expect? They wait for the hottest day in August to come along and then they hogtie themselves into garments of steel, canvas and whalebone such as I saw in there," he pointed, "they squeeze their inwards, compress, impound, circumvest and generally pinch and strangle their viscera until — " He stopped. "Why didn't you cut her infernal corset strings?" he demanded.

The husband flinched. "I wasn't there," he said.

"Next time, do so instantly! Cut them before she faints. Better still, cut them before she gets the damnable thing on in the first place. Next time — "

Mr. Morelewski took his handkerchief out and weakly patted his forehead. "There's not going to be any next time," he said. "No more sightseeing trips and wandering around in the hot sun and all that. No more of that nonsense." He turned to his nephew. "I'm sorry, my boy. I know you were planning — I can imagine your disappointment."

In a flood of relief but little less than his responsible for the safe delivery of the Punjab Kohinoor when Victoria's short fingers finally closed over it, Teige said, "I'm sorry, too, Uncle Joe. It's really a shame."

Out in the kitchen Dorney lit the fire and put the teakettle on. Mr. Morelewski had said the Queen would want tea as soon as the doctor had gone. He said "My wife," of course, not "the Queen," and took time to be pleasant, upset and nervous as he was. Dorney liked the hurried glimpse she had of him and the way he introduced himself. "Dorney, hello, we miss each other every morning, don't we? By inches, you might say," before he went on to explain how the Queen had had a fainting spell up at Fort Douglas. Mr. Desmond had already told her that, as had the Queen herself when being helped to lie down, but Dorney said, "Did you ever hear of such a thing?" as though his was the first report of the affair. She thought he looked much older than the picture that was not hung up yet, but that was because the enlarger had tinted his hair a burning brown instead of gray and smoothed his face so that the wrinkles around his eyes didn't show. The photograph also made him look bad-tempered and puffed up when he was not like that at all.

She was standing, wondering what to do next, when the sound of the hose being dragged around the house reminded her that she had business with Mr. Sodaquist and she went to get from their hiding place under the bench on the back porch the pair of shoes she had taken from Mr. Desmond's room.

"Set 'em on the steps," the gardener said. "I got to get this hose set up."

"I brought your money, Mr. Sodaquist."

"You can pay me later."

Back inside the house, she looked to see if the fire was burning, adjusted the damper and then went over and pushed the chair Crystal had sat in under the table again. There was something she had been going to do — what was it? — when Crystal arrived. Oh, yes, spread some newspapers down on the damp floor. But it was dry now. She gathered them off the chair seat and started for the coal shed, collecting the mop, broom, dustpan and basin as she went. No wonder the kitchen had looked so untidy, although kind Mr. Morelewski had never said a word about it. When the broom began to slide out from under her arm and she made a grab for it, the papers scattered all over the porch. She was down on her knees picking them up when she saw the headline:

WILD BUNCH LEADER THOUGHT TO BE
IN DENVER VICINITY

She leaned closer, looked again.

Wild Bunch leader? Like a note-wrapped rock shattering the grilled window of a locked room his name tumbled into her consciousness and lay under her eyes.

Butch Cassidy!

She took up the paper and sat back.

Denver, April 30

The notorious outlaw, George Leroy Parker, alias Butch Cassidy, was seen today with four companions in the Fairlop Saloon in this city. He was recognized by Mr. J. S. Silk, 68, who resides at the home of his daughter, Mrs. Lester Figg, 126 Fourth Avenue. Mr. Silk, employed as a guard at the Wyoming State

Penitentiary at the time Parker alias Cassidy served 1½ years of a 2-yr. sentence for cattle rustling in that prison, sent word to the Sheriff's office, but the outlaw and his companions departed before they could arrive to make the arrests. Mr. Silk borrowed a gun, ran to the street, fired after the retreating horsemen and is thought to have wounded one of them.

A Sheriff's posse and a posse of private citizens set out immediately in pursuit but at a late hour tonight no news was forthcoming as to whether any of the five men had been apprehended. All roads are being watched. Mr. B. W. Morgan, 85, Haverstock Hotel, who overheard some of the conversation of the fugitives while in the Fairlop Saloon, believes that Parker, alias Cassidy, leader of the Wild Bunch, said to be the largest gang of outlaws in the west, for whom a large reward is offered, was planning the robbery of a local bank.

When her friends brought word to spirited Flora in the Tower of London that he had landed on the Continent out of reach of his enemies, her Bonnie Prince, the tale goes that she turned her back to hide her millennial face. Dorney did not have to hide hers, for she was all alone. He was alive, he was well! And he had most certainly escaped. They never in the world caught him, never. This very August afternoon at ten after four by the clock, he was somewhere, no matter whether on Diamond Mountain, in Mexico or in between the two, somewhere, as certainly as Mr. Desmond was in the parlor.

The fact of this, by some strange pursuance, made actual the hazy coexistences of others, and all in a vagrant visionary moment Dorney could grasp their unquestionableness. President McKinley dipping his pen in the inkwell on his desk in the White House, her own lost father shaving himself before a looking glass, a woman and child strolling in big Chicago, were real, as Butch Cassidy was real. Now! while she sat here on the porch floor, while the Queen lay wanly on her bed, while over on Eighth South Jetta swung back and forth in her swing, while Clara in the Palace Laundry ironed bosoms, they lived and breathed, as he lived and breathed. The old wild longing to go and find him assailed her. No need then to go home to the hot attic, the round pillow, sulky Crystal and displeased Madge. No need then to chafe and yearn for she knew not what and think the time would never pass.

In sudden restlessness, she gathered up the papers and got to her feet.

It *would* pass, then, the time, because —

"I come — " somebody said behind her.

She whirled and saw Teige Desmond.

" — to inquire for the cup which cheers but not inebriates," he said. "For her gracious majesty."

"The — what?"

"The tea." He held out a large square parcel done up in brown paper.

She looked at it and then at him. An adjustment had to take place in her eyes before she could verify him, a matter of a few absent-minded seconds, and when she could, she thought, He looks so much like somebody I used to . . .

"With my compliments," he said, putting it down on the bench beside the door, "providing I have your faithful promise not to become a blue-stocking."

She groped backward in time for the tantalizing reminder. Like a minnow, it was there and, when she nearly had it, not there, but if she could just . . .

"Books," he said. "For you."

"Books?"

The almost captured clue darted away in memory's deep river.

"You mean that package?" she said. "You mean — ?"

"I hope they will serve you."

She took a step toward them. "Serve me?" she whispered.

She did not hear Mr. Sodaquist come up the back steps but when he shook the screen door, she heard that.

"Here they are," the gardener said, holding up the large pair of shoes.

She turned in agitation.

"Shined up like a nigger's heel."

There was nothing to do but take them, and pay him.

Dorney did so as, before an Edinburgh policeman, Dr. Knox in his dissecting chamber might have paid his body snatcher, Burke, for dumping down two green cadavers. When the transaction was completed she put the shoes and the newspapers on the railing and turned to meet the dancing eyes of Teige Desmond. "The Queen said I was supposed to shine them every day," she said, "but I — but I — "

"How much do you pay him?"

"A nickel," she said miserably. "And it's not because — "

"You don't say," he said. "How is it that you can do many hard and disagreeable household tasks, but when it comes to polishing a pair of shoes — ?"

"Well, you see, it's just — " She turned away, swallowing.

"Just what, would you say?"

"I can't exactly explain, exactly, Mr. Desmond."

"Can't you?" he said, and quoted softly,

". . . from morn
To noon he fell, from noon to dewy eve,
A summer's day; and with the setting sun
Dropped from the zenith like a falling star
On Lemnos, the Agean isle . . ."

Her eyes beginning to brighten, she turned back to him.
"Who fell, Mr. Desmond?"
He smiled. "Have a look at your books," he said.

18

THE YOUNG MAN LOUNGING ON NEIBAUER'S MOON-
lit doorstep scratched a match into flame with his thumbnail and
lit the damp-spotted cigarette. "And that was about the size of it,"
he said, finishing his tale. "Naturally, after this old guy started
hollering and shooting and the whole damn town took out after us,
we couldn't get near the recruiting station. There wasn't nothing to
do but blow." He tossed the match away. "Oh, well," he said. "I
guess the army can get along without us." He smiled one-sidely.
"If they try real hard."

"*C'est la vie,*" the straight-backed Austrian said, his large dark
eyes on his visitor's face.

"Yeah, I guess so," Butch Cassidy said. "We split up outside
Denver," he added.

"They must be up to the Roost by now," the Tall Texan said,
raising his voice as was his involuntary habit when addressing a man
with a foreign accent. "We're on our way there, me and Butch."

A slender young squaw rounded the corner of the house bearing
a tray on which was coffee and brandy. She came noiselessly on her
bare feet, her red shining like a banked fire, her beads glistening.

"Place it here," the Austrian ordered. She put it down beside him
and walked off lightly.

Butch reached out and caught a handful of Kilpatrick's shirt.
"Oh, no, you don't," he said, under his breath.

"I got something important to tend to," the Tall Texan whispered
back.

"Oh, no, you ain't."

"Ze cowboy, he admires ze little Cheyenne? She is name Woman-
Afraid-of-ze-Lightning."

"She might be named woman afraid of something else if Kilpatrick ever gets out in back there."

Neibauer threw back his head and laughed. "He likes the ladies,
no?"

"He likes 'em yes," Butch said.

"You have company, my friend Kilpatrick. I, too."

The Tall Texan emptied his brandy glass, set it down on the step and got to his feet. "I got a little business to tend to." He tightened his belt, pushed his hat to one side and strolled off in the moonlight toward the stable.

Butch laughed. "Soon as he gets out of sight, he'll cut back and see if he can't meet up with that little Cheyenne somewheres around in back of the house," he said, looking after him. "I never seen such a guy. Why, he'll —" He broke off. "Say, she don't happen to be a particular friend of yours, does she? Because, the doggone son of a gun, I'll have to go put a bug in his ear if she is."

"He is a nice young man, zis Tall Texan."

"As white as they come," Butch said. "But he's dead set on the ladies. He'll take out after darn near anything."

"Do not concern for my sake," Neibauer said, "she is not ze particular friend of mine. She is ze particular friend of ze big Indian, Dry-Grass-Catch-Fire. She is his wife." He looked up. "Ze western stars," he said dreamily, "always do they delight me. Zey do not look like zis at home."

"Uh, Neibauer."

"Yes, *mein* bandit."

"This Indian, where would he happen to be right about now, for instance?"

"Zey live in ze small cabin behind. Ze poor homeless Cheyennes, always when zey come, I occupy ze squaws. Zey wash, cook, clean, but ze braves, zey will not, how you say? turn over ze hand."

"Well, if he ain't old enough to take care of himself by this time, I don't know when he will be." Butch gazed in the direction in which Kilpatrick had disappeared. He took his hat off, ran his fingers through his hair and put it back on.

"You fear ze scalping?"

"It ain't that exactly. But if that old Dry-Grass-Catch-Fire ever blazes up, the Texan might get a little singed." Butch sighed. "That'll learn him, though, maybe."

"You like ze ladies, yes, too?"

"Sure, I like 'em. Who wouldn't?"

"I inquire. You will marry someday?"

"I ain't thought much about it."

"Ze beloved, you have found her?"

Butch glanced upward at the moon. "Once in a while I kind of get a picture in my mind," he said softly, "of a —" He broke off. "No, I ain't," he said, looking down again. "I haven't. Not yet."

"Now, tell me," Niebauer said, "you are not no longer ze leader of ze outlaws, ze Wild Bunch?"

"Not any more."

"But since you could not join ze army in Denver because ze man recognized you and made ze hue and cry, could you not go back, ze same as before?"

"Maybe. Maybe not. I don't know."

"It was ze *big* bunch?"

"It wasn't exactly little."

"Now you start, you commence once more by yourself?"

"Well, not by myself. There's the five of us — me and the Texan, if he don't get burnt to a crisp, and Deaf Charley, and Sundance Kid and Elza Lay."

"Zem, I like."

"Yeah, the Kid and Lay was with me the last time I come down. I remember now. They was, wasn't they? But you ain't seen Deaf Charley. He's a card, that Charley."

"You sing cowboy songs." Neibauer began to hum the tune and Butch, leaning back against the wall, listened a moment and then sang the words:

> "Goodbye, Old Paint, I'm a-leaving Cheyenne.
> Goodbye, Old Paint, I'm off to Montan'. . . .
> My foot in the saddle, the reins in my hand,
> Good morning, young lady, my horse he won't stand. . . ."

He broke off. "Wait till the Texan comes back," he said, "and me and him'll sing it for you together. We been practising to harmonize. When we get to the part that goes good morning, young lady, why, then we — "

"It is lovely song."

"Yeah," Butch said. "I'll be riding along and I'll catch myself singing it, I won't even know it till all of a sudden I'll catch myself. The boys'll say, old Cassidy and his tune."

Neibauer smiled, studying him. "In my country," he said, "we do not have ze outlaw. We have ze, how you say? crooks, but not ze *Banditten*."

"Your country must be quite a place."

The Austrian nodded. "Ah, yes!"

"I ain't never thought about going there," Butch confided. "But once in a while I get a notion, maybe I'll go to South America someday."

"So?"

"A fellow was telling me there's some of the best range land in the world down there. And that's where I'd go to start ranching, if I ever quit this business." He added as though to himself, "The trouble is, they won't never let you."

"You would not like to start ranching here?"

"Where?"

"In Utah? Or, perhaps Wyoming?"

"Oh, I'd like it all right. Sure, I'd like it."

"Better zan Souse America?"

"Sure."

"Zen why not?"

Butch laughed. "Because I'd be took up and swung very pronto, that's why."

"But if you tell zem you now, how you say, go straight?"

"That wouldn't make no difference."

"But if you go under anozzer name, not George Parker, not Butch Cassidy, but maybe somesing else?"

"That wouldn't make no difference either."

"You would like to go straight, my friend?"

"That was why I was so damn anxious to take the boys into Denver and join the Army," Butch said softly. "Of course, I wanted to help whip the Spaniards just to learn 'em, and because, well, by God, any man has got to stand up for his country, but way in the back of my mind," he said, "I was thinking that if I — well, you know, went to work and fought, and maybe — "

"Become a hero, yes?"

" — why, that would even the score and I could start over. Quit all this roaming around and get me a ranch someplace and settle down like anybody else. I've had my fun by now. Of course, a guy's got to pay up someways for his deviltry and I guess I was going to settle up what I owe by — " He stopped. "It sounds awful damn small," he said, "to have a personal reason like that! Even something on the level a guy tries to do, it looks like old Number One is standing there grinning like a damn spook right in back of him all the time, no matter what."

"But you would have died, if need be?"

"I'd of took what was coming."

"For your country, yes?"

"How do I know what for? When I was blowing off steam in that saloon where we had our meeting, trying to get the guys to go with me to Denver and join the Army, it seemed like I was thinking of something besides old Number One, but how do I know I was? How do I know? God, I get disgusted."

"You would be more zan a man, I sink, my friend Cassidy, you would not have ze human failings. Zis is ze agony of ze idealist."

"It ain't that. It's just that a guy ought to be able to do something once in a while where he don't figure, no more than a stranger. Don't it look like to you?"

"When ze guy dies, zat day will come." Neibauer thought scowlingly. "Like Mani, Savonarola, Pascal, you would forget Number One. But I ask you a question you will understand. Would you forget your horse? Never. And for why? Because he carries you

187

everywhere, he stands, he waits, he is endurable. No hour goes by but what you sink of your horse. Do you blame yourself for zis? You would blame yourself if you did *not* sink of him, rather! And so it is wiz ze body. Ze soul, zis is ze cowboy. Ze body, what you call Number One, zis is ze horse. It is so simple. Do not deplore what ze *Gott* have devise. Do not regret. Now," he said briskly, "we will speak of ze straight going. Why cannot zis be accomplish?"

Butch smiled. "If you'd of seen what happened when that old guy run out of that saloon in Denver blazing away and hollering Cassidy loud enough to wake the dead, and how we had to hump to get away from that posse, you wouldn't ask," he said.

"But you are not a murderer!"

"No, but you don't just have to kill somebody to rile people up and I been riling 'em up for quite a while now, you want to remember." Butch looked toward the dark stable. "I don't hear nothing," he said. "Maybe that Indian has really went to work and cooked the Texan's goose." He reached for the string of his tobacco sack.

"What about ze amnesty?"

"The what?"

"Ze amnesty!"

"I don't savvy."

"In my country is such a possibility. Is not here?"

"What is it?"

"Ze general pardon for ze past, how you say? badness. Ze declaration zat all is forgiven. All is wipe out. It never was. In my country, ze Sovereign, he may declare zis on political offenders and such."

"Now, that sounds right handy. Damned if it don't." Butch lit his cigarette and flipped the match away. "Too handy. They don't have nothing like that in this country that I ever heard of."

"But zey do!" Neibauer's face brightened. "Ze Mormons, was not ze general pardon declared on zem for ze crime of polygamy?"

"Come to think of it, they did come to some kind of a agreement," Butch admitted. "But I didn't know that was what they called it."

"Ze amnesty. But yes. You have not committed ze murder. Could you not go to one in ausority and say, Now I am sorry, I settle down, I go straight?" Neibauer said. "Could you not say, We make ze deal — I will give up ze outlawry, you will give up ze persecution. Yes? Could you not say?"

"To who, for instance?"

"Well, to ze Governor, for instance."

"Of Utah?"

"Of Utah, yes, why not?"

"Why not, he says. Butch Cassidy walks up the marble steps of the Capitol Building as big as life and pays a call on the Governor. Why not? All a guy's got to be is loco enough, that's all."

"But you would like?"

"Like what?"

"Ze amnesty to be declared?"

"Sure, I'd like it. But there ain't nothing easy like that, or the papers would of been full of it. I'm kind of afraid that's got all the earmarks of a pipe dream, Neibauer."

"We will find out."

"How, find out?"

"I have ze friend in Salt Lake City, ze big lawyer. When first I come to zis country, I am ze guest of his neighbors beside him. We become acquainted, because zis lawyer, he likes to hear of Europe. We have many talks together. I could write to him and say, What about zis amnesty for Butch Cassidy? I could tell him, Please ask ze Governor. For zat man, he knows everyone!"

"Well, that's damn nice of you, Neibauer," Butch said, "but I wouldn't want you to give somebody the idea we was mixed up together some way. I could maybe ask him myself sometime."

"Do so, my friend! Do so at once! Zis lawyer is name Judge Alexander Towers. He lives at Six Twenty-Five East Souse Temple. See him, truly. It might be, all your troubles would be over."

"Well, I got to go up to the Roost first, and then me and the boys was talking about a little trip down to Mexico, and I got to get me a bigger stake beforehand," Butch said. "But I'll be coming back this way, and the next time I do, I sure as hell will go on in to Salt Lake City — there won't be nobody recognize me there, I don't think — I been there before and there wasn't nobody recognized me — and damned if I won't ask this lawyer if there is any such doodad as this amnesty proposition and what about it."

"I will write down ze name and ze address."

"Judge Alexander Towers. Six Twenty-Five East South Temple. You don't need to, Neibauer. I got it down pat."

"Hey, listen a minute." He cocked an ear. "There's the Texan." Neibauer listened. "What does he whistle?" he asked.

"Love, Love in Disguise."

"Well, he is not scalped then, you see."

The Tall Texan lounged up, sunk onto the step again and leaned back against the post, whistling softly to the end of the tune.

"Beautiful," Neibauer said. "Ze cowpuncher, he have se beautiful songs, but always so *triste*, I observe, so very sad. Why is zis, please?"

"You'd be sad, too, if you was a cowpuncher," Kilpatrick said, drawing a sigh.

"Why?" Neibauer asked, smiling.

"You'd be sad if you was him, the Texan means," Butch said.

"Say, Mr. Neibauer," Kilpatrick said, reaching over to pluck the tobacco sack out of Butch's breast pocket and dodging back to escape a good-natured poke, "who's that big Indian you got corralled out in back?"

"You mean Dry-Grass-Catch-Fire?" Neibauer winked at Butch.

"He sure shot out a few sparks there for a minute, I can tell you."

"What got him started?" Butch inquired innocently.

"Well, he's got this boil on the back of his neck, see," the Tall Texan said. "And when I get out there, he's crouched down and he's got this little Cheyenne squeezing it. She'd squeeze, and he'd give her hell for squeezing. Then she'd stop, and he'd give her hell for stopping. Finally, he looks up at me and says, 'You want buy squaw? Me sell. Five dollars!' " He paused.

"Kilpatrick, he bought?" Neibauer inquired.

"Kilpatrick, he bought."

"Now, listen here," Butch said. "Don't you get the idea you're going to come dragging some squaw with us up to the Roost and down into Mexico and no telling where all, because you ain't, you great big flapping-eared stand-up-and-bawl-for-buttermilk. Not by a jugful you ain't!"

While he spoke the Tall Texan whistled "Goodbye, Old Paint, I'm a-leaving Cheyenne" under his breath.

"But before I could fork over the money," he continued calmly, when silence fell, "be damned if she didn't get the core out. I'm telling you, it popped like a cork out of a bottle and shot clear over to there." He pointed. "And the pus come a-hissing out in a regular stream. Well, sir, you never heard nothing like it, the way that Indian began enjoying himself. He grunted and he gurgled and he carried on till it would of made a cat laugh to hear him, the pot-bellied son of a gun. After that, of course, he wasn't sore no more at Woman-Afraid-of-the-Lightning, so he decided to hang on to her. 'She good squaw,' he said. 'Me keep.' " Kilpatrick laughed. "And then you sit there and wonder why a poor damn cowboy don't never sing nothing but sad songs!"

19

BEFORE SHE STARTED UPSTAIRS TO TAP ON MR. Desmond's door and tell him the table was set and breakfast would be ready in a few minutes, Dorney slipped out to the back porch to collect the brown-paper parcel. "These are the books," she explained as she went past Mrs. Morelewski who was standing on tiptoe peering into the dark corners of the second shelf for the cinnamon. The Queen at that instant spied the little green can and brought it down. "All right," she said, paying no attention. Then she turned and glimpsed the package. "What in the world is that?" she asked in astonishment.

"These are the books," Dorney repeated, stopping in the doorway. "The ones Mr. Desmond got for me yesterday."

"Well, what are you going to do with them?"

"Give them back to him."

"But why? Don't you like them?"

"Madge won't let me keep 'em."

"Why not?" Now the Queen was on her toes again before the cupboard hunting the powdered sugar. She found it, but it was on the third shelf and she had to ask taller Dorney to reach it down for her. Dorney put the books on the woodbox and obliged.

"Now what was that again, about your sister not letting you keep the books?" the Queen asked. "That's really too bad."

"She would have," Dorney said bitterly, "if somebody else hadn't butted in and spoiled everything."

"Well, that's too bad," the Queen said again. "Did you happen to see the sifter any place?"

Dorney got it for her, from the cabinet under the flour bin.

"Tell Mr. Desmond breakfast will be ready in about fifteen minutes. And remember," she said, "remember to ask if there is anything you can do the way the Eti— the way I told you."

"All right, Mrs. Morelewski," Dorney said, mounting the stairs.

The door opened before she could knock, and Teige Desmond standing in the doorway with folded arms, recited, " 'Oh, is it surely blown, my martagon?' No," he said. "No. For were the purple lily burgeoned, Asolo would behold another face than this. Wherefore, Mademoiselle?"

"Wherefore what, Mr. Desmond?"

"This immeasurably dejected countenance?"

She held out the package.

"These are the books you gave me yesterday," she said, not lifting her eyes. "I took them home and Crystal said — and then Madge said I couldn't keep them, and so this morning I had to bring them back, and so here they are."

He took it and put it down on a chair beside the door. "I see," he said. "No, I don't see, at all. Why shouldn't you have them? What utter nonsense! I suspect we are being confronted by an outrage of some sort. Tell me."

"Madge said I wasn't supposed to take presents from anybody."

"Presents?" His eyes flashed. "Presents! These are books. By the Lord Harry! Who is this Madge?"

"She's my sister that I live with. First I lived with Wanda, and now I live with her."

"You really liked them, didn't you?" he said. "You would have enjoyed them very much?"

"Yes, Mr. Desmond."

He proffered his handkerchief and she chased the rapid tears with one tiny corner of it at first, economically, but they were too many and fell too fast and soon she had to make use of it all.

"Yes, sir, an outrage," he said. "As the scholars of Vienna said to one another in eighteen-forty-eight, we shall have to take up arms!"

She tried to smile.

"Liberty, equality, fraternity! Right?"

She did smile now, drying her wet lashes. "I guess so," she said.

"Tippecanoe and Tyler too. Tell me where you live, Dorney."

"Around the corner on Eighth South. There are three houses just alike and I live in the middle one."

"In full panoply, expect me."

She stared. "You mean, you're coming to where I *live?*"

"Tonight, for fifteen minutes or so to expostulate with benightedness, remonstrate against grievance and extol the virtue of learning."

"Tonight?"

"In full panoply. And that reminds me. Sometime today, the Queen will issue orders to the effect that henceforth the shining of the shoes of Mr. Teige Desmond will no longer incur as a responsibility of the Lady in Waiting." He winked. "How does she, by the way?"

"You mean the Queen? Oh, she's up, and breakfast is nearly ready."

192

On her way home that evening she met Schooner Bill wearing an untrimmed white fur-felt hat so large it rested on the top of his ears. He hopped off to the side, doffed it, bowing, and hopped back. "Friend," he announced.

"Friend," she said. More than ever did he seem that today, and she stopped gratefully. A moment's chat would keep her from home that much longer, her tidings to herself, that Mr. Desmond was coming to call. She had not decided whether to tell Madge and Crystal the news at all, and was glad to put aside the problem that had troubled her much during the day, whether to let them know, or not. Crystal could make so many complications!

"Well, Schooner Bill," she said. "You're just going to work and I'm just getting through for the day."

"Like him," he said, pointing to the red sun in the west. "He's just getting through for the day. We think he's always going to be on the job, don't we? But he ain't. One of these days he's going to up and quit and then we better be careful! She wants him to, she keeps after him, only don't tell anybody I said so."

"Who wants him to, Schooner Bill?"

"Her." He looked craftily over his shoulder at the transparent disc of white high in the eastern sky. "Then she'll be the boss. That's what she wants, so bad. You know what will happen then?"

"No, what?"

"We'll all turn white as snow, even the darkies and everybody. And after a while, we'll all be dead!"

Not until Madge came home at seven-thirty did Dorney come out with the information that Mr. Teige Desmond was going to pay a visit.

"If that isn't the meanest thing I ever heard, waiting till now to tell a person!" Crystal flew off into the bedroom and banged the door behind her.

"You and her just can't seem to hit it off together, can you?" Madge said sadly.

Last night, Madge had not stormed at Dorney about the books. She had merely taken the stand that as long as her little sister was under her roof, she was going to watch over her as their own dear mother would have done, and protect her from those who would come along and try to cause her downfall. A young man, she said, from New York, didn't give the hired girl where he was staying, expensive presents, if —

"They're not expensive," Dorney wailed. "The prices are still in them. Look, Madge, please, please look!" She flipped back the cover of the Geography. "See, this one cost thirty-five cents! It's written right here." She pushed it over and reached for the Tales from *Shakespeare.* "And this one cost," she looked, "a — a dollar." This came out in a whisper for the sum was more than she expected. "And this one cost — "

"Men that give hired girls expensive presents ain't up to no good," Madge repeated, patiently and kindly.

"No," Crystal said.

"I'm *not* a hired girl!"

They both laughed. "What are you then, you silly billy?" Madge said.

"I'm a — "

"You're a hired girl, and he's a man from *back East,* and I'm not making you take the books back because I want to be mean. I'm making you take them back because, after all, blood is thicker than water."

"Mamma's got to make you take them back, like I told her," Crystal said gently. "You don't know what men think of you, does she, Mamma? when you take expensive presents. You wouldn't want Mr. Desmond to think of you what he would be bound to think, if you took those books. That's all we're saying, Dorney. Good heavens, the way you stand there and look at us, you'd think we were your enemies!" Her amiability puzzled Dorney more and more.

Why, for instance, had she treated Dorney's lie about the Queen's whereabouts, her statement that Mrs. Morelewski was in the bedroom taking a nap instead of up at Fort Douglas, where she really was, as a matter of no importance, almost a joke? Dorney, crawling home with Mr. Desmond's gift at ten past six, had prepared herself for either a holocaust or a frozen waste of dead-quiet resentment, but never for a duped and imposed-upon Crystal saying, "Hello! We're going to eat in fifteen minutes!" as if nothing had happened. If she had met a wounded buffalo behaving the same way in the kitchen, Dorney could not have been more surprised.

Of course her loving-kindness had had to be paid for very soon by giving thought to and answering in detail her impertinent questions about the Queen's seizure and many other things, which Dorney did, feeling like a traitor. Strangely enough, Crystal did not mention Mr. Desmond during this catechism and seemed only to be reminded of his existence when Dorney undid the parcel of books on the kitchen table and explained how they had come into her possession. Then she had merely said, "He looks like a New Yorker all right," and went on to speak of the Queen's gown and how extraordinarily slender it had made her appear, as though seeing him had been a trifle, not worth discussing at greater length.

When Madge came home Crystal had not given her time to take

off her hat and coat before she told her she wanted to see her in the bedroom. They were in there a good while, with the door shut, talking in low voices and when they came out, nervous Dorney was surprised to descry on her sister's face the same expression of benevolence and impassibility that Crystal had met her with, earlier.

"I hear somebody has been giving you presents," she said cheerfully.

"Mr. Desmond gave me some books, that's all," Dorney said, on guard.

"Yes. Well, that's something we're going to have to have a little talk about right now," Madge said, "because, like Crystal has been saying in there in the bedroom, if we don't watch over you and protect you, who else will?"

Dorney went down vanquished. Against their steady patience, unwavering good humor and cumulative dialectics, she had not a leg to stand on. Did she weep? Their sunlight dried her dew. Did she beg, plead, protest, promise? Her twitter lost itself in their blue sky. . . .

When it was all over, Madge had wrapped up the books in the same paper, tied up the parcel firmly with the same piece of string. "There," she said, putting it on the end of the drainboard, "there it is for you to take back to fine Mr. Desmond in the morning. Now, don't forget it, honey."

"If she does happen to," bland Crystal said, "I'll be glad to run over to the Morelewskis' with it, myself, tomorrow."

"I won't forget!" Dorney said bitterly.

Madge looked at the shut bedroom door. "Really," she said, "you will have to try to be a little more thoughtful with Crystal, or you and her will never hit it off. She tries to be nice to you, Dorney, but you always rub her the wrong way." She got up and took a rag from behind the pantry door, rubbed it briskly over the already shining surface of the stove, put it away and stooped to pick up a fleck of nothing off the swept piece of carpeting under the table. "It's a good thing the house looks fairly decent," she said, "with company coming. Why didn't you say something right away? instead of waiting until I got home. No wonder Crystal got her dander up. After all, she's the one that takes care of the house! After all, it's her that things reflect on!"

"What kind of things?" Dorney sat by the table, drawing moodily on the tablecloth with her fingernail.

"Don't do that, honey," Madge said. "Open that window by the stove a little wider. It seems to me I can still smell that cauliflower smell. Why, everything," she continued in answer to the question.

"It reflects on her if the house don't look right up to snuff when company comes. It's a good thing we got Jetta put to bed, at least! That I can be thankful for."

Crystal's anger at not being told before that the young man was coming to call vanished in the bedroom under the beamy thought that somehow yesterday as she walked past the carriage he was helping Mrs. Morelewski out of, Mr. Teige Desmond had seen her, found out what her name was and where she lived, and was now paying this visit expressly to make her acquaintance! It was not long until she could be heard singing some bars of the music she had been assigned at her last lesson. When she came back out into the kitchen she was wearing the red and white striped dress of yesterday and had combed her hair softly down around her heart-shaped face. She danced across the floor and, holding her skirts out, made a little whirl and bow.

"How do I look?" she said.

"You look just like Mamma's Aunt Ann," Madge said, studying her. "She was the prettiest one in the family, with that very same black hair and arching eyebrows and kind of a dimple in her chin. You're the only one that looks like her," she said. Turning to Dorney, she added, "Aunt Ann was supposed to of caused all kinds of battle royals in her day and one man was said to of tried to kill himself over her, only the bullet didn't hit a vital spot or something. I've forgotten how Mamma said it was."

"I'd like to see a picture of her," Dorney said. "I've always wanted to."

"She never had her picture took," Madge said. "She was only twenty-three years old at the time she died, sewing on a dress to wear to some big dance."

"Dorney doesn't think I look like her, I guess," Crystal said teasingly. "She wants proof."

"Of course you look like her," Madge said. "Haven't I heard Mamma describe her a thousand times?"

"Don't you, Dorney?"

"Don't I what?" Dorney looked up blankly, thinking of how sorry Aunt Ann must have been to die when she did, right in the midst of everything.

"Want proof. Mamma, honestly, did you ever see anybody moon like Dorney does?" Crystal surveyed her with mock severity, smiling the while. "I wish I could sit and moon like that."

"I wasn't mooning. I was just thinking how sorry Aunt Ann must have been to — "

"Be still!" Crystal put her finger to her lips.

"Somebody on the porch," Madge said, getting to her feet.

They all listened for the knock at the front door which seemed to come nevertheless as such a surprise, at least to Crystal, that she gave a great start and almost paled.

"It will look best if I go, maybe," Madge whispered, "and you girls follow right along behind me."

Sighing, Dorney prepared to do so but Crystal grabbed up the lamp and hurried to the small square of mirror over the sink. "You two go," she said breathlessly, "and take him in the parlor and when he gets sat down, why, then I'll come in!"

"All right," Madge said. "Come on, Dorney."

While Madge kept up a steady stream of talk, about train traveling, the East, the West, Mr. Desmond's relatives the Morelewskis, vacations in general and the Paris Café, asking crowded questions with pauses after them too small to squeeze an answer in, and laughing from time to time in a way very unlike herself, Dorney uneasily perched on the piano stool, looked about her at the parlor she had not been asked to sit in since the evening of her arrival. She had glimpsed it often through the door and assisted in cleaning it on two occasions, but tonight she had the feeling she had never seen it before. Mr. Desmond, sitting on the slippery horsehair sofa, looking taller than at the Morelewskis' and as handsome in the lamplight as the illustration of grown David Copperfield courting Dora, made it seem so unfamiliar that she wanted to pinch herself to see if she was not dreaming.

Crystal stopped in the doorway, a light white hand on either side of the door frame, in pretty confusion, interrupting her mother's excursus on Mormon people as neighbors — if you let them alone, they let you alone — with a half-muffled, "Oh, pardon me."

"This is my daughter Crystal," Madge broke off to say radiantly. "She plays."

Teige Desmond got to his feet and inclined his head. "How do you do," he said.

"I'm pleased to meet you," Crystal said, advancing gracefully. She took a seat on the other end of the sofa and he resumed his former one, while Dorney looked for a place to move to, since the stool she occupied would soon be called upon, and decided on the armchair with the footstool before it. Indeed, there was no other choice, for Madge had taken the uncomfortable chair with the claw feet that matched the sofa. Dorney left the piano stool to move to it as unobtrusively as possible. She had not dared to take it earlier, in case Mr. Desmond or Madge might want to sit there, but it was all right now, especially since Crystal had not taken it either, making the rejection of it unanimous. She settled back with a little sigh, for it was the most comfortable chair in the house. I wish I could sit here every day, she was thinking when she caught Madge's frowning glance and the almost imperceptible shake of her head. Now what? What was the matter? She looked anxiously to the right, the left, turning her head as far as it would go both ways and then in front of her. Her feet? Of course. One of them had crept up onto the footstool! She brought it away quickly and looked back at Madge, who slightly smiled and nodded. Crystal paused an instant to see what was going on between her mother and Dorney and then continued with what she was saying, that it certainly was a treat to meet somebody from New York. Her dream, she said, was to travel someday and if she had been born a gypsy it wouldn't have hurt her feelings a bit. In fact, she said, she often imagined that it would be the most wonderful thing in the world to have been born a gypsy.

If only they would let him talk! What was it he had been going to do? Dorney tried to remember. Expostulate with something, remonstrate against grievance and do something connected with the virtue of learning, she could not recall the exact word. Ex — extol, that was it. But when Madge wasn't talking, Crystal was, and sometimes they both came out with something together, in which case Madge always stopped after a few simultaneous words and said, "You tell it, dear," and let Crystal go on by herself.

Madge had just said this, and Crystal was going on. "I have always loved music," she was saying, "and that was why Mamma started me out in the first place. I have been taking lessons since I was twelve. That's five years!" She stopped and flushed charmingly. "Now you know how old I am," she said, as though the secret had slipped out in spite of her.

"Seventeen," Teige said. "A delightful age to be." He looked across the room. "Dorney, how many summers have you grown in sun and shower?"

She looked up guiltily to meet his dancing eyes. "I'm going on fifteen," she said.

"Next March," Crystal said. "That's quite a ways away." She shot a merry, confidential look at Mr. Desmond. "But about how I got started with taking from Mrs. Million — "

Dorney bit her lip and put her hand up to her hot cheek.

"Fourteen is a delightful age, too," he said. "Shakespeare must have thought so, to make his loveliest heroine no older." He read the question in her eyes and answered it. "Her name was Juliet."

"I saw that play at the Salt Lake Theatre," Crystal said hurriedly. "At least, I'm sure I did. Mamma, you remember when I went to the matinée that time and came home and told you about the balcony and everything, and how they both took poison at the end. The leading lady looked lots older than fourteen, though," she said, frowning. "In fact, if I'm not very much mistaken, she looked about Mamma's age."

"Also delightful," the caller said gallantly, inclining his head in Madge's direction.

She said, "Why, Mr. Desmond, you know perfectly well I'm an old woman!" and looked for an instant so like the rosy auburn-haired Madge of long ago that Dorney was startled. Madge had been pretty, and it was no wonder that even 'Dair Yandle had loved her and married her. . . .

"Do you like the theatre, Mr. Desmond?" Crystal inquired archly. She did not wait for an answer. "I suppose you go so often to the wonderful theatres in New York that you won't want to go here to either of our two, the Salt Lake or The Grand," she said. "And I wouldn't blame a person."

"Your Salt Lake Theatre is quite famous," he said, "you would be surprised. We are going tomorrow night. Mademoiselle Anna Held is playing in *The Cat and the Cherub*. My uncle tells me everybody has been here at one time or another. Maurice Barrymore, Daniel Frohman, Effie Ellsler, Lillian Russell — "

"This is a personal question and you must forgive me," Crystal said, with a flutter of her lashes and a little catch in her breath, "also for changing the subject, but isn't your aunt *beautiful?*"

The visitor looked rather surprised. "She certainly is," he said.

"She was the Queen of the Jubilee," Madge said.

"So I heard."

"She was *beautiful*," Crystal said. "I said to Mamma at the time, didn't I, Mamma? I said, 'Mamma, did you ever see such a sight in your life as her up there on that float with that white dress and that crown on? and just think,' I said, didn't I, Mamma? 'a week ago she was in the kitchenware department at Auberbach's and now — ' "

"Linens," Madge said.

"Well, whatever it was. I said to Mamma at the parade, I said, 'A week ago, look what she was doing, and now look where she is.' "

"And that same summer she married your uncle, Mr. Desmond. Two years ago last month," Madge put in.

"The family was very pleased," he said.

"I don't know whether I ever heard," Madge said, "but does Mrs. Morelewski play the piano?"

"No," Dorney said in a low voice.

Crystal ignored her and said, "Oh, she must, Mamma. She simply must!"

"Dorney is right, Miss Yandle. My aunt does not play."

"Oh, Mr. Desmond, that simply doesn't seem *possible*. Anybody so beautiful and —"

"But you do, Miss Yandle, and when I have made a certain explanation which I would like to do now," he turned to Madge, "with your kind permission, Mrs. Yandle, I will ask your daughter to play something for me."

"I don't know what it would be," Crystal said, going to the shiny music cabinet and pushing back the fern-printed silkaleen curtain with a little rattle of rings sliding along the metal rod. She began to go through the neatly stacked music.

"Go right ahead, Mr. Desmond," Madge said, watching her daughter with a look that said she must spring to her aid if the need arose and that she hoped her visitor would excuse her concern and not lay it to inattention. "Go right ahead."

"Mrs. Yandle, I am Assistant Professor of English Literature at Columbia University," he said. "Books are the tools of my trade. Yesterday, I gave Dorney some books, and today she brought them back to me, saying you found them inacceptable. I approve of and honor your scruples, but perhaps if I explain how I came to do this, you, as her kindly, intelligent, sympathetic and broad-minded guardian, will allow her to keep them. Suppose," he said, "I were a carpenter, and Dorney, not a young lady at all but a boy of fourteen, had wandered into my shop. It would not take me long to ascertain that my tools, my lumber, the work I was engaged in, interested him more than a little. I would know almost at once — would I not? — by the bent of his questions, the way his hands would stray to this and that, the very look in his eyes, that here was a potential confrère. If then," he said, "having found this out, I happened to give him some pieces of wood, a handful of nails, a tool or two and he went home with them — to you, say, Mrs. Yandle — you would not, I think, be offended."

"Well, no, I really wouldn't, if it was a case of something like that. I see what you mean. Of course, Crystal and I wasn't really offended. It was just that Dorney is inclined to be kind of — anyway — and my sister Wanda raised her, you see, and Wanda was not one to — and so we thought that — but naturally we wasn't *offended*, Mr. Desmond." She gave him a quick cordial glance and then turned back to her daughter, who had lifted a stack of music to the top of the stand and was going through it there. "Find the one where you got to cross your hands over every little while," she said. "Will you, Crystal?"

"Then I may take it that I have your gracious permission to return the books and Dorney your leave to accept them?" Teige Desmond winked at Dorney, who took a deep breath and very carefully settled back in her chair.

"Why, I guess so, Mr. Desmond, since you put it that way, about the carpenter and the tools and everything. I never thought of looking at it like — " She broke off. "It's the one with the wild roses on the front, or else the bluebirds, I forget which," she called out to Crystal.

"Oh, Mamma, I'll never find anything if you keep after me all the — oh, here's one." Crystal held up "Saltarello" by Potestio. "But I'm sure Mr. Desmond doesn't really want to hear me." She pouted enchantingly, pressing the booklet against her bosom. "He must have heard so many wonderful pianists in New York — "

"Miss Yandle," he said, "please play. I should like it very much, I assure you."

"Well — " Crystal twirled the stool up once, down one-half and seated herself, spreading out the music on the rack in front of her at the same time. "Don't pay any attention to the middle part, please," she said over her shoulder. Then she poised her hands over the keys for an instant and began to play.

It sounded spectacular to Dorney, and she guessed that Mr. Desmond's face must be a study of dazzled approbation, a sight she tried hard to keep from seeing. If only she could do something he would esteem, but what? She looked at Crystal's flying white hands and then down in her lap at her own before she slid them out of sight between the arms and seat of her chair.

It had happened. . . .

Crystal had met Mr. Desmond, what she had wanted so much to do, and there was every chance in the world that he would fall in love with her, especially now that he had had a chance to hear her play! Dorney could resist no longer a quick, sidelong glance, but Mr. Desmond had his elbow on the arm of the sofa and his hand was shading his face so she could not see his expression very well, except that it was serious. She looked back at Crystal, who turned a page with such speed that she snatched a little piece out of the edge that fluttered to the carpet like a snowflake. Would he ask Crystal to marry him? Would he take her to New York? Suppose he asked me . . . suppose I had a chance to go with him? That thought cleared the way for another as audacious. Or, suppose . . . just suppose . . . I could go with Butch Cassidy instead . . . which one would I go with? Suppose I had my choice . . . ? She looked down at the rosette of brass nails in the corner of the footstool and began to think about it as seriously as if it were a true dilemma.

She could see herself dressed like Amy, Duchess of Leicester, in the first picture in *Kenilworth*, where she had the jeweled corset on and the veil hanging down from her cap and the pet bird was taking a seed from her lips. . . . Generally in dreams she made herself older but Mr. Desmond had said Shakespeare's loveliest heroine, Juliet, was only fourteen, so she was contented, at least for the moment, to be that age, and even to look almost like herself.

There she was, then. . . .

And there was the Assistant Professor of English Literature in a windowed alcove, reading a book. And there, outside by the green hedge on black Little Dipper, was the great outlaw. "As well try to catch the wind, as catch him," Grandpa Bannon had said long, long ago. But Grandpa Bannon was mistaken because Butch Cassidy was beckoning, as plainly as could be, to her. She started for the door. Teige Desmond called something after her. What? "Don't go, Dorney." She halted . . . turned back . . . her veil blowing first this way and that. . . . Then Teige Desmond got up and left the book and came toward her, but at the same time, outside, she could see through the window, Butch Cassidy jump lightly down off Little Dipper and approach the door, his wide hat pushed back, his spurs jingling . . . and she chose . . .

Crystal ended "Saltarello" with a flourish that made everything on top of the piano quiver slightly, the two thin vases with curled rims, the tiny bust of a sullen man named Beethoven which Mrs. Million had given her for Christmas, a wood engraving of a peacock, a plated candlestick without a candle and the small disqualified clock.

With difficulty, Dorney looked up, but nowhere in Mr. Desmond's vicinity.

"That composition is new to me, Miss Yandle," he said. "You play vivaciously indeed."

"Don't she, though, Mr. Desmond? I just wish you could hear what her teacher has to say about her sometimes. Really, I wish you could."

"Oh, now, Mamma." Crystal whirled about on her stool so that she could face them, breathing somewhat quickly from her exertions. She laughed. "Mamma always wants to — " She stopped, her eyes widening, her color failing, her hand creeping to her throat. "Mamma," she whispered.

They all turned at the same instant, to see in the doorway pygmy Jetta in her wretched nightgown, barefooted, her head tipped to one side.

Madge, with a smothered, "Excuse me just a minute," jumped up from her chair, rushed over and hurried her out of sight.

"That's Jetta," Dorney said. "She's — "

"Yes," Crystal interrupted. "She's a poor little unfortunate girl Mamma's taking care of, for some people we know." She glared at Dorney, daring her to speak.

"May I add, Miss Yandle," Teige Desmond said smoothly, "that I thank you very much for the pleasure?"

She glared once more at Dorney and turned to him with a brilliant smile.

"Oh, you're welcome," she said. "You're welcome as can be."

20

ALMA MORELEWSKI ASSURED HER WORRIED HUS-
band every morning and every evening that she had never felt better
in her life and that there was no sense in becoming an invalid and
hiring a cook and housekeeper just because she had happened to have
a slight heat stroke up at Fort Douglas two weeks ago and keeled
over in a faint. Mr. Morelewski got Teige's solemn promise that he
would not ask his aunt to accompany him on any more of his sal-
lies and Alma's that if he did, she would politely decline.

She promised, because sightseeing was a little wearing, and because, when she considered, she knew she would appear much prettier reposing on the shady porch in the wicker chair or half reclining in the corner of the wicker sofa behind the flower-graced table,
when Teige came back to the house in the late afternoon, than if she
had clomped all over creation from early morning and was worn entirely out.

She had a great deal on her mind. She had always given careful
study to what she was going to wear up to the restaurant because
the customers looked at her and the headwaiter bowed so low and
Joe was so proud, but never before had her costumes mattered so
much.

It was not enough to try on clothes at bedtime and once or twice
during the day. Alma Morelewski found that if she also lay quietly
and thought of them, imagining herself wearing this and that, inspiration would come and she could sometimes devise and discover
wonderful new combinations, such as, to change the lace vest from
the blue Jacquard to the olive-green wool, and the shoulder knot
with the hummingbird in the center from the bronze taffeta to the
white louisine. She would have intuitive flashes: the gray Perinette
jacket needed red buttons, not jet, the white hat a plume instead of
flowers, and when they came, would stare a long time at the ceiling,
fancying these combinations and changes, breathing through parted
lips.

She had to think about herself, too, how changed she was. Mamma
and Papa would be surprised next time they came, which she hoped

would not be soon, to see she was as thin as a rail and had no appetite at all. She would not tell them Joe had the strange idea in the first place to starve her until she could wear the turquoise dress, but would pretend she herself had lost all interest in food. It was true, now. If the faintest stirring of hunger came, all she had to do was think of Teige and it vanished. It was only lately that she had discovered this, at the close of the day she fainted, to be exact. That evening, after her ordeal, she had been close to famished, and when Joe brought a magnificent dinner tray to the bed was going to sit up and eat it as of old. But as she took up her fork, she thought of the ride home from Fort Douglas in the carriage, her head drooping against Teige's shoulder and his hands holding her left hand, and her stomach shut so tight, her throat filled so with gladness and excitement that she could only stir the food and pick at this and that.

Such being the case, she could never get fat again because she would always think of him, always with the same consequence, and therefore always be thin! It was quite a relief to her, and she realized that her appetite and inclination to put on weight must have worried her more than she was aware. She need never worry again, that was sure. Fat wasn't such a terrible problem. Now when she saw hugely corpulent women on the streets, she wanted to say, You don't *have* to be fat, honestly. All you have to do is just — but they couldn't all say Teige's name, or imagine him.

Joe was concerned because the matter had been taken out of his hands, but he too was pleased enough with what had mysteriously happened not to press her to eat more than the little she seemed to require. It was like changing a stream in its course, he thought, somewhat in awe, for he had not supposed it could be done with such ease. Once that's done, it flows as happily the new way as the old. Sometimes, however, he regretted the deflection and wondered uneasily if he had done right, she felt so clammy-cold to the touch, slept so uneasily and the pupils of her eyes were so big and black. Ought he to try to send the stream back into its old bed? No, he thought selfishly, gloating over the shape of his wife posturing in front of the glass in her ribbon-strung petticoat and black velvet hat as if she had been a Tanagra figurine.

"Does Teige think I'm beautiful?" she asked, looking deep into her own eyes.

"Turn around here," he said.

She did, and approached him.

"Does he?" he said. "What man in his right mind wouldn't?" He sat up and groped for her but she danced backward just out of his reach.

"Does he, though? Tell me," she demanded.

He reached out and she moved a little farther away. "Of course he does."

"Did he say so?" she wheedled.

He swung his feet to the floor, came after and seized her gently, as was his way. "Of course he did," he said, trying to kiss her.

"What did he say?" She pressed her hands against his chest and leaned away.

"Why, he said — he said — let me see — "

She twisted out of his grasp and fled beyond him. "Well, what?"

"Oh, darling," he pleaded, coming after her.

She stamped her little stockinged foot. "Tell me!" she said sharply.

"Tell you what, sweetheart?"

"What he said."

"Why, he said — "

"What?"

"Why, that you are the most beautiful woman in the world."

At that she let him gather her to him in a tight embrace, saying against his lips, "Did he really?"

She did not think Joe might have exaggerated, because Teige looked at her as if he thought she was, and gave her dozens of compliments about how she looked in her clothes. She had never worn the same thing twice, even when most successful, as for instance, the blue maline, which Teige declared was the loveliest dress ever invented. He said every day she was beautiful, and always in a clever, new way, not like Joe who said the same thing over and over.

He loved her, of course, how could he help it? Had she ever once worn the same costume, morning, afternoon and night? No, always something different, always something wonderful. Of course, soon she would have to start putting the same things on again, but enough time would have elapsed so that he wouldn't notice, except the very memorable dresses like the blue maline and the pink crêpe. And her hair, too. She had combed it twenty different ways already and would comb it twenty more. Besides, she had such good taste, Mr. Morelewski said so all the time, and was so mannerly, and had a lovely disposition, too. How could he help loving her? He couldn't. Therefore he did. She knew by the way he looked at her, knew by the compliments he gave her, that the die was cast.

What she had so urgently to think of each day, and every night tossing on her pillow beside Mr. Morelewski, was not that, not the fact of Teige's love. It was what to do when he asked her to leave her home and husband and come with him to New York. That was what she had to turn over and over in her mind, so that when he brought the subject up, as he would sooner or later, she would know what answer to give him and not be caught by surprise with no plans made or packing done or anything.

The first time she thought about it, she decided to yield to his plea because he was so handsome, only two years older than she was, lived in the biggest city in America and especially because of the way she felt when she was with him. That way, as she would have confided to a close chum, if she had one, which she didn't, was the way a person feels with two hundred dollars to buy an Easter outfit with, only even better. In fact, she could not describe it. She resolved to say yes. But then she remembered another important point, which she talked over with her husband, an aspect with so much bearing on the case that she had to take the time, as she did every day now, to weigh and consider it and thus save herself a lot of future grief and trouble.

Mr. Morelewski had just fallen asleep when she remembered that other important point and while she hated to wake him, she did, very gently, by tugging at his shoulder.

"What is it, my darling?" he mumbled.

"Wake up, Joe."

"I am awake. What is it, sweetheart?"

"Nothing, only I just wondered if the wind was blowing too cool in the window and if we might not get cold."

"Shall I close it?"

"No, don't. It feels good after such a hot day."

"You say when . . ."

"Joe."

"Yes, my angel?"

"I was just wondering about college professors."

"Oh . . ."

"How much they make and everything. How much do they?" She had to give another little tug at his shoulder to make him answer.

"Who, sweetheart?"

"College professors. How much money do they make?"

"Money? . . . depends on how old . . . and how long . . . and what degrees they . . ." He dug his nose deeper into the pillow and pulled the sheet up around his ear.

"Joe, tell me. Don't keep falling asleep like that."

" . . . not falling asleep . . . wide awake. . . ."

"How much does Teige make, for instance?"

"Why, he makes . . . young, you know . . . only teaching a year or two . . ."

"How much?"

" . . . believe he said . . . hundred a month. . . ."

"Counting summers?"

He snuffled a dim sound.

"Do they pay him through the summer?"

He did not answer and she let him sleep. Teachers didn't get anything through the vacation, she was sure.

She figured up. School started in September and ended the first part of June. She counted on her fingers, naming over the months, including May. Nine months, nine hundred dollars. And he didn't own a house, he just lived in two rented rooms, didn't own any furniture, either, probably. Of course, his father was well enough off to retire, but he had married again. When the father died, of course, Teige would probably inherit something, but he was only about Mr. Morelewski's age, he might live another forty years or even longer. Of course, Teige might get a raise later on but even so, it might be years and years before he made as much as Mr. Morelewski.

It was a real problem, Teige's love when looked at from that standpoint, and it was no wonder that Alma Morelewski had to do some hard meditating.

After all, she had not lived off the fat of the land all her life. If she had met Teige Desmond *before* she met Mr. Morelewski, when she was making sixteen dollars a month, she might have accepted him without a second thought, but as it was, she had had two years of real luxury with which to compare what he would offer her, and two years can make all the difference in the world.

The cream-colored brick house on Fifth East for instance, that was all paid for, not a penny owed on it. It was not a mansion such as could be seen up on Brigham Street, but she was still as proud of it, still admired it as much, with its awnings and porches and hedged-in lawns, as the day Mr. Morelewski had first brought her to see it. Inside it was even nicer than outside, papered and painted, with electric chandeliers in every room and a real bathroom next to the bedroom. Could she give up her house? She loved her things, too, curtains, pictures, rugs, furniture, dishes, silverware, cut glass, ornaments and house plants. Could she give up all of them for two rooms full, as Teige said himself, of books?

There would be other losses. A hired girl, for instance. She would have to do everything herself. And no Paris Café to be carried to in a livery-stable carriage at the same hour every evening, there to dine at a palm-shaded table, with the owner himself. She would have to make her dresses out of cheap goods, trim her own hats, carry her own groceries home, put up fruit in summer, make pickles, wash and iron, the way her mother did. Maybe she would even have several children! No time then to rise at ten, pose before the glass, nap, sit, read the pretty magazines, lie in the tub for an hour at a time, dress and undress twice, three times a day.

She thought perhaps she would miss Mr. Morelewski, too. He petted and babied her so much, paid her so much attention, brought her things, took her to the theatre, let her buy nearly everything she wanted. Besides, he never spoke to her without calling her darling, sweetheart or angel, never gazed at her without looking as if he could eat her up. In fact, he loved her so much that even if nobody else on earth had loved her, she would have felt surrounded with affectionate feelings on every side because of him. She supposed she might miss all that, the case, the lavishment, the love.

Sometimes she almost felt like crying, because Teige had come and fallen in love with her and was going to ask her to leave Mr. Morelewski, and because she was in love with him and would most certainly have to go.

She must be in love, if the thought of him could shut up her stomach and narrow her throat the way it did, for not even when she was elected Queen did she feel any such effects as that, and she had been stirred up enough then, heaven knew. She must be in love, if she wanted, intensely, painfully, to go, as she did, to marry him, even on nine hundred dollars a year, and give up everything, possessions, joys and pleasures for him. . . .

Did she, really?

Oh, yes!

Really?

Well, maybe she would have to think about it a little longer. . . .

Because it was quite a sacrifice.

But still, you know, love.

A little longer. . . .

Every morning and every evening, Alma Morelewski, thin, empty, weary from lack of sleep, excited, agitated, restless, with a great big problem on her mind to settle, told her husband when he asked her, that she had never felt better in her life.

And she could look him right in the eye, too, when she said it, for it was Gospel truth.

21

IT WAS SATURDAY NIGHT, A WEEK AFTER MR. DES-
mond's visit, and Crystal dressed up after supper as she had been
doing for the past six nights, and waited. Sometimes she took the
lamp into the parlor and played the piano, played, not practised, but
broke off in the middle of the piece, took up the lamp and came out
into the kitchen again. Sometimes she said to her mother, "Let
me sew on that," and took her work out of her lap. But she no more
than settled down in the circle of light and took a few stitches, then
she tossed the sewing back and got up and went over to look critically at herself in the mirror above the sink, or sighed and strolled
to the back window and stared out on nothing.

The clock struck nine and Crystal came over to the table and sat
down, frowning. She began to take the pins out of her hair and
arrange them in a straight line across the tablecloth. "Dorney," she
said, "I just can't imagine — are you sure you didn't tell him about
J-e-t-t-a?"

Dorney lifted preoccupied eyes from her book.

"Now, Crystal, you know she gave you her promise." But Madge
looked questioningly at Dorney. "You didn't tell, did you? What
would of been the point of telling?"

Dorney blinked. "I didn't, Madge. Cross my heart and hope to
die."

"Did he ever *mention* you-know-who?"

"No," Dorney said. "Honestly he didn't. I'd tell you if he did,
honestly."

"I can't help but think, Crystal," Madge murmured, "that maybe
you made a mistake to tell him that f-i-b like that. After all, just
because somebody in the family has something r-o-n-g with them,
doesn't mean that there's something r-o-n-g with everybody. He
wouldn't of thought any the less of you if you had come right out
and —"

Crystal took up and began twisting one of the hairpins. "You just
don't understand," she said bitterly.

"Sure, I understand. I understand enough not to allow no traipsing around the neighborhood and parading before everybody."

"I'll never get any place with h-e-r around here. She ought to be p-u-t in some kind of an i-n-s-t-i— some kind of a h-o-m-e for people like that."

"Crystal, you don't mean such a thing," Dorney whispered.

"Don't I, though!"

"You've had all kinds of chances, as you very well know," Madge said soothingly. "You could of been just as popular as could be. Why, I could name seven or eight boys right now without even thinking. They knew about J-e-t-t-a and it didn't make a particle of difference. That front door was always being knocked on and you had invite after invite, and could of gone all kinds of places, if you just would of. The boys — "

"Boys! Who were they, I ask you? Horace Blood and Lew Fleming and Hike Christianson and Bill Luby and — "

"Now, Crystal, you can't expect the President of the United States's son, or John Jacob Astor, Junior, when you happen to live in — "

"That's another thing. This town! If we could just go to some place where a person would have some kind of a chance for once in their life! and not have to sit around and wait for accidents."

"Now, honey."

"Dorney, are you sure you didn't say anything to him? Maybe not realizing it, like. You can tell me. I won't be mad, I promise."

Dorney shook her head. "No, Crystal, I didn't. I never said one word." She looked up, turned the page.

"One word," Jetta repeated. She edged over close to Dorney's knee and carefully placed the moth on it. When she took her hand away, it did not flutter off but lay still. "Look," she said.

Dorney inspected it, smiling. "My, what a pretty one. Look, Madge, at Jetta's moth. Look, Crystal. Did you ever see such white wings or such big red eyes? And look at this velvety streak of black down here across the back."

"Big red eyes," Jetta said proudly.

Madge squinted at it a moment, then leaned over and brushed it into her hand. "Nasty things," she said. "Lay eggs. Eat everything full of holes." She got up, carried it over and dropped it in the stove.

A shrill wail burst from Jetta's lips.

Dorney's hand went out to her. "Don't cry," she said, feeling the loss herself with sorrow and regret. "It was dead anyway."

"No! No!"

"You hush, now," Madge said. "Or you'll be in bed so fast, you won't know what happened. It's your bedtime anyway."

The wail turned to a whimper and stopped as Dorney gently undid Jetta's hair ribbon and began to unbraid her little knot of hair.

"What has he *said* to you the past week? I know he must have said *something*, at least," Crystal said.

"What about?"

"About anything!"

"I haven't hardly talked to him, really I haven't. He goes out in the mornings and then when he comes home he sits out on the porch with the — with Mrs. Morelewski, and then he goes upstairs, and then pretty soon the carriage comes and they go up to the restaurant. And at six o'clock I come home."

She knew what Crystal wanted to hear, that Mr. Desmond thought she was beautiful and could play the piano better than anybody. But all he had actually said about his visit was, "Well, we took our objective, didn't we?" and Dorney couldn't tell Madge and Crystal *that*. She couldn't tell them, either, that she had had a long talk with Mr. Desmond just yesterday, because they would ask what it was about and somehow she wanted to keep that conversation to herself as the Queen had kept her chocolates.

She was sitting by the newspaper-spread table cleaning the silverware when Mr. Desmond pushed the kitchen door open and stuck his head in.

"Thy mistress, Lady, wends upon what progress? Or art thou sworn to utmost secrecy?"

"She's gone to the dressmaker's, I think she said, Mr. Desmond."

"Could I have a cup of coffee?"

She pushed back her chair and got up smiling. "I'll bring you some as soon as I can make it," she said. "It doesn't take long."

He wandered away but came back to the kitchen just as she was ready to set out with it in search of him.

"Here's your coffee," she said. "Where do you want it?"

He considered. "On the drawbridge over the moat? No. On the dais in the grand ballroom? No. How about right here?"

"Where?" she said.

He took the cup and carried it around the table, drew up a chair and sat down. "Here," he said, taking a sip. "Now, tell me. How's the reading going? And what are you going to do after you finish those four measly books?"

"They aren't measly!" she said, sitting down, picking up a heavy cake server and beginning to scrub it with a little brush over the pan of blackish water. "They're wonderful. They're just wonderful."

"There's a library up in the City and County Building," he said, "but it doesn't amount to much, and it's only open Mondays, Wednesdays and Fridays from ten to five."

"I'm glad to find out about it," she said. "The worst trouble is, Sunday's my day off." She rinsed off the silver, dried it, laid it carefully in the case from which it had never been removed except for polishing, and reached for another piece. "But I thank you for telling me just the same." She looked up. "Mr. Desmond," she said, "I was thinking about how nice it was of you to come and explain to Madge. . . ."

"The pleasure was all mine, Dorney."

"I've been wanting to ask you — a potential confrère. What is that, just exactly?" She had been practising the two words so as to be able to say them without stumbling.

"Well, potential means possible, or in the making. And confrère means a colleague or fellow worker. An associate, in other words."

"I was hoping it meant something like that, ever since then."

"Why?"

"Well, because, you see — " She scrubbed away hard at an engraved *M* in a wreath of flowers. "Mr. Desmond."

"Yes, Dorney."

"You know what you told Madge about if you had been a carpenter and I was a boy?"

"None too good, alas, but the best example I could think of at the moment."

She raised her eyes. "Well, I wish it was all true," she said.

"That you were a boy?"

"Not that I was a boy so much, but that you really *did* have a shop and I could work there and learn — not how to be a carpenter, naturally — but oh, different words, and about books, and what you mean when you say different things. I'd rather learn how even to be a carpenter, though, from you, than not to have you teach me anything, if I had my say."

"I have got a kind of shop, Dorney. My classroom. But you can't come there. . . ."

"No, I couldn't come there."

He put his cup down. "No, you couldn't."

"I was thinking all the time, *how* I wish — and do you know something? I wouldn't care a bit about shining your shoes. Not a bit! If only I could be where I could listen to you."

"Nearly eight centuries ago, now, in France, a young lady named Héloïse said almost those very same words to a certain teacher. At least they meant the same. Guide me, she said. Teach me. Her eyes must have looked very like yours." He got up and went to the window, stood looking out. "He couldn't say no, to that, any more than I — " He swung about. "But they order the matter better, there. You'd have been young enough to adopt or you'd have been old enough to — not betwixt and between this way. What am I to do with you?"

Madge said, after she came back from tucking Jetta in bed, that she was so tired she couldn't keep her eyes open, but long after Dorney went to bed she heard the murmur of her voice and Crystal's in the kitchen.

"We've just got to do something," Crystal said fiercely when she and her mother were alone. "I just *know* he liked me. I *know* it. I could feel it in my bones."

"He hardly took his eyes off you," Madge agreed.

"Well, why hasn't he been back then?"

"Maybe the Morelewskis — "

"I know why, well enough! Either because Dorney has been talking to him behind my back — "

"Why would she, now?"

"She's so jealous of me she can't see straight."

"But she doesn't like Mr. Desmond!"

"Doesn't she! She just worships him, that's all."

"Only because he gave her those books, and you heard what he said himself. He said he would of give 'em to her just the same if she'd of been a boy. *That* don't mean nothing. You know very well she wouldn't stand a chance in the world alongside somebody like you. Besides, she's too young."

"You heard what he said about Juliet."

"That don't mean nothing."

"She's pretty, though, Mamma, you have to admit." Crystal clicked her thumbnail and the nail of her middle finger together, scowling.

"Not alongside of you."

"She's got prettier eyes."

"Oh, pooh."

"Her waist is littler."

"Pooh."

Crystal's face cleared. "But he wouldn't look at Dorney, anyway," she said. "Not with Mrs. Morelewski around."

"There you are!" Madge said with a beaming smile. "Worrying over nothing. Of course he wouldn't! Not with the most beautiful — I mean, after all — he wouldn't have much time for Dorney."

"But suppose he's gone to work and fallen in love with her!"

"With who?"

"Mrs. Morelewski!"

"If you don't beat all," Madge said. "She's a married woman. Of all the notions. That's a fine way to do, I must say. Come to pay a visit and walk off with his uncle's wife. Did he strike you like that? You know very well he didn't! That Mr. Desmond is a very, very nice, honest boy and you know it."

214

"Well, why doesn't he come then, Mamma?" Crystal buried her face in her hands. "I kept thinking and thinking —"

"It beats me."

"I *know* he liked me! I just *know* it. I could tell."

"Of course he did."

Crystal looked up. "It's that Jetta. That's what it is. I just know that's what it is."

"But he doesn't even know she's your sister!"

"Mamma, I'll never have a chance with her around. Never. Not if I live to be a thousand."

"Oh, now, Crystal."

"It's true! People look at her and they think being the way she is runs in the family, and they think —"

"All that's the matter with Jetta —"

"They do! You know they do!" She drew a quivering breath. "Why can't we put her in a home where somebody like she is belongs?"

"That costs money."

"Mamma, let me tell you something. We've just got to!"

"Now, see here," Madge said. "You can go so far and no further. I ain't got money to put Jetta in a home and even if I did, I don't know whether I'd want to give up my baby girl just because —"

"Your baby girl," Crystal sneered.

"There's no sense in being snippy."

"Nobody's being snippy. All I'm saying is —"

"Because it's all very fine to sit there and talk, but you want to remember that the tables might just as well of been turned. Jetta might of been you, you know, my fine lady, and you might of been —"

"Oh, Mamma, don't say such mean things!" Crystal slipped to the floor, slid over and buried her face in her mother's lap. "I'm just *miserable*."

Madge laid a scarred hand on her daughter's warm hair. "Oh, now, honey, you ain't, either."

"I am, too!"

"But you got it better than lots of girls. You got nice clothes. You don't have to get out and work. You can practise —"

"Don't think that's not work!" Crystal's shoulders shook.

"I ain't said it wasn't. Do you think I don't know? But I'm just telling you. You're pretty as a picture. You ain't sickly. You get to take music lessons twice a week — that amounts to quite a bit. I'm just trying to make you stop and think — why, honest, Crystal, in comparison with most girls, you got the world by the tail!"

"In comparison with the Daly girls, I suppose! With the Kearns girl, I suppose!"

"But honey, their fathers is millionaire miners. Naturally, they can afford to dress 'em — and give 'em — and send 'em — but they ain't got your looks, not by no means. You want to think of that."

"What good's it going to do me?" Crystal reached for a handful of her mother's apron and used it to soak up her tears. "What good is it, if I'm pretty or if I'm ugly? I might as well be dead."

"Somebody'll be coming along one of these days and then —"

"Mr. Desmond came along! and look what happened." She wiped her nose and sniffed.

"He may surprise you yet. But even if he don't, for some reason, there's just as good fish in the sea as ever's been caught, you want to remember. He ain't the only pebble on the beach."

"Mamma, why can't we *go*?"

"Go where, honey?"

"Go where a person would have a chance to meet somebody — maybe Chicago —"

"I don't know what we'd do in Chicago."

" — or San Francisco. I could set up as a teacher there — I could meet somebody — you and I could rent a nice flat — it wouldn't be like this town. I'd have a *chance* for once. I just know I could meet a rich —"

"I don't know what we'd do it on."

"We've got nearly three hundred dollars in the bank."

"We'd need more than that, I can tell you."

"No, we wouldn't. We could start all over. I'd be happy there, I'd accomplish something, I'd be somebody. I just know it, while here I'm so miserable, I can't hardly —"

"What about Jetta? And Dorney?"

"Dorney's not a little child, after all. She's bigger than I am. You could maybe get her a job at Judge Towers's or somewhere, where she could get her board and room. *She'd* be all right. Besides, she's Grandpa's responsibility, not ours, you've said so the whole time!"

"I know, but she kind of grows on a person and I can't help but feel a kind of a soft spot —"

"And Jetta would be *happier* in a home, I just know she would. She'd be *lots* better off. You could get a job in San Francisco, the same as here. I could set up as a music teacher —"

"Three hundred dollars wouldn't be a drop in the bucket," Madge said, musingly. "It would be spent before we could turn around, and what if I couldn't get no job? You're just nervous and tired to-night, and kind of disappointed. Tomorrow things'll look —"

"They'll look just the same," Crystal said. "Just like they always do. Hopeless."

"Oh, no, they won't."

216

"We've *got* to make a change, Mamma. Or I might just as well kill myself right now and get it over with."

"Why, Crystal!"

"I mean it. One of these days you'll see I meant it. You'll see I wasn't fooling."

"We'll be making a change. You see if we don't."

"When?"

"We don't have to do it *tomorrow*, do we? But we'll think about it, and the first thing you know — "

Crystal lifted a happy, flushed face, shook back her damp hair. "I could do lots better than any old Mr. *Desmond* in San Francisco, you can bet your boots."

"Sure you could."

"I could do wonders."

"I know you could."

"Let's leave then, Mamma. What are we waiting for?"

"There's no big hurry," Madge said soothingly. "We got plenty of time. We'll have to start trying to save some money, and then we'll have to decide — and we'll have to think — "

She put out her hand and touched her daughter's cheek. "You just be patient, lovey."

"I'll try, Mamma. But not forever, because human flesh and blood can just only stand so much and then — "

"Not forever. Of course not." Madge looked at the white forehead under the waves of soft hair, wanting to press her lips to it. Sometimes it was hard to stay mad at 'Dair Yandle, considering that even though he had broken her heart, he had left her so sweet a companion, so beautiful and talented a child. . . .

Dorney threw back the sheet and moved to a cooler place on the edge of the narrow bed, thinking of the girl Mr. Desmond told her about, the one in France eight hundred years ago, who had asked that teacher to let her learn from him. Héloïse, her name was, Mr. Desmond said.

Eight hundred years ago was an awfully long time. It hardly seemed possible that there were people then, just like the people now.

That girl — What was it she had wanted to learn so particularly from that teacher?

Had she learned what she wanted to know? And then, did she die? Of course she did. But soon? Or when she was an old woman? It didn't matter much, one way or the other — considering that it was nearly a thousand years ago. Someday, just for example, it would be eight hundred years since she herself, Dorney Leaf, told Mr. Desmond . . . and eight hundred years since he said to her . . . and that long, since Crystal dressed up after supper and waited for him to come again . . . and that long, since Clara went . . . and Schooner Bill wore . . . and Butch Cassidy rode . . . and the Queen . . .

Sleepily she thought, It will be. It actually will, someday, although people can't really believe it down in their hearts. And then it will be *sixteen hundred* years since Héloïse said to Mr. Desmond . . . said, Mr. Desmond, guide and teach me, and he looked at her and said . . . but what good was it all when the pupil must die, and the teacher must die, anyway? There must be some reason behind it. Mr. Desmond, if you'll explain everything, I'll shine your shoes and . . . I'll do . . . whatever you want. . . .

22

IT WAS NOT UNTIL THE TUESDAY BEFORE TEIGE'S departure on Saturday that Alma Morelewski made her final determination in regard to him. Before, she had wavered, one day deciding that yes, she would go away with him and the next day changing her mind and concluding that no, she would not, it was asking entirely too big a sacrifice. She settled the problem for sure the day they went out to Saltair, or rather, the evening of that day, and after that there was no more irresolution.

She and Teige went in the carriage to pick up Mr. Morelewski at four o'clock. At the restaurant, one of the waiters came staggering out with a big picnic basket and put it on the seat beside the coachman, then Mr. Morelewski came out and they drove to the Salt Lake and Los Angeles Railway station and boarded the train for the resort. She was wearing a gray India mull trimmed with white Languedoc lace, with a rose-colored taffeta sash, not the pink dress with the Spanish flounces, and she was glad because at least two other young ladies on the cars had on pink. Her hat was rose-colored velvet and her shoes were gray kid. Everything was new.

She had her bathing dress with her, a cunning affair of blue and black striped stockinette with trousers like a harem lady's and a tight tunic. With this went a blue turban and India rubber shoes. She knew it was becoming for she had tried it on at least half a dozen times in the last twenty-four hours, but when they arrived at the bathing resort, she was not very anxious to go into one of the bathhouses and put it on and bathe with Teige and Mr. Morelewski after all. They had to beg her for some time while she eyed the lake and the rows of dressing cubicles. Maybe she couldn't hang her clothes up and they would get mussed. Besides, there was probably a tiny mirror that she couldn't see in. And how could she be sure of ever getting her hair done up right another time, or putting her hat back on the way she wanted it. Too, the salt water might get into her eyes and make them red. There were other hazards. It had been rumored that on Pioneer Day last year, some vicious child had gone into the bathhouses and cut all the ladies' corset strings.

This ghastly trick Alma did not recall until the very moment her companions were coaxing her to accompany them into the water. Then the remembrance of it gave her palpitations. If anything like that happened to her, she might as well be dead, for she could never fasten the taffeta sash, never, or hook up her dress, and what she would do she could not even imagine.

What made her decide to take the bull by the horns and bathe in spite of all perils was Teige turning his head to look after a girl in a ridiculous green swimming dress, a great dark creature with no cap on and a bounding front she should have been ashamed of, instead of showing it off like it was something wonderful, on her way to the water.

"All right, I'll take a dip," she said.

When she came airily out on the odd-feeling rubber soles and went down the boardwalk to meet them, she saw by their faces that it had been worth the trouble even if, as she had feared, the bathhouse mirror was no more than three inches square, there was only one clothes hook and the bench was crusted with salt. That is, the look on Teige's face was worth it. She glanced only fleetingly at Mr. Morelewski whose open mouth and worshipful eyes made her feel more impatient than pleased.

Teige chanted softly, "But what was shocking . . . shocking . . . her small snow feet had slippers but no stocking. . . ."

"Isn't she wonderful?" Joe said.

"Oh, I am not." She said this reprimandingly to him, but smiled at Teige.

"You look like Haidée," he said.

Possibly because she was so happy she did not mind the aggravations of getting dressed again in the miserable little closet and managed the ordeal so deftly that when she went to the lunch pavilion through the long corridor hung with mirrors, she could see in them that she looked as well or even better than when she set out from home. So the bathing had not done any harm. In fact, her hair looked almost prettier than before and so did her eyes. Really, it had been fun. It was no good trying to swim in the water, even if one knew how, which Alma didn't, it was so salty that the best thing to do was to sit upon it and make little circular pushing movements with the hands to keep upright and bob around like a cork. Of course, one had to take care, for one's feet could fly up and one could lose one's balance and swallow a quart of brine and blind oneself momentarily and have a horrid, even a frightening, time. But when Alma had begun to somersault, Teige was right there and grabbed her around the waist. He could perceive how slender and supple she was under the thin stockinette, she knew. All the time she was dressing afterward she thought how glad she was that she had gone to bathe, and even when her corset was back on and laced as tightly as it would go, she could feel his large warm hands encircling her, bringing her close to him and then carefully balancing her on the water, as though on top of a high and narrow wall, holding her elbow, touching the small of her back now and again, until Joe floated over and took her other arm.

They ate their picnic supper in the luncheon pavilion by a Moorish arch overlooking the Lake, under the great dance floor upon which children could be heard running and sliding. In the blue twilight, they sat and watched the stars come out. Teige smoked his pipe, Mr. Morelewski puffed a soft black cigar, and Alma, as the evening breeze began to blow in from across the water, grew cold enough to need a wrap. She shivered in it, as Teige talked about getting his doctor's degree in Europe, and tucked her chilly hands in under her arms to warm them.

Teige had not mentioned going abroad until now. He wanted to go next spring, he said, when college was out, and stay for a year. He thought he could go to Oxford or perhaps Dublin or maybe he would go to Leipzig. It confused Alma to listen to him. What did he want to be a doctor for all of a sudden, when he was already a teacher? She must ask Joe about that, casually, as if it did not matter much. Maybe a doctor made more than a teacher, that was why, unless he had a lot of poor patients he couldn't collect from. But if he was going to take a notion like that, why didn't he go to medical school in the first place instead of wasting so much time? And how would that affect her, if she decided to go with him to New York and divorce Mr. Morelewski and marry him?

It grew darker and darker and then the lights came on, all the incandescent and all the arc lights, and up above them, more and more people gathered on the dance floor and a horn began to tune itself and then a violin and then another horn. The dance started to the music of "Over the Waves." Alma couldn't worry any more about her problem then. "I'll bet they're not cold," she announced brightly, giving a little shiver and wrapping her cloak more tightly about her.

"You are!" her husband said, jumping to his feet. "We must go, my darling. We can't have you getting pneumonia."

"I should say not," Teige said.

She ignored Mr. Morelewski. "I mean the people upstairs in the dance pavilion," she said. "They're not cold, because they're dancing."

"Ah, ha! The child wishes to dance," Mr. Morelewski said, delighted. "She hints, you hear. Come, sweetheart, we will go and have a waltz."

She felt intensely annoyed until she considered that if she danced first with her husband, she could dance the next time with Teige.

It was in his arms, feeling as if she was made out of pure electricity and he was, too, dancing with him for the first time, that she knew once and for all that when he asked her, as he would at any moment (for he was leaving on Saturday), she would have to go, knew she loved Teige Desmond as a woman loves but once in her entire life and that nothing mattered but love. She grew quite faint, coming to her last and irrevocable decision like that, and the other dancers' faces and forms blurred all around her, but her feet did not falter. She only clung to her partner a little more closely and soon her giddiness passed.

She wanted to slip out of the bedroom that very night and go out onto the porch and find her tablet and pencil and compose her farewell note to Mr. Morelewski, but she waited until the next day when she was alone to sit down and write.

"Dear Joe,

I am sorry to go away and leave you like this after you were so nice to me and gave me so much. But all that is important is love to a woman so please forgive me. I hope you will not get too excited the way you do as there is no use in crying over spilt milk. I never took only just my clothes but if you send me my looking glass later on, I would appreciate it very much. Don't water the plants too much as too much water kills them. I hope you won't have any hard feelings against me because I — " She could not think exactly how to end it so she tore off the page, folded it and slipped it into the front of her dress beneath her corset cover, to finish later.

That was on Wednesday. At breakfast with him alone, at tea with him alone, in the restaurant with him alone, while Mr. Morelewski was called away to the kitchen and left them sitting together at the table, in the box at the Salt Lake Theatre alone, while Mr. Morelewski had to go down to the lobby and see a man about something, in the carriage . . . in the parlor . . . out on the cool side porch in semi-dark while Mr. Morelewski was preparing the midnight snack in the kitchen . . . though her eyes did nothing but inquire, Teige did not declare himself. He went on acting the same as always.

Thursday came, morning, afternoon and night, and he did not speak.

Friday morning, Mr. Morelewski told his wife that if she did not sleep tonight, he was going to bring the doctor down to see her. She had tossed and turned for two nights now, he said, and hadn't slept half an hour. Something was terribly wrong and he had never been so worried in his life. He did not tell her, but he feared that her symptoms, appearing as they did out of a clear sky and totally without warning, denoted the last stages of galloping consumption, for which he blamed nobody but himself. Fool that he was, he couldn't be satisfied with the most beautiful and wonderful wife a man ever had, just as she was and would by her nature and constitution be. Not him! He had to start meddling. She put on a little weight (the thirty-two pounds became a trifle, nothing) and what did he do, wretch that he was? Did he let well enough alone, reconciled to the will of the All Powerful? No. He persuaded her to starve herself — painfully starve, in the midst of plenty — so he could gloat over her like a goatish god with a new-fledged nymph. The fat had melted away, yes, but the result of his fetishistic tampering was, that in her defenseless emaciation, she had fallen prey, as he might have foretold, to the deadliest of diseases.

He felt a little better when he told Teige the whole story at lunch on Friday, from the beginning nearly three months ago when she couldn't get into the dress, until the present moment when, thirty-five pounds lighter, she was almost certainly at death's door. Teige cheered him by reminding him of the Chinese who lived on a cup of rice a day, and not that, when there was famine, and suggesting to him that hers was probably not an illness at all but a nervous crisis brought on by unaccustomed fasting, something that would pass as soon as she began to eat again.

Teige felt comforted himself by his uncle's confession. Alma's strange behavior the past few days had puzzled him, but the mystery faded when he knew what lay behind it, that she was of an essentially plump genus coerced and bedeviled into masquerading as thin. No wonder her eyes had looked so odd, no wonder she was so nervous. He would have liked her much better as nature had intended her to be, he thought, and hoped she would soon return to her right condition.

The Etiquette book with its full directions for conducting every social transaction from making a Protestant Bishop acquainted with a Catholic cardinal, to how to place one foot behind the other and sink upon the floor at the Court of St. James's failed utterly to tell how to induce a lover to say, I love you, come away with me, the words Alma Morelewski waited in agony to hear while there was still time to purchase sufficient luggage and pack decently. Not one of her magazines told her, either, and she had no friend to ask.

On Friday afternoon when Teige came back for tea, she did not pretend to be a pretty invalid, half reclining on the wicker sofa. She was one. Her hand shook when she poured out the tea and she did not meet his eyes. When would he speak? When? She knew he loved her. How could he help it? She was perfectly beautiful, as her mirror had told her not fifteen minutes ago. Did he fear to ask her to share his poverty? It would seem that, true, by the side of what Mr. Morelewski had given her, but love could rise above botherations of whatever kind. As the poem said in this very copy of *Leslie's*, "One throb of love is worth all the stars above." She glanced nervously at the clock. Not twenty-four hours until the train pulled out of the station! She would be forced to throw a few things in a suitcase and go like a gypsy — or remain behind, let him go first and then follow in a few days. When he disclosed his feelings, that was what she would tell him, explaining why, at this late date, she had better stay here for the present and come along later. In fact, that was probably a much better idea than to try to go with him — it would give her time to do everything with care and system, even have a new lining put in her broadcloth coat, which she would be glad of later.

She drooped against the cushions with a sigh of relief. There was no big hurry, a week . . . two weeks . . . time to give a person a little breathing space.

Suppose he did not speak at all?

She stiffened and sat up. The thought was so frightful that her heart stopped dead still for an instant and then began to race like somebody fleeing a ghost through a deserted building.

She tried to lift her cup but her hand was so unsteady, she left it in the saucer.

Never. As long as she lived.

Some, in her place, would themselves have spoken, Alma Morelewski knew, but this recourse, to the true beauty, was unthinkable. Besides, she had been a Queen. She saw herself riding on the royal float, sceptered, crowned, enthroned behind four white horses, rolling between the rows of her subjects. A born beauty — and a Queen! It would take more than love for her to forget herself so far, to stoop so low as to offer herself to any man.

But he was speaking!

She turned her head very carefully, as though favoring a stiff neck or a painful shoulder.

"My dear, dear Alma."

One hand crept to her throat, the other began to stretch out to him.

He took it in both his own. "Somebody told me once," he said, "that the acceptance of himself is a man's hardest job in life."

"This comes — as rather a surprise," she whispered.

"None of us are satisfied," he said. "We always think we could be better, richer, wiser — in your case, whimsical as it seems, more beautiful. We discover a limitation in ourselves about the way a Simon Legree discovers laziness or thievery or lying in a slave. We reach for the blacksnake whip. We oughtn't to do it, Alma. Improve, yes, if we can, unceasingly, no lifetime is long enough in which to learn compassion, generosity, love — but outside of that — "

She stared at him in bewilderment. "Love?"

"Just as the groom takes his bride, just as she takes him, so should every man and woman take himself or herself, for better or for worse. Why, if people would just be reconciled to *themselves*, half the misery on this earth would — "

"Teige." She wet her lips. "Are you asking me to — do you want me to — I don't understand exactly what you're — "

"Why, all I'm saying is, I'll bet you were just as beautiful three months ago as you are today. Alma, be what you are."

"I don't quite — "

"The noticed want to be inconspicuous, the shy, bold, the short, tall, the fat, thin. Think of the precious hours of precious life wasted that way — crying for the moon. And only one life to live."

When Mr. Morelewski proposed, he came right out with it. He said, "Alma, I love you, I want to marry you." She fingered her throat uneasily. "I know," she said. "That's what I've been telling myself." What was he talking about? It was the strangest thing how he could go along speaking plain English for the longest while and a person would have no idea what he was driving at, yet every separate word was comprehensible and even familiar.

"I want you to know what a delightful time I've had, how very much I have enjoyed my visit here," he said. "I shall think of you very often, Alma, here on this porch, looking so lovely, drinking your tea." He looked around. "It suits you wonderfully," he said, "your bower, the vines, and the charming way you have arranged — but you can't sit out here in winter, can you, in spite of its being glassed in? Isn't it too cold?"

"Yes, it's too cold," she said.

"Where shall I imagine you sitting then, when the snow falls?"

She drew her fingers out of his grasp, gently. "Why, I don't know," she said. "In the parlor, I guess."

He smiled. "Eating bread and honey? Being a Queen, you know."

"Oh, I'm not a Queen," she said. "Not by any means. . . ."

She stared down at her hand as once, long ago in childhood, squatting by the side of the road, she stared down on a shut-eyed bird killed by a boy with a rock. No more than then over that did she cry now over this, what was small and slain, but forlornly studied it. Too bad . . . too bad . . . how sad.

Dorney tapped at the half-open door. "Mr. Desmond, your last breakfast is nearly ready," she said.

"My last breakfast!" He opened the door wider and stood smiling down at her. "A cheerful pronouncement."

"I mean, in Salt Lake City."

"Never you think it," he said.

She caught her breath and her face lighted up.

"I am coming back someday."

"I hope I will be about sixteen then," she said, after a little consideration, as one would say, I hope I will have come into my fortune by then. She did not add but thought, I also hope I will be beautiful. "I'll save up things to ask you, if you won't care if I do."

"Maybe you will have learned so much, you won't need to ask me anything, Dorney. Perhaps I should begin to save up things to ask you."

"Oh, no," she said, shaking her head.

He looked at her. "It's a pity one can't put a glass globe over certain curious Ladies-in-Waiting — keeping their hair," he lifted a strand of it off her shoulder, let it fall again, "their sweet smiles, their guileless and lovely eyes, their manners and modesty, unspecked, beyond peril." He glanced at the walls, the ceiling, then back at her. "But this house is nearly like a glass globe. Mrs. Yandle's, too. I think I may safely leave my scholar here, since there is nothing else I can do with her, impecunious bachelor that I am, facing a trip that has to be made, abroad. There is no other choice. You remember what potential means?"

"It means, something that could be."

"And confrère?"

"I remember everything," she said gravely.

"Well, I do, too," he said.

"Goodbye, Mr. Desmond."

"I touched her not, alas, not I . . . I did but see her passing by . . . and yet *I — something — till I die,"* he said softly. "Like Alice, I'm testing out my memory by repeating a — " He stopped, smiling, and put his hand out.

She gave him her hand.

"Goodbye, Dorney. We shall meet again."

23

THAT SATURDAY AFTERNOON, THOUGH IT WAS
only four-thirty, when Alma Morelewski came home from the railway station, she went into her bedroom, took her clothes off and
went straight to bed. In the evening, her husband brought Dr.
Bacon to see her. He didn't, he said privately to Mr. Morelewski,
like the looks of her tongue at all. However, with supervised recum-
bency, plenty of good nourishment and the taking of the elixir he
would prescribe, three times, the Blaud's pills he would suggest,
twice, and the tamarinth curds he would order, once a day, he had
every hope that she could be pulled through.

All Alma herself knew about her illness was that it had come on
with alarming abruptness. She and Mr. Morelewski had seen Teige
off for New York and then had gone in the carriage and returned
home. She had come into the bedroom and was going to pick out a
dress to change into, to wear back up to the restaurant. She opened
the wardrobe door and was standing there looking accidentally at
the mull dress with the white Languedoc lace, the one she had worn
out to Saltair, when with no warning whatsoever this pain took hold
of her. She tried to tell the doctors when they asked her to describe
it, but it was no easy matter to explain. "It started here, and it came
right up my chest, oh, just terrible, like a —" but it was silly to say
a big plowshare making a deep furrow in the ground and throwing
the dirt to either side, so she did not tell them that. "It was just
terrible," was all she could say. She didn't know whether to go
or stay or what to do and then she was in front of the mirror and
that was when her feet and hands felt so numb and her throat refused to swallow even a little saliva, while she stood there staring,
hardly able to breathe with this pain, looking in the glass, thinking
that she was at the height, the very summit of her beauty, as beautiful as a living woman could be, and it wasn't worth a nickel, it
didn't amount to a hill of beans. "It was just terrible."

She had, very naturally and sensibly, taken her clothes off and
gone to bed. Did the pain continue? It did for a few days, she
politely told her questioners, and then it went away little by little.
But she didn't feel at all well yet.

Mr. Morelewski was hunting for a light wrap to put about his wife's shoulders while she sat among her pillows trying to sip a little soup when he found the note on the closet floor and absent-mindedly picked it up and put it in his pocket. It was not, however, until she was better and could be up and around that he happened one day in the restaurant, rummaging for a match, to run across it again by chance and opened and read it. At first it made no sense at all, and he almost called the headwaiter over to him and asked him to read it, and see what he could make of it. For a minute he thought it must belong to some customer, until he remembered distinctly the day he picked it up at home. It was in his wife's handwriting, that was sure, and the dear Joe — who could that be but him? Why, though, would Alma be writing a letter to her own husband when they lived right together in the same house?

He nearly carried it to the cashier's cage, too, to see if he could figure out what the joke was, for of course that was all it could be. Then it dawned on him that it was a farewell note.

Nobody in the Paris Café knew what made the boss make a jump in the air and tear out that way without his hat, leaving the front door wide open though he harped nothing but closing it to keep the flies out. If he had not come back an hour later looking as if nothing had happened, they would have imagined he went crazy, but since he did, they didn't. Old Moffat, who had been with him longest, was the only one with nerve enough to ask him what bit him and he said nothing, he had had to go to the bank. "That's how I'd make a beeline for it, too," the old waiter said when telling the others, "if I had a bank account like he's got."

He was halfway home before he slowed down enough to think, and then he didn't go home after all, but turned down Third East and headed in the direction of the Park. She wasn't gone. The note hadn't been written today! It was at least a month old. She wasn't going, either, not in her weak condition, and besides, hadn't she told him only last night, when he mentioned the robbery up on Brigham Street, to take her jewels for her and put them in the restaurant safe? A woman hung on to her valuables when she was going to run off. Besides, she said that next year she wanted a carpenter to come and glass in the front porch so it would match the side porch, and a woman wouldn't do that if she was going to fly the coop. She wouldn't take any interest. He fished for the note, brought it out, read it again and looked up flabbergasted. Not only had she been going to leave him for somebody else, but she said right here, *all that is important is love*. Alma! It was practically impossible.

Joseph Morelewski had passed his forty-fifth birthday when he married Alma Carlyle. He understood women. At least, if he didn't, he was more of a dunce than he looked, for enough keys had dangled one at a time on his key ring through the years to open enough front doors on enough of the ladies' natural history to give him a pretty fair idea of the subject, the study of which he had pursued not only on their premises but on his own, under all and any circumstances and everywhere. He ought to understand them, and he did. One look at a woman and he knew what category she belonged in, as well as the butterfly expert knows whether what has alighted up ahead on the fence is an Angel Wing, a Red Admiral or a Great Sulphur.

Alma, of course, did not belong in any category, because she was his wife, and she was his wife because she did not belong in any category. To him, from the beginning, her beauty had set her apart from judgment as did something else, her uncanny resemblance to the unknown princess of his boyhood. Added to this, that he should have first beheld her wearing a crown of sovereignty in the democratic wilderness of western America and it is not to be wondered at that he needed no other sign from heaven.

When he knew that he had not so much married a spouse as got into his keeping a rare possession, like the "Virgin with the Pomegranate" by Botticelli, he did not, as he would have done a very few years before, gnash his teeth and chide cruel destiny. He sighed a little but that was all. Sooner, later, men and planets cool.

He walked more and more slowly, reading the note again and rubbing his forehead. The painted Venus does not step from the frame, the marble Psyche does not hop from the pedestal and run away with a lover. Maybe once when the world was young these fictitious fair ones had done such things but they didn't now. They stayed where they were.

Suddenly he began tearing the note into little shreds and letting them flutter off one by one. Leaving . . . love . . . lover. She had not gone. This was all that concerned him! She was not going, either, or why would she give him her jewels to take care of, why would she want the carpenter next year? She didn't say anything about the year after next, though . . . or the year after that.

He stood still, thinking.

She might take a notion, then. . . . There was no guarantee she wouldn't take another notion. . . .

He must prevent it! at any cost, put strong locks on every door and bars to every window. While there was still time he must make preparations, build a place, a stronghold in which to keep her fast. But if she wanted to get away bad enough, she would escape, no cage, no cell could restrain her. She would go. He would come home and find her gone. He considered the matter all the way down Third East to Ninth South where he turned right and went toward Main Street. But there was one kind of prison she couldn't take French leave from, one kind of barricade she could never climb over! He breathed more quickly, thinking of it. There most certainly was! her own flesh piled layer upon cloistering layer. That would hold her. Let the lovers come then. Let them! They wouldn't even know she was there. She could signal with her eyes, drop a note outside, cry out to them, do anything, and they wouldn't know. He alone would be aware of what was locked behind those deep downy walls, the tender beauty enthralled there, the slender sylph entrammeled. And that would be enough. Perhaps that would be enough after all. It was enough for the man who owned the Golden Chalice of Iona to know he owned it, though nobody saw it, hidden as it was from vandals in a dark cave, hardly himself saw it from one year's end to the other.

Teige was the man in the case, of course. Teige was the man she loved, the man who had loved her. Mr. Morelewski pondered that calmly. He must have been blind as a bat not to see what was going on under his very nose. But it did not matter. When Teige came next time, she would be inviolate, undiscernible, as buried as the dead under a mound, as lost as an unmined opal, with a wall all around her. Let him find the way to tumble that masonry. Let him try it. Just let him try. . . .

Alma Morelewski was sick in bed for three weeks before she began to mend. As the time comes when the sorely wounded can place a gingerly palm upon his satiny scar and feel no pain, so the day arrived, the hour, the moment, when she could think without wincing that her love had been unrequited. From then on, she began to look with a flicker of interest at her tray when it was placed in her lap — but no, she wasn't really hungry, or if she was, all she had to do was whisper a chaotic phrase and her hunger fled. This, composed of three words, Teige, myself, never, possibly because she had thought of it so often, gradually dulled, as a knife will dull, and finally did not cut so deep. Eventually it did not cut at all.

Whether it was the elixer, Blaud's pills or the tamarinth extract, which she was still faithfully swallowing — she could swallow anything now without distress, while at the beginning even a bite of bread gave her trouble and she would have to chew and chew until it melted quite away into saliva before she could get it down — that brought back Mrs. Morelewski's appetite, she never knew, but one of them or the combination of all three must have been responsible, for it returned as good as new or perhaps a little bit better. She did not dine at the Paris Café, being as yet too delicate, but Mr. Morelewski came home every night at six o'clock and cooked dinner for her. When they were first married, her husband's talent for cooking did not appear to her mind an aptitude of which to be very proud and she would have apologized for it more than once had the occasion arisen, but as she saw it unfold now in grandeur not previously manifest, she could not help feeling stirred. She had thought cooking was woman's work, but when it dawned on her that no woman could cook the way he did, she admired his genius more every day.

"I thought you were the one who wanted me to be thin," Alma would say when, some culinary wonder was set before her. "You're the funniest man. Here you expect me to starve for weeks and tell me what you're going to buy for me and do for me and where you're going to take me if I just have a waist this little," she put the tips of her middle fingers and thumbs together and showed him the circumference he had ordered, "and then I do what you want, and you turn right around and start feeding me like those geese you told me about in — wherever it was."

"Strasbourg," he said, laughing. "To make the pâté de foie gras. But you see, my darling, I learned my lesson. Besides, I will make a confession. You were not so beautiful, I discovered, then, as you are when you — "

"But I'm thin now," she said, putting down her fork. "I'm as thin as I was when Teige was here. Maybe not quite, but nearly, and you said just this morning that you never saw me look so beautiful! I've a good mind not to eat this at all!"

"Sweetheart!"

"Well, I have. Besides, you know I bought so many new clothes while Teige — I bought so many new clothes before I got sick — Madame Blanche fits everything so tight a person can hardly breathe anyway — and suppose I can't get into them any more?"

"What of it?"

"They cost money!"

"What of it?"

"Well, I can't throw away a whole closet full of clothes."

"Small damages to pay for the folly of us both."

"What do you mean by that remark?"

"I mean, go and buy whatever you want, when you have need, my angel."

She resolved not to have need. If her clothes became unfashionable, that was something else again, then would be time enough to replace them, not before. "Good heavens, I'm not going to turn around and get fat, don't ever think."

"Fat, thin, what does it matter?" he said soothingly.

"That's a lot different talk than last spring when you had such a fit because I couldn't get into that dress! You should have heard yourself then, how you carried on," she said. "You'd have thought I committed a crime or something! And now listen to you."

"A man learns wisdom." Slyly he helped her to another portion

231

of Parisian *Profiterolles au Amandes,* dropping a generous spoonful of whipped cream on the top.

"Anyway, I'm not going to get fat, I can tell you." She looked grimly at the pleasant sight for at least a minute before she took up her fork. "So you don't need to worry."

When he brought home the box of Schramm-Johnson's chocolates, she did not tear off the wrapping for three days. Then, in her room one day, preparing to lie down for an hour and read the October issue of *Peterson's Magazine,* she decided she would unwrap them and nibble just one. Having eaten an ample lunch, she wasn't hungry, and she had long ago lost her taste for them, she felt sure. She waited until she was on the bed with her shoes and dress off, the two pillows behind her back, before she inspected the ribbon-tied box. It was very pretty, worth saving, with a pompadoured girl in a low-necked dress on the cover, in profile, a round gilt moon behind her. The chocolates under the pressed wadding and clear tissue had a richer smell and looked bigger and brighter than usual. The O's, M's, S's and other curlicues like musical notations, bass or treble clefs, marking the top of each one, seemed to stand out in bolder relief, too. She chose the first carelessly, a melting vanilla cream with a nut in the center, the second, a thick caramel, not so carelessly, and the third, only after intent and frowning speculation. This proved to be one of her great favorites, a rough almond paste suspended in lustrous brown liquid, and she hunted quickly for another like it, having forgotten to note its identifying swirl. She tried and discarded in the old dissolute way three others before she ran across it again, observing with close attention this time the sign on top and the general size and shape so she would know it again. A prudent search, necessitating the removal of wadding, tissue and cardboard between the two layers, revealed in the bottom under a heap of tumbled chocolates two more of the same, and when she had eaten them, she pushed the box aside, got up and went to the bottom dresser drawer for a large yellow book, *The Etiquette.*

Good heavens, she thought, re-establishing herself in her soft nest, opening the book and groping for an oblong piece of candy (they were always butterscotch), my life isn't over just because of what happened. How could I have thought such a thing? She looked dreamily over the book, reflecting upon the foolish past, with a tiny smile on her lips. If she could find one of the ones with the pink coconut centers she would be glad. It seemed to have had a little O with a kind of tail on it but she might be mistaken. . . . She was not, it had, and biting into it delicately she turned to page 126 and began to read her favorite chapter: The Grand Ball.

That was the afternoon she fell into the blissful slumber of former days, the book slipping out of her grasp. She roused herself enough to pull one pillow out from under her head and push the box of chocolates away, but nervelessly and unheeding. . . . When she woke in perfect contentment an hour and a half later it was as though to see for the first time her room, how lovely it was, how many things she owned. What a fool she had been! to consider giving up all this, and not only this but what lay beyond the polished door, the house, the wide garden, the best and kindest husband who ever lived, money in the bank, a big restaurant. Why, she must have been out of her mind, but no matter. Her good angel was watching over her all the while. She stretched, turned over and slid forward, reaching for the bonbons. She would just see if she could find one of the ones with the greenish crumbling stuff inside, and then she would get up and take her bath and dress. O happiness! that need not ever pass.

Once more, at ten or ten-thirty in the morning, Alma Morelewski in her bright wrapper with her ribbons and her hair flowing, stepped into the kitchen and prepared her breakfast. Once more, the sticks of bacon sizzled, the eggs bubbled, the thick toast browned, the red and purple jelly quivered, the coffee boiled. At noon, lunch was meal enough to fill the sink with dishes. And she did not now content herself with a cup of afternoon tea and a crumb of cookie but prepared a handsome tray and carried it out to the porch or, on gray and windy autumn days when the weather was too cold, to the window seat in the dining room.

He oughtn't to do it, she said scoldingly, when Mr. Morelewski brought home another box of chocolates, another, another, another . . . she really didn't want them.

The day she could not get into the mull gown, she stopped taking the elixer, though she kept on with Blaud's pills and the tamarinth extract. An appetite was all very well but you could have too much of a good thing. She was shocked about the gray dress until she reminded herself that it was the most recent addition to her wardrobe. She could easily get into the black velvet and blond lace. Not easily, to be quite truthful, but at least it came together in front. Two days later it refused to meet, but she blamed her corset for that and yanked at her corset strings so hard that she broke one and had to sit down and thread in another pair. Maybe she would have to have all her spring and summer dresses let out a little although she hated to go to Madame Blanche and ask her to do it. The dressmaker would be sure to click her tongue and look sad, when before she had done nothing but envy and admire and say, "So slender! so graceful! so soignée!"

When she went to buy some new clothes, she did not go to Madame Blanche. Actually, she did not like her very well anyway, she was so

233

haughty, and had been going to find a new dressmaker for a long time. She went, not to a glittering establishment this time, but to a small dwelling she had often passed on Sixth East, with a sign that said "Dressmaking and Alterations" in the dining-room window. There she dealt with a large-knuckled old maid wearing glasses and a black sateen apron, Miss Peacock, who did not care whether a customer was big or little, soignée or frumpish, ordering two modest frocks, a transaction that proved extremely pleasant.

Her milliner, Colette, she had liked much better than Madame Blanche but she abandoned her also, for fear she might say something to the girls in the workroom. She might even let them peek at her through the back portières. Auerbach's had pretty hats and she was about to drop in to the millinery department when she remembered that she was acquainted with nearly everybody in the store and they might make remarks behind her back, too. Many clerks in the Z.C.M.I. knew her so she did not go there, either, but had the coachman drive her to Walker Brothers where she had never traded and where, consequently, nobody could be smart and say anything about Mrs. Morelewski.

Walker Brothers did not have very fashionable hats, but she found one that would go with the green silk Miss Peacock was making and was so pleased at finding it, and especially at being a total stranger, that she decided to trade there all the time.

Miss Peacock's dresses were all right but they didn't seem to have much style to them, even if she used the latest patterns. They didn't make much of an impression up at the restaurant. In fact, hardly a head turned any more, and sometimes it would be fifteen or twenty minutes before Mr. Morelewski complimented her on her appearance. What she was going to have to do eventually, of course, was take off some weight and go back to Madame Blanche, whether she liked her or not. Nobody else's gowns could hold a candle to hers. But that would take time and she could not face the modiste's sharp eyes before she had recovered her figure. In the meantime, why not do what Mr. Morelewski had always wanted her to do? Hire a cook and housekeeper. That way, she wouldn't have to dress up every night in Miss Peacock's dismal frocks and go uptown to the Paris Café, but could stay home. Later on, of course, when she looked like herself again and could wear something worth a second glance, she would let the cook and housekeeper go and return to the old way of living, but in the meanwhile why not try something else for a change? It might be very enjoyable, now that the weather was growing so very cold.

24

MADGE ASKED DORNEY SEVERAL TIMES IF SHE WAS quite sure she hadn't displeased Mrs. Morelewski in some way — to be let go like that, out of a clear sky — and Dorney said she couldn't think how, to save her life. Mrs. Morelewski didn't feel like going up to the restaurant every night the way she used to do and so she hired a lady who could cook as well as do the housework. That was all. She had seemed sorry to have to tell Dorney she didn't need her any more and said that sometime in the future when things got back to normal, she might have her again if she was available. "You were a very nice little Lady-in-Waiting," she said, "and if it wasn't on account of my health and needing somebody in the house all the time that can cook and take complete charge, I wouldn't let you go."

Before she left, Dorney roamed around pretending to search for a missing dustcloth but really taking leave of the parlor, the elephant-eared begonia, the dining room, hall, the familiar bedroom, the pantry and kitchen. She mounted the stairs, too, wandered into the guest room, looked all around and came out, and looked back at the doorway, imagining Mr. Desmond in it, standing there. Now when he came back, she wouldn't be here. She wished there was some way of making a mark that would be a message for him: Come and find me, don't forget me, please.

She wanted to ask the Queen for a photograph of herself wearing her crown and royal robes, but didn't, took her leave, went down the steps and then turned back. This time, having been dismissed from service and not working there any longer, she had to knock on the back door like a stranger. Not again would she open it and go right in. When Mrs. Morelewski appeared, Dorney asked her if she could have a photograph of her dressed up like a queen because that was the way she wanted to remember her, as the Queen of the Jubilee. She smiled and looked pleased but she said, "I don't know where they are right now so why don't you come back sometime and I'll be glad to give you one."

"If it wouldn't sound silly, I'd say, 'Goodbye, your Majesty,'" Dorney said shyly.

"Not goodbye, Dorney. You're coming to get the picture, and anyway you'll come and see me sometimes. You live so close." Feeling vaguely sad because a certain time had come to an end and another was beginning, Alma Morelewski thought, Maybe I could give her some of the clothes I can't wear. . . . But she decided against it because she would need them again herself.

Madge said that the least Mrs. Morelewski could have done would have been to give a person two weeks notice. That was a fine way to do! Without telling Dorney, she knocked at the Morelewskis' door a night or two after, on her way home from Judge Towers's.

The variegated porch light went on over her head and then the door opened and Mr. Morelewski said, "Good evening?"

"I'd like to talk to your missus," Madge said.

Mrs. Morelewski, when she appeared in the doorway, assured her visitor that Dorney had not done anything to displease her. The child did everything she was told, and more, too, and was just fine. Mrs. Morelewski's illness had made it necessary for her to get maturer household help, that was all, she said. Otherwise, she would have kept Dorney on, and in fact when things got back to normal she might send for her again.

Madge told Crystal about the call she had made. "My, that Mrs. Morelewski looks different," she said. "It may of been what she was wearing or not having no corset on or something, but she looks twice the size she did, it seems to me."

"How could she?" Crystal asked with great interest. "The last time I saw her, she looked *thin*, and that's only about three months ago. How could she have changed that much in that length of time? It doesn't seem possible."

"I said so from the beginning," Madge said. "You remember I did. I said at the time, when her picture come out in the paper, I said, I bet anything she'll fade quick and lose her shape. I know that kind of good looks, I said. Why, I bet when she's my age — "

"Wouldn't that be terrible?" Crystal said sadly. "Anybody as beautiful as that? Why, it would be a perfect shame!"

Clara Tofflemire got her on and Dorney went to work as a shirttail ironer for three-fifty a week in the Troy Laundry the day of the big snowstorm the first week in December. Madge let her keep a dollar fifty of her salary, but since she had bought winter clothes for her at a cost of over fifty dollars, she expected to be paid back at the rate of a dollar twenty-five a week, and Dorney was right back where she started from, with a quarter a week spending money.

She was pleased with her new clothes although they were more for use than beauty. Saturday evenings, the stores kept open until nine o'clock, and it was on a Saturday evening that she and Madge went shopping. She could have gone forever up and down the crowded streets and in and out of the bright lighted stores, but Madge knew right where to go and what to buy and in two hours they were back on the Fifth East car with their packages, riding home. Everything they bought was dark, heavy, warm and substantial, but as Madge said when Dorney got her eye on what belonged in a different category, the main thing was to guard against pneumonia and not come down sick with something that would take a lot of nursing and throw everything all out of kilter. Later on, when she had got these clothes paid for, she could buy something else, maybe pretty and light, Madge said. Dorney agreed with her but she found it was easier to do if she averted her eyes from certain objects and pretended they did not exist, like the white fur muff and blue velvet cape.

At home, the purchases looked better and Dorney, up in her room arranging and rearranging them, began to feel quite proud. How lucky she was to have such a kind sister! Right now, out in the falling snow, there were orphan girls who didn't have anything, not even a roof over their heads, and here she had all these new nice things and a good home and everything. With some embarrassment, she caught herself feeling smug for having the virtue to be thankful, almost preening because she was not without gratitude but knew how to be obliged, like Ellen Montgomery in *The Wide, Wide World*. She tried to stop it, the feeling smug, but when she did, sternly, the other thing began to go, too, the sense of indebtedness, and she had as much struggle to banish the one and keep the other as a man has to pat his head and rub his stomach at the same time. She sat down, took up one of the shoes and sniffed its newness, thinking that if you could just be good and not know it, why, then you were really good, but the minute you knew it, you weren't so good any more. The trick was not to know. Like Wanda's oldest little girl. Pearl could sing like an angel when she was out in the yard by herself playing and didn't think anybody was paying attention, but the minute she thought somebody was, she showed off and then she didn't sing half so well any more. That's the way it was with feelings of generosity, or thankfulness, or sorrow, or anything. The minute you got to noticing, then they weren't true any more, like Pearl singing to an audience. Why do we have to notice? I wish I could ask Mr. Desmond, she thought lonesomely. I wish he lived around here so I could ask him that, and a lot of other things.

On Sunday afternoon she put all the new clothes on and went clomping through the snow over to Clara Tofflemire's, to show them to her. Both she and Mrs. Tofflemire thought they were beautiful, especially the coat, and Mrs. Tofflemire said she bet it would last ten years. The lining, of course, she said, would wear out sooner but it could be replaced and then the coat would be like new again.

Clara's eyes were red, as though she had been crying, but she explained that they had been itching and she had been rubbing them and that accounted for it. There was a more eerie hush than usual in the house, and Dorney did not discover why until she observed that mother and daughter were not speaking to each other. They spoke only to her. A small white stocking with a hole in the heel hung out of Clara's work basket but Clara did not work on it or on anything else for the Mudge children. Two or three times she made a little motion toward it, but each time drew back and folded her hands in her lap.

"Well, how do you like the laundry?" Mrs. Tofflemire asked brightly, looking straight at Dorney as though she had blinders on and would not trouble to try to see to either side. "I hear tell you're a shirttail ironer."

"I like it just fine."

"How do you like Mr. Horsefeldt?"

"Well, he scares me a little bit."

"He's supposed to scare you," Clara said softly. "Because he's the boss, that's why. Bosses are supposed to scare you. That's why they're the boss in the first place."

"Some men," Mrs. Tofflemire said, pretending that nobody was in the room but the caller, "couldn't scare a fly and don't amount to *nothing*, but some *women*, they like that kind, because they can't get nobody else, and in fact they ain't got a Chinaman's chance even with *them*."

Dorney cast about desperately for a change of subject. "My, the snow looks pretty, doesn't it?" she said. "All over everything?"

"It sure does," Clara agreed, gazing straight through her mother as if she had been made of air. "It looked awful pretty a little while ago, when I was out."

Mrs. Tofflemire leaned her head on the back of her chair and stared upwards. "Some people," she philosophized, "don't like nothing better than to make fools of theirselves."

"Mrs. Tofflemire," Dorney said quickly, "did you ever happen to visit the laundry?"

"No, I never did."

"Well, it's certainly big."

"I've worked there seventeen years," Clara said, "and it don't seem big to me now."

It was nearly dark when she took her leave, but the Tofflemires' clock had said it was only four o'clock so she decided to go around by Mrs. Morelewski's house on her way home.

She turned in at the gate and went up the front walk, recalling how the white garden full of white bushes had looked in summer, and up the steps to the front door. Everything looked strange, the windows, the lace curtain she had pulled back to see Mr. Desmond and the coachman helping Mrs. Morelewski out of the carriage, the day when Crystal had come calling, the lock and the doorknob she had polished so often, the mailbox that Mr. Desmond's letter had been dropped in so long ago . . . all strange, all unfamiliar.

Not so the parlor into which Mrs. Morelewski invited her. Yet it was different, too. Dorney remembered it as rather forbiddingly elegant, but that was because she had never seen the lights turned on behind the rose-shaded lamps or a bright red fire dancing in the base burner stove. In winter, it was the coziest room in the world, which it was not in the summer. The mahogany chairs and table looked redder and the carpet yellower and bluer. An enlargement and softening had taken place, too, in the warm air and pink light — even the Queen, who had once been tight-furled was open now, widespread as a full-blown rose. She was wearing an unfamiliar wrapper of silk and lace and had tied a ribbon around her hair.

"You couldn't have come at a better time," she said. "A package came for you yesterday."

"For me?" Dorney said in disbelief, clutching the arms of her chair.

"It's out on the back porch. I'll have Mrs. Hopple get it for you." The Queen stood up. "Isn't that a funny name? But she's just wonderful. Keeps everything done up like magic — everything — and imagine, she cooks so well, it even suits my husband. Imagine. He comes home now, at night, to eat with me, and he hardly makes any changes with the dinner at all after he gets here. Of course, he tells her what he wants her to fix, so that makes some difference."

Dorney had supposed she would be an elderly woman but Mrs. Hopple, who brought in a large brown package, set it on the floor and instantly departed, proved to be as young as the Queen herself. She looked sinewy and preoccupied and there was a smudge of flour across one thick black eyebrow.

"She's wonderful," Mrs. Morelewski repeated, looking after her. "Never says boo." Then she turned back to her guest who had got up, gone over to the package, stooped down and was reading what was written on it. "You probably want to wait to get home to open it. I was saying to Mr. Morelewski, it's probably books. You remember Mr. Desmond, don't you?"

"Remember him?" Dorney turned and gazed at her former employer. "Oh, I should say I do." She thought to herself, How could anybody forget him, if they lived to be a thousand years old?

"Did you read the books he got you that day?" The Queen had

folded her arms on her breast and was softly smoothing her left shoulder with her right hand as though it had been a kitten.

"Yes, ma'am, I did," Dorney said. "But it took me quite a while because I don't have much time. I'm starting in on them all over again."

"Have you got another job?"

"Yes, ma'am. At the Palace Laundry."

"What do you do there?"

"I'm an ironer." She did not say specifically which kind. "Clara Tofflemire got me the job."

Alma Morelewski thought again of the clothes she could no longer wear. Maybe she should give them away where they would do some good — Dorney would look wonderful in the gray-green or the salmon-colored, with the sleeves lengthened and the hems let down — and not let them go to pieces in a trunk. The only trouble was, she wasn't done with them herself! not by any means. She decided not to be rash.

"Mrs. Morelewski, did you find the picture?"

"Why, yes, I did, Dorney." She bent forward and opened the drawer of the table, the slight exertion flushing her face and making her draw a short breath. "It's right here." She handed it over.

Dorney took it and looked down at it with soft eyes. "It's beautiful," she said. "Whenever I think of you, I'll always think of you looking like this."

"I didn't get to keep the robe of state, or the crown, either. I guess I told you before. They belonged to the city."

"Well, here, you got to keep them," Dorney said. "Here, you'll always be wearing them, and have this thing," she pointed to the scepter, "in your hand and you'll always be — you'll never change, or anything."

"That was taken right after the coronation," Alma Morelewski mused. "And that night was the Queen's Ball. And the next morning I could hardly open my eyes, but of course I had to, because that was the morning of the big parade. It was supposed to be over a mile long but of course me there up on the royal float I didn't have any idea how long it was. . . ."

Dorney put the photograph in her pocket. "Thank you," she said, quite soberly, as if she had been given the picture of somebody who was dead, as a keepsake. She felt that way, as if Queen Alma was as dead and buried as Queen Elizabeth.

"That package might be kind of heavy. But if you leave it, I'll see if I can't get somebody to —"

"Oh, no, it isn't heavy! Really, it doesn't weigh hardly anything!" Dorney slid her fingers in under the stout cord, lifted the box as if it had been a feather. "Really, it's *light*."

240

Before she got home she was staggering and both hands felt as if they had been sawed through. She had to set the package down on the bottom step and catch her breath before she could carry it on into the house.

He sent twenty-two books. In one, *Alice in Wonderland*, was a folded note written in large carefree black letters: "Dorney Leaf. You will read these and write and tell me what you think. Sending the 'fair copy.' Something — whatever — does not alter when it alteration finds but you will kindly keep out of the days and dust all the same. You are looking forward to birthdays fifteenth, sixteenth. Mind you grow no older until the coming of the Cocqcigrues! Then, no objection will be raised by your partisan and friend, Teige Desmond."

At first in her smarting hand and under her dazed eyes, it looked like a communication in Greek, but then it began to be more understandable, up to a certain point. Luckily, one of the books was a Webster's Dictionary and she looked up Cocqcigrues, but the word was not there. She meant to show Crystal and Madge the note, but when Crystal stopped practising and came into the kitchen she did not say anything to her about it, and when Madge came home, she did not say anything to her about it, either. Several times after, she thought she ought to show them what he had written her, but somehow, she never did.

Crystal said, taking up this book and that one and inspecting them all in her amused way, that they certainly weren't new. That was plain to be seen. And half of them were spoiled, too, by that little card pasted in. Ex libris Teige Desmond. What did that mean, anyway?

Dorney, red-cheeked, her heart beating fast for fear she could not find it, turned the pages of the dictionary unhandily and after what seemed a long while discovered it! It was actually there. "Ex libris!" she read aloud in a muffled triumphant voice. "A bookplate, often bearing the words *ex libris*, from the library of, preceding the owner's name." She put the book down, giving it the proud look a mistress bestows on her pet when it has performed some clever trick at her command.

"It seems funny he'd send a lot of second-hand books," Crystal said, unimpressed.

"College professors don't make much money," Madge explained.

"Who said so?" Crystal inquired with interest.

"I forgot to tell you," Madge said, "but just for the sake of fun, I asked Judge Towers how much they made, and he said they don't make much. An assistant professor, I told him."

"How much, Mamma, just for the sake of fun?" Crystal's look said, There, you see, Miss, but it was lost on Dorney who had taken up a book called *The Oxford Book of English Verse* and was staring at the cover as if it had diamonds and rubies imbedded in it.

"Well, he said it depended on which school, but it wasn't much, he said. A good plumber makes as much or more."

Mother and daughter cast each other a Cheshire cat glance.

"How was your famous Queen?" Madge asked indulgently.

"What?" Dorney gazed up with so blank a stare that Crystal burst out laughing.

"I asked you, how was your famous Queen?"

"Fine."

"Dressed fit to kill, was she?"

"Oh, yes."

"Put on any weight lately?"

"Oh, no. None that I could see." Dorney told these lies dauntlessly, in memory of old allegiance to a once great and fair sovereign.

"I'd like to see her when she's my age," Madge said.

"How does she like her cook?" Crystal asked.

Dorney's guilty eyes slid to the open book and an incomprehensible line of poetry, *Whan that Aprille with his shoures soote.* "She likes her fine," she said.

"How about Clara?" Madge inquired jovially. "Was she home, or was she off chasing poor little Mr. Mudge as usual?"

"Let her read, Mamma," Crystal said. "Can't you see she's too busy to talk to ordinary human beings?"

Madge glanced at the clock. "Bedtime," she said. "Five-thirty comes along very early in the morning, and I know a young lady that I had to call twice, yesterday."

Upstairs, Dorney read the note again, and again, and then once more before she blew out the lamp and climbed into her ice-cold bed. After she got warm and could stretch out, she began to answer it in her mind, in the dark. At first the words were in her best handwriting across a white page and then they turned to a stream flowing past with a murmuring sound that said: Mr. Desmond . . . I thank you . . . I don't work at the Queen's any more . . . I work in the laundry. . . . Mr. Desmond . . . I wish I could send you something to repay you. . . . I looked up Cocqcigrues in the dictionary but I couldn't find it. . . . I always wanted to have a dictionary . . . Miss Littley had one . . . even if it doesn't tell what Cocqcigrues is . . . one thing it had was ex libris and I was so glad. . . . Now, Mr. Desmond, I want to tell you that . . .

25

DORNEY ALWAYS STOPPED FOR CLARA AND WALKED
to work with her. They walked fast because it was so cold and it
would still be dark when they went up the alley and in at the back
door of the laundry at a minute or two before seven. If they had
walked just a little more slowly or turned back once to look, they
would have seen how the day followed. They saw it later, but inside the building through windows so high up in the whitewashed
walls that a tall man had to stand on tiptoes to reach the window
sills, it did not seem quite real. Even at along toward noon when a
shirttail ironer gazed hopefully up, it looked like anything but day.

The laundry's permanent smell was of wet cement, moss and
naphtha, but temporary whiffs went back and forth through this, of
boiling starch, hot linen, hot oil, hot machines, perspiration and, at
noontime, coffee, garlic in baloney and summer sausage, and un-
aired lunch boxes. It was worse to look at than smell, illuminated
by bare electric light bulbs that would put the eyes out as quick as
the sun, but that was because everything in it, including people, was
for application. Except for an escaped trill now and again of flighty
song, or snatch of female chatter cut short almost as soon as begun,
its steady noise said, Keep at it. The grumbling washers in the basement rumbled it like thunder, the wide belts clicked it like teleg-
raphy, the mangles whirred it like quail, the casters under the haystack piles of white clothes squealed it like fiends, and the light soft
flip! of the rigid collars flopping into the collar ironers' baskets told
it like the drip from a faucet. Work, for the night is coming fast.

Two stations over from Clara, who often sent her an encouraging
look, Dorney worked. The first week, a leery novice, she did not
dare to lift her eyes from her machine, for a bone-dry and ironed-
down wrinkle, she soon discovered, in a shirttail, was almost as
ineradicable as the same thing on a human countenance, but now,
with practice, she could glance around between whiles, let her mind
wander and mangle just the same.

In spite of being daubed like a Comanche with white stuff, there
was a face that was restful to the eyes over in the corner in the

hand-ironing department, and Dorney liked to look at it once in a while. It belonged to a widow named Phoebe something — Clara couldn't think of her last name because she hadn't been working very long, only five or six months — who was said to have two children. She was thirty-five or even older but she looked young. Naturally round-shouldered, her back bowed more and more as the long day wore on, though she often threw her shoulders back as if this time she was going to stand straight or know the reason why. She never did, for more than minutes, over her coffin-shaped ironing board, possibly because her spine was weak. Her back must have ached for she could be seen sometimes slipping a hand to the small of it and wincing but she smiled all the same so that her dimples flashed clear across the long room. Dorney made up her mind that as soon as gratitude and loyalty to shy Clara would allow her to stray elsewhere now and again, she wanted to know Phoebe, who had a haunting resemblance to Wanda. She wanted to be friends with her, more than anybody else, except perhaps the two Danish girls of her own age, The Giggler and Moonface, who ran the handkerchief mangles and couldn't speak a word of English.

At lunch time Clara, as she had done ever since her friend Sophie quit work to marry Joe Mudge, liked to go to the narrow bench in the quiet unoccupied corner beyond the starching department and eat there. Dorney, of course, ate with her, but she hoped gradually to persuade her to join the others who, when they brushed the crumbs off their laps and shut up their lunch boxes, took out their embroidering or crocheting and laughed and talked their heads off. So far she had never said a word about it for fear Clara would be hurt. There were two large lunch groups, either of which it would have been a pleasure to sit in with, Dorney thought. The one beside the glassed-in office room — emptied, during the noon hour, of Mr. Horsfeldt and unpopular Tamer Camomile, the black-eyed bookkeeper suspected of being responsible for many of Mr. Horsfeldt's calling-downs, a stylish girl with silk arm garters, a pompom behind either ear and a yellow pencil stuck in her round black hair — always seemed to be having the most fun. But Phoebe was in the other and so were The Giggler and Moonface, who crocheted nothing but black lace, and Dorney planned that when she could get Clara to do it, they would join that group, the one by the folding table near the stairways at the far north end of the room, at least at the beginning. Clara said that the reason it didn't seem as lively as the other bunch was because Hester Walp was in it.

During their first lunch together Clara told Dorney who everybody was and what they did. Hester Walp, she said, was a hand-ironer — you could always tell them because their faces blistered so, they had to plaster on that white paste around their noses and on their foreheads, chins and lips — it wiped right off, though — the sour-looking one with the pinched-on glasses, she was so religious and preachy and ranted such a lot against crimped bangs and everything else that every once in a while one of the girls would have to land on her hard with both feet, and then she would get mad and eat up in the ladies' toilet for two or three days by herself. Then she would come down and eat with the same bunch until somebody had to land on her again, generally old Harem Winfrey or Oda Partridge who had bad dispositions anyway. Oda — just to give you some idea — was so mad at her husband over something when he died that she wanted to have him buried twelve feet deep instead of six, but the graveyard sexton wouldn't allow it so she got mad at *him* and called him a goof and everything else she could lay her tongue to. They would have had a real set-to if some relative hadn't stepped in, softpedaled Oda and patched things up.

What made the bunch over by the office partition sound so lively, Clara said, was Lela Galloway, although the way she buckled down and worked, a person would never think she was so full of fun. The minute the twelve o'clock whistle blew, she started in cutting up and nobody could beat her for that until the whistle blew again and it was time to go back to work. Then, she shut up like a clam. She did the same kind of work that Dorney did.

Shirttail ironing was a beginner's job, but Lela liked it so well that although she had been in the laundry nearly two years, she preferred to keep it and let others in the shirt department advance as they would, to more exalted positions, such as bosom-ironing, neck- and cuffband-ironing, sleeve-ironing and finishing. Why should she worry her head over promotions? she said, when she was happy where she was. They all got paid the same! except the two foreladies, Harem Winfrey and Aurilla McCann, and who would trade places with them? except somebody not in their right minds. Lela Galloway, from Ogden, was on the slender side as to body, but she had the legs and arms of a fat woman. She was about forty and had never been married, but she did not seem in the least like an old maid. Her brother was the famous Ogden heavyweight boxer, Jib Galloway, renowned throughout Utah, who had almost got a match with Sullivan but didn't, for some reason. He lived and drank up all he made, so Lela had to support their old deaf father, a still older and deafer aunt, besides a houseful of mysterious children, four or five, by herself. The eldest was said to be big enough to care for the household, and Lela, after moving her flock to Salt Lake City, had come to work at the Palace. The children were mysterious because one time she said they belonged to a widowed brother, one time to a dead sister and one time they had been willed to her by friends, so what was true, nobody knew. When caught contradicting herself, she only laughed and went right on with what she was saying as though it did not matter in the least. She was the biggest cut-up in the laundry during the noon hour and had been embroidering on the same pillow top of brown linen with a pattern of shaded oak leaves ever since she started. It was going to be beautiful.

Clara said that eventually, after she got used to the work, the time would seem to go faster, but Dorney, three weeks after she began there, had to confess that she could not see much improvement. "The main thing is," Clara said, "not to look at the clock. Not just because Tamer Camomile tattles on people, but because that makes it even worse."

"Which do you hate the most," Dorney asked, "Morning or afternoon?"

"Well, now, that just goes to show," Clara said. "The first eight or nine years, I used to hate from seven till twelve the most and didn't so much mind the afternoons, but now I hate from one to six most, and don't so much mind the mornings. So you see a person changes."

"The afternoon is ten times the longest," Dorney said.

Stealing a glance over her shoulder into the glassed-in office to see what time it was, the thought came to her that clocks were just like the people they belonged to. Take Mrs. Diltz's, for instance. The cuckoo in it was noisy and quarrelsome and sprang out with its head feathers mussed up, looking as if it wanted to pop over and pick out one of your eyes. Or take the Queen's, all golden, with that soft tick, and the hand-painted flowers in a wreath. Or Wanda's, twinkling at you when you looked at it to see how long the cake had been baking. Possibly the very ugliest clock in the world was the one hanging on the wall high above Mr. Horsfeldt's rolltop desk. When you turned to watch it, it was watching you with a steady malevolence, swinging its long pendulum back and forth as a policeman his club when he strolls along looking for criminals. It had a slow-witted look but was not slow-witted. For example, it would say five minutes to six o'clock, time to go home — and word would come from Mr. Horsfeldt or Tamer Camomile that the clock was ten minutes, or twelve minutes, or seventeen minutes, fast! That was one of its crafty tricks. It never ran slow, to give somebody some pleasure for once, or stopped, never in its long history, though its hands would seem to point to the same identical second for minutes at a time.

The custom was, on payday, when work ceased at six o'clock, for Tamer Camomile to go from station to station and deliver the pay envelopes. But tonight (Dorney's third Saturday) a change was announced.

Tamer Camomile said they should gather together, she would call out the names and they could walk up and get their checks. Clara paled and then flushed, so reluctant was she to stand forward alone in plain sight of everybody, but when her name was announced she steeled herself and advanced bravely enough. Dorney was proud of her and gave her arm a squeeze when she came back, at which the breath went out of Clara and her face took on the relaxed glow his does who has made a difficult speech or done some other dreaded thing before an audience, and now may settle back and enjoy himself.

The envelopes were not in alphabetical order and Dorney had to wait for hers.

"Julia Mullicane."

"Oda Partridge."

"Phoebe Bannon."

So that's what that nice hand-ironer's name is, Dorney thought idly, as she watched her go up for her pay, take it and start down the long room for the stairways.

Phoebe Bannon. BANNON?

Quick as a flash Dorney was racing after her, leaving bewildered Clara behind.

"Oh, Mrs. Bannon. Wait! Wait a minute, will you?"

The woman halted and turned around, grasping the newel post. "I bet I dropped something," she said.

"I just wanted to tell you," Dorney panted, "I happened to hear what your name was back there and I wanted to ask you — you see, I knew a — Mr. Bannon one time, in Rock Springs, Wyoming — Grandpa Bannon — and I — are you any relation?"

"Well, I'm not, exactly, but my husband — he was born there — his name was Bluford Ban — "

"Blufe!" Dorney breathed, her face radiant. "Oh, I just can't believe it."

"Did you know him?" the widow asked in some surprise.

"I didn't. Not very well, that is. But Grandpa Bannon used to talk about him so much that it seemed as if I — you see, we lived right next door, and Grandpa Bannon and me, we used to be the best friends. He told me, oh, so many things, all about when he came across the plains, and all kinds of things — about Blufe and — " She moved back without being aware of it, to let Amy Unthank and four or five other women go by and came forward again, "and Butch Cassidy."

"My husband died a year and a half ago," Mrs. Bannon said quickly, putting a hand out and drawing her into the corner, so people could get past. "We was living in Star Valley at the time, but there wasn't no way to earn nothing there so I took the kids and come down here. I got a brother here, see. He's a barber. Me and

247

the kids stay with him and his wife. She looks after the kids while I work, mine and hers. She used to work here in the Palace herself one time, before she and my brother got married, and that's how I happened — "

"I just can't believe it," Dorney repeated, as though in the presence of a miracle. She couldn't take her eyes off Mrs. Bannon, who knew, who had seen and spoken to him! Why, she had been in danger of forgetting him, with Mr. Desmond, and the books, and all that, in danger of not believing in him any more, almost, and here was Mrs. Blufe Bannon, who knew him, to tell again how real he was, tell all over how Butch Cassidy was the bravest, best and boldest outlaw who ever lived! "Mrs. Bannon," she said, "please tell me. Is Butch Cassidy — "

"You know," the widow broke in, "I had the funniest kind of a feeling about you ever since you come to work here, I don't know why, like as if — I can't explain it, but it was the funniest feeling — and here it turns out you lived right next door to Blufe's folks, so no wonder. I mean, you did have some connection in a way. So no wonder." She slid a hand to the small of her back and pressed against it, biting her lip. "I wish I hadn't of said I could do hand-ironing," she added. "I'd be lots beter off on a mangle."

"Mrs. Bannon, did Butch ever — "

"I got to run now," the woman said, looking nervously around. "What's your name? Didn't I hear somebody call you Dora one time?"

"Dorney. Dorney Leaf. Mrs. Bannon — "

"Well, you and me will have to get acquainted." Mrs. Bannon lifted her wool shawl up over her head and folded it in front under her chin. "You'll have to come and see me and the kids sometime. We live on the corner of Seventh South and Second West, in a 'dobe house with a green gate in front. In fact, come tomorrow, why don't you?"

On the way home Dorney told Clara why she had run after the little hand-ironer that way and had so much to say to her. "Imagine," she said. "I've been looking over there at her and we've been smiling back and forth at each other for three weeks and it turns out she's Mrs. Bannon! Blufe's wife! Grandpa Bannon's own daughter-in-law! I just can't believe it even yet."

Clara was greatly interested, having heard several times, on the way to and from work, all about the Bannons. (But not about Butch. Whether the old cross-my-heart-and-hope-to-die promises to Grandpa Bannon were what sealed her lips even now, or whether he was more hers when she kept still about him, Dorney had never talked of Butch Cassidy to anyone). "She looked kind of afraid about something, I thought, from where I was standing," Clara ventured.

"Did you ever hear of anything so nice?" Tomorrow she would go to Mrs. Bannon's and talk about him to her heart's content. He was more real than Mr. Desmond! At least, today he was, since she had somebody to say his name to. And he would stay real, not fade into nothing. "I'd rather have met her than anybody else in the whole world."

"I thought she looked kind of afraid," Clara repeated, "some way or other."

"She was just surprised," Dorney said. "Like me."

Madge, when she came home from Judge Towers's, took the news calmly. "Them things will happen," she said, "but why should you get so excited over it? Lots of people run into people that they never any more thought of running into than fly to the moon. That ain't so unusual."

"Excited? I wish you could have seen her when she came in that door there," Crystal said. "You'd have thought she just found a million dollars!"

"Dorney is glad," Jetta said. In winter she could not swing in her swing on the porch but wandered uneasily about the kitchen, often dropping down to sit on the floor by the stove but sometimes climbing onto the deep window sill and looking out, drawing a slit to peak through in the film her breath made on the glass. "Mrs. Bannon," she added, to show the new word she had learned.

"That's right," Dorney complimented her. "But only just imagine," she said, turning to her sister. "All this time, three whole weeks, and I had no idea!"

"How come you pay so much attention to it?" Madge asked. "Was Wanda so thick with the Bannons or something?"

"Well, you see, Grandpa Bannon and I — "

"That terrible old murderer," Crystal said. "His very name makes me shudder. I couldn't sleep for a week after Aunt Wanda sent Mamma that piece out of the newspaper telling about that awful murder. Could I, Mamma?"

"Grandpa Bannon was a good old man," Dorney said, her eyes blazing. "And old Mrs. Bannon never let up on him for one minute, for years and years and years!"

Jetta pursed her little yellow lips and nodded wisely.

"Well, he didn't have to kill her, after all," Crystal protested. "After all, a person doesn't have to go around killing people."

"He didn't kill people. He only killed her! And if you'd have heard how she tormented him, you wouldn't blame him, either. So there!"

"Crystal, don't tease her," Madge said. "And Dorney, you be nice now, like a good girl." She looked at the clock. "Anyway, it's nearly bed time," she said, "and five-thirty comes along awful early in the morning."

"Not tomorrow," Dorney said. "It's Sunday."

"Sunday's the same as every other day to me," Madge said, yawning and stretching. "I got to work just the same."

"You get Wednesdays off," Crystal said touchily, as though answering a criticism. "Every day's the same as every other day, to me, around *this* town!"

"Can I go and see Mrs. Bannon tomorrow?" Dorney asked softly.

Madge smiled. "We won't make a steady thing of it," she said, "but I guess so, if you're home before dark."

Mrs. Blufe Bannon had four rooms with an outside doorway into them in the adobe house on Seventh South and Second West. She had three children, she said, but Dorney saw only one of them, a tiny thumb-sucking girl of three. The other two were playing with their cousins.

Her visitor was no more than seated before the cheerful coal fire in the grate, than Mrs. Bannon, taking a seat opposite, said breathlessly, "I wanted to explain — please don't tell anybody at the laundry about Blufe's father. Because that was such a terrible thing, him killing Blufe's mother and then doing away with himself, we don't want it to get out where it might be a detriment to the family. I ain't told the kids about it, and I ain't going to, either, if I can help it. I was afraid you was going to mention it yesterday and somebody would hear and, in fact, I was on pins and needles."

"Oh, I won't tell anybody," Dorney said. "Anybody else, I mean. I happened to tell Clara Tofflemire about it once, but she won't tell."

"Which one's she? The tall homely one you eat your lunch with?"

"She's not homely," Dorney said. "Not when you get to know her."

"Well, maybe you can kind of ask her not to spread around what you told her about what happened."

"I will," Dorney said. "But I know she wouldn't say anything anyway."

"And another thing," Mrs. Bannon said. She got up, tiptoed over and leaned against the door, but it was already shut tight. When she came back and took her seat, she spoke in a whisper. "You mentioned somebody — "

"Butch Cassidy!"

"Well, that's another thing," Mrs. Bannon said. "I don't want *that* to come out, either. My brother knows I know him, and the connection between him and Blufe — but my sister-in-law, she don't, and I don't want her to, either. Fern, her name is. Fern is goodhearted but she's one of these that would be throwing it up to the kids every day, that their dad rode with Butch Cassidy's outfit."

"I knew they were friends," Dorney said, "but I didn't know Blufe was one of the — " So that was how Grandpa Bannon had known so much about everything! she thought, because Blufe had been an outlaw, too.

"I thought Grandpa must of told you if you and him was such good friends. When you mentioned Butch Cassidy yesterday, you looked like you knew the whole story. Well, it don't matter," Mrs. Bannon said. "He's dead now, so it don't make no difference. But please don't say nothing to nobody."

Dorney's heart gave a plunge. "Dead?" she said. "Why, he just can't be! Butch *can't* be."

"Why not?" Mrs. Bannon said. "Ain't he human, like anybody else? Is he supposed to live forever?" The troubled half-angry look went off her face and she smiled. "No, he ain't dead. It was Blufe, I was talking about. The last I heard was from some friends in Star Valley that he tried to get the whole Wild Bunch to ride into Denver with him and enlist in the Army and go to war. Butch, I mean. But there wouldn't only three or four do it. That sounds like Butch all right. It sounds like something he'd do." She brooded on the straight falling snowflakes beyond the bluish window. "Blufe would sure laugh. He always used to say, 'That doggone Cassidy.'" She turned and looked at her guest. "But what do you care for, whether he's dead or not? Was you and him acquainted? Did you ever see him?"

"Yes," Dorney said, and then, "no, not actually see him. I didn't actually see him, only — " She couldn't say *only in my mind* because Mrs. Bannon might not understand how that way could be as real, almost, as seeing somebody face to face. Even now, it was. She could see him come toward her, smiling, and nobody else's face, not Mr. Desmond's himself, was clearer than that one! In fact, Mr. Desmond's was not as clear.

"In other words, you only heard Blufe's father talk about him?"

"Has he still got Little Dipper?" Dorney asked. The memory came back of how, as a child, she had got it into her head that Little Dipper was Fiji, that somehow 'Dair Yandle's black horse that was never seen or heard of again after 'Dair was shot and killed, had got into Butch's possession. I wonder how I got a notion like that in my head? She thought, that Little Dipper and Fiji were one and the same?

"Well, he won't ride nothing but a black horse and he always calls him Little Dipper, but whether it's the *same* horse as he used to have when he used to come up to Star Valley, I don't know. I don't imagine so. He rides 'em hard. Him and his boys gets their

251

horses from some rancher down in southern Utah, some foreigner that talks broken. But what I wanted to say," Mrs. Bannon said, "was, I just didn't know what to say yesterday when you come running up to me and started mentioning Blufe's father and Butch Cassidy like that, because them's the last two things I want known in this locality, as you can imagine."

She sounds just like Madge, Dorney thought sadly.

"You won't say nothing, will you?"

"I'll cross my heart and hope to die, like I used to do for Grandpa Bannon, if you want. Every time he'd go to tell me about some train holdup or some big robbery — "

"Shhh," Mrs. Bannon said, putting her finger to her lips.

" — why, I'd have to — " Dorney crossed her heart and hoped to die, to demonstrate.

Over a cup of coffee and a plate of gingersnaps, Mrs. Bannon said it seemed funny that somebody who had never seen somebody could take such a liking to somebody just from hearsay! "You *would* take a awful shine to him, though, I guess, if you seen him. Everybody does," she said. "Butch is one of these here that's just naturally the friendliest — but it ain't that, either. Not his friendliness, so much. It's just that he's — well, it's hard to explain. He's got this way with him whether he's a outlaw or not, and the minute you get around him, things start to brighten up some way. Everything starts to brighten. Whatever you got to say, he'll listen, like he takes a interest, and he does take a interest, too. You can see. Or, he'll sit back and tell something himself — and if he happened to run along for a whole hour, or even longer, it wouldn't seem like more than about five minutes."

Like Mr. Desmond, Dorney thought. It's the same way with him. "What does he talk about?" she asked.

"Oh, all kinds of things, but mostly he'll tell about different kinds of people," Mrs. Bannon said. "See, there never was nobody like Butch for getting his eye on the ones that's got something kind of out of the ordinary about 'em."

"Like how do you mean?"

"Well, like for instance some Indian, say, that can't go near a horse without sneezing himself half to death. Or, some white man that — well, that's maybe been hung and lived to tell the tale. Or, some Chinaman that's got his brother's bones stacked like a armful of kindling in the kitchen by the stove. Anybody kind of out of the ordinary."

Dorney's eyes sparkled.

"I've heard him tell — I just wish you could hear him tell about the different peculiar ones he's met. But not like people do, I wouldn't want to give you the idea, not by any means," Mrs.

Bannon said, "that ridicule and poke fun. He don't do that. He'll tell about what's out of the ordinary about people like it was wonderful, like he respects 'em because they got something different about 'em that sets 'em apart from other folks, and he even sounds like he thinks the world of 'em someway. It's hard to explain."

"I think I understand," Dorney said, "because I — "

"And then he'll sing one of his songs — "

" 'Goodbye, Old Paint,' maybe?"

Dorney was so happy to be sitting here with this woman who knew him, talking about him, that she would have felt like singing it herself if she had known the tune. "Grandpa Bannon said he liked to sing that."

"That, or 'Billy Venero,' or one of them. He don't really look like — he'll be sitting on the ground with arms around his knees, and he don't no more look like a outlaw — not like you'd imagine somebody that was running the biggest bunch of outlaws in the country would look, no more than nothing! He looks just like any cowboy! with them old dusty boots and that old dusty big hat — but his looks'll fool you. There ain't nobody quicker or tougher or that can shoot strai— but he ain't never killed nobody, that's one thing sure and certain." Mrs. Bannon handed a cookie to her three-year-old, who pulled from her mouth the thumb that had kept her quietly entertained. Before the cookie was gone she had the thumb back in and was sucking it, chewing at the same time, a dangerous-looking trick she performed expertly. "He could dance! Oh, you ought to of saw him," Mrs. Bannon said. "And he'd dance with fat old Mrs. Pingree and me and everybody, not just the young girls. I wish you could of saw him. They was crazy about him, the girls. Wherever he goes, I guess, they're always crazy about him."

"Will he ever be coming back, do you think?"

"Him? The last I heard he was down in Texas and somebody was saying he was going to stay there or go down into Mexico. Somebody was saying he's quit the outlaw game. It wouldn't surprise me none. I always had a hunch he was going to, one of these fine days. He ain't naturally — even when I was so mad at Blufe when I found out he was riding for him, rustling and raiding and all like that, I couldn't be sore at Butch. Nobody can, for very long. And one thing I will say, when I raised Cain, Butch backed me up and wouldn't let Blufe ride for him no more. Blufe was awful hurt about it but like Butch said to him, 'Blufe,' he says, 'you've made enough of a stake to do you, and a married man with a wife and kids ain't got no business taking a chance on getting himself put out of commission. No, sir,' he says. Blufe did have a stake, too," she said, "but with him being sick so long and everything — he was sick better'n two years with yellow jaundice and I don't know what all —

why, when he died and the doctor bills and funeral expenses was paid, I didn't have only just enough left to pack up the kids and come on down here to my brother's. How do you like it at the Palace?" she asked suddenly.

"Why, I — " but her fancy had carried her too far away to hear the question and Dorney, returning in some confusion to her surroundings, had to beg that it be repeated. "Mrs. Winfrey has worked there thirty years," she said in answer, "and Clara's been there almost twenty, and Amy Unthank has been there even longer. And what I don't see, I don't see how they stood it."

"To hear my sister-in-law, Fern, talk, you'd think it was wonderful. She claims how well she liked it when she used to be there before she married Ed. That's my brother. I guess I might not mind it so bad if it wasn't for my back," Mrs. Bannon said, "but I fell off a porch when I was little and to this day half the time I feel like it's going to break in two. Sometimes I just don't know whether I'm going to be able to stand it or not. But I got to work, and jobs ain't so easy to get."

"The worst thing is having to wake up when it's still pitch-black night," Dorney said, getting to her feet. "Like outside right now. Don't you think?"

"The worst thing is all of it, from beginning to end," Mrs. Bannon said. "I just don't like that laundry!"

26

ON CHRISTMAS EVE THE STORES KEPT OPEN UNTIL
ten o'clock and Clara said that then you could get everything so
cheap, they practically gave it away. That was why she was waiting
until the last minute, she said, to do her Christmas shopping. She
was so excited about it that she could hardly eat her lunch and she
kept feeling every little while in the front of her dress where she
had some bills and a handkerchief with some loose change tied in
the corner stuck down in her corset cover. Dorney was as excited,
because with the money from the Jenny Lind dish, she was going
to do her Christmas shopping, too, with Clara. Madge had given her
permission that morning. Nobody was really calm, especially from
about two o'clock on, there was a fever and a hurry in all they did,
but it was quiet, not like the tail end of Saturday, because Mr. Horsfeldt did not go out even for a breath of air on the loading platform.
He made the rounds more assiduously and often than ever, as though
tracking down the smell of smoke.

At six o'clock it was all over but there was some little delay, first,
because the announcement came that it was not really six o'clock at
all but six minutes to, and secondly, because Tamer Camomile had to
distribute, one to each employee, with the compliments of the season from Mr. A. F. Horsfeldt and the Palace Laundry, the stiff and
handsome calendars, shining with strewn-on mica, with a sort of
pasteboard pocket or bin beneath for holding odds and ends, that
were given each year. This was the prettiest ever, everybody said,
and so it was, with a glossy raised picture, half an inch deep in spots,
of a barefooted boy with fishing pole over his shoulder and a dog
bounding along at his heels.

They started off without supper, because as Clara said, why should
they waste time when they could always get a bite of something in
some restaurant or somewhere? She did not say how anxious she was
not to sit down at her mother's table with a guest — who might not
be welcome, there was no telling — and be scolded for past follies
and those to come, and Dorney did not tell Clara that Crystal would
be wild if she took company home to eat, because of Jetta, who was

255

not supposed to be seen. Each pretended that they could have invited the other to sup had they not been so eager to get uptown and agreed that much the better scheme was not to stop off anywhere beforehand. Clara wanted to carry the calendars along with them, for fear Mr. Horsfeldt and the Palace Laundry would get their feelings hurt, but Dorney ran upstairs to the ladies' room and put them on the high shelf in the corner where they would be safe until the day after Christmas. It was a good idea, for they were clumsy and might get bent, but Clara said Mamma would be disappointed as she always looked forward to the Palace's calendar to see what it would look like. However, it couldn't be helped, this year.

"Now what I'm going to buy for Georgie," she confided as they made their way in the darkness against the wind up Fourth East, holding on to each other to keep from slipping on the shoveled sidewalks and stumbling into the high snowbanks, "is a hammer and nails. His father won't let him touch *nothing* in the line of tools and he's just dying to hammer."

Dorney blew on her mittened fingers. "Oh, look," she said. "Look." She clutched Clara's arm. "There in that window! She's lighting the Christmas tree." They stood a moment and watched a dim woman set firefly after firefly alight in a pyramid shape against a long lace-curtained windowpane, dull red with lamplight, while dim children danced around her.

"Joe's going to get a tree," Clara said, ducking her head against the cold. "Me and the kids got popcorn strings all made and the kids has been cutting things out of paper. Last year he never got one because of not wanting to be reminded of Sophie. She always put this certain angel up on top and he couldn't stand it, see, to have a Christmas tree and her dead. But this year — "

"It's so pretty in there," Dorney whispered. "Look how pretty it is and warm-looking and everything. Look, they've even got a cat, up there on the window."

"But this year," Clara continued, "he said he would. He seen what me and the kids was doing — and I mentioned how nice it would be — and he kind of nodded his head, so I know he'll have a tree there tonight when we stop in. It won't take long to decorate it!"

Dorney did not know how empty she was until they got to the corner of State Street and Third South and the door of the small bakery opened and a man emerged into the street, leaving the wide-flung door to close so slowly behind him that the white-aproned woman attending the shop came forward and banged it angrily shut. That let enough smell escape, of crusty and warm, soft and icinged bakery goods to tantalize a hibernating black bear. But when they came to busy and day-bright Main Street Dorney forgot her pangs and her mouth stopped watering.

It was at Walker Brothers, in the toy department, that she noticed with astonishment and pride Clara's self-possession and her bravery in dealing with the beardless male clerk who attended them. She could say No! almost sharply when the need arose, ask questions, demur, request with hauteur (or a good imitation of the same) to be shown this or that and even turn up her nose at something she didn't like. It was remarkable.

Once only, in Auerbach's, was her newfound poise shaken, by the proximity of another shopper, a sweet-scented, veiled and velvet-hatted lady in a shining beaver cloak who coolly purchased a wax doll the size of a real girl of six or eight years for the sum of *twenty-five dollars* which she took from a beaded bag with a French kid-gloved hand. When the long wrapped box was offered to her, she declined it, motioning to a uniformed coachman already loaded down with packages to step up from behind her and take it. That performance seemed to shoo Clara back into her old shell, where she had to keep clearing her throat and could scarcely look a clerk in the eye, the same as ever. But she came forth again, composed and elevated, when she found a tool chest for George with a bent hinge in back and a sprung lock in front, otherwise perfect, that was so much of a bargain that anybody would be out of their head not to buy it! It even had an auger and a ruler shaped like a T! to say nothing of everything else, and it was marked down to almost nothing! After that *coup de maître* nothing could daunt her. The red-enameled express wagon for Alfred, which Dorney was grateful for since they could put the heavy tool chest in it and pull it along, was still a bigger bargain than George's present, Clara insisted, although of course she did not say so to the limping clerk at the Z.C.M.I. who served them. She pretended not to be very impressed and said she hadn't intended to get Alfred a wagon, fooling even Dorney, until the purchase was actually made, when she blazed out in glory like General Miles at the surrender of the Nez Percés and left the toy department so fast that Dorney had to run to keep up with her.

As good as given away though these treasures might be, they cost considerably more than Clara had intended to spend, and she had to shop long and hard for Ruby's doll as a consequence, until she found the one, almost by a miracle (at the moment Dorney was ready to sink down in the middle of the aisle with weariness and never rise again), that a series of accidents had put within reach. This vision had a missing little finger, yes, a lost shoebuckle, yes, and her wig would have to be glued down again, but she was golden-haired, her blue eyes opened and shut and she was wearing a silk dress — just what Ruby had prayed for every night since before

Thanksgiving. Clara said she would have never given up looking till she found that very doll at a price she could pay, and Dorney believed her.

They were very tired, after the long day at the laundry, the cold walk uptown and the immense shopping. They were hungry, too. Clara's legs trembled under her and the dark circles around her eyes were darker than ever. In the mirror behind the perfume counter at Auerbach's where Dorney stopped to buy a bottle of eau de cologne for Crystal, she saw that they were both as pale as linen. Neither one knew where to go to eat a bite, but Clara said that as soon as they got through with their shopping, they would see if they could find a place to have a bowl of soup. Dorney suggested that they might go into the Paris Café, she had been longing to see it, but Clara said regretfully that it would cost a fortune, and that she had heard when you went in there you had to order a whole complete meal. If Mr. Morelewski was on the premises, they wouldn't, Dorney said, because she would explain to him that they didn't want much. When they went past the restaurant she looked in the plate-glass window beyond the glazed little pig, and the plaster of Paris cornucopia spilling out its fruits including a bearded pineapple, and the vase of artificial asters, but he was nowhere to be seen. It was just as well, for Clara had gone on ahead anyway, pulling the wagon, and a quick glimpse of a fashionable late diner or two within, at pink-lamped white-clothed tables, quelled Dorney enough so that she did not persist in wanting to go in.

On Second South, just off Main Street, they saw a tiny restaurant called Ogg's Chophouse, and Clara thought that might do. They were starting for it, Dorney full of anticipation, for this would be the first time she had ever been in an eating house, when the woman accosted them. Whether she stepped out from a doorway or passed and turned to face them, they never knew, for in the midst of a rapt discussion about their purchases, they happened to glance up and see her standing in front of them.

"Please, ladies," she said.

They stopped in some surprise because she was addressing them, and looked at each other to discover whose friend she was. Nobody's! it seemed. Then they looked back at her.

"Could you give me a little something?" she said, her head quaking on her neck in a perilous way.

A beggar, Dorney thought wonderingly. A real true beggar. Somehow, she had thought a beggar would be a long-haired old man, like Little Nell's grandfather, leaning on a staff, or a thin and shivering child like Poor Little Joe in the old song, not a heavyset, middle-aged woman with rouged cheeks and beady black eyes, wearing a picture hat laden with blighted ostrich plumes, and more of the same, wilt-

ing and delapidated, wrapped around her in a boa over a tat-
tered silk dress. She seemed to be dizzy for she would no more than
take her hand away from the Commercial Building wall than she
would have to reach for it again, to steady herself.

"I've got twenty cents left," Dorney whispered. She could feel
the warm coins in her palm under her mitten. Her first beggar!
There was nothing to do but pay up.

"We don't need to eat nothing, I guess. It won't kill us to wait
till we get home," Clara whispered back. "It's bad luck to turn 'em
away, though Mamma don't think so. I've got about the same
amount or maybe a nickel more," she said. "We don't need to ride
on the streetcar, do we? It ain't far." She was feeling in under her
shawl as she spoke and soon there was a little chink of coins. "We
got nearly four bits between us, I guess," she said timidly to the
woman. With her final Christmas purchases, her new brave personality had melted away like mist and the old one had come back
again, more abject than ever.

"No more, ladies? No more?" their petitioner said.

Dorney with the forefinger and middle finger of her right hand
was raking out the money from her left glove. "Here," she said.
"Merry Christmas." She wished she could have added "my good
woman," to see how the phrase really sounded, that read so well on
the printed page.

"Here," Clara echoed.

The woman came close to them and they dropped their coins into
her hands, purple with the cold, not without flinching, for with her
creaking hair, her white bird's eyelids, and jet beads, like scales upon
her front, she looked a kind of myth, incantatory and wild.

"Come on," Clara said fearfully, tugging at Dorney's sleeve.

In the street traffic, they heard a "Whoa!" and the screech of a
wagon brake. Two gray-helmeted policemen jumped down out of
a heavy black wagon like a hearse that stopped beside the curb. They
stepped swiftly over the banked snow to the sidewalk and had the
feathered woman caught like a bird between them before she could
fly. She screamed and clawed at them.

"Now, Mary," one of the policemen said, "don't you know they're
anxious to see you down to the station house? Don't you know you
got to get your stocking hung up?"

"In a pig's eye."

"Sure, you have. Ain't Santy a-coming down the chimney tonight?"

"In a pig's eye."

"Ain't this Christmas Eve?"

"You son-of-a-bitches."

There was laughter and Dorney turned bewildered eyes to see that a crowd — not all amused for some looked sad and solemn and whispered what a shame it was, poor thing, or looked indignant and said that it wasn't any laughing matter, it was a perfect disgrace, on the public streets like this — had gathered to watch what was happening.

"Come on," Clara said in an agitated voice. "We've got to go home." She hastened around Mary and her captors, the little red express wagon rattling, and Dorney went, too, quickly.

"Ladies!" the woman called.

They kept going without looking back though Dorney wished she might have said goodbye, or some word of cheer, or that she had waved, at least.

"Ladies! Your dreams will come true!"

Whoever had laughed before in the crowd, laughed some more, while the same who had murmured, murmured, and the same who had been indignant were indignant over again.

"The two of the both of you. They will! God's truth!"

They did not slow down till they crossed State Street and started up Third South.

"She was drunk," Clara said sadly. "I might of known that if I had just used my head for one minute. But here I thought she was sick."

"Me, too," Dorney said, who would not have been coming home more affected or enkindled from a performance by Effie Ellsler of *The Noble Outcast* at the Salt Lake Theatre. "I thought so, too, when she staggered that way, and kept reaching out for something to hold on to."

"Wasn't she a sight, though?"

"All those plumes and things."

"Did you notice her eyes?"

"She gave us a blessing, Clara," Dorney said, in awe. "At least, it was nearly the same thing. That's the first time anybody ever gave me a real *blessing*, or practically the next thing to it."

"When was that?"

"Didn't you pay attention? It was when she said, 'Ladies, your dreams will come true!'"

"Oh, you call that a blessing? I can imagine how my dreams will come true," Clara said wryly. "I can just imagine. One thing, I'm glad Mamma wasn't watching out of the window at us! If we'd of waited just about a half a minute longer, and not been so quick on the give — why, we'd of had our money and could of ate a bite and rode home on the streetcar, too. Although, maybe we couldn't of got this wagon hoisted up onto it very easy," she added.

"But we wouldn't have got to see her so close and we wouldn't have had our blessing!"

The two changed sides, so as to grasp the handle of the wagon with different hands.

"Oh, well, I don't guess it makes much difference, now. I ain't so hungry but what I can wait a little longer or so tired I can't walk a few blocks."

"Me, either. And you know, I'd rather have seen her and given her my twenty cents than *not* have seen her, any day. Wouldn't you, Clara? But of course it's too bad, just the same."

"What is?"

"That somebody would be drunk like that and have to be put in jail on Christmas Eve, when people are getting ready for tomorrow and everything," empty Dorney, chilled to the bone and so weary she could hardly keep going, said. "The *fun* she's missing."

"It is too bad," Clara said primly. "But then, it's her own fault."

They heard the footsteps behind them and crowded over to the edge of the sidewalk to let the pedestrian by, but he slowed up beside them and fell into step. "Friends," he said, bobbing forward into a bow and bobbing back again straighter than ever.

"Schooner Bill!" Dorney said, feeling all at once very much better and not so tired any more. Under the corner street light she could see that he was wearing a cowboy hat and it was as if a sign had come from somewhere, a message, she could not have told how, a greeting, that lifted her heart up.

"Dorney," he said. "Clara." He was carrying a small jug under his arm with great care.

"We have been doing our Christmas shopping," Clara explained.

"Is that wagon for your kids?" He looked back at it, taking three sliding polka steps forward.

"I ain't got any kids."

"That's a nice hat," Dorney said quickly.

"Yes," he said. "Old Man Henderson, he sleeps in his."

"Somebody up at the saloon, probably." Clara explained in a soft voice. "Some man he knows."

"Old Man Henderson," he said, "that me and him had our heads together just today, and he was saying, Christmas comes but once a year. That's who."

Dorney smiled and looked at the high curved hat against the starlight.

"But when you're dead, it don't, he was saying," he added.

"Don't what?" Clara asked.

"Come but once a year! It don't come never," Schooner Bill said solemnly. "Christmas don't. So — live according. That's what Old Man Henderson says. Live according."

In front of the Mudges' gate, he carefully unstoppered his jug. "Here," he said offering it to Dorney with a low bow. "Tom AND Jerry, that Ike give me, that was left over."

She looked at Clara, who said, "A swallow can't hurt you none."

"Say, 'A health, gentlemen. Let it go round,' " Schooner Bill directed. "You're always supposed to say something like that, every time. You're supposed to drink to something."

Dorney nodded, remembering to have read that there was such a custom.

"He's learned them things up in the saloon," Clara elucidated. "That's the way the men do, I guess."

"A health, gentlemen. Let it go round," Dorney obliged, and lifted the jug to take a long swallow of pure ambrosia that fell down her gullet glacially but in her stomach turned hot as a layer of red coals, warming her cold ribs.

Schooner Bill now passed the jug to Clara. "Say, 'Here's to the land we love, and the love we land,' " he suggested. "If you want."

She paused, with it halfway to her lips. "Well — "

He lifted his cowboy hat, scratched his head and set it back on again. "Or, 'Here's to old Kentucky,' " he said, " 'the state where I was born, where the corn —' That's more of a funny one, if I could remember it."

"I thought — wouldn't something more Christmassy — ?"

" 'May the blossoms of love never be blighted, and a true-hearted young woman never be slighted,' " Schooner Bill offered after a moment's deep thought.

"Drink to that," Dorney said. "Oh, Clara, please do!"

After saying it once over to herself to be sure she got it straight, Clara did.

Then it was Schooner Bill's turn, and after he had proposed rather bewilderingly, "To Scots who hay," at least that was what it sounded like he said — and taken his swallow, he put the stopper back and pressed it in. "Christmas comes but once a year," he repeated.

"Ain't that the truth?" Clara laughed suddenly, a free, girlish laugh that rang like a bell.

Joe Mudge said that in another five minutes he would have been in bed. He brought the lamp out into the kitchen and opened the back door for them. Clara had been afraid that if they went in by the front way the children might wake up and have their surprise spoiled.

"What you got there?" the weak-chinned young man said, standing back while Clara lifted the front wheels up over the threshhold and pulled the wagon into the kitchen. "You shouldn't have got the kids nothing," he added sternly. "There wasn't no call for that."

"Where is it?" she asked in a loud whisper. "In the parlor?"

"Where's what?"

That this was the tired, hungry, white-faced woman she had seen under the streetlight on the corner but a few minutes ago, Dorney could scarcely credit, she looked so different now with her tinged cheeks and bright eyes.

"The Christmas tree," she said. "I got to trim it, unless you took a notion yourself — "

"What Christmas tree?"

"Why the kids', of course, that we made the strings out of popcorn for, and cut out all the — "

"I never got no tree." He looked sulky but at the same time injured as though accused of a crime he didn't commit. "Wait till you lose the bottom right out of your life sometime. Just wait," he said. "And then try trimming a tree and all that kind of stuff, with her angel up on top, and all, and see how you like it, once. See how easy it is to stand, once, the knife a-turning in your heart. You just try it."

Clara dropped to a chair, put her elbows on the bare kitchen table and her face in her hands. She did not say a word.

Like a man who has been injured by someone else's carelessness, Joe gazed at her sulkily, and then turned to Dorney, who had taken her own two small packages off the top of the wagon and was stuffing them in her pockets. "What's she so put out about?" he inquired.

"Come on, Clara," Dorney said softly, bending down and putting a hand on her humped shoulder. "Let's go home. You've got such lovely presents for the kids, they're not going to miss a Christmas tree! They'll be playing so hard with their toys, they won't even notice."

"Won't they, though?" Clara said in a choked voice. "Won't they! You don't know kids."

"What's she so put out about?" Joe demanded.

"Honestly, Clara, they won't even notice!"

Her pale lips shook. "The baby — Sophie — she ain't ever saw a Christmas tree in her whole life. This was going to be her first one! The kids was going to watch how she'd carry on when she spied it — and I was going to watch, too — and we was all going to — be so tickled when we seen how she — " She bent her head first and then buried it in her arms on the table. Her shoulders did not shake but Dorney knew she was crying.

"Well, God Almighty, Clara — " Joe Mudge stood looking down at her in glum disquietude. "When the bottom drops out of somebody's life, what do you expect 'em to do? Act like everything was all right again? Decorate Christmas trees and stick Sophie's angel up on top like she was — like nothing had happened?"

She stayed the way she was, without moving or answering, and Dorney wondered what to do, whether to go or stay, while she tried to feel sorry for the widower instead of wanting to hit him with a piece of stove wood.

"Why, God Almighty, Clara. A man that's been slashed to the quick, he can't turn right around and — you want to think of that, once — a man ain't made out of *iron*." He snapped first one suspender and then the other and came forward an uneasy few steps. "After all."

Dorney took hold of the handle of the wagon and pulled it a foot or two off to his right so he wouldn't bump his shins against it.

"Clara, I ain't never seen you take anything so — you're the one that's always smi — that always sees the bright — when other people are down in the dumps." He put his hand out as though he might be going to touch her, while Dorney held her breath. But he drew it back and put it to his mouth, catching his lower lip between forefinger and thumb while he looked at her as if it was beyond him, what had got into her to make her act this way. Suddenly he seemed to think of something, for he snapped his suspender as though to say, There, I've got it! and backed to the pantry. He turned on his heel and stepped into it, coming out almost instantly with something in his hands that he carried over and set down in front of her. It was a birdhouse, painted strawberry pink and green, with a steep roof and a round doorway. "Remember the one you said you thought was the prettiest that time?" he said. "Well, it's yours. It's a Christmas present, see." He put his hand out again and did not draw it back now before he had let it rest a moment on her rough knitted cap. "Ain't you even going to take a — squint at it?"

She was, she did, her head coming up off her arms the way a tree springs into being for a magician. After a long moment of seeing it like a casque of pearls, she whispered, "Why, I never expected — never dreamt — "

"This here's the one, ain't it, that you claimed you liked that time?"

"It's the one, all right."

"Well, merry Christmas, then."

She had blotted away her tears with her palms, but her eyes filled again and wetted her cheeks in an instant.

"Now quit," he said, "will you? because maybe I can scrape up a tree somewheres tomorrow before the doggone kids get up. You know, if you're so dead set on it and nothing else ain't going to suit."

"Joe — "

"A fellow ought to be able to scrape one up *somewheres*."

"Joe — "

"You claimed you liked that there birdhouse," he said severely. "Or I could of maybe made you a sewing box or something more along that line."

"I didn't need no sewing box!" She was horrified. "No more than I need a extra — I don't know what."

"Well, anyway — " He looked at her, snapped his suspender and looked away. "It's for finches," he said, "and listen, Clara, you want to try and hang it pretty high."

Jetta had been put to bed, but Crystal and Madge were still up when Dorney got home. The fire was blazing in the stove, and it did not take her long to stir up a bowl of cornmeal mush and eat it with milk and sugar, eat a piece of cold fried liver left over from supper and a piece of custard pie, too, like a starving Armenian. Something, at least after her hunger was appeased and she had got warm, made the room seem decorated and holiday-like, Dorney could not think what. Maybe Jetta's empty stocking, the end of which was weighted down by the flat-iron to keep it from slipping off the warming oven, hopefully hung by the chimney, maybe the remembrance of Clara carrying her present home all shielded and protected as if it was alive and might get cold . . . or the thought of the Christmas eggnog drunk by the Mudge's gate with Schooner Bill in the Christmas starlight . . . or there by the window the handful of holly on the top of the woodbox beside the hammer somebody had forgotten to put away . . . or, on the end of the table, the naked goose covered with bluish and human-looking gooseflesh (to be on the morrow the immemorial crisp and crackling bright brown Christmas bird, spurting like a fountain at the prick of the fork). . . . Whatever it was, something made it seem so, surely, like true and genuine Christmas that comes but once a year.

She had her foot on the stair when Crystal called to her. "This little package came for you this afternoon, Dorney! From your famous Mr. Desmond."

She hated to have to open it in the kitchen under their eyes but she found herself having to do it for courtesy's sake, with hands Crystal laughed at for being rattled, and a face whose incandescence she shook her hair around to hide.

In a blue pasteboard box it proved to be two or three quires of letter paper, some stacks of envelopes, and there was a card on top that said Best wishes to Dorney from her friend Teige Desmond. That was all. Madge said that, of course, since it was just paper, nothing else, she could keep it, but if it had been jewelry or anything valuable, it would have had to be returned.

"Jewelry?" Crystal said, looking pleased. "What do you think Mr. Desmond is, for heaven's sake? A banker?"

27

TEIGE DESMOND HAD SAID IN THE ONE AND ONLY
note he had ever written her (which he had placed in the *Alice in
Wonderland*, to be found there) that when she read the books, she
was to tell him what she thought of them, but gratitude would not
let Dorney wait that long to write. When the Christmas writing
paper came, that occasioned a second letter, and it was in this one
that she told him how she had come to leave the Queen's and go
to the Palace Laundry, where she worked on a mangle.

In March, she wrote him a third time, to say she had got through
all the books now except the one called *The Complete Shakespeare*
and was enclosing her opinions of the same as he had asked her to.
She did not stop with that, for there was much more to be said. For
one thing, she had to apologize because it took her six months to
read even that much, without counting the Shakespeare, and then,
she had to thank him once more, and then, she had to mention that
today was her fifteenth birthday!

"I did my hair up this morning," she wrote, "for the first time, so
it does not hang down any more. It makes a person's neck stiff.
Crystal made me a birthday cake but she did not put any candles on,
but I did not care. There it was on the table when I came home and
Jetta was sitting watching it. It was a marble cake, pink and black.
I think it was nice of Crystal to make it. I will take a piece to my
friend Clara Tofflemire tomorrow, that I told you about in my last
letter, and also to my friend Mrs. Bannon, that I told you about,
too. Her back pains her very much. She hurt it when she was a
little girl and it always bothers her."

Her letter was several pages long when she got through. And then
she had to tell him one more thing! about "La Belle Dame sans
Merci" in the *Oxford Book*. She had memorized it, to have something to repeat to herself while working — it made the time go faster.
She was going to commit some more to memory, she didn't know
just which ones. She had recited "La Belle Dame Sans Merci" to
Clara one morning on the way to the laundry and Clara said the
knight-at-arms sounded just like poor Joe Mudge! alone and palely

266

loitering. Of course, if he could get back on at the cabinet works, he would feel a lot better.

She ended her letter by saying that it was not dark any more, except one morning when it rained, when she and Clara went to work. It was broad daylight and everything looked so pretty. The snow was almost gone, just little patches here and there.

She wanted to sign her letter a certain way she had seen letters signed (as in *Vanity Fair*)— Yr. humble and obedient servant, but after long consideration she decided to leave the humble and the servant out, and just say: Yr. obedient Dorney Leaf.

28

WHEN DRY, WARM, LEAFY SPRING CAME, EVERY-
body, even the older women like Harem Winfrey and Aurilla Mc-
Cann, with touches of rheumatism, took their lunches outside to eat.
sitting along the wide grassy ditchbanks in front of the laundry beneath the box elder or poplar trees under the clear blue and white
sky. The foot-deep ditches that ran along both sides of every wide
street were originally for the purpose of irrigation but later there
was not much use for them, except to look at. That was use enough!
most thought, in desert country. There were those, of course, who
objected to the poll tax of three dollars levied for their upkeep,
amounting to a stiff twenty-five cents a month to be paid in cash
or in one day's labor a year (there were always little bands of men
at work on the ditches, especially in early spring and at the end of
summer, cleaning out the culverts or repairing the footbridges that
spanned the gutters, sometimes two or three a block) and said they
ought to be abolished. Many a complaint would have been forthcoming if they had been! for the ditchbanks were the playgrounds
of Salt Lake City, and had not the clear water been rippling beside,
half the attraction would have been wanting, not only in summer
when it was soft and murmured as it went, but in winter when it
froze over and made wonderful sliding places, emerald green in the
lavender daylight.

Everybody went outside the first hot day in April, and Dorney
wanted to go, too. The two Danish girls had trotted out like ponies,
and everybody was gone, even Mrs. Blufe Bannon, whose back had
ached so during the morning she had to keep wiping away beads
of sweat. She would have lain down on a bench, she said, and spent
the time that way, but Julia Mullicane, the collar starcher, said that
if she let the beneficial sun strike down on her back that would do
more good than anything.

Clara wouldn't go outside because she said everybody would be
congregated out there by and by, sitting around or strolling up and
down, all the markers and the people from upstairs and the ones
from the basement, too, the sorters, the washers, as the men who ran

the big washing machines were called, the flannel washers, the dryers and everybody, even the drivers, such of them as were about the building. "They're liable to make remarks," she said.

"What kind of remarks?"

"Really," Clara said, "you don't have to stay inside with me. Before you come to work, I used to always be by myself — after Sophie married Joe, I mean — and I didn't mind it none, honest I didn't."

"But it's so pretty outside, while in here," Dorney glanced up at the high windows, "we can't even see anything, except — "

"Except little squares of sky like quilt blocks cut up ready to sew together," Clara said, also looking up at the windows and then turning away and beginning to spread out her lunch under the naked light bulb that dangled overhead. "I know. That's why I wish you wouldn't pay no attention to me and go out with the others."

"Oh, I wouldn't leave you all by yourself, Clara." But Dorney did, when her sandwiches were eaten and the crumbs brushed off her lap, Clara threatening to be as mad as a wet hen if she did not go around the block for some fresh air at least once before the noon hour was over.

"Won't you come with me?" she pleaded as she stood up to go.

"I always stay in," Clara said.

"We can just sit on the ditchbank by ourselves. We don't need to walk in front of anybody."

"I can't."

"Please, Clara."

"I always stay in. That's easier."

"Easier than what?"

"You go, though."

"I was thinking," Dorney said, "that now that we eat lunch with the others — you were so brave about that, Clara — I was thinking that maybe you wouldn't mind doing the other things, like going outside, for instance."

"That's different. Outside there's them fresh drivers and washers and everybody — and how do I know? They might take a notion to start in and make all manner of fun."

"What over?"

"Me. How I look. How I — look, and everything."

"Oh, Clara! they wouldn't. Nobody would, because you look just as good as anybody else. In fact, better."

Dorney saw Ishmael when she stepped out onto the loading platform. He was sitting far down it, by the big double doors, with his back against the wall and his feet stretched out in front of him, reading, and he did not look up at her in the side doorway.

Clara had pointed him out to her long ago, but except for exchanging a nod and a smile with him now and then, she did not know him as yet. In winter he spent his noon hour in the basement in the corner between the warm dryer and the big tumbler, an inaccessible place.

The old gray-headed roustabout turned the page without looking up and said, "Come here."

Dorney glanced back but there was nobody behind her. There was nobody on either side of her, either. She went toward him curiously. "Were you talking to me?" she said. "Did you want to see me?"

He nodded. "Tofflemire woman came out here like a scared rabbit few months ago — says some friend of hers wants to know where to buy books, where the public library is and all that. You, wasn't it?" He squinted at her.

She nodded, putting her chin up.

"Don't believe in 'em myself," he said. "No worse folly in the world. Form of suicide. Always advise the young — get out and live, don't read — don't even learn *how*, if you can help it. Only difference between reading and drinking — reading's cheaper, unless you figure time as money. Same proposition. Got no use for 'em whatever."

"Use for what, Mr. Buckingham?"

"Books. Always advise the young — keep away from 'em. Me, I bummed my way from Bridgeport, Connecticut, to the Sacramento Valley with a hundred pounds of books on my back one time. Didn't have any better sense, then. Threw 'em to the four winds, after."

"What's that you've got in your hands right now, I'd like to know?"

"This?" Ishmael laughed. He closed the book upon his forefinger and held it up. "Well now, this is a little bit different. This is something — the *one* book, in fact — that a man can't get along without."

She stooped and read the faded gilt letters down the spine. "E-p-i-c-t-e-t-u-s. What's that?"

"All the library a man needs. Only book I ever look at any more."

"I read anything I can get hold of," Dorney said, wishing she could borrow it and wondering what Mr. Desmond would have to say about the matter.

"What for?"

"Well — you know. To learn things and to — "

"Suppose you were wise. What good would it do you? I'm wise, and look at me."

She thought a moment, biting her lip. "Well — for one thing — I'd know what to say to Clara."

"Say to Clara about what?"

"You see, she doesn't want to — she thinks people — today, for

270

instance. Everybody's out around in front along the ditchbank, but Clara, she stays upstairs there and won't come down for fear somebody might make fun or — she thinks she's homely, you see."

"She *is* homely," Ishmael said cordially. "About as homely as they come."

"She is not!"

"Well, no, maybe she isn't. I'm thinking about Hester Walp, maybe. Ashamed of her looks, you say? Shy over that?"

"I guess so. If only there was some way to make her not mind, and not pay any attention."

"How about this?" Ishmael said, thumbing through Epictetus for the place he wanted, finding it and flattening the book with his hand. "Something like this. Wouldn't this straighten her out?" He began to read:

" 'What then makes a man beautiful? Is it on the same principle that a dog or a horse is beautiful?'

" 'The same.'

" 'What is it, then, that makes a dog beautiful?'

" 'That excellence which belongs to a dog.'

" 'What then a horse?'

" 'The excellence of a horse.'

" 'What then a man? Must it not be the excellence belonging to a man? If, therefore, you would appear beautiful, strive for human excellence.' "

"Well — " Dorney said softly, frowning a little, "I'm not quite sure whether — She might think you were hinting she looks like a horse."

"Maybe the simplest would be just to give her some remedy from old Albertus Magnus. How to make the ugly beautiful. Take the eggs of a raven, boil them hard, put them back in the nest where you found them. Mother Raven will come home, discover the catastrophe, fly across the ocean for a certain flat stone which she will fly back with to lay over these eggs, to soften them again. Then, all you have to do it to sneak up and take this stone, crush it, grind it to powder, mix it with — " he stopped. "Don't look like today was the Fourth of July. It's not. You don't imagine that stuff will work, do you?"

"Oh, wouldn't people be happy!"

"Wouldn't they be miserable, you mean."

Ishmael got to his feet, stuffed his book in his back pocket and started off. "Come on," he said, over his shoulder.

Dorney scrambled up and ran after him. "Where are you going?"

"Listen," he said. "You go on back upstairs, and in a minute I'll come up, accidently like. And I'll tell that Tofflemire woman a little story."

271

"Yes, sir, ladies," he said, hoisting himself farther back on the folding table, crossing his legs and hooking his hands around one knee, "this all happened a long, long time ago. It's about a beautiful princess in a castle, naturally, like all good stories are, that are worth the paper they're written on or the breath it takes to tell 'em. This beautiful princess," he said, "had a cruel stepmother, and a flock of cruel stepsisters — always had had, ever since she was a babe in arms. Her father, the King, was never home. Well, sir, this cruel stepmother and these cruel stepsisters did nothing from morning till night only to tell this beautiful princess that she was the most awful-looking sight on the face of the earth. The servants were trained to do the same thing. So that's all she ever heard. 'You're a fright,' they said over and over. 'You're the homeliest creature on the face of the earth.' Well, the beautiful princess, in spite of mirrors and her own two dapper eyes, she believed them, and she crawled and she slunk and she hid and there was nothing she liked so well as to stay in her darkened room and only come out by nightfall. Did you ever hear this story before?" Ishmael demanded.

"No," Clara said nervously.

"Never," Dorney said.

"Well, it's Gospel truth." Ishmael pulled the long lobe of his ear. "So, anyway, all of a sudden who should arrive on the premises but a handsome young prince! She saw him and of course she fell desperately in love with him but she stayed under cover. That night when it was all dark, only moonlight all over everything, the beautiful princess slipped out onto the parapet and there she stole up and down for her evening constitutional like a pickpocket afraid of the police. She was quite muffled up in shawls and one thing and another, but in spite of this, the prince was watching from the windows of the guest chamber and he saw she was a sight for sore eyes such as he had never seen in his life before. By daylight, as she lay asleep, he made sure of it by pussyfooting into her room and looking at her. The way he said Oh! and Ah! woke her up. He fell to his knees and begged her to be his bride. She cried and shook her head. 'Why not?' he pleaded. 'Because you are the handsomest man ever to draw the breath of life,' she said, 'but look at me.' 'You?' he said. He was astonished. 'Why, you are the most glorious princess in the whole wide world. Look, only look,' he said, taking her by the hand and leading her to the mirror, 'all I ask is that you look at yourself.' 'I have,' she said sadly, 'many times.' 'And what did you see?' 'I saw what I see now, a monster, an eyesore.' Beg as he would, she turned him down because she had been so long coerced and deceived that it was a habit she could not break. She thought she was too homely to be his bride, and so she sent him away!"

"She must of been a half-wit," Clara said sharply. "Anybody knows how they look!"

"You think so?" Ishmael said. "Well, you may possibly be very much mistaken. I haven't come to the end of my story yet."

Dorney silently hoped that it would improve.

"No, indeed," Ishmael said, "I haven't come to the end of it. Not by any means. Because you see, there's another princess in it. This one," he said, "was without a doubt the most hideous creature ever seen. Her eyes were — her hair — her nose — but I won't describe her, because I'm not capable of it. I haven't got the vocabulary. She was a terror, though, that's all I can say. But what should she have but a papa and a mamma and a big bunch of brothers and sisters who told her, one or the other of 'em every minute of the day from the time she got up in the morning till she went to bed at night, how beautiful she was and what a treasure she was, and they never told her anything else, never, from babyhood on. The servants, too — they had their orders. Well, sir," Ishmael said, "this terrible-looking princess, in spite of mirrors and her own two amphibious eyes, believed them, and you should have seen how she went around! Like Napoleon, like Sullivan, like — I don't know who all. Head up in the air! Back straight as a string! Bold as brass."

"She got took down a notch, I'll bet," Clara said severely.

"You think so? Listen," Ishmael said. "This same prince came there to the castle where she lived. She saw him, she loved him — all the ladies loved him the minute they saw him, you understand — and she wanted to marry him. 'Why, I wouldn't have you, if you were made out of solid diamonds,' he said — he was horrified at the very thought — 'for you are the homeliest creature I have ever laid eyes on. Come,' he said, unwilling to touch her hand but picking up an end of her sash and using it to lead her to the mirror, 'only look in there and you will plainly see why I cannot bear the sight of you!' 'Cannot bear the sight of me?' this princess said. 'I do not comprehend.' She looked at herself up and down in the glass, as puzzled as could be. 'What do you see?' the prince asked curiously. 'See?' she said. 'Why, what I have always seen, of course — a raving, tearing beauty.' "

"So then what happened?" Dorney ventured after a few moments of silence so profound that the dishonest clock above Mr. Horsfeldt's rolltop desk could be heard ticking. "How did it end?"

"It didn't," Ishmael said. "The beautiful princess went on imagining she was homely and the ugly princess went on imagining she was beautiful until the cows came home — it's all habit, you see, and all chimera — and the prince continued his travels until he wound up marrying a woman who imagined she was the best cook and

273

housekeeper in all the Middle West, with whom he imagined he lived happily ever after."

"How about the homely ones who imagine they're homely and the beautiful ones who imagine they're beautiful? How about the beautiful who imagine they're beautiful and then get old and ugly and don't know it? Or the homely who get beautiful all of a sudden for some reason and don't ever find out?" Dorney asked breathlessly. "And how about —"

"The mind, the mind," Ishmael said, tapping his forehead. "Right in here, the whole kaboodle, space not any bigger than a teacup, whole blame thing."

"Well, thank you," Dorney said. She was smiling when she turned to Clara.

"Let's go outside and sit on the ditchbank, shall we? or walk around the block?"

"It's all very well to talk," Clara said, but she got to her feet and reached for her shawl.

"You don't need it," Dorney whispered.

"Maybe I don't," Clara said. "Maybe I really don't." She looked at it thoughtfully.

"Listen," Ishmael said. He took his book out of his pocket and opened to the page he wanted at the first try. He read:

"'Conduct me, Zeus, and thou, O Destiny . . . Wherever your decrees have fixed my lot . . . I follow cheerfully; and, did I not . . . wicked and wretched, I must follow still!'"

"It's all very well to talk," Clara repeated, but her eyes had begun to brighten and her chin had come up an inch or two.

"And listen," Ishmael went on, "to this! 'When we are invited to an entertainment we take what we find; and if any one should bid the master of the house set fish or sweets before him, he would be thought absurd. Yet in the world we ask the Gods for what they do not give us; and that though there are so many things which they have given us.' How did you like my story?" he inquired, putting *Epictetus* back into his pocket.

"Fine," Clara said.

"Oh, fine," Dorney told him. "Did you read it somewhere or did you make it up yourself?"

"Come on," he said. "I'll walk as far as the platform with you."

"A little sun wouldn't hurt you," Clara said timidly, "any more than it would hurt us. You're welcome to come with us."

Ishmael shook his head. "I'd get sunstroke sure," he said, winking at Dorney. "Never go near the sun when I can help it."

"It's all your imagination," Clara said, as the three started for the door.

Dorney shot him a grateful look.

274

"Think so?" Ishmael said.

"Why, sure. The only kind of people that the sun hurts is albinos, and you're not an albino, are you?"

"Not that I know of."

"Then what are you afraid of a little sunshine for?"

"There you are," Ishmael said. "Imagination. Waly, waly, woe is us!"

29

IN THE HOTEL ROOM, THE TALL TEXAN GOT UP from his seat on the edge of the bed and went over to the little writing desk, opened the drawers one after another, and looked into them. "Somebody's left a whole outfit here for writing letters — pens, and a bottle of ink and everything." He held it to the light and squinted at it. "Black," he said. "I never thought to look in here yesterday, did you? That being the case, I guess I'll write me a bunch of letters. Why not? Instead of just sitting around."

"Who to?" Butch said idly. He was sitting on the wide window-sill in his striped shirtsleeves looking down on State Street. A sweatered young man rode his bicycle between a butcher's wagon and a fancy rig and Butch's eyes followed him to a dangerous left-hand turn on Third South. He said, "Whew!" when he disappeared from sight. "Them guys sure take chances." He stood up to lean out the window so he could look farther up the street and the dusty lace curtain looped up over the famous picture of Washington (the one where his nose looks like it belongs to a jack-o'-lantern) sagged down on him. He tried to shrug it off the back of his neck, then drew his head in and stepped back to loop up the drapery still higher. "B-o-h-e- something," he said, leaning out again. "B-o-h-e."

"What you trying to do? Fall out on the pavement and bust open your head?" the Tall Texan said, making a dive for Butch's new suspenders.

"I was just trying to see what that sign says, plastered up there on the corner of the Salt Lake Theatre."

The Tall Texan pushed him back from the window and he too tried to read the playbill, leaning out so far that Butch made the same kind of grab for him.

"Now who's falling out on the pavement and busting open their head?"

"Damned if I can make it out, only them four first letters." Kilpatrick said, bringing his head back in. He wiped his perspiring face leaving a smudge over his eyebrow. "We going to the show tonight?" He went back to the desk and took the chair beside it,

276

tipping himself back until his head touched the wall and hooking his heels over the middle rung of the chair.

"We're going someplace," Butch promised. "That is, if you don't write no letters."

"How do you expect a guy to keep up with his correspondence?"

"Who with?"

"Well, for one, with a girl in Abilene I met one time. That is, she was more of a woman — had one of these — general delivery, I can send it. Flossie, her name was. Bryant or some such name. Ryan, that was it."

Butch sat down on the bed and fished in his left-hand shirt pocket for the package of tailor-made cigarettes, shook one out and stuck it between his lips. "She must of made quite a deep imprint on you," he said, scraping a match alight with his thumbnail.

"Oh, she did," the Tall Texan said, going through the same motions and flipping his blackened match out through the open window. "She sure did. And then there's one or two others — Thelma — no, Velma — "

"No letters," Butch said gently.

"Why not?"

"For the simple reason, that when it comes to the ladies — well, you've heard tell of this guy Samson that some woman cut off his hair and he got weak as a cat — couldn't so much as lift his hat no more, ain't you?"

"You think I'd tell 'em about what we was doing up around Wilcox, Wyoming, two weeks ago tonight."

Butch blew a ring of smoke into the hot motionless air. "You can tell 'em all the news you got to tell 'em, when you see 'em."

Kilpatrick looked defiant a moment or two and then his face changed.

"Yeah, I guess I can, at that. Save myself a little trouble." He let down the two front legs of his chair and edged it forward so he could tip it back at a still more perilous angle. It squeaked alarmingly as he settled himself into it. "Wasn't that old moonlight bright, though?" he said reminiscently. "And didn't that old Overland Flyer pretty near double up on herself coming to such a quick stop when she seen our red lantern on the tracks? I'll never forget the fireman's face. We done all right, didn't we? Thirty thousand dollars for only one night's work and only five of us to share and share alike. Too bad that expressman wouldn't open the safe and we had to blast it open like that. Wasn't that a sight when all that paper money and all them bonds come a-floating down out of space like a regular snowstorm?"

"Deaf Charley thought we'd blew somebody to kingdom come for a minute there, and I did, too, when I seen — "

"You mean all the blood." The Tall Texan threw back his head and laughed.

"It sure as hell looked like it, didn't it? Didn't it, though? I thought — my God."

"But all it was was a little old shipment of raspberries." Kilpatrick's face sobered. "Wasn't that pretty early for raspberries?" he asked.

"June second?"

"Wasn't it?"

"All I know is, they was ripe. They sure looked redder'n life blood anyway after the blast went off. Give me quite a jolt there for a minute."

"Me too."

"Neibauer was sure surprised to see us, wasn't he? He thought we was still down in Texas."

"This judge you're going to see — he's a guy Neibauer knows is all right? He won't try no funny stuff?"

"Judge Towers?"

"Too bad he wasn't home last night."

"He'll be back tomorrow or next day, according to that woman that come to the door when I knocked."

"You think it's going to do any good?"

"What is?"

"This amnesty business. Is there honest to God such a thing?"

"Ain't you heard tell of it before? I have."

"Maybe if that Judge Towers can work out a proposition like that for you, maybe he can work out a proposition like that for me," the Texan said.

"First time I heard tell of you wanting to try the straight and narrow!"

"Try anything once. Even getting married someday, maybe."

"What I'd do, if there was anything to it, I'd get me a little ranch right down in Circle Valley," Butch said, musingly, "or else — "

"You figure a guy can ever go back to where he started from?"

"He don't never know . . . till he tries it."

"Funny how a guy *wants* to go back, after he couldn't get away fast enough. How come, do you think?"

"Born that way — don't know what else." Butch leaned back and put one of the limp pillows under his neck. "I'm kind of anxious to get it over with now," he said.

"Get what over with?"

"This confab with this friend of Neibauer's, this judge. Wouldn't you know he'd be gone off to Denver?"

"You was right when you figured how none of them Wyoming posses or Pinkerton's men or nobody would think we'd head for a big town like Salt Lake. Nobody has paid us no attention. Too bad

278

Elza Lay and old Deaf Charley and Sundance Kid wouldn't come along but made for the Roost instead. They'd of had a right good time." Kilpatrick looked wistful. "That is, they would, if you'd let a guy strike up a acquaintance with one of them nice girls like I seen up on Commercial Street yesterday. The one in the green hat."

"Not this trip."

"Or have a friendly little game with somebody, or get a kind of a little edge on, to celebrate, like."

"Tell you what we'll do," Butch said. "We'll maybe go to the Salt Lake Theatre tonight. We'll — " He stopped and sat up, cupping a hand around his ear. "What's that? Don't that sound like a Fourth of July band?"

"It sure as hell does." Kilpatrick leaped from his chair and rushed to the window to look out. "Maybe there's a circus come to town!"

"I don't see nothing yet — " Butch had gone to the other window, but it stuck some inches from the bottom and he could not get his head out.

"The people is all looking in that direction." He pointed down towards Third South, "so it's coming up that way. And see them kids a-running."

"Here they come!" the Tall Texan shouted, hopping from one foot to the other. Butch rushed to join him and together they shared the sooty windowsill, both leaning far out. "Look at that high-stepping fella in the swallow-tailed coat — look at them gold teeth a-shining!"

"Look at that little guy playing that horn with the glasses down on the end of his nose and his head held back so's they won't fall off!"

"Doctor Ferdon's Grand Free Attraction," the Tall Texan read aloud as the big banner went by, skipping the words he couldn't pronounce. "Big Show Tonight. Eight P.M. Ferdon's Herbal World Beater Tonic. Ten Big Acts. Ten. Murdo, the Magician, Mademoiselle Flowerdew, the Minstrel Seven, Snelgrove the Mighty — Hey, Butch."

"What?"

"Let's us go to this here instead, shall we?"

"Instead of the Salt Lake Theatre?"

"Hey, look at them *ladies*."

"Well, well."

They leaned out farther and waved and beamed, catching the roving eye of first one pink-and-white-faced black-eyebrowed woman and then another, crowded facing each other in the dusty barouche with the top folded back, three to a seat, corseted within an inch of their lives, elegantly holding up on slender necks their heads under great cushions of hair on which rode hats with crowns big enough to fit down over prize-winning pumpkins, and fruit, flower and feather trimming enough to keep a milliner in business six months — hats for giantesses.

"We got to go see that show, Butch!"

The women looked up and waved wispy handkerchiefs with kid-gloved fingerless little paws. They smiled, made a remark or two to each other, laughed, looked back up, and there was a glitter across them in the blazing sunshine, as though they had been rained on with bits of a broken mirror, or glass, or pure diamonds, and their colors had a wet glisten.

"Did you ever — ?" The Tall Texan breathed in awe.

"Hey, look!" Butch said. "Look what's coming now, back of them darkies with the big bowties. That fellow there, breathing out fire. Look at him, Kilpatrick, if you want to see something."

"Did you ever in your life — ?"

Butch made a grab that kept his dazed companion from tumbling out of the window. "Must be Murdo, the magician, or whatever the banner said his name was."

"Who must be?"

"You've saw all there is to see about them ladies, you big long limber lunkhead," Butch said sternly. "Now look at the rest of the parade. That guy breathing out fire, I'm talking about."

"Breathing out what?"

"Fire, damn it. All you can see of him is his back, now! Right up there, in the purple coat. Why didn't you look when you had a chance?"

"I seen him. What do you think I am? Blind?"

"How does he do it, you figure?"

"Do what?" Kilpatrick leaned forward again and craned his neck, trying to follow the maidens in the barouche around the corner like a human periscope.

"Breathe out fire like that?"

"Fire? Who's on fire?"

"A big lubbering Texan," Butch said, starting for the pitcher of water on the washstand. "But his flames is about to be renched, drenched and quenched."

Mrs. Luby was standing out in front of her gate when Dorney and Clara came down Sixth East on their way home from the laundry.

"You girls about cook today, did you?" she asked cheerfully, wiping her own perspiring face with her apron. "Sure was a scorcher. I'm out here calling Thornton in to supper. He's off playing someplace. THORNTON!" Dorney gave a start and clutched the arm of her companion, who, being Mrs. Luby's neighbor and long familiar with her clarion calls, remained unaffected by the yell that could have been heard in the middle of Liberty Park.

"Here he comes." A blur whizzed through the hedge, across the yard and around the house. "I knew he wasn't far. Tonight, that is. Sometimes I'll have to scream my lungs out. But I knew he was close around tonight. Promised the kids I'd take 'em to the big medicine show up on Fourth South. You been hearing about it, of course?"

"Hearing about it?" Clara said. "Till we was green in the face, that's all."

"All during the noon hour," Dorney said. "Everybody was talking about it."

"I'd like to get some of that medicine that man sells and see if it would help Mamma's dizziness," Clara said. "She keeps getting dizzy."

"Well, why don't you girls come and walk along with me?" Mrs. Luby inquired. "A friend of mine come to see me today. She went to it last night. Claimed it was the best show she ever seen in her life! She laughed so hard when she was telling me, I thought she was going to go into convulsions — them minstrels — and that woman dressed up like a little girl and singing that song. It ain't only funny, see, either. There's this man gives this lecture about what ails people — and there's these tapeworms in these big bottles and everything. And a real human skeleton, from a actual person, not imitation or nothing. It really lived at one time, but I don't know if they can tell whether it was a man or a women."

"I'd just love to go," Dorney exclaimed, clasping her hands together. "Wouldn't you, Clara?"

"I sure would."

"Say, Clara." Mrs. Luby was eying her. "I've been meaning to mention — you look like you feel real good these days, for a change."

"Oh, I do!"

"I mean, like you've been laying around drinking eggnogs and maybe went to work and put on a little weight or something. Your color ain't so peaked no more. You look — different, somehow."

Dorney looked at her friend proudly. Not only did Clara look different, she was different. At the noon hour, now, she went outside when everybody else went outside, and sat on the ditchbanks and ate her lunch. Afterward, she was willing to sit and chat or stroll up and down quite freely, without her shawl. Ishmael thought his story and what he had read out of his book were responsible for the change, but he didn't know what else had happened, planting Clara on a peach-colored cloud from which she had not as yet descended though weeks had gone by since the momentous occurrence.

Joe Mudge had called her honey! When she told Dorney, in strictest confidence, she said that she wasn't taking this at face value by any means — it was very likely an accident, maybe he didn't even know he had said it, it was easy for a word to slip out and a person not know it — but he *had* said it, in perfectly plain English. The way it had happened was this. She had gone over, as usual, after supper, mended some pants, baked up a batch of oatmeal cookies, bathed Sophie, got all four kids to bed and was just going to take her leave — when Joe stuck his head in at the back door and asked her whether she would mind giving him a hand out in the shop. He was changing things around and he wanted a little help in moving his work bench. That is, it had to be lifted, not pushed, so as not to disturb some other things — and Clara was maneuvered into the corner where the roof slanted down and where that shelf was hung on the wall — and she had stooped forward and was straightening up when he hollered, "Look out, honey! You'll bang your head!" and sure enough she did, he spoke too late, and she went ahead and banged it — but she didn't even feel it! "I never felt a thing!" she told Dorney. It was after that that the real change took place.

Ishmael gave himself and Epictetus the credit and Dorney did not argue with him but privately she thought that Joe Mudge's one word had more to do with it than all the wisdom and philosophy in the world put together. She had every hope that it had not slipped out unnoticed by the speaker and that it would again drop from his lips. What would not Clara transform to then, if it did, or if that pearl of pearls rolled out — darling?

"What time is the performance?" Clara asked.

"Eight o'clock," Mrs. Luby said, "but I figure we'd ought to go soon after seven if we want to get a standing place close up to the platform. I like to know what I'm looking at."

Crystal said that her mother would be very mad if Dorney went traipsing off to a medicine show without asking. It was just as low and vulgar as could be and nothing but the riffraff went to it. Dorney said that Clara and Mrs. Luby weren't riffraff and that she was going with them.

"Well, I'd hate to be you when Mamma finds out about it," Crystal said. "That's all I can say."

"I'll bet she won't care."

"Won't she, though! Won't she!"

So ominous did she sound that Dorney almost grew fainthearted but then she remembered what had been said at the laundry about the show, and how Mrs. Luby's friend had laughed so hard she almost went unconscious. The more she remembered the more she longed to see the Grand Free Attractions and by seven o'clock she had changed into the white graduation dress, tied a length of pink sash tightly around her waist, rubbed the toes of her shoes, brushed her hair, put on her old hat and was ready to start.

Jetta whimpered a little to go along. "I don't get much pleasure out of life. . . ."

"What would it hurt?" Dorney couldn't help asking Crystal. "Nobody knows me, or her, either, and they say it's dark out in the audience. Nobody would see us. She could just stand there and watch the show like everybody else. I'd hold tight to her hand. Nobody knows us. Nobody would see."

"You can cause," Crystal said with blazing eyes, "all the trouble you want to for *yourself* by going to a low, vulgar, silly, foolish, free medicine show if you want — but when you start trying to cause trouble for me — "

"I'm only saying — "

"It looks like you would have learned your lesson about Jetta long before this! You know what Mamma said when you took her out around the block that time."

"But, Crystal — "

"Show," Jetta pleaded in a chant. "Show, show."

"You know very well, missy."

"It's too bad all three of us can't go together," Dorney said wistfully, "like — relations, and friends." She turned to Jetta. "Don't feel bad," she said. "I'll tell you about it when I come home, if you're still up, or tomorrow. How it was and everything."

Crystal spoke to the ceiling. "It can't last forever," she said. "It'll all be over *sometime*."

"Story," Jetta said, solaced.

"That's right. About the medicine show."

"Surely," Crystal continued, "it will. *Surely*. While I'm still young. Before I'm an old woman and dead."

Mrs. Luby was glad to see Dorney and said she hoped Clara would be able to go, too, but very likely she wouldn't. Old Mrs. Tofflemire would probably put the kibosh on it some way. To their surprise, when they reached the Tofflemire gate, before Mrs. Luby had time to send Althea around the house for her, Clara was discovered to be just running down the front steps, girlishly, with a flower-laden hat on and her hair quite loose and pretty around her face. Rupert padded after her. "You go back," she ordered firmly, turning around and stomping her foot.

"Let him come, too! Let him come, too!" Thornton and Althea begged, leaping like Comanches, while small and tottering Herman tugged at his mother's hand to get free and make for the big dog. "Yes, let him, why not?" Mrs. Luby said. "Ain't there a saying that a cat can look at a king? So, why can't a dog look at a medicine show?"

"Oh, he's got to stay with Mamma," Clara maintained, and stomped again, pointing, pointing once more with such emphasis that her long hand creaked.

"What for?"

"Why, to protect her."

Mrs. Luby shrugged.

"Rupert ain't got no *teeth*," Althea argued plaintively.

"No, but he can bark." This time Clara's stomp told Rupert she meant business and he turned and padded up the walk without looking back, not humbled or obliged but with his nose up in the air as if it was his own idea not to depart from here. He lay down before the front door and put his head between his paws, ignoring all of them at the gate. Thornton called softly, "Rupert! Here, Rupert!" as they started off, but his mother made him stop it with a gentle box to the side of his head.

Clara said, as they came up Seventh South, that she would just run in and find out if Joe Mudge and the children wanted to come along with them! Would the Lubys and Dorney mind? "No, indeed, if it don't take all night," Mrs. Luby muttered under her breath. But she needn't have worried. Clara must have been over earlier in the evening to warn them, because she had no more than run up the front steps and knocked on the door when out streamed — washed, brushed, in their best clothes, hats on, eyes straight ahead — Alfred, Ruby, George — and, behind them, with baby Sophie in his arms, the young widower Joe Mudge himself.

Both Mrs. Luby and Dorney, singly and in concert, tried to manage things so that Clara and Joe would have to walk with each other, but there were seven kaleidescopic children to see to, five on foot. To their dismay, when the procession took final shape and got under way, Joe Mudge bore Mrs. Luby company, flanked by little Alfred; overjoyed Clara walked ahead between Thornton Luby and Georgie Mudge; and Dorney, at the rear, was accompanied by Althea Luby and Ruby Mudge. Two or three times during the walk, Mrs. Luby, a born matchmaker hating to waste that sentimental hour of evening when the stars popped like popcorn one by one and the air was the color of a strawberry fizz, tried to remedy this regrettable state of affairs — to no avail. They stayed apart. However, she did not feel discouraged, as she said later.

Dorney did not, either. For the first time she had the feeling that Clara might really have a chance with Joe Mudge. Wasn't he shaved as slick as a whistle? Wasn't he wearing a straw hat? Didn't he have his white shirt on? Wasn't he — one might almost say — escorting Clara to the medicine show? whether they walked together or not. It was as exciting as when, at a race, the slowest horse inches forward, inches forward, ahead of this one, that one, and all of a sudden there it is! Out in the lead. Clara might win, after all. If they get married, I won't just put in with the Palace Laundry collection, Dorney thought. I'll buy her a present all to herself. Suddenly, she wanted to skip, as Althea and Ruby were doing every once in a while, because to see a life's dream *that* close to coming true must make anybody want to give some little demonstration.

Dr. Ferdon and his outfit had landed on an empty lot on a corner of Fourth South and Third East. It was a soft place to the shoe soles for it had been weeded and worked over with rake and hoe and left dusty and deep. All the weeds had been burned in big piles days before, but there was a faint smell of smoke upon the air yet that reminded and saddened until one bethought oneself: 'Tis but grassy summer; winter, and death, are far from here. The big tent was pitched on the lot as the monogram is stitched to the handkerchief, in one corner, and this was cut diagonally across by the platform on which the Grand Free Attractions were shown. Lit by flaring gasoline torches, it was as bright as day, buoyant and island-like, seeming to float upon the surrounding darkness. Behind this stage hung a backdrop, a yellow canvas curtain that rippled like muscles when somebody walked behind it, on which a red, green and blue sentiment painted in white-edged baroque letters declared that Dr. Ferdon's Herbal World Beater Tonic was a Chalybeate and Corroborant Catholicon! Corrective and Cleansing! with Help for All! These words hovered above the life-size figures of a burnt orange Indian and a spirit-white white man reaching across a platterlike blue lake, some stretches of lilac desert, a bright green mountain nightcapped with snow and a drift of florid sky, to shake hands. The paint was somewhat cracked with age and hard usage but that only made the picture more categorical, like "The Last Supper." The stage was empty except for a small round table covered by a rubbed red velvet cloth on the right-hand side, two large green glass bottles, each containing a wired and vertical tapeworm and, in the background, apocryphal and occult, a human skeleton hung as carelessly as an overcoat on a nail.

"So that's what it was!" the Tall Texan said as they stepped out of their hotel into the gauzy evening.

"That's what what was?" Butch Cassidy wanted to know.

Kilpatrick pointed up the street. "*Bohemian Girl.* Playing at the Salt Lake Theatre." He accented the second syllable. "That you and me was trying to read the sign from out our window."

"Want to go there, instead of to the medicine show?"

285

"And have them ladies' evening spoiled, that was riding in the parade, if I didn't show up? Ain't you got no more heart to you than a gila monster?"

Butch laughed.

They started down the street, two cowboys by walk, aspect, bearing and deportment, but clad in city clothes, even to wearing neat bowler hats.

"Pardner, where's the big show?" Butch asked a paper boy, tossing him a quarter for his answer.

"Down to the corner, mister. Turn left and straight ahead. You can't miss it."

It's about to start. It's about to begin.

"Ain't you a-going, kid?"

"Seen it six times already."

"Good, is it?"

"Good ain't the word for it."

Hurry. Hurry. Hurry.

30

"LUCKY FOR US WE COME EARLY," MRS. LUBY SAID, throwing drowsy Herman over her shoulder as if he had been a sack of flour and letting his head and arms dangle limply behind. "Look at this crowd, would you. It's kind of disgusting to watch people flock, when something's free, ain't it. Now, where are they?"

"Where are who, Mrs. Luby?" Dorney asked.

"My kids." She looked back into the darkness hung with dim transparent faces beyond reach of the coruscating torches. "With Clara, or Joe Mudge, likely."

"I had hold of Althea and Ruby up until a minute ago," Dorney said, "but then they broke away."

"Probably edging up closer to the stage. Oh, well, they're old enough to find their way home, I should think. Or else they'll get lost, one or the other. When the show's over, I'll holler for whoever's missing," placid Mrs. Luby promised. "You don't happen to spy Clara and Joe nowheres together, do you?"

"No, I don't, Mrs. Luby." Dorney stood on tiptoe and looked all around, saying, "Excuse me," to the young man on her left when she accidentally bumped his arm.

"That's all right, ma'am," Butch Cassidy said, taking off his hat and putting it back on again.

Next to him, the Tall Texan took his hat off, too, placed it over his heart and smiled until he was commanded in a whisper to replace it, which he did gloomily. "Ain't we made her acquaintance somewheres?" he muttered under his breath.

"No."

"Hold your horse now, I once knew a girl in San Angelo one time —"

"Not this one, you didn't."

Kilpatrick peeped around him. "Had the same kind of a —"

"Oh, no, she didn't."

The Tall Texan heaved a sigh. "Guess she didn't at that," he said. "This one's got her beat, maybe."

"Ain't that one of your parade ladies?" his companion asked suddenly.

That was all it took. "Where?" Kilpatrick said, looking off to the left. "Where?"

"There. Going around the tent there in that brindle dress. Ain't it?"

"Which direction?"

"Right there. You watch. She'll be showing up again."

Out of the corner of his eye, Butch looked at the girl next to him once more. Kilpatrick always had the feeling he'd seen them before, in Cheyenne, San Angelo, Denver or Abilene. A regular joke, it was, how he always thought he'd seen them before. But this time Butch Cassidy was the one it was happening to, the one who was having the uncanny feeling that somewhere, sometime, he himself had been acquainted with a girl, with this girl, or somebody so like her, it was ghostly. In Vernal? Star Valley? Telluride? If so, she had been a little kid, then . . . in Dubois, Lander or someplace, at some Saturday night dance, sitting on her pa's lap hiding her face against him or snooping out from behind her ma's skirts. . . . Maybe he had let her ride in to supper on his shoulder, jounced her on his knee, helped her to a formal somersault or let her swing from his thumbs . . . he was a great one for kids . . . but he wouldn't know her now, would he, years later? Blossomed out? Standing there in a white dress? With one of them chins the hand hankered to slide in under and tilt upward? And those eyes? And that hair?

He looked away with regret. No, no more than the Tall Texan ever had, he hadn't. Known her. Seen her before in his life. Like a cold, like a fever, he had caught it off incurable Kilpatrick, that homesick kind of feeling, that doctored up remembering, that half a wish and half a blindfold hope . . . that they had met before, were meeting now like auld lang syne, would meet again.

"I think the battle is as good as won," Mrs. Luby said into Dorneys' right ear, "and Clara is going to catch Joe Mudge after all. I didn't think so but I've changed my mind. Not that he's such a bargain, especially not working steady and with them four kids."

"Wouldn't that be wonderful?" What good was love if the lover didn't live happily ever after? That was the purpose of it all!

"Wonder how old Mrs. Tofflemire would take it?"

Herman woke with a start, raised his head, stiffened and began to slide downwards. His mother caught him, turned him around and sat him up on her right arm. He was squirming to get down, and ready to burst out with a snuffle and a sob when something caught his attention, a hush, an expectancy, and he kept still. An almost imperceptible tremor went out under the ground, the flames in the torches seemed to leap higher, on the platform the skeleton rustled, the gold fringe on the table cover quivered, the green bottles rattled, and out from behind the billowing yellow canvas curtain in tight-fitting citified clothes and bowties nearly a foot across tramped the Minstrel Seven chanting, "Say, Brothers, will you meet me?" some of them going shush, shush, whoosh, whoosh like a train softly running or a river slapping the sides of a sandy beach. Except for two who were empty-handed, they were playing musical instruments — castanets, a tambourine, two banjos and a concertina — as well as singing:

> "Say, brothers, will you meet me,
> Say, brothers, will you meet me,
> Say, brothers, will you meet me
> On Canaan's happy shore?"

At the sight and the sound of them people went wild — cheering, clapping, whistling. Here's the way it starts, see. This is the beginning. Don't cost nobody a penny! How can Ferdon do it? High class show, high class singers that could go on any vaudeville stage in the land — and all free. There's a mystery. Well, his medicine don't only set him back two or three cents, they say, including the bottle, and he charges a dollar. But even so . . . even so. . . . The song was half over before the thrilled and excited audience managed to quiet down enough really to listen.

"Say, Brothers, Will You Meet Me?" ended with a woo-oo, woo-oo like a faraway train whistle or a loon call and so faint a shush, shush, whoosh, whoosh that the sounds were like a memory. It brought such tumultuous acclaim that the Minstrel Seven had to start right in again. This time they sang "Then I'll Come Back And Keep My Loving Promise," and after that the middle of the line shuffled backwards to make a half circle and they began tossing jokes at each other very much as if they had been playing a fast game of beanbags — whiz, zip, plop. "How'd you like that there lecture at the Chautauqua last night, about the law of compensation?" "Law of compensation. Where the man explains if you loses one eye, other eye gets stronger — loses one ear, other ear gets sharper — loses one arm, other arm gets powerfuller?" "That's right." "Believe it." "Believes it, does you?" "Believes it, yessir. Noticed it myself. Take somebody with one short leg. Nine times out of ten his other leg will be a little bit longer!" STOP IT, BOY. "Before my wife and me was married we agreed I'd have the say in the major things, she'd have the say in the minor." "How'd it work out?" "Well, so far, no major matters have come up!" BEHAVE YOURSELF, BROTHER. "What was it that man come up and ask you yesterday?" "Asked, what's the extreme penalty for bigamy." "What IS the extreme penalty for bigamy?" "Two mother-in-laws!" QUIT IT, BOY.

The funny stuff over, it was time for two of the performers to bound out of line, run forward and begin to step dance with such speed, lightness and elegance that it took the breath away, while the castanets, tambourine, banjos and concertina sounded like a full-grown orchestra behind them. When the Minstrel Seven were through their performance and filed off, they weren't allowed to stay behind the curtain but were clapped, cheered and whistled back on half a dozen times, to bow, grin, pat the sweat off their foreheads and upper lips with their handkerchiefs, and scamper off only to be commanded to return, until finally they wouldn't do it any more.

After that the stage was left empty for a few moments to whet the appetite for what was to come — a skit called "Heinie's Dream." This was put on by a young man, disguised as an old shoemaker with silver-rimmed glasses on the end of his nose, and a small wrinkled woman — Mademoiselle Flowerdew — dressed terrifyingly like a schoolgirl with morbid red curls bounding at her shoulders and cobalt-blue eyelids. The way the act went was this: the man came on alone, took a seat by the table and pretended to be cobbling a shoe. His actions made one imagine the whole shoemaker's shop. Then he nodded and fell asleep over his work, and dreamed his partner was a vision who burst out from behind the curtain, skipped rope all around him and came forward to sing to the accompaniment of the concertina and a fiddle, neither instrument being anywhere in sight, a song that went,

"Heinie,
I'm tiny
Alongside of you,
But I've a heart that is
Big and true.
Heinie, oh, Heinie,
If you will be mine-ee,
I'll yump in the ocean
And swim out to you!"

Why she pronounced it "yump" was not known. All this woke the shoemaker and what should he do when she started in on the second chorus, but get to his feet and start in performing with her rope. Well, if ever there was a rope skipper upon this earth it was that one! He did things with that rope that had never been done before, turning it into a whirlwind, a tunnel, a waterfall, a cocoon, a tree and a bridge, his feet like hail on a tin roof all the while. He wasn't more than half through when people started clapping and they kept it up to the very end when the velocity of his invisible rope made it sound like an east wind whistling down through Cottonwood Canyon and he seemed to be jumping backward and forward at the same time. That his partner, put so completely in the shade, could ever recover her ascendancy after this triumph didn't seem possible, but recover it she did by the rendition of a simple ballad with this chorus:

> "We have got a boarder
> And the boarder's stuck on Ma.
> I wonder why?
> I wonder why?
> Pa don't like the boarder
> And the boarder don't like Pa!
> I wonder why?
> I wonder why?"

It had ten or twelve verses, each one funnier than the last, and when she got done singing it, the fickle audience could be heard clear up to the Capitol Building.

Snelgrove, the Mighty, appeared in long tights and a sweater that together would have looked like a suit of long woollen underwear only that the outfit was peacock blue under a kind of panther-skin apron, with a massive belt of Mexican silver slung around his middle and odd high shoes on, with straps buttoned all up and down across the front like a ladder. He lifted weights and bent bars of iron and did many more things too. The way he ended his act was just to stand there, instruct his trained muscles and grow to twice his natural size. Far from making him look more dangerous, however (he had looked very dangerous indeed part of the time), the more he swelled, the lighter and rounder and softer, the less able to inflict any damage and the liabler to soar off into space, he appeared, like a balloon. People did not clap much for Snelgrove.

There had been six beauties in the open carriage, riding in the parade, but the truth was there were only two female performers with the show. The other four ladies did not act and in fact two of them were local girls, one a waitress and one a chambermaid, both dressed up in Mrs. Ferdon's clothes, who did not belong with the troupe at all. The others were Mrs. Ferdon and a close friend of Snelgrove, from Butte, Montana. The two actresses were Mademoiselle Flowerdew, Heinie's "dream," with the red hair and blue eyelids, and Flossie O'Brien. Flossie was Murdo the Magician's wife, a thin Irish girl with wild black hair and wild black eyes, like a Balkan witch, and teeth meant to last for centuries, that she would never begin to get the good out of, for she would be dead of consumption in a little more than a year.

After Snelgrove diminished to his right size and backed off bowing, Mademoiselle Flowerdew and Flossie came on stage wearing ordinary street dresses, with yachting caps rakishly cocked to one side of their heads. In identical soprano voices they sang,

> "In the far off land of Australia
> Lived a dear little kangaroo-oo

She found her a beau
But the folks said, No!
We've made other plans for you-oo.
So she danced on her tail
In a home-made jail,
And every night here's what she'd do, (pause)
She'd say (pause):

· " 'Oh, moonbeam light and airy,
Oh, moonbeam soft and blue,
Be my good kind fairy —
I've work tonight for you.
Go to my distant sweetheart,
Fly swift as Cupid's dove,
Give him my heart's kind message:
YOU'RE THE ONLY ONE I LOVE!' "

This, with an encore, brought the show to the halfway mark and the dramatic moment when Dr. Ferdon stepped forth with a bottle of his medicine held high, like a flambeau. He appeared from behind the yellow curtain the way everybody else did, but a certain crackling conspicuity about him alerted the audience no less than if he had materialized in a bolt of lightning, sprung from a puff of livid smoke or been shot out of a cannon. "Ladies and gentlemen," he began.

It was rumored afterward that he talked for a solid twenty-seven minutes, but if so, he knew how to make the time fly. In fact, more than one said afterwards that Dr. Ferdon himself was the star performer of the show, which he was, of course, or there wouldn't have been any show in the first place.

Wearing a café au lait suit, hat and spats to match, black patent boots, white ruffled shirt, black satin cravat and an amethyst stickpin as big as a crab-apple, Dr. Ferdon was a silver-haired man with a steamy carnation-colored complexion, a great many reconstructed brown and white teeth, bent hands scaly as a lizard's and thick bronze fingernails. For eloquence, he had been compared to Daniel Webster, but that great American talker would have had to get up pretty early in the morning to outshine him. His message was simple — Ferdon's Herbal World Beater Tonic would cure anybody of whatever it was that ailed them — but it did not sound simple. That is, it did and it didn't. It contained a sufficiency of big long words like prophylactic, antispasmodic, helminthiasis and effluvium but little words a-plenty fenced them in and kept them close to home.

Toward the end of his speech, he made use of the skeleton, a dreadful example, bringing it forward as if it had been a living man, one arm about the neck, one hand resting companionably on the fellow's humerus. Alas, he had known him well, the human being whose framework this was, once, had Dr. Ferdon. Told him on many an occasion that a stitch in time saved nine, told him much more, for the sake of boyhood friendship, all free gratis. Even offered to give him a bottle of Herbal World Beater Tonic, wouldn't have cost him a dime, all free gratis. And how did he react? Like a mule, a stubborn onry unlicked army mule. Well, it was no wonder. Look at this here obstinate jawbone. Look at the bullhead slant of this here skull. With this here mandibula and this here particular cranium, was it any wonder that he was pigheaded, mulish and contrary? Not the slightest. "Take a few bottles of Herbal World Beater Tonic, Virgil," how many times had not Ferdon put himself out to go to the trouble to suggest to him? (His name had been Virgil.) "No, thanks, Ferdon." "But it will be the saving of you, Virgil!" "No, thanks." No, thanks! Well, here he stood this very evening, to show where stubbornness could land a man if he wasn't careful.

Dr. Ferdon also presented the two tapeworms, first the one in the right-hand bottle and then the one in the left, as though they had been the thieves on either side of the Saviour, leaving them in the mind as unforgettable characters. He ended his lecture magnificently, with a coda neither too long nor too short. His final phrase — "that flesh is heir to!" — was the signal for his troupe to come forth from the tent behind the platform with their arms full of bottles, to mingle with and sell to the crowd. (Performers off the stage! their doggerel and portent and tints beneath Malaga frost! Those eyes of rock crystal, of jacinth, emerald, sapphire, onyx! their sacred language!)

Dorney turned to Mrs. Luby. "Let me hold him now," she said. "You must be tired." She had asked if she couldn't hold him before but Mrs. Luby said "Shhh!" sharply and shook her head, afraid to move him for fear he might wake up and cause her to miss something of what was going on.

The man standing by Dorney removed his bowler hat and leaned over to speak to Mrs. Luby. "Excuse me, ma'am, but you've got quite a load there, ain't you? I'd be glad to hold your little boy for you, if you want."

"Well, now," Mrs. Luby said, "that's very nice of you but — " She turned rather helplessly to Dorney. "We don't need help, do we?"

"I'll be glad to hold him," Dorney repeated.

"Thanks just the same, mister," Mrs. Luby said to the stranger, about whom there was something, as she mentioned later, very gentlemanly and likable. "But that would seem like a imposition, I'm afraid."

"I don't see why." Putting his hat back on, Butch murmured,

"Excuse me, miss," and reached in front of Dorney for all-gone Herman, whom he took expertly.

"Hey," the Tall Texan announced, tugging at his sleeve, so intent on watching the actors go through the crowd with their medicine that he did not see his companion now held a small sleeping boy against his right shoulder. "Hey, listen. If that lady with the red hair don't get over in our neck of the woods, I'm going over in her neck of the woods. Why shouldn't I buy my tonic offa her if I want, kindly tell me?"

"What will you do with it?" Butch said. "You don't need no medicine. You ain't never been sick a day in your life."

"Didn't you hear what the man said? Them's the kind that's got to watch out the carefullest! Them's the ones that goes out like a light." Kilpatrick had his hand in his pocket and was fumbling for a silver dollar. "You don't happen to have — " He stopped short. "Hey, there she is! I'm going to mosey on over and buy offa her, why not? Ain't no law against it."

"Behave yourself, now."

"Oh, sure."

"And mosey on back."

"Oh, sure."

Butch sent a rueful glance after the Tall Texan and turned to Dorney. "Great guy for — " He paused, realizing that he was speaking to a very young lady. How young, anyway? Fifteen? Sixteen? He changed what he had been going to say to something else. "For moseying off," he said, and smiled. Her answering smile sent an unexpected pang through him.

"You give him back to me or Dorney here," Mrs. Luby said, bending closer, "any time he commences to feel heavy."

"The kid, you mean," he said stupidly. So her name was Dorney. "Oh, he ain't going to commence to feel heavy, ma'am. Don't you fear for that."

Dorney.

He looked at her.

As though he had said her name aloud she looked back at him and smiled again, and again the pang shot through him.

"Buy dis medicine and save yo life!" One of the Minstrel Seven had got close enough so they could see the whites of his eyes.

"I want some," Mrs. Luby said, shutting her purse with almost as loud a bang as if she had shot off a pistol, causing several in her vicinity, including Dorney, to start. "Will it help drinking, sir?" she inquired respectfully, paying her money and taking the bottle.

"Saves yo life, mist'ess," the Negro said, while Dorney kept large eyes upon him. He was one of the two dancers, coal-black, but with a great aduncous nose like that of a Lebanese, or an Assiniboin chief.

"But will it help drinking?"

"Don't know about it helping, mist'ess. Know it ain't going to do no *hindering*." He scratched his head.

"Oh, dear me —"

"Less'n yo take some mighty big doses," the Negro added hastily, in the midst of laughter. He moved on. "Save yo life."

"Oh, it ain't for me," Mrs. Luby explained to the young man who was holding Herman. She put one hand on Dorney's sleeve and stretched out the other to rest it lightly on her son's dangling right leg, making a private circle for the three of them, the stranger, Dorney and herself, almost like a room with walls where they were all alone, friends of many a season, visiting together. "It's for you-know-who," she said to Dorney, who nodded and looked apologetically at Butch Cassidy because he was not let in on the secret. "My husband," Mrs. Luby decided to reveal graciously. "The children's father. One of the best men that ever lived, except for that one thing."

"I'm sorry, ma'am," Butch said, more to Dorney than to her. "That's a dam — a doggone shame, doggone if it ain't."

"Oh, she's no kin to us," Mrs. Luby explained. "Just a friend, you know. A neighbor." She looked from Butch to Dorney and back to Butch. "Don't drink steady, understand. Mr. Luby, I mean. Just goes off on one of these jollifications every so often. Smashes — But he always buys me something new to take the place of what got busted so I shouldn't really holler. Do you suppose something like this here tonic would work? When the man was talking up there, I just stood here and said to myself, Why not try it on Mr. Luby?"

"Can't see where there would be no harm in it, ma'am."

"It might," Dorney ventured hopefully.

I got to ask her where she lives, Butch thought. I got to find out some way.

"It cures everything else, so why not drinking?" Mrs. Luby said. "What I think maybe I'll do, is —"

What for? Butch shifted Herman and ran his forefinger around the inside of his collar. What do I want to know where she lives for? What would I do if I did know? Go up to her front door with a bunch of posies in my hand? Hello, kiddo, here I am, on the run, more guys after me than you could shake a stick at, stack of chips this high offered for my arrest — Butch Cassidy, honey, holding out his arm for you to take ahold of, asking you to —

"Looks like it's starting, don't it?" Mrs. Luby said.

"What is, ma'am?"

"The show, again."

Is it, again?

The second half of the show started off with the Minstrel Seven tramping on as they had before, whoo whooshing, shush-shushing and singing "Dear Old Girl" and "I Went to the Animal Fair." Then they formed their half-circle again and told some more jokes, just a few this time, and their last song was,

> "Can she bake a cherry pie, Billy boy, Billy boy?
> Can she bake a cherry pie, charming Billy?
> She can bake a cherry pie
> Quicker'n a cat can wink its eye
> But she's a young thing and cannot leave
> Her mother . . . ."

A skit came next.

This time the wrinkled woman with the morbid red curls and the blue eyelids acted out the part of a schoolteacher sitting at her desk, the desk being the round table with the rubbed velvet cloth, admonishing the young rope skipper, supposed on this occasion to be a pupil kept in after school, for some mischief. Before the act began, one of the Minstrel Seven brought out and opened up a stepladder, which everybody, including the skeleton (who seemed to be taking notice of all that was happening), knew was going to be used for *something*. It was. Before long, at the request of the teacher, the pupil had to run up it and supposedly take a picture down off the wall. Now, there was neither picture, nor wall, nor roof overhead, only the open air and star-sprinkled sky, but somehow he appeared to be in a real room taking down a real picture from perilously near a real ceiling and several squeals and many groans were heard when he almost dropped the heavy frame and splintered the large glass! That a man could do on a stepladder what he did did not seem humanly possible. He stood on his head on top of it, he walked up and down the rungs on his hands! he balanced on it, his whole weight on a toe or a finger. Pretending to slip and fall backward, pretending to slip and fall forward, he made his audience's hair stand on end. People clapped till their hands stung when he got down. How does a man get started with something like that anyway? A common ordinary everyday stepladder!

What the eerie music was, where it came from, nobody knew, but it started when Murdo the Magician, with long strands of dingy hair combed from the tip of his left ear up over his bald dome to the tip of his right ear, came out in formal but dust-streaked black broadcloth clothes and a white shirt stiff as a china plate, and began to perform. While he talked, his spitty speech itself like a sleight-of-hand trick, the music died down, then swelled again when he was silent and did his miracles. From a flute, those sounds? a little drum beat with the hand? something strung with tiny bells giving those jingles? a lute, its strings not stroked but plucked? Strange, foreign, riddle-me-this melody, it yet had phrases one knew, or thought one knew. Butch Cassidy fancied he heard *good morning, young lady, my horse he won't stand* a time or two, the notes of this, before they faded and disappeared like smoke on the air.

Murdo's marvels with rabbit, water pitcher, card deck, flowers and American flag disposed of, Flossie O'Brien, his wife and assistant, came on stage. She was blindfolded, and the magician, a cold and awe-inspiring Mephisto, went through the audience pointing out objects and calling to her to identify them. She never missed, even objects that would stump almost anybody — an ear trumpet, for instance. Next, people silently thought of questions to ask her and she answered them aloud: "A lady, initials R. P. It was not *lost*, but *stolen*." "A gentleman, initials W. M. It was her you saw in the carriage, all right." "A young girl, initials F. S. I am sorry to tell you, but your fears are justified, the answer is — yes."

Up there on the stage, Flossie O'Brien looked pale and exceptional, no simple Irish girl but a veritable White Lady, a familiar spirit, with ferine hair and scarab eyes, that sent chills rippling down the back of the audience. Like a cat, did it sense that she was not long for this world? Or what? A cool, almost chilly wind nosed in and out among the crowd, and many a vain young woman wished she had carried a wrap over her bare arm when she left home and ran into the red June evening. The sky was black now, the stars greenish, at ten o'clock or past. It had turned cold.

People felt better when Murdo made them laugh, when he called for volunteers and the bold but sheepish young men, the two giggling middle-aged women who dared each other to go up on the platform, the stubble-haired boy and the old man with the skeptic face presented themselves to be hypnotized. Of course, it was all a trick of some kind. Whatever incantation it was the magician droned, those passes he made with his hands, such stuff wouldn't make anybody *really* sleep and *really* imagine what these ridiculous people were told to imagine — that they were hot, cold, thirsty, hungry, in love and, finally, running off with their sweethearts. . . . They were disguised members of the troupe, no doubt, paid by Ferdon (except the old man with the I'm-from-Missouri look on his face, and the stubble-haired boy who senselessly bolted off the stage almost as soon as he got up there) to pretend to be hypnotized and believe what the magician told them. Naturally, they didn't *really* believe it, even if they were going through those hilarious dreamy motions of packing suitcases, tiptoeing around, waiting, listening and so on. It was all a trick, of course.

To account for what singularly happened or seemed to happen then, Dorney told herself afterward it was because she had been up since five-thirty in the morning. She had worked all day at the laundry, walked no telling how far and watched the medicine show for nearly two hours without once sitting down and she was tired, that was all. Tired enough so that sometimes her knees trembled. She must have turned somewhat light-headed. The magician wasn't responsible for it, or his assistant, either, sorceress though she might be.

Butch, when he came to himself and rubbed his eyes, thought that the whole pipe dream could be laid to his shoes. He was wearing new bluchers instead of the high-heeled cowboy boots he was used to. And standing around like that, with a sleeping kid against his shoulder, would make anybody get to feeling peculiar. No cowboy ever just stood! He slouched or leaned, against fences, walls, posts. Never did that when he could squat back on his heels. Never did that when he could stretch out nice and lazy, flat on the ground, his hands under the back of his neck and his eyes only about half open. That was what was behind it, of course, the damn low-heeled shoes, and standing right out in the open with nothing to lean against. Naturally it'd make a guy's head seem kind of empty and far-off like it didn't hardly belong to him no more but to some other fellow listening (with that funny crawling along his spine) to them peculiar sounds of — what was it, anyway? Did they call that music? More like a hive of bees swarming, more like somebody blowing through thin tissue paper on a comb, more like . . . It made him sleepy to listen to it and be staring into that gasoline torch like that, flickering and jumping. He'd ought to fix his eyes on something else, or shut his eyes, so he could remember better.

Remember what? What did he have to remember, now that he was here at last, safe and sound? Nothing. Not remember, any more. Not, that is, if she was waiting. But would she be? Some girls promised one thing and did another and a guy never knew for sure whether *his* girl . . . He'd know now, in about a minute.

You hold the fort, Little Dipper, while I go in. Some ride, wasn't it, pardner? Them posses was like leeches onto our tail, the miles got to lengthening out till it seemed like they stretched to the moon, but we shook 'em, we covered 'em, didn't we, though? (While the years blew by.) Well, either she's stayed or she's vamoosed, my friend, and there ain't but one way to find out.

The old man in the rocking chair there, on the side porch, with the newspaper on his lap and his glasses shoved up onto his forehead, that must be her grandfather. Come to think of it, he looks kind of familiar.

Granddad, where would she be?

"Where *would* she be now, Butch Cassidy?"

298

Where *would* she be, only standing there, waiting?
Not standing long, for sure!
Not her!
Making a beeline for his open arms, colliding against him. . . .

Funny how she had been imagining all the time that Grandpa
Bannon was dead. He's not! or he wouldn't be sitting and looking
exactly the same as ever. And the ground all around the lilac bush
wouldn't be wet from the dishwater he threw out just a little while
ago when he finished the dishes, and came outside to cool off in the
shade. Dorney, in her old place on the bottom step, sometimes looks
up at him — he wears his glasses on his forehead, so he is fixing to
tell her something — and sometimes across the pale empty yard to
the spot where a house used to stand. Whose it was, what it looked
like, she can't remember, but it was built right there on that lot,
where nothing is now, but dust clouds moving over. A little girl
used to play out in back of it by the chicken house, on an old gray
blanket with a doll.

Well, an occasion like today is no time to grieve over the natural
order of events, that's certain, and take on because death, because
change —

"An occasion like today, did I hear you say?"

Yes, Grandpa.

"Today ain't no occasion."

Oh, yes, it is. It's my wedding day.

"Kep' it very mum, didn't you? Kep' it very mum!"

Now don't be mad, Grandpa. I never did it on purpose.

"I guess not. I guess not."

No, really. I had to wait till he came back, you see. He said, "I
touched her not, alas, not I . . . I did but see her passing by . . . and
yet I . . ." He said, "Goodbye, Dorney. We shall meet again." Was
merely that a guarantee? *He might not have come back.*

"Who said? Who might not? A likely story."

Him, there. Galloping up the road, halting his black horse by the
gate, jumping down, coming around the house on the dead run . . .

"Ain't nobody but 'Dair Yandle."

Look again, Grandpa!

(For an instant, oddly enough, it does seem to be 'Dair Yandle
through her tears of gladness, but that is some trick of memory.)

"As I live and breathe — "

Recognize him now, don't you?

"Butch Cassidy!"

That's who it is.

The only trouble, his face is sometimes like the blur a whirling top

299

makes at the height of its spin, as though one was staring at a photograph in which the sitter had looked in another direction just at the crucial moment. If she didn't know for sure, for positive, for absolutely, that it was he, there would be moments when his smile, the flash of his brown eyes, would puzzle and bewilder and make her think it was somebody else. But of course there was nobody else it could be, except . . .

Let her look closer and she will tell! Alas, the closer she looks, the more of a haze, the more misty and dim his countenance, though his arms are real enough, his beating heart is real enough.

"Changed, have I?"

No. Oh, no.

"She's a young thing and cannot leave her moth-er," sings the old man in the rocking chair slyly.

"Now, Grandpa!"

This time, I ain't going to leave you behind, never fear. This time, I couldn't leave you behind, no more'n I could leave behind my two eyes to see with.

" . . . can-not leave her moth-er. . . ."

"Goodbye, Grandpa, goodbye!"

We're a-leaving, sir, you might as well know it. Ain't stirring nowheres less'n she's with me. Couldn't, no more. A drownded cat for feeble and weak, a stillborn pup for flimsy and limp, I'd be. Nothing more no-account never. (But listen, I'm Timpanogos in her arms.)

Clutching him, she thinks that his famous horse could go even faster and she would not be afraid, although it is a long way down to the swift moving ground of river and blue-eyed grass. If they suddenly soared through the air, she would not be afraid. She lays her cheek against his solid back and shuts her eyes. Not to sleep. She does not shut her eyes to sleep but only to think of him the better, and think of love.

He turns in the saddle.

Hey, kiddo. You ain't drifted off, have you? You ain't said nothing in a long time.

"I was thinking."

Happy, kiddo? But you don't have to tell me. How about we make camp here? There's a nice little stream and some willows. . . .

On the ground he reaches up for her and she slides down into his arms. Night has fallen but when he looks in her eyes he can see what color they are.

Even when it's dark I can see the color of your eyes.

The never-before-heard voice may be the wind. "What's all this about a *wedding* day?"

Mine, if you please.

"You don't say! Now pray tell me. Who is that man over there by the fire, with the firelight shining on his face?" (The bright, the leaping fire.)

Him, you mean. Why, that's —

"Who, child, who? We haven't got forever."

Why, that's —

"Who?"

Pardon, I beg of you. But the difficulty arises when the face is part of the darkness, you see. When the stars shine through it. When one cannot make out for sure whether it's he or whether it's somebody else, you know. Somebody like —

"Yes? Yes?"

Another. Or, for that matter, the stranger.

"The stranger? What stranger?"

At the show that time, you know.

"The show? What show?"

Doctor Ferdon's Great Free Attractions that time.

"Oh, that, you mean. Him, you mean. The cowboy."

He wasn't a cowboy!

"No? Well, take a good look."

I *am* looking.

"Don't you think I'm right?"

It is Mrs. Luby who is tugging at Dorney's arm. "Don't you think I'm right?" she says.

"About what, Mrs. Luby?"

"About hypnotism?"

"What about it?"

"That it's all in people's minds? I mean, that it's all in a person's imagination. Of course, when you come right down to it, where else would it be?"

From the stage the brave volunteers trouped jocularly down, the middle-aged women out of breath, the young men more sheepish than ever, the old skeptic looking as triumphant as though he had certainly put one over on somebody, and they lost themselves in the audience.

Everybody clapped loud and long and the show was over.

The great Ferdon had left the premises soon after intermission and it fell to Murdo, now no dangerous wizard but, after a suitable pause, a fast-talking Friend of Man, to make a last decrescendo pitch, and blather genially to the departing crowd. "That's all, folks! That's the show for tonight! There isn't any more. Tell your friends and neighbors. Another grand free performance at the same time tomorrah night. Few bottles left of Ferdon's Herbal World Beater Tonic right down here to the side of the platform! Hurry. Hurry. Hurry. One dollah. Yes, sir. That's right. Here you are, mister. Save your life."

Flossie O'Brien, an apparition of dread no longer but a scrawny young lady with circles under her eyes, helped him. (The rest of the actors were nowhere to be seen.) They did not do a very thriving business, however.

Now that it was over, people wanted to get home.

The Tall Texan had had so much to look at, he didn't see that Butch was holding a small boy until the moment he handed him back to his mother. By that time, it was too late. They were all beginning to move as in an eddying stream. "Well, for God's sake," he said, removing his hat quickly, trying without success to stop in his tracks. Maybe Butch had struck up a friendly acquaintance, for a change! Maybe they'd get invited to a fried-chicken dinner, get to sit in a parlor, get to look through a stereoscope.

Butch jabbed him in the ribs and he put his hat on, hurt and indignant.

"I certainly thank you for your kindness," Mrs. Luby called, being carried farther and farther away.

"Don't mention it, ma'am!"

"I notice you got your hat off," Kilpatrick hissed into his ear.

"That's a different proposition." When she was lost forever, when Butch knew he would never see Dorney again (that was the name the woman had called her, wasn't it?) he put his hat back on, slowly and drearily.

Mrs. Luby and Dorney met the others on the corner, Clara carrying Sophie, Thornton and Althea, Joe Mudge carrying Alfred, George and Ruby, so nobody had to be hollered for or a lot of fuss made, after all. In such a mob it seemed almost a miracle that thus without misventure or worry, the eleven of them should be reunited. To run across anybody they knew even though just by sight belonged in the same category, and it was but natural that when Clara — such a changed, happy, bright-eyed Clara — caught a glimpse of the Queen, arm in arm with Mr. Morelewski, passing in under the streetlight, she should grow rather excited about it and give a smothered little scream. "Ain't that the Queen?" she begged of Dorney.

Mrs. Luby, thrown off because Clara, knowing it was bad manners to point with her index finger, had used her less censurable little finger, which curved, barely saw her, and did that only by accident and the greatest good fortune. But she didn't need to look all day, Mrs. Luby didn't. One quick peek was enough for her. She said flatly that it wasn't the Queen and that she would be willing to bet a dime that it wasn't. "Look at the size of her," she scoffed. "Why, that woman was so fat she fairly waddled and Mrs. Morelewski ain't fat! Besides, she's a stylish dresser. She don't go around in black like that, wearing a black lace shawl over her head like a — like a — a Armenian widow."

"I seen her face," Clara persisted gently. "The light was shining right on it for a minute." She had fallen into step with Joe Mudge, and they were leading the procession home, a circumstance that Mrs. Luby drew Dorney's attention to by a convulsive grab at her sleeve and a gloating twitter. Clara glanced back over her shoulder. "Wasn't it, Dorney? Wasn't that Mrs. Morelewski?"

"Well, I didn't get a very good look at her, but — yes, it was. I think so, anyway. That was Mr. Morelewski, I know for sure. So who else could it have been, only her?"

But Mrs. Luby would not hear of it.

Neither, surprisingly enough, would Joe Mudge. And when he took a firm stand and denied it, Clara began to waver. If Joe said it wasn't Mrs. Morelewski, how could it be? Ruefully she gave over and confessed that her eyes must have been playing her a trick.

It was the once transcendent and beautiful Queen, Dorney knew, feeling with sober sadness some trenchant but obscure misfortune brought home, sensible of personal loss. She did not insist on it but let the subject drop.

"That magician was a big fake," Joe Mudge said cordially. He turned and repeated it to those straggling along behind. "They always are," he added. "And so was that strong man. From the word go."

"I don't see how you figure," Mrs. Luby said after some thought, pushing Althea farther behind her to keep her off her heels. "Either you got muscles or you ain't. I can see how the magician might fool people — but not the strong man. Everything's right out there in the open. He's either strong, or he ain't."

"There's tricks to all trades," Joe said deeply, while Clara nodded in profound agreement.

"I guess we're gazing on a perfect picture of it," Mrs. Luby whispered out of the corner of her mouth a few moments later, "and it's just a matter of time from now on."

"Picture of what?" Dorney whispered back.

Mrs. Luby gave her a jubilant poke in the ribs. "Double l, double o, double v, double e," she breathed. "As plain as the nose on your face!"

31

FROM MRS. LUBY'S DORNEY HAD TO GO THE REST
of the way by herself. It was not far, less than half a block, and she
covered it at a run. At first when, panting, she flung herself in at
the gate, she was relieved to see that the house was all dark. She had
been heedless of Crystal's warning all evening, but now it came back
to her in full force. Madge was going to be mad for more reasons
than one (not least among them that the hour was close on to
eleven) and when she saw that everybody was in bed, Dorney hoped
to be able to postpone her reckoning until tomorrow. By morning,
it might lose some of its sting. It did not occur to her to shrug
off Crystal's admonishment. Crystal always knew exactly how her
mother was going to take anything, almost as though she had second
sight, and if she said Madge was going to be mad because Dorney
went to the medicine show, she was going to be mad, that was
certain. But not tonight, thank heaven. That is, not if she was
asleep.

Dorney then remembered, stifling a groan, that every door and
window would be locked tight, and she would have to knock for
admittance! Wanting to turn and run in the other direction, she
groped her way around to the rear. There was a light, however, in
the transom above the back door, and her heart leaped. She would
not have to get anybody out of bed to let her in! Then it fell. Oh,
dear, there was no postponing *anything* until tomorrow!

Standing with one foot on the bottom step, looking upward disconsolately, it came to her by degrees that the back of the house
seemed changed and unfamiliar. Why it should appear so took a moment's frowning thought. The shades, that was it! They were pulled
clear down to the sills of both windows. She went gingerly up the
steps, aware for the first time how they creaked, and when she
hastened across the porch on tiptoe, it creaked, too. Should she tap
on the door very lightly or turn the knob and walk in, as always?
She tried to do the latter, but it was locked. She bent her head
and listened. Had she heard a murmur of voices just then or hadn't
she? She would be so much better off if Crystal was in bed and

Madge was up by herself. She listened again. No, there was no sound. She raised her hand to knock.

"Who's there?" came a frightened voice.

No such luck. Think of the devil and he's never in bed asleep. Crystal was awake.

"It's me, Crystal."

"Who?"

What a preposterous question. "Dorney, of course."

The key grated in the lock, the bolt was pushed back and the door opened a mere crack. One of Crystal's eyes looked through it. "Oh, it *is* you," she said, opening the door wide enough for Dorney to slip through. Then she shut, bolted and locked it again, quickly.

"What's the — " Dorney began in astonishment.

"Look," Crystal said, pointing.

Dorney turned and looked at Madge stretched out full length on the lounge, and instantly flew to her. She went down on her knees. "What's the matter? What happened?" Madge's hair was toppled, a long bloody scratch shent her pale cheek, there was a bruise on her temple and a swelling over her eye.

"You should have seen her," Crystal said, "when she came home. I just wish you had been here to see her, that's all I wish. You'd have absolutely fainted, that's all."

"What happened?" Dorney pleaded.

"I looked just terrible," Madge said weakly. "I thought Crystal was going to go down in a heap when she seen me. Jetta hid under the table. She was afraid of me! So you can just imagine how I looked."

Crystal nodded. "He had beat her and scratched her something terrible," she said. "I wish you could have seen her. She looks like nothing now, in comparison."

"Who did?" Dorney said in agony, suddenly feeling very sick at her stomach.

"This fiend in human form that jumped out at me."

"Oh, Madge!"

"Isn't that awful?" Crystal went around Dorney and took a stance at the end of the lounge where she could possessively smooth her mother's pillow now and again. "Mamma says, Mrs. Towers had a bunch of ladies, her Birthday Club, to supper tonight while the Judge is still gone, he's in Denver on a trip and isn't coming home till tomorrow, and hates to have a lot of women around. So that made Mamma a lot of extra work and dishes and everything, so she was late. So here she was, just coming up Second South as usual, only quite a lot later, when — "

Dorney, on the floor, tucked her knees in under her and settled back.

"There's a big high hedge along that piece of property there," Madge said in a new weak way, "and there's all these trees — "

"Now whether he jumped out from behind a tree or from behind a bush," Crystal put in, "Mamma don't know, but — "

"I screamed bloody murder and started to run — "

"He grabbed ahold of her coat!"

"Nearly tore it off my back!" She pointed to the thin black alpaca coat hanging on the nail back of the door.

"He hit her with something, maybe a baseball bat for all we know!"

"And grabbed my purse!"

"In fact, he nearly jerked her arm off!"

"And banged me, and choked me and hit me — " She panted, shuddering.

"Oh, Madge," Dorney said, wringing her ice-cold hands together. "How awful — how terrible — why, that's the most terrible thing that ever was."

"She had two seventy-five in her purse."

"He's welcome to that," Madge whispered. "I'm surprised he didn't kill me. I believe he would have, if them people hadn't run out to see what all the hollering was about."

"The people who owned the property where it happened run out and found her."

"I couldn't quit screaming for the longest time — "

"I should think not!"

"And they took her in the house and called the police, and the police brought her home." Crystal made her mother lift her head so she could pull the pillow outward an inch and shove it back under half as far. "What was it you told the police you thought he looked like, Mamma?"

"Tall and thin, but so strong, it was like having a grizzly bear jump out and pitch into you." She shivered and rubbed her eyes as though waking from a nightmare.

"One thing I know," she said. "Never again will I walk home alone after dark, never, until that murderer is safe behind bars. Because I know he was a murderer just as sure as I know that God made little apples!"

"If I were you, I never would," Dorney said earnestly. "I'd always ride on the streetcar!"

"Who said anything about a streetcar when the place is within walking distance and I can't earn thirty-five cents a week that I'd have to spend for carfare one way, easier? Besides, what would be the advantage to have to transfer and stand and wait on a pitch-dark corner where anybody could be laying in wait and ready to jump out, I'd like to know?"

"But I thought you said — "

"Mamma means that you and I have to go up to Judge Towers's every night and walk home with her."

"How about leaving Jetta alone?"

"Oh, she'll be all right."

"Until that fiend is caught," Madge said. "I'll never rest any other way."

"How will you know when they've caught him?" Dorney asked.

"I'll know, all right."

"You don't *mind* doing that little favor for Mamma, I should hope?" Crystal said, not so much sneering as preparing to, later on.

"Of course I don't mind." That was better than having Madge murdered! but it would be a long walk every night after the long day in the laundry.

Before Dorney went upstairs to bed, Madge asked her if she had had a good time and if the entertainment had been worth putting her loved ones to a lot of worry and why she had taken it upon herself all of a sudden to be so high and mighty and go off without permission when Crystal plainly warned her it would mean trouble? Before, however, Dorney could formulate an answer, Madge went back to her own personal experience, the assault, to add something she had previously forgotten — that the man had grunted "Ow!" So maybe she had managed to inflict some punishment on him without knowing it. Let's hope and trust so, she said thoughtfully. After that, she seemed disinclined to go back to the topic of Dorney's defection, only to say that tonight, being alive when she might just as well be laying dead in the morgue, she could only forgive and forget. But that did not mean she would do the same thing another time. No, indeed. Let Dorney put *that* in her pipe and smoke it.

Upstairs in bed, on the verge of going to sleep, it came to her that she must write to Mr. Desmond, even if she didn't owe him a letter, or else she would fairly burst, there was so much to tell. (She wouldn't have to send it until it was proper and she had a good excuse.) Otherwise she might forget some of the things that were happening and he would never get to hear about them. The medicine show, for instance. About Clara, too, and Joe Mudge, and how he had suddenly grown so agreeable, it looked as if *maybe* she was going to get her heart's desire after all. Also, the way Mrs. Luby was going to try out Ferdon's Herbal World Beater Tonic on Mr. Luby, to see if it would keep him from drinking. That was worth mentioning, first, because it was extremely interesting, and second, because if it worked, Mr. Desmond might have a friend who could be helped to stop the habit by the same means.

Then, there was having seen the Queen tonight. She had looked straight at Dorney for an instant, but did not nod or smile. Had she known her, or not? How she had changed, the Lady in Waiting of yore, constant yet, would not go on to say. It would pain him to know it and besides, maybe when he returned (had he not said, "We shall meet again"?) Alma Morelewski might have changed back to her right self of beauty and grace once more. If a spell had been cast over her, might she not break it?

She would tell him how, whenever she had a minute to spare, she was always picking up one or the other of the books he had sent and reading or rereading them, but she still had several more plays to read in the *Complete Shakespeare*. In fact, she had only read *The Tempest*. But she could recite at least a dozen poems by heart now. Wouldn't he want to hear what Ishmael had said about the whole duty of man? Much happened at the laundry every day that was worth repeating. And is there such a thing as hypnotism? she would inquire.

Because Mr. Desmond knew all about everything.

If so, Mr. Desmond, is it a perfectly blank sleep? Or does one dream at the same time?

Because, you see, here we were at this medicine show — truly, it was remarkable, the Minstrel Seven, and Heine's Dream, and Snelgrove the Mighty, and this magician — Murdo, his name was — in a swallow-tailed coat — and he came out and did various tricks and pretty soon he called for these people to come up on the stage and be hypnotized, and all of a sudden I was just standing there, Mr. Desmond, and it seemed as if I wasn't there at all, but back in Rock Springs, over at Grandpa Bannon's, sitting there talking to him, and all of a sudden . . .

Dorney was awed when she and Crystal, going to escort Madge home, got to the proper address on East South Temple and she saw what a big house Judge Towers had! Anybody would be. It was three stories high except on the left-hand side where a round turret with a roof like a dunce cap added another story. She wished they could have approached it from the front without having to go around to the back because she would have liked to walk respectfully up onto the tremendous vine-shaded porch as rich as a jungle with plant-filled buckets, barrels, hanging baskets, urns, troughs and jardinières and furnished with enough willow porch furniture to seat an entire W.C.T.U. Chapter, and knock at the door. On either side was a stained glass panel and the transom was also of stained glass.

"I'll bet the doorway looks pretty with the light behind it," Dorney said. "I wish it was dark, so the lights were on and it would show off better." Shading her eyes she looked at the low sun in the west.

"I don't care for it," Crystal said. "By the way, take a peek at the curtains, but don't act like you're looking. I'll bet you never saw anything like them before, did you?"

They were of tan silk, shirred, scalloped and tasseled. "Only in a hearse," Dorney said, meaning no disparagement. She would have lingered by the gate to stare but Crystal said to come on. Going up the long narrow sidewalk she mentioned wistfully that she had always wanted to knock at somebody's front door and have a butler or a housemaid open it to her, to see how it felt!

"Well, you've been a housemaid yourself, and that ought to be enough," Crystal said, unable to keep from laughing at her own joke.

Dorney decided not to take this up. There was too much to see to have her attention distracted by a tiff with Crystal. The cellar windows, for instance, such of them as she could view among the thick shrubbery that filled the space between the sidewalk around the house and the house itself. They were barred over with massive prison bars, which must indicate that immensely valuable things were stored below stairs! The back yard contained besides what looked like an acre of lawn and several outbuildings, a small mossy orchard and, near the house an ornamental iron and glass structure, the use of which Crystal did not know other than that Mrs. Towers sometimes sat in it, well wrapped, for even on a hot day like today it was cool and damp.

Madge let them in. "I'm going to be late again," she said. "Come on in and grab a dishtowel — they're hanging right there by the pantry door."

"Why, you look even worse than you did last night!" Dorney exclaimed, shocked and concerned. "Don't she, Crystal?"

Crystal eyed her mother. "I believe you do," she said. "More swollen, and black and blue."

"I do?" Madge said, rather gratified than not. "Well, I don't feel bad. Except when I chew or blink my eyes. I knew I was all right to come to work this morning, so I'm glad I didn't stay home, the way things turned out."

"What did Selma Ankerstrand say?" Crystal inquired, taking up a silver knife off the wet towel on the drainboard and, as she dried it, examining it with something very like disdain. Selma Ankerstrand was the other servant in the Towers' establishment.

"Why, she never come to work for some reason. Probably sick or some of her folks sick. I might know something like that would happen just on the day the Judge come home from his trip to Denver! Whenever he comes home, there's an awful stir around here for a little while. Mrs. Towers," she lowered her voice and both girls had to bend nearer to hear her, "just seems to go all to pieces, for some reason. You'd think it was one of these here royal I don't know what, coming home! He had to eat his supper alone," she went on, "because Mrs. Towers took to bed about five with one of her sick headaches. She does that. Lays there with the blinds all pulled down and a towel soaked in vinegar on her head and can't swallow a mouthful till it's over. One-sided, her headaches is, she claims. Claims just the one side aches."

When the front doorbell rang, Madge had her hands in the bread dough that was going to be left to rise all night, and she couldn't answer it. "You go," she said to her daughter, thinking she looked very pretty even when she was sulky and that it would do no harm for her to be seen by one of the Judge's rich clients or friends. To Madge, they were all rich. She herself did not get to see many of them but Selma Ankerstrand, whose duty it was to admit callers, used to describe their fur collars, canes, diamond stickpins and seal-hung gold watch chains heavier than a handful of rocks as though they were all J. P. Kearns in person. Who knew? Maybe a miracle would happen and Madge would wake up some fine morning with just such a wealthy son-in-law on her hands as Crystal could accidentally meet at this very front door!

"No," Crystal said, taking a cold seat on the edge of the marble-topped kitchen table. "Why should I?"

"Please, Madge," Dorney begged. "Let me go." She wanted badly to get to see the handsome rooms beyond the pantry door.

The bell rang again.

"Go, then. But don't trip over nothing. Watch where you're going and don't touch none of the china ornaments. Judge Towers, he's in his study. That's right there by the entrance. The big mahogany door there, you can't miss it. Whoever it is probably wants to see him. And get back here. Don't take all night."

"I won't!" Dorney fled, as the doorbell rang a third time and did not stop.

Once she got through the pantry door she was in the great high-ceilinged dining room, hazily full of brass, decanters, giant furniture, velvet hangings, spears, shields, wax fruit, clusters of unlighted candles and two-foot-wide picture frames around black pictures. She jumped from the carpet here to the carpet in the vast entrance hall, overstepping the slick expanse of hardwood between as though it had been a deep canal she was afraid of falling into. That hall! with the great black staircase coming down it, the rubber plants, the mirror as wide as a barn door, the white marble statue like a ghost in one corner. It seemed a block long, and she looked to first one side and then the other as she sped down it, so as not to miss anything.

Somewhat nervously, she took hold of the heavy silver knob of the front door and turned it. She began to sweat when the door wouldn't open. How clumsy the man outside would think her! She could see the shadow of him standing there through one of the stained glass panels. She made an apologetic little moue through it as though to say, Am I not ridiculous? so clumsy, but have patience a moment, if you please. Finally she discovered it was locked and found out how to unlock it. Blushing and smiling she flung the door open and said, "Good evening. I bet you thought I'd never — Won't you — ?" If a chair had been by, her knees felt suddenly so odd, she would have sat down in it hard, right then. "Why, it's you!" she said.

All Butch Cassidy could do was to look at her as if she was Little Dipper coming cantering across a field to him, not dead and gone at all, but alive and kicking. Or whom, that he was so glad to see, he had to laugh out loud? "Well, if this don't beat the Dutch!" he said. "Is he your granddad?"

"Who?" she asked, laughing too, unaccountably so happy she could have danced.

"Alexander Towers? The Judge?"

"Oh, no," she said, shaking her head. "My sister Madge works here. She's the cook."

He tossed his hat onto the slippery taboret, sending a small silver tray crashing to the floor in a snowstorm flurry of little white cards. They both got down to pick them up, he on one knee, she on all fours, and when the cards were all back where they belonged, on the tray, Butch reached across and returned it to the stand and Dorney started to rise.

"Wait," he said, stopping her gently. Wide-eyed, she sat back on her ankles and he took both her hands in his. "Dorney," he said.

She was not surprised that he knew her name, and did not beg, How is it that you know it? but he told her anyway, as if she had asked.

"I heard what that woman called you last night at the medicine show."

(Even afterwards, it did not occur to her that since he was a stranger she ought to have drawn her hands away.)

He looked at her, not a steady but a transient gaze like a ray of light that scanned her hair, brows, lashes and lips and every line of her face, tracing between herself and him in air an invisible perfect likeness of what he saw, before his eyes fixed on hers. "Listen," he said. "Some things is meant to happen and got to happen, everybody in the world knows, and maybe this is one of 'em. When I looked through the pane of glass there a minute ago and seen you

311

come through that archway and come running towards me, to open up the door, I felt like I was seeing a — I can't tell you what a feeling went up the back of my neck and up over my scalp — and while you was fiddling with the lock there, I kept saying to myself, It ain't, it can't be, all it is, is somebody else that happens to look like the kid, because — it just ain't her, I said. Maybe I better explain, except that in a case like this, that's a whole lot easier said than done. You see, last night when I first laid eyes on you, I had a kind of a hunch right then that somehow — but time is mighty short and there's a lot to — one thing you got to hear, though, and that's this. Last night when the show was over and I looked around and you was lost in the crowd, why, I didn't make no attempt — and I wouldn't of never made no attempt — to find you — even if — because a guy like me — and somebody like you — like a sego lily blooming out of the rocks — not on your tintype, I says to myself. No, siree. But this seems to put a — a kind of a different slant on things."

"What does?" she whispered, dazed.

"Tonight does." He spoke so rapidly and softly, she could hardly hear. "Me ringing that doorbell and you answering it. You. It begins to look as if — "

"Please," she said, "tell me your — "

"I got to talk fast, I got to," he said. "I come here tonight to see Judge Towers on business, to see if he can do something for me that a friend of mine thinks he can. I ain't going to get my hopes set on it though, before I see it done with my own two eyes! But *if* he can, why — " He broke off. "How old are you?" he asked abruptly.

"Sixteen, my next birthday."

"About what I figured, and prettier'n the lining in a new hat." He smiled, and unexpectedly let go of her hands. "But what I started to tell you. If what I've come to see Judge Towers about — he's here, ain't he? He got back from Denver all right?"

She nodded.

"If what I've come to see him about," he repeated, "turns out the way I'm hoping, why, then I'll have a bug to come and put in your ear — only, listen." The smile left his face. "If it don't, what can I do but tell myself you wasn't nothing but a mirage, like in the Salton Basin or on the old Yuma road or up in the Jimjam Valley of the Sierra Magdalenas — something I *thought* I seen that wasn't there at all? What else, honey? Only make tracks? Only hightail it away where — ?"

A voice said — but perhaps it said nothing, only coughed. At any rate, it made some sound and they looked up to see the great red mahogany door on Dorney's left swing open and a polished blue-gray head poke out. "I heard the doorbell ring some while since. Did you arrive together?" Judge Towers said, pleasantly gazing down at them as though it was the most natural thing in the world to find callers sitting face to face on the floor in front of his study.

"No, sir," Dorney said. "I opened the door for him. He's your company."

Butch got to his feet lightly and pulled her up with him.

Judge Towers lifted one blue-gray eyebrow and reached up to twist an end of his blue-gray mustache. "Now where would such a dryad come from, I wonder?" he muttered as if to himself, and then, more loudly, "You, sir! Are you the man I think you are, by any chance?"

"Who is it, Alexander? Is something the matter down there?" a distraught female voice called from above stairs. All three looked in the direction from whence it came floating down the shadowy stairwell.

"No, Vida," Judge Towers said. "Everything's fine."

Butch turned to Dorney and she turned to him at the same instant.

"Listen, kid — remember — "

"Please — "

He caught up her hands once more, pressed them to his chest and let them go.

"Are you sure, Alexander?"

"It's just a caller, Vida. I'll be up in a little while. Take another pill and go back to bed." He stepped forward and laid his hand on Butch Cassidy's shoulder. "Come on in, young fellow," he said. "You don't have to tell me who sent you. I know all about it. I had a letter from him."

As Dorney went down the hall she thought she heard the Judge say, "Well, up until now I classed you with specters and the Black Rider of the Plains. I supposed you were a legend . . ." before he shut the door.

"What's the matter with you?" Madge said, as she came out into the kitchen. "You look like you had a start or something. Who was that at the door?" She smoothed the thick pad she had placed over the top of the pan of bread and moved to shut a cupboard door that was a little bit open.

"A man."

"What'd he want?"

"To see Judge Towers." She drew a quivering breath.

"Well, did you usher him in like I told you?"

"Yes, Madge."

"What kept you so long?" Crystal asked idly, buffing her fingernails on the bosom of her dress and inspecting them through narrowed lids.

"Why, I — "

"Gawking, I suppose."

"You never disturbed nothing, did you?" Madge asked anxiously. "Mrs. Towers, you can't move a antimacassar a fraction of a inch but what she knows it, nor breathe on a paperweight nor nothing else, not even peep through the curtain but what she can tell right where you been and what you done. I never seen such a woman."

"I didn't touch a thing, honestly I didn't."

"Well, it don't hurt to look. There's sure plenty to see — and dust and clean. Poor Selma is forever making the rounds and there's never no end to it." With a sigh, Madge walked down the long clean kitchen and reached behind the door into the broom closet. "Well, I'm glad *this* day's over," she said, hanging her coat over her arm. "And I sure hope Selma comes back tomorrow, so I won't have to tackle them dirty shirts."

The next day Selma did come back and the next evening if anybody came to the front door, it was she who saw who it was. Dorney and Crystal were just starting up the back steps when Madge opened the door and came out to meet them, and so there was no occasion for them to go into the house. The night following, they had to wait ten minutes, and longer the night after that, because there had been company. That meant all the silver had to be put away in bags and in the silver chest, which always made Madge late starting home. But Dorney did not get beyond the pantry door again, and if he ever came back, she did not know it.

For some days, even at the laundry, she believed she would look up suddenly and see her friend standing beside her. She always called him that in her mind. My friend. Not the stranger, any more. He had said — what was that he had said about — ? It was hard for her to remember what he *had* said. Strangest of all was at the beginning. "Well, if this don't beat the Dutch!" And then, "Is he your granddad?" Funny that he would connect her with a grandfather and say a thing like that.

Every day she looked for him, from the time she left the house in the morning until she came home at night, everywhere, no matter who she was with or what she was doing. If upon the ditchbank at noon sitting, every shadow that fell across her made her look up wide-eyed, with her heart in her mouth, and think it was he. When she strolled around the block with Clara, she thought every pair of footsteps behind her belonged to that approaching friend.

She told Clara about him, the little there was to tell, after she left out the waking dream during the hypnotist's act and what had happened when the card tray fell on the floor. If Clara was disappointed with the way the promising story, begun so breathlessly and told with such bright eyes, limped up a blind alley that led nowhere, she was too polite to show it. It boiled down to something hardly worth telling, Dorney was afraid Clara thought, and perhaps she did. Just that Dorney had stood beside a certain man at the medicine show when she and Mrs. Luby had got separated from the others. Young? or old? Clara wanted to know. Neither. At least, well — neither. And the next night she and Crystal had to go up to Judge Towers's, because Madge was afraid to walk home alone after having been so scared the night before. And Selma Ankerstrand, the housemaid, who always answered the door, didn't come to work that day. And the doorbell rang. And Crystal wouldn't go and answer it. So Dorney went. And who should be standing there outside on the porch but that very same man again! Now, wasn't that a coincidence? If Dorney could have gone on and recounted what had happened after he and she got down to pick up the tumbled calling cards, Clara might have understood better why she was so stirred by the event, but something made her keep mum about that and break off short there. It was as unsatisfying a story as "Drink to Me Only with Thine Eyes" is a song when hummed or played without the words.

In the middle of July, a purse snatcher was apprehended not far from where Madge fell afoul of her attacker, and when she saw his picture in the *Salt Lake Tribune* she identified him absolutely. That was him, she said, the only man on earth she was afraid of. She had no doubts about it. How did she know? Woman's intuition! and when he was sentenced to prison for five years, she was her old self again, not leery of anything. Nobody had to walk home from Judge Towers's with her, she went back and forth by daylight or dark as if nothing had happened, except that never again could she be induced to pass that one particular corner where she had been pounced upon. Occasionally, she worried about when the five years would be up and the dangerous criminal put back in circulation again, but Crystal reminded her that by that time they would be far from here, either in California or Chicago. If not, Crystal said, she hoped that she herself would be out of her misery because she couldn't stand it around here much longer.

Little by little, what had seemed real began to seem less real. Dorney shut her eyes, the best way to see the friend, and could glimpse him but transparently, insecurely. He moved like fog. Not only what had happened during the hypnotist's act but the whole medicine show began to seem nebulous. Judge Towers's house grew mythical as Camelot, though Madge worked there every day. The doorbell rang without a sound, she sped to the front door without touching the velvet floor . . . and he . . . If she could remember what he had said, word for word, then everything might take on actuality. But she never could. And he had no name! Gradually, she began not to look for him to come up behind her, did not expect to turn a corner and meet him, did not think that if a knock came at the door, even over at Clara's — he would be standing there.

When Mr. Teige Desmond's half-page letter came from Trinity College Dublin, Ireland, saying not much except that never was there a greener, wetter place, this particular summer at least, than the county of Eire, nor ever more of a hoax than a tiny red fire of sea coals, nor anything colder than the Irish sea . . . that some men studied for doctor's degrees while other men had sense enough to drive camels over the hot Peraean plains . . . and that it was inconsiderate of her not to be made out of Chelsea-Derby biscuit like the little milkmaid on his mantelpiece . . . and when she answered it, asking him all the questions she had been saving up, except the one about hypnotism, if there was such a thing (which she was positive by now there wasn't), telling him all the news she had been intending to tell him, and more, too, she did not mention Murdo the Magician, nor what transpired up at Judge Towers's the night following the night of the medicine show. The reason she didn't was because by the time the letter got written, and a fair copy made, and the hard-come-by information was got about how many stamps to put on a thick envelope going to faraway Ireland, and she finished *The Merry Wives of Windsor* so she could put *that* in, the important piece of news about her friend, the man Judge Towers said he thought was a legend (or had she dreamed that?) had got lost like a sand painting in a playful breeze. And what he had said to her, she could no more repeat than if it had been in pure Latin or Greek. All that stuck was "Is he your grandad?" and that inkling about the Jimjam Valley of the Sierra Magdalenas.

She had to steam the letter open, even though it was a good deal of trouble to do it neatly, and then make up a drop of flour paste to stick the flap down with again, to add a most important postscript. Two, in fact. One to say that Mrs. Tofflemire's condition was unchanged, and a second to tell about the death of one of the Negroes with Ferdon's Great Free Attractions. It was in the newspapers and everybody was talking about it at the laundry. He performed with the Minstrel Seven, both as singer and as one of the two dancers. Imagine, to die among strangers like that, of whatever it was he died of, and not get to be shipped home! The medicine show pulled up stakes and left, but the poor minstrel, he had to stay right in Salt Lake City, Utah, forever. He was buried in Mount Olivet cemetery. The funeral procession went past the laundry and everybody crowded to the windows and looked out, whether Mr. Horsfeldt liked it or not. He didn't. He said he was going to dock them all for fifteen minutes, but really, they only looked out about five minutes all together, or perhaps seven or eight, until the parade was out of sight. There were two or three open carriages with Dr. Ferdon and a very pretty lady sitting in one, and Murdo the Magician and the thin black-haired woman that looked sort of scary, like a witch, in another, and the actress with the red curls. The Minstrel Seven — only six of them now — walked, looking very woebegone, with black neckties on. One of them was seen to say something to the man nearest him and smile a little, but he stopped right away and looked woebegone again.

The hearse was black with waving plumes. It had such big plate-glass windows on the sides, almost the entire casket could be seen. The casket was a deep lavender color, trimmed with gold. Some of the ladies said that wasn't much of a recommendation for Ferdon's Herbal World Beater Tonic, was it? To have somebody who you might say was fairly swimming around in it all day long and half the night die like that, and made a few feeble jokes of like nature, but mostly they just watched and kept quiet. It was a hot, sultry day with lots of dust blowing around. That night there was a heat lightning storm and the rain poured down in buckets.

Dr. Ferdon's show only gave two more performances and then picked up and left. It had been there on the corner of Third South and Fourth East for five weeks altogether.

Mr. Horsfeldt did dock them — two cents apiece! And gave Tamer Camomile all kinds of trouble, she had so much small change to handle on payday.

32

"WHAT YOU CAN SEE IN THAT OLD MAID IS MORE than I can tell," Madge said. "Why don't you sit down and read some of your famous Mr. Desmond's books, if you're supposed to be such a scholar?"

Dorney sighed. If she said that on this last night of July her room, though quiet enough with the door shut tight, was insupportably hot and in fact would not be fit to sleep in for hours, Madge was capable of taking the explanation as a personal insult. If she confided that when Crystal banged away in the parlor with gymnastic monomania like that, as she always did before a lesson next day with Mrs. Million, nobody but the stone-deaf could so much as hear herself think, Madge might suspect her of jealousy and take her to task for it. She did this from time to time, a painful few minutes Dorney was glad to avoid if she could. To hint that she regretted Jetta's early bedtime and wished she might be allowed to invent another story for her would be rash, as the subject of Jetta was ever a touchy one — and to suggest that Madge was somewhat less than entertaining when Crystal was not by, for whom alone she made any effort to descend to particulars and relate something interesting, would not only be foolhardy but unkind. "Maybe Clara won't be an old maid much longer," Dorney said, rather irrelevantly.

Madge stopped fanning herself with the stiff paper fan printed The Autoharp, Easy to Play, Easy to Buy, and looked interested. "Has he popped the question?" she asked.

"Well, no, not exactly, yet."

"Then what makes you think so?"

"I wish you could see her, that's all, how changed she is and happy and everything. Lela Galloway says it's just a pleasure to see how Clara has come out of it."

"Come out of what?" When Dorney opened her mouth to speak, she held her hand up, shaking her head. "Hush a minute," she said. "Listen to that long run there. I wonder the child's fingers will move that fast. Listen." Dutifully cocking an ear, Dorney had a vision of a tiny creature running down a long slope. Near the bottom, she stumbled and fell, rolling over and over, then picked herself up and slowly and painfully climbed the hill once more to the very top. This time she tripped down the acclivity as though descending a long flight of stairs, with no mishap. Repeated this haughtily. Repeated this saucily. Lost her balance! Fell! Turned end over end! and had to start from the beginning.

"Now, where was we?" Madge asked, her eyes shining. "If that ain't talent, I don't know what is."

"We were talking about Clara Tofflemire."

"Well, don't wear your welcome out over there." Madge hitched her chair over closer to the open back door, rolled her sleeves up higher, undid her band collar and fanned hard, as though to make up for lost time. She glanced at the clock. "It's eight now," she said. "Don't stay much past nine, and I mean that."

Clara had a length of white Henrietta cloth pinned all over the pattern shapes, laid out on the bare dining-room table which, with all its leaves in, would seat a large company, and was in the midst of cutting out a dress.

"I want your honest opinion," Mrs. Tofflemire said, when Dorney had taken the chair pointed out to her. Tossing her head, she handed across a large envelope printed with a picture of the frock Clara was making. "Don't that look to you like somebody was out of their mind, I'm asking you honestly?"

"Mamma thinks it's too young for me," Clara said, smiling. "She objects to the ruffles and the short sleeves." She did not look up but went on about her business, snipping around a campaniform piece of tissue and then with forthright whacks of her long scissors attacking a semilunar one nearby.

"I object to people making fools of theirselves, is all." Mrs. Tofflemire reached for the heart-shaped woven fan on the window seat and began to wave it rapidly before her moist face.

"Oh, I think it's beautiful," Dorney said, studying the illustration. It was. Not an everyday dress by any means but something for a real occasion. She took a quick peek at busy Clara and looked back at the picture. Had Joe Mudge asked her to marry him? Up to this morning, he hadn't, Dorney was sure, for Clara had merely repeated herself which she would not have done if she had had something new and significant to say, and on the way to work dwelt on Joe's kindness and how much more friendly and cheerful he seemed ever since the medicine show. Just last week, she said, she had sent Georgie out for an armful of kindling and who should come bringing it into the kitchen but Joe himself! with Georgie right behind him, grinning for all he was worth, like the two of them were playing a joke of some kind on her (she never found out what it was). She put up a crate of strawberries Joe had bought off a peddler and he said he never knew but two women who could make better jam, his mother and Sophie, and even they wouldn't beat her by more than a hair's breath. And he said she ought to set up a school to learn ironing to them that didn't know how! And only last evening when she was over there mopping up the kitchen floor, she happened to look up and there he was standing in the doorway! And what did he say? Why, he stood there as big as life and said, "How soon before a fellow can dast to step across your clean floor?" Her clean floor, if you please! The way a man would say it to — but Clara stopped there superstitiously and did not say to whom.

No, Joe Mudge had not yet proposed, Dorney was sure, and she hoped he would hold off for a while, so that Clara would have a chance to enjoy her assumption. Reassured, comforted, emboldened, in a state of grace, she did not seem like the same person any more, but could look straight into another's eyes, speak without clearing her throat beforehand, laugh without looking shamefaced and she no longer muffled herself up like a Bedouin when she went abroad. She had discovered that asset, her small waist, and had taken to wearing sashes. A few shy curls were commencing to appear on her forehead. The last two or three paydays, when Tamer Camomile called her name, she went up for her check matter-of-factly, not as if she was going to the gallows, and she did not shake all over like a leaf when she came back with it. Yes, Clara was a changed woman.

Lela Galloway wondered if she hadn't sent for and wasn't using some new face wash or cold cream. They were inventing new things all the time and the advertisements claimed they could do wonders. Aurilla McCann gave it out as her opinion that Clara had fallen heir to some cash, which there was nothing like it, Aurilla said, for putting a backbone into anybody. Even an angleworm, with money, had gumption enough to turn right around and spit in your eye. Ishmael told Dorney that he had noted Clara's metamorphosis with great satisfaction and was convinced that the philosophy of Epictetus was responsible for it. Those first snatches he read aloud to them up in the shirt department and the later selections as they wandered by the loading platform and stopped to chat a moment on their way out to the ditchbanks these summer noons, she and Clara — they had been like chunks of ripe red beef and mugs of porter to an invalid, building her up and putting her on her feet again. There was nothing like Epictetus for what ailed a man, Ishmael said, proud as a doctor who has cured a patient of bleeding ulcers. Nothing like a dose of philosophy! Hester Walp said that either Clara Tofflemire had found her Redeemer and finally set her gaze on something Higher than this puny earth or else she was very much mistaken. Hester was, Dorney knew, but she did not tell her so, any more than she straightened out Lela Galloway or Aurilla McCann or Ishmael in regard to what was really responsible for Clara's transformation. Let them wait until the happy day they had to chip in for a wedding present! Then might the revelation come, that love was the only answer.

Mrs. Luby had taken to strolling around the block with her children after their early supper and Dorney, after Clara had said good-bye and turned in at her own gate, often met her. She was waiting as eagerly for word that Joe Mudge had proposed as Dorney was. "Has he?" she had been saying almost every night for the past two weeks and Dorney had to shake her head and say no, not yet. But both knew it was just a matter of time. The evening before, Mrs. Luby had said of the fascinating change, "If I wanted to write my daughter Mary about it, for instance, I'd have a hard time, because Clara ain't a ounce lighter or heavier, or a fraction of a inch shorter or higher . . . and it's hard to put a person's finger on any particular . . . I declare," she said, "if it don't seem like nature ain't behind the whole thing!"

"How do you mean, Mrs. Luby?"

"If there's any way around it at all, nature don't want no old maids! I've noticed it many and many a time. She just naturally slips something into their blood someway at the last minute if not before to smooth 'em and tint 'em and shine 'em and sparkle 'em till they're like mallards with them little oil sacks in their skin that makes their feathers glisten. That's what nature's went to work and took a hand and done to Clara, as sure as fate, ever since that medicine show!"

Perhaps she had, for true love's sake, Dorney thought as she sat watching Clara cut out her dress.

"That won't last, I can tell you," Mrs. Tofflemire snorted. She folded her hands across her big stomach, the fan sticking out, and began to rock back and forth in her squeaky chair.

"What won't, Mamma?" With each cut of her scissors Clara bit down softly on the end of her tongue.

"Such a fad as that. Short sleeves. Long gloves! Naked elbows sticking out in the weather. I never seen nothing sillier in my life." She snorted again. "How's your sister Mrs. Yandle?" she demanded suddenly of their visitor.

"She's fine, thank you."

"Still afraid to walk home alone?"

"Not now. You see, the man, he's been arrested and put in jail, so now she goes and comes just the same as ever."

"What did he look like?"

"You've heard the whole story over and over," Clara said. "I don't know how many times." She turned to Dorney. "Mamma took a notion she had to hear all that you told me the next day after it happened, over and over, till I've been practically blue in the face."

"Mamma knew very well why," Mrs. Tofflemire said mysteriously. "Mamma ain't in the habit of doing nothing without a very good reason. What's got me stumped," she said, "is that Mrs. Yandle never woke up with snow white hair the next morning, that's what's got me stumped. After a fright like that. From what Clara tells me, the fiend nearly killed her. What did he look like?" she repeated.

"Well, he was tall and thin, but terribly strong. Madge didn't get to see him very well, but she said — "

"Then how does she know it's him that's been arrested?" Clara's mother said with triumph. "Kindly tell me that, will you?"

"His picture was in the paper."

"But you just said she didn't get to see him very well!"

"She's pretty sure, though," Dorney said. "You see, he was arrested right up in that very neighborhood, practically in that same block, for knocking a woman down and grabbing her purse, the same way he did with Madge, and so of course — " She stopped and looked with some curiosity at Mrs. Tofflemire who had been shaking her head in disbelief and a kind of sly jubilation and continued to do so.

In the silence, Clara looked up. She laid her scissors down, "Now, Mamma," she said.

"Don't you Now-Mamma me," Mrs. Tofflemire said, looking sternly at her. "Anybody that Now-Mamma's me has got to have quite a bit more authority than you got, I can tell you that much. They ain't caught the one that's to blame! You know it, and I know it. Everybody else that halfway uses the sense they were born with, knows it!" Her large face and neck darkened. "Tall and thin! Superhuman strength! Lay in wait and jump out on innocent women! Choke 'em! Beat 'em! Nearly murder 'em! Who does that description fit, I want to know? Who, I ask you?"

"Mamma gets quite worked up over — " Clara began, turning uneasily to Dorney.

"Schooner Bill, that's who!" the old lady said.

"Oh, no, Mrs. Tofflemire!"

"Now that's just silly, Mamma, as I have told you every day since it happened."

Mrs. Tofflemire ignored her daughter. "I have said over and over again — in fact, if I had a nickel for every time I've said it, I could retire right this minute and live off the fat of the land — I have said — Schooner Bill Cursoe is a terrible danger to girls and women! I always have. I never said nothing else but. He's crazy, that's why, crazier than a peach-orchard bore. And he's a man, that's why, and any man, no matter who or where, is just naturally dangerous because he *is* a man which both of you may look back some day and mark my words and say I was right all the time. Just naturally dangerous! because of his nature! But you take a crazy man at the same time and there ain't nothing worse on the face of the earth. And I ain't fooling, either. I mean every word I say. It was Schooner Bill that jumped on your sister and almost done her in, you can be as positive as you are that the sun's coming up tomorrow morning!"

"Mamma gets her head set on something like that," Clara murmured, "and nothing will faze her."

"Madge would have known if it was Schooner Bill," Dorney said. "Really, she would. But it wasn't, Mrs. Tofflemire. Cross my heart and hope to die, if it was."

"Of course it wasn't," Clara said.

To Dorney came the memory of the strange cowboy-hatted man unstoppering his jug and offering them a sip of Christmas cheer by frosty starlight, repeating the toasts he had heard up in the saloon where he worked, making them smile, making them feel better than they had before.

The old lady looked at them narrowly. "Why the two of you would want to band together and stick up for a ugly customer like that is more than I can see. But it's not going to do either of you any good, or him either."

"You can't just accuse somebody of something like that. You've got to have proof," Clara said, a sharp note creeping into her voice. "And besides, I thought we had been all over that and it was settled once and for all."

"Maybe I can get some proof."

"What for?" Dorney asked, worried.

Only last Sunday afternoon on her way to call on her friend Mrs. Blufe Bannon, she had met him. He was wearing a sea captain's dark-blue gold-braided cap, exceptional to see so far from any ocean. As ever, he had stopped short, sidled off to the right, bowed and tipped his cap, danced back and said, "Friend." How he did lift the heart! even when, as on that occasion, he spoke of death.

"Mrs. Dearing had her canary bird to die last night," he said. Mrs. Dearing was his landlady. "Eleven years old, Fonsie, its name was, bawled the whole night long, she did."

"Poor lady," Dorney said.

He beckoned to her, she bent her head nearer and he whispered almost into her ear, "Death ain't what they think it is, by no means."

"What who thinks, Schooner Bill?"

"People and everybody."

"What is it, then?"

"It's lots different than *that*, for sure." He batted his small clear light eyes. "First, it's a law," he said. "And a law means, it's got to be. So no use to holler about a *law*. Then, how do they look? Like somebody sleeping their head off dead to the world, snug as a bug in a rug. No use to holler about nothing so *snug*. Then, what they missing? That's what I says to Mrs. Dearing this morning! What they missing, Mrs. Dearing? I says. She says, Everything. I says, Everything is right. Hitting their crazy bone! Throwing up their heels! Getting knocked for a loop! Being give the go-by! Winding up busted! Nobody can name what all. You hit the nail on the head, Mrs. Dearing, I says. Everything is right, Mrs. Dearing!"

Dorney had been looking serious but when Schooner Bill smiled then, a bright rubbery smile, she smiled back at him.

"So that's what I say," he said. "And so now I'll tell you a secret."

"A secret?"

He nodded. "There ain't but one way to do about death, no matter what nobody says about it, even somebody as smart at the Fire Chief."

"What's that?"

"Play like you never heard tell of it. And that's the secret!"

"What for, Mrs. Tofflemire?" Dorney asked again. "Proof for what?"

"Why, evidence — so he can be put in the asylum, that's what for, and women and girls can walk the street in safety. For the rest of his natural life."

Clara plucked a pin out of an oblong piece of pattern and ran it in again more to her liking. "Who feels like a nice cold glass of lemonade?" she said.

"I've talked all I'm going to," Mrs. Tofflemire said. "Now I'm going to get busy and do a little acting for a change! I'm going to the authorities and I'm going to have that man put behind bars if it's the last thing I do. All it takes is somebody determined enough, to do a mighty lot, all by theirself! and I'm going to show this neighborhood that if *they* won't do it, *I* can. One determined woman, that's all it takes! without no help from nobody."

"A man that's never harmed a flea — a man that can't help it if the Lord happened to make him kind of — tell me, what satisfaction will it give you, if you can do it?" Clara said softly.

"I can do it, all right. All a person has to be is determined enough." Mrs. Tofflemire shut her lips tight together and Dorney, watching her, thought she had never seen anyone look so like a big toad. "I'll get up a petition and have it signed. Take it before the Mayor. One lone woman can do a mighty lot, when she's got right on her side, believe me! I'll call on people and explain to 'em and rally 'em round. We'll fix it. We'll legislate some safety for poor women and girls walking the streets taking their life in their hands or know the reason why!"

"Just because you took it into your head you don't like him! If everybody was locked up that people didn't happen to like — why, there wouldn't be nobody left! The whole blame world would be looking out from behind bars!"

"You'd lock me up quick enough!" Mrs. Tofflemire said. "I can tell by that look you're giving me." Suddenly she grinned. "Wouldn't you?"

Clara picked up her scissors and began to cut through the Henrietta cloth again.

"Wouldn't you?"

Dorney felt her heart begin to beat faster.

The scissors stopped where they were. Clara gazed levelly at her mother. "Why should I?" she said.

"Why should you?" Mrs. Tofflemire grinned once more. Her already red face had turned purplish, ugly, and shone like an eggplant.

"Don't start something, Mamma, that's all I'm asking you," Clara said, licking her lips. "Let Schooner Bill be. He ain't doing you nor nobody else no harm. He works for a living. He behaves himself. Why should you take it on yourself to try to spoil his life for him now at this late date? Not that I think you'd get to first base. But let him be."

Please, Mrs. Tofflemire, Dorney thought. Please. She was convinced that if the relentless old woman was resolved to get up a petition and go to the Mayor and move heaven and earth, Schooner Bill, like the albatross in the much-marked poem in Mr. Desmond's *Oxford Book of English Verse*, was doomed.

"Probably a dozen people — or no telling how many — can swear that the night Mrs. Yandle had that awful thing happen to her, Schooner Bill was right there in the saloon where he works!" Clara went on. "This is a free country. You got to have some proof. You can't get busy and railroad somebody into a asylum just because you don't happen to like their looks and the way they act, you know!"

"Maybe you got a little surprise coming about what a little determination can do, if a person keeps after something and don't let up," Mrs. Tofflemire said, breathing as if she had run around the block, "when they've got right on their side! And if I ain't, wanting that lunatic put where he belongs before it's too late, I don't know who has! and I think I'll get quite a few to agree with me."

With an effort, Clara pulled her eyes away from her mother. "I'll make us all a glass of cold lemonade," she said with difficulty, and started for the kitchen door.

"Wait a minute," her mother said. "Wait just a minute there."

325

Clara halted.

"What was you going to say, I want to know? Say it! if you ain't too much of a coward and waiting to say it to somebody behind my back instead."

"I wasn't going to say nothing."

"Oh, yes, you was. I know you, when you get that look on your face. I know you! I know that look, too. You ain't changed. You might put on airs and think so, but you ain't. Them curls, instead of wearing your hair decent the way a woman going on for forty ought to, they ain't changed you, never think. I know you."

"Thirty-four," Clara said between her teeth.

With wonder Dorney thought, Will I ever be that old? Is it possible? With time dilly-dallying the way it does? with it taking forever to be next month, Christmas, March, my birthday? She was careful not to let this show in her face, for fear of wounding Clara who stood clutching the table.

"Them curls! I ask you, do you think he's going to do anything but laugh at 'em? at you? with that green sash around your waist? No man could help it, if Joe Mudge can be called a man — to see the demonstration *he's* seen, of just how big a fool a woman can make out of herself over somebody that wouldn't walk half a block for her. Half a block? Not the length of this room! How could anybody help but laugh? at a demonstration like that — a woman that never could get no kind of a beau of no kind or description whatever — of such a one, making such a spectacle over herself for somebody that wouldn't touch her — that wouldn't spit — that can't stand the sight — that can't see her for dust!"

"What you're so scared of, you can't see straight," Clara said in a hushed voice, "is, you're scared he *will* see me for dust. Because maybe he will, someday! And I'll be happy for once! and get out of your clutches! and be able to call my soul my own, which I ain't been able to, never for five minutes, since the day I was born!"

Mrs. Tofflemire reached out and gave a twitch to the material hanging down from the dining room table. "What do you call this?" she said. "A wedding dress? excuse me a minute while I bust out laughing."

"You're so scared, you're shaking in your shoes."

"Too bad your mother's dead," Mrs. Tofflemire said to big-eyed Dorney. "Because here would be your chance to take a lesson in how to talk to her when she's a poor old lady!"

"A poor old lady!" Clara laughed bitterly. "When didn't you let me think so! Twenty years ago when you started me to work at the Palace Laundry, you wasn't by no means a poor old lady. You was forty-seven years old. That wasn't so old you had to lay back and never do a tap again in all your life, only just what you took a notion, while somebody else walked to work and stood on their feet and sweated and walked home, winter and summer, summer and winter, and kept you going while you — "

"Too bad your mother's dead," Mrs. Tofflemire repeated to Dorney. "Because this here's the finest lesson in the world in how to talk to a mother that had done everything in her power to make the best out of — and try — and never leave a stone unturned — You've heard tell of the Ten Commandments, I imagine. Well, they're just silly, especially the one that goes, Honor thy father and thy mother that thy days may be long upon the land which the lord thy God giveth thee!"

"Honor my father," Clara murmured. "I did honor him! but you, I'll never forget if I live to be a thousand years old, how you — I used to sneak alongside of him and say, Papa, why don't you — ? why do you — ? and Papa, he'd shake his head and say, She's only tired, she's only nervous, she don't mean it. . . . But you did mean it! You hated him. Was it because he — ? I've wondered lots of times. Maybe because I loved him! Maybe because he loved me!"

"You," Mrs. Tofflemire said. "You should have heard what he said one time about you."

"If the brother that died before I was born had lived, would that — ? Or what would? Was it because Papa was a man and you hate men because they're men and you hate men? Or what, in God's name? I honored my father. And for all I know, you might have honored your father! but one thing sure and certain, you never honored your *husband*. The time you found them tickets to the turkey raffle in his pocket, I can see it like it was yesterday, I'll never forget as long as I — how you — what you — while poor miserable Papa, God love him — "

"Hell hath no fury like a woman scorned," Mrs. Tofflemire said elaborately, once more to Dorney. "I knew somebody one time that used to say that, and they was right, too. It's true. Hell hasn't. A woman scorned is as full of poison as a swole-up and wiggling mean old rattlesnake."

"Scorned!" Clara said. "Who says I'm scorned?"

"Who says she's scorned?" Mrs. Tofflemire said, giggling in Dorney's scared direction. "She wants to know, who says she's scorned? When that weak-kneed, chicken-livered, chinless, bulgy-eyed, jobless, penniless thing of a Joe Mudge wouldn't touch her with a ten-foot pole, wouldn't have her at any price, who says I'm scorned? she says!" Mrs. Tofflemire burst out laughing.

Clara stood there by the table, the fingers of her right hand closing around the long scissors. She grew taller as smoke grows taller chimerically and her eyes somehow disappeared. That she spoke and could speak came as rather a dumfounding thing. "Ever since," she said, "Sophie died, and I started going over there to do what I could for them little motherless kids —"

"Ever since Sophie died and she started going over there to lally-gag all over that poor excuse of a man Sophie left, she means," Mrs. Tofflemire said loudly behind her hand to Dorney, "that poor little nibbling nothing of a rabbit that would have to get down on his bended knees and beg and plead with any other woman to get her to so much as look at him! a man that's fixed the way he is, out of work, kids squirming all over the place —"

"— why, you been after me," Clara said. "But then, you always been after me! I never knew a time when you wasn't after me and I guess I never will. You had excuses enough, maybe — I wasn't no prize — maybe I wouldn't of been quite so bogus or quite such a fizzle, I mean — but that ain't either here or there, now. You had excuses enough, and if you hadn't of had, you would of made 'em, but the best one you ever had was since Sophie died and I been going over there doing for her loved ones."

"Her loved ones," the old lady mimicked.

"That was right down your alley," Clara said. "If I hadn't of give it to you free gratis, you would of paid out money for a excuse like that, and you've sure got all the good there was to get out of it. But now I got a little news for you. I'm sick of it, see, I'm sick and tired of it, and I'm going to put an end to it once and for all."

Dorney's eyes slid to the scissors.

"She's going to put an end to it," Mrs. Tofflemire said pointing with her thumb in Clara's direction. Then she turned and looked full at her daughter, sneering.

"Yes, I am."

"And how, if I may make so bold as to inquire?"

Their visitor began to rise.

The blades when closed together made a sharp and long weapon.

"I'll tell you how," Clara said.

Dorney was out of her chair now, frightened.

"By killing me, I suppose," Mrs. Tofflemire said, "which I have always thought you was capable of. It certainly shouldn't come as no shock to me when I consider how you've took pleasure in being as contrary as you knew how to be, all these years! So that would be only what anybody would expect, I guess."

"No," Clara said, shaking her head, a smile playing about her lips.

"In fact, when I look back —"

"You flatter yourself, Mamma dear, that you're worth somebody's everlasting soul! Who do you think you are? No, what I'm going to do, I'm going to take your fine excuse away from you and leave you

328

high and dry the way I should of done, months and months ago."

"Oh, you are, are you?"

"I'm going over there and ask Joe Mudge to marry me!" Still clutching the scissors, Clara started for the open back door.

"Shut it!" Mrs. Tofflemire screamed, and Dorney, close by it, automatically did so. "You ain't! Never! Not while I got the breath of life in me! A daughter of mine, to go over there like somebody out of their head and prostrate theirself and lay theirself down in the dirt, and roll over like a nasty pup, and plead — and let their tongue hang out — and prostrate theirself — and *be turned down cold.*"

"All that's the matter with you, Mamma dear, you're afraid I *won't* be turned down cold!"

Dorney, fearful as in the midst of lightning and thunder, stared at Clara, who for the first time in her life looked like a monarch.

"Just you dare, that's all!"

"You're afraid I'll be took up on it, and he'll *have* me, and I'll get to be a real live woman after all! Because that would put such a crimp in you and all your schemes that you'd never get over it."

"You go and I'll promise you this much — you'll never get back in this house as long as you live!"

"Wish me good luck, Mamma."

"I flatly forbid it! and I promise you this much, if you go, I'll —" Mrs. Tofflemire got out of her chair with such force that if it had turned a complete back somersault behind her, it would have come as no surprise, approached headlong on unsteady legs, pushed Dorney away from in front of the door and took a stance there with her back against it, barring it. Her purple burned like wine held up to the sun.

"This ain't the only way out," Clara said. She wheeled and headed for the parlor. "There's a front door, remember."

Mrs. Tofflemire was after her in a flash. She grabbed her, clung, seemed to clamber, slid on the ingrain carpet, forced her around.

"I'm going," Clara said. "You got to find some other excuse than Joe Mudge and them little kids because that one ain't going to hold good no longer. I'm going to find out once and for all whether he *would* touch me with a ten-foot pole or whether he wouldn't, because I've heard for the very last time that he wouldn't and I'm going to find out!"

"Don't you do it! Don't you dare! Don't you dare go near that man and prostrate yourself and roll in the dust and ask him to — that rabbit — that nasty silky-haired jobless penniless — with all them squirming — I forbid it — don't you dare! Don't you dare!"

"Let go of me, Mamma."

The words were hardly breathed before Mrs. Tofflemire did let go, to put a fumbling hand to her temple. She took a queer staggering step backward and said, "Now where would anybody get such a pain in their head, if you please? Where?"

Clara blazed for a long moment, and then the fire went out and she looked scared and inquisitive. "Mamma?" she said. The scissors still in one hand, she reached out and took hold of the sagging shoulders. "What's the matter with you?" She shook her. Her mother's head hung to one side as though her neck were broken. "Mamma? Tell me! . . . Dearest?"

On her way over to Second East for the doctor, with tousle-haired and swollen-eyed Thornton Luby, whom his mother insisted on rousing from a sound sleep and dressing in trousers, shoes and the baby's shawl, to accompany and protect her, Dorney stopped in at Madge's to tell the news and say where she and her little escort were headed.

"Mrs. Tofflemire has had an awful spell of some kind and Thornton here and I are going to the doctor!"

"What kind of a spell, for goodness sake?"

"She got a terrible headache and put her hand up to her head, and then she began to do this way," Dorney swayed back and forth, "and Clara caught her or she would have fallen right down on the floor and I helped too — she was so limp, she couldn't stand up, and she was covered with perspiration but she was as cold as ice — and Clara and I, we got her to the lounge and then she didn't know anything, honestly, and her eyes rolled right back in her head. She could hardly breathe, and she turned such a funny color, like paste — "

"I suppose I'd ought to go over and see if I can do something."

"Oh, Madge, that would be so nice! Mrs. Luby's there but Clara is awfully upset and maybe you'd know something to do."

Crystal lifted her glass and took a last swallow of milk, then carried it over and set it down on the drainboard. "I don't know why you should," she said. "Dorney's the one that's so thick with the Tofflemires, not us."

Dorney set her lips.

"And besides, you promised to finish my dress tonight."

"They're neighbors," Madge said, looking at the closed sewing machine, then at Crystal and finally at her young sister. "But of course if Mrs. Luby is already over there . . . and if the doctor's coming . . ."

"And Dorney is representing the family," Crystal said smugly.

"Maybe I could do more good later on. You tell Clara," Madge said, "you tell her that if I can do anything, to feel perfectly free to call on me, any time that I'm home."

"All right," Dorney said.

330

Dr. Reach was a prosperous-looking man who wore a pair of spectacles on a black ribbon around his neck. They kept him occupied, fixing them on his nose with the utmost care only to flip them off and let them plunge down and dangle against the third and fourth buttons of his vest. He did not appear to need them when, for instance, he removed his coat, rolled up his sleeves and went to work, cutting open the vein in the cradle of Mrs. Tofflemire's arm and watching the blood drip out drop by drop into a fluted sauce dish until he thought it was full enough, then bandaging up the wound. But when he stood lost in thought, he did, and very opportune they made him appear, prudent and long-headed. The stroke of apoplexy the patient had suffered was a severe one, of which she might yet die, he said, bespectacled. Her brain had ruptured on the left side. Down fell the glasses when he pulled back her eyelids, examined her eyes and squeezed the fingers of her right hand hard, but he had to put them on again to address his solemn audience — Clara, Mrs. Luby, Dorney and Thornton, who refused to turn in at his own gate and go back to bed — and announce that he prescribed head elevation, hot water bottles at the feet, and a whiff of ammonia from time to time. To write out certain secret characters on a little piece of paper, his own eyes served, but not when he handed it to Clara and said she should get it filled at the druggist's the first thing in the morning and administer according to directions. One more careful scrutiny of the patient (glasses off) and Dr. Reach was ready to take his leave (glasses on), announcing that he would call round tomorrow.

In the middle of the night when Clara, politely refusing assistance, went out into the kitchen to make coffee and fix a bite to eat, Mrs. Luby whispered to Dorney that the poor thing didn't seem so much like a daughter whose mother had been taken with a stroke as somebody that had seen some terrible calamity take place and couldn't get rid of the picture of it in the back of her mind. "Like when I was a girl," Mrs. Luby explained. "I knowed a woman that seen the ground cave in on her two boys that was digging a well, and when they was excavated a day and a half later, why, she had a certain look on her face. It was froze on, you might say, for it never really left her ever after although she lived to be as old as the hills, in fact she just died not long ago. And Clara, she seems to be kind of the same way, somehow. Like she seen some awful thing that was printed on her brain. But there's quite a lot of difference in being the daughter of a old lady that has a natural stroke, and being the mother of two fine strapping boys that gets buried alive in a well. So she'll get over it. . . ." She reached across and turned the low flame of the lamp still lower. "She sure looks sick, don't she?" They both looked at the stricken woman, still on the lounge in the shadows, and listened to her labored breathing. "I wouldn't be surprised but what she'll die. It's a shame." Mrs. Luby said, careful not to be overheard, and with a glance at the closed kitchen door. "But at the same time, maybe it will make things easier between Clara and you-know-who. I often wondered if he wasn't kind of leery of somebody, not to mention any names, and if *that* wasn't maybe holding things up."

Thornton, on a low stool at Dorney's feet, pressed his chin into her knee and gazed up at her. For a long time past he had been thinking that he liked her very much and that when he grew up he would perhaps ask her to marry him, but of course as became a boy of eight he had only run and hid when he saw her coming, or screamed outlandishly, or leaped upon and throttled a playmate, or crazily flapped his arms. But catastrophe and the incredible hour, heretofore conjectural, freed him of embarrassment, as war does, or a comet. Ignoring his mother, he said softly, "I wouldn't be a-scared to go in a graveyard no matter if it was as *dark as pitch*."

Dorney, in the act of shivering a little in the cold breeze blowing in through the half-open window, that did not mean the coming day would not be hot, leaned forward to lift the end of his shawl, and wrap it more closely around him. "Most kids would be," she said. "And grown people too."

"Not me." He wanted to whisper something in her ear then, so she bent down and let him, pushing her hair up out of the way. She could feel the movement of his warm lips. "I can walk all up and down where the roof of the coal shed comes to a peak but Mamma don't know it. . . . I'll walk for you. I'll tell you my secret hiding place. I'll give you a piece of glass. It's blue. . . ."

"Hoity-toity," Mrs. Luby said to motionless Rupert who lay by the stove with his head between his paws, his eyes worried and watchful. "So it goes."

Clara appeared in the doorway. "It's ready," she said. "Such as it is. I must say, I'm ashamed to ask company to sit down to nothing no better."

Dorney looked at her, looked again. What had she done to herself? She was not changed any more. No one would ask now, was it a miracle-working face wash? money? religion? love? that wrought so great a transformation? for no transformation was wrought. She was just the way she had been, her old self again, the same as ever, ugly and sad. So ugly and so sad that if she went to Joe Mudge and asked him — but she would not go to him and ask him anything. Not him, nor God, nor anybody. And ask them anything. Ever.

33

MRS. LUBY SAID THAT THE WORST THING ANYBODY of the caliber of Clara could do was to quit the laundry. After all those years she didn't even go there to say goodbye, but let Dorney carry the message that she would not be back! and the Palace lost the best bosom ironer they ever had. Some people, Mrs. Luby said, needed worse than others to be forced by circumstances to get out and mix with the world. It wasn't going to do Clara a bit of good to stay home instead of going on with her job and hiring somebody to nurse her mother. In fact, it was going to do her a terrible great lot of harm! And the truth of the matter was, it already had.

Harem Winfrey, Oda Partridge and several others came to call a time or two, but by the end of August, Mrs. Luby and Dorney were Clara's only visitors, except for those, few and far between, who saw the sign she had stuck in the window, Plain Sewing, and brought work for her to do.

That is, not counting Joe Mudge!

Some two weeks after Mrs. Tofflemire's seizure, Dorney, on her way home, saw him coming toward her from the direction of Clara's house and knew he had either paid a call on their friend or come very close to it. Few sights would have refreshed her more, for many was the time in the past few days that she and Mrs. Luby had wondered whether he would come, or not, of his own accord!

Long since, she would have run over there to tell him what had happened had not Clara forbidden it. "I'll never forgive the one that goes to Joe Mudge and even so much as mentions my name," she said. Mrs. Luby, told of this injunction after she expressed the opinion that Joe Mudge ought to be notified of developments, decided upon consideration that maybe such a course of action was not of the dumbest. What Clara very probably had up her sleeve, Mrs. Luby said, was to find out if he cared the snap of his finger about her, and how could she find out better than by waiting to see what he would do if she never went near him? As the days wore on, however, and Clara continued to backslide and put about until it took an effort to recall how close she had come to the splendor of being both fair and beloved, and nobody saw hide nor hair of Joe Mudge, her two friends grew more and more anxious. Only the evening previous to his call, Mrs. Luby had threatened, "We may have to take things in our own hands before the situation goes too far!"

But now, here was the desideratum himself, plainly hailing from Clara's!

It was no wonder that Dorney wanted to give a hop, skip and jump when she caught sight of him until she got near enough to see how pensive were his large pink and blue eyes. They were enough to sober her.

Luckily, he began to speak at once of what was as much on his mind as on hers, so she did not have to cast about for a way to broach the subject. "The groceryman told me what happened," he said. "But the first week, as you may imagine, I was left in the dark."

Dorney felt she deserved his reproachful look, took it flinching a little.

"I didn't know what could of happened," he said. "Didn't have the slightest idea. See, she'd been coming so steady, never missed a day, morning and evening, Sundays and holidays, and she's one of these, folks get used to. We could always depend —" He took his plaid cap off and scratched his light golden head. "Ever since my wife died, see, leaving a man with four kids and the oldest not six, and me nor Sophie with kinfolk around, Clara'd been on the job. So you can imagine — All of a sudden she don't show up! Morning comes, no Clara. Night comes, no Clara. The kids bawl, they been used to this fussing, see, and hair-brushing and all that, and they fight and carry on. I can't hardly do nothing with 'em, so I thinks to myself, Is she sick or what's happened? So when it gets dark and I get the kids to bed and they get to sleep, why, I sneak over there. The front of the house ain't lit up but I go around to the back and I look in the kitchen window, and there's Clara, standing by the stove stirring something. So she ain't sick. I say to myself, She ain't sick, she could of come." He looked at Dorney.

"Why didn't you let her know you were there? She'd have been so glad. Her mother had that terrible stroke!"

"That's what the groceryman was telling me last week."

"If you had just given her the least inkling that you were there."

"I kept thinking she'd come back, like always, see. A fellow don't like to go and tell a woman how much — and how the kids — they get the swell head awful easy, if a fellow don't watch his p's and q's."

"Who does?"

"Women." He put his cap back on. "But anyway, today I says to myself, I guess this won't look like I'm rushing things if I go and

334

see Clara and find out what's what." He thrust out his small chin. "I must say, I got a cold reception."

"Oh, no, Mr. Mudge! Why, Clara thinks the world and all of — of the children and — and —"

"A fellow without no steady job, he's got his hands tied behind him," he said belligerently. "It looks like certain people would just naturally realize that and that a house wouldn't have to fall on 'em! It looks like certain people would get it through their heads once that certain things takes *time*."

"I just can't imagine Clara giving anybody a cold reception, Mr. Mudge." On her face was the look she wears who has almost put her hand down over a bird only to have him give a shake of his feathers and spring away.

"I guess I know a cold reception when I see it. Why, she never even asked me to walk in. Chewed the fat with me through the screen door, never even opened it! *Mind you!*"

"She's — had an awful lot to contend with the last few — But I'm sure that the next time —"

"There ain't going to be no next time! I thought about sending the kids over, once, letting Georgie carry Sophie, but now —"

"Oh, Mr. Mudge, please do! please!"

"Not now, by a long shot."

"Why not?"

"Listen," he said. "I know I ain't a catch like some old tobacco-spitting millionaire with a mansion up on Brigham Street, but just the same there ain't no necessity for a man to bow down to the ground."

There was no doubt about it, Joe Mudge's touchy feelings had been badly hurt!

After supper, when Dorney went over to Clara's she came right out with it. Why had Clara treated Joe Mudge that way? Didn't she see how he had shaved and spruced up? and that he most certainly had had a haircut? and was wearing his white shirt? and was making a very big concession for a man like Joe?

Clara, who did not meet another's eyes now, quite, but in the old way fixed her gaze a little beyond or to the side, with no curls upon her forehead, with no bold green sash about her waist, tired and red-eyed from her sleepless nights, said, "You was here. You know what happened."

"Happened when? I wasn't here!"

"The night Mamma had her stroke." The scowl between her brows did not come and go but stayed like an engraving of the letter W, scratched deep enough to last. "You know who was to blame for it."

"*What* was to blame, you mean," Dorney corrected her. "The

335

same thing that's to blame when anybody has a stroke! What the doctor said. A rupture in her brain."

"Me, I mean. I was what caused it. I killed her. Just as surely as if I took the scissors and jabbed it right in her juggler vein."

"But she's not dead, Clara. She's alive. And the doctor says she can live for years maybe."

Clara shook her head. "You was here. You saw it. You know." She wrung her hands together. "So anyway when a knock comes at the door today and I answer it and who should it be but Joe, well, my first thought, you know how I feel about him, you can imagine how I would — I nearly — my heart almost jumped out of my — But then I hear this awful voice, her voice, see. It come to me so plain I'm surprised he didn't hear it too! *Don't you dare go over there, I forbid it, don't you dare*, this voice said. Her last words! Just like she said 'em when she was right there on that spot," Clara pointed, "hanging on to me, the minute before she — So what can anybody *do* but carry out the last wishes and orders of their poor dead heartbroken mother?"

"She said for *you* not to go over there. She didn't say anything about forbidding *him* to come over here!"

"It's all the same."

"Why, it's nothing of the kind!"

"Oh, yes, it is."

All this was bad enough but Dorney and Mrs. Luby did not really despair until they saw, by degrees, how the care of her mother absorbed Clara, and saw something worse, that she was behaving uncommonly like a rapt new mother with a precious new baby. No one could mistake those actions, motions and fond rueful looks!

"I declare if it don't send chills down my back," Mrs. Luby said, "to listen to her talk baby talk when she goes to feed Mrs. Tofflemire or change her nightgown or comb her hair. Regular chills! You listen sometime."

Dorney did, and wondered why it sounded so wrong and so dreadful. Clara whispered, cooed, sang and burbled this strange language. Not once did she address the sick woman as Mother, but only crooned an endless variety of pet names. If "Mrs. Tofflemire" or "your poor mother" was mentioned to her, she seemed to have to stop and think, to guess who that might be.

It had to be admitted, of course, that there was more than a casual resemblance between Mrs. Tofflemire and a newborn infant. Certainly she was changed from what she had been. Although by now recovered so far as to be able to sit up briefly in her old rocking chair, she did not know who or where she was. What she saw through the window, Clara's work in the house, Rupert's drowsy torpor — he had decided there was nothing to be worried about, after all — meant less than nothing to her. She had forgotten how to talk but she could make a few unearthly noises and smile, flickeringly. In her bedclothes, she seemed much larger than before, and without her teeth, soft and billowing. Her eyes, now that they were uninhabited, looked prettier, as rooms will sometimes be seen to be fairer and larger than one supposed after the furniture is moved out and they are stripped of what it was that made them appear small and mean, and they rested as happily on the wooden bedpost as on a vase of autumn roses or a live face.

"If it goes on like this," Mrs. Luby said, moving over and patting the step beside her, "I don't know how it's going to end."

"I don't, either," Dorney said, taking the place Mrs. Luby indicated.

"The moonlight's so bright, I could see you as clear as day when you come out of there. How is she tonight?"

"Mrs. Tofflemire, or Clara?"

"Both."

"The same. Mrs. Tofflemire was just lying there looking up at the ceiling — till she shut her eyes a little while ago — and Clara was taking a hem down."

"She'll never make a living that way. There's too many seamstresses in business already. In the last month, there ain't been three people pay no attention to her sign and go in there with anything for her to do. Of course, she's probably got a little something laid by, enough to last a month or two — I'm worried about her, oh, every way, ain't you?"

"Yes, I am," Dorney admitted.

"And here six weeks ago we were patting ourselves on the back thinking it was all over but the shouting, thinking Joe Mudge was going to pop the question and Clara was going to be sitting pretty. Not that he's any great bargain, but — "

"No, but — "

Mrs. Luby nodded. "Right," she said, as though Dorney had expressed herself at length. "He ain't, but anything, nearly, would be better than having things the way they are now — Clara carrying on over her mother, like she was her own *baby* — I never seen nothing to equal it — and Mrs. Tofflemire not knowing nothing about it, no more than if she was a sack of potatoes, which that's the worst, it gives me the goose pimples, don't it you? There wasn't no love lost between 'em, *I* at least know, that has lived neighbors to 'em all these years! And now to listen to her! When she starts that lovey and lambie and dolly talk, you'd think everything had been apple pie between 'em from the start and that to have the care of that big heavy sprawling thing that don't so much as know which way's up was all she ever wanted!"

"Of course, it doesn't seem like it is Mrs. Tofflemire any more," Dorney said thoughtfully. "It seems like a perfect stranger."

"But not a babe in arms!" Mrs. Luby said. For the twentieth time she asked, "What made Clara get on her high horse that way with Joe Mudge? Sick mother or no sick mother, she could of asked him in, couldn't she? Why didn't she do it?"

Dorney swallowed. Circumspection and discreetness had obliged her to keep silent about what had happened the night of Mrs. Tofflemire's visitation, and her firm intention, not unworthy the knights of the Round Table, those pure fictional people, Ellen Montgomery and Sydney Carton and the good opinion of her preceptors, Wanda, Miss Littley and Mr. Teige Desmond, could they but know, was to carry the story locked in her breast to the grave. Now, however, the thought came to her that if Mrs. Luby was let in on what had taken place, she might think of some way to help Clara, but she couldn't do much if she was left in the dark!

First begging her listener to cross her heart and promise never to breathe a word of what she was about to hear — Mrs. Luby did both with alacrity — Dorney proceeded to tell her all she knew about Clara and her mother on that fatal last night of July.

When she had finished, Mrs. Luby drew a deep breath. "And so *that* was what happened," she said. "Well, that throws a little light on the subject! So when the blow fell, Clara was about to go over and ask Joe Mudge if he would — " she nodded when she saw Dorney's finger go to her lips, "I won't mention it," she said, "never fear. And her mother forbid her, and wouldn't let her out the back door, then run and grabbed ahold of her when she tried to get out the *front* door. And in the midst of everything Mrs. Tofflemire keels over with a stroke. Now, don't it seem to you like maybe God had a hand in it?"

"You mean, to keep Clara from — ?"

"You said the old lady was going to get on Schooner Bill's trail the next day," Mrs. Luby said, "and I wouldn't put it past her, once she got her mind made up, to really have maneuvered things till she got the poor fellow put in the asylum! A few years ago, she got her head set that she was going to get rid of a family out of this neighborhood and she done it, too! though they had bought their house and wasn't renting — someday I'll tell you how she worked it, it was a terrible thing and Clara don't know half of it and I ain't had the gumption to tell her — so if she come out flatfooted, Mrs. Tofflemire, I mean, and said she was going after Schooner Bill, why, that was what she was going to do, and he would of had about as much chance against her as a little baby chick against a big black hawk! And that's what I mean when I say maybe God had a hand in it, because you know in the old country lots of people believe that anybody like Schooner Bill is God's special pet that He don't want no harm or hurt to come to, because He has made all the natural idiots like they are 'and set 'em apart for some special purpose. It could well be," she said, "that that was why the old lady was stopped in her tracks, I wouldn't be a bit surprised! But tell me. Do you honestly believe Clara would of asked him? And what would he of said?"

"Asked Joe Mudge?" Dorney considered the question with knitted brows. "When I got there she was cutting out that dress — "

"She ain't took a stitch on it since," Mrs. Luby said.

" — and she was smiling and laughing and looking the way she did the night of the medicine show, or even nicer because of her hair being curled in front. If she had asked him right then, he would have said yes! But by the time her mother got done saying all those mean things and had had her stroke — and by the time you got over there and the doctor came, Clara had started to look like she used to — before, and if she had asked him then, why, I don't know."

"Well, from what he said to you when he met you up on Seventh South, about he might not be no ketch like some millionaire but that didn't mean he had to bow down to the ground, shows that his mind must be running along a certain line, or else why would he think of himself as being a ketch if he never thought about Clara ketching him? Or his mind was running along a certain line, at least," Mrs. Luby said. "But whether it is now, after a turn-down like he got, and the way Clara must of looked like something the cat drug in when she went to the door that day, is something else again. Maybe things is spoiled permanent, for all we know!"

"Oh, I hope not," Dorney said in dismay.

Mrs. Luby sighed. "Well, if Clara keeps on the way she's doing now, she's going to get awful awful strange, that's all I can say, and besides, she never was no beauty to start with. A few more weeks and months of neglecting herself and acting like she's acting ain't going to work a very big improvement on the girl, at her age, that's sure and certain. So all in all I'm just as downcast about everything as can be."

"Couldn't we do something?"

Mrs. Luby cocked her head and listened.

Behind the open mosquito-netting windows of her small house, all was still. A black vine scraping across a white moonlit wall was what had made her think her children were awake inside. When it made the same sound again she knew what it was and stopped listening. "Do something about what?" she said. "About Clara acting like her mother was her own little baby? Or about getting her and Joe Mudge together again? If she would just call Mrs. Tofflemire

339

Mother like she used to and not come out with that pitty and petty and ducky — and if she wouldn't fondle her and twine that creepy old hair around her finger trying to see if she can make a ringlet. It makes my blood run cold. I don't believe Clara's said the name of mother once since Mrs. Tofflemire took sick."

"She thinks her mother the same as died, that night, because she's so changed."

"That's what you said. And thinks she killed her, poor thing." Mrs. Luby clicked her tongue. "But it's no good crying over spilt milk. What we'll have to do is, we'll have to see if we can't straighten things out."

"I thought maybe I'd stop in and see Mr. Mudge," Dorney ventured, "and kind of apologize and tell him Clara wasn't herself that day. Of course, I *did* tell him that already, the day I met him, and it didn't do any good."

"He's one of these stubborn ones," Mrs. Luby said. "Maybe it would be best if *I* went and seen if I couldn't do something."

"Oh, it would, Mrs. Luby! I'm sure of that. I'm sure you could fix everything."

"Two things I got to straighten out in my own mind first," Mrs. Luby said, after thinking hard. "And one is, how in the world to explain to Joe Mudge — I know he imagines he ought to have a gold crown for how he humbled himself to go over to Clara's in the first place — how to explain to him why it was that Clara didn't invite him in! He can't ever be told the real reason, that she imagined she heard Mrs. Tofflemire's voice telling her not to have nothing to do with him, or he's liable to think she's weak in the upper story and that *would* throw a monkey wrench in the works, forever! because it stands to reason a man don't want a crazy woman, either as a wife or as a mother to his kids. So we got to steer clear of that!"

"And the second thing, Mrs. Luby?"

Mrs. Luby blinked. "Why, the second thing," she said, "why, that's really something that ought to come *first* by rights."

"And what's that?"

"What it is, is this, Dorney, if you want to know," Mrs. Luby said. "It's merely that I got to straighten out in my mind whether we shouldn't just let well enough alone. Clara's already got her hands full taking care of that sick mother, and you know the doctor said she would maybe live for years. Now, to saddle the poor soul with *four kids* that there ain't no end to what's got to be done for 'em and no rest from one year's end to the other — besides that sick old lady — if that wouldn't be just too much of a good thing — that is, if we could work it — I just don't know! I just don't know which way's the kindest — to try to do something or to let sleeping dogs lay where they are."

340

"She loves the kids so, and she said once that she wouldn't want anything more in life than just to be their mother and take care of them. I know she meant it. I'm just *sure* she did!"

"And him with no job," Mrs. Luby went doubtfully on, "and none too sweet a disposition — and he was so crazy about that wife of his — I just don't know. Maybe it would be best not to butt in, and let this thing between him and Clara die a natural death." She tapped the end of a fingernail against a hard white eyetooth. "But on the other hand, even so, wouldn't him and his kids with all their troubles and aggravations be better for Clara than to go on the way she's doing? staying with her mother day in and day out? talking that foolish baby talk? getting deeper and deeper into her shell till you couldn't pry her loose? The minute she quit at the laundry, I said to myself, Now Clara's went to work and did something very foolish. I just don't know. . . . It'll take some figuring. . . ."

It did. Every day for the next week Dorney saw Mrs. Luby and every day Mrs. Luby still had not decided what to do.

Dorney began to fear that there was nothing to be done and that Clara who had come so close to integrality and fulfillment had lost her chance of happiness forever. In panic, while Mrs. Luby bethought the problem, Dorney went to Ishmael with it. She told as much as she needed to tell and no more. He had helped once before with his quotations and the fable he made up for Clara's benefit. Perhaps he could help again.

Down at the far end of the loading platform, where the shade was, she found him sitting on the end of his spine, with one of his heels higher than his head. He waved it lazily in the air while he speculated. "Let's see," he said, "let's see." He had been reading but he bent down the corner of the page of his familiar little book, shut it and laid it on top of his narrow chest. Then he clasped his hands under his head and squinted upwards. "Maybe — " He closed his eyes. "No," he said, opening them. "Maybe — ? No. You say he came to call and she turned him away? Hurt his feelings?"

She nodded. "Just terribly," she said.

"And among other things you want me to think how to account for the way she treated this Mr. Joe Mudge who might otherwise go along for the next fifty or sixty years without forgiving Clara or doing her the honor to call upon her?"

She nodded again.

"The simple remedy is, why doesn't *she* go to *him?*"

"Her mother," Dorney said, and *illuminati* that Ishmael was, he understood without further specification, as the Indian by the bruised leaf knows the unseen man who has traveled before him so well that if he happened to meet him on a crowded city street he could go right up and say hello.

"Waly, waly," he said. "He is, of course, ignorant, vain, opinionated, balky and hidebound. Also deaf, dumb and blind. Still, where nothing else will penetrate, philosophy might just be the . . . and yet, I will tell you something, Dorney, a thought I have had lately." With his left hand he lifted and dropped the cover of the book on his diaphragm as though it had been the hinged lid of a box.

She sat down on the edge of the platform, began to dangle her legs, and waited.

"It just came to me lately, the thought that philosophy does a man good only so long as his eye is fixed on a printed page of it. Like I went to a concert in Frisco once and sat by this little Dutchman. They played this long piece for the French horn and orchestra, by Mozart, I think it was, and when it was over this little Dutchman turned to me and said, 'If my two ears could just be listening to that every minute of the day, I would never have a care in the world.' I had forgot that concert and that fellow all these years, but now I remember because it's the same proposition with philosophy. As long as you've got your eyes glued on it, it works, it's good, it will solve all your problems, you'll learn something, you've got some chance not to be an imbecile for the rest of your life. But just you look away from that printed page of Plato or Aristotle, yes, or Epictetus, either," he rested his hand on the book, "or Spinoza, or Voltaire, or Kant, and you're like the little Dutchman when the French horn stops blowing. Boom, down you drop. You may say, yes, but he can whistle the tune of Mozart's composition any time he wants to, and you may say that the reader of philosophy can repeat by memory what he has read and thus have it ever by him. I say, No. And that, in case you have wondered, is the reason there are so many philosophies! because no man can make another man's philosophy his own except by permanently riveting his eyes upon the words of it written down in black and white, and that being a physical impossibility, eventually he gets around to formularizing his own philosophical principles, *for* himself and *out of* himself."

"Is that really true?"

"Of course it's really true, and that explains why all the philosophies of the world don't really amount to a hill of beans. But to get back to our lover's quarrel, and what to — how about something like this?" He brought Epictetus up close to his eyes, thumbed over several pages and then read aloud, " 'Demand not that events should happen as you wish; but wish them to happen as they do happen, and you will go on well.' Or this? 'The condition and characteristic of a vulgar person is that he never looks for either help or harm from himself but only from externals. The condition and characteristic of a philosopher is that he looks to himself for all help or harm.' Or — ? 'But if, poor wretch, you envy, and fear, and pity, and yearn, and are jealous, and tremble, and never cease a single day from complaining of yourself and the gods, why do you boast of your education? What education, man? That you have learned syllogisms? Why do not you, if possible, *unlearn all these*, and begin again?' No, wait a minute. I know something better. Right over here towards the front, right here where it says — "

Just then the warning whistle blew and Dorney scrambled to her feet and brushed off the back of her skirt. "Thank you, Ishmael, ever so much," she said, feeling that on this occasion at least, philosophy had failed them miserably.

"The main thing to remember is, it's all relative." The wise man sat up, stuffing his book in his back pants' pocket. "You remember that and nothing will stick in your craw very long."

"Relative?"

"Yes." He thought a moment and then his shoulder shook with silent laughter. "I myself never had any," he said, "and if you think I'm sorry, you got another think coming."

Clara could be certain of one caller every afternoon, Mrs. Luby, and one every evening, Dorney, even if nobody else came near. Madge said that after six weeks there was no sense in it for Dorney to run over to Clara as though Mrs. Tofflemire had just had her stroke yesterday, and Dorney had a hard time to think up excuses. Such abstractions as a sense of duty, compassion and affection could not be mentioned, with Crystal on hand to be amused, but every night she thought up some plea or other, concluding with the remark that she would not stay long, and so far Madge had let her go. "But the first time the clock strikes nine and you're not home," she said, "this visiting will be a thing of the past. What you can see in that old maid is a mystery to me. And speaking of old maids, I thought Mr. Mudge was going to propose to her one of these fine days! What happened?"

"Nothing," Dorney said, pretending to have trouble getting the door open.

"I'll bet something did, too."

"No, honestly."

"Why do you ask, Mamma?" Crystal said. "That was just a pipe dream in the first place because who in the world would want to marry a homely and gloomy old thing like Clara Tofflemire?"

Clara did not look gloomy. On the contrary, she wore a cheerful mien that was worse to see than its opposite would have been, for it was as hard, slick and canonical as a rolling pin. When once she had disclosed all her heart, now she kept mum, and Dorney, sitting on the edge of a chair in the Tofflemire dining room, felt like one stranger talking to another. They had hard work of it to carry on a conversation, those two, once so congenial, and the visitor was generally more relieved than not when a peek at the clock told her her visit might now be terminated.

Clara was too civil to leave all the floundering for something to say to Dorney, and she did her share of it more than usual tonight as she sat putting an elbow patch on an ugly gray dress. "Who do you chum around with most, now?" she said, in her unfamiliar chipper way, glancing up with lifeless eyes that said if her dozenth question of the evening was left unanswered it would mean as little to her as that eleven had been answered to the best of uneasy Dorney's ability.

"Mrs. Bannon, mostly. I mean, I sit by her to eat lunch, but of course we don't walk together because she lives in the opposite direction." Dorney was considering if anything more might be added when a knock came at the back door and Mrs. Luby poked her head in to announce that she had gone through a trunk and some bureau drawers and found some of Thornton's and Althea's things that she thought Georgie and Ruby Mudge might be able to wear. What she wanted to know was, did Clara think that Joe Mudge would be offended if she took them over?

Dorney looked at Mrs. Luby with alarm. Clara had made it plain long since that the name of Joe Mudge was not to be mentioned in her presence and they had humored her, afraid, as Mrs. Luby had expressed it, that she would "crack" otherwise with grief and pain. Now, however, caution had been thrown to the winds and Dorney's surprised eyes went next to Clara to see how their neighbor's temerarious statement was affecting her.

No way! unless that was a quiver so slight it could hardly be seen in the corner of her lips? "I'm sure I don't know." Clara said, the W between her brows growing smaller while she appeared to be speculating on just who the Mudges might be, "whether he'd be offended or not."

Mrs. Luby settled down in Mrs. Tofflemire's rocking chair, on the very edge, her shoulders not touching the back. "Clara, I want you to tell me truthfully and honestly if — " she was beginning, when a funny, small cry came from the dark bedroom.

Clara put by her work, got to her feet, lit the lamp on the sideboard and carried it in where her mother lay. "What's the matter wif the doll baby?" they heard her say. "Does she wiss a drinka watey? Is the footies cold? Here, sweetheart, let me see."

"When I was over here this afternoon," Mrs. Luby said rapidly, "I heard enough of that," she raised her eyebrows and inclined her head, "to make me realize that things had went far enough, so I'm going over to see Joe Mudge tomorrow!"

344

"Good," Dorney whispered, beaming. "Do you know what you're going to say to him and everything?"

"It come to me, you might almost say, like a inspiration." Mrs. Luby settled back in her chair and began to rock.

"What — ?"

"Shhh. Don't ask me till the time comes."

Without being able to understand what she said, they heard Clara's soft mumble. When she came back after some moments and took her seat again, she announced, "I think her little footie had gone to sleep," and picked up her sewing with a queer melting glance at the wall behind which Mrs. Tofflemire lay in her bed.

"Clara, what happened to that dress you was cutting out the night your mother took sick?" Mrs. Luby asked sternly.

"Why, it's rolled up in the drawer. It ain't all cut out yet. Some of the pieces is still pinned to the goods."

"Let me see it."

Clara — Clara still so far as courtesy went — returned on tiptoe to the bedroom where she was heard opening first one drawer and then the other before she came back with an armful of white goods shining with pins. She put the bundle down on the table at her visitor's elbow. "Bless her pretty heart, she's sleeping like a little angel," she said.

Mrs. Luby and Dorney exchanged unhappy glances. It was the former who opened her mouth and spoke. "Clara, I've knowed you — how long is it? Long enough, you'll grant me. And all them years, I've minded my own business, now ain't I? more than maybe I should of," Mrs. Luby added before Clara could reply, "which ain't nothing to be proud of because there was times when, as a friend of yours, I could of butted in. But you know what the truth of the matter was, that your ma was one of these neighbors you want to give a wide berth to, because she was one of these women that — "

Clara's cold lips turned upward in a stiff smile. "She was, you say. So you think of her just like me. She's dead, that's why. Was!"

Mrs. Luby looked grave. "Who's dead, Clara?"

"My mother."

"And who's that in the bedroom?"

Again that stiff smile. Clara turned stony eyes in the direction of the half-shut door and back to her caller. "The naughty girl!" she said. "Do you know what she done today? Here I had a spoonful of nice gruel right up to her mouth when — "

Dorney bit the tip of her right thumb and looked away.

"Clara, you've got to be told this sometime and it might as well be here and now. It's wrong, it ain't normal, it ain't right and it shouldn't be, for you to go on like this. I've got to come right out

and say it. That old gray-headed woman in there ain't what you've
took a notion to pretend, and you know it, you ain't lost your senses.
She's your mother! and it won't hurt to remind you that she
wasn't the best mother a girl ever had, either. I've lived next door
to you long enough that I ought to know! But now she's had a
stroke, poor thing, and nobody ought to hold the past against her.
That ain't what I want you to start in to do, God knows! now that
she's on her back and helpless — have you take a notion to pay her
back for all she done to you and your pa and I don't know who all
else. No. All I'm saying is, take care of her and do for her, like any
daughter would, but quit acting and talking like she was your baby!"

Clara put her work by and clasped her rough hands together on
her lap. "My baby?" she said, in a dreamy voice. "Yes, of course.
I didn't realize. But sure! That's so. I should of knew all the time
that was the kind of a trick God was going to play on me. I might
of knew it, all the time. You had a-plenty of Mamma? says He.
Have I? says I! she sucks my life blood, she eats me up alive like
a sow her piglet, she smothers me, rolls on me, I can't breathe. Have
I had enough! says I. Well, no more Mamma, says He. Breathe
easy! So then He says, look what I've give you instead, Clara!
What, dear God? What you've been a-hankering after, a baby,
looky here. She slobbers, she spits, she weighs as much as a sofa,
she's got bristly hairs on her chin, and she's older'n the hills but —
here's your baby, Clara! 'Dance a baby ditty . . . what can mammy
do wit 'e . . . sit inna lap . . . give 'un some pap . . . dance a baby
ditty. . . .'" Clara's voice broke and her hands went to her face.
"He laughed," she droned, taking them away an instant after. "He
nearly busted his sides laughing at the big joke He rigged up! because, you see, a million years ago a certain child gets born to a
certain woman. All right! Well, now, says He, we'll hocus-pocus
and fix it so that very same woman gets born to that very same child!
All in fun! says He. Ain't it a lark, though? Ain't it rich?"

A low growl came from sleeping Rupert, whose ears went up.

"I never realized it, till you mentioned it," Clara said, "but that's
the ticket. That's it. If I act like she's my baby I act like it because
she *is* my baby, that's why. She had me, and then, I had her! There
won't never be no end to it, neither. Never! For when she grows
up," Clara's face grew so eerie and her voice rose to such a shrill unearthly pipe that Dorney wanted to squeeze her eyes shut and stick
her fingers in her ears, "she'll turn right around and have me, and
when *I* grow up, I'll turn right around and have her, and she'll have
me, and I'll have her, for all eternity, see saw, Margery Daw, dance
a baby — " Clara's head went down and her arms came up over it as
if she was shielding herself from falling stones, "ditty," she moaned,
"ditty, ditty."

34

WHEN DORNEY TURNED THE CORNER ON HER WAY
home from the laundry, there was Mrs. Luby strolling toward her.
She had Thornton, Althea and small Herman in tow, but after she
stopped, said something Dorney was too far away to hear, turned,
pointed and looked as if she meant business, she lost the first two.
Althea was sulky about being banished but she followed orders,
grabbed insulted Herman, who flatly refused to budge, by the hand,
jerked a time or two on his arm while he braced himself with his
short legs spread wide apart, and then she appealed to her mother,
who gave her a little push. "On second thought, go on by yourself," Mrs. Luby obviously said, "and I'll keep care of Herman."
The small girl let go of her brother with such suddenness that he
staggered and had to be clutched by his mother, and made off with
haughty head-tossing and kangaroo leaps, her two braids flying up
in the air, not deigning to look behind. Thornton departed with
greater willingness, but he gazed wistfully over his shoulder in
Dorney's direction, then made a quite hideous face at her which she
answered with a smile and a wave of her hand before he dodged
from view behind the hedge.

"Well, I've been and done it," Mrs. Luby announced when she
came up close enough to be heard. "And when I think about last
night — and poor Clara — I never felt so sorry for anybody in my life
— I could kick myself all around the block for waiting so long."

"How is she?" Dorney asked eagerly. "I've been wondering all
day."

"Right back where she started! About like she was before she
broke down. Same frozen-halibut look, same silliness with her
mother. I thought maybe that blow-up and bawling spell last night
would of cleared the air. You know for a while, before we left,
after we talked to her and you put your arm around her and helped
sop up her eyes, it seemed like she was going to come out of it,
but — "

"I was hoping so, all day, Every time I looked over and saw her

347

machine, that Aurilla McCann runs now, I thought about her, and hoped — "

Mrs. Luby shook her head. "No such luck," she said. "I went over this afternoon and I could see right away there wasn't no improvement. And what I hated worse, she tried to make it seem like we had just *imagined* what happened last night. Any time I'd come anywheres near the subject, she'd change it just as slick as a whistle — she'll do the same thing with you tonight, you watch — but I let her and didn't light into her or nothing because I knowed I was going over to Joe Mudge's. Once he's pacified, I says to myself, and the strings pulled so that he'll be over there knocking on her door again, why, Clara'll be all right! So I just set there and let her do as she would. And after I left, away I went and made a beeline straight for his place, to tell him a thing or two."

"You really did!"

"Of course I really did."

"I can't imagine what you *said*, Mrs. Luby."

"Didn't I tell you I had a inspiration about the one and only excuse that would repair all the damage? Because naturally I couldn't come out with the truth! that Clara thought she heard her mother's voice. Because that makes her sound like she's crazy and a man ain't going to marry a crazy woman if he can help it, especially when he's got a family of kids."

"No, you couldn't tell him that."

"And everybody knows how touchy he is, so *that* had to be considered."

"I just can't imagine what in the world you *said*."

"I said — " Mrs. Luby let go of Herman's hand and let him trot off toward a gray cat out for an evening's stroll, who, looking him straight in the eye, stopped and waited to see what his intentions might be. "I said — " But it was not Mrs. Luby's way, like the tabid author of a puzzling tale, to commence any way but at the precise beginning. "First of all," she said, "when I left Clara's bound and determined to take the bull by the horns, and when I got over there to the Mudges'," she said, "ready to do or die, who should I see but Joe Mudge just coming out the front door with his cap on!"

"Well!"

"He was on his way to the cabinet works, he said, because he had some kind of news about some foreman or somebody he didn't use to get along with. To tell you the truth, I didn't pay much attention to what all he did tell me because I was so busy figuring out how to say what I had in mind."

"I don't wonder!"

"First," Mrs. Luby said, gratified, "I come right out and told him that I had these things I thought Georgie and Ruby could get some good out of! and he wasn't a bit offended. I could of saw if he was, right away. In fact, he thanked me for the kind thought! Then he offered just as nice as could be to go back inside the house if I wanted to come in and set down, but I said no, I'd just as soon stroll along with him for a ways. The kids," she said, "I didn't see, but I heard 'em, so I guess they was playing around in the back yard." She eyed small Herman on the ditchbank reaching for the gray cat who backed away from him in a circle. Finally the boy sat down hard, the cat three paces off sat down, too, and they looked at each other. "So we strolled along and mentioned this and that, and all of a sudden, lo and behold, I took it on myself to lead up to Clara!"

Dorney pressed her hands together and waited.

"That is, I didn't lead up to Clara, exactly, but here's the way I did. 'Mr. Mudge,' I said, 'I'm a married woman, as you know.' 'That ain't no news,' he said, smiling polite-like. 'Well, the reason I mention the fact, Mr. Mudge,' I said, 'is because by rights what I got to say to you today, couldn't be said to you by nobody else *but* a married woman.' "

Dorney's face began to feel unaccountably flushed and there was a strange buzzing in her ears. What in the world of life's and the world's great mysteries was she about to hear? She was glad of the fast-falling twilight.

"Well, he batted them big blue eyes of his at me," Mrs. Luby continued, "and cleared his throat sort of and said, 'Oh?' kind of squeaky like. 'You'll understand what I mean by saying that nobody but a married woman could of took it upon herself to clear up this matter and explain how it all happened, when I tell you what I purposely come to tell you today,' I said. 'What matter?' he said. 'What happened?' 'Now don't you think, Mr. Mudge,' I said, 'for one instant, that Clara sent me, for she didn't,' I said, 'because as far as *she's* concerned, she's that ladylike and decent and delicate-minded, that her heart could be broke right in two because of what happened, and the rest of her life from now till she's a old decrepit lady could be entirely *ruined* — because there ain't a man in the world she respects like she respects you, Mr. Mudge,' I said, 'and there ain't nobody living that she loves like she loves them children of yours, either — but before she would open her mouth and say boo,' I said, 'and explain such a embarrassing and unfortunate thing,' I said, 'she would reconcile herself to never seeing hide nor hair of none of you again!' Joe Mudge," Mrs. Luby said, sighing, "is a nice enough man, I guess, but he's inclined to be awful dense — "

Like me, Dorney thought, thoroughly mystified.

" — and all he said was, 'What unfortunate thing?' 'From Clara's place you run into Dorney Leaf,' I said, 'and told her about it. She come straight to me, all upset, because you said Clara had never showed you no hospitality. Me and her talked it over, saying how peculiar it all was, because Dorney knowed and I knowed what store Clara set by the kids, yes, and you, too, Mr. Mudge. So the next step was,' I said, 'for me to go over to Clara's to see if I could find out what in the world had happened! And what do you suppose I found?' I said. 'What?' Mr. Mudge said. 'Why, I found Clara's heart broke right in two, that's all,' I said, 'I found her sitting there crying a gallon of tears, that's all, biting her handkerchief, walking up and down, wringing her hands, that's all.' 'What was the meaning of that, Mrs. Luby?' said Mr. Mudge, batting his eyes at me. 'What was the meaning?' I said. 'Why, what would it be, but that you, Mr. Mudge, that she holds up higher than any man in Salt Lake City, in Utah, in the whole United States — in fact in the whole world — mind you, the husband of the woman that was her best friend, the father of the four children she cares more about than if they was each one either a diamond, emerald, ruby or gold mine,' I said, 'you, if you please, that was kind enough and thoughtful enough to pay her a call, should *have to be treated like you was treated!*' 'Why was I treated that way then?' he said, and he got one of these mulish looks on his face that makes a man with such a little chin look so funny. And at the same time he looked like he was going to pucker up and cry. 'She didn't even open the screen door, but kept it hooked tight,' he said, 'like I was a tramp she hadn't never saw before in her life, or a bagman she was afraid was going to get his foot inside the door, that's how she treated me, left me outside in the cold, standing there without a leg to stand on, looking like I don't know what kind of a half-wit! so what could I do but say goodbye and leave?' 'Listen, Mr. Mudge,' I said, 'I said to Clara, I asked her what in the world happened? Well, sir, I'm telling you, Mr. Mudge,' I said, 'even though I'm a woman, and a old friend, and a neighbor,' I said, 'Clara is that ladylike and decent and deli- cate-minded, that it was like pulling teeth — pulling teeth,' I said, 'to get her to come out with it and say what had caused all the trouble. And when I heard, well, I didn't wonder at it — nor you won't, either,' I said. 'And a good long while went by before I could see how I could ever bring it over my lips to tell you, because *I* wasn't brung up in the lowest dredges of society, either,' I said, 'Mr. Mudge. *I'm* ladylike and decent and delicate-minded, too. *But,*' I said, 'while my lips was sealed and the time run along, and I watched, what did I see? I'll tell you,' I said. 'I seen how Clara just fairly drooped away, being deprived of your kids and everything, like a fish pulled out of the water and left to flop on the shore. So then I had it out with myself. Things had gone on long enough! What's decency, I says, what's being so ladylike, what's being so delicate-minded if somebody has to suffer, that otherwise wouldn't

350

have to suffer? What does them things amount to? I says to my-self.'"

"And what did he say?" Dorney asked in bewilderment, hotter faced than ever, her breath coming short.

"Don't pet the kitty," Mrs. Luby called to Herman, who, not making any attempt to do so, seemed contented just to let fly little bits of grassy turf in the implacable cat's direction, amiably and inaccurately, from time to time. "He might scratch you." She watched a moment, but her mind was plainly somewhere else. "Why, he said," she said, turning back to her listener, "'Mrs. Luby,' he said, 'you could of knocked me over with a feather when Clara Tofflemire let me cool my heels on her porch and never even unhooked the screen to me!' I never seen nobody more hurt, or stubborner about nothing, than he was about that. 'Well,' I said, 'Mr. Mudge, we're getting down to cases now and the mystery is about to be cleared up, because,' I said, 'I had it out with myself, Mr. Mudge. I said to myself, Rhoda, the time has come to tell him the whole story, because after all you're a married woman and if you can't tell the whole story, I don't know who can!' So, then I took the bull by the horns and waded right in. 'Mr. Mudge,' I said, 'you know what a invalid is,' I said, 'and when I tell you that old Mrs. Tofflemire ain't herself at all no more, and she ain't never going to be herself no more' — I thought I'd just give him the comfort of *that* news while I was at it — 'and don't know no more about what's going on than a tiny baby,' I said, 'why, you will understand that there's quite a good many things that has to be done for such a invalid that somebody of the category of Clara would sooner be tore apart limb from limb by wild horses than tell to a man, or let him come in and find out himself. You know what a lady is! Well, without beating further around the bush,' I said, 'the truth of the matter is, when your knock come, Clara was BUSY and there wasn't nothing she could do, only to turn you away right at that particular moment, which you, that knows how ladylike, decent and delicate-minded Clara is, certainly can't wonder at! Now, can you?' I said. Well, sir, Joe Mudge stopped dead still and then he turned to me and said, 'So that was what was in the wind, was it, Mrs. Luby?'" She nodded her head to show how she had nodded it at him. "'That was what was in the wind,' I said. 'Well, now I'm beginning to see a little daylight,' he said."

Dorney put her hand up to her cooling cheek. Her pulses had slowed down. "I don't see how you ever —"

"I told you it come to me, just like a inspiration," Mrs. Luby said. "Anyway, him and me meandered to the corner and then we parted company and he went on to the cabinet works, or at least I think so because that was where he said he was heading, and I come on

351

home with a big lie or two and several little ones to my conscience that I ain't started to regret yet at least, and don't think I ever will!"

"When's he going to go and see Clara?"

"That remains to be seen."

"Tonight, do you think?"

"No telling when. Maybe not for two or three days, or a week, but he's forgave her and he'll be calling, you mark my words."

"Maybe I'd better not go over, then, tonight." Dorney said.

"You little dumbhead," Mrs. Luby said gently, "do you want the same thing to happen all over again that I had so much trouble about and had to lie myself blue in the face to fix up in the first place? If you're a real friend of Clara's you'll go earlier and stay later than ever, till all this is settled, and during the day I'll go over as much as I can and keep my eye peeled on the house, too, because if he happened to come and she turned him away *again*, well, I don't know how I could whitewash another such mishap. I really don't know!" Rolling her eyes at the seriousness of the thought, she happened to glimpse her son. "Herman!" she called. "You get up off that ground and let that kitty alone."

Since the small boy had never been closer than six feet to the gray cat that now for no special reason streaked away and disappeared in the shadows, he began to wail softly, not so much because the cat was gone, Dorney thought, as because of his mother's heedlessness and inattention, which, depending on who it is that hasn't really *seen*, can sometimes sting worse than a birch rod.

It seemed too much to hope that Joe Mudge would come that night — at least, until his children were in bed and asleep — but Dorney did not want to take any chances, and so, even before Madge came home from Judge Towers's, at ten past seven, she hung up her dishtowel and made a dash for the door, murmuring that she was going over to Clara's and would not stay very late.

"I should think you'd want to wait and say hello to Mother at least," Crystal said, "and see whether she gets home safe, without being practically murdered the way she almost was that one time, but of course if you care more for somebody like Clara Tofflemire than you do about putting your mind at rest about your own flesh and blood, why, then of course, you'll just have to do as you please."

Tiny Jetta took a stiff-legged step toward Dorney. "Tell the story," she said.

Dorney, contrite, went and knelt down beside her, tilting the sharp little chin upwards with a gentle forefinger. "I've just *got* to go tonight," she said, "but maybe your mamma will let you stay up till I come home, and then I'll tell it."

"You know what Mother said about what will happen if you're

not home by nine o'clock — even five minutes after, and she meant it, too. After all, you're only fifteen years old, you're not of legal age, and Mother has a *little* say over you, and you ought to be glad, too, since nobody else in the world cares anything about you or takes the least bit of interest in you, only her and me, and why you should want to go off every night and leave the only two people that cares the slightest bit in the world about you, for somebody that's no more to you than the man in the moon, is more than *I* can see."

Dorney sighed.

Jetta fastened a cold little claw to the front of her dress and repeated, "Tell the story."

"And Mother doesn't like filling her up with all that stuff you tell her, either, every night, about her having two servants, one as little as a fly and one as big as a giant that will do everything she asks, and that swing she's supposed to have that swings five miles in either direction, and all that stuff."

Jetta turned, gazed owlishly, then stomped away on her stiff little legs to the dusky back porch to scramble into her swing and push herself off into space. Plus the sound of the small thud of her feet, came the wild little cries that in a few moments died away.

"Now, she's mad at me," Crystal said, laughing. "But just the same it's true. Mother doesn't like you to fill her poor little mind up with all those stories." She began to flex her fingers, exercising them, which she did whenever she thought of it, to improve her piano playing.

"She loves to listen," Dorney said. "It doesn't hurt her."

"That's for Mother to say," Crystal said, "and she's been meaning to speak to you about it."

"I'll tell her something else, then," Dorney said quickly, "some other story that Madge won't find any objections to, about — about flowers or something."

"She shouldn't hear any stories at all. They only make her worse than ever and Mother doesn't like it. And she's not going to be very pleased about you being gone tonight, either, before she even has a chance to get home and say whether she wants you to go or not, I can tell you that much."

"I won't stay long."

"You'd better not."

Dorney on her way out went up close to where Jetta was flying back and forth, her matchstick legs pressed tight together. She spoke so as not to be overheard by Crystal. "I'll come home as early as I can," she said, "and don't worry. I just know your mamma will let me tell you the story the same as always. So don't you feel bad, will you?"

Jetta cast a quick look to the side and then gazed straight ahead again, the way she always did when swinging, as if she was guiding some vehicle that might come to calamity if she did not keep her mind on her task. Her little yellow face was engrossed and happy.

"Will you now?" Dorney repeated, but Jetta did not have time either to nod or shake her head.

Mrs. Tofflemire sat in her rocking chair by the dark window, not rocking, for she had not the strength nor inclination for that, but quiet and still, wrapped in a pretty shawl of white and pink, with her softened hands laid in her lap. That she had ever once been an ogress, a Fury, a bogie, a lady lion on the loose, a ripsnorter, a hell tooter, hell on wheels and the Devil's grandmother, deadly, grudgeful, obstructive and petrifying, seemed beyond the bounds of reason. For all the threat she was now, she might have been shaped up out of marshmallow, and often Dorney glanced at her, with wonder and awe that such a thing as had happened to Mrs. Tofflemire could happen to anybody. Sometimes, when she moved her head plan-lessly, her eyes sparkled like pale blue glass.

Dorney had come early but not so early that Clara's supper dishes were not all done, the floor swept up, and she herself settled by the dining-room table sewing. She had been talking to her mother — Dorney heard her through the open door as she came up the back steps — "Izza doll baby warm enough? does she wiss somefing around the little footies?" — but she hushed when Dorney cleared her throat and shook the screen. Clara had to come and unhook it for her, and she did, smiling in a way that made Dorney feel worse than if she had not smiled at all. It took no more than seconds to ascertain that Mrs. Luby was right, last night's tumult had not cleared the air and Clara was right back where she started from. Dorney's heart sank until she remembered that this time was only temporary, for help was on the way. Thanks to clever and kind Mrs. Luby, Joe Mudge would come back again, sooner or later, and then — but what then?

Glancing sidelong at Clara, she hoped he wouldn't come tonight. Clara was anything but at her best, grayish pale, in her most hapless dress, with her hair skinned back until her dull and heavy eyes had new moon corners from the relentless wrench to her scalp. "Lela Galloway," Dorney began in desperation, "had her hair fixed a new way today and it looked just beautiful. It was — " She got up and went across to Clara. "I could show you, if you'd like to see," she said.

"Can't you show me, on yourself?"

"I could easier show you on you."

"Does it take a lot of hairpins? because — "

"Not many. But I'll need your comb."

354

Clara went into the bedroom and got it. "Here." She took her seat again and called across to her mother, "Is oo all right, petty?" receiving not so much as a blink in reply. "Izza baby tired, wisses go beddy-bye?"

Clara's hair when let down to a point just below her shoulder blades and combed, looked lighter in color than when it was braided and confined, and there was a pretty ripple in it.

"Isn't it a shame," Dorney said, combing and admiring, "that all the ladies can't let ther hair hang down their back instead of doing it up? People could see how pretty it was, then. Lela Galloway said the other day that we'd all ought to just let our hair hang down and start a new fashion. Hester Walp nearly died at the thought."

"It ain't been so long since you was wearing your hair down," Clara said, "in fact, just a few months ago, so it wouldn't be nothing so strange to you, but as many years as I had my hair up, I don't know what I'd feel like — I guess like a wild-eyed gypsy or something."

Sleeping Rupert woke up and raised his head. He pricked his round ears and his black nose twitched.

Dorney saw his movements and thought she heard a slight sound outside. Was it only Mrs. Luby? or — ? She drew a quick breath, held it and tried to listen without appearing to do so, exhaling little by little.

The old dog growled.

"What is it?" Clara said, holding her hand up for Dorney to be silent.

Far from being so, Dorney began to talk as if her life depended on it. Clara reached for the hairpins, but Dorney swept them away, she wanted the comb, Dorney put that in her pocket, chattering away for all she was worth.

Rupert growled again, not portentously, but as though to say, I might be old but I'm not so old that I don't know that somebody or something is on my very own back porch! or coming up my very own back steps, one or the other.

Clara, alerted, her eyes growing big and black, catching her hair up in two shaky hands and trying without success to twist, roll, poke it in and make it stay up off her neck without pins, implored, "Dorney, for heaven's sake, what did you do with the hairpins?"

Traitorous Dorney, seeing that if she could do nothing else she could do this at least to make Clara look prettier (for she did, with her hair flying all about, even if she still had that excommunicated, cut off, hopeless look) said, "The hairpins! yes, let me see, I had them just a minute ago — "

Mrs. Tofflemire made a little sound. Clara dropped her hands and let her hair fall. "Poor little lovey, tired and wisses go beddy-

355

bye," she was saying, starting for her side, when the knock came at the back door.

"I'll go," Dorney said, remembering Mrs. Luby's dread of another setback, perhaps irremediable. She hurried to the screen door which she unhooked as if her life depended on her dispatch. "Come in," she said, first to the ectoplasmic shape that wavered behind the wire mesh and then to the bigger than lifesize actuality that, when the door was thrust open, proved indeed to be golden-haired Joe Mudge come to rectify and restore (*immensum gloria calcar habet*). "Oh, do come in!"

He tossed his cap in his hands and made no move to accept the passionate invitation. "Where's Clara?" he said, not gazing beyond into the lighted room but looking back over his shoulder into the darkness and seeming to listen for something behind him.

"She's here. She's right in here." Dorney might have reached out, got hold of the caller and dragged him in bodily, so bent was she on admitting him, had he not at that moment stopped looking and listening, faced her and decided to step across the threshold without assistance.

"Clara," he said, "I happened to be passing and I thought — "

Happened to be passing and he thought!

What had he been trying to see out there in the blackness, and trying to hear? Dorney wondered. She pushed the screen open wider, letting in bugs and moths with gauzy wings that made straight for the lamp, and stuck her head out. It was very dark outside. A little breeze in the drying leaves, a man's faint voice on Fifth East, a frog croaking, the bark of a dog far off, otherwise stillness. And yet, nothing, nearby. Unless just around the corner of the house? — some muffled — ? But no.

Clara did not faint. No doubt because she was already so white it was an utter impossibility, she did not even pale perceptibly. That her hair was swishing about her shoulders like a wild-eyed gypsy's appeared to have slipped her mind. What had not slipped that mind? along with knowledge of how to work those eyelids, move those spellbound hands, shut that staggered mouth?

Dorney rushed to bring Joe Mudge a chair and took, not easily, his plaid cap out of his hand. Then she hastened to Clara's side and led her to a chair opposite him. That she was participating in something histrionic, inflorescent and ultimate, also a matter for history, she knew without words, and stepped back so as not to impede anything or be in anybody's road, wishing she knew the secret of invisibility. When, some moments after, she discovered that the cap was still in her hand, she reached behind her and laid it on the sideboard as spiritually as she could.

356

"I got my job back today," Joe Mudge said, giving himself a mighty flip with his suspender.

"Your job?" Clara was beginning to recall how to swallow, wink, bring her senseless fingertips together, and she practised all three gingerly.

"At the cabinet works."

"Oh?"

Mrs. Tofflemire made a slight sound and Clara, after thinking hard about it, sent her a concerned glance. "Yes, lovey," she murmured. That was all she had to say to her mother, no long string of pet names, no fanatical baby talk, and when she looked back at her visitor, Dorney who in her apprehension had stopped doing so, could breathe again.

"That son of a gun of a foreman got fired," Joe Mudge said. "Done some dirty work, got caught and got fired, like I could of told 'em long ago. So old Mr. Dannals, he's the owner himself, mind you, he put me back on."

"How wonderful." The word wasn't nearly good enough and Clara looked as if she knew it, so she tried again. "How —" she began. Whether she could have done better on that second attempt must ever be veiled in mystery, for she was interrupted.

" 'Course that'll mean I got to leave the kids alone all day," Joe said, "and naturally I'm gonna — you ain't forgot 'em, have you, Clara?"

"Forgot the kids?"

All of a sudden, Joe Mudge reached in his back pocket and with a crackling sound that would make anybody who was not expecting it, and nobody was, give a start, pulled out a small striped paper sack, leaned over and presented it.

"What — what's all this?" Clara said with an effort.

"Candy," Joe Mudge said.

She blushed such a scarlet that the heat could almost be felt across the room, took it, in agitation opened it without looking down inside, held it out blindly. "Have one?" she entreated with extreme urgency.

"No, thank you," Dorney said. The sack was not aimed at her but she said it anyway, for sociability's sake.

It was not aimed at Joe Mudge, either, but he shook his head with great courtesy and said, "Keep 'em to eat later on." Then he added, "A fellow without no steady job, he's got his hands tied behind him, and I said," he turned and looked fiercely at Dorney who dodged a little as from the path of a wasp, "I said to this young lady right here — didn't I? — that day I met you right outside here? — didn't I say, that it looked like certain people would realize certain people's predicament and that a house wouldn't have to fall

357

on 'em! Didn't I?" His face was as stern as Zola's when he sat down to write *J'Accuse.*

Dorney gulped and nodded.

"And I said — didn't I stand right out on the street and say? — I said, it looks like certain people would get it through their heads once that certain things takes time. Didn't I?"

Feeling dreadfully guilty of some dereliction and not daring to look in Clara's direction, Dorney nodded again.

"And furthermore I said — didn't I? — that I knew very well I wasn't no catch like some pot-bellied millionaire — "

"Yes, Mr. Mudge."

" — with a mansion half as big as all outdoors — "

"Yes, sir."

" — but just the same, whether I'm that kind of a catch or not, I said, there ain't no necessity for a man to bow down to the very ground." He looked huffily at Dorney and as huffily back at Clara. "I never figured on you having company," he announced. For the first time then, he caught sight of Mrs. Tofflemire. Shrinking, he said, "Good evening," to her, but his voice in the meanwhile had changed. It was as if Punch had opened his mouth and Judy's woodnote wild had come out. This disconcerted him not a little.

"She — don't know that you've said it," Clara, now red, now white, said.

"No?" Joe Mudge, regaining his composure, looked back at her like a man who has been told that the bear looks so alive, isn't at all, but is only stuffed and couldn't harm a flea. He believed, and did not believe, as the man does, and doesn't, until he has surreptitiously sidled up a little closer and maybe poked one of the bears' glass eyes. "Well — " He looked away, looked quickly back again as if he would detect some briskness, some tell tale sign of dangerous life, then away, satisfied that Mrs. Tofflemire was verily no longer the creature who had once struck terror to the hearts of men. Snap! went his suspender, and for the first time since his arrival, he smiled. "Well, I guess a fellow can't just pick his own time and place, right down to the dot," he said, "so — Clara, will you marry me?"

Dorney was not sure that Clara, with such an odd familiar look of — what was it? — on her face, had heard him, but she heard something, that was sure. Those last cruel words — no — no — I forbid you — again? that quenched voice as good as from the grave? to mar her life forever? Dorney sprang to her side. "Clara, it's not real — don't remember!" She spoke in a whisper. Could Mrs. Luby help? Would she dare to leave and run for Mrs. Luby? She took Clara by the shoulder, shook her.

358

"I know I ain't a catch like some people I could name, but will you?"

Clara's hand went out to push Dorney away. She looked baleful, ill-disposed, inclement, as cruel and heartless as her mother had looked that dreadful night.

"Clara, truly — "

"Well, old girl?"

She got to her feet with care, flicking her hair back. She opened her mouth. "Joe," she said.

Dorney, ready to burst with anxiety, had been wishing for Mrs. Luby, for Ishmael, for anybody old and wise to come and save the day, but when at that moment the children — four of them and what might as well have been a Trojan Horse, it looked so big, and was, in fact, the biggest birdhouse for the horned lark, or any other kind of a songbird, that Joe Mudge had ever made — two stories high, with windows all around, and balconies, chimneys and a slant roof painted blue — no laughing matter to carry — when they assailed the castle, stormed the agitated and billowing screen door, attacked, rode full tilt at it, struck home — when the children, out of the darkness, came, stampeded by what signal? affrighted by what noise? impelled by what? with cry, clamor and hullabaloo — when they were let inside — Ruby in a tarantella to shake off wombat Sophie — Alfred moaning, stuck by the thorns of half a dozen elegiac roses — Georgie so vulnerable until he dropped the birdhouse — clatter! — and leaped over it with as glad a howl as a Riccaree over his campfire — when they, admitted by who but quickened Clara — who but she to din of whom but them? — Clara, down on her knees, enfolding them all in her arms, in her hair, in her laugh, her belighted tears, in the shine of her, yes, of her beauty — when they hove on the scene — when she did welcome them — who better to the rescue? Pray, pray, tell.

They might have been tidier. Their father said so, after his pains. Had he not made an inspection? Alfred! one o'clock. Hiked up petticoats? Wiped off hands and faces? Sophie with that licorish!

And they might have waited for the signal. The signal? They did wait! They didn't. They did. They didn't. They did.

Now, hush!

"How about it, Clara?"

This sticky blindfold kiss from Sophie and pinwheel eyes of Ruby spinning with love? Alfred's gift of roses? (Against thy skirt their scratch of thorns the sound of "many sleeping Saints, that russled their Dust together and gat up.") This birdhouse, sweetheart?

Taking on a man? a boy? and life? Clara.

"We ain't much of a bargain."

(*Still, in green and golden summer — *)

359

"But a steady job should make some difference."

(— the horned larks?)

Mrs. Tofflemire gave a little whimper.

"Shouldn't it?"

Clara stood up.

"Honey?"

The whimper came again, and she swept everything out of her way, harming or jarring nothing, even limpid Sophie, melting with sleep, who washed against her sister. Then, very tall and sure-footed, she started forward.

Dorney watched her as she would have watched a comet cross the sky.

At the invalid's side, she lifted the soft shawl and matter-of-factly rearranged it, tucked in a pillow and pulled the chair a bit to the right.

Then she spoke.

"What can I do for you, Mother?"

35

"SHOULD NOT ZE LEADER TAKE ZE LION'S SHARE?" Neibauer, the Austrian rancher and former member of Crown Prince Rudolph's staff, asked of his guest, taking a sip of brandy.

Butch Cassidy lit a cigarette and flipped the match away into the moonlight. "We shared and shared alike," he said.

"And all have separate, one from ze ozzer?"

"Well, me and Sundance Kid stuck together because he wants to get him a ranch down in South America, too, the same as me."

"And ze big cowboy zat was wiz you here last spring — not last spring, but ze year before — ze one zat like to be friendly wiz ze little Cheyenne?"

"The Tall Texan? He'd like to be friendly with anything that wears skirts. Him? Why, he made a beeline for New York City."

"Such a western man like zat in *New York City?* For why?"

"Well, he figured that was the biggest town in the U.S. and naturally there'd be more ladies there than anywhere else, that a fellow could kind of circulate amongst."

"Circulate amongst!" Neibauer clapped his hands to his head and moved it back and forth, pretending great pain. "Ze lamb to ze, how you say? massacre!"

"You ought to seen him. Bought this black broadcloth suit, but wouldn't wear nothing but high-heeled boots with it. Said he'd be crippled if he did. And wouldn't wear nothing but this big fine Stetson hat. Tell you what he looked like when he got ready to vamoose — "

The door opened and a pleasant-faced cowboy, plain to be seen in the clear night, came out into the low stoop. "How about you guys riding in to Price with me to the dance?" he said.

"I think I'll turn in early," Butch said. "Quit, when your feet get to blistering. Don't do like you done that time up in Star Valley."

When Sundance Kid had gone, Neibauer said, "He will not say to ze pretty daughter of ze Mormon bishop or to ze pretty daughter of ze Constable or to none of ze ozzer sweet girls in ze town, zat he is

Harry Longabaugh, ze Sundance Kid, if zey ask, yes? when he is in ze tender mood?"

"He's too anxious to get down into South America and get him a ranch down there. He ain't going to risk nothing."

"Why does he go to zis Pioneer Day dance zen?"

"Oh, he's restless. Maybe he'll go to the dance and maybe he won't. Maybe he'll just ride around through the town and circle past the dance pavilion and then larrup out over the open country till him and old Bess gets tired. I know him."

"But he takes a chance by zis action, no?"

"Yeah, I guess so. But not much of a one."

"And you, my friend Butch. Do you not take a chance by going once more to Salt Lake City at ze end of ze week?"

"Oh, I don't reckon anybody's going to recognize me. We ain't going to be riding. I'll have some city duds on. Me and the Tall Texan was there a year ago right about now and nobody recognized us."

"But why do you not go from here to Galveston, Texas, and embark for Argentina?"

"I got to see Judge Towers again."

"But he make it so evident he is helpless in zis matter. Zere can be no amnesty."

"Neibauer," Butch said, swallowing, "I've spoke of what I'm going to tell you now, to the Texan — in fact, he was with me at the time — and Sundance Kid, he knows, but I ain't told nobody else. But the real truth is — "

"Yes, my friend?"

"The real truth is, I'm kind of figuring on taking somebody with me down there to South America. I mean, besides Sundance Kid. A — a girl."

The Austrian looked startled. Then his face began to beam. "A girl? A little friend? Ah, charming, charming!"

"She ain't said she'd marry me yet, you understand, but — "

"You mean, you will marry?"

Butch looked indignant. "Didn't I just say I was figuring on taking her with me? Could anybody but I don't know what kind of a sneak do such a thing *without?*"

Neibauer opened his eyes wide. "But you have had ze — ze warm friendship of ladies before."

"This is a entirely different proposition."

"Ah?"

"She's just a kid."

"So?"

"Why, hell, yes."

The Austrian nodded. "Now, tell me," he said.

"Tell you what?"

"From ze beginning. You have lately been in Texas — no, wait! — ze most recent is in Montana. You find her there, yes?"

"Judge Towers has got some woman doing his cooking. And Dorney, she's her sister. Her and me happened to stand side by side each other at this medicine show that me and the Texan went to. And from the minute I laid eyes on her — well, I don't know how to say, but I'm telling you, Neibauer, I never was so pulled out by the roots towards anybody before in my life like I was towards that girl. And then — well, you see, the last act was — this magician come out up there on the platform and started this hypmatism and — and — this girl was with this woman, see, and this little boy — I kep' a-looking at her standing there in this white dress she had on. You never seen such a — she was watching and listening to the show — and her eyes — and then she'd laugh with these pretty white — and every move she made was — and she was so — but I said to myself, What kind of a guy am I to get mixed up with somebody like her? me, I said, no place to light, nothing to offer nobody, a big reward hanging over my head — "

"Big? It is immense!" Neibauer reminded him. "Since zese last sree big robberies."

"I know," Butch said ruefully. "Anyway, like I'm saying, I wanted to make her acquaintance — I held this woman's kid for her and everything, the woman she was with — but I didn't. I figured, what could it lead to? Nothing. And she was so damn won — well, anyway, then this guy was supposed to be some kind of a hypmatist — do you believe in hypmatism? — when the show was over, I grabbed the Texan and away we went. I tried not to even look back. You should of seen the crowd. Just as well try to find a needle in a haystack as ever find her again, either there on the show lot or anywheres in town. After all, Salt Lake ain't the size of Vernal or Price! The Texan, he was pretty sore because I wouldn't let him go nowheres afterwards — you know what kind of a sociable cuss he is — but I wouldn't. Me and him went back up to the room, and he was so put out, he went right to bed and right to sleep and snored as loud as he could, but me, half the night I was sitting on the window sill looking outwards, thinking of how she looked, and thinking that if only I had went to ranching and cowpunching in the first place — and never — why, her and me — . Then I remembered what I was going to try to get Judge Towers to do for me — get me pardoned — but that was worse than ever, because, my God, if I was in a position to go a-looking and then couldn't find her, why —

"Well, the next night here I was up at Judge Towers's again, to see if he had got back all right from Denver."

"Zis, I have heard."

"But you *ain't* heard who it was that come a-running down the hall after I rung the bell, like the lightest-stepping, most, most — I could see through the panel on the side of the door — "

"Ze girl!"

"I'm telling you, Neibauer, when I seen it was her — she couldn't get the door open, and she stood there fiddling with the lock, giving me these little tosses with her head and these smiles — she didn't know it was me outside there, see, for the porch was dark while the hallway was light — why, I'm telling you — when she throws open that door and sees it's me, why, her face just fairly — and so when I step in and — "

"You embrace, yes?"

"We do what?"

"Embrace?"

"You mean, her and me?"

"Who else?"

"Why, we ain't even been introduced!"

Neibauer smiled. "A sousand apologies."

"The first thing, I accidentally knock over a tray of cards, and then, both of us are down on the floor picking 'em up and laughing — and then, all of a sudden, here I am telling her — "

"You have not been introduced, I remind you."

" — telling her that what I'm there for, I'm there to try to get the Judge to do some particular thing for me — and I'm telling her that us meeting again — her and me — like this — the way we're doing — why, that *means* something — it ain't just accident. And then I'm saying to her, that if the Judge can do this thing — why, her and me has somehow got to — "

"And what does she say when she knows it is ze great Butch Cassidy who speak zese matters?"

There was a silence. "She don't know it," the outlaw said.

"She do not know it?"

"No. I didn't only have time to tell her just that — and she never got to say hardly nothing back to me — because right then Judge Towers opened up his door, and her and me stood up, and the first thing I knew she was running away down the hall and gone. And when me and him had had our confab and I left there about ten o'clock, why, I was feeling very low down, because he as good as said nobody could do nothing. He went and saw the Governor the next morning and then he sent some young fellow over from his office to the hotel with this message in this sealed envelope — "

"Addressed to whom?"

"Jim Lowe. That was how I was signed up in the hotel register."

Butch took out a folded envelope and looked at it. "Ain't it funny how a guy will pack something around with him? This envelope. I threw away what was written inside. All it said was, the idea of getting an amnesty was good but it was hopeless and that the Governor said he couldn't do nothing." He crumpled it lightly into a ball and made as if to toss it away, but then smoothed it out on his knee, folded it as before and put it back in his pocket. "So then me and the Texan picked up and left town."

"You did not say goodbye?"

"Who to?"

"Ze girl?"

"You mean this Dorney? The way things turned out, what good would it have done? What would of been the point of it?"

"And zis is all happen one year ago?"

"Nearly to the day."

"And now, after all zis long time, you take ze great risk to go back to Salt Lake City for zis mademoiselle zat, first, might not be living, second, might be married, sird, that you have behold but two times, and forse, zat does not even know wiz whom she have dealings?"

"That's about it."

"For why, my friend?"

"Because I ain't forgot her, that's why. Because every day and every night, no matter where I am or what I'm doing, I keep picturing her in my mind, and if I don't never see her no more, well, all I can say is, I ain't going to be worth a nickel."

"But what paradox, what inconsistency is zis? for in ze meanwhile — since zis time — you lead ze perpetration of ze biggest criminalities in ze whole career! Two train robberies and ze, how you say, overrow of a bank! All, in less zan a year. So, you are a worse, how you say? scalawag to meet zis girl now zan ever before. Is zis not true?"

"It is and it ain't," Butch said. "The way I look at it — if I'm going down to South America to start over — if I ain't going to do nothing crooked no more — if I'm going to start raising cattle and working hard and being as honest as any other guy — well, why ain't I got just as much right to go to the girl I want and say to her, kiddo — "

"But two brief meetings! How can one be sure zat zis is ze kiddo? worse risking everysing for, to return to ze dangerous city?"

"I know, that's all. I don't know how I know. I just know."

When Sundance Kid came around the house from the corral and saw the red glow of Butch's cigarette, he said, "Hey, are you guys still gabbing?"

"Too hot to turn in," Butch said. "How was the dance?"

Sundance Kid dropped to the step and sprawled there, pushing his hat onto the back of his head. "I didn't go in. I just watched through the window a while."

36

THAT SATURDAY AFTERNOON, THE LAST IN THE month of July, was memorable to Dorney for more reasons than one! First, the shirt and handkerchief department ran out of work at two-eighteen by the knavish clock (it was really two-thirty-one) and were sent home, docked three and a half hours' wages. Nobody objected, even Hester Walp who wondered with great innocence if Mr. Horsfeldt and Tamer Camomile would be lonesome or if they could find something to amuse themselves with there on that big lonesome second floor all alone.

"You've sure got a nasty mind," Lela Galloway said, very glad of the layoff. She was feeling the way she looked, somewhat green around the gills. In another two or three weeks she would be handing in her resignation and "The Baby," so called, now aged three and a half, of her mysterious brood of five at home, was to have his nose put out of joint by the addition of a newcomer who would succeed to that title sometime in December. The remark that never-wedded Lela would make to Aurilla McCann at the hour of leave-taking was to assure her imperishable fame in Palace Laundry history. "Yes, sir," she would say, in all soberness, "I tell you something, Aurilla, I'm really going to be glad when my child-bearing days are over!" But perhaps she would have been famous anyway, considering how near her brother, Jib Galloway, who so kindly helped to support his contraband nephews and nieces, had come to having a bout with the great John L. one time.

"I don't know why you say I've got a nasty mind," Hester Walp complained. "I never said nothing."

When Dorney came home before three o'clock, Crystal could scarcely credit her story, that the second floor had run out of work. "I thought maybe you found out some way that that old one-eyed man was here," she said. "And couldn't wait to find out what he wanted."

"What old one-eyed man? What who wanted?"

"The one that takes care of Mrs. Morelewski's yard."

"Mr. Sodaquist? You mean *he* was here? What did he want?"

"He said to say Mrs. Morelewski wants to see you one of these days."

"Honestly?"

Dorney had not seen the Queen for over a year — since the night of the medicine show, to be exact, when she had caught the hurried glimpse of her, half hidden in a black lace shawl, on her husband's arm. She had not called on her because in her free hours, after seven-thirty at night (when the dishes were done) and Sundays, she knew Mr. Morelewski was at home, but she often thought of going there, for the sake of the old times, to inquire how Mrs. Morelewski did. Sometimes, on Sundays, she walked past the cream-colored house with the striped awnings, but the thick green hedge surrounding the property had grown very high and she could no longer see enough of the side porch to tell if the Queen was on it or not, in her great wicker chair, or see into the sprinkled garden, to glimpse her strolling there or in the act of snipping roses.

"What could she want, I wonder?" she mused.

"I thought maybe she wanted you to work for her again. In fact, that's why I thought you came home early today, because you had quit the laundry, on account of Mrs. Morelewski."

Dorney laughed. "How would I know she wanted me? No, we ran out of work." After a moment's thought she decided that there was no time like the present, and departed for the Queen's house.

When she had gone, Crystal remembered that a letter had come for Dorney in the morning mail. She took it down off the clock shelf and looked at it. It was from Mr. Morelewski's nephew in New York. Even now, after two years, she felt a pang of something very like remorse that changed sharply almost at once into resentment when she recalled how she had spent her wiles on him — her, so attractive and gifted — and he had been unimpressed. He had called that one time and never again. Well, who cared? Who was he to put on such airs? Judge Towers, when asked, didn't suppose he made more than a hundred a month, if that! She held the letter up to the window and frowned through it. It wasn't very thick. She could see the writing on the thin sheet of paper but it was folded so that it could not be read. What in the world did he have to say to her? Something about books, maybe, or some silly thing. Not worth reading. There didn't seem to be more than about one sentence. She turned the envelope over to see if anything was written on the back flap and then put it up on the clock shelf. When Dorney got back from Mrs. Morelewski's, she would give it to her, watch if she wouldn't act silly and blush. Crystal glanced out through the open back door at abstracted Jetta swinging back and forth. Then she returned her gaze to where the letter was lying. It probably wasn't worth reading — in that bold smart-alecky writing — but maybe Dorney would hand it over to her to read, all the same. Restless and bored, she strolled back into the parlor, though she had stopped a long session of practising only half an hour ago, and settled down at the piano again, but this time she rested her elbows with a discordant clatter in the middle of the keyboard and put her chin in her palms. Now, what did Mrs. Morelewski want with Dorney? She thought she was smart enough already, now that she was sixteen, learning those big words from that silly dictionary and all that — but if Mrs. Morelewski was going to ask her to a party or something, maybe a garden party with Japanese lanterns hung out in the trees and everything, why, she would be just simply insufferable.

When Alma Morelewski woke in the morning, the instant her eyes opened, before she quite knew anything or remembered, she felt as free as a bird. But then, almost before she had time to blink once, it all came back, that something was amiss, something had happened to her, something she most particularly did not want certain people to see. Sometime — soon — it would be mitigated, and she would be what she had been, but in the meantime there was every reason to keep out of the public sight and lie low. That spoiled the fine free feeling, the minute it all came back.

Not then, in the morning, for morning found her full of hope, did she shed tears of dissatisfaction. The grief came, if it came (confinement did not always chafe, sometimes it seemed preferable to any latitude), in late afternoon, especially during fall and winter when it got dark early, in the slow hours between four when she had roused from her nap and had her coffee, and seven, when Mr. Morelewski came home. Once or twice he had found her in quite a dreadful state in the dark bedroom, devastated, face downward on the bed, both hands twisted in her tangled hair — the pillow and spread and herself as soggy damp as if she had spilled a cup of tea all over everything. She couldn't eat a bite till nearly nine-thirty! But such upheavals did not happen very often, thank heaven. And what had been the cause of all this anguish? Because she was sick of staying home and wanted to go out, that was what it was! Go out where? To the Paris Café once more at the dinner hour, as she had been used to do for those two happy years, of course, in the carriage, with Mr. Jump driving, all dressed up, and sit at the old palm-shaded table again! Come on, then, Mr. Morelewski had said. What was to prevent it? He could be as dumb as any human being that ever lived. Prevent it? Imagine how the waiters would whisper to one another, Mr. Moffat especially! They would probably pass the word and even the cooks and the kitchen help would come and peep at her from behind things and have all kinds of remarks to make. What kind of remarks? What kind! About what? About what! About how fat Mrs. Morelewski was, that was about what! About how she certainly had changed, if anybody on God's green earth ever had.

Foolish, foolish girl — where else would she want to go? To Madame Blanche's again, that was where, and come away with a handsome frock in one of the stiff pink boxes everybody on the streets of Salt Lake knew came from her establishment. Sometimes she longed for this so morbidly that it was like one of the pilgrim ladies longing to go see old England once more before she died. What was stopping her? She had a big checking account, didn't she? All she had to do was buy whatever she wanted? Stopping her! Well, what was? What! Why not go there? Go there! Why not indeed! — and have that sharp-tongued beady-eyed dyed-haired wasp-waisted Madame Blanche with her Polish accent — her and her silly shop girls that never had a thought in their minds only clothes and who had a good shape and who had a bad shape, like that was the only important thing in life — make all manner of fun of her behind her back? Maybe Madame Blanche would even give her some jolt right to her face, she wouldn't put it past her. No, sir. She was too smart for that! Not until her waist was the exact same size it used to be, or maybe even an inch or two smaller.

She was homesick for the milliner's as well, yearned to sit in the cozy elegant parlor and try on hats, but that province, also, was lost to her! Why? Why! Because Colette, that sour red Swede with her made-up French name, would bat her stubby white eyelashes and tell nothing but one lie after another, and purse her lips, and make an excuse to go behind the mulberry velvet curtains into her work-room where there was a buzzing and chattering going on — and soon, the noise would all stop, there would be silence, and then whispering, and Alma Morelewski, her spine crawling, would feel first one pair of hidden, amused, incredulous eyes on her and then another. . . . Yes, she would! She was not very likely to be fool enough to go there. Not changed like this, the laughingstock of the whole city, whose ruling sovereign she once had been. She couldn't even go to Walker Brothers, for the clerks knew her and said things to one another — she could tell, by the looks on their faces — or to the theatre — people plucked at nearby sleeves and inclined their heads in her direction — or to the band concert in the park, where the un-wavering eyes of profound little girls or boys with their thumbs in their mouths might be disconcertingly encountered.

It wasn't that she was a hideous old hag. She was still beautiful. She often thought when, after she had pushed aside her breakfast tray and got out of bed (the floor creaked, which showed that the brick house was not so solid and well built as a person might imagine) and had gone as was her wont, every morning without fail, to the three-paneled mirror to look at herself, that she was more beautiful than she had ever been in her life! if one didn't pay any attention to — her hair looked like an advertisement for an expensive imported shampoo, and far from darkening as some blond hair did, it was as fair as in childhood. Her eyes looked like a great big china doll's, just as blue as the sky. And her skin! it was like a baby's. Actually. Talk about lilies and roses, peaches and cream. And her teeth were absolutely perfect, perfection itself, not a cavity, not a blemish, as white or whiter than pearls. What did people expect, for heaven's sake? A lot of women, thousands of women, hardly weighed anything — but how many of them had looks at the same time? Fair and honest now, how many? Practically nobody! while she was nearly snowed under with beauty.

She did not know exactly what her weight was, but she was a little heavier — a very little — than just before Labor Day last year. That was when, on her way over to Miss Peacock's for a fitting, she had ill-consideredly stepped on the scales out on the sidewalk in front of that awful feed store on Fourth South! It happened to be also the last time she had gone out. Now the arrangement was that Miss Peacock came to her.

She had thought no one was anywhere around — the premises and sidewalk seemed to be deserted — then was a good chance to step quickly on the — her cheeks burned when she thought of the impudent grizzled old man in a sweat-stained calico shirt who popped up out of nowhere to stand at her elbow and begin sliding the weight jigger back and forth, and edging the other thing over, to make the scales balance. "Say!" he said, giving a long loud whistle. "Quite a armful, ain't you, girlie? But that's what the fellers like. That's what the fellers like!" She never did find out what she weighed for certain — the top thing was stopped at an impossible number but a true balance hadn't been reached when she stepped off the scales without a word to that frightful old man, who kept on laughing and talking about what the fellers liked, and got away from there as fast as she could with her chin pointing upward and a funny booming sound in her ears. Why she had done such a thing in the first place she didn't know. Trying to weigh herself on a feed-store scale. Queen Alma!

She was a teeny bit heavier now. At least, the dress Miss Peacock had tried on her that unfortunate day would have to be let out, now, if she wanted to wear it. But she didn't want to wear it. Miss Peacock had many virtues, one being that her dull old introspective expression never changed, no matter whether the tape measure said thirty-three or forty-nine. She had, however, no style at all and that made things rather hard.

Mrs. Hopple — what a jewel that woman was — seemed to know not only when she was awake, but when she was going to wake, for hardly had Alma Morelewski's eyes rested more than long enough on the lowest six inches of window pane, under the pulled blind, to ascertain whether or not her day was going to be fair, when the housekeeper tapped at the door and here she was with a magnificent breakfast. This morning, she brought, all very nicely arranged on a tray, a plateful of little rolled pancakes full of currant jelly, dusted over with a powdered sugar, and a dish of fresh stewed pears. Wasn't that lovely?

No young woman who has ever worked for a living can look upon Saturday as merely a day, like any other day of the week, and Alma Morelewski was no exception. Saturday was different, there was no question about it! Somehow, on Saturday mornings, drinking a second cup of Mrs. Hopple's delicious coffee and letting her eyes roam around the room, she felt still more full of hope and confidence than on other mornings. She couldn't help it. Certainly she felt that way this day. She was not very musical but a song bubbled on the back of her mind, like a teakettle on a stove, something about letting the punishment fit the crime, but she couldn't remember it well enough to sing it out loud. (It simmered there for hours until it boiled away.)

There was no reason for her to have to stay home all the time and never go anywhere. All she had to do was not be fat any more and then she could go to the Paris Café, the theatre, Madame Blanche's and Colette's, the same as ever! and that wasn't very difficult. All she would have to do was to go hungry — quite hungry — in fact, agonizingly hungry — for a few weeks, but that was nothing. It wasn't half as hard as saving up for a new pair of shoes had been when she worked at Auerbach's. That had seemed almost impossible! But a little thing like this? The main thing was one's attitude and she had been feeling weak and helpless about something that all she had to do was be determined about and it was licked! Imagine cringing before it, as if it was something she couldn't handle! She needed a paddling, that's what she needed, not to have seen it in its right proportions long before this! People could do anything they wanted in this life but they had to be stubborn. They had to be like a bulldog, dead set. Alma Morelewski pushed her tray away, threw back the thin sheet that had been covering enough through the hot night and stepped out onto the creaking floor. Ritualistically, she went to her mirror but was too preoccupied to stay there looking more than three or four minutes.

Her first resolution was to eat no lunch, but it would be two hours before she could put that into effect. She got into the dainty blue and white Mother Hubbard Mrs. Hopple had gone up town and bought for her at the Z.C.M.I. and combed her hair neatly. The housekeeper was a very trustworthy shopper. Later in the day she would dress up and wear her shoes, but for a beginning she would just wear these lovely soft moccasins that Joe had bought off an Indian peddler who came into the restaurant. She hoped he would be able to get another pair like them some day. They were so comfortable! One scarcely knew one had anything on one's feet at all.

Alma Morelewski did a lot of things that morning. One job was to go carefully through her clothes, making various decisions. She posed a question to herself. Suppose — just suppose — that she was not going to wait two or three months but was going to go out to-day, right this minute, or tonight — what would she wear? Not wait! Go now! Anybody who didn't like the way she looked could go jump in the lake. The thought was so convulsionary that she felt rather nauseated, as in an earth tremor, and when she reached out to shut the wardrobe doors her hands were not steady. Her heart began skipping a beat every now and again, too, so there was nothing for her to do but have Mrs. Hopple bring her a fresh cup of coffee and sit down and take a rest in the wicker chair on the cool side porch. The climbing vines were very thick there — one had to step to a particular corner where there was an opening if one wanted to see into the garden — and it was always moistly cool even on a scorching day like today.

The yellow Etiquette book lay close at hand (one good thing about Mrs. Hopple was that she couldn't seem to tell one book from another) but Alma Morelewski seldom read it now. She didn't seem to get the enjoyment out of it anymore that she used to. One reason was that her opinion of Society had changed through the years. She was somewhat critical now and when she read, read sardonically. All those childish little manners and customs. So much fuss over nothing — fish forks and fruit knives, gloves on or off, the way cards ought to be printed, toasts, pews, handshakings, opera parties, cotillons, patronesses, horses, traveling abroad, deep mourning and all that — grown people, you know, carrying on so about trifles! It was almost laughable. From old habit, Alma Morelewski still sometimes let her eyes rove over a few pages here and there, but she would be making mental remarks like, Is that so? You don't say. Is that a fact? Do tell! and other fine ironies. She no longer dreamed of living a famous social life. What would that amount to? Nothing! It was a waste of time even to think about it. Now, she dreamed of something far, far above the haut monde (that meant high life in French) not only of her own city but of New York, the hautest of the haut. She imagined herself to be in another land entirely, almost like on some star.

It wasn't a very big land. In fact, it was rather small, about a hundred and sixty acres all laid out like a park, with little paths and fountains here and there, and statues, and tiny cottages like doll houses scattered about, where respectful laborers lived, with their respectful wives and cunning respectful children. In the middle was a great big castle, about as big as the City and County Building, looking rather like that, of stone, with battlements and towers but of course no clock. And in there, the Queen of that land, she lived, Alma Morelewski. She was very slender and she always wore the robes of state she had worn at the Salt Lake City Jubilee, only of course much more costly than those, and a crown that in spite of being loaded with jewels was as light as a feather on her head. Except for fifty servants, she lived all alone. Sometimes, however, when she was bored and tired of looking at all her possessions, and was walking up and down out on the great stone balcony and the moon was as big around as the big wheel of a bicycle, a King would come and keep her company! He was from another land very like hers and he wore robes of state, too, and almost as expensive a crown as her own. The only thing he talked about was, he told her how beautiful she looked, pleaded with her to marry him and said he was so wretchedly in love that he could neither eat, drink nor sleep. He said this as they strolled back and forth, back and forth, in the moonlight and then sat on the balustrade holding hands and looking at the beautiful dim land until it fell away into the haziness at the edges. He was such a handsome young fair-haired blue-eyed king, almost like an identical twin brother. . . . In comparison with delight and satisfaction like that, Society was two for a penny indeed! not worth bothering one's head over, let alone feeling bad because it gave one the coldest of cold shoulders.

The realer it seemed, the vision, for it was more or less a clear steady vision and not just a flitting daydream, the crosser she felt when Mrs. Hopple took it on herself to come and disturb her. (The truth was, she didn't like Mrs. Hopple very well. Having her around was too much like having a senseless machine around that didn't know how to do anything, or know anything, but work.) She wanted to know what to prepare for lunch! Even when she felt irritated, Alma Morelewski had a hard time looking or sounding so. "Don't bother about lunch for me," she said. "I don't want any." The trouble with Mrs. Hopple was, she took that statement as though it didn't surprise her, and that was somewhat annoying.

Well begun is half done! no lunch today. In two or three weeks, or a month, she could return boldly to Madame Blanche's hemisphere, to Colette's, to — She could — her eye fell on the handsome red pasteboard box tied with pale yellow ribbon. It stood on a pile of magazines on the wicker table. The chocolates Mr. Morelewski had brought home to her last night! She had forgotten all about them, what with two helpings of warm apple dumplings with cream for dessert last night and English Monkey before she went to bed. It was an awfully nice two-pound box. Too bad that when she had the chance she didn't take advantage of it, before it was too late. Because now it was too late, and all that lovely candy would have to go begging.

Weren't men the most strange and mysterious creatures in the whole world? Here Mr. Morelewski had starved her so cruelly just two years ago now, got her to where she was only skin and bones, and now his greatest pleasure in life seemed to be to stuff her. It certainly looked like it, anyway — teaching Mrs. Hopple how to cook all those fancy dishes, rushing home himself every night to put the finishing touches on their dinner, bringing home those rich pastries of all kinds and descriptions from the restaurant and wheedling her to eat them, feeding her every midnight with snacks that were the same as a whole meal, and then, never forgetting to keep a supply of chocolates on hand. Long ago, she had stopped even trying to save the boxes. There were so many that if she hadn't put them out on the trash pile the house would be overflowing with them. Of course, if an especially pretty one came along, she saved that, but she had grown very discriminating and it had to be extremely artistic or out it went.

That husband of hers! Sometimes when she was grieving, she would say, "Look at me! Look at me! Why don't you *help* me instead of doing the way you do, poking the food down me? Sometimes I think you do it on purpose!" Then she would glare at him with tears standing in her eyes, and she would want to rip and tear off her flesh as if it were a blanket a foot deep she was accidentally wrapped hand and foot in, helpless, like a papoose in one of those husks on its mother's back or Jonah down inside the whale. That was a terrible feeling when she felt like that. It almost made her frantic. She could hardly breathe. She wanted to jump right out through the window or do any wild thing so she could get away. "Can't you *see?*" she would pant and cry, gasping for air. Then he would set to work and soothe her. He knew how to say just the right thing and soon all her frenzy would pass and she would be feeling much, much better and after a while she would be eating some delicious morsel and wondering what in the world she had felt so bad about, with every comfort and not a care in the world! Men were funny, though. One of these times she was going to pin him down and ask him what in heaven's name he meant when he talked about how a treasure could be concealed and thieves and vandals walk right by within arm's reach of it and not know it! after sitting and studying her maybe for ten or fifteen minutes at a time while she went about her own affairs. She asked him what he was talking about but he only laughed and said he didn't need locks and bolts and chains and bars! "Never changing, always fair, always beautiful!" he said, too. "Eternal, in ice, in amber." She didn't like that kind of talk, it sounded crazy and made her nervous and besides she had requested that he wouldn't look at her so much. But she didn't really mean that.

Since she couldn't eat the candy herself — she wouldn't even so much as take the lid off — she might as well tell Mrs. Hopple that she could take the box upstairs to her room with her and enjoy it. But she didn't have to do it today. (Actually, Mrs. Hopple was one of those unsympathetic people who eat because they have to, not because they take any particular interest in food, and that was strange considering that she was a good enough cook to please even Mr. Morelewski!)

Alma Morelewski was full of plans and ambition today. The lunch hour found her going through a trunk of clothes she had been meaning to inspect for a long time, taking the dresses out one by one and deciding what to do with them. Two or three could be let out — she must have Miss Peacock do that. The best parts of two could be combined to make quite a pretty frock. And then, there were the last of the crop of Madame Blanche dresses — had she truly ever been able to get into them? when she held them up to her it didn't seem possible. Of course, in two or three months, she would be able to wear them again, but the question was — would she want to? After all, there was no reason for her to wear dresses two years old — she had plenty of money — she would buy a whole new outfit. Start fresh, in other words. She would have to wear stylish clothes that would put anybody's eye out when she started going back up to the restaurant every night for dinner, not something that had been mouldering away for months. Not that they were actually mouldering away. The moths hadn't got to them and they were as good as new. Too good to throw away — nice rich material like this — if somebody could get some good out of them. Mrs. Hopple? but it would be like hanging them on a clothesline pole. And the colors were all wrong. She'd look awful in them and besides Alma Morelewski didn't want to have to see them around anymore. They made her feel vaguely bad and uneasy, especially the gray mull trimmed with white Languedoc lace, with the rose-colored taffeta sash. (But she kept that, putting it in the bottom of the trunk.) She heard Mr. Sodaquist outside, the snip of his garden shears, and thought that same moment whom to give them to. She went to the window, pushed it open and stuck her head out.

"Mr. Sodaquist."

"Yes, ma'am."

"Would you mind going through the alley to the middle house of those three houses on Eight South and tell the girl that used to work here that I'd like to see her sometime when she can get over?"

"All right, ma'am." He looked at her with his white eye and turned away.

She stood by the window a moment, breathing in the fragrant warm air, feeling harmonious, pertinent and capable. Here it was past lunch time and she wasn't even hungry. All one had to do was take the reins in one's hands and sit up in the driver's seat oneself for a change, and make things happen just the way one wanted. A prisoner? What kind of a notion was that? Talk about going to Madame Blanche's and Colette's — why, if she wanted to go to China she could go! She could do anything.

From clothes, Alma Morelewski went into interior decoration. At two-thirty, she was pacing about with flushed cheeks and excited eyes, nibbling a sleek fingertip, while she decided how, when she was no longer heavy and could go out and go shopping again, she would have the parlor and dining room done over with new paper and paint, new carpets, new everything! Of course, the carpets weren't really very worn and the furniture was almost as good as new, but maybe she could make an arrangement with Dinwoodie's Furniture Store where she could trade all this in. At three o'clock, however, when the knock came at the door, she was feeling rather fatigued and was sitting on the window seat, turning over the pages of her scrapbook, not reading the clippings but idly looking at them and taking a breathing spell.

Her intention was to pay close attention to Dorney's face when she opened the door, but a carriage with the top down and two very dressy ladies in it was just passing that very instant down Fifth East, and behind her Mrs. Hopple in the parlor archway had to be told that she didn't have to bother about answering the door because the lady of the house was doing it herself, so when Alma Morelewski was able to pay heed to her visitor's expression, it had had time to alter into what showed neither surprise nor consternation. She wished she had not been distracted and could have seen it as it was in that first flash, if it was different then from what it became, friendly, shy, pleased and open-eyed. Dorney was quite a young lady now. Some people would think she was very attractive.

It was worth having her come and get the dresses if for no other reason than to hear how she remembered them, each and every occasion that she knew about, of their having been worn. It was amusing. You would think Alma Morelewski was a celebrated actress and these gowns had been worn when she played different immortal roles. She had the feeling she was giving them away to a museum where they would be placed in glass cases with little printed

377

cards propped up against them telling their history. It amused her so that if she hadn't thought they might still be wearable on occasion, she would have given Dorney some hats, too. She was a nice girl. Those were happy days, when she was a Lady in Waiting. . . . Alma Morelewski started a smile but did not finish it. Why was the past always so much better than the present, even when itself had once been a present less good than a still earlier (and earlier) past?

"Have I changed very much?" she begged.

"Not a bit, ma'am, truly." Dorney gave answer quickly, without stopping to think, as she would have given her hand to a strolling companion fallen, to help her to her feet.

"But don't you think I'm — ?" Alma Morelewski stopped without mentioning her size. It was only temporary, anyway. An upwardly spiraling sound only she could hear came from the region of her empty stomach and it felt squeezed as by a hand, faintly. What was Mrs. Hopple cooking out there in the kitchen? It smelled like . . . that was a delicious . . . once in a while a whiff of it would . . . She thought of the full box of waiting chocolates. Perhaps, when Dorney had gone, she would just sit out on the side porch and read the new issue of *Peterson's* Magazine, and eat a vanilla crème with half a walnut on top. That wouldn't hurt anything. One vanilla crème. It wouldn't spoil her appetite for sup — dinner. Not that she was going to eat much of *that*. What was it that Mrs. Hopple had on the stove? If she could just identify it, it wouldn't be so tantalizing. . . .

Alma Morelewski was sorry she had waited so long to give all this joy and pleasure. She wished she could have a picture of Dorney's face. "There's an old superstition," she said, "that a dead person's clothes don't last very long. They're supposed to drop to pieces right away, even if they're good material. So if that's the case you won't have to worry about these things not wearing. . . ." The faint squeeze came again, this time followed by a tiny pang. Maybe a chocolate-covered cherry would be better. The only trouble with that kind was, if you poked or bit into one of them, you had to pop it into your mouth and eat it whether you felt like it or not or it was so liquid it would run all over everything.

At the door, saying farewell to Dorney, saying not to mention it, really not to mention it, it wasn't worth talking about, really, she noticed that a letter had come in the afternoon mail and fished it out of the box and looked at it. She knew without excitement who it was from by the writing, without reading what it said up in the left-hand corner. It was addressed to Mr. and Mrs. Joseph Morelewski. Once they had got a letter from him from Ireland. This was postmarked New York. Without excitement she slipped it into the pocket of her dress. She must change her shoes before she sat down, not go around the rest of the afternoon and evening in these moccasins. Of course nobody was coming, and there wasn't much sense in making yourself deliberately uncomfortable in weather like this, as hot as it was. She would start in tomorrow morning putting her shoes on the first thing, when she got dressed, but as far as the rest of today was concerned . . .

"You're most welcome," she said, and "Do come again," in a way of which the editor of The Etiquette of Today would have been proud. While she said goodbye, her tongue was beginning to float as in water and her pulse was speeding up. After all, she had not been lazy but had been busy ever since she got up. Surely she had earned a little rest and refreshment. She saw herself sitting down with her feet on the footstool, the weighty box in her lap, taking off the yellow-ribboned red lid, lifting the sheet of wadding, turning back the rustling clear tissue. Round and rich stood the rows of chocolates while their smell rose up like incense. She might have to bite into several before she found the kind she wanted, but she would eat only one. . . .

Even Mother would not understand this. She might think she was jealous of Dorney! But it wasn't that. How could she possibly be jealous of somebody who worked in a laundry, who couldn't play a note on the piano, who — who —

Crystal stifled a sigh and turned over on the parlor couch, flinging the coverlet by.

The point was, certain people could get their heads turned by the least little thing, and from now on Dorney would probably not be fit to live with! If anybody ever put on airs or acted ridiculous, it was her tonight, dancing around in those silly dresses with her hair all tumbled down and her eyes just nothing but black pupils. As if that was anything to get so excited about! And then, she had been so impudent, too, arguing that Mrs. Morelewski didn't give the dresses away because she was too big to wear them any more but just because she had so many clothes she didn't know what to do with them all. It was common gossip that Mrs. Morelewski had got fat. Everybody knew it. So why couldn't Dorney just admit it instead of fibbing and trying to pretend it wasn't so? It was the most disgusting thing. One of these days Crystal was going to scheme out a way to see Mrs. Morelewski face to face and then she would tell Dorney what she thought of those that beat around the bush and couldn't speak an honest word!

The way she paraded in those dresses was almost more than human flesh and blood could stand. There was no question about it, Madame Blanche dresses were prettier than other dresses. They were terribly stylish and had these artful little touches, and the difference between their colors and materials and the colors and materials of

379

other dresses was the difference between real gems and artificial ones. Even so, that was no excuse for Dorney to show off the way she did all evening! just because somebody had given her an armful of old clothes. Actually, it was an insult to have anything like that handed to you. Nobody would ever have the gall to try to give Crystal Yandle a lot of old second-hand wearing apparel. They'd hear something, if they did. When she wore a Madame Blanche frock — and she would wear one someday, life couldn't be so cruel as to deny a truehearted girl so passionate and fervent a wish — why, she would go in and buy it with her own money. Or rather, with her rich husband's money, which was the same thing.

Crystal, sweating, sat up in the dark, her mouth feeling parched. If she was going to get a rich husband, she had better start doing it! because she would be twenty-one her next birthday. Nobody had forever! Nobody. No matter how pretty or how talented they were.

She saw Dorney blazoning forth in front of Mother and Jetta. Jetta thought it was all so wonderful. Every time Dorney came running downstairs in another dress, Jetta would make those funny little sounds and have to stroke and pat and lay her cheek against it like it was alive. Like it was the kitten she was always begging for! Past eighteen and she had the mind of a little child! It was simply awful. Saddled with her, who could ever hope to accomplish anything? Men were afraid of a peculiarity like that in a family. They thought whatever made her like she was might crop out again sometime in a later generation. They were afraid to marry into families where everybody wasn't exactly normal, or if they weren't, their relatives were and fought against it tooth and nail.

If only Mother would let Jetta be put in an institution where she belonged! If she didn't want her to go to the state asylum there was a private home for backward or feeble-minded children, located between Warm Springs and Beck's Hot Springs. That would do just as well and in fact the only disadvantage was that it cost twenty dollars a month to keep somebody there. It was easy to reach. Crystal had found out all about it. You took the Center Street car out to Warm Springs, and from there you went on the Bamburger Dummy Line to one mile this side of Beck's Hot Springs. It was a lovely location! And after that, nobody would need to know that a creature like Jetta had ever existed, unless maybe one of the neighbors would tattle. And the way to get around that was to pack up and leave and go where they and their family history had never been heard of.

If only mother wasn't so stubborn. She thought that three hundred dollars in the bank and some furniture wasn't enough to go somewhere new and get started over again in life! But it was! She would rather let her daughter wither away here where everybody was against her, than make a change. Even her music teacher was awfully unsympathetic lately. Why couldn't she have a recital? even if she did have to have the music up there in front of her? Was a recital a test of memory or was it to show how well you could play the piano? What if it wasn't customary? She had no chance here whatsoever. None in the world. But somewhere else, she could amount to something.

The horrible thought struck her that Dorney might get married before she did! and the still more horrible thought — suppose she married a millionaire! Suppose she accidently happened to get acquainted with someone and gave him one of those little smiles of hers, and that toss of her head, and opened her lips and said some interesting thing she had read or heard, that would make him imagine she was interesting . . . and he turned out to be rolling in money.

Agonized, Crystal could see her again in the dresses, one by one, the bronze taffeta, the cream-colored Surah printed with little pink roses and green leaves, the sleek grey ottoman with the ruffled shoulder cape, the mauve albatross, the soft green satin. . . . Maybe in her work dresses, or her skirt and waist, or that decrepit yellowing graduation dress, nobody would pay any attention to her, but in clothes by Madame Blanche they could hardly help paying attention! The sleeves and hems had to be taken down but otherwise they fitted perfectly and even as they were, without any alterations, they looked good. There was no doubt about it, this business with the clothes was going to get her started. Nobody knew how it would end, but just imagine the stark horror of it if all of a sudden she was announcing her engagement to a millionaire!

To have to sit back and watch something like that happen and be utterly helpless and not able to do a single, solitary thing to prevent it — she might as well be dead. Human flesh and blood can only stand just so much.

That busybody of a Mrs. Morelewski! Why couldn't she have minded her own business and realized how easy certain people's heads were turned? She thought she was very smart, just because she happened to be the Queen of the Jubilee that time! But that wasn't so clever. There were a lot of things a whole lot cleverer than that.

It was so dark, she had to grope her way into the kitchen for a glass of water, but out there the moonlight coming in the east window made the room so bright she could see everything, even what time it was. It was ten minutes past one . . . and Sunday morning. . . .

Funny, she hadn't heard the hour strike. Maybe the clock had stopped. . . . But no, it was ticking.

All of a sudden she thought of Dorney's letter underneath the clock on the wall shelf, the one that had come today from that smart-alecky nephew of the Morelewskis'. In the excitement about the dresses, she had forgotten to mention it.

She took it down and looked at it. ·

Now, what did he have to say?

Something to give Dorney more of a swelled head than ever?

By the parlor lamp turned down as low as it would go and the chimney off in order that she could give one little quick puff and the flame would be out in case she heard some sound, she read, "Cometh not the Cocqcigrues next Tuesday night to see Miss Dorney Leaf but her curious friend, Teige Desmond."

Well, if that wasn't ridiculous! Not worth wasting a stamp on.

She read it twice more before she destroyed it, smiling to herself.

What a way to express a person's self.

He must be coming out west to visit the Morelewskis again.

Tuesday night, hmm?

Well, well, well.

37

"HOW DO YOU FIGURE THAT WOULD BE?" SUN-
dance Kid inquired, stopping before the gate post in front of the
gabled Lion House. Upstairs, all the windows of the house were dark
but downstairs a few lights burned behind drawn shades.

"What what would be?" Butch Cassidy said.

"Having maybe forty or fifty better halfs. He kep' 'em in this
house, and in that one," he pointed to the neighboring mansion,
"and that there one across the street." He turned and looked at
the great dark Gardo House on the landscaped corner lot. "Ain't
nobody home there, I guess."

"He never had that many."

"How many did he have?"

"A sight, but not that many."

"Must of been quite a skylark just the same."

Butch laughed and walked on, up South Temple, his husky companion lingering behind and then catching up with him at the Eagle
Gate.

There was a sound of running water in the darkness, and overhead the leaves of the linden and mulberry trees that edged the
street, fluttered in the fresh mountain breeze.

"Butch."

"What?"

"One woman can be just as bad sometimes as a whole herd. You
know that."

"So I hear tell."

"I sure hope to God you know what you're doing."

"I know what I'm doing."

"What I can't understand is how you could see a gal two times
for about five minutes and then take a notion and chase all over
hell for her!"

"Listen, Longabaugh. Down in Circle Valley when we first went
there to live, why, there was this couple that used to go to the
dances. He sparked her for twenty years before they finally got married. And what do you think? A week after the wedding, here she

was back with her pa! which she ain't never left since. And her sweet patootie, he's a-batching it out on his ranch the same as ever. So you can't tell nothing about how *nothing's* going to turn out. All you can do is make as good a guess as you can and leave the rest to luck."

At the end of Judge Towers's long sidewalk, looking at the house and the way the light sparkled through the stained glass of its windows and door panels, Sundance Kid said in awe, "Maybe she's going to want to think twice before she leaves something like this for South America!"

When the doorbell rang, Selma Ankerstrand, hurrying to answer it, heard her mistress's step on the stairs behind her and caught a whiff of vinegar, that sovereign remedy for headache. The maid switched on the overhead porch light and opened the door. "Good evening," she said.

Both men removed their bowler hats. One stepped forward.

"Good evening, ma'am. We come to see the Judge," he said.

"He ain't here."

"Where is he?"

"Gone to Ogden on a case."

"When's he coming back?"

"Monday or Tuesday."

A pale elderly woman in a handsome dress emerged out of the shadows by the staircase. Her face had a drawn look and the fingers of her right hand were pressed against her temple. "Who is it?" she asked, though she could see as well who was standing on the lighted porch as her maid could. "At this time of night?"

Selma Ankerstrand looked around at her.

"Two men that want to see the Judge," she said, returning her gaze to the visitors.

"Tell them he's not here."

"That's what I'm doing, ma'am."

The elderly woman gazed fixedly at the foremost of the callers.

"Well, I wonder then," he said "if I can see the lady that does the cooking around this here outfit, please?"

"He wonders if he can see *whom?*"

Selma Ankerstrand peeked uneasily around again to say, "Madge Yandle."

"Why, she's gone home!"

"She's gone home," the maid turned back and repeated.

"More than an hour ago," Mrs. Towers said, to a spot just above the handsome mirror that hung on the wall opposite her.

"Where does she live?"

"Five thirty-two East Eighth Sou — "

"Selma!" her mistress said sharply.

"Does she have a sister by the name of Dorney?"

"Yes, she makes her home with her. She's a orphan."

"Selma, that will be enough."

"What was nipping on the old woman?" Sundance Kid asked as they went down Fourth East.

"I wouldn't be surprised but what that was the Judge's wife. Must of been quite a pretty girl in her day."

"Well, what was nipping on her?"

"God knows."

"She sure give you the once-over."

"I noticed that."

"Too bad the Judge wasn't there."

"Yeah, he's a very nice fellow. I'd of like to of made you acquainted with him. But it don't really matter. All I wanted was, to find out about the kiddo."

"I thought you wanted the names of a couple of the Judge's friends he's supposed to have down there in Argentina."

"Oh, I would of asked him for 'em, and chewed the fat with him a while if he'd of been home, but it don't really matter."

At the corner of Sixth South, Harry Longabaugh gave a little chuckle. "This is sure going to wake up the green-eyed monster in poor old Mary," he said. "You out sweethearting another girl like this."

"Mary who?"

"The old buzzard that cleans up, at the hotel. That took such a liking to you this afternoon when we got to town and took the room and there she was making the bed. She was telling you her whole life story and everything."

"Oh, her," Butch said.

"How many times was it she said they locked her up?"

"She didn't say."

"Sure she did."

"Guess I must of missed that."

"I wouldn't be surprised but what she thinks she cut quite a wide swath with you, you giving her a ten spot like that."

"It must be damn tough to be old like that and not have nobody."

"Probably thought maybe you was a-going to take her out tonight, on your arm. You sure encouraged her."

"Well, by God, when somebody ain't only held one job down in ten years and they're a-trying to straighten up and keep out of jail —"

"Listen who's talking." Sundance Kid gave his companion a little nudge in the ribs.

385

From across the street they looked at the middle one of the three small houses. A crack of lamplight showed beneath the blind in the front window. They could hear music coming from that room, piano music, the kind that is being practised, not the kind that is being played for an audience. Even to untutored ears, the difference is unmistakable.

"You figure that's her, banging away on the pianforte?" Sundance Kid inquired.

"Search me," Butch said.

"Maybe she'll want to cart the thing along with her!"

"I'll buy her one, when we get there."

They stood, looking and listening. "Well, now what do we do?" Sundance Kid said, putting a tailor-made cigarette between his lips and lighting it.

"Hey, wait." Before he could toss the lighted match away, his companion bent forward and lit his own cigarette on it. "Damned if I know," he said.

"By God, that's something new to hear from Butch Cassidy."

"Well, her and me ain't so acquainted that the circumstances is such that I can go up there and knock at the door like we been sparking for years. Besides, it's pretty late by now. Must be nearly nine."

"Late? Guess you must of lost track it's Saturday night! Where I come from, Saturday night at nine o'clock things ain't even started getting warmed up yet. Its just like the middle of the afternoon, where I come from."

"We would of got going earlier if you hadn't of thought you knowed that guy that was camped there in the lobby of the hotel."

"I know I knowed him," Sundance Kid insisted, "and he would of knowed us, too. Remember the guy in Vernal with the drugstore, where the Texan bought the epsom salts for Deaf Charley that time he had the colic? That's who it was."

"That's what you said. But even so, he wouldn't of knew who we was if we'd of just went on about our business and walked past."

"We was standing right alongside of the Texan that time! And everybody in Vernal knowed Butch Cassidy and the biggest part of the Wild Bunch."

"He wouldn't recognize us now. Elza Lay went back all right."

"I recognized him, didn't I? so who's to say he wouldn't recognize us? I'd hate to take a chance on it."

"Well, he sure had staked out a claim on that old rocking chair there by that post and that spittoon. Begun to think he wasn't never going to vamoose." Butch Cassidy looked up and down the dark street, quiet except for the music, and then back at the small house. "This is the first time since I was knee-high to grasshopper, seems like, that I don't know which card to lay down."

"Maybe she's out to some shindig."

"I got a hunch she's in there."

"Let's go have us a look in some of the windows, why not?"

"Huh-uh. That wouldn't be no way to do."

"Let's go on up and knock at the door!"

"No, wait." Butch laid his hand on Sundance Kid's sleeve. "I ain't figured out just exactly what I'm going to — whether to say who I —"

"Play like you're selling stereopticons."

"If I could just see her away from that house."

"Let me go and deliver her a message, telling her to meet you somewheres. You can write it, down there at the corner under that there street light."

The outlaw fingered the folded envelope in his pocket. "That might scare her," he said. "Besides, if she come, maybe some of her folks would come with her, and then what kind of a excuse would I have, in front of them?"

"There must be some way to do," Longabaugh said, moving over to lean back comfortably against a tree.

"Sure, there's some way."

"What is it?"

"Give a guy a chance to think, why don't you?" Butch tossed his cigarette into the ditch water. "If she'd just come along down the street right about now."

"How would you know it was her? Supposing she did. It's mighty dark right along here even if the moon's a-shining."

I'd feel it in my bones, Butch thought.

"How about —" Sundance Kid paused, and looked in the direction of the house. "Listen," he said.

"Yeah, I hear."

"Whoever that was in there has quit a-banging on the piano-forte. . . ."

"And there goes the light. . . ."

"Yeah. Now what?"

Butch took his hat off, ran his hand through his hair and put it back on. "Tell you what I'm going to have to do," he said.

"What's that?"

"Going to have to come back by daylight. There ain't no other way around it."

"Now's a fine time to figure something like that out, after people's feet's practically bleeding in these damn dudified shoes."

"I think I'll try it alone, too," Butch said apologetically.

387

"Well, I would of drifted anyway, once you and her got past the how-you-been."

"I know you would. . . ."

"But, it don't make no difference to me."

"You can run down plenty of entertainment, and a guy don't need to worry when it's the old Sundance Kid like as if it was the Tall Texan."

"Entertainment like what kind?"

"Well, like — for one thing, you can go down to the station and buy the tickets for Galveston, and another thing, you can — "

"It holds, don't it, what you said?"

"What's that?"

"That we're taking the train out of here tomorrow night?"

"Why shouldn't it hold?"

"Supposing she ain't said by then she'll come with you?"

"We're taking that train."

"I think I'll get them tickets the first thing in the morning," Sundance Kid said thoughtfully. "One for you and one for me. You can get hers when the time comes."

He was as good as his word. When he returned to the hotel room the next morning, he found Butch shaving. "Well, here's our tickets," he said, patting his upper coat pocket. "The train pulls out at 'leven fifty-five tonight and there ain't going to be no delay, either. So I know one *hombre* that's got to work pretty fast."

"You see your friend downstairs?"

"The old geezer from Vernal? No. But I seen Mary down the hall, sweeping out a room. You should of saw the dust clouds. Know what she asked me?"

"What?" Butch bent over the wash basin and splashed his face, then reached for the dingy towel.

"Wanted to know if Mr. Jim Lowe was married."

"What'd you tell her?" The words came out muffled.

"Told her you was. Are, ain't you, very nearly?"

"Bust her all up, did it?"

"In little pieces. Know what she said?"

"What?"

"Said if she'd of met somebody like you forty years ago, she wouldn't be where she is now."

"Me, neither," Butch said, laughing. He hung the towel around his neck and reached for the comb.

"Said a ten spot from anybody else she would of had it all diluted long before this and down the hatch — that is, if she hadn't of turned over a new leaf — but a ten spot from you she's keeping as a souvenir." Sundance Kid went over to the window and let the shade up. "Look at the doggone day you got, would you? Hot, but prettier than a hatful of nuggets. Guess the way you was sitting nearly out on the roof half the night last night smoking, you got things figured out to the fine points now, about doing your sweethearting."

Butch nodded, but did not meet Harry Longabaugh's eyes.

"I'm beginning to get kind of anxious to see who it really is that's finally throwed their lasso over Butch Cassidy. There's been some experts try it, me and the boys remember, even if you don't. When I think of that little beaut up there in Missoula that time — " Sighing, Sundance Kid took a seat on the wide window ledge. "Know what's always stumped me?" he said. "How come it is that the gals always fall all over theirself for the guy that don't hardly pay no attention to 'em whatever, while the guys that comes a-faunching with their tongues hanging out a mile, like the Texan, or — "

"What you going to do to while away the time?" Butch asked, reaching for his hat.

"Maybe climb up and rub noses with that gold angel up on top of the Temple. Only he's a man, ain't he?"

"How the hell should I know?" Butch's white teeth flashed in a smile. "Listen, Longabaugh."

"Yeah, Boss."

"How about we meet at the restaurant where we et last night. At that same table back over there in the corner under the big green plant."

"What time?"

"Right around six-thirty. See, in case she's along with me, I don't want to take a chance on coming to the hotel and maybe running into that old bird from Vernal that you claim would know us, in case he's back on his perch again."

"He would know us. You'd find out quick enough if he spotted us." Sundance Kid moved to the unmade bed and sat on it, but too restless to stay there, got up and wandered on, to lean against the golden oak bureau. "I can't say I'm going to be sorry when that old train gets to rolling out of the station tonight," he said, feeling for a cigarette. "For that matter, I ain't going to be sorry when that old boat pulls away from shore, that's going to take us to Argentina. Fact, I ain't going to breathe perfectly easy till we get there, and I got me the deed to my ranch in my back hind pocket and I'm sitting on my own veranda smoking my old pipe — "

"You don't never smoke a pipe."

"Don't I, though! You ain't never saw me when I'm a honest respectable South American rancher!"

Butch laughed. "The Paris Café right around six-thirty," he said.

Sundance Kid shook hands with himself. "You're going to have to step mighty lively, amigo."

At the head of the stairs Butch Cassidy met the old charwoman.

"Good morning, Mr. Lowe," she said, coquettishly smoothing back a lock of dead black hair and patting her wrinkled pumpkin-red cheek as if it belonged to somebody else. With her discolored left hand she twisted the long string of jet beads that swung down over her patched calico apron. "Except that it's closer to noon," she added, cackling as at a very funny joke.

"How's the world treating you?" Butch said cordially as he started down the stairs.

"Mr. Lowe."

"Yes, ma'am?" He halted and turned, his hand on the banister.

She came over and took hold of the newel post, smoothing the top of it as though it had been the bald head of a small man of whom she was fond. "You know I explained to you about taking the pledge — and going to work, and how I was telling you all them different things — "

He nodded, his eyes lenient.

"Your friend claims you're a married man and I was wondering — why couldn't I come and work for a nice goodhearted friendly young feller like you and your ladylove instead of having to stay here and work in a dump like this? Why couldn't I, now?"

"Supposing her and me don't live in the United States of America?"

"You ain't no foreigner," she scoffed.

"No, but supposing we live in a foreign country."

"I'd be game for it."

"How about if I talk things over with the missus and then sit down and write you a letter sometime, huh? How about that?"

"M-a-r-y B-r-o-c-k-e-t-t." The old woman spelled it childishly. "Write me in care of this here Temple Hotel. Wait a minute and I'll step in one of these rooms here and write it down for you on a piece of paper, so you won't forget."

"I won't forget, honest. I'm in kind of a hurry," Butch said. "How about giving it to my pardner?"

"He's a nice goodhearted friendly young feller, too."

"Sure he is."

"But I'd rather give it to you, personal."

"All right, you do that. That'll be great."

"Mr. Lowe."

Again he halted and looked back, smiling.

"That wouldn't be Ireland, now, would it?" she asked wistfully. He shook his head. "No, ma'am, not Ireland."

"I couldn't hardly conceive so," she said. "You know why not?"

"Why not?"

" 'Cause you said a foreign country."

390

It was a quarter to one when he took up his stand across the street from where the girl lived. He had been sure that this was the proper hour and that there was nothing more sensible to do than what he was doing, but the sight of her house by daylight shook him, and he felt weak with doubt. How could he have been so careless as to leave the premises unguarded throughout the night? All kinds of accidents could have happened, not least among them that, before breakfast, somebody came and carried her off on a picnic! from which she might never return. The bull in the soft meadow! The treacherous rill! The poisonous snake! The dislodged boulder! These could make a picnic hazardous as a battle, everybody knew. Had she gone? Would she come safely back?

After twenty minutes to half an hour of keeping watch, he began to have a peculiar sensation along the nape of his neck.

He looked behind him. Someone within the house directly opposite hers, was standing back of their lace curtains — there was a twitch to that one — wondering who he was and what he was doing. This neighborhood was not the place for a long vigil unless, when asked, it could be accounted for. Slowly he commenced to walk on, thinking of an ideal world where everybody minded their own business.

His hope had been, and still was, that all of a sudden she would be coming down those front steps. He would appear to be passing, they would look and know each other and presto! things would start happening. The difficulty was, in a quiet locality like this, a stranger who just stood and didn't do anything, or walked up and down smoking, had about as much chance of not being noticed as a green and orange zebra jumping around on its two hind legs. Soon some shirt-sleeved property owner would challenge him. "Hello, mister. How about it? You lost?" No, he wouldn't put it off any longer. Once around the block, to give him time to decide just what to say and how to say it (and what to do about the matter of his name) and he would go up there and knock on that front door.

At the corner, he crossed Eighth South and started up shady Sixth East. A middle-aged woman with a boy of three or four was coming down it, taking an afternoon saunter.

She looked at him so sharp a glance that he found himself looking as hard at her, and then she smiled! the pistillate red smile of the nearly toothless, as if she knew him. But she did not stop, and he, tipping his hat warily, did not stop, either. When after a dozen steps or so he decided to look around at her, she was doing the same thing. Shocked, he brought his gaze to the front once more. Good God! did she know him? Was she going to put somebody on his trail?

A pair of children, a small girl and still smaller boy, were solemnly climbing the gate in the fence at his left. "Hello," they said.

"Hello," he said, relaxing his shoulders and letting the hand in his left coat pocket slowly open. Well, if she was, she was. No use to start running like a kid past a graveyard at midnight, till something was really swooping down on him. He halted to watch a woolly old dog, brown as coffee, with round black ears and a black nose, amble down the walk and drop down close to the children, putting his head between his paws. His ancient eyes watched steadily, without animosity.

"Did you come to see us?" the small girl inquired. She was dressed for Sunday in a white dress with a flounce around the bottom, and her hair had been put up on rags. To call attention to it, she pulled a tight ringlet, let go and it bounced like a spring.

"No, miss, I regret to say I didn't."

At first Butch thought the massive old woman sitting in the rocking chair on the porch, muffled in a shawl, was staring at him, but she wasn't. She appeared not to blink.

"We're going to have chicken and noodles and raisin pie," the boy announced. He, too, was dressed in his best for Sunday.

"Good for you." The outlaw looked back down the street again and saw that the woman and her child were now well into the next block, slowly sauntering along. Maybe he looked like somebody she knew, that was all. That could happen.

A small blond man with arm garters on, came out of the house, banging the screen door behind him. Catching hold of the rocker, he maneuvered it gently backward a foot or two into the shade. "How's that, Mother?" he said, giving her a smile which she did not return.

'That's Grandma." The small girl looked over her shoulder. "She had a stroke." She said it proudly.

Butch Cassidy did not go around the block. Instead, he continued down Seventh South to Main Street, and there walked along the main thoroughfare. From mulling over a jumble of matters, he came to the thought of love, which reminded him of something. When he was still small and hung about the womenfolks, Ma and her sister had talked about the yearnings of certain ladies. Menfolks couldn't have them. He had asked and they said no. Just certain particular ladies. They craved strawberries in the dead of winter when there wasn't none, mustard pickles when the supply was all ate up, cinnamon drops when it was four miles to the crossroads to get some, lemonade when they might as well of been asking for pink champagne, they'd of had that much chance of getting it. Nothing never possible, nothing right at hand, nothing easy. He found out later on who those quirky ladies were and what was ailing them but that didn't explain their notions. Why had they got that hankering after just what they hankered after? Wasn't love in the same category? Craving this or that? Why not the girl in Missoula, Montana? Or somebody else? Why Dorney?

In love. He pondered. Love. It seemed so valuable. Like that flower the little Swiss fellow was telling about that used to board at Mrs. Peipinbrink's in Telluride. Grew clear up on top of the alps, he claimed, little flower, sweet smelling, but not so much, not really, the hardest thing in the world to get hold of — people died, or got their backs and legs broke, trying — but that didn't stop 'em. They had to climb up them perpendicular mountains just the same, just to pick one of them flowers . . . that seemed so valuable, like love, and the one you loved. Idle something, they was called, idle something.

The streetcar whose coming the humming of the trolley wires had been announcing for many minutes and which could have been seen far off, for the long street ran as straight as a die down from its hilly northern rise, had not the playful breezes swirled up dust in clouds to obscure it, lurched into view clanging cheerfully. Butch looked at it with the same comradely urge to take his hat off and wave it he felt when, riding out in lonesome country, he heard a train whistle and looked up to see a train rounding the bend, but he stuck both hands in his pockets.

Even when he was too far away to be entirely sure it was she crossing Main Street on Eighth South, going west, he was entirely sure. At first he broke into a loping run and then slowed down to a walk, while his heart reeled and his mouth felt as dry as chaff. This was what he had been hoping against hope for, that she would come out and he would meet her on the street and by George, it looked like if a fellow just wanted something to happen bad enough, it up and happened. Maybe, like Ma used to say so long ago, a guy really had a guardian angel flapping his wings over him all the time, that arranged things the way they ought to be. He had often felt so when time after time he and the boys had backed out of some bank or jumped down from some stalled baggage car with a feed sack full of money, without firing a shot, that something was watching over him and his affairs, just the way Ma had claimed. Not that Ma had any idea what he was up to — she'd have a conniption fit if she did, her pa being a preacher. But . . . by George, didn't it look like it? Already, his eyes on the girl ahead, he was censuring his unspoken words. No more of this cussing every breath. He'd have to put a bug in Sundance Kid's ear about that, too.

By God — by George, rather — wasn't she — heavenly days in the morning — say, wasn't she?

She went down Eighth South. He followed and soon overtook her.

393

Phoebe Bannon, out by the green gate trying to call her youngest in for a nap, saw them coming. She blinked, rubbed her eyes and looked again, looked harder, commenced clinging to the fence in a most odd fashion. She got so pale and looked so queer that Dorney ran the last few steps of the way. "What in the world's the matter, Mrs. Bannon?" She looked back at the man who had come with her and saw that he looked almost the same, except not pale, and not scared. But he was flabbergasted, too, the way she was. "Mrs. Bannon — " she began. The woman, white as wax, looked up and down the street, looked back at the double house, opened the gate and said hurriedly, "Come on." She did not wait to see them accept her invitation but hastened up the walk. They went after.

Inside the house she did not speak until she had closed the windows, pulled the shades of the windows facing the street nearly down to the bottom and made sure for the second time that the door was not only shut but bolted. Then, "Take chairs," she said, shortly. Her agitation had kept them silent. She looked at Dorney. "I guess you thought that was very smart, pulling my leg all this time. Sounding me out! hearing all I had to say on the subject! Well, I hope it was worth your trouble. Maybe someday you'll tell me what the purpose was, and the big joke, so I can laugh, too."

"What are you talking about?" Dorney asked in bewilderment.

"My, we're innocent, ain't we?" She looked at the man then. Her face softened. "Of all the people," she said. "Butch Cassidy."

Dorney reached for an edge of the table.

She would never have known in a million years. No extra sense, no perception inward said: fabled, unparalleled, stalwart, Jason and the Golden Fleece, Jack the Giant Killer: here he is. Dull clod! Log of wood! Now the din of his fame sounded in her ears. Now the rays of his glory stabbed her eyes. But she did not know him of her own accord. St. Joan knew her King. She knew not her hero! She held on tighter and wondered how outlandish it would look if she sat down on the floor.

" 'Tell me about him,' " Phoebe Bannon mimicked. " 'I never seen him in my whole entire life. I don't know him.' Not much. I guess not! What was up your sleeve? That's all I want to know. Let me in on the fun, too, now the joke is over! Or is there more to come?"

"You mean," the man spoke carefully, "the kiddo here — you mean, she already knows something about Butch Cassidy?"

"Knows something about you? She knows your whole life history from one end to the other, up and down, right and left. Maybe better'n you know it yourself!"

He looked incredulous. "Here I was arguing with myself whether to — " That guardian angel! flapping his wings, manipulating affairs the way they ought to go. Here he was arguing with himself whether to tell her that once upon a time there had been a wild and woolly outlaw by the name of George LeRoy Parker alias Butch Cassidy who had done a good many things he might better not have done — and she knew it already! "How come?" he said. "When she don't know me from Adam?"

Phoebe Bannon stared. "Don't know you?" she said. "Then how — ?" She looked at Dorney. "Didn't you honestly have no idea that this was — was — him?"

Dorney opened her lips, shut them.

"Well, who did you think it was, then? How in God's world did you get together?"

Dorney, listening, blinking, did not answer. Why hadn't she known? Why didn't she guess? For two hours, she had stood next to him at the medicine show. Sometimes, their pleased eyes sociably had met. And then when the hypnotist was pretending to hypnotize . . . He had knelt in front of her on Judge Towers's floor! He had said something, now forgotten, never understood, rapid, mysterious, but he had spoken. He had taken her hand in his. Had pressed it to his beating heart. And she had been deaf and blind! No trumpet blasted, no lightning flashed, to tell, to instruct: Dorney: the hero of all your days: behold him here.

Why that unbroken stillness? Why that unbroken dark?

Because this man was not Butch Cassidy! no more the tapered, telescopic, brown and dark outlaw she had seen since time's beginning in her mind's eye, than the highest magnifico of Venice.

This man was as blond as a crocus: blue-eyed as sky.

He was about as tall as Thomas Diltz, who was five feet eight inches in height.

But he did not look it, being of a stocky build.

How could she have been so mistaken? Imagining all these years that Butch Cassidy was —

So other!

— when he looked like this?

Grandpa Bannon was the most terrible liar!

"What does he look like, Grandpa?" Little and young once more, there she sits on his back step twirling her tasseled braid.

"Look like? He looks — well, how would you figure? How would you guess?"

"Well, I would figure — I would guess — "

She tells him, down to the fine points. He listens, musing, studies her. "That's him!" he decides. "You hit the nail right on the head!"

So, after all, Grandpa is not the most terrible liar. He does not chime in with her, to be mean. He thinks she has about as much chance of ever meeting Butch Cassidy as she has of meeting the

395

man who invented the balloon. Then let her say how she wants him to look! thinks Grandpa. Let her choose and say. What's the hurt? What's the difference? The doll of a child's life, let her point it down off the toy shop shelf. The hero of her life . . . let her pick out his eyes, his hair, his stature, for the day will never come, will never never come, when he'll turn up.

The genuine article.

Dorney let go of the table by degrees.

The real outlaw!

She looked him full in the face.

La, no.

Not him!

Any more than . . .

Until — while she gazed — his personality, and fame, and the two together, began to blend with blueness and flaxen and . . .

Butch Cassidy smiled! like a beam of sun.

Then she knew him.

Oh, then she knew him.

Very well!

38

PHOEBE BANNON, HER HAND PRESSED TO THE
small of her back, more from long habit than because it hurt her —
for on Sunday, when she could get off her feet now and again, it
was better than other days — watched them through the window
as they went down Second West.

If that wasn't the funniest thing, that Dorney should really meet
the one she had taken such an interest in so long! Grandpa Bannon would be entertained by it. In fact, anybody would be entertained. It almost made a person half believe that nothing in life
is accidental — it's all planned, down to the very last particular.

He was only a little bit taller than she was but they made a nice-
looking couple. He was — let's see, how old would Butch Cassidy
be now anyway? She was thirty-seven and Blufe had been four years
older and Butch was ten years younger than Blufe — so he was —
let's see — thirty-one. And Dorney had turned sixteen — or was it
seventeen? — when she had her birthday last spring. Fifteen years
wasn't too much difference in age in case Butch finally had it in
mind to settle down . . . but of course it didn't look like he was
going to do much settling if he was leaving tonight for Texas, and
then going to go to South America. Funny that he would invite
Dorney out like that, to go to Liberty Park. That didn't seem to tie
in with Butch. He didn't say what he was doing in Salt Lake, only
that he and Harry Longabaugh were stopping at the Temple Hotel.
It would have been nice to see Sundance Kid again. It was nice to
see Butch. Of all people. Too bad they weren't going to stay longer.

They had passed from view now, the rather thick-set blond man
and the slender brown-haired girl, but Phoebe still stood in the
window, lost in thought. What a happenstance, if he and Dorney . . .
Well, he wouldn't be going very far wrong to pick a girl like her if
that was what he had taken a notion to do. From the time they
stepped in the house and Phoebe Bannon had let the cat out of
the bag about who he was, he had looked like if he could just take
the kid in his arms that would be all he wanted. That was sure a
new side to Butch. At least one or two girls around Star Valley would

397

be very much surprised to hear it. They thought that if he wouldn't take a fancy to *them*, he wouldn't take a fancy to any woman living — but it looked like they were mistaken. Well, that new lavender dress she had on was certainly becoming . . . if her sister Madge had made *that* she had missed her calling. The only trouble with Dorney she was kind of dreamy but she'd outgrow that, likely. And yet, some people never changed.

Butch, for instance. He was still the same doggone fellow . . . same smile . . . same way of talking. And still taking chances . . . there would be hundreds of people in the park . . . and how was he so sure somebody wouldn't spot him and point him out to the nearest policeman? There must be quite a reward offered for him now. He mentioned, himself, that there was. "I'm about twice as dear as I used to be, Phoebe!" Years ago, the authorities were offering five thousand dollars reward for him. It must be ten thousand or even more now. But he didn't pay any attention to that. Liberty Park was a pretty place to go and that was where he wanted to take Dorney. Who cared about hundreds of people? That was Butch for you.

She began to rub her back absent-mindedly. It was beginning to ache a little now, the way it always did when she stood too long. In the laundry, where she couldn't sit down, it would start like this and then hurt worse and worse until the sweat would be standing all across her upper lip and she would be sick at her stomach. She really should have it operated on, wherever the trouble was, in her spine, the way the doctor said. How quickly Sunday passed! before you could hardly catch your breath, here was horrible Monday again. Why couldn't Blufe have left her a little insurance? enough so she could stay home with the kids. They needed her so. Fern didn't know how to handle her own, let alone anybody else's — they were getting wild and impudent. What they needed was a firm rein, a mother at home, not one off working in the laundry.

Wrapped in thought, Phoebe Bannon took up a corner of apron, moistened it with her tongue and began to rub off a tiny speck on the windowpane. She could keep house the way a woman ought to, then. Not give things a lick and a promise. She had always liked to keep house. That was what women were made for. If she had to do nothing but that from morning till night, and take care of the kids, in spite of her back, she would never complain. If Blufe had left her a little money! Not ten thousand dollars, naturally — like the reward for Butch — he could never have paid on such a policy — but enough to make ends meet while the kids were little. She'd like just for the curiosity of it to see an amount like that reward all together sometime — ten thousand dollars. It would probably fill the washtub . . . or two washtubs and the water bucket. . . . It would last a long time. One thing sure and certain, it would solve each and every problem of Phoebe Bannon's life.

They had been talking a long while there, that couple on the grassy ledge in behind the wild rose bushes under the chestnut tree. The small girl, left to her own devices by the bigger children who ran away and wouldn't let her follow them, came and peeped at them sometimes when she got tired of amusing herself in other ways, such as dabbling a leafy branch of willow in the creek. She belonged to the picnic party at the nearest rustic table some seventy-five yards through the trees.

Sometimes the couple saw her peeping at them and smiled at her. Once they motioned for her to come closer but mostly she could look and not be heeded, for they had so much to say to each other, it kept them too busy to pay attention to anything else whatever. They had been talking, oh, the longest time. She couldn't hear what they said but it must have been very interesting. Now it was beginning to look late. The sunlight came in long yellow rays through the trees and there were more bugs dancing in the air. The small girl noticed that she wasn't so full as she had been and went and teased for something to eat and her mother lifted the lid of the picnic basket and dug down under the fringed dishtowel and brought out a bread and butter sandwich. "That will have to hold you till supper," she said. "When evening comes." "That's pretty long, Mamma." "No, it ain't. An hour or two."

The young lady looked like a picture on a candy box, almost. She had such a pretty dress on. It was the most beautiful color. The sunlight hit her hair and made it look like religious people's hair on a Sunday School card printed in colors — that thing around it.

The man was not very good-looking but he was a nice man. He looked nice whenever he smiled or laughed.

The small girl watched them from behind the trunk of the box elder while she ate her bread and butter. Then she wiped her fingers on her voile dress and wandered away. An hour or two till evening was a long time.

"Well, now you really know more about me than I know myself," Butch said.

"And you know all there is about me." (Except the most important part, about Mr. Desmond and the books, but so far, the time to mention them hadn't come.)

She could look at him and he was just her oldest friend, the one she had known longest and loved most, as familiar, now, after three hours, as the back of her own hand, until, out of nowhere, that name would burst like a clap of thunder and reverberate in her ears, or flash before her eyes in great headline letters — BUTCH CASSIDY!

Then, warm as was the July day, gooseflesh would form along her outer arms and something would be tugging and dragging her scalp upward from the region of her neck. She was wide awake and she was sitting here with — him! There was no Little Dipper any more, and had not been, for a long time — he had got his leg broke and had to be shot. Butch had another horse now, called Prince, a roan. Butch had on citified clothes, too. But mounted and dressed like himself or not, he was himself . . . sitting two feet away, arms hugging his knees. His face was bent toward her. His story fell from his lips! Nothing could beat that for wonderful — unless the Deerslayer should reappear in the flesh and tell what happened after he said goodbye to Chingachgook for the last time and left the country round about the Glimmerglass! Yet, it was all quite natural, too — whenever Dorney looked into his eyes, she thought it was — and so, between feeling with skin ripples and a lifted scalp that it was an apocryphal situation, for Butch Cassidy *couldn't* be sitting there, and knowing that he was, and taking it for granted, too — Dorney wavered, once complacent, once overwhelmed.

"Yes, sir," he repeated, reaching down to pluck a blade of grass, "more than I know myself."

"You forgot — Mrs. Bannon heard that you wanted to take the Wild Bunch and go to and join the Army when the war was on. She heard that you tried to persuade them, and that you even — "

"Uncle Sam didn't need no help. Whipped 'em in six months. Didn't need us." He changed the subject quickly. "Too bad I can't remember Blufe's old man. I wish I could."

"He was so proud when you shook hands with him that time in the butcher shop in Rock Springs. He told over and over again how you and he had had quite a conversation."

"Old guy, hmm?"

"Real old, and kind of stooped over, and he used to frown so, and his eyes were so small you could hardly see what color they were — "

Butch shook his head. "No, honey, I just can't remember. But — funny thing — I connected you with a old man, someway. Now, how did I come to do that?"

"You asked me if Judge Towers was my grandfather. That night, you know."

"I know. . . ." He looked about him. "You like this place? This park, I mean?"

"Oh, yes!"

"Last year me and the Texan hired us a rig and drove around it. Last night, thinking where you and me should go, I thought of it. And — " He looked at her, thinking that she was going to speak but she kept silent. "And so we come here," he said. "You and me.

And got everything straight between us — about getting married, and leaving for Galveston and going to South America. . . . "

She did not speak but crossed her arms over her chest and held her elbows in her hands as though she was cold.

"Happened just like I was a-wishing — even better than I was a-wishing. Because you knowed all about me already."

"Butch."

"Yeah, kiddo."

"That night up at Judge Towers's. That was strange."

"Spooky, almost. But it stamped your face on my mind so that it went clear through to the other side. And if I'd of never saw you again there wouldn't of been no way to rub it out . . . and I'd of been . . . "

"You said something about — what was it you said about mirages?"

"Did I? I guess that I thought you was one when I seen who it was, going to open the door!"

"I always wanted to see a mirage."

"They can sure act peculiar."

"Can they?"

"Say for instance — you'll look out over the desert. It'll be so hot and bright the air looks like it's jiggling up and down — and here will be some fellow driving a cow towards you. You know how long that old cow's legs will look? Maybe twenty feet long!"

She laughed.

"The commonest, most ordinary kind is to see lakes and pools with big high grasses growing around 'em. They'll seem so real you can very near hear the fish a-flapping and see the ducks a-swimming and animals coming to drink. Kind of a light pale blue color, the water'll be, and it'll go to shimmering and sparkling and the wind'll come over and cause little waves and ripples in it. . . . Everybody out on the desert some time or other has saw that. The kind of mirages that tickle me are the ones — well, there'll be a little antelope, say, about as far off as that footbridge down there over the crick," he pointed, "but it won't no more look like a antelope than I do."

"What will it look like?"

"Not like a antelope, that's sure — and it'll be about the size of a overgrowed Percheron. You'll start walking towards it — if you know — otherwise if you're a greenhorn, you'll turn and run for your life. — and you keep a-going till you get past a certain point — and it's a antelope, like it was all the time! You know something?"

"What?"

"Going back to them lakes and pools. Cattle can see 'em, and horses, just like men. That can be awful pathetic. Horses, you can put a bug in their ear, but cows . . . " He stopped.

"How many kinds of mirages are there?"

"More kinds than you can shake a stick at. Once I seen a freighting outfit that I found out later was nearly a hundred miles away at the time. That's God's truth. Seen the wagons, the mules, the drivers, everything — seen a fellow spit tobacco juice, seen another guy wipe his face with a red bandanna hankachiff, seen the mules waggle their ears — like the whole outfit wasn't no farther away than just through them trees over there. That's one kind. Seeing actual things that's really too far off to see. But then there's another . . . I heard a guy tell about this war party he seen a-coming. All of a sudden here they was making a beeline for him, jogging along on their cayuses, painted within a inch of their life, spoiling for a fight. . . . While he watched, his eyeballs popping, for they had come so quick, with no warning, they commenced to rare up on their horses and gallop, waving their rifles around. Well, the way their mouths was open and the way their horses was a-flying, there should of been such an amount of yelling and commotion that you couldn't hear yourself think. But instead of that, they was just as quiet as death. Their horses never made no sound, them yelling braves never made no sound, and the first thing this guy knowed, they started to get transparent so he could see through 'em, and got more and more so, and the first thing he knowed had just naturally melted away. Sometime I'll have to tell you about once when I was on the Mojave, I seen a . . . Oh, I got lots to tell you. The Indians don't like mirages."

"Don't they?"

"They think they're bad medicine. Wherever they can see 'em especially strong, they stay away from that place. They're mighty superstitious, Indians is. You know where there's mirages take place that would scare a Indian out of seven years' growth? In fact, there's white men that needed a little bracer when they come out of there. The Jimjam Valley, that's where."

"That's the place you mentioned that night! I remember now," Dorney said.

"Where we're a-going, you and me, there's mirages, too, a fellow was telling me, this fellow from Argentina. Every country has their own kind. Did you ever stop to think of that?" Butch lay back and stretched out on the warm grass, then turned over on his side to face her, his left arm doubled under his head. "That South America sure must be something to lay eyes on. The pampas. That's what they call the plains there. The pampas. A house, that's called a estanchia."

"Estanchia. . . ."

"We'll have us one that's a daisy! Cool, it'll be, on the hottest day, with this fountain sprinkling out in the back yard. 'Stead of chickens, you'll have a henyard full of peacocks a-spreading their tails, and when you and me ride along the river, we'll see these big old long-legged birds, pink as the wild roses — as your cheeks — and they'll be flamingos. Sometimes you'll wake up in the night in a terrible fright, I should guess. What's that, Butch? you'll say, and you'll be quaking and shaking. Then I'll put my arms out like as if you was a baby daughter 'bout three years old and take you in 'em and hold you. That? I'll say. Why, that ain't nothing, lovey, only a little old brown October owl."

She listened, rapt.

"Everybody's got hired help there. All shapes and sizes. Sometimes, when there ain't nothing else to do, I'll start 'em to fanning out and hunting flowers for you. This fellow was telling me about these lilies — the Tears of the Virgin, they're called — and all this hired help will go after 'em and bring home enough so you can have a carpet of 'em if you want to. They'll smell up the house. . . . There's all kinds of flowers."

She clasped her hands tight together.

"You think you could make a omelette out of a ostrich egg?"

Dorney laughed.

"Well, let me tell you something, kiddo, you'd have to have help if you did. And you know how many 'twould feed? No? Well, us, and our kids, and our next-door neighbors, and their kids, and two or three other people besides! The yolk is yellow, like a hen's egg, and this fellow says it tastes fine." Butch put a cigarette between his lips, lit it, tossed the match away and continued. "Now, where was I? Oh, yes. Well, every day you and me will have us a ride over the pampas. I won't do like some of them gauchos this fellow was telling about, lay out a dried horsehide and tie it to the saddle with my lariat, set a stool in the middle of it and have you sit on that and drag you along the ground — fast, too — amidst the dirt and big clouds of dust. Some of the ladies go a-visiting that way. No, you'll have you a snow white horse, and you'll ride right along side of me. . . . Know something, honey?"

"No, what?"

"That's mighty pretty country, this fellow said. The willows is as red as roses. And the alfalfa — that grows down there, too, just like it grows here — when it's a-blooming and looks blue instead of green — why, here'll be these butterflies dancing all over it, big walloping things every color under the sun. Sometimes. . . . we'll go to town to stock up on supplies," he said, "and then you can see how the city folks live. They got mansions there, just like here. But the walls around 'em is different."

"Different, what way?"

"Well, from far off, maybe, you'd think they was white stones, but they ain't. They're cows' skulls."

"Cows' skulls!"

"Yes, sir. They're laid together one on top of the other just like as if they was stones, maybe even with mortar between, I ain't sure. The horns all point outwards."

Dorney shivered.

"It ain't a terrible sight 'cause there, things grow so fast that before you know it, greenery and creepers and flowers is growing all out of the eyes and everywhere, and you can't hardly tell what they are, no more. . . ."

The small girl, called from the creek by her mother to come and eat supper, stopped by the box elder to see the couple, because they were leaving now, she would never see them again, in her life. The nice man stood up first and reached his hands down to the young lady. He held to her, then.

"You didn't sing any of your songs!" the young lady said.

"What songs?"

"Oh, 'Billy Venero' and the one you always . . ."

He smiled and began to draw her closer to him, little by little. "I'll sing 'em to you, while we're traveling along . . . sing 'em while we're traveling . . ."

"And you didn't tell me . . ."

"I'll tell you all about everything, through the years, till there ain't a day, a hour, a minute, you don't know about. . . ."

"The people you take a shine to . . . that aren't like other people . . . you didn't tell me . . ."

"My funny ducks, you mean," he said, pulling her nearer and nearer. "I'll tell you about them. The guy that talked to his morning-glories like they knowed what he was saying. Tried to learn 'em lessons! The guy that had special pockets built in his clothes, so they wouldn't bust out nowheres when he weighed 'em down with rocks so big they bent him clear over. And he wasn't saving no mineral specimens, either. He just wanted 'em to weigh him down. The woman . . . Sure, sweetheart. While we're a-traveling. Ain't nothing I like to talk about better. Like Grandpop used to say — I ever tell you my grandpop was a preacher? — oh, wonderful are the works of His hands! I'll tell you . . . all there is to tell."

The small girl watched the man reach out and take hold of the young lady's shoulders and then gather her into his arms. He put his hand under her chin and tilted it up. His lips came close to hers and anybody would have thought he would kiss her on the mouth instead of on the forehead. After that he squeezed her again with a kind of soft sound — and put his hands under her chin that way once more and tilted it up — and anybody would surely have imagined that *this* time — but he smiled — and gave her a little flickering wink of his eye — and pinched her cheek — and then, like pulling teeth, stepped back and let her go.

"I seen some spooners!" the small girl screamed wildly when she ran back to the picnic table, for the benefit of the children who might have returned from greater adventures than hers.

"Pooh," said one of them, stealing a slice of hard-boiled egg off a dish of potato salad and having her hand slapped just enough to make her drop it where she found it. "Everybody sees them."

"But these was gypsies!"

"Gypsies?"

"Where, missy?"

"Right — over — there!"

One of the boys ran to investigate, but nobody was anywhere in sight behind the rose bushes under the chestnut tree on the grassy ledge above the creek. . . .

This time, when they left her house, they went in the opposite direction, and again Phoebe Bannon at the window watched them go. They would separate up on Main Street, likely. He was going to meet Sundance Kid and tell him the news and she was going to pack her things. They had eaten a piece of cake and drunk a cup of coffee and both of them complimented her on the cake — but Phoebe Bannon was sure they didn't know whether it was white or chocolate. For that matter, if she hadn't made it herself, she wouldn't have known what it was either, for the excitement. She did not watch them out of sight but turned from the window and went over to clear the table of the coffee cups and small plates, leaving the sugar bowl, spoon holder, salt and pepper shakers and the little cruet of vinegar in the center of the table, for the next meal.

Lucky Dorney! some people had all the luck. Butch Cassidy might be very notorious and all that but he had a lot of good qualities at the same time — better than a lot of men who had never stolen so much as a pin in their whole lifetime. He would make a mighty good husband. Besides, now he had a stake and was going to go straight from now on. Dorney would never have another care in the world. Phoebe Bannon could imagine what kind of a married life they'd have, especially where it was a case of him being that much older. He'd carry her around on feather pillow, that was what he'd do, give her the world on a silver platter. They'd have this big cattle ranch down there in South America — she'd never have to lift a finger. Never. Hired help was very cheap down there. Butch was smart — he'd show those foreigners a thing or two about ranching. Pretty soon he'd be rolling in money — they'd have all kinds of fancy things in the house, be dressed fit to kill, and they'd be taking trips on these big passenger ships, everywhere.

Why couldn't she have found a guy like Butch? Phoebe Bannon thought resentfully. But no, not her, with her luck. She'd have to take up with a guy like Blufe Bannon — good as he was, God rest his soul in peace — but just the same, to be sick like that — and then die off, and leave somebody all soul alone with three little kids to raise. . . .

She opened the side door a little wider as she went past to the kitchen. But there wouldn't be any breeze until the sun went down. Out in the kitchen she began cutting up bread into cubes for the children's supper of bread and milk. She could hear them around at the other side of the house, playing with their cousins, their shrill voices. The kitchen was extra hot but then it would be, facing west, even though she hadn't had a fire in the stove since noon. She reached up with her left hand and tried to pull the shade down a little farther to keep from being blinded by the sun, and it stuck. She pulled harder and down it came out of its brackets, knocking the plate of liquid butter she had forgotten to put away in the pantry off the drainboard. The dish did not break but the butter splashed all over everything and somehow or other during the mishap she managed to slice her finger with the knife. It wasn't a deep cut but it bled and bled. She didn't know flies liked butter but they buzzed around it worse than if it was a bowl of meat gravy she had spilled, and while she was down on the floor cleaning it up they kept settling on her wet face and neck. She rolled up the blind, climbed on the rickety kitchen stool, stepped onto the drainboard and fixed it back at the window, then jumped to the stool and down to the floor again. This time, when she pulled on the blind, it came down all right, came down rapidly as far it it would go — but it wouldn't go back up! She couldn't budge it. There was only one thing to do — she would have to climb up and take it down again — the spring would have to be rewound. She was rummaging in the drawer for a fork when her eyes flooded over with tears — for no reason — and she couldn't see anything. She was sobbing out loud, too, but she stopped that so that Fern wouldn't hear her and come in and want to know what was the matter, and groped her way back into the sitting room. She sat down gingerly on account of her back and wiped her eyes with her blood-spotted apron. That silly cut! she had wrapped her handkerchief around it. It would probably matter and act up and she would have an awful time with it before she got through. She unwound it to see if it was still bleeding — it was, oozily — and wrapped it up again. Angrily she brushed a motionless fly off her wet forehead. Sometimes, they didn't seem just to touch you with the tips of their feet but seemed to lay down flat on you so you could feel the whole nasty things, wings and all.

Well, July would soon be over, thank God!

But August was even worse.

Lucky Dorney! tomorrow when everybody else in the laundry was working, when the shirt department was standing over those scorching hot machines — so hot that the ironed linen would burn you if you grabbed hold of it without giving it a second or two to cool off — when the poor hand-ironers had their faces daubed with paste — when everybody was stewing and cooking in their own juice in that bake oven of a second floor under that tin roof — when some people were wanting to turn right around and spit up the water they drank — and getting spots before their eyes and a buzzing in their head — and they never had hardly a dry stitch on them — and others had the most terrible agonizing backache that a human living being could have — why, she — just because she was one of the lucky ones and right at the heighth of her bloom — why, Dorney would be riding along in the lovely train on a plush seat, with the windows wide open and the lovely breezes blowing back her hair. She'd be with Butch Cassidy and Sundance Kid — talking back and forth, or listening to 'em sing, watching the pretty scenery, planning her wedding. The first thing Butch would do when they got down there in Texas, he would buy her such a bridal outfit as never was seen, because he was a great spender, Butch was. Money didn't mean anything to him. Easy come, easy go. Maybe it would mean something to him now, that he was going straight and fixing to start ranching, but it didn't used to. Would they find some woman to stand up with 'em, or just have Sundance Kid? Butch would be mighty particular who she associated with. Afterwards, they'd have this big celebration supper, with a great big bottle of cool sparkling golden champagne or whatever color it was. They'd be happy, all right. . . . They'd really be happy.

She had kissed Dorney on her warm cheek and kissed Butch, too, on the cheek, and wished them all the happiness in the world. It's the most romantic thing I ever heard of! she said. It was romantic, that was no lie — an elopement — running away together at midnight. Butch didn't want Dorney to tell her folks and she promised she wouldn't. He didn't say so, but Phoebe Bannon knew he was thinking of the reward and how money can be a very great temptation to some people. A big reward like ten thousand dollars. A very great temptation. Some people couldn't withstand it. Phoebe Bannon had promised that tomorrow night after supper she would go over and tell Dorney's sister Madge that Dorney had eloped, was going to get married and would write a long letter soon. She had eloped with a man from Star Valley, Phoebe Bannon was going to

say, a nice fellow named Jim Lowe that I introduced her to. . . .
They probably wouldn't care much. From what Clara Tofflemire
said, her sister and her sister's girl were as cold as a couple of fish —
just the opposite from Dorney.

Butch was going to hire a rig and he and Sundance Kid were going down to Dorney's house to get her at ten-thirty, so they'd have
plenty of time to get her ticket and get settled on the train.

Phoebe Bannon, untying her apron and fastidiously rolling it up,
offended by the stains of blood from her cut finger, glanced at the
clock. Six-fifteen. Dorney was home now, already — and Butch was
at the hotel, or he would be, in a little while. Sundance Kid was
slapping him on the back. . . . The nerve of the two of them, coming into town as bold as brass. There must be detectives on their
trail — Butch hinted that they had done three big jobs since spring
— weren't they afraid of anything? After all, what made them think
their luck would never run out? Who said it wouldn't? Everybody
else's did, sooner or later. Why not theirs? Maybe there would be
somebody on that night train that used to know Butch back in Circle
Valley . . . and he'd spill the beans . . . or maybe somebody in the
railroad station . . . It was a funny proposition, how some people's
luck held, and held, while other people, it ran out before it even got
started! For that matter, how did Butch and Sundance Kid know
but what the *hotel clerk* had recognized 'em? That was possible, for
heaven's sake. Why wasn't it possible? Hotel clerks traveled around,
they kept their eyes and ears open — they weren't so dumb. Maybe
the one at the Temple Hotel had spotted them right away but bided
his time so as not to lose out, just when he had them. If he hadn't
already done it, he would probably do it pretty soon now — turn
them in and get that big reward! whoever got a-hold of a pile of
money like that, they could certainly afford to quit work and get a
little enjoyment out of life for a change. If the man had a wife
and children — maybe a sick wife who needed an operation — why,
it would be just the saving of all of them, that's what it would be,
that reward. The saving of them all.

There was nothing lower on the face of the earth than somebody
who would do a trick like that, sneak around behind somebody's back
and turn somebody in. It wasn't so bad if it was a complete stranger,
but if it was an old friend, why, then that was just terrible. People
around Star Valley wouldn't touch somebody who had done a stunt
like that with a ten-foot pole! Blufe thought they were lower down
than a lizard. For that matter, Phoebe Bannon thought so herself.
Of course, it wouldn't go so hard with Butch as if he was wanted for
murder. Murderers were hung or shot. But just being wanted for robbing banks and holding up trains — maybe the authorities couldn't
even rustle up proof enough to convict him! — that wouldn't bring

408

him a very heavy sentence. Maybe only five or ten years. Maybe not that long. In fact, they were both such sociable, likable guys, Butch and Harry Longabaugh, that they would probably get paroled in just a little while.

It didn't hurt to amuse a person's self with imagining what a person would do with a whole lot of money, in case it fell down in a person's lap by some accident. After all, relatives died and people inherited money every day of the world, somewhere, or — or — Phoebe Bannon rolled the bloodstained apron into a tighter and smaller roll, let loose of it, rolled it tight and small again. One thing she wouldn't do — she'd never invest in something with the idea in mind of trying to make money out of money. You had to have plenty more where that came from, to pull something like that! And she wouldn't squander it on a lot of silly things she didn't need, either, like a Peerless steam cooker or a Miller lamp or an Orchestrion just because they were new, handy and useful and other people were reading the advertisements and buying them. No, sir — a penny saved is a penny earned. What she would do was this: she would buy a little home out in the country on three or four good acres of ground. She might be very much tempted to buy a parlor carpet, perhaps — actually, all the parlor furnishings had ought to be new — and a new kitchen stove with a big reservoir on one side, one of the ones where they gave away a whole set of new utensils as a premium at the time of purchase. Then, she would have her back fixed — no, she would do that first — and then, she and the children would go out there and live on that pretty place in the country. They would have a vegetable patch, fruit trees, chickens, berries, a cow named Bossy. . . . She could almost manage it so that they would get almost their whole living off the place and she wouldn't have to touch any of the seven thousand or sixty-five hundred they still had in the bank. She could be at home with the children all day long. She could keep house, make garden, be happy. No more backache. No more laundry. No more impudent kids left to their Aunt Fern who didn't know any more about bringing up young ones than a cat knows about Christmas. . . .

But it would be the hotel clerk, or some detective, that would cash in on all that, not her. Not her. Never her, for any of the easy pickings of life. . . . And the haunting thing was — whoever it was that did it, they might really be doing Butch a favor! Nobody knew what the future had in store. Maybe if he was just left to go and do what he wanted — why, he would be walking into terrible trouble, while if he was put in prison for a year or two (they wouldn't give him a very big sentence just for robbery) he would be kept safe and sound. That train he and Dorney and Sundance Kid were leaving on at midnight tonight — who knew but what it might run off a grade and half the passengers be killed outright, including those three? Suppose they got down there to Texas! Suppose they really got on that ship. Maybe it would sail into a hurricane and tip over and sink and everybody get drowned! Or if they ever arrived in South America, maybe some band of foreigners would waylay Butch and clean him out, or he would get thrown from a rambunctious horse and have his neck broken. Or Dorney would die in childbirth. Maybe somebody was supposed to come forward and prevent such things, as an instrument of Providence. Maybe Phoebe Bannon was supposed to be that instrument, and come forward, else why did the whole thing pop in her mind in the first place? Maybe she was supposed to go now and throw this bloodstained apron — the handkerchief, too, for the cut had stopped bleeding — in the dirty clothes. Then go and change her dress and tidy her hair and put a hat on, and tap on Fern's door and tell her to keep an eye on the children for half an hour or so while she was away on an errand. Then go out and catch the streetcar and go up to — let's see, where was the station house? — oh, yes, on First South between State Street and Second East. And walk in there and ask to see whoever a person should see, that wanted to tell the police that the robber and outlaw, Butch Cassidy, and his friend Sundance Kid, were right in the middle of Salt Lake City, at the Temple Hotel, and if they wanted to nab them, now was their time.

While the steamy big-faced man in the blue uniform with the brass buttons was writing down the whys and wherefores, the informer, in the chair beside his rolltop desk, heard the clock in the City and County Building strike seven through the open window that looked on a grey wall red with evening sunlight. It seemed to take a long, long time to get done. She counted the strokes.

When the man finished scribbling, he got up and came around the desk and walked to the door. Before he went out of the room he said, "You just sit here for a minute."

She would have, anyway, even if he hadn't told her to — would have sat there. Her stomach did that again, seemed to rise up and turn over. She put her handkerchief to her mouth and thought she might have to find a place to . . . but after swallowing once, and twice, and thrice, and shutting her eyes, and resting her forehead against her now queerly chilly hand, and breathing deep and trying to think anything, anything at all, she began to feel a little better, and then considerably better, and then she was . . . just fine.

39

AT SUPPER DORNEY ATE SO LITTLE, AND HAD SUCH a hard time doing it, that Crystal wanted to know what ailed her. Didn't she like the cooking, or what was the matter? The cooking was lovely. Where had she been? Visiting Mrs. Blufe Bannon. Maybe she had caught some disease off of that band of children! Oh, no, they were all well. It would be too bad for her to bring home smallpox or something like that! Associating with so many . . . people . . . like that . . . such a thing wasn't an impossibility by any means. Crystal eyed her narrowly two or three times — her eyes seemed to be fuller of light than usual but at the same time darker, and her cheeks were red just along her cheekbones, under her eyes. She might be feverish. When Mother came home, Crystal was going to ask her if Dorney didn't look to her as if she was coming down with something. Mother would be an hour or two late tonight because Mrs. Towers was having her Ladies' Club for supper, using the time that Judge Towers was away, a custom of hers. But when she came home, Crystal was going to point out Dorney's almost delirious looks. If I get smallpox, she was going to say, and get scars all over my face, just on account of her and the trash she associates with, and have to kill myself, well, somebody's going to be sorry, I can promise you that!

After the meal, Jetta went out and climbed into her swing once more. The way she spoke in greeting it might have been a play-mate who had patiently waited for her to go and eat and then come back and play again. It moved, therefore to her it lived. Sometimes she would bring her face over close to the rope, just beneath where her hand clung, and mumble as into a living being's ear.

Crystal and Dorney did the dishes, Dorney talking in a light-headed wandering way, Crystal thought, about schooldays, and Geog-raphy! Did Crystal remember the lesson about South America? Peo-ple kept peacocks there, instead of chickens; their fences were made of the skulls of cows! "We never had that in our book," Crystal said sternly. Snakes carried on conversations amongst themselves! Would Crystal be seasick if she went on a boat? Could she imagine

411

people who had to see clear to the horizon in every direction or they got nervous and went on wild rampages? If she could have a horse, would she choose a white one or a black one? "A white one," Crystal said. "Me, too," Dorney said, flirting the dishtowel and giving a little skip. "What's wrong with you?" Crystal asked. "Nothing!" But Crystal knew there was and made up her mind that when Mother came home she would have her look at Dorney carefully and see what she thought she was coming down with.

The first fifteen or twenty minutes after she heard her go upstairs, Crystal, in the parlor, kept one ear cocked in the direction of the attic stairway, so she could hear if Dorney stormed downstairs and accused somebody of trying on those dresses of Mrs. Morelewski's. She had accidentally torn a button off the bronze taffeta — but tucked it into a fold of the cuff so that when the dress was handled, it would fall out on the floor — and burst a seam of the china silk lining in the Surah skirt — but that was no great harm! She wasn't going to admit she had been up there! If Dorney came stomping down, Crystal was going to tell her a thing or two about false accusations and unjust suspicions. She was going to make her curl up and shrivel away. She didn't come, though, and the musician, glancing at the ceiling and holding her breath while she listened a little longer, opened the thick book of music upon the piano rack and began to play.

Dorney, in the attic room, sitting on the edge of her bed, leaned over and wiped the sweat off her face with an edge of the pillowcase on the round sofa pillow. She didn't dare to pack anything as early as this for fear that by some accident Crystal or Madge would discover what she was up to. If they went to bed at the usual hour, ten o'clock, she would have plenty of time to get ready and steal outside by the time Butch came for her. It was seven-thirty now, or had been a few minutes ago when she looked at the kitchen clock. And he was coming at ten-thirty. That meant she had three long hours to wait. It was too hot to stay up here. When it got dark and the wind started to blow, it would cool off, but right now it was terribly hot. She was afraid to stay downstairs. Crystal had acted suspicious and kept looking at her. If she really put her mind to it and tried to worm out what was afoot, it would be hard to resist her, hard not to drop a hint. When Madge came home, that would be worse than ever, because she would be wanting to tell Madge, down in her heart, and was ashamed to be going away without telling her, like someone who didn't know what gratitude and sisterly love meant at all. But she would write her a long letter and tell her. . . . And then, kind Mrs. Bannon promised to come tomorrow night. She could spend a little of the slow time by going over to Clara's and Mrs. Luby's. They would not know it, but she would be bidding them goodbye, her dear friends. And then she would . . .

The telescope suitcase would easily hold everything she owned, including the Jenny Lind dish. She looked down at the books arranged in two rows at the back of the dresser, one row in front of the other. They would be pretty heavy and take up quite a lot of room but she had to pack them. Rather leave her clothes, except just the gray silk to get married in, and leave Mamma's dish, and trust to luck that Crystal would let Madge forgive her enough to send them on, but never leave these. Almost, rather not go than leave them.

She took one up at random, *The Handy Volume Shakespeare, with Glossary,* laid her cheek against it, then put it down on the dresser and opened it. *Ex Libris* Teige Desmond! Out of the books of him. Leave this? As soon the hand she now began to turn the pages with. The more lines of poetry he had underlined, the more X's he had made in the margins of paragraphs, the better she liked it. For she knew she was going in the right direction then, knew he had been this way before her, that she was following the right trail and was not lost, and that somewhere ahead, he was, and if she kept going and did not stop to rest . . .

Sometimes he wrote words along the edge of the page, lightly, with pencil. He had, just here. Dorney bent nearer to read them: *the reason.* They stood beside the underscored lines:

> She loved me for the dangers I had passed
> And I loved her that she did pity them.

This play was *Othello.* She had not read that. In fact, she had only read *Macbeth* and *The Merry Wives of Windsor* and *A Midsummer Night's Dream.* At first, it was hard to get used to Shakespeare. She wasn't used to him yet. She had a lot of questions to ask Mr. Desmond. One thing she wanted to know especially was . . .

But she was going away now, to marry Butch Cassidy, and she would never get to ask Mr. Desmond anything.

Not anything.

Because she would never see Mr. Desmond again as long as she lived!

Smoothing the page the way one smooths the nap of velvet, her eyes suddenly clouded over and began to sting, while a great Adam's-apple she didn't know she possessed commenced to press against her windpipe. Not a day or a night for the past two years had she not thought about how he would be coming back to Salt Lake City and how pleased he would be because she had read the books and looked up so many words in the dictionary and because. . . . But now, she would be gone from here and whether he came or not, was the same. The same, if he stayed away. The same if he was changed to some-one else, unkind. The same, if he perished. Oh, not the same! She put her hand up to her throat. Dear Father in Heaven, she prayed, shutting her eyes tight, surprised when tears squeezed out and ran down her face, don't let Mr. Desmond die till he's an old man, older than Grandpa Bannon!

"And I loved her that she did pity them." They must have talked a lot different in those days than people talk now, she thought, wip-ing her eyes with the back of her hand. And yet this wasn't hard to understand the way some of it was. Some of it, you could read on for an hour and not know any more than when you started, but this was easy. All it meant was, that this girl . . . whoever she was . . . loved this boy . . . Othello . . . for all the close calls, the close shaves he had had, the times when he had just barely got away by the skin of his teeth . . . and this boy loved this girl because she "did pity" all that. Funny that he'd use the expression "did pity." Maybe what he wanted to express by that was, "And I loved her that she sympathized with me for all the scrapes I got into and very nearly didn't get out of!" She might have been one of these girls that wished she had been born a boy. That could account for her having so much sympathy, and being in love, for such a reason as because of what he had been *through*. Or she . . .

After all, the two lines weren't so simple as they looked right at first. Slowly she closed the book, pushed it aside and went to stare out the window at the fast falling twilight. "She loved me for the dangers I had passed." Having thought upon them, they seemed to mean more than they exactly said. Lines of poetry often did that. A long time after, they would suddenly pop out in full bloom in your head, surprising you the way certain bushes did in spring that one day were bare and the next day were covered with roses. In season they budded and they bloomed.

At first she went right past Jetta swinging in the half-dark and then, with her hand on the screen door, turned back. "Why don't you stop?" she said. "And you and I will have a nice talk?" She glanced into the dark kitchen in the direction of the door that led to the parlor. Crystal was playing softly and drearily. "And then I'll tell you a story."

Jetta did not leave the swing in motion but stopped it dead-still with great care before she stomped stiff-leggedly over to sit on the overturned clothes basket while Dorney took a seat above her on the porch railing.

"Would you miss me if I went away?" she asked.

The hooded lids came down over the protruding eyes, lifted, the tiny lips pursed together. Jetta put a narrow paw out and touched Dorney's skirt. "Pretty," she said.

"I thought we'd all love each other," Dorney murmured, as if to herself. "I hoped we would. I guess it was my fault in lots of ways that we didn't, but you know, Jetta, it's been going on three years now since I came here, and I don't seem to know Crystal and Madge any better or feel any closer to them than the first day I got here. Why was that? Was it because — ?" But she knew the little creature did not understand or know why. Still, she had to talk to someone. The moment had come when she had to.

"I want a kitty," Jetta said slyly. "I don't have much pleasure out of life."

"Oh, yes, you do, too, now. You swing, and you watch out the window, and sometimes your mamma brings you nice things to eat from Judge Towers's — "

"I want a nice kitty." Jetta began to whimper.

"Listen," Dorney said, "and I'll tell you a story. Once upon a time there was a girl, and sometimes she used to cry and be lonesome. But she had a friend. He was a wonderful cowboy that everybody in the world had heard tell of. Whenever this girl would be crying and lonesome, this cowboy would come riding up to take her away. Little Dipper was the name of his horse. It was black. It would run faster than the wind. He would take her up behind him and they would gallop off just as fast as could be."

"Me, too," Jetta said, nodding wisely. "I'd go, too."

"But, he was not real, the way you and I are. See, you can feel my hand and I can feel yours. You couldn't feel his. It was just like air. He only *seemed* real. He was tall and he had brown eyes and black hair and he looked — " Dorney paused, and considered. "He looked like someone I seem to remember, except the trouble is I *don't* remember, only that — it's like when you know a word, but you can't think what it is, except that you're sure it starts with a certain letter."

Jetta nodded again, still more wisely.

"Well, anyway, then something that you could never guess what, happened, just this afternoon! She saw him! She met him on the street! and it was him. I mean, *he was real.*"

The small yellow lips opened and Jetta yawned.

"He didn't look like a cowboy, because of the way he was dressed. He didn't look like himself! He wasn't tall! only about the size of Thomas Diltz. And he had blue eyes instead of brown, just as blue as blue. And yellow hair instead of black and — and — she could hardly believe that it *was* him. But it was! And then, after a bit, she could believe it. Now she knows that he looked like that, all the time. It seems natural! It really does, at least when he's right

415

in front of her, sitting there talking. It seems the most natural then, and — and — she's going to — he's — they're going to — oh, Jetta!" Dorney said, reaching out for her, but when she stiffened and drew back, letting her go again. She clasped her hands together. "I never thought when I got up this morning . . . She never thought . . . I'm a little bit scared, Jetta."

"Ghosts scare people."

"There are no ghosts. Whoever told you that? Jetta," Dorney said, her voice suddenly breaking, "what could I have done for you? How could I have been better, and loved you more? now that — you and I — will never — "

"I want a kitty."

"I brought you one! Remember how mad your mamma got because we put milk in a good pie tin? and then it disappeared. Remember?"

Jetta gave a trembling little sigh.

"Did you ever think, how things keep coming to an end, Jetta? It seems as if they're going to last forever, but they never do. They end. Like me living with Wanda. Me living here with you and Crystal and your mamma. Or working at the Queen's. Or in the laundry. Everything seems to end. What's going to happen now, it doesn't seem as if that would end — him — and the horses — and the pampas — and what he said, but — oh, Jetta, I feel so sad tonight! I feel happy but I feel sad. Maybe it's because it's — you know — evening, and the evening always seems sad." In the parlor the music suddenly ceased but she did not hear it. She stood up and Jetta slid down off the clothesbasket and turned toward the swing. Suddenly Dorney knelt beside her, and put a hand on her thin little arm. "Goodbye," she said. "I wish . . . If I had a wand that was magic, I would . . . Sometimes, will you think of me? I promise to think of you. Goodbye, dear Jetta!"

"Goodbye?" Crystal said, laughing in the kitchen doorway, a hand on either side of the frame. "Where in the world do you think you're going? New York City?"

Jetta did not look at her sister but hopped birdlike away to her swing and climbed carelessly into it, as the engineer climbs carelessly into the cab he knows better than he knows himself. A tight clutch on the ropes, three small steps backward, a swish forward and she was swinging again.

Dorney stood up and brushed off her skirt. She was glad for the darkness. "I'm just going over to see Clara for a little while," she said.

"I should think you had done enough visiting for one day."

She called her when she got to the bottom of the steps and Dorney halted and looked back.

"You didn't say goodbye to me before you go on this long journey of yours over to Clara Tofflemire's!"

"Goodbye, Crystal."

"Be sure to write!"

"I will."

"If you see anybody from the old home town, give them my regards." She laughed again, teasingly.

When Dorney went around the corner of the house and passed the east window, light began to shine in it. Crystal had lighted the lamp in the kitchen. She nearly turned back, but didn't, to look into the room where, tomorrow night, she would not be, to see it without her. How things come to an end! There was not only death. . . .

Old Mrs. Tofflemire, whose habits had changed, was already in bed and fast asleep. Before, she had not used to sleep well, but she did now. Sophie was in bed, too, being the youngest of the family, but she was not asleep. She was standing up, hanging on to the bed railing, wondering where everybody had gone to. No voice in the dining room or kitchen, not a footstep, not a sound anywhere. That was a fine how-do-you-do. She began to cry and then stopped that to set about climbing up and over the railing and getting out of bed.

Dorney expected to see the Mudge family sitting on the porch, enjoying the twilight hour, and that was where they were. They called out greetings and as she came up the walk, asked her to come and join them. She could make out Joe, in shirt sleeves, there by the railing — Georgie and Alfred with Rupert between them — and there was Clara, in her mother's rocking chair, with Ruby in a white dress on her lap.

"Hot enough for you?" Joe said, à la mode.

Choosing a place on the step, Dorney was about to sit down and answer that it was, when a great yell, or bellow, or war whoop, that if heard in desolate Blackfoot territory would have frozen the blood solid, came from down the street. It grew to a hideous yodel that almost rattled the windows in their frames, and Dorney, her hair standing on end, half sat only, to be ready if disaster overrode them in the form of landslide, runaway locomotive or tidal wave.

Clara held up her hand. George and Alfred, who had been chattering, shut up. Rupert barked once, then looked to his mistress for orders. "He's come back," she said. "I knew he would. I didn't think that scheme of hers was any good. To lock him out that way."

"Who?" Dorney asked.

"Mrs. Luby," Clara said, raising her voice. "He never come home from work this morning like usual, so she got set for a performance! He was gone all day! Then about half a hour ago here he come home! She thought she would try locking all the doors and windows for once! She never had done that!"

"How did it work?" Dorney said.

"Fine! He must of thought he was at the wrong house or something for after trying the doorknob two or three times, he just wandered away!"

"But now it must have dawned on him that that was his house," Joe said. "So now he's come back to give her another try."

"She was hoping to save things from getting smashed and busted," Clara said only a little louder than usual. The uproar had died down, as a lull comes in a storm. "She told me she was going to send for the police the minute he showed his face. I seen Thornton run by here a while ago but I don't know whether he was going to try to get the police or not. I don't know if she'd really send for them. I thought maybe that was just a threat. Every other time the police come, some of the neighbors sent for 'em — Mr. Popma, or somebody — not her."

"I seen Thornton run back home," Georgie volunteered.

"Listen!" Joe said. "Ain't that lively? He's sure a-banging on that there door over there. Trying to bust it down, I guess. Listen!" He laughed a little, as when watching an acrobat do some impossible-looking stunt. "By golly."

It was no wonder he was impressed. How one man, with the usual number of hands and feet, and one head, could make a hullaballoo like that was hard to understand. He might have a big stick, but even so! Thud! Bang! Whack! Clatter! Boom! Anybody to hear him would have thought he was a whole posse.

"I'm scared!" Alfred said, getting up and stumbling as fast as he could over to the safety of his stepmother's arm. She put it tight around him. "I'm awful scared."

"No, you ain't," Clara said. "Because that's just Mr. Luby. And you know how nice Mr. Luby is, to all you kids in the neighborhood. Don't he give you a jawbreaker every little while?"

Alfred nodded, but without much conviction.

They heard glass breaking, the smash and shatter of it into a million pieces, heard the splintering of wood. Mr. Luby kept on kicking, pounding and thumping. There was a loud crash. He roared out something.

"He's in!" Clara said. She pushed Ruby gently off her lap and tried to rise but Alfred clung to her. "No! No!" he cried, in panic.

"Where do you think you're going?" Joe asked sternly.

"Over there," Clara said. "Poor Mrs. Luby — "

"A woman in your condition?" he inquired. "You sit right back down! What's wrong with your head?"

Dorney's heart leaped. He must mean — why, that was wonderful. It was just *wonderful*.

"I'll go," Joe said manfully. "This here ain't nothing to fool around with."

Dorney recalled with relief that Mr. Luby was a small man, quite a bit smaller than Clara's husband. But what a commotion he was making. It was remarkable. People were beginning to gather here and there on the street. Under the streetlight on the corner was a cluster of several, looking over in the direction of the Luby's house, talking and pointing.

Just then a piercing scream split the air.

"Papa! Papa! Papa!"

Mrs. Luby, being murdered.

Dorney raced down the walk, Joe Mudge ran down the steps and pounded along behind her.

"Hey!" he cried. "You stay here. You go back!"

One window, the one on the left of the front door, had a light in it. The rest of the house was in darkness. With Mr. Luby there inside, thumping, slamming, banging, lunging and plunging, it seemed to be rocking on its foundations. He or a herd of elephants was breaking dishes, smashing chairs, overturning tables, yanking pictures down off the wall and jumping in the middle of them. The very walls seemed to bulge outward.

"The police are coming!" Dorney heard from the peopled gloom as she turned in at Mrs. Luby's gate and flew up the walk. She ran up the steps, across the porch and through the open doorway beside which the splintered door hung on one hinge. "Mrs. Luby! Mrs. Luby — ?" The room where the light was, the parlor, in shambles, was empty. Dorney hastened through it. "Mrs. Luby!"

In the dark room beyond that, taking up half the floor space, a thing writhed, making inhuman noises and buckling and contorting itself. Dorney, her heart in her mouth, her eyes straining to see what it was and where it intended to squirm, had taken a scared step in its direction when a small figure hurtled out of the shadows, leaped on the monster and began pelting and pummeling it. "Stop hurting my Mamma!" Breaking in two, the top half raised up, spun around, made a grab, the bottom half rolled away and clambered up, howling.

"Papa, let him go! Let — him — GO!"

There was a rush of feet, the sound of men's voices. "In there!" somebody shouted.

Mrs. Luby and Dorney pulled together, on what Mr. Luby had got possession of, if that was really he, and he let go of it so suddenly that they, with it, staggered and almost fell, then he backed away and went out through the window.

"Heaven preserve us," Mrs. Luby moaned. That it was she, Dorney turning to her, could hardly credit. Someone had brought a lamp upon the scene. She was killed, it appeared — she must be killed — with all that blood about her — and on the floor, white and still, limp as a wet shirt, Thornton, the boy whom they had torn from his father, lay killed, it appeared, too! Mrs. Luby knelt and drew him to her and Dorney, helpless, knelt beside. "My baby — my poor little baby — trying to save his ma!"

It was about eight-thirty that Mr. Luby got away out of the window and fled into the darkness. A policeman came and looked the situation over. He asked Mrs. Luby some questions and then went out and tromped up and down in the high grass in the empty lot on the corner. He stayed around in the locality for nearly an hour but Mr. Luby had disappeared.

Joe Mudge told him a thing or two, policeman or no policeman. "Why the hell don't there enough of you to do some good come a-running when the call comes through that there's a maniac on the loose? What's one policeman good for? He goes in one door. The maniac runs out the other. What kind of business is that?"

"Maybe the force has got something better to do tonight than run their legs off because a man happens to get drunk and let off a little steam," the officer said.

"Whams his wife with a bottle and damn near cuts her head off and damn near chokes a little boy to death and you call that letting off steam." Joe Mudge told him, so he knew he'd been told. Clara, carrying barefooted nightgowned Sophie, coming there in the midst of the other three children, heard that much, and her heart swelled to bursting with pride, to see the way her man could handle a policeman. They were having an historic discussion out on the sidewalk in front of the Lubys' house.

"Where the hell was that old Black Maria?" Joe inquired loftily. "The taxpayers spend their money and buy the thing and then where is it when it's needed? Up in front of the police station, some damn fool polishing up the brass trimmings, that's where it is, instead of where it might come in handy for a change."

"Maybe you'd be surprised where it is," the officer said. "There might be a lot bigger fish to fry tonight than a measly drunk that happens to bust a piece of chinaware!"

"Happens to bust in a woman's skull, you mean," Joe Mudge said with fine scorn.

"Oh, Joe, is she hurt? did he hurt her?" Clara interrupted. "Oh, I've just got to go in there!"

"You just try it," Joe said firmly, stepping over to take her by the arm. "What you got a man for if he can't watch over you when you need watching over? She ain't hurt bad, just cut a little around the face and neck. And the kid come to all right. There's women in there with her, two or three, now. And Dorney's in there. You ain't needed. You come on home, where you belong, for the Lord's sake." He looked back at the policeman who had been fanning himself with his helmet but now put it back on, forthrightly, squaring his shoulders and putting a hand down onto the club that swung against his right thigh. "Wait till elections," he said. "Maybe the taxpayers want things run with a little more *system* around here for their money."

"Maybe they do," the officer said cordially, spitting in an arc onto the grassy curb.

"Joe," Clara whispered in a fright, "don't talk to the man that way. He's in a position — he might *arrest* you."

"I wish he'd try it," her husband, bold and brave as a lion, said. "I just wish he'd try."

"Go ahead and try it!" George said to the policeman. For his pains, his father gave him a painful flip on the head. "What are you trying to be?" Joe Mudge said armipotently to his son. "A hooligan?"

They got the blood stopped — the wounds were only scratches — but to dry up Mrs. Luby's tears was a much more complicated business.

"In all these years, it's the first time he's ever touched me," she sobbed. "It's the first time he's ever touched one of the *children*. So if he starts in like this, I don't know how it's going to end! In all these years of busting and breaking, he's never touched us. And now he starts!"

"What you'll maybe have to do," her neighbor said, the homely and old-looking one of the two Mrs. Vertrees. "You'll maybe have to take a lesson out of the book of a woman I heard of once, that had a drunken husband on her hands, that abused her and the children. What she done, she snuck up on him one time and tied him up to a post and then she went to work and beat him nearly to death with a rawhide whip. That learned him something, you can bet. He was a good dog after that, for she threatened to do it every time he fell off the wagon." She was still wearing her churchgoing clothes, a murmuring black silk dress and handsome pointed shoes.

The other Mrs. Vertrees, who was pretty and young-looking though both women were about the same age, must have changed her clothes after coming home from evening services in the Second Ward meetinghouse, for she was wearing a full gingham skirt, a loose basque and soft low slippers. These ladies and their husband,

421

Mr. Vertrees, lived just down the alley in the small house so covered with green vines that only the door and parts of the windows showed. Dorney had seen them seldom and she wondered on each occasion, as she did now, whether it was the homely one who, long ago, according to legend, had cut off the pretty one's hair, or vice versa. Strangely enough, the homely one was wife number two. They each had the same number of children, all of whom were grown and married now. "Well, I don't know," the pretty Mrs. Vertrees said. "That may work, but I heard of a woman once that done just the opposite. She commenced to baking the most delicious big pies and cakes and cookies and puddings and she developed her hubby's sweet tooth till it got to the stage where he wouldn't even so much as look at booze no more. But the only trouble about that was, a few years later he took with the sugar dybeetus and died, so that may of not been such a good idea." Tenderly she proffered her own handkerchief for Mrs. Luby to use in drying her tears, but that stricken woman shook her head and continued to use her apron.

The clock struck nine.

Dorney, sitting on the edge of the sofa holding tight to pale excited Thornton's hand, looked at it with a start. But she had plenty of time — a whole hour and a half. What with pot lids, a neatly folded stack of clean laundry, a stray rubber boot, a milk pan full of peaches, the day's newspaper and a wadded up shawl, and Thornton, stretched out at full length, there was not much room for her but she sat as she could, holding his hand. When revived from the curious shivering and mewing unconsciousness he had sunk into as or before his father let go of him, he had wept passionately but when Dorney came close to him and sat and took hold of his hand, he stopped. She said she had been a witness to what a brave boy he was, and that she would never forget it as long as she lived. The pupils of his eyes were very big and he didn't get his color back for a long time. His hand felt wet in hers. Once when she looked down at it, something about it made her swallow hard, its autocracy yet babyishness.

"I'm going to kill my papa," he confided to her proudly.

"Oh, no, you're not, Thornton."

"I am if he does anything to Mamma."

"He won't do anything, any more."

With the one he loved sitting beside him holding his hand, hero that he was — had not Althea hid in a closet? had not Herman climbed up in bed and buried himself under the covers? but of course Herman was not four yet — the small boy could hardly contain himself. "He choked me terrible," he said happily.

"I know, Thornton. You were the bravest boy in the world!"

"No, I wasn't. Soldiers is braver."

"Soldiers are not!"

He prolonged the argument a little, then gave way gallantly and let the lady have her say.

" — and his father being a letter carrier there in Liverpool like that," Mrs. Luby was saying, still weeping, but the tears growing fewer and farther between, "wearing that nice uniform and being looked up to by everybody, and his mother's people being in the store business, which they was all looked up to, too, and then *him*, you know, poor Mr. Luby, their direct descendant, coming along and taking up such a *different* line of work, that *ain't* looked up to, why, I can't help but say there's a excuse for him! poor dear." She put the end of her apron down only to take it up again and start dabbing at her eyes with the opposite corner.

"Something that helps to keep the city so sanitary like that, I can't see why he would feel no shame about doing that," the homely Mrs. Vertrees said. "There ain't nothing dishonorable about *that* work. *Somebody's* got to give 'em a cleaning once in a while."

"What if he was a hangman?" the pretty Mrs. Vertrees asked.

"I believe I'd make him cool his heels quite a while before I'd take him back into the fold," the former suggested, removing a darning basket, a pasteboard shoe box without a lid and with four marbles rolling around inside, and a lady's hat from a chair seat so she could sit down on the front half of it.

"I'm sure he'll be just as sorry as can be when he sobers up," the latter said comfortingly.

"Sorry?" Mrs. Luby ran a soft boneless finger lightly over the fast-drying cuts on her cheek and along the scratches on her neck. She blinked away the last of the tears and began a faint smile. "Sorry?" she said. "You mark my words now. I guess I'd ought to know the man after having had seven children by him — two dead, two married and three little ones at home — and living with him for more than twenty-seven years! I'd ought to, I guess. So now you mark my words."

Dorney leaned over to pull Thornton's pillow half an inch downward, and they smiled. His color flooded back.

"Everything he busted," Mrs. Luby continued, "he'll buy twice as good — for he may be a lot of things, but he ain't cheap, and when Mr. Luby buys something, it's good, in fact it's the best, or he don't buy it. And as for what he done to me and Thornton," she said, "well, I nearly hate for us to be the child and me for the next few weeks, for how good he's going to be and spoil and make over us! Why, we'll be all wore out with kindness by the time he gets done, if he ever does! That's all I can say."

"When will he get up enough gumption to come on home?" the homely Mrs. Vertrees asked.

Mrs. Luby wiped her nose on her apron, then pinched it while she meditated.

"It ain't a matter of gumption," she said finally. "Nobody needs to worry about Mr. Luby and gumption. They can worry about Mr. Luby and pneumonia and Mr. Luby and a slick customer and Mr. Luby and a lost shovel, but they don't need to worry about Mr. Luby and gumption. No, sirree!"

40

THE WINDOW OF THE JEWELRY STORE CAUGHT
the eye of the smaller of the two men and he stepped aside
to look in it while his companion, chewing on a toothpick, went on
a few paces, then stopped, turned and wandered back. "Now what?"
said Sundance Kid.

"Nothing. But it's too damn bad the store ain't open." Butch
Cassidy gazed wistfully at the handsome display, the watches, gold
chains and lockets, some open, some closed, on the soiled blue velvet,
the wide-eyed wax doll propped in the center, dressed in a Sunday
gown of the latest fashion, exhibiting bracelets and a lady's amethyst
necklace, the turban on her frayed hair bearing a costly diamond
brooch.

"You got plenty of time to get it when we get to Galveston."

"Get what?"

"The wedding ring."

"Oh, I ain't worried about that. But look there." He pointed at
a tiny watch on a pearl and ruby pin.

"How could a thing that size keep time?" Sundance Kid brought
his own heavy gold timepiece out and looked at it, then glanced at
the bauble again. "It's a bilk," he said, putting the watch away.
"Don't never lay out nothing on a bilk like that." He slapped at a
mosquito on his neck and scratched the spot with his index finger.
"It's five past eight," he added.

Butch pointed to the row of six clocks of various shapes and
dimensions behind the opulent doll, all telling the same time almost
to the second. "News," he said, smiling.

"Come on, boss."

"We ain't in no hurry. We got plenty of time." But obligingly
Butch strolled on and Sundance Kid matched his own steps to his
friend's.

"How we going to kill the time?"

"Ain't much to kill."

"More than two hours! That's a plenty, specially where everything's shut down tighter than a drum. I might of knew that there

425

restaurant would be closed. Know how long I was keeping a eye out in front there for you? Damn near a hour! By God, I thought you got caught in a bear trap. When I seen you coming without nobody in tow I thinks to myself, Well, sir, here's once old Cassidy has hung fire or he's missed his mark, I says. But then I seen how high you was stepping and the look on your beezer and I says, No, sir, he ain't. He's won the day."

"I'm telling you, Langabaugh, she's the blestest, brightest — "

"I know. That was the tune I et my supper to, remember." Sundance Kid felt for a cigarette. "Say, that wasn't such a bad dump, that chophouse." With his thumbnail he scratched a match alight and inclined his face to it.

Butch caught his arm and lit his own cigarette before the match burned out. "No, it wasn't," he agreed.

"What do you know about it? You didn't no more know what you had in front of you than if it was a plateful of puppy dogs' tails. What was you a-eating on?" he demanded.

Butch frowned and considered, drawing on his cigarette. "Now, wait just a minute. . . ."

"See there?" Sundance Kid laughed. Then his face sobered. "Why couldn't you of had her meet us at the station? That going down there for her ain't sensible."

"Why not?"

"Because you would of been the first one to say so your own self before you got this bee in your — Imagine if the Texan had wanted to pull such a — "

"We got all kinds of time to do it in."

"It ain't sensible. She should of come on up to the station."

"Wait'll you see her," Butch said.

"What's that got to do with it?"

"You'll see. She's — "

"Hey, boss." Sundance Kid plucked at his companion's sleeve. "Do you glimpse what I do?"

"Where?"

"Just come out of that doorway there. She's coming toward us."

"My God," Butch said.

"Hello, my fine gentlemen!" a hoarse voice called.

"Why, it's Mary, the lady from the hotel."

"Looks like she's busted your ten spot and went to celebrating."

Butch removed his hat as he neared her, and Sundance Kid, with a puzzled side glance, did the same.

Thick white powder filled the wrinkles of the woman's face, round red moons stood upon her cheekbones. Her dark irises seemed to have run at the edges into the dingy whites of her eyes, giving them a blurred, smoky look. Upon her dead black hair a wide hat sat rakishly, heavy with ostrich plumes, and more of the same, with a smell of camphor about them, fluttered about her in a once splendid boa. Gone was the patched apron of her servitude. She wore a beaded waist, a spotted skirt banded with rubbed velvet, and a tasseled bag swung from her discolored hand. With the erumpent social grace of even the shyest when caught looking her very utmost best without possibility of improvement, she smiled, then spoke suavely. "Good evening, boys."

"Well, if you ain't a sight for sore eyes, ma'am," Butch said.

"Go on with you now." She flipped him lightly with her purse. "I was hoping you'd be coming along this way. You see — I don't know whether either one of you has got nothing on your *conscience*, but — when somebody does me a good turn once, why, then I try to turn around and do them a good turn."

The two men exchanged glances.

"Meaning what, ma'am, if you'll excuse a guy's dumbheadedness?"

"Meaning the hotel's swarming with policemen."

"That don't worry us, ma'am," Sundance Kid, stiffening, said.

She laughed and they could tell she was wearing another perfume besides the camphor — whiskey.

"No, ma'am," Butch said, giving her a wink. "Not us."

"Little after seven here they was, a whole flock of 'em, searching the rooms, going through folks' baggage, poking around in the closets. Now they're hid around here, there and everywhere, like Easter eggs, which their heads is about the same proposition. They're laying for *somebody*, that I know."

"Wonder who for?" Sundance Kid said innocently.

"Not you, my downy ducks! not you, of course. But anyway I thought I'd tell you, so if you don't happen to like their smell, you don't have to smell 'em."

"That's mighty white of you, ma'am." Butch took his hand out of his pocket, reached out, caught the tasseled bag she was swinging, opened it, dropped something in it and closed it again. "Taking all that trouble to do a couple of guys a favor."

"I was praying you'd come by this way."

"We ain't going to forget it in a hurry."

Sundance Kid was beginning to look up and down the street.

"Well, I wanted you to have my name," she said, "and the place where you could write me, wrote down in black and white, like we talked about this morning, so when you talk things over with your missus, you can write to me." She handed him a folded piece of hotel stationery. "Tell her I'm a respectable hard-working woman. Tell her she could go lots farther and do lots worse. Ain't a lazy bone in my body. Go to church, behave myself, keep outa jail, stay sober. . . ."

Butch tucked the paper inside his coat.

Sundance Kid said, "Come on, boss. No use in standing around asking for it."

"Sober as a judge," the woman said, brushing a purplish hand across her eyes as though to clear them of cobwebs. "You tell her."

"I sure will, ma'am."

"Come on," Longabaugh repeated, more sharply. "This here's Main Street, damn it." He started for the alley, came back and took Butch by the arm.

"You tell her," she repeated.

"I will. You bet."

"You're a mighty downy duck, you know, Mr. Lowe."

"Take care of yourself, ma'am, won't you?"

"Come on, boss. What you trying to do?"

"Mr. Lowe, honey."

"Yes, ma'am."

She pointed, giving a flip to her purse. "Him too. He's a nice young bucko."

Sundance Kid halted, and looked around.

"Darlings!" Her hoarse voice cracked. "Your dreams will all come true." Again her hand brushed at her eyes. "The two of the both of you. God's truth!"

When they were out of sight she went unsteadily to the wall of the Constitution Building and leaned against it. "You see," she explained carefully to some people then passing, an elderly man, a younger man and a well-dressed woman, "they really will come true, because . . . Well, you see, everybody's dreams comes true . . . because . . ." She finished the sentence to a startled boy with a bicycle clip on his right pant leg who detoured outward to the curb when he saw her. "Because we die, don't we? Don't we die?"

"If that wasn't a gray helmet up there at the corner, I'll eat my hat," Sundance Kid said, pulling on the reins.

"It's the middle house," Butch reminded him. "I'll get out here, though. It don't matter. We won't be long."

"You better not be. What do you figure's going on up there?" He leaned forward and peered through the gloom.

"I never seen no policeman."

"Listen, you make it fast. That's a crowd up there at the corner. I don't like the looks of it. Maybe they know about the kid here. Maybe they're planted all over hell. Maybe when you go up and knock on that door . . ."

Butch laughed. "Maybe that's a constable playing the piano in there. Who knows? Plays mighty sprightful, don't he?"

"Go get her, will you? You can crack the funny jokes later on. We should of left town. You could of wrote her a letter at Neibauer's. By God, *he'll* be surprised to see us back there wanting horses again, when the next time we was supposed to meet was supposed to be down there in Argentina." The last words he said to himself. He could see a moving shadow on the girl's front porch, heard a knocking. The music broke off. "Giddup," he said, and clucked his tongue. The livery stable horse plodded ahead, the well-greased wheels of the buggy did not creak. "Whoa. This here's all right."

A pretty dark-haired girl with a heart-shaped face opened the door. "Yes?" she said. Darkness had scarcely fallen but she brought a lamp with her and now shaded it with her hand, directing its beams. She smiled when she saw the caller was a young man, a stranger, and not without attraction.

"I'd like to speak with a young lady that lives here. Dorney. Dorney Leaf, her name is."

Crystal surveyed him, thoughtful.

"It's important."

"She's not here."

"But — where did she go? I — got to find her, see."

Her nose went up and Crystal's smile died away.

"That is — please, miss — you see, I got a message for her, and I got to find out where she is, because — "

"I don't know anything about it."

"But you live here. You must know. Couldn't you — ?"

"She's gone."

"But where to? Didn't she say — ? didn't she — ?"

"She just went. I don't know anything about it, when she left or when she's coming back or anything."

"Maybe somebody else here could tell me — "

She shook her head and began to shut the door little by little. So they had begun pounding on the door asking for Dorney, had they? So it was beginning, was it? The big flurry. Well, maybe it was and maybe it wasn't. This was a crude young man, not a born gentleman, but looks didn't mean anything. Maybe he was a rich man . . . maybe he was the one who was going to give Dorney a chance to lord it over everybody else . . . make everybody else's life miserable. . . . Crystal's eyes narrowed.

"I've just got to find her, miss!"

"She's not here. But I'm a relation of Dorney's. May I ask why you want to see her?"

He looked at her a long instant, measuring, weighing. "Something personal, miss. Real personal."

Her lip curled.

"You see, miss — " He spoke to the closed door.

Out in the street again Butch climbed into the rig and sat down

429

heavily. "She ain't there," he said. "But it ain't the kiddo's fault. See, I told her ten-thirty and it ain't only nine or so." He struck his knee. "By God. There ain't nothing to do but wait, I guess."

"Wait? For a hour and a half? With maybe a posse collecting up there at the corner, and half the police force down around here ready to spring?"

"This ain't a cow town like Lander or somewheres," Butch said. "They don't congregate posses in Salt Lake City."

"Listen a minute," Sundance Kid said, "what I'm going to say now, I don't mean no offense — but are you sure she never went to work and give the good word to nobody? Because, after all — "

"I got reasons — good ones and more of 'em than you could shake a stick at — to know you mean it when you say you don't mean no offense," Butch said softly, "or I wouldn't take to it kindly. I wouldn't take to it kindly a-tall."

"Well, how about — Mrs. Bannon? Would she go to the law?"

"Her? You remember her, from up in Star Valley. Nicest little, best little — "

Sundance Kid meditated. "No, she wouldn't," he agreed finally.

"Besides, we ain't the only pebbles on the beach. Maybe them policemen up around the Temple Hotel was laying for somebody else!"

"I got a strong hunch they wasn't."

"Me too."

"That old geezer from Vernal must of put 'em wise."

"Somebody must of."

Sundance Kid turned and looked at the blur that was Butch's face in the darkness. "We got to hightail it out of here, boss, or we're going to find ourselves staying. A lot longer than we want to, maybe."

"I know it. I know we got to." Butch took his hat off, ran his fingers through his hair and set it back on. He gazed at the house. They could hear the music faintly.

"Who the hell is that playing all the time?"

"That's my girl's sister's girl. She's the one that come to the door."

"And she wouldn't say where your girl had went to?"

"Didn't know."

"Wouldn't say when she was a-coming back?"

"Nope. But Dorney was telling me about this here one that plays the piano. Crystal, her name is. She's — "

"I'm telling you we got to make tracks!"

"Let a guy think a minute."

"Send her a telegram."

"Where from? We can't go back uptown."

430

"Write her a letter."

"She'll be waiting. I can't let the kid wait on me, and me not show — "

"Write something and leave it here. That's all you can do. We got to get moving!"

Butch opened his coat and felt in his inner pocket, brought out the worn and crumpled envelope in which Judge Towers's message of last year had been delivered, and the piece of paper on which Mary Brockett's name and address had been written. He unfolded it, turned it over, smoothed it on his knee and searched for the stub of pencil.

"I might of knew we'd have to ride that old outlaw trail down to Texas again, instead of going on the train in style. I did know it!" Sundance Kid muttered to himself. "I felt it in my bones."

"You and a old lady in Telluride one time. Soon as she found out how something was going to turn out, you ought to of heard her prophesy. Knew all about it! And that's the way with — "

"In my bones," Longabough repeated sadly.

"Hold a match over this, will you?"

In the still warm air, one, two, three matches burned one after the other with a steady flame behind Sundance Kid's cupped palm. Butch wrote in an unpractised hand. *Come to Galveston the Laurel Hotel wait for me plans changed love Butch.* "There," he said. "Give me one of them train tickets."

"But, boss — "

"We can't use 'em, you lunkhead."

Unwillingly Sundance Kid found what Butch wanted and handed it over. He stuffed it into the wrinkled envelope, along with the note, started to get down and sat back.

"Now what?"

"She can't go far without money."

Harry Longabaugh groaned.

"She's got to eat, ain't she? And maybe we'll be delayed, you and me."

"We will be, for from twenty years at hard labor, to life, if we don't get to traveling, so that thought don't come as no big surprise."

"A kid her age — where's she going to get a trunk and the like of that? And she'll need things — maybe new shoes — no telling what all." He had peeled off several bills from a big roll and now began stuffing them into the envelope. He paused, considered and peeled off some more.

Sundance Kid watched, frowning. "For the Lord's sake, Butch. You ain't took a lesson from the Texan, have you?" He had been searching for something in his pocket. Now he found it and handed it over. "Everything comes in handy if a fellow just hangs on to it long enough."

"What this?"

"Remember that box of pills the time Deaf Charley had the colic?"

Butch laughed, and snapped the rubber band around the envelope. "Light another match, will you? I got to write her name here in front." Again the steady little flare, in which to scratch out Judge Towers's handwriting — Jim Lowe, Knutsford Hotel — and scrawl beneath it, *Personal Dorney Leaf.*

At the foot of the front porch steps he decided not to trust the dark-haired young lady after all. Not if there was any other way. Something about her made him leery. Instead, making no sound, he started around the side of the house, making for the back entrance. Perhaps he would find someone else, who would tell him where to find Dorney or with whom he could more safely leave his message for her. Pulse quickening, he halted beneath a dimly lighted window and looked in to see a kitchen, to all appearances empty, then went on, found the back steps and went up them to tap at the screen door. It squeaked when he opened it. He shut it with care, tiptoed across the dark porch and tapped at the back door, where he waited, hardly breathing. No answer. He turned the knob, opened the door a crack and peered through it. Nobody home! But yes, there was a little child, a little girl over there by the sink, getting a glass of water. She turned, the half-empty glass in her hands, and stared at him.

"Don't be scared," he said quietly, stepping in, leaving the door open behind him. "Please don't, because I ain't nobody to be scared of. I'm hunting for a girl named Dorney." The child, still staring, set the glass on the sink and began to come forward on stick-like little legs.

"She lives here, so you must know her. Don't you?"

"Dorney."

He could see now, that this was no little girl and remembered suddenly that Dorney had said her sister's youngest girl had something wrong with her. This must be the one — Betty, Jessie — no, Jetta — the one she had told him about.

He came and knelt on one knee beside her. "Where did she go, Jetta?"

The strange hooded eyes surveyed him without blinking. The tiny yellow lips moved.

"Where did she go?"

"Gone."

The music stopped and Butch began to rise, but it took up almost at once and he knelt down again. "Are you a big enough girl that if I give you something to give Dorney, you'll give it just to her and won't give it to no one else?"

The hooded lids came down, lifted.

"Listen, I'll send you a peacock — not a stuffed one but a real live one — I'll send you a pony — if you'll just do me this one little favor."

"I want a kitty."

"Is that all? Listen, I'll send you a dozen." He held out the thick envelope. "She's got to get this. It's a matter of life and death. Now, you're a big enough girl to understand what that means, ain't you?"

Jetta nodded slowly, reached out and took it in an unready nerveless little claw.

"Hide it," he said uneasily. "Don't let that girl in there that's playing the piano get ahold of it, no matter what, now will you? Here, honey. Here's the way." He snatched up the envelope, unbuttoned two buttons of her dress, thrust it in against her chest, cinched her belt tight and buttoned her up again. "Now, when Dorney comes, you give her that and mind you don't do it in front of nobody."

"Yes," she said clearly. She fastened her hands over the secret.

"I'm depending on you. You see that she gets it."

"I want a peacock."

"Sure, hon, sure. Providing you give that to Dorney. Just to her and no one else."

"Yes."

He stood up and began backing to the door. "Tell her . . ." For the first time he looked about him, at the room he was in. That table, that was where she ate. The lamp, it shone on her. The chairs — the stove — this floor — the window — a longing to see her, though it had been but a few hours since they parted, so great he felt weak in the knees, shook him. "Tell her — listen, you tell her Butch was here and say — no, wait — listen. Say Butch was here and says for God sakes hurry, kiddo."

Madge did something very unusual. She opened the door that led into the parlor and interrupted Crystal while she was in the middle of a piece of music. "Have you had company?" she called, in agitation.

Crystal did not like to be interrupted but her mother's voice sounded interesting. "Company?" she said, hurrying out into the kitchen. "No, why?"

"Who did that rig belong to, that drove away just now as I come up the street?"

"In front of our house?"

433

"Right smack in front."

"Well, a man came here a while ago, asking for Dorney. But that was at least ten or fifteen minutes ago."

"This happened just this minute!"

"He must have sat out there and waited. I don't know what else."

Neither noted that Jetta had got down on all fours and crawled behind the sofa.

"You say he asked for Dorney?" Madge took off her hat, stuck the hatpin in it and hung it up on the nail of the door. "Wait till I tell you the most peculiar thing I heard today!"

"What?"

"You tell me first about this man and then I'll tell you."

"Well, all there is to tell — he wanted to see her."

"Where is she?"

"Over to Clara Tofflemire's."

"What did you tell him?"

"I said she was gone."

"What did he look like?"

"Blond. Medium-sized. Blue eyes. Sunburned-looking, kind of."

"That's him, as sure as God made little apples!" Madge pulled out a chair and sat down hard by the kitchen table.

"That's who?"

"Listen," her mother said. "Remember last year? Remember when I was scared to come home by myself and you and Dorney had to come up there to Judge Towers's and walk home with me? Remember the first night you two come up there, and Judge Towers was just home from Denver, and Selma Ankerstrand wasn't there, and Mrs. Towers was upstairs with a sick headache, and I was finishing up the dishes — and the doorbell rang?"

Crystal nodded. "You wanted me to go."

"That's right. But instead, Dorney went!"

"What's that got to do with — "

"Now wait till I tell you. Last night, just after dark — Selma Ankerstrand was telling me — why, the Judge's doorbell starts in to ring. Mrs. Towers was just coming down the stairs, so she stopped where she was, in the hall, to see who it was, and she stood there the whole time, and the porch light was on so she got a good look. And here was these two young fellows, one kind of off to one side, but this light-complected one, he was standing right in the doorway. And what should he do politely but ask for Judge Towers!"

"Now don't take a week to get to the point," Crystal said impatiently. "What has somebody that wanted to see Judge Towers got to do with — "

"Wait a minute. Hold your horses. Selma told him the Judge had went to Ogden. And *then* who do you think he wanted to see?"

"Who?"

"The cook!"

"The cook? Why, that's you!"

Madge nodded triumphantly. "I know it," she said.

"What did he want to see you for?"

"That's what I say! What did he? So anyway, Selma said I didn't live there but went home nights, so then he said, where does she live? and he asked if I had a sister named Dorney! so Selma give him our address."

"Last night, you say? Well, who was it?"

"There you are! Who was it? I *think* it was the very same man that was here tonight asking for Dorney. And I ain't the only one that thinks so, either."

"What are you talking about?"

"The most peculiar thing of all is, Mrs. Towers thinks she recognizes him. She thinks he's the same one that come to see the Judge about a year ago."

"Why should that be so peculiar, I'd like to know?"

"He's the one that Dorney went to the front door that night and let him in!"

"I still don't see — "

"You will see when I tell you that Mrs. Towers happened to be going to the bathroom and she looked down over the upstairs balustrade and what should she see down in the entrance hall but Dorney — she didn't know that's who it was till later — and some man — she naturally supposed it was the man that had rung the doorbell — down on the floor together as big as life."

Crystal's eyes widened. "You mean — her and this man she let in — down on the floor together?"

"Did you ever hear of such a thing? Dorney was sitting back on her feet and he was kind of kneeling in front of her — and he had ahold of her hands! He was holding her hands!"

Crystal gasped.

"So anyway right about then the Judge opened his door and called this fellow in, and Dorney come on back out to the kitchen. Did you ever hear of such a thing in your life? And not a word to us about it. I remember she was gone quite a while — "

"I do, too, now . . ." Crystal said musingly.

". . . but I never no more could imagine . . . I thought she was looking at the ornaments in the china closet, and like that. I never dreamt of such a thing!"

"Did Mrs. Towers tell you about it the next day?"

"Wouldn't I have told you if she had? I don't know why she didn't," Madge said, "but she never said a word. She had such a terrible headache that night — maybe she thought she was kind of

435

delirious. Anyway, she never said a word till last night when this same man come *back*. Then she told Selma about what she seen last year down there in the entrance hall, and naturally when I got to work this morning, Selma fell all over herself to tell me! and then about noon here comes Mrs. Towers into the kitchen to talk about our company supper tonight and she told me, too."

"I bet you felt just like a *fool* to have a sister like that!"

Madge looked rather startled. "The most peculiar part of all," she said, "is that she recognizes him!"

"Mrs. Towers does?"

"See, the Judge told her last year, when he went upstairs after this fellow had gone, that he was a very famous character."

"That this man was, you mean?"

"That's what he said!"

"Well, who was he?"

"I believe I've told you," Madge said apologetically, "that lawyers has very funny notions about keeping secrets about their customers. Selma was explaining it to me. Catholic priests is supposed to be the same way. The members of their church confide in 'em certain things and the saying goes you could tear 'em apart with wild horses and they never would tell what it was they had heard. So it's the same way with lawyers. The Judge never told Mrs. Towers who this man *was*, but he did ask her if she got a good look at him and when she said yes, he said, 'Well, you've saw a pretty famous character!' but he wouldn't say no more about it."

"A pretty famous character?" Crystal echoed. "Oh, that sneak," she whispered, "that dirty little sneak." Why, he might be a famous actor at the Salt Lake Theatre, on tour from New York! He might be a millionaire!

"Some kind of a criminal of some kind."

Crystal's face began to clear. "A criminal!" She took the chair nearest her mother and hitched it still closer. "What kind of a criminal?"

"Selma didn't know. But Mrs. Towers says she knows that was what the Judge meant, because he defends lots of criminals and they're the ones he's the closest-mouthed about. Selma was thinking it might be Jesse James, but Mrs. Towers said he never was around this territory and anyway he's been dead for quite a while."

"Who's a famous criminal?"

"How should I know? I don't read that kind of stuff. When Selma brings the newspapers out to throw on the trash heap, I just read the —"

"Imagine!" Crystal said, clinching her hands. "That little sneak. When we've been so *good* to her — and gave her a home — and tried to do everything under the sun — and she goes around behind our backs like the lowest sneak in the world — and takes up with *that* element of society! Why, it makes me *sick*."

"How did she meet somebody like that? is what's worrying me," Madge said mournfully, "And where? Maybe he come here to try to get her to *hide* him! The police are after him, of course — must be — they might come here asking all kinds of questions." She bit on a hangnail, tugged at it, brushed something off the tip of her tongue with one finger. "Maybe the whole story about 'Dair — about your dad — will all come to the fore again and all be revived and — "

"That won't matter!" Crystal said bitterly. "My life is ruined anyway!" She gave a harsh laugh. "In this town — with Jetta for a sister — with an aunt that associates with scum and criminals — with no chance to give a recital just because that jealous Mrs. Million thinks people can't play before an audience unless they learn their selections by heart and I can't *learn* anything by heart in this town! — why, what's the difference if it comes out that Daddy was a thief and a cattle rustler and got murdered? What's the difference?" She dropped her head in her arms on the table and began to sob.

"Now, darling . . ." Madge knew better than to try to touch her at the moment.

"Ruined — absolutely ruined!"

"Now, sweetheart . . ."

"I might as well be dead!"

It was safe now and Madge put a gentle hand on Crystal's hair. She smoothed it softly. "What I can't understand," she murmured, half to herself, "is how in the world they *met* because God knows I've tried to watch over her. If Mamma could look down, she could see I've kept my eye on her — she's never been away from home a night since she come from Rock Springs — she ain't been allowed to run all over town — the only place she goes visiting is to the neighbors or that Bannon woman from the laundry."

Crystal raised her head slowly, sniffing and rubbing her eyes. She drew a quivering sigh. "Maybe that's just a bluff," she said.

Madge put her hands in her lap and tried not to show how relieved she was that the crying spell was over so soon. "It couldn't be a bluff," she said. "I'd know. She sits and talks to me lots of times when you're practising. She practises a few big words and comes out with ideas every once in a while that sound — smart — but at the same time she's very much of a — you know, a little girl, too. I'd know if she had some — some *criminal*, mind you, on the string. I just know I would!"

"Maybe you would and maybe you wouldn't," Crystal said. "I could tell you a lot of things about your precious Dorney that would make you sit up and take notice!"

437

Madge got up suddenly and went to the back door. She looked out on the unlighted porch and came back and looked around the room. "Where's Jetta?" she asked.

"I could tell you something about your precious Dorney that you would never — "

"Where is she?"

"Who?"

"Jetta."

"Why, she must be here. I didn't put her to bed."

"Well, where?"

"How should I know?"

They looked for her everywhere. It was only by accident and just when Madge was going to go and look for her somewhere outside in the darkness that they discovered and dragged her from her hiding place. She looked wild and disheveled, and when her mother pulled her hands down from the front of her dress, she put them right back up again, clutching and gripping.

"What in the world's the matter with her?" Madge asked, looking from one daughter to the other.

"Don't ask me!"

"You didn't punish her, did you? You know you gave me your solemn promise never to punish her, no matter what she did." Madge tried to pull Jetta's hands down again but this time she edged backward so recklessly it seemed she must fall.

"I hope you're not accusing me," Crystal said, beginning to pale. "Because I never even touched her! I never went near her! She was swinging and I was practising! Dorney might have hurt her someway, but as God is my witness — "

"Look at her," Madge said. "Look at the way she's doing. What's the matter, baby? Does something pain you? What in the world —?" She went after, caught and squatted down beside her.

"Dorney acted so strange at supper, I thought she was coming down with smallpox or something, so maybe Jetta caught it and that's what's the matter!"

"Her color looks funny. Her eyes . . . Jetta, tell Mamma. . . ."

The tiny creature, struggling to get away, flailed out and struck her mother. "A peacock," she wailed.

Madge held onto her, ducking back to miss another ineffectual blow. "What's she talking about?"

"That's those silly stories Dorney makes up for her!"

"I've never saw her act this way. I can't imagine. Her chest must be hurting her or else why should she . . . ?" She was hard to hold but Madge hung on. "She's buttoned up wrong. See, this button should go in this — "

Jetta, kicking and screaming, slid to the floor. She jerked and twisted, trying to escape.

"Well, did you ever see such a — "

"No! No! No!" Jetta bit into her mother's hand sharply enough to draw blood, and Madge gave a squeal, letting go.

Clumsy as were her stiff little arms and legs, Jetta crawled away with surprising swiftness and disappeared under the table. It was angry Crystal who dragged her out, in no very mild way, giving her head a severe bump in the process.

That aroused Madge. "Crystal Yandle!" she said. "What do you mean by — "

"What do I mean by what?" Crystal cried in a fury, while her mother pulled mewling Jetta to a chair, sat down and lifted her up onto her lap.

"There, there," Madge soothed. She seldom made over her younger daughter in this manner because it disgusted Crystal and made her irritable, but she was so worried she didn't care. Perhaps the child really was ill or had suffered some painful injury. She held her close and even dropped a kiss on her hair.

Jetta stopped her shrill piping and settled contentedly down in her mother's arms. Her tiny yellow hands relaxed and fell away from the bosom of her dress and Madge, without difficulty, began to unbutton it.

Meanwhile Crystal's rage had been growing. "To dare to accuse me!" she breathed. "To dare say that I — "

Madge looked up, queerly. "Now what in heaven's name?" she said, probing and feeling.

"What is it?" Crystal came close.

"I — don't — know."

Jetta said "No!" again but this time without much conviction. So welcome was it, so pleasant, to be snuggled against her mother's breast that she forgot how it was she had come to be there and wanted but to stay undisturbed, forever.

Madge, as though it had been a live thing that might bite, drew out the thick envelope. She stared at it, astonished. "*Personal Dorney Leaf*," she read, and looked up. "Now where in the world did Jetta — "

"Who is it *from*?"

"There's no — it doesn't — "

"Give it to me!" Crystal snatched it out of her mother's hand.

"Where in the world could Jetta have got it?"

Crystal slid the rubber band off, lifted the flap of the envelope and took a peek at what was inside. Her eyebrows shot up and she gasped. Quickly she closed it, snapped the band back on and stuffed it in her pocket. "Come on," she said. "We've got to get Jetta to bed before Dorney comes home!" She was white, red, white, and trembled where she stood.

"But, Crystal — "

"Come on." She started for the hall door. "We've got to pretend to be in bed, too!" Her eyes glittered.

"But what *is* it?" Looking dazed, Madge put Jetta down, got to her feet, took her tiny daughter by the hand and followed.

"We can talk — in the bedroom!" Crystal said. "All of us has got to be in bed by the time Dorney comes. We've simply got to!"

"But I've got a bone to pick with that young lady about a lot of — "

"Come on."

"For God's sakes hurry, kiddo," Jetta said clearly.

Madge looked down at her, bewildered. "Crystal, did you hear what Jetta just said?"

"If you don't want to spoil *everything*, come on!"

Dorney could not have been more surprised to find a grand ball in progress than to find, when she got home at twenty minutes past nine, that everybody had gone to bed! This was so extraordinary that it scared her a little. She had crawled along at a snail's pace from the Lubys', thinking of ways to get out of the house in case Madge and Crystal stayed up later than ten o'clock, as they frequently did, but now the path had been cleared as if by magic.

She was halfway upstairs when the thought came to her that maybe some tragedy had happened while she was absent, to account for such a state of affairs. Some terrible thing — and she was rejoicing when she might better be decently grieving. Maybe they were gone and she was here all alone! That sent her scurrying down again and she tiptoed through the kitchen and groped her way down the hall to the shut bedroom door. Usually it was open. She bent close to it and listened. Not a sound. Her heart began to beat so that she could hear it in her ears. Lifting her hand, she rapped lightly.

Dead silence. She was about to turn the knob and walk in when Madge cleared her throat.

"Who is it?" she asked in a muffled voice.

"It's me. Are you all right?"

There was a whisper, a long pause, another whisper. "Of course I am," Madge called finally. "You'd better go to bed."

"I am, Madge. But you're sure everything is all right?"

"Of course. Don't go in and bother Crystal, though. She was ready to drop tonight, she was so tired." Crystal slept in the parlor.

"I won't," Dorney said. She never did, so she was not likely to begin now. "Madge . . ."

"What?"

"Good night." This was her goodbye. A fine way to do to a sister who had provided the best home she could, who had been as kind as she knew how to be. A fine way to do! But she would write. She would send her presents from South America. She would . . .

"You go to bed now."

"I will, Madge. Good night. . . . I'm going."

Upstairs, she did not begin at once but sat down and waited for what seemed a long time, until she was sure it was safe, and then, in stocking feet, set about packing. Ten minutes later, she could see that old Mr. Diltz's telescope bag really was going to hold all the books — thank the dear Lord for that — but nothing else except one petticoat! however, that was no disaster. Her clothes — the Queen's lovely dresses — would have to be carried some other way, that was all. Wiping her damp forehead, highly pleased not to have to worry any more about the books, she stood and wondered how she was going to . . . but of course! No sooner said than done. All she had to do was tie her clothes in a sheet and drop the bundle out of the window! People in the railroad station might think it was somebody's washing, or gypsy baggage, but that couldn't be helped. She had to take the books.

They were so heavy that she thought she would never get the suitcase downstairs without bumping it on every step, but somehow she managed to do it, and managed to get it outside and around to the front of the house, where the sheeted bulk she had already pushed out of the window lay in the middle of the sidewalk.

Sitting on her handkerchief spread out on the next to the bottom step, catching her breath, she noticed how the muscles in her right hand and arm were jumping and quivering. Quite a long while after, when she reached up to see if her brown straw hat was on straight and if her hair was smooth, her hand was still trembling. Why did lifting something heavy make a person shake that way? What would Butch say when he went to pick the suitcase up and felt how much it weighed? He would wonder if it was full of stones!

Butch . . . she felt impelled to explain who that was, not aloud but silently to herself. Butch was . . . Butch Cassidy. Not him in a dream she was going to wake up from. Not him as a mirage that would go away if she rubbed her eyes. Not him made up and imagined, the way he had been all the times before, but Butch Cassidy as real as the step she was sitting on, the fence, that tree across the way, the late and lazy moon.

This time he was really coming and she was really going.

She could see him as she had seen him this afternoon down in the park, his blond head inclined towards her, his blue eyes looking

441

deep. She could see him laugh. She could hear him too, talking. The fact of the matter was, he was her oldest and best friend. She was not going away to far South America with an unknown stranger. Whom had she pondered as long in her life, loved more, loved better? She wanted badly to explain that to someone. She longed for the pen in her hand, the smooth paper under it, to be telling, to be explaining, because all of a sudden then the picture in black and white would begin to glow in its natural colors. To write it down was to put the finishing touch on any event, see what it was, what it meant, what it stood for. To put anything into words was like pouring melted wax on top of cold glasses of jelly, to harden there and preserve and keep what was underneath like new.

You see, Mr. Desmond . . .

But there would be no more writing to him, no matter how important the occasion, or what she had to tell or what she had need to inquire. If she read *Othello*, if she learned to jump her white horse over the moon, if a flamingo went for a stroll with her, if she saw . . . if she heard . . . if she wondered. . . . Not again, drawing a happy sigh, would she begin a letter *Dear Mr. Desmond*, because . . .

When the clock in the tower of the City and County Building began to strike she counted the strokes, and then got up and hurried out to the street and looked up and down in some excitement. It was eleven o'clock.

He was late, but he would come.

At midnight, when the clock struck again, she walked out and wandered almost up to the corner, and then ran back, for fear she would not know when he got there. He was so late they had missed the train and would have to catch another.

Back on the step, she drooped tiredly, yawned, put her knees up, leaned her forehead against them, her arms circling her head.

She was awake when it was one o'clock, and one-thirty.

You see, Mr. Desmond . . .

No need to worry even if the train has gone . . . and even if . . .

For he will come.

The same as always.

Oh, yes!

At first he will be far off and then he will come nearer — and nearer — and nearer —

(How he does run, Little Dipper! How he does tear!)

And now, you see, he is at the gate. Tall as a cliff and dark-eyed and dark-haired Butch Cassidy jumps down from the black horse. Hear the jingle of his spurs! The bold cowboy, the outlaw of old, is come for his own true love. Hear there his song?

She never was worried a minute!

For this time it's true.
This time it's real!
This time there's no doubt about it.
She flies, she dashes —
And flashes through him, as through the smoke of frost. . . .

41

MADGE CALLED HER AT THE USUAL HOUR, AND DOR-
ney crawled with difficulty from the heavy quicksand of sleep. It
took some while for her to realize that this was her old room, and
home, and Monday morning, and that the yellowness of the early
sunlight told how the day was going to be hot, and that she had to
go to work at the Palace Laundry the same as ever. Blind with
fatigue as she had been the last night when she crept in at something past three, first with the heavy suitcase and then going back
for the bundle of clothes in the sheet, she had tiptoed about unpacking, hanging up garments and placing the books back on the
bureau before she undressed, shivering, and climbed into the warm
attic bed, where she dozed off instantly. Somehow, she knew it
was no use to stay ready. He was not coming. He would never come.
When she got up and started to dress she felt crushed and baffled,
but strangely reconciled. She might have stayed awhile and shed
some proper tears for the lost land, for love disavowed and the
dream gainsaid, but she had no time to waste.

She dreaded to face Madge. Surely, everything would show? had
been stamped there for all to see? her wild intentions, her blighted
hopes, even his kiss upon her forehead? She ran down the stairs and
out into the kitchen trying to seem the same as ever, but she felt
so culpable that a finger pointed at her would have buckled her
knees.

It was Madge's habit to light the fire and prepare the simple
breakfast of toast and coffee. Generally, she was all dressed and
ready to depart for the Towers' when Dorney came down, but this
Monday morning, already seated at the table, she was in her nightgown, with a dressing sacque over it, and her gray-streaked hair hung
in a long braid down her back.

"Come on," she said. "I've got the coffee poured." She lifted her
cup in a somewhat unsteady hand and took a sip.

Dorney, surprised, sat down opposite her. "Did you get the day
off?" she asked.

"I've got news for you," Madge said.

444

"News?"

"Yes, it's — you see, I — we've decided — well, I've quit my job up at Judge Towers's."

Dorney's mouth opened, closed.

"I've got a chance for a better job in — California, so I'm going to take it."

"But what — but when — "

"You see, I didn't mention it, but the Judge had this rich man there one night, and he ate supper, and he liked the cooking so well, and — before he left he offered me a job at his home in San Francisco at real good pay — real good — so — at first I didn't know, but Crystal and me has been talking it over, and we decided — so now I'm going to take it."

"But Madge, you never said anything about — "

"No use crossing a bridge before you come to it!"

"Well, I never was more — "

Madge looked puffy, tired and pale. She seemed to be irritated too, about something, at least there was a coldness in her eyes and a sulkiness about her lips, as on the occasion that Jetta had been taken out for a walk around the block, that said she considered herself ill used, and yet she appeared timid and uneasy at the same time. She held and set her cup down into the saucer with both hands. She spoke coldly and sulkily but there was nervousness in her voice. "I thought maybe you'd be surprised," she said.

Dorney's own concerns were forgotten as, stirring her coffee and breaking a piece of toast in half, she surveyed her sister. "My goodness," she said. "Surprised! Why, I'm just flabbergasted."

"We're going tomorrow."

"Tomorrow!"

"Well, Crystal thinks — "

Crystal spoke for herself. "She most certainly does," she said, coming into the kitchen in a wrapper. She went to the cupboard for a cup and saucer, came back to the stove and poured out some coffee.

"Good morning," she said blandly, looking at Dorney. "Well, what do you think of the good news?"

"I think it's — "

"We're leaving tomorrow."

"I never even dreamed of such a thing!"

Crystal laughed. "It was a big secret."

"I just don't know how you think we can do all we have to do in a matter of twenty-four — " Madge began.

"Talk lower," Crystal said crossly. "Do you want to wake up Jetta?"

Dorney looked at the clock. "I'll stay home and help," she said, "and then this afternoon I can go and tell Mr. Horsfeldt that I have to quit because we're leaving. I haven't got any money coming because Saturday was payday — " The thought came suddenly that whoever might in future seek her here would find her gone. A pang of regret shot through her.

Crystal looked at her mother.

"You're not going," Madge faltered.

Dorney moistened her lips.

"A ticket costs quite a bit of money," Crystal said.

For some reason, Madge reddened painfully.

"Anyway, you've got a good job here, and you've got lots of friends at the laundry and around the neighborhood here. Like Mother and I were saying. You can board someplace. Lots of girls live in boardinghouses and they like it just fine."

"But I — but what about — "

"Sometime later on you can save up enough money and then you can come down to California, too, if you want. Like Mother and I were saying. Either to — to us, or to Grandpa."

"Maybe I could borrow — maybe I could write to Papa and ask him," Dorney said, "if — " She looked anxiously at Madge whose eyes were on the lines she was drawing on the table cloth with the blade of her knife.

"The rent won't be due here for a week," Crystal went on. "That will give you plenty of time. We'll just move our stuff out, but the stove belongs in the house, and the furniture upstairs and the parlor sofa and this table, so the place won't be stripped entirely bare. And then when the rent's due you can go to a boardinghouse. You'll get along fine. Nobody needs to worry about you. Like Mother and I were saying." She pushed her chair back.

"But what shall I — "

They heard the bedroom door squeak as it was pushed open and Crystal, rising to her feet, said "Jetta!" almost as if in alarm.

Madge said, "I'll go! You stay here!" and hurried clumsily out of the room.

"What's the matter with Jetta?" Dorney asked, she, too, rising. "Is she — has something happened?"

"No, of course not." Crystal sat down, reached over and gave Dorney's dress a little tug. "Sit down," she said. "Come on. Sit down."

"Well, what made Madge — ?" Dorney looked at the doorway through which her sister had disappeared.

Crystal whistled under her breath. "My!" she exclaimed. "Look at that clock, would you! You're going to be late if you don't hurry."

Dorney started slightly. A glance told her it was later than she had supposed.

"You can't risk your job now, can you?" Crystal said sweetly.

"Since you're going to be dependent on yourself after this? Isn't that right?" She got up and trailed across the floor to the stove and pulled the coffee pot over to the hottest part of it. "Goodbye, honey," she said over her shoulder. "We can do the rest of our talking tonight!"

If they had known where Dorney was the night before, that she was sitting out on the front steps waiting, until past three, nearly an hour after Crystal had crept from her mother's room to her own bed on the sofa in the parlor, they need not have spoken in whispers and might have left the door open and let a breeze blow through. But Crystal and Madge supposed that Dorney, after she tapped at the door and said good night — a disagreeable few moments — had gone upstairs to bed as usual. They were hampered and made uncomfortable accordingly.

Crystal's first concern, when she, her mother and sister were safe in the bedroom, was to find out what Jetta knew. But her impatience and annoyance so intimidated the little creature that she could not or would not speak, and there was nothing for it but to let Madge ask the questions while Crystal paced the floor. A man had come. He left a letter for Dorney. He put it in Jetta's dress. He was going to send her a peacock someday. That was all. That was really all. Jetta, handled gently, repeated the same story several times. When she fell asleep, as she did soon, within her mother's arms, too enraptured in that uncustomary refuge to more than make a few sounds expressive of her bliss, Crystal stopped pacing. She took out the packet and was about to empty it at the foot of the bed when they heard Dorney come in.

With the windows closed, the blinds pulled down tight, the door shut, the crack under it stuffed with a towel and the keyhole with a handkerchief, the bedroom grew oppressively hot, but they had seclusion and privacy and a light could burn. Not once, during their whole ensuing conversation, even when it grew violent and one or the other was tempest-tossed, did they speak above a whisper.

They did not speak at all, for longer than a minute, when what was in the envelope lay spread out and revealed upon the bed for them to gaze at. They knew that there existed hundred dollar bills, but neither had seen one in her life before. Now they were looking at nine of them. At nine hundred dollars. At enough crisp green deceptive money (for it looked very like one-dollar bills) to go — to do — to buy almost anything in this life! They stared at it. They gawped at each other. Taking turns, they fingered it. It was some time before they could pay heed to the pink railway ticket, and the note. Crystal read it first. "Oh, that sneak," she said in warm indignation. "That sneak. Listen to this, would you! *Come to Galves-*

447

ton *the Laurel Hotel wait for me plans changed love Butch.* Butch!
Imagine such a — such a — "

"That's him, of course. The man. That criminal. Oh, what
Mamma would say!" Madge reached for the note, read it with
shocked eyes. She looked up. "I don't suppose it could possibly be
the one that everybody's — Butch something — Cassidy — "

"What?"

"The bank robber and outlaw. Every once in a while there'll be
some big long mention in the papers. You must of noticed, once
in a while. . . ."

"It couldn't be!" Crystal recalled the name and looked stunned.

"Why couldn't it?"

"Well, where in the world would a little nobody — where would
somebody like Dorney meet anybody like *that?*"

"The Judge told Mrs. Towers that this fellow was a very famous
character, and the name sounds like it might be — "

Jealous Crystal shook her head. "It's not," she said. "I'm positive!" She thought, pinching her cheek. "But *if* it is, why, that's
all the more reason why we've got to keep it!"

"Keep the money?" Madge blinked. "It ain't ours. It's Dorney's.
Why, we ain't got no right — "

"You always claim you've got to watch out for Dorney on account
of your mother looking down from heaven. Well, what's Grandma
going to think of you if you let Dorney have this money, that has
probably been stolen in the first place, and go down there to Texas?"
She waved the ticket disdainfully. "And take up with a man *who
doesn't say one single word about marrying her.* Why, she'd be
ruined! For life! Your conscience would never give you another
peaceful minute if you allowed that!"

"I'll talk to her . . . tell her . . ."

"You have talked to her! You've been wonderful. Just like a
mother to her! And how does she turn right around and pay you
back? By sneaking! By lying! By deceiving! By getting mixed up with
criminals! Why, she was only fifteen years old when Mrs. Towers
saw her with her own two eyes sitting down on the floor with that
terrible man — letting him hold her hands! And now she's sixteen
and — oh, Mother, don't be blind!" Crystal sputtered. "Here is
nine hundred *dollars* right under your nose! Enough to buy a house
with, a whole house and a piece of ground. And here's an expensive
ticket to Galveston, Texas! What does that tell you, I want to know?
What does that tell anybody? Men don't hand out things like that
for *nothing!*"

"I just can't believe . . ."

"Look at the way she behaved with the Morelewski's nephew
when he was here. That smart-alecky Mr. Desmond or whatever his

name was." She remembered the note she had got rid of, saying that he was coming to call on Tuesday, and hoped spitefully that Dorney would be absent. If not, how she would chatter to him, showing off until it would be just sickening. "Giving her those books," she said. "Books! Why books, do you think? Because he's a poor schoolteacher. Because he didn't have money to hand out."

"Oh, Crystal!"

"Some people — you know you've said so yourself — are just naturally — there just naturally isn't a decent bone in their body!"

"Now, you wait a minute. You're going a little too strong there. She works at the laundry. She must work or she wouldn't be able to come home with her pay every week. And she's home every night! except when she runs over to Clara's or Mrs. Luby's, so I don't see when she's going to do all this — this — "

"I suppose Mrs. Towers lied, then! I suppose she didn't see Dorney and this criminal together in her own entrance hall sitting down on the floor holding hands!"

Madge's eyes wavered.

"Why didn't she tell us about that? Why didn't she tell us what it meant, explain herself, be open and above board about it? Did she say one word to me, that has tried every way I knew how in the world to befriend her and win her confidence and be her friend? Did she say one word to you, that has been so kind and has sacrificed — "

"No," Madge admitted.

"No. You bet not! And now tonight the man comes here as big as life. This note!" Madge gave it an angry flip. "This note telling your precious innocent little sister — about as innocent as a — I don't know what — to come to a *hotel*. This expensive ticket!" She threw it toward her mother. "This money — all this money — nine hundred dollars — I suppose that's imagined! Why, you must see," she said passionately, "you must see that she's been a liar and a cheat and a sneak and I don't know what else, ever since she came here to live. But now we've found her out, thank God, and we know how to deal — "

"Maybe I should go to the police," Madge said miserably.

"The police! Why? You don't know who the man is — you might make a guess, but you don't know — and he's gone by now anyway! He's left town. They'll never catch *him*. You don't want your sister arrested and have the whole family of us bothered and questioned and everything published in the newspaper, with no telling what damage and trouble all that would cause!"

"We'll send it back to him, then. At that — " She picked up the note and read the name again. "At this here place — this Laurel Hotel, in Galveston."

"And what would that accomplish, I wish you'd kindly tell me?"

"Why — "

"Nothing, that's what! It probably isn't his money to start with — it probably belonged to some big bank or some company that will — will just raise their interest, and get it all back that way."

"But — "

"Mother," Crystal said rapidly. "If we keep the money, if we pick up stakes right now — tomorrow — and clear out — why, that will probably do more to bust up whatever there is going on between Dorney and this awful man than any other single thing we could do!" She drew a quick breath and her eyes sparkled. "We'd be saving her from disgrace and no telling what misery! so you would never need to think Grandma was looking down at you and reproaching you for doing something wrong in regard to Dorney. And at the same time we would be helping *ourselves*. In fact, Mother," she said, "my idea is — I think — well, whatever happens is supposed to happen! If I — if we — got hold of this money, it's because we were supposed to get hold of it! We're supposed to leave this town just like I've been praying to do every day and every night for the past two years! We're supposed to start over! This is our one and only chance to — "

"Now listen here, young lady!"

"Three hundred dollars wasn't enough to get us a start," Crystal continued, refusing to be interrupted, "just like you always said, I grant you that. You were perfectly right! But *twelve hundred dollars* certainly is! Now, isn't it, Mother? We can go to San Francisco. We'll rent a nice flat. I know I can memorize my music there — I'll have a recital. Pretty soon I can set up as a teacher. I'll meet people! the kind a person doesn't need to be ashamed of. And there's all kinds of millionaires there — "

"They ain't no easier to meet there than they are here!"

"Aren't they, though! You just wait and see." Crystal looked proud, smug, confident, handsome.

"Maybe I couldn't find a good job like I got at Judge Towers's!" Madge began to lay a fold in her skirt as carefully as if she were going to take a needle and thread and run a tuck in.

"Sure you can!"

"What will I tell them? They've been such nice people to work for."

"Tell them you got a telegram that your father is very sick."

"What will we say to Dorney?" She laid the fold as far as it would go and then smoothed it out.

"What would she have said to us?" Crystal pointed to the ticket. "She would probably just have up and gone! Not that I'm so mean I want us to do her the way she would have done us! We'll take her into our confidence and explain. We'll say you have a chance for a lots better job down in California and you feel like you owe it to yourself to accept it. Remember that time that man was visiting the Towers and came out in the kitchen and offered you a job? Something like that could have happened!"

"It ain't going to be easy to transplant Jetta. She's so used to her swing, and — " Madge leaned over to pile the sheet higher so that the wizened yellow face was more in shadow. She paused to move a limp lock of hair with one finger.

"We're not going to transplant *her*."

"What do you mean?"

"You know that home for backward children I told you I read about, the one between Warm Springs and Beck's Hot Springs, that costs twenty dollars a month, that you go out there on the Center Street car?"

"But she ain't no backward child! She's past seventeen!"

"That doesn't make any difference. Look at the size of her! Why, seven- and eight-year-old kids are bigger than she is. And she'd be happy there, Mother! I know she would. She'll have the time of her life."

"Why, I would no more consent — "

"We can hire a hack and take her out there and be back before noon. And then all we have to do is pack and have the expressman come, and the piano mover, and we'll be all ready to go on Tuesday."

"Why, do you think for one minute that I have so little mother's heart in me that I would consent to leave a poor little helpless — "

"I didn't mean forever! I just mean — until we get settled. And then we can send for her! Somebody can bring her. That way, she won't have to be uncomfortable in hotels and here and there while we're hunting for a flat to live in. Why, anybody would say that's the only way to do! for *her* sake more than ours."

Madge, worried, began taking the hairpins out of her hair. "But why does it have to be tomorrow? Why does everything have to be so soon? When anybody takes a big step like this, they want time to consider."

"You grant that Dorney mustn't see Jetta under any circumstances? Because if they get their heads together, Jetta's liable to say something and the first thing we know — we've got trouble on our hands. They simply must be kept apart, that's all there is to it, until Jetta has had time to forget. You grant that?" Crystal spoke patiently.

Madge got up and walked to the bureau where she laid the hairpins in a small tin tray, then turned and walked back. "You don't seem to realize — " she began.

"Oh, yes, I do!"

"But, Crystal — look, honey." Madge clung to the brass knob of the bedpost. "Listen. What you're asking — is — is — practically an impossibility!"

"What is?"

"Put youreslf in my place for a minute. You want me to quit a good job I've had for more than six years! You want me to put Jetta in a home. You want us to pack up a household full of stuff and move in one day from a house we've lived in now for — and all this is supposed to happen tomorrow, mind you! and the very day after, we're supposed to leave for California. Why, it's the craziest, fool-ishest — "

"Is it?" Crystal said. "Well, now I want to ask you something. How long has it taken you to save up three hundred dollars? Don't answer that because I'll tell you. We came down here to Salt Lake from Reliance ten years ago, and you started working at that overall factory right away — and you've worked at one job or another ever since — so — it's taken you ten years! At that rate, if somebody doesn't name you as their heir, it's going to take you — three times ten — thirty years — to save up just the exact same amount of money that I'm holding right this minute, right here in my hand!" She waved it gaily. "You'll be sixty-seven years old!"

Madge looked from the greenbacks she seemed to be seeing for the first time, to her daughter.

"And what if this man comes back?" Crystal said. "There's no guarantee that he won't, you know. And if Mrs. Towers is right, and he really is a well-known criminal like she said, he's very likely not the kind that's going to enjoy it very much to have a monkey wrench thrown into his schemes! and he won't relish it very well to have money that belongs to him walked away with."

"It don't belong to him if he give it to Dorney," Madge said uneasily.

"He's not going to relish it," Crystal repeated. "And he might come back! And you ought to know, if anybody in the world should, what crooks and criminals DO when they think they've been tricked or cheated out of something that was theirs, or been hoodwinked some way! You certainly ought to. The same kind of an element shot Daddy, didn't they? your own husband! shot him in the back and brought him home in that wagon."

Madge bit her lips, and sat down weakly.

"And maybe what he did was a whole lot less than what we're — "

"But you're asking me to — you just don't realize — starting all over — of course I ain't a old lady, but even so — It ain't that I don't want to consider it, I don't mean to say by that, but — "

"There's nothing else to do!"

"But where will Dorney — ?"

"That little sneak? that has repaid all you've done for her the way she has? *She'll* thrive, never you fear for that. You mark my words. And in the meantime, she can go and board someplace."

"But she only makes — "

"Has anybody ever offered me nine hundred dollars? Or you? No, you bet they haven't! and she's only sixteen years old. What will she be when she's my age, I wonder? Or yours? You certainly don't have to worry about her! She'll be all right."

"Mrs. Towers is going to be very much upset about me leaving."

"There's nothing else to do," Crystal repeated. "We don't want to live in constant fear that every time we step out of the house we're going to be shot at and maybe killed. This is money, remember — nearly a thousand dollars. And some people are more concerned over money than if it was their own flesh and blood. Especially criminals. And I happened to get a good look at this one, remember. I know what he looked like! I know what he looked capable of! Murder, that's what. So all I know is, we've got to get away from here, and we can't waste any time doing it, either."

"Now wait a minute — just you wait — "

Crystal stood up. "I'm tired of arguing," she said. "What do I want to argue for? The truth is, I'm going anyway. Whether you go or not. If you want to stay, you stay. But I'm going. This is my chance to make something of myself and my life, and if you think I'm going to let it slip by me, you've got another think coming!" She waited and then added, "You'll never see me again as long as you live!"

Tears welled in Madge's eyes. "I dont' know why you would want to say such a thing," she whispered, "and turn a knife in my heart like that when you know what you mean to me — when you know how all through the years you've been my life and soul and I been so wrapped up in — and so proud — of your playing — and how smart you are — and how pretty — I always tell Selma — I'm always saying — " Madge buried her face in her hands and her shoulders shook. "You're all I got," she wept, "and all I had to live for since 'Dair — you don't remember — but that was the cruelest meanest thing that ever a living woman had to go through!"

"I do remember," Crystal said coldly.

"If I lose you, I might just as well go out and — "

"You're not going to lose me." Madge's daughter sat down next to her on the edge of the bed and put an arm gently around her. She took out her handkerchief and began to dab at her mother's streaming eyes.

"Look at me," she said dimpling.

Madge, sodden and red-eyed, looked.

453

"Why, you're not going to lose me, you silly thing! Why, you and I are going to San Francisco and we're going to have the most wonderful new life that anybody ever *heard* of. It will be just simply wonderful. But I can't help it," she said beguilingly, "because everything has happened so fast! Now, can I? It's not my fault. *I* didn't plan it. It just happened that way, that's all! You know that old saying, don't you, that opportunity only knocks once? Well, that's true, it really is. So you just pay attention to Crystal now, and you and I will use our heads a little and take it on ourselves to have the happiest — nicest — pleasantest — "

Madge blew her nose softly, and listened, thinking how lovely her child looked when something interested her bright mind and caught her roguish fancy, and soon she was nodding, and then she was nodding again, and then she was saying, "Well," and "Maybe . . ." and "Yes, dear."

If Mrs. Bannon had come to work and been available for a parley at the noon hour, the day might not have seemed such an eternity, but she was absent. Dorney, longing to speak of what was foremost in her mind to the one living being who knew something about it, decided to go to Mrs. Bannon's house on her way home and find out if she was sick. Having slept so little the night before, she was plagued all afternoon with sleepiness, which, with the intense heat, her mood of dejection and the staggering amount of work to be plowed through under the sharp gaze of Mr. Horsfeldt (Tamer Camomile had a stye on either eye), gave such an aspect of unreality and vaporousness to that long Monday that half the time she felt she was dreaming.

After she had knocked at the door several times and no Mrs. Bannon appeared, Dorney went to the other side of the double house. The front door there was open and through the screen door thick with flies she could see beyond the parlor and small passageway, to a horde of children in a back room at a long table. From the smell, not unappetizing in spite of the weather, they were supping on cabbage and fried potatoes. Two or three of them wanted to jump down and see who was at the door but someone forbade them and came herself, shutting them off from sight by drawing a curtain. This was Fern Cruver, Mrs. Bannon's brother Eddie's wife. She was a broad young woman who had curled her bangs so recently that perspiration had not yet begun to take the crimp out. Her curling iron had been too hot, that was certain, for an odor of burnt hair hung about her, and on the other sleeve of her clean blue cotton dress a boat-shaped scorch of pale sepia proclaimed that recently another warm implement, her flat iron, had been in use. She seemed pleased to see a caller for her sister-in-law and stepped outside, jarring the flies loose as she opened the screen only to have them settle back where they were as she closed it behind her, to divulge the information that Phoebe had had an accident and was flat on her back in bed.

"Yes," she said, folding her broad arms across her chest and pushing a dirty rag doll with button eyes away into a corner of the porch with the toe of her shoe, "we all got a fright. The first thing I knew, here was her oldest boy — in fact, all three kids, screaming loud enough to wake the dead, running through the house bawling that their mamma had fell down and broke her back — "

"Broken her back!" Dorney said in horror.

"No wonder they thought so! Me and Eddie thought so, too, when we went to get her up off the floor and she hollered like we was pulling her wisdom teeth — but when the doctor come, he said it wasn't. She'll have to lay in bed quite a while to rest it, but it ain't broke."

"When did it happen? I was here just yesterday afternoon — "

"I know," Fern said. "I seen you. I inquired who you was when you and him left the first time, you, and your gentleman friend, and Phoebe was telling me you was a girl from the Palace — I used to work there myself before I got married — I was a marker — one of the best, if I do say so myself — and she said the fellow with you, why, her and Blufe used to know him in Star Valley. Jim Lowe, she said his name was."

"Yes," Dorney said, coloring. "Was it last night or this morning that she — "

"Last night," Fern said, moving to the door frame and rubbing her left shoulder against it. "She went out on a errand yesterday evening about seven, and when she come back she was fixing the kids a bite to eat before she got 'em to bed when the oldest boy took it on himself to let the blind up over the sink. Well, it wouldn't go up because it stuck and what should he do but give it a hard yank, down it come! and banged the littlest girl's head, and she yelled, and Phoebe was rushing to see what the damage was, when she slipped in a streak of butter or grease or something — you know there ain't nothing sliprier — and up went both her heels and down she come full force right on the middle of her back. It's the biggest wonder in the world she didn't break her backbone right in two! Well, it sure must of hurt her plenty, because when I got in there, she was whiter than pie dough and her lips was blue and the sweat was rolling off of her, and I tell you, we had something on our hands to get her up and get her to bed."

"Why, that's just awful," Dorney said. "Maybe I'd better not — maybe it would be better if I came back some other — "

"Oh, company won't hurt her," Fern said. "It'll do her good. Last night the doctor give her some kind of medicine to make her sleep.

455

Me and Eddie, that's my husband, we was hoping," she lowered her voice, "she'd be all right this morning and could go back to work but the doctor has got her bandaged up and he claims it'll be a month or more before she can get out of bed. That's going to work a hardship on us, as you may imagine. Eddie ain't John Jacob Astor by no means and we got five kids of our own. I wasn't strong on her coming down here in the first place . . . like I told Eddie, relatives is all right but not under one roof, there's no house big enough to . . . but she's his sister and he felt called upon . . . you know how it is." Fern sighed. "And now this descends on us, so there you are. Her kids is in to my place, eating. I give her her meals. I took her supper to her. I guess she's ate it by now." Going to Mrs. Bannon's door, she threw it open and looked over her shoulder. "Right through the parlor and out into the back hall and it's the first door to the left," she said.

"She's lucky to have somebody like — like you."

"That's what I was telling Eddie. Not that I mean to brag or nothing, but, well, she is, ain't she? somebody to keep care of things and see that the wheels go round." A kindly smile spread across Fern Cruver's broad face. "I spout off," she said, "but me and her kids get along fine, and besides, the way I figure — supposing it was me? People ought to figure that way. Supposing it was them? Because nobody ever knows."

There was a strong odor of liniment in the small gloomy chamber. Mrs. Bannon, looking ill, propped stiffly against her pillows, in a hot-looking long-sleeved and high-necked muslin nightgown, said "Oh!" as if scared by an apparition when Dorney appeared in the doorway.

"It's only me," Dorney said, advancing into the room. "Your sister-in-law was telling me about your accident and I — "

"I thought you was going! I thought you and — him — was leaving last night. How come you're still here? Where's Butch? I worried how I was going to get the message to your sister Madge. What happened? I've been terribly — "

Dorney stopped at the foot of the bed. "He didn't come," she said. She had dreaded to speak the words aloud, but they came more easily than she supposed they would. She could not have said more, however, for something clutched at her throat.

"What do you mean?"

She waited, regaining her composure. "I got ready," she said, finally. "You know he was supposed to come at ten-thirty. Madge and Crystal went to bed early. I was very glad about that because — "

"Sit down," Mrs. Bannon said. "Bring that chair up to the bed and sit down."

456

Dorney did as she was bidden.

"Now, tell me."

"There's nothing to tell. I packed my suitcase and went outside and sat on the steps and waited and he didn't come." She clasped her hands carefully together on her knee. "I don't know what could have happened, unless maybe they arrested him. I was thinking that I'd better go up to the jail or somewhere and ask if — if — "

"Oh, no!" Mrs. Bannon cried. "Don't do that. That would be the worst thing you could possibly do because that might *really* get them started on his trail, when otherwise they wouldn't even know he'd been here! Besides," she added feverishly, "besides, I sent out for the *Tribune*, and if they had caught either him or Sundance Kid it would of been spread all over the front page! See, here it is." She reached under the sheet and brought out an untidily bunched-up newspaper. "It would of been printed in letters three inches high." She pushed it away and it slid down over the far side of the bed. "No, I hope you will never be so foolish as to play him a thoughtless trick like that, no matter what."

"Could he have got hurt, do you think?" Dorney asked, after a pause.

"Him?"

"Maybe he was taken to the hospital! I should — "

Mrs. Bannon, forgetting her injury, tried to turn on her side, to be closer to her visitor, but white-faced and panting, had to desist and stay as she was. "Dorney," she said, "there's something I'd just about rather have my tongue cut out than have to tell you, but — you see, honey — Butch Cassidy's a very nice likable fellow and all that, and everybody that knows him thinks they can trust him with their life, but — "

"Mamma," said a childish voice.

Dorney turned to see a small girl about the age of Ruby Mudge standing in the doorway, bearing a cup and saucer in both hands. Her eyes fixed on it, holding her breath, she inched forward to the bed. "Aunt Fern says here's more coffee," she announced, drawing a sigh of relief when her mother took it out of her hands.

Mrs. Bannon set it unhandily on a straight kitchen chair the seat of which was already somewhat crowded with a large comb, an empty soup bowl with a spoon in it, a crumpled handkerchief and a glass of stale water polka-dotted with tiny air holes. "Thank you, Floy," she said, "and you tell Aunt Fern that Mamma says thanks."

"She says she can have some, too, if she wants," the child said, pointing to Dorney.

"No, thank you," Dorney said, smiling. "I can't stay very long. But tell her I said thank you just the same."

When Floy had gone, Mrs. Bannon repeated, "Yes, sir, I'd rather

457

have my tongue cut out than have to tell you what I'm going to but there ain't no way around it. When you and him left here yesterday — not the first time, when you went to the park, but the second time, after we had cake and coffee and bid each other good-bye, as we thought, forever — when you and him got ready to leave I wondered to myself if I shouldn't ought to take Butch to one side, and say to him, 'Butch, I hope and trust that this ain't going to turn out like that other time!' but when I seen how your eyes was a-shining and I seen how he — "

"What other time?" Dorney said.

"The time that him and that poor girl up in Star Valley — about your age, she was, maybe a few months older — he likes 'em young — the time that him and her was billing and cooing like turtledoves and had the date all set — "

"You mean, to get — married?"

"She thought so, anyway, and nobody could blame her."

"You didn't mention — I never knew — I thought — "

"I never felt so sorry for anybody in my life as I did her. Why, she was right down in bed with grief. I thought of her yesterday when you and him told me your news. I felt leery."

"You didn't look that way. You didn't say — "

"I didn't," Mrs. Bannon said solemnly, "because I wanted to give him the benefit of the doubt. And besides, it seemed so romantic — you knowing all about him ever since you was a little kid, and you and him finally meeting — like one of these here love stories — so I put the thought right out of my mind. He won't do such a thing again, I said. He just wouldn't have the heart to do it! not in a case like this."

Dorney spoke with great care. "I wonder if you happen to know if he talked to her about — about South America?"

"Very likely. And anything he talks about, he can charm the birds right out of the trees. He asked her to marry him, that I know, she said yes, the date was all set, — and then — one bright morning — what should he do but turn up missing!"

"What did she look like?" Dorney asked.

Mrs. Bannon took up her crumpled handkerchief, pinched her nose with it and put it in the sleeve of her nightgown. "Well, that's another thing," she said, "another reason why I didn't really figure he would do the same thing again — because you see, this girl was very sweet and all that and she had a very pretty complexion and pretty eyes and she was very well liked, but she wasn't," she swallowed, "beautiful — the way you are."

"Beautiful?" Dorney said dumbly.

"Sure," Mrs. Bannon said. "You're going to be a beautiful

wom — in fact, you're a very beautiful — Harem Winfrey says
wouldn't be surprised but what — "

"I — am?"

The invalid nodded. "So that's why I thought this one time when Butch Cassidy wouldn't be able to *help* himself and you and him would get married and leave the country and live happy ever after. But, I was mistaken." She drew a deep breath. "Well, he's spoiled. The women flock after him. That spoils a man terrible. They been doing it a long time. This girl in Star Valley . . . and there's been so many others, I bet he couldn't sit down and name 'em off without forgetting more than half. He means well — but he's just naturally footloose, the footloose kind. How many times ain't Blufe and me set with him outside the shack of an evening and heard him say — "

Dorney rubbed her eyes as though waking from a deep sleep.

" — a rolling stone gathers no moss. I bet if I heard him say that once I heard him say it a thousand times. He just can't help himself. When the time comes, to tie the knot and settle down in one place and saddle himself with responsibility, why, he just don't have what it takes to do it with. He thinks twice, and then he thinks some more, and then — he don't do it. He lights out!" She stirred her by now cool coffee, seeming to gaze past and beyond her listener. "I feel sorry for him. The honest truth is, I feel sorrier for him than I feel for you. Because you'll get over it. Your life's only beginning. He wasn't the guy for a girl like you anyway, which I would of told you yesterday if I hadn't of been took so by surprise. Why, he's pretty near twice your age, and besides — well, you read books and you don't talk the common language — while him — he's just the opposite — and he don't care for nothing only to keep moving and have a high old time. You didn't really love him! Now, did you, honey?"

A little cat chill ran down Dorney's back. *I loved him for the dangers he had passed,* she thought suddenly. Like that woman loved Othello! *And he loved me that I remembered them . . .* the cattle-rustling, the long night rides over the Outlaw Trail, the train hold-ups and bank robberies, the time he was shot, the times he . . . That was the answer, from William Shakespeare. That was the reason.

She thought of his fame, his glory, the legend of his valor. "Is it true love," she whispered, "if you love somebody because they — "

Phoebe Bannon shook her head. "No," she said. "True love ain't connected with *because*." She took a sip of coffee and made a wry face. "She forgot the sugar," she said, putting the cup down. "Fern did. She'd forget her head if it wasn't fastened to her. Would you mind stepping out and getting the sugar bowl off the table?"

Dorney came back with sugar bowl in one hand and a hundred

dollar bill in the other and when Mrs. Bannon saw what it was she stopped breathing and said, "What's that?"

"It was under the sugar bowl!"

"Under the sugar bowl? How did it get there?"

"I don't know," Dorney said.

The invalid took it. "It's real," she said. "It's a real one, anybody could cash this without no trouble whatsoever." She looked up. "Why, he must of — Butch must of — yesterday — when we wasn't paying no — "

Dorney nodded.

"It couldn't of been nobody else! It's the kind of a trick a person would expect of that doggone — "

Mrs. Bannon's face began to twitch as she looked down at the bill again.

"That doggone — "

Her mouth grew square and ugly and she sobbed.

42

"I GUESS NEIBAUER THOUGHT WE WAS DEPARTED spooks coming back from the beyond," Sundance Kid said, breaking a long silence. He wrapped the reins around the pommel of his saddle and reached for his cigarette papers and sack of tobacco. "He sure never expected to see us no more after us telling him so-long Friday night."

Butch Cassidy slowed his horse down to a walk. "Long old day, wasn't it, till it got dark?" he said.

"Oh, I don't know. Snoozing passed the time, and chewing the fat with Neibauer. I didn't so much mind it." Sundance Kid flipped the lighted match away into the darkness.

"It seemed mighty long to me." Butch, too, rolled and lit a cigarette.

Sundance Kid sighed. "Well, that old train for Galveston is chugging right along through the night, I guess. More'n half way there already. Nice plush seats . . . water cooler . . . genuine beds. . . . And here we are right back where we started from, riding the old trail again. But it's the last time, ain't it? That ought to be some consolation."

Butch squinted upwards at the stars. "What do you need consolation for?"

"Me?"

"Yeah, you."

"'Cause I'm out here in the saddle with the wind a-whistling through my coattails —"

"You ain't got no coattails. And there ain't wind enough to blow out a match."

"I had my neck bowed for a beefsteak in that fancy dining car with them darky waiters two-stepping around —"

"You'll live through it."

"And besides —"

Silence fell, broken only by the sound of their horses' hoofs clip-clopping over the hard ground. The night was black but over in the

east, beyond the mountain peaks, a lighter sky foretold the moonrise.

"Boss," the Sundance Kid said.

Butch turned his head.

"Would you mind telling a guy? How about if we get where
we're going, to that hotel, and she don't happen to be there?"

"I ain't worried."

"How long we got to hang around and wait for her?"

The outlaw considered, then shrugged.

"Because — supposing she don't show up?"

"That don't even enter my mind."

"Well, all I want to get straight is, would you leave the country
and go down there to South America without her?"

"She'll show up."

"But what if she don't? Women is pretty well known for changing their mind, you know, and sometimes," Sundance Kid chose his
words with care, trying hard not to put his companion out of countenance, "sometimes a chunk of jack will change it for 'em. And
— that was quite a chunk, so far as I could see. But you could write
her a letter, I guess, and tell her — "

"She'll be there, I ain't got no more doubts than I got that you
and me is heading south, but *if* she ain't, why, the first thing I'll
do is, I'll write and ask Phoebe Bannon for news, for she's one of
the kiddo's best friends. She'll give me the word."

"I wish I could of saw Mrs. Bannon this trip."

"She's a fine little woman."

"Yep. A number one." Sundance Kid cleared his throat. "I wish
I could of saw your girl," he said. "Because then I'd know whether
— I believe I'd be able to tell if — "

"You'd know you seen somebody," Butch said. He saw her clearly,
saw himself reach out and draw her close, only to let her go again.
Weak and nerveless with longing, he called to remembrance the
scene in the shady park. Three more days!

"Just so you don't let it throw you, boss, whatever happens."

"Nothing ain't going to throw me."

"Because you know what old Neibauer says."

"What's what?"

"Say la vee."

"Yeah. Say la vee."

"What the hell does that mean?"

"Damned if I know."

"But that's the ticket, anyway, boss. Ain't that so?"

"Sure it's so. Say la vee."

There was plenty of moonlight all of a sudden, the hard-packed
trail was plain ahead, and the two men put their horses to a gallop.

Somehow, in a house so still, there was something that made the flesh creep about Jetta's empty swing on the dusky porch. Yesterday, to Dorney's great surprise, Madge and Crystal had taken her out to a private institution beyond Warm Springs, where she was to remain for an indefinite stay. They had been unbelievably active, these two, and when Dorney returned home on Monday evening she found many changes. The furniture, all that belonged to Madge, had been carted away for shipment, dishes and household goods had been packed in barrels and boxes and they were filling a trunk with clothes and linens when she came in. She felt as if she had got into the wrong house.

Little given to showing affection, even to her favorite, Madge on the eve of leavetaking was so cold and forbidding that Dorney, whose conscience stung, did not dare to approach and inquire how she had offended. Madge went to bed while it was still daylight and Crystal told Dorney, carefully shutting the hall door and speaking in a low tone of voice, that she shouldn't blame herself for the way Mother was acting. All that was the matter with her was, she was upset by the huffy way Mrs. Towers bid her goodbye, Crystal said, and because Jetta had been put where she belonged. She would get over it in time! but she cried all the way back to town.

"I thought she'd never stop," Crystal said. "And here it was such a lovely place, with nice green lawns and everything. Mrs. Glasscock, she's the lady that runs it, says nobody would be ashamed of having anybody there. Do you know what she says?"

"No, what?" Dorney said.

"Well, she says she would bet that we would be very much surprised if we knew who some of those backward children out there are. There's one man, sixty-seven, that crawls around on his hands and knees. She says he belongs to one of the finest and wealthiest families in town! And it's the same way with several others. Imagine that. So that was some comfort. She says she's noticed through the years that the better class some people are, the more apt they are to have a backward child. Just to hear what Mrs. Glasscock had to say should have cheered anybody up, but Mother —"

"Did Jetta cry much?"

"Well, no, she didn't," Crystal said. "She had a fine time going out there, looking at everything and — no, she didn't cry. What she did was, just when we got ready to go and she saw we were leaving her there, she fell into some kind of a fit, like. She stiffened out just like a board, and didn't pay any attention even when Mother tried to — like she was deaf and dumb."

"When can I go out and see her?"

"Mrs. Glasscock said that was really better than screaming. She was more encouraged, she said, and she knew right what to do for her. She was going to do it as soon as we got gone. What did you say?" She inquired with great politeness.

"I said, when can I go out and see her?"

"Not for at least a month," Crystal said. "Because that will make her homesick and upset all Mrs. Glasscock's work. She said that's one of her strictest rules — no visitors for several weeks. And the kind of woman she is, I doubt if she'd let the President in if she didn't want to! so don't waste your money on carfare until later on."

Crystal sought her bed soon — they had hardly lighted the lamps before they were blowing them out again — and when Dorney went upstairs she thought she had misjudged her niece and regretted that they must part, for in spite of her exhaustion Crystal had never been friendlier or more communicative or showed more, how charming she could be.

While she was eating her lonely supper on Tuesday night, Dorney shut the back door so she couldn't see the swing. It appeared to move a little now and then and that was eerie. Madge, who had said goodbye with a peck on the cheek but added no heartening instruction to be good, and Crystal, both were gone to California and would not return, but somehow it seemed different with Jetta. It seemed as if she was dead and had a ghost that might come back, a smaller than life-size ghost on tiny legs, stomping and tottering noiselessly, who once more would hoist herself into her swing, take three solemn steps back and then come swooshing down. . . .

She wandered into the bare parlor, sat down on the horsehair sofa, the only remaining piece of furniture, and looked at the squares of new-looking wallpaper where the pictures had hung. She was glad the piano and piano stool were gone. There were no such things as specters, certainly not of living persons, but it would be horrid to hear — or fancy one heard in the dead of night — Crystal playing a ghostly trill, as she had done so many hours and years here in this room, so that the very air had the habit of repeating the sound of her music and must rehearse it, now and again, forever. She had never before in her life faced the prospect of being all alone throughout the night and it made her feel not only excommunicated but blockaded. Now it was early, and still light, the red rays of the setting sun came through the bare window, but it would be dark, and then . . .

Dorney got up and walked back out into the kitchen, her own pair of footsteps on the squeaky board floor sounding as if another stepped just behind. Perhaps she should go over and ask Clara if Ruby could come and keep her company, or borrow Althea from Mrs. Luby, but the trouble was, to have to wake them up and send them home so early in the morning before she went to work, and

464

then, there was no milk and what would she give them for breakfast?

She considered whether to pay a visit in the neighborhood, but the thought of returning and entering the empty pitch-black house all by herself made her decide to stay at home. She had never noticed the smell of the wallpaper before, and the smell of dust and stale coffee, but she did now, and then, how loud the clock ticked and what a whirring of wheels there was before the half hour struck.

Her room was unchanged, as the little furniture in it belonged to the house, and she went upstairs, thinking she might stay up there and read, but it was too hot. She was about to go down again, having chosen a book when she decided to look at her dresses.

The gray silk was to have been her wedding dress! She fingered it, lifted the sleeve and brought it up to her cheek thoughtfully. Had Grandpa Bannon known, and not revealed, that great Butch Cassidy would play no man false, and no woman, either, except his betrothed bride? That he would jilt her and leave her to wonder and weep? But she had wept at Mrs. Bannon's and upon first coming home to Madge's desolate house . . . not for him, so much, for the blue-eyed outlaw, the lover and stranger, but for the loss of the dream she had had so long that it was a habit, like reading one sweet book again and again, one *Wonderland*, one *Old St. Paul's*, the single copy in existence now dismantled and destroyed.

She pushed the gray dress aside and reached for the soft green satin, thinking to put it on for consolation and company. Doing so, she reflected on how long it took to go by train from Salt Lake City to Galveston, Texas. They had left Sunday night at midnight, and tonight was Tuesday. Were they there yet? And from Galveston to Argentina, how long did that take? When she looked in the mirror she seemed to be looking out of a window at a purple plain where a white horse and a black horse grazed and peacocks trailed, but that melted away . . . and then she could see herself, standing in her own room in the green dress. It was becoming. It made her look nice. She remembered what Mrs. Bannon had said, or as good as said, about her being beautiful. Was she, indeed?

Dorney had never had any trouble imagining that she would be, one day. Young women know in their hearts that if they do their duty they will be so, for beauty beseems them. Therefore, hers had been long expected . . . and now, like the rightful heiress to the Manor come to claim her own, was she here? had she arrived? Dorney bent closer and looked, her heart beating a little faster. Well, the freckles hardly showed any more. The brows that had been light were darker. The . . . the eyes . . . She began to smile a smile of welcome, then sobered and turned away. Not yet. And if love could fail and the dream could fail, perhaps never . . .

For coolness, she piled her hair in a topknot on her head, and, still wearing the green dress, carrying a book in her hand, she went downstairs. The rooms, even the light parlor, were darker now, and she concluded to go out and sit on the front porch for the last of the daylight, and try to read there. If she could not read, she would think, and perhaps she should think in any case, for it came to her that it was time she did. The blind kitten sees after nine days. After sixteen years, or woefully more, or awesomely less, the blind young human being blinks in the light and says, Who am I? how came I here? If not now, then soon, Dorney knew she would have to mull over the matter of who she was, and what she was in the world for. She needed food to eat and clothes to wear and a bed to sleep in, but the soul, had that not corresponding needs and what were they? She had to think of them. Life itself she must ponder, to guess what it was going to make of her. Or was that her own business? What people were, what they became, were themselves responsible? She sat on the top step with her book in her lap, gazing far away.

The clock in the City and County Building had struck three times before she started to reckon the hour, so she counted wrong. Five? When all the summer stars were shining down?

After three days' coach travel with the tall cowboy in the seat opposite him, the young New Yorker had a feeling he knew him quite well. His name might be Bill Jenkins, as he claimed in his Texas drawl, but something made Teige Desmond doubt it. A slouching long-faced man of perhaps thirty-five, he was wearing a once handsome but by now sadly rumpled black broadcloth suit, the trousers of which were tucked into cowboy boots, a white shirt, black string tie, and on his head a wide cowboy hat that looked new and costly. He had not, so far, drawn a sober breath. Where he procured his liquor, Teige Desmond did not know. The bottle he drank from, and politely offered, looking unoffended when it was declined, seemed never to empty. Inebriation did him no harm and may have worked an improvement on him, as proper pickling will make of a cucumber something superior to what it was in its natural state. He was silent and pensive, courtly and slow. In short, he was the perfect traveling companion. He had a small imitation leather Old Testament which he tried unsuccessfully to read from time to time. It had been given him, he said, by a "saint in human female form" whom he had run across on Water Street when sightseeing, and he intended to read it from cover to cover before he was done. Teige Desmond had already picked it up twice off the floor and handed it back to him.

Bill Jenkins would smile dejectedly from time to time. The train was not crowded but there seemed to be quite a number of women aboard and these passed by sometimes, two or three together, or one, looking straight ahead and catching hold of the worn emerald-green plush backs of the seats to find their balance when the car lurched. Strangely enough, this oppressed the cowboy. He would be overcome with what seemed very like misery and, tears filling his eyes, would turn his head and stretch his neck forward to look after them, and then, heaving a sigh, would gaze out of the window. On one of these occasions, observing his neighbor's sympathetic if amused brown eyes upon him, he volunteered the information that he had sworn off women. "Too rich for my blood," he said. Soon after, he explained that he had come east with enough money to buy a city block, but that he had met up with a — He stopped and did not say what. Later, he said that he was a cowpuncher and was going back to cowpunching to try to build up another stake. He had lost the one he had in the stock market, he said. He used to have three or four mighty good friends, the best damn friends a guy ever had, but now they were scattered to the four winds, and no telling what had become of them or if he would ever see them again. It made him even more melancholy to speak of them than it did to see the ladies go by.

Sometimes he fell into a quiet doze, flat on his back on the plush seat, with his fine hat over his face, and slept for a long time. He slept that way on Monday, the last afternoon of the trip. Teige Desmond reached over, plucked the small Bible from the seat and looked at it. On the flyleaf was written precisely, with violet ink, "Yet if any man suffer as a Christian, let him not be ashamed. I Peter, 4–16," and beneath it, "From your sister in Christ, Drusilla E. Goodhue." A name for a Water Street mission *religieuse*, for sure! whom poor Bill Jenkins had met too late.

Like him, the young professor had every intention to read the Bible through someday, and a fine *Doctor Litterarum* he was, he thought, not to have done it long since! Today, however, was not the time to begin it, and he was about to replace it when he recalled the silly superstition that one could foretell the future by means of it. Shut your eyes, open the Bible, point to a certain verse and look!

The book he landed in was the Song of Songs which is Solomon's, Chapter Five, Verse One, beginning, "I am come into my garden, my sister, my bride." Surely not much of a prophecy! Smiling slightly, he leaned across and laid the Bible on the seat opposite, under the limp hand of the sleeper, then settled back and looked out at the Wyoming landscape.

My sister, my bride.

467

The words echoed in his mind. He came back to the thought he had had over and over. Would she be greatly changed? She was only fourteen when he last saw her. Now she was past sixteen. Sometimes maturity worsened. The possibility existed that whatever it was he had thought he had seen in her, grace and virtue, might have vanished. She had written half a dozen letters that would have done honor to Miss Fanny Burney in her young, innocent days, and he had hope for her. If she would study, if she would apply herself . . . But suppose, oh, any number of things. Suppose she had a sweetheart. The notion came as an unpleasant shock. For that matter, she was old enough to marry!

I am come into my garden.

Bill Jenkins, as he had the night before, and every night of the trip, when darkness fell and the low lights came on in the car, began melodiously and mournfully to sing. He was singing when they pulled into Cheyenne at nine o'clock on Monday night and singing when they pulled out. It happened to occur to him that the words of his song, "Goodbye, Old Paint, I'm a-leaving Cheyenne," were singularly appropriate to the occasion and he pointed out the fact in pleased and childish astonishment. Once in a while he sang about a man named Billy Venero and something about love in disguise, but he always returned to his favorite lay. "Me and the boss — me and my pardner — " he said, "we used to harmonize on this here. Many's the time me and my pardner, we harmonized." The song had a pretty tune. The cowboy had sung it so many times that Teige Desmond knew it by heart now, every verse.

It was about two in the morning when he woke up cramped and cold. He sat up straight and rubbed his face, yawning. Next year, if he traveled, he could go in a little better style than this. That raise, starting in September, was going to make a lot of difference. The landlady wanted him to take the big flat in the front of the building and move out of his two small rooms and he was going to do it.

Once more, the Westerner in the seat opposite was sound asleep, lying flat on his back with one long leg draped over the outside arm of the seat and the other jackknifed against the back. Cradled in his arms against his breast like a living creature was the mysteriously ever full whiskey bottle. His wide cowboy hat had fallen on the floor.

Teige Desmond bent forward and picked it up. He brushed it off and was going to restore it to the cowboy's face when something made him keep and look at it with curiosity. He had never had hold of one of these hats before. They were quite a sly invention, devilishly becoming. It appeared to be about his size, too. He looked up and down the shadowy car to see if anybody was stirring and then, not without embarrassment, first smoothing down his black hair, tried it on. It felt fine. He turned his head from side to side. All of a sudden he wondered how he looked in it and tried to see, in the window, but the moonlight was too white and bright outside. The glass wasn't dark enough for a good reflection.

Smiling at himself for his foolishness, he got out of the seat without disturbing the sleeper or falling over the part of him that encroached into the aisle and made his way to the men's washroom. It was even darker there than in the coach but a light burned beside the small mirror and he could view himself fairly well, by stooping, for he was tall.

He didn't look half bad in a cowboy hat! In fact, if this one belonged to him, he just might wear it tomorrow night when he went to pay his call. Wouldn't the little quondam Lady in Waiting laugh, though? to see a professor looking like a . . . He began to sing under his breath, while he straightened it, tipping it to the left a trifle, to the right, forward and backward, then let it stay.

He ought to have a hat like this, for a souvenir of the Wild West. When in Rome . . . The truth was, he should buy one tomorrow. So far as that went, to really enter into the spirit of the thing, he should hire a horse from a livery stable, a black horse, like the one he had learned as a boy to ride in Brooklyn Park, and do a little riding. It would be the last thing she'd ever in the world expect, to see Mr. Teige Desmond come cantering up to her gate on a black horse (*I am come into my garden, my sister, my bride*) singing — how did it go now?

> Goodbye, Old Paint, I'm a-leaving Cheyenne,
> Goodbye, Old Paint, I'm off to Montan',
> My foot in the stirrup, the reins in my hand,
> Good morning, young lady, my horse he won't stand.
> I'm a-leaving Cheyenne, I'm off to Montan',
> Good morning, young lady . . ."

That ought to be a pretty big surprise.

— THE END —